Avaryan Rising

By Judith Tarr from Tom Doherty Associates

The Hound and the Falcon

AVARYAN RISING
The Hall of the Mountain King
The Lady of Han-Gilen
A Fall of Princes
Arrows of the Sun
Spear of Heaven

HISTORICAL NOVELS
Lord of the Two Lands
Throne of Isis
The Eagle's Daughter
Pillar of Fire
King and Goddess
Queen of Swords

AVARYAN RISING

The Hall of the Mountain King

The Lady of Han-Gilen

A Fall of Princes

JUDITH TARR

A Tom Doherty Associates Book
New York

AVARYAN RISING

This book is printed on acid-free paper.

An Orb Edition
Published by Tom Doherty Associates, Inc.
175 Fifth Avenue
New York, NY 10010

Tor Books on the World Wide Web:
http://www.tor.com

Library of Congress Cataloging-in-Publication Data

Tarr, Judith.
    Avaryan rising : The hall of the Mountain King, The Lady of
Han-Gilen, A fall of princes.
        p. cm.
    "A Tom Doherty Associates book."
    ISBN 0-312-86388-8
    1. Fantastic fiction, American. I. Title. II. Title: Hall of
the Mountain King. III. Title: Lady of Han-Gilen. IV. Title: Fall
of princes.
PS3570.A655A94   1997   97-19556
813'.54—dc21   CIP

First Orb Edition: November 1997

Printed in the United States of America

0 9 8 7 6 5 4 3 2 1

CONTENTS

A Note on Pronunciation

With regard to the pronunciation of the names herein, the most useful rule is that of medieval Latin, with the addition of the English *J* and *Y*. The result is an accent somewhere between that of Ianon and that of Han-Gilen. As for Asanian, which is a tonal language written in complex and highly precise characters, my transliteration is, of necessity, highly simplified. I have adapted it to the usage of names in the eastern languages, and to the limitations of the English alphabet.

To be precise:

*Consonants are essentially as in English. *C* and *G* are always hard, as in *can* and *gold,* never soft as in *cent* and *gem. S* always as in *hiss,* never as in *his.*

*Vowels are somewhat different from the English. *A* as in *father:* Vadin is pronounced VAH-deen, Sarevadin sah-ray-VAH-deen, Aranos ah-RAH-nos. Long *E* as in Latin *dei* (approximate, but not identical, to English long *A):* Elian is AY-lee-ahn, Han-Gilen hahn-gee-LAYN. *I* is much as the English *Y:* consider *hymn* and the suffix *-ly,* and the consonantal *yawn:* hence, Ianon is YAH-non; Alidan ah-LEE-dahn; Ziad-Ilarios zee-AHD-ee-LAH-ree-os; Hirel hee-REL. *O* as in *owe,* not as in *toss. U* as in Latin, comparable to English *oo (look, loom):* Uveryen is oo-VER-yen, Umijan OO-mee-jahn, Uverias oo-VAIR-ee-ahss.

Y can be either vowel or consonant, as in English; before a vowel it is a consonant (Avaryan is ah-VAHR-yan, Odiya OH-dee-yah), but before a consonant it is a vowel (Ymin is EE-min, Yrios EE-ree-ohss).

Ei is pronounced as in *reign* (Geitan is GAY-tahn). *Ai,* except in the archaic and anomalous Mirain (mee-RAYN), is comparable to the English *bye:* Abaidan is ah-BYE-dahn, Shon'ai SHOWN-eye. Otherwise, paired vowels are pronounced separately: Amilien is pronounced ah-MEE-lee-en, Asanion ah-SAH-nee-on.

THE HALL OF
THE MOUNTAIN KING

For
Meredith

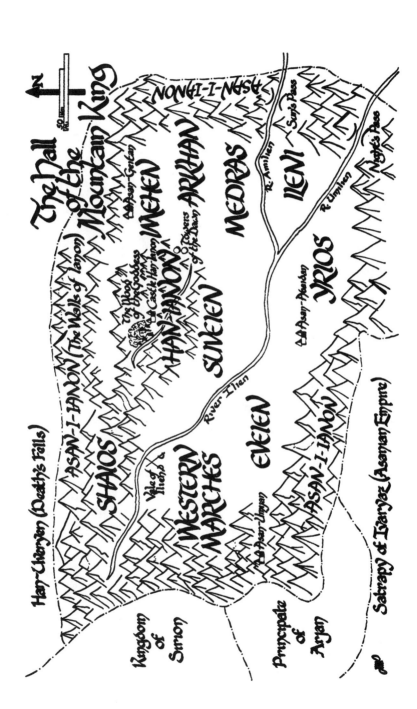

One

THE OLD KING STOOD UPON THE BATTLEMENTS, GAZ-
ing southward. The wind whipped back his long white hair and
boomed in his heavy cloak. But his eyes never blinked, his face never
flinched, as stern and immovable as an image carved in obsidian.

The walls fell sheer below him, stone set on stone, castle and crag set
in the green Vale, field and forest rolling into the mountain bastions of
his kingdom. North and west and south, the wall of lofty peaks was
unbroken. In the east lay the Gate of Han-Ianon, the pass which was
the only entrance to the heart of his realm. On either side of it rose the
Towers of the Dawn. Gods had built them long ages ago, or so it was
said; built them and departed, leaving them as a monument, the wonders of the north. They were tall and they were unassailable, and they
were beautiful, wrought of stone as rare as it was wonderful. Silver-grey
under stars or moons, silver-white in the sun, in the dawn it glowed
with all the colors of the waking sky: white and silver and rose, blood-
red and palest emerald. That same stone glimmered still under his feet
although it was full morning, the sun poised above the distant Towers.
An omen, the priests would say, that the dawnstone had kept its radiance so long. Against all reason, against all the years of hopeless hope,
he yearned to believe in it.

From his post at the southern gate Vadin could see the lone still figure
dwarfed by height and distance. Every morning it stood there between

sunrise and the second hour, in every weather, even in the dead of winter; it had stood so for years, people said, more years than Vadin had been alive.

He swallowed a yawn. Although sentry duty was the least strenuous office of a royal squire, it was also the least engrossing. And he was short on sleep; he had been at liberty last night, he and two more of the younger squires, and they had drunk and diced and drunk some more, and he had had a run of luck. In the end he had won first go at the girl. This time, at the thought of her, it was a smile that he swallowed.

Swallowed hard and as close to invisibly as he could. Old Adjan the arms master asked very little of the young hellions in his charge. Merely absolute obedience to his every command, absolute perfection in hall and on the practice field, and absolute stillness while on guard. One's eyes might move within the sheltering helmet; one might, at regular intervals, pace from portal to portal of the gate, which was when one could glance upward at the flutter of black that was the king. For the rest, one made oneself an image of black stone and lacquered bronze, and made certain that one observed every flicker of movement about one's post. It had been excruciating at first, that stillness. Raw boy that he had been, brought up wild in his father's castle in the hills of Imehen, he had imagined no torture greater than that of standing in armor with his spear at one precise angle and no other, hour upon hour, while the sun beat down upon his head or the rain lashed his face or the wind bit him to the bone. Now it was merely dull. He had learned to take his ease while seeming to stand at rigid attention, and to set his eyes to their task of observation while letting his mind wander as it would. Now and then it would wander back to his eyes' labor, contemplating the people who passed to and fro in the town below. Some approached the castle, urchins staring at the great tall guards in their splendid livery, one at each of the lesser gates and half a company at the Gate of Gods that faced the east; at servants and sightseers and the odd nobleman passing within or going out. At the very beginning of Vadin's watch, the Prince Moranden himself had ridden out with a goodly company of lords and attendants, armed and accoutered for the hunt. The king's son had had a glance for the lanky lad on guard, a flicker of recognition, a quick smile. A proud man, the prince, but never too proud to take notice of a squire.

Vadin glanced at the sun. Not long now before Kav came to relieve him. Then an hour of mounted drill and an hour at swordplay, and he was to wait on the king tonight. A signal honor, that last, rarely granted to any squire in his first year of service. Adjan had been sour when he announced it, but Adjan was always sour; more to the point, the old soldier had appended no biting sarcasm. He had only growled, "Pick up your jawbone, boy, and stop dawdling. It's almost sunup." Which meant that he was pleased with his newest and most callow recruit, gods alone knew why; but Vadin had learned not to argue with fortune. While his mind reflected, his eye had been recording on its own, independent of his will. The Lady Odiya's elderly maid scuttling on an errand; an elder of the council with his followers; a gaggle of farmfolk come to market, taking time to gape at the glowing wonder of the castle. As they wandered back down toward the town, they left one behind, a man who stood still in the road's center and stared up at the battlements.

No, not a man. A boy perhaps Vadin's own age, perhaps a year or two younger for his beard was just beginning, very erect and very proud and patently no rustic. He could not but be Ianyn, blackwood-dark as he was, yet he was got up like a southerner in coat and trousers, with a southern shortsword at his side. Vadin would have called him a paradox but for the flame of gold at his throat, the torque of a priest of the Sun, and the broad white browband that marked him an initiate on his seven years' Journey. This one was young for it, but not overly so; and it explained the Ianyn face atop the dress of the Hundred Realms. No doubt the trousers were a penance for some infraction.

The priest left off his staring and began to walk, drawing closer to the gate. Vadin blinked. The world had gone out of focus. Or else—

If Vadin's training had been beaten into him even a little less thoroughly, he would have laughed. This boy with the face of a mountain lord, who carried himself as if he had been as high as all Han-Ianon, was hardly bigger than a child. The closer he came, the smaller he seemed. Then he raised his eyes, and Vadin's breath caught. They were full of—they blazed with—

They flicked away. He was only a ragged priest in trousers, standing not even shoulder-high to Vadin. And Vadin was flogging himself awake. The boy was almost through the gate. With haste that would have won a scowl from the arms master, Vadin thrust out his spear to bar the way. The stranger halted. He was not frightened; he was not visibly angry. If anything, he seemed amused.

Gods, but he was haughty. Vadin mustered his harshest tone, which was also his deepest, booming out in most satisfactory fashion. "Hold, stranger, in the king's name. Come you out of the Hundred Realms?"

"Yes." The priest's voice was as startling as his eyes, a full octave deeper than Vadin's but eerily clear, with the soft vowels of the south. "I do."

"Then I must conduct you to his majesty." At once, the order went, without exception, without regard for any other order or duty. Beneath the stoic mask of the guard, Vadin was beginning to enjoy himself. He had the immense satisfaction of collaring an armed warrior, a full knight to boot, and ordering him—with all due respect—to hold the gate until Vadin or his relief should come. "King's business," he said, careful not to sound too cheerful. "Standing order." The man did not need to ask which one. The torque and the trousers made it obvious.

Their bearer looked on it all with the merest suggestion of a smile. When Vadin would have led him he managed to set himself in the lead, striding forward without hesitation, asking no direction. He had a smooth hunter's stride, barely swaying the black braid that hung to his waist behind him, and surprisingly fast. Vadin had to stretch his long legs to keep pace.

The king turned his face toward the cruel sun. Again it was climbing to its zenith, again it brought him no hope. Once he would have cursed it, but time had robbed him of rage as of so much else. Even the omen of the dawnstone meant nothing. She would not return.

"My lord."

Habit and kingship brought him about slowly, with royal dignity. One of his squires stood before him in the armor of a gate guard. The newest one, the lordling from Imehen, for whom Adjan had such unwontedly high hopes. He was standing straight and soldierly, a credit to his master. "Sire," he said clearly enough, if somewhat stiffly, "a traveler has come from the Hundred Realms. I have brought him to you as you commanded."

The king saw the other then. He had been lost in his guard's shadow, a shadow himself, small and lithe and dark. But when he lifted his head, the tall squire shrank to vanishing. He had a face a man could not forget, fine-boned and eagle-proud, neither handsome nor ugly but simply and supremely itself. The eyes in it met the old man's steadily, with calm and royal confidence; almost, but not quite, he smiled.

Almost, but not quite, the king returned his smile. Hope was rising once more. Swelling; quivering on the edge of fear.

The boy stepped away from his guard, one pace only, as if to shake off the intruding presence. Something in the movement betrayed the tension beneath his calm. Yet when he spoke his voice was steady, and unlike his face, incontestably beautiful. "I greet you, my lord, and I commend your liege man's courtesy."

The king glanced at Vadin, who was careful to wear no expression at all. "Did you resist him?" the king asked the stranger.

"Not at all, my lord. But," the boy added, again with his almost-smile, "I was somewhat haughty."

From the glitter in the squire's eyes, that was no less than the truth. The king swallowed laughter, found it echoed in the clear bright eyes, and lost it in a dart of memory and of old, old grief. He had not laughed so, nor met such utter, joyous fearlessness, since—

His voice came hard and harsh. "From the Hundred Realms, are you, boy?"

"Han-Gilen, sire."

The king drew a slow breath. His face had neither changed nor softened. Yet his heart was hammering against his ribs. "Han-Gilen," he said. "Tell me, boy. Have you heard aught of my daughter?"

"Your daughter, my lord?" The voice was cool, but the eyes had shifted, gazing over the southward sweep of Han-Ianon.

The king turned, following them. "Once on a time, I had a daughter. When she was born I made her my heir. When she was still a young maid I consecrated her to the Sun. And when she reached the time of her womanhood she went away as all the Sun's children must do, on the seven years' wandering of her priestess-Journey. At the end of it she should have returned, full priestess and full wise, with wondrous tales to tell. But the seven years passed, and seven again, and she did not come. And now it is thrice the time appointed, and still no man has seen her, nor has she sent me word. I have heard only rumors, travelers' tales out of the south. A priestess from the north, Journeying in the Hundred Realms, abandoned her vows and her heritage to wed a ruling prince; but nay, she spurned the prince to rule as high priestess in the Temple of the Sun in Han-Gilen; she went mad and turned seer and proclaimed that the god had spoken to her in visions; she . . . died."

There was a silence. Abruptly the king spun about, swirling his black cloak. "Mad, they call me. Mad, because I stand here day upon day, year upon year, praying for my daughter's return. Though I grow old and soon will die, I name no heir, while yonder in my hall my son leads my younger warriors in a round of gaming, or sleeps deep beside his latest woman. A strong man is the Prince Moranden of Ianon, a great warrior, a leader of men. He is more than fit to hold the high seat." The king bared his teeth, more snarl than smile. "No man should grieve so for a daughter when such a son has grown to grace his hall. So men say.

They do not know him as I know him." His fists clenched, hard and knotted, thin as an eagle's claws. "Boy! Know you aught of my daughter?"

The young priest had listened without expression. He reached now into his scrip and brought forth a glitter of metal, a torque of gold twisted with mountain copper.

The king reeled. Strong young hands caught him, helped him to a seat upon the parapet. Dimly he saw the face close above his own, calm and still; but the eyes were dark with old sorrow.

"Dead," he said. "She is dead." He took the torque in hands that could not still their trembling. "How long?"

"Five winters since."

Anger kindled. "And you waited until now?"

The boy's chin came up; his nostrils flared. "I would have come, my lord. But there was war, and I was forbidden, and no one else could be spared. Do not fault me for what I could not help."

There had been a time when a boy, or even a man grown, would have been whipped for such insolence. But the king swallowed his wrath lest it destroy his grief. "What was she to you?"

The boy met his gaze squarely. "She was my mother."

He had gone beyond shock, beyond even surprise. For that tale too had come to him, that she had borne a son. And for a priestess wedded to the god to conceive a child by any mortal man, the penalty was death. Death for herself, for her lover, and for their progeny.

"No," said this young stranger whose face in its every line spoken poignantly of her. "She never died for me."

"Then how?"

The boy closed his eyes upon a grief as stark and as terrible as the king's own; his voice came soft, as if he did not trust it. "Sanelin Amalin was a very great lady. She came to Han-Gilen at the end of its war upon the Nine Cities, when all its people mourned the death of the prince's prophet, who had also been his beloved brother. She stood up in the midst of the funeral rites and foretold the fate of the princedom, and the Red Prince accepted her as his seer. Soon thereafter, for her great sanctity, she was taken into the temple in Han-Gilen. Within a year she was its high priestess. There was no one more holy or more deeply venerated. Yet there were those who hated her for that very sanctity, among them she who had been high priestess before Sanelin's coming, a proud woman and a hard one, who had treated the stranger cruelly and been deposed for it. In the dark of the moons, five winters past, this woman and certain of her followers lured the lady from the temple with a tale of sickness only she could heal. I think . . . I know she saw the truth. Yet she went. I followed her with the prince hard upon my heels. We were just too late. They threw me down and stunned me and wounded my lord most cruelly, struck my mother to the heart, and fled." His breath shuddered as he drew it in. "Her last words were of you. She wished you to know of her glory, of her death. She said, 'My father would have had me be both queen and priestess. Yet I have been more than either. He will grieve, but I think he will understand.' "

The wind sighed upon the stones. Vadin shifted in a creaking of leather and bronze. In the world below, children shouted and a stallion screamed and a tuneless voice bawled a snatch of a drinking song. Very quietly the king said, "You tell a noble tale, stranger who calls himself my kin. Yet, though I may be mad, I am not yet a dotard. How came a high priestess to bear a son? Did she then lay aside her vows? Did she wed the Red Prince of Han-Gilen?"

"She broke no vows, nor was she ever aught but Avaryan's bride."

"You speak in riddles, stranger."

"I speak the truth, my lord grandsire."

The king's eyes glittered. "You are proud for one who by his words is no man's son."

"Both of which," said the other, "I am."

The king rose. He was very tall even for one of his people; he towered over the boy, who nevertheless betrayed no hint of fear. That too had been Sanelin, small as her western mother had been small, yet utterly indomitable. "You are the very image of her. How then?" His hand gripped the boy's shoulder with cruel strength. *"How?"*

"She was the Bride of the Sun."

So bright, those eyes were, so bright and so terrible. The king threw up all his shields against them. "That is a title. A symbol. The gods do not walk in the world as once they did. They do not lie with the daughters of men. Not even with the holy ones, their own priestesses. Not in these days."

The boy said nothing, only raised his hands. The left had bled where the nails had driven into flesh. The right could not. Gold flamed there, the disk of the Sun with its manifold rays, filling the hollow of his palm.

The king slitted his eyes against the brightness. A deep and holy terror had risen to engulf him. But he was strong and he was king; he reckoned his lineage back to the sons of the lesser gods.

"He came," said this child of the great one, "while she kept vigil in the Temple of Han-Gilen where is his most sacred image. He came, and he loved her. Of that union I was conceived; for it she suffered and came in time to glory. You could say that she died of it, by the envy of those who reckoned themselves holy but could not endure true sanctity."

"And you? Why did they let you live?"

"My father defended me."

"Yet he let her die."

"He took her to himself. She was glad, my lord. If you could have seen—dying, she shone, and she laughed with purest delight. She had her lover at last, wholly and forever." He shone himself in speaking of it, a radiance touched only lightly now with sorrow.

The king could not partake of it. Nor, for long, could the stranger. He let his hands fall, veiling the brilliance of the god's sign. Without it he seemed no more than any other traveler, ragged and footsore, armored with pride that was half defiance. It kept his chin up and his eyes level, but his fists were clenched at his sides. "My lord," he said, "I make no claim upon you. If you bid me go, I will go."

"And if I bid you stay?"

The dark eyes kindled. Sanelin's eyes, set with the sun's fire. "If you bid me stay, I will stay, for that is the path which the god has marked for me."

"Not the god alone," said the king. He raised a hand as if to touch the boy's shoulder, but the gesture ended before it was well begun. "Go now. Bathe; you need it sorely. Eat. Rest. My squire will see that you have all you desire. I shall speak with you again." And as they moved to obey: "How are you called, grandchild?"

"Mirain, my lord."

"Mirain." The king tested it upon his tongue. "Mirain. She named you well." He drew himself erect. "What keeps you? Go!"

Two

THEY CALLED HER THE QUEEN WHO WAS NOT. IN LAW she was the king's concubine, captive daughter of a rebel from the Western Marches, mother of his sole acknowledged son. In her own country that would have sufficed to make her his wife, and her child heir to throne and castle; here where they had cast aside the old gods and the great goddess to become slaves of the Sun, a concubine was only that, her son always and inescapably a bastard.

She did not stoop to bitterness. She held the highest title these apostates allowed, that of First Lady of the Palace; she had a realm of her own, the women's quarters of the castle with their halls and their courts, barred and protected in proper fashion, with her own eunuchs to stand guard. Though those were aging, alas, and his majesty would permit her to buy no more; when she had been so unwise as to suggest that he send her young slaves of his own choosing and a surgeon to render them fit for her service, his rage had come close to frightening her.

They were turning barbarian here. They had few slaves, and no eunuchs. In a little while, no doubt, they would put on trousers and shave their beards and affect the dainty accents of the south.

She contemplated her reflection in the great oval mirror. It had been her father's shield; she had had it silvered and polished at extravagant expense, that she might never forget whence she had come. The lovely maiden it had once reflected was long gone, she of the wild lynxeyes and the headlong temper. The eyes were quiet now, as the lynx is quiet before it springs. The face was beautiful still, a goddess-mask, flawless and implacable.

She waved away the servant with the paints and brushes, snatched the veil from the other's hands and draped it herself. Doliya tarried overlong in the market; damn the old gabbler, could she never perform a simple errand without dallying in every wineshop along the way? Not but that the woman's delays had often proven profitable; secrets had a way of escaping when wine loosened men's tongues, and Doliya's ears were wickedly keen.

"Great lady." The voice of her chief eunuch, thin with age. As was he, a gangling spider-limbed grotesque of a creature, who had never learned to creep and cringe and act the proper servant. His father had been her father's enemy; it had amused the old monster to slaughter all that line save the youngest son, and to have the child cut and trained and given to his daughter as a slave. It was a crooked comfort to see how old he was and how much younger she seemed, and to know that she was a full year the elder.

He was accustomed to her brooding stares, and unafraid of them. "Great lady," he repeated, "there is that which you should know."

His level tone, his expressionless face, told her much. Whatever tidings he bore, he rejoiced to bear them; which meant that she would not be pleased to hear them. Such games he played, he her bitter enemy, he the perfect faithful servant. Impeccable service, he had told her once when he was still young enough to blurt out secrets, could be a potent revenge. She would never dare to trust him completely; she would never dare not to. She had laughed and taken up his gauntlet and made him the chief of her servants.

"Tell me," she bade him at last, coolly, sipping iced wine from a goblet of tourmaline and silver.

He smiled. This was bitter news indeed, then, and he was in no haste to reveal it. He sat in a chair the twin of her own, commanded wine and received it, drank more slowly even than she. At last he set down the cup; laced his long withered fingers; allowed himself a second smile. "A stranger has come into the king's presence, great lady. A stranger from the south, a priest of the burning god." For all her control, she tensed; his amusement deepened. "He brings word of the king's heir, of her who departed so long ago; some would say by your connivance, although that surely is a falsehood. You may rejoice, great lady. Sanelin Amalin is dead."

The lady raised a brow. "I am to be surprised? Vain hope, my old friend. I have known it for long and long."

He continued to smile. "Of course you have, great lady. Have you also known that she delivered herself of a son? A son of her god, bearing the Sun in his hand, wrapped in divinity as in a cloak. With my own eyes I saw him. He has spoken with the king; the king's folk serve him; he lodges, great lady, in the chambers of the king's heir."

She sat very, very still. Her heart had stopped, and burst into life again, hammering upon the walls of her flesh. Ginan smiled. She thought of flesh flayed living from bone, shaped the thought with great care, and thrust it behind those glittering eyes. They dimmed; he greyed, his smile died. But his satisfaction could not so easily be vanquished. All her care and all her plotting—all the women who came to the king, who could conceive no children to supplant her son; the one whose spells sufficed to conceive a son but not to bear him alive, who died herself in the bearing—all for naught. Because she had not gone so far as to dispose of the heir herself, trusting to the Journey and, if that failed, to the priestess' vows. Sanelin would never know man, never bear a child. If she returned, if she took the throne, how easy then to cast a spell, to distill a poison, to assure that Moranden son of Odiya of Umijan became king by right of all Ianon.

Almost, almost, the lady could admire her. Insufferable little saint that she had been, still she had found a way both to thwart her enemy and to keep her name for sanctity. It seemed that the barbarians had believed the lie; the whelp had been suffered to live. Unless . . .

Ginan knew her well enough to read the flicker of her eyes. His smile returned undaunted. "No, great lady, he is no impostor. He is the very image and likeness of his mother."

"Dwarfish and unlovely? Ah, the poor child."

"As tall as he needs to be, and well above any need of beauty. He is a striking young man, great lady; he carries himself like a king."

"Yet," she mused, "a priest."

"A priest who is a king, great lady, may marry and beget sons. As indeed some had speculated that the princess might do if she were ruling queen, for the kingdom's sake. As it seems that she did."

"He is not king yet." Odiya said it with great care. She refilled her cup and raised it. "Nor shall he be while I have power in this kingdom. May the goddess be my witness."

Vadin did precisely as he was bidden. It kept him from having to think. He did not understand half of what he had heard on the battlements; he was not certain that he believed the rest. That this foreigner should be the son of the king's daughter, of a woman so long mourned that she seemed as dim as a legend, yes, perhaps he could credit that. But that the boy should have been sired by a god . . .

Mirain bathed, which truly he had needed, and he let the king's servants carry away his ragged trousers and bring him a proper kilt. But he raised an uproar by calling for a razor. First they had to find one; then he insisted on shaving his face as smooth as a woman's. Vadin's own twitched as he watched. The servants were appalled, and the eldest of them ventured to remonstrate, but Mirain would hear none of it. "It's hot," he said in his mincing accent. "It's unlovely. It itches." He grinned at their shocked faces, shocking them even further, and sat to the repast which they had spread for him. Perched on a chair that had been carved to Ianyn measure, devouring honeycakes and laughing still at the servants' outraged propriety, he looked even younger than he was. He did not look like the son of the Sun.

He finished the last drippingly sweet cake, licked his fingers, and sighed. "I haven't eaten so well since I left Han-Gilen." The eldest servant bowed a degree. Mirain bowed half a degree in return, but lightly, smiling. "I commend your service, sirs."

It was a dismissal. They obeyed it, all but Vadin. He kept his post by the door and said nothing, and won his reward: Mirain let him be.

As soon as the men had gone, Mirain's face stilled. He no longer had the likeness of a child. Slowly he turned about, his right hand clenching and unclenching, his brows drawing together until he was the very likeness of the king his grandsire. His nose wrinkled very slightly. Vadin could guess why. Although the rooms to which the king's men had brought him were rich, clean and well swept, they breathed an air of long disuse. No feet but servants' feet had trod that splendid carpet out of Asanion in time out of mind; no one had leaned upon the window-frame as now he leaned, looking down into a sheltered garden or up over the luminous battlements to the mountains of Ianon.

He turned his hand palm up upon the casement. Flecks of blinding gold played over his face, over the walls and ceiling, into Vadin's eyes. They vanished as his fingers closed; he turned his eyes to the sun which had begotten them. "So, my lord," he said to it, "you led me here. Drove me, rather. What now? The king grieves, but he begins to rejoice, seeing in me the rebirth of his daughter. Shall I heed my fates and prophecies and his own command, and stay and be his death? Or shall I take flight while yet there is time? For you see, my lord, I think that I could love him."

Perhaps he gained an answer. If so it did not comfort him. He drew a long breath that caught sharply upon a wordless sound. A cry, a gasp of bitter laughter. "Oh aye, I could have refused. Han-Gilen would have kept me. I was no foreigner there for all my foreign face, eagle's shadow that it was amid all the red and brown and gold; I was the prince's fosterling, the priestess' child, the holy one, venerated and protected. Protected!" That was certainly laughter, and certainly bitter. "They were protecting me to death. At least if I die here, I die of my own folly 'and naught else."

He turned from the sun. His eyes were full of it, but it had no power to blind them. As they caught Vadin he started, as if he had forgotten the squire's presence. Probably, Vadin thought, he had hardly been aware of it at all, no more than he was aware of the floor under his feet.

Unless, of course, it rose and tripped him. His scrutiny was both leisurely and thorough, taking in the squire as if he had been a bullock at market. Noting with due interest the narrow beaky face with its uncertain young beard; the long awkward body in the king's livery; the spear grounded beside one foot, gripped with force enough to grey the prominent knuckles.

Mirain's eyes glinted. In scorn, Vadin knew. *His* body was hardly awkward at all, and he acted as if he knew it. He had a way of tilting his head that was both arrogant and seeming friendly, and a lift of the brows that a courtesan should have studied, it was so perfectly disarming. "My name is Mirain," he said, "as you've heard. What may I call you?"

Dismissed, Vadin wanted to snap. But training held. "Vadin, my lord. Vadin alVadin of Asan-Geitan."

Mirain leaned against the casement. "Geitan? That's in Imehen, is it not? Your father must be alVadin too; my mother told me that Geitan's lord is always Vadin, just as Ianon's king is always Raban like my grandfather, or Mirain."

Like this interloper. Vadin drew himself up the last possible fraction. "It is so, my lord."

"My mother also taught me to speak Ianyn. Not remarkably well, I fear; I've been too long in the south. Will you be my teacher, Vadin? I'm a disgrace as I am, with a face like mine and a Gileni princeling lisping out of it."

"You're not staying!" Vadin bit his tongue, too late. Adjan would see him flogged for this, even if the foreigner did not.

The foreigner did not even flinch. He took off the band of his Journey and turned it in his hands, and sighed faintly. "Maybe I should not. I'm an outlander here; my Journey is hardly a year old. But," he said, and his eyes flashed up, catching Vadin unawares. "there is still the geas that my mother laid upon me. To tell her father of her glory and her death; to comfort him as best I could. Those I have done. But then she commanded me to take her place, the place her vows and her fate had compelled her to abandon, for which she bore and trained me."

"She placed great trust in blood and in fate," a new voice said. Its owner came forward in the silence. A woman, tall and very slender, robed all in grey with silver at her throat, the garb of a sacred singer. Her face was as beautiful as her voice, and as cool, and as unreadable.

"So she did," said Mirain as coolly as she. "Was she not a seer?"

"Some would say that she was mad."

"As mad as her father, no doubt. As mad as I."

The woman stood before him. She was tall for a woman, even a woman of Ianon; his head came just to her chin. "My lord gave you her rooms. His own son has never had so much."

"You know who I am." It was not a question.

"By now most of the castle knows it. The servants have ears and tongues, and you have her face."

"But she was beautiful. Not even charity could call me that."

"All her beauty was in her eyes and in the way she moved. No carved or painted likeness could ever capture it."

"Nor any in flesh." He shook off the complaint with its air of long use, and regarded her, loosing a rare and splendid smile. "You would be Ymin."

Strong though she was, she was still a woman, and that smile held a mighty magic. Her eyes warmed; her face softened a very little. "She told you of me?"

"Often and often. How could she forget her foster sister? She hoped you would win your torque. The loveliest woman and the sweetest singer in Ianon, she said you would be. She was a true prophet."

Almost Ymin smiled. "Your own torque, my young lord, could as easily be silver as gold. Was it our blunt-spoken Sanelin who taught you such courtesy?"

"She taught me to speak the truth."

"Then the sweetness must be the legacy of Han-Gilen, which we singers call the Land of Honey."

"Sweet speech is certainly an art much valued there, although they value honor more. The worst of all sins, say they, is the Lie, and they raise their children to abhor it."

"Wise people. Strength is greatest here, of the body most often, of the will but little less. There is no place in the north for the gentle man or for the weakling."

"Hard as the stones of the north, they say in Han-Gilen."

Mirain turned back to the window. Ymin set herself beside him. He did not glance at her. "Why did you depart?" she asked him.

"It was time and past time, though my lord prince would have had me wait longer, till I had my growth and an army to ride with me. But the god has no care for manhood, or for the lack of it. I left in secret; I walked in secret until I had passed the borders of Han-Gilen. It was a very long way to go afoot, with winter coming and a long cruel war but lately ended." His voice changed, took on a hint of pride. "I fought in it; well, my lord said. I was his squire, with his son, the Prince-Heir Halenan. He made us both knights and armed us alike. I was sorry to leave them. And the princess, Halenan's sister . . . she helped me to slip away."

"Was she very beautiful?"

He stared at her, briefly speechless. "Elian? She was all of eight years old!"

Ymin's laughter was sudden and heart-deep, a ripple of pure notes. He frowned; unwillingly his lips twitched. "Maybe," he admitted, "someday she will be lovely. When I saw her last, she was dressed like a boy in ancient tattered breeches and a shirt of mine—much too large for her—and her hair never would stay in its braids. Still, that was splendid, like her father's and her brother's and no one else's in the world: red as fire. She was trying to look like a bold bad conspirator, but her eyes were all bleared with crying, and her nose was red, and she could hardly say a word." He sighed. "She was a living terror. When we rode off to war, we found her among our baggage. 'If Mirain can go,' she said, 'why can't I?' She was six years old. Her father gave her a royal tongue-lashing and sent her home in disgrace. But he gave his steward orders to have her taught weaponry. She had won, in her way, and she knew it."

"You loved, it seems," she said, "and were well loved."

"I have been fortunate."

She looked at him for a long moment. Her face had changed, grown cool again. "My lord, what will you do here?"

His hands rested on the casement, the fingers tightening until the knuckles greyed. "I will remain. When the time comes I will be king. The king who drives back the shadows, the son of the Sun."

"Your will is firm for one so young."

"My will has nothing to do with what must be." His tone was faintly bitter, faintly weary.

"The gods' love," she said slowly, "is a torment of fire."

"And a curse on all one cares for. Hold to your coldness against me, singer, if you would be wise."

She laid her hand upon his arm. Her eyes were clear again and steady upon him, as steady as her voice. "My lord, do you know truly what you are doing? Can you? Your mother raised you and trained you and commanded you to be what her fate had forbidden her to be, high ruler in Ianon. But the place for which she shaped you is twenty years gone."

"It is known even in far Han-Gilen that the King of Ianon has no chosen successor. That he awaits the return of his daughter."

"Is it also known that he keeps his vigil all but alone?" She spoke more rapidly, less calmly. "Kingdoms can rise and fall in a score of years. Babes then unborn have since borne children of their own. None of whom has any memory of a priestess who set forth on her Journey and never came back.

"But they do know, they do remember those who remained here. Your mother had a brother, my lord. He was a child when she left. Now he is a man and a prince, and his father has never let him forget that he is not judged worthy of the name of heir; that he is bastard seed, acknowledged, endured, even loved, but never equal to the one who is gone. Whereas to the people, who have no care for the passions of kings except as they breed war or peace, he is their sole and rightful prince. He has dwelt among them all his life; he is one of their own, and he is strong and fair, and he wields his lordship well enough. They love him."

"And I," said Mirain, "am a foreigner and an interloper, an upstart, a presumptuous stranger."

Vadin's thoughts to a word; the squire knew a stab of superstitious dread. And another of annoyance. All of it should be obvious to the merest child, which Mirain most certainly was not. He seemed undismayed by it. He was not stupid, Vadin was certain; very probably he was mad. It was in his blood.

He prowled the room, not precisely as if he were restless; it seemed to help him think. He was doing it again, that witch's trick of his, filling the wide space, towering over the two who watched him. When he halted and turned, he shrank a little. "Suppose I leave quietly, singer. Have you considered what that might do to the king? It could very easily kill him."

"It will kill him to have you here."

"One way or another." Mirain's head tilted. "You could be speaking for my enemies."

"If so," she said unruffled, "they have moved upon you with supernatural speed."

"It has happened to me before."

"Were you ever a child, my lord?"

He stood back on his heels, eyes wide and ingenuous. "Why, lady, what am I now but a babe scarce weaned?"

She dropped her mask and laughed aloud. It was not all mockery. Much of it was honest merriment. When it passed, her eyes danced still; she said, "You are a match for me, I think. You may even be a match for the whole of Ianon." She sobered fully. "When you are king, my lord, and more than king, will you let me make songs for you?"

"If I forbade it, would that prevent you?"

Ymin looked down, then up, a swift bright glance. "No, my lord."

He laughed half in pain. "You see what kingship I can claim, when not even a singer will obey me."

"When it comes to singing," she said, "I obey only the god."

"And your own will."

"That most certainly." She stepped away from the window. "The god calls me now to sing his office. Will you come?"

Mirain paused, a breath only. Then: "No. Not . . . quite yet."

She bowed her head slightly. "Then may he prosper you. Good day, my lord."

When she was gone, Mirain sent Vadin away. None too soon for the squire's peace of mind. He was soul-glad to be back among his own, comfortable, sane and human kind, driving his body until it was all one mindless ache. He drove himself so far that when Adjan called him out of the baths, he could only think that he had earned a reprimand somewhere on the practice field. That was terror enough, but he had survived the old soldier's discipline before. It was only pain; it passed, and everyone forgot it.

Adjan inspected his damply naked person with no expression that he could discern. In spite of himself he began to be afraid. When Adjan roared in rage, all was well. But when he was silent, then it was wisest to run.

Vadin could not be wise. He could not even cover his shriveling privates.

After an eternity the arms master said, "Dry yourself and report to me. Full livery. Without." he added acidly, "your spear."

Vadin dried himself and dressed with all the care his shaking hands could muster. He was beginning to think again, after a fashion. He kept seeing Mirain's face. Damn it, the foreigner had sent him away. Ordered him in no uncertain terms, and barred the door behind him. What had the little bastard done, brewed up a mess of sorceries over the bedroom hearth?

He braided his hair so tightly it hurt, flung the scarlet cloak over his shoulders, and went to face his master.

Adjan was standing in the cubicle that served him as both workroom and bedchamber. On the battered stool that the squires called the throne of judgment sat the king.

Vadin came very close to disgracing himself and all his house. Came within a twitch of turning and bolting, and if he had, he would not have stopped until he came to Imehen. Pride alone held him back, pride and Adjan's black grim stare. His body snapped itself to full attention, and stayed there while the king examined him. He was raw with all the scrutiny, and growing angry. Was he a prize-colt, that all these people should memorize his every line?

His majesty raised a brow—gods, precisely like Mirain—and said to Adjan, "He has promise, I grant you. But this demands performance."

"He can perform," the arms master said, no more smoothly or politely than he ever did. "Are you questioning my judgment?"

"I am pointing out that this task would challenge a seasoned soldier, let alone a boy in his first year of service."

"And I say that's to his advantage. He'll keep up his training; he'll simply be assigned to a different duty."

"Day and night, Captain. Whatever befalls."

"Maybe nothing."

"Maybe death. Or worse."

"He's young; he's brighter than he looks; and he's resilient. Where an older man would break, he'll bend and spring back stronger than before. I say he's the best choice, sire. You won't find a better in the time you're allowing."

The king stroked his beard, frowning at Vadin, hardly seeing him except as a tool for the task. Whatever it was. Vadin's heart was pounding. Something high and perilous; some great and glorious deed, as in the songs. For that his father had sent him here. For that he had prayed. He was no longer afraid; he was ready to sing.

"Vadin of Geitan," the king said at last, his voice like drums beating, "your commander has persuaded me. You shall continue to train among my squires, but you are no longer in my service. Henceforth you are the liege man of the Prince Mirain."

Vadin was not hearing properly. No longer serving the king—serving the prince—Moranden? There was only one prince in the castle. There could not be—

"Mirain," said the king relentlessly, "stands in need of a good and loyal man. He has come late and all unlooked for; he is godly wise, but I do not think that he knows truly what he faces here. I call on you to be his guide and his guard."

High. Honorable. Perilous. Vadin wanted to laugh. Nursemaid to a priestess' bastard. He would dare death, oh yes, death by stoning or poison when Ianon turned against the upstart.

The king was not asking him to choose. He was a thing; a servant. A half-trained hound, mute and helpless while his master handed his lead to a new owner.

No, he thought. *No.* He would speak. He would stalk away. Go home, no, he could not do that to his father or his poor proud mother, but maybe the prince would take him. The true prince, the man who had time to smile at a guard or to speak to a squire in the market or to greet a boy coming new and homesick and scared into a city greater than he had ever dreamed of. Moranden had taken the edge off his terror, made him feel like a lord and a kinsman, and better yet, remembered him thereafter. Moranden would be glad of his service.

"Go now," the king said. "Guard my grandson."

Vadin gathered himself to cry out. Found himself bowing low, mute, obedient. Went as, and where, he was commanded.

The foreigner was gone. For a blissful instant Vadin knew that he had changed his mind; he had escaped while he could. Then Vadin thought to go to the window Mirain had seemed so fond of, and there were the braid and the torque and the girl-smooth face, exploring the garden. Vadin took a long moment to steel himself. At last he went down.

Mirain had folded himself on the grass, bent over his cupped hands. When Vadin's shadow blocked the sun he looked up. "See," he said, raising his hands a little, carefully. Something fluttered in them, small and vividly blue, with a flash of scarlet at the throat and on the iridescent wings. The dragonel scaled the pinnacle of Mirain's forefinger and coiled there, wings beating gently for balance. Mirain laughed softly. The creature echoed him four octaves higher. With blurring suddenness it took wing, darting away into a tangle of fruitthorn.

Mirain stretched and sighed and smiled his sudden smile. "I never thought northerners were a folk for gardens."

"We're not," Vadin tried an insolence; he dropped beside the other, full livery and all. Mirain chose to pay no attention. "The king had it made for the yellow woman—for the queen. She pined amid all our bare stone. Herdfields weren't enough, and the women's courts were too severe with their herbs and such. She had to have flowers." His lip curled a little as he said it.

"The yellow woman," Mirain repeated. "Poor lady, she died before my mother could know her. I understand that she was very beautiful but very fragile, like a flower herself."

"So the singers say."

Mirain plucked a scarlet blossom. He had small hands for a man, but the fingers were long and tapering, with a touch as delicate as a girl's. They closed over the flower. When they opened they cupped a hard green fruit. It ripened swiftly, darkening and swelling and speckling with gold.

He held the thornfruit under Vadin's nose. Thornfruit in spring, real as his own staring eyes, with its sweet potent scent, its suggestion of a blush. "Yes," said Mirain, "I am a mage, a born master; I need no spells to work my magics, only a firm will."

A sun kindled in his hand. The fruit vanished. Mirain clasped his knees, and rocked, and regarded Vadin, and waited. For what? Abject submission? Cowering terror?

"Plain acceptance," the mage said, dry as old leaves.

Vadin gave him red rage. "Get out of my mind!"

Mirain raised a cheer. "Bravo, Vadin! Obey my grandfather, endure me, but keep your rebellion alive. I do detest a servile servant."

"Why?" demanded Vadin. "One word of power and I'm your ensorceled slave."

"Why?" Mirain echoed him. "By the king's orders you're mine already." He sat erect, suddenly grim. "Vadin alVadin, I do not accept unwilling service. For one thing, it hurts my head. For another, it's an invitation to assassination. But I will not stoop to win your willingness with my power. If your loyalties lie elsewhere, go to them. I can settle matters with the king."

Vadin's anger changed as Mirain spoke. He had been close to hate. He was still, but to a different side of it, a side much closer to his pride. Instead of roaring or howling or striking out, he heard himself say coldly, "You're a supercilious little bastard, do you know that?"

"I can afford to be," Mirain answered.

Vadin laughed in spite of himself. "Sure you can. You're planning to be king of the world." He stood and planted his hands on his hips. "What makes you think you can get rid of me? I'm a good squire, my lord. I served my master loyally; my master gave me to you. Now I'm your man. Your loyal man, my lord."

Mirain's eyes widened and fixed; his chin came up. "I refuse your service, sir."

"I refuse your refusal, my lord." *I am an idiot, my very unwelcome lord.*

"You most certainly are." That stopped Vadin short; Mirain grinned like a direwolf. "Very well, sir defiance. You are my man, and may the god have mercy on your soul."

Three

THE KING'S SUMMONS CAME AT EVENING, AND WITH it a robe of honor, royal white embroidered with scarlet and gold. Someone had been cutting and stitching: it fit Mirain admirably. He preened in it, vain as a sunbird; and he did look well. He had his hair braided differently, Ianyn prince's braid, although he had not let the servant add the twist that marked the royal heir. "I'm not that yet," he said, "and I may never be."

Vadin restrained a snort, which Mirain pretended not to hear. The servant struggled with the heavy black mane. Freed, it was as outrageous as its bearer's moods; it curled with abandon, and it had a life of its own, a will to escape the grimly patient fingers and run wild down Mirain's back. A brand of his Asanian blood, like his smallness, like his dancer's grace.

At last the servant won his battle. Mirain applauded him; young man that he was, he broke into a smile, swiftly controlled. It was almost amusing to see how easily these bondmen fell into Mirain's hand. His glittering golden hand.

The king sat enthroned in the great hall with before and below him the lords and chieftains of his court, gathered for the evening feast. He rose as Mirain entered; the rest rose perforce, a royal greeting.

Mirain stood straight in the face of it and met the old king's gaze, that was dark and keen and quietly exultant, filled with a welcome as fierce as it was joyous. "Mirain of Han-Gilen," he said in a ringing voice, "son of my daughter. Come, sit by me; share the honor of the feast."

Mirain bowed and advanced down the long hall through a spreading silence. His back was erect, his chin up. Unconsciously Vadin, following in his wake, matched his bearing and his steadiness.

The king's hand clasped Mirain's and set him to the right of the throne, in a seat but little lower. The heir's place. Eyes glittered; voices murmured. Not in thrice seven years had that chair been filled.

Mirain sat very still in it, as if the slightest movement might send him leaping into flight. Vadin could almost taste his tension. Surely he had planned for this. But now that he had it, it seemed he was human enough to have a doubt or two. His fist had clenched in his lap. A muscle had knotted in his jaw. He raised his chin another degree, to imperial hauteur, and held it there.

The king sat beside him. A sigh ran through the hall as the court returned to their seats. Their lord raised a hand.

The door of the hall flew open. Figures filled it. Prince Moranden strode through them, resplendent in scarlet and in mountain copper. Tall even for a northerner and broad with it, he towered above the seated nobles. The men with him, lords, warriors, servants, passed insubstantial as shadows. But their eyes gleamed.

He stalked to the dais and halted before the king. "Your pardon for my lateness, sire. The hunt kept me away longer than I had looked for."

The king sat too still, spoke too gently. "Sit then, and let the feast begin."

"Ah, Father," Moranden said, "you waited for me. It was courteous, but you had no need."

"Indeed, sir, we did not. Will you sit?"

Still the prince lingered. As if for the first time, his eyes found Mirain. Stopped; widened. They were all innocent surprise, and yet Vadin's blood ran cold from heart to clenched fists. "What, Father! A guest? You do him great honor." His eyes narrowed; his lips thinned. "Nay, nay, I had forgotten. The boy who came this morning, the little priest from the south with the news we've all dreaded for so long. Shouldn't we be mourning instead of feasting?"

"One does not mourn a priestess whom the god has taken to himself." Mirain's voice was soft and steady, but higher than it should have been, the voice of a boy just come to manhood. It was well feigned. A stranger would have heard the youthful tenor with its hint of uncertainty, as if it would break on the next word, and seen the clear-skinned beardless face, and taken it all for what it seemed.

It seemed that Moranden did. His tension eased. The fire of wrath sank to an ember, swiftly banked in ash. He walked easily around the dais to settle beside the heir's place. It was not his wonted seat. Even in the lower chair he dwarfed his sister-son. "Well, lad," he said with hearty good humor, "are you pleased with the hospitality of Han-Ianon?"

"I am well content," Mirain answered him, as ingenuous as he, "and pleased to greet you at last, uncle."

"Uncle?" asked Moranden. "Are we kin?"

"Through my mother. Your sister Sanelin. Is it not her place I sit in?"

Moranden had taken half a loaf of bread and begun to break it. It crumbled in his tensed fingers, falling unheeded to his plate. "So," he said, "that's what kept her. Who was her lover? A prince? A beggar? Some fellow pilgrim?"

"No mortal man."

"I suppose everyone believed that. At least until she died. Or did they kill her?"

"They did not." Mirain turned slightly, with an effort Vadin could just see; he took up a bit of meat and began slowly to eat it.

"She left you alone then," Moranden said, "and you came to us. Not much welcome anywhere for a priestess' bastard, is there?"

"I am not a bastard." Mirain's voice was as calm as ever, but it had dropped an octave.

The king stirred at his left hand. "Enough," he said, low and harsh. "I will not have you coming to blows in my hall."

Moranden lounged in his seat. "Blows, Father? I was only exchanging courtesies with my sister's son. If so he is. Ianon is a rich prize for an ambitious wanderer."

"I do not lie," Mirain said in his proper tone at last. His nostrils were pinched tight below the haughty arch of his nose.

"Enough!" rapped the king. Suddenly he smote his hands together.

Although Ymin had sat among the court, she had not been eating with them. She rose now with fluid grace and went to a low seat which the servants had set before the dais. As she sat, one handed her an instrument, a small harp of golden wood with strings of silver.

It was common enough that she should sing so in hall. But this was a new song. It began softly as a hymn of praise to the rising sun. Then, as the court quieted, caught by the melody, she changed to a stronger mode, that half-chant which told the deeds of gods and heroes. A god tonight, the high god, Avaryan whose face was the sun; and a priestess, royal born; and the son who came forth from their loving, born at the rising of the daystar, god's child, prince, Lord of the Sun.

Mirain forsook even his feeble efforts to eat. His fists clenched upon the table in front of him; his face set, expressionless.

Silence was strange after the long singing. The king's voice broke it, concealing no longer his deep joy. "As Avaryan is my witness," he said, "it is so. Behold the prince, Mirain alAvaryan, son of my daughter, son of the Sun. Behold the heir of Ianon!"

Hardly had the echoes died when a young lord leaped up: Hagan, who would embrace any cause if only it were new enough to catch his fancy. And this cause was the king's own. "Mirain!" he cried. "Avaryan's son, heir of Ianon. Mirain!"

One by one, then all together, the court joined in his cry. The hall rang with their homage. Mirain rose to meet it, raising the fire of his hand, loosing his sudden, fierce elation. The old king smiled. But Moranden scowled blackly into his wine, as all his hopes vanished, shattered in that great wave of sound.

Four

VADIN OPENED HIS EYES AT THE STROKE OF THE
dawn bell. For a moment he could not imagine where he was. It
was too quiet. None of the muted clamor of the squires' barracks, growing not so muted as the more vigorous pummeled the sluggards out of
bed. Nor ever the warm nest of his brothers in Geitan, with Kerin's arm
thrown over him, and Cuthan burrowed into his side like an overgrown
pup, and a hound or four doing service for the blankets that the baby,
Silan, had a way of stealing for himself. Vadin was very much alone,
cold where his blanket had slipped, and surrounded by unfamiliar walls.
Walls that glowed like clouds over Brightmoon. He peered at them.

A figure barred them. Memory flooded. Mirain stared down at him as
he lay abed in his new room, a fold of the wall between the prince's
bedchamber and the outer door. He scowled back. His liege lord was
dressed in kilt and short cloak, girded with his southern sword, with no
jewel but the torque he wore even to sleep. Much as he had drunk, late
as he had feasted, he seemed as fresh as if he had slept from sunset to
sunrise. "Come," he said, "up. Would you sleep the sun to his nooning?"

Vadin sprang erect, scouring the sleep out of his eyes. Mirain held up
a kilt, the king's scarlet livery. He snatched it. "You are not to do that!"

Mirain let him wrap it and belt it, but when he looked up again he
saw a comb in the prince's hand and a gleam in the prince's eye. He
leaped; Mirain eluded him with animal ease, then startled him speech-

less by setting the comb in his hand and saying, "Be quick, or I'll keep no breakfast for you."

A squire did not eat with his lord, still less share a plate and a cup. "The servants have a thing or two to learn," Mirain observed as he passed the latter.

"My lord, you are not to—"

The bright eyes flashed up. "Do you command me, Vadin of Geitan?"

Vadin stiffened. "I am a squire. You," he said, "are Throne Prince of Ianon."

"So." Mirain's head tilted. "Formality is easier, is it not? A servant need have no feeling for the man he serves. Only for the title."

"I am loyal to my lord. He need have no fear of treachery."

"And no hope of binding you with friendship."

Vadin swallowed past the stone in his throat. "Friendship must be earned," he said. "My lord."

The prince rose slowly. He had no excess of inches to make him awkward. His body fit itself; he moved with the grace and economy of an Ishandri dancer. A little tight now, like his face, like his voice. "I would explore my grandsire's castle. May the throne prince take that liberty?"

"The throne prince may do as he pleases."

Mirain's brows went up. With no more warning than that, he strode to the door. Vadin had to scramble for cloak and sword and dagger, and don them at a run.

At this hour only squires and servants were awake. The high ones liked their sleep after a hard night's feasting, and the king never left his rooms until the last bell before sunrise, when he mounted to the battlements. Save that this morning he had no need to stand watch; Vadin wondered if he would, by sheer force of custom.

Han-Ianon's fortress was very large and very intricate, a labyrinth of courts and passages, halls and chambers and gardens and outbuildings, towers and dungeons, barracks and kitchens and the eunuch-guarded stronghold of the women. Only the last eluded Mirain's scrutiny, and that, Vadin suspected, only for the moment. Mirain approached the guard, a creature less epicene than most of Odiya's monsters, who might almost have been a man but for the too-smooth face; but the prince did not either speak or attempt to pass. He simply looked at the eunuch, who retreated with infinite slowness until he could retreat no more, for the door was at his back. The prince's face wore no expression at all.

Still without a word, Mirain turned on his heel. Afar atop the tower of the priests, a single piercing voice hymned the sunrise.

Mirain descended through the Chain of Courts to the outer ward and the stables of the castle. There at last the tension began to leave him. He brightened as he wandered down the long lines of stalls, among the grooms whose high calling left no time for gaping at princes, past broodmares and colts in training, hunters and racing mares and chariot teams, and, set apart, the great fierce battlestallions each in his armored stall. Here and there he paused. He had a good eye for senel-flesh, Vadin granted him that. He ignored the haughty spotted mare for the drab little dun stalled beside her, making much of that least prepossessing and most swift of all the king's mares. He stood his ground when Prince Moranden's stallion menaced him with sharpened horns, and the tall striped dun retreated in confusion. He persuaded the whitehorn bay to take a tidbit from his hand.

As he turned from the bay to Vadin, he was close to smiling. "Show me yours," he said.

Vadin had not known how disarmed he was, and how easily, until he found himself standing in the lesser aisle among the squire's mounts. His own grey Rami lazed hipshot midway down the line. Her rump was only a little less bony than his own; but the tassel of her tail was full and silken, and her legs were long and fine, and her neck was serpent-supple as it curved about, the long ears pricked, the silver eyes mild. Vadin melted under that limpid regard.

"She is beautiful," Mirain said.

Vadin congealed into temper. "Her ears are too long. She's ribby. She toes out behind."

"But her gaits are silk and her heart is gold." Mirain was beside her, and she was suffering him to touch her. Even her head. Even her quivering ears. She blew gently into the foreigner's shoulder; and Vadin knew his heart would burst with jealousy.

"She is mine!" he almost shouted. "I raised her from a foal. No one else has ever sat on her back. Last year she won the Great Race in Imehen, from Anhei to Morajan between sunrise and noon, and straight into the melee after, where all the boys vied to become men. She never faltered. Never once. Even against horned stallions."

Mirain's hand had found one of the scars, the worst one, that furrowed her neck from poll to shoulder. "And what was the price of that?" he asked.

"She tore out the beast's throat." Vadin shivered, remembering: the blood, and the stallion's dying scream, and gentle Rami wilder with war than with pain. She had carried him to the victory, and he had hardly noticed. He had been too desperate with fear for her.

"Ianon's seneldi are famous even in the Hundred Realms," Mirain said, "for their beauty and their strength, and for their great valor."

"I've seen southern stock." Vadin did not dignify them with a sneer. "A trader from Poros used to haunt Geitan. Every year he'd come. Every year he'd pay emeralds for our culls. Geldings, and now and then a stallion the gelders hadn't got to. One year he tried to steal a mare. After that we made sure he didn't come back."

"My mother said a Ianyn lord could forgive the murder of his first-born son, if properly persuaded. But never the theft of a senel."

"Firstborn sons are much less rare than good seneldi."

"True enough," said Mirain. Vadin could not tell if he was jesting. He bade Rami a courteous farewell, left the stall, looked about. The aisle led into waxing morning, the stableyard and a paddock or two, and the training rings. One or two colts were out, but Mirain did not tarry to watch them. He had heard what the squires called the morning hymn: the belling of a stallion and the hammering of hoofs on wood and stone, and piercing through it at intervals, a shrill scream of seneldi rage.

Mirain advanced unerringly to the source: in a corner of the wall a high fence, and within that a small stone hut. Its windows were barred. Triple bolts warded the door, trembling under the ceaseless crashing blows.

"The Mad One," Vadin said before Mirain could ask. "The stable used to belong to the king stallion when he came up from the fields to cover the king's own mares. But the old herdlord died in the spring, and there'll not be another till the last of this year's foals is born. Meanwhile the Mad One has a prison to himself. He's the king's own, bred from the best of the herds, and my lord had high hopes for him: he's as fast as a mare, but he has a stallion's strength, and his horns are an ell long already. But he's proven to be a rogue. He killed a stablehand before they locked him up. If he's not tamed by High Summer, he'll be given to the goddess."

"Sacrificed." Mirain's voice was thick with revulsion. The Sun's priests did not worship their god with blood. He leaned on the gate. Within the prison the Mad One shrilled his wrath.

Before Vadin could move, the prince was over the fence, running toward the hut.

Vadin flung himself in pursuit. And struck a wall he could not see. It held fast against him, rage though he would, and left him powerless to do more than watch.

Mirain had shot the threefold bolts. As the door burst open, he sprang aside. The Mad One hurtled out, foaming, tossing his splendid mane. He was more than beautiful. He was breathtaking: an emperor of seneldi, long and slender of leg, deep of chest, with the arched neck and the lean small-muzzled head of the Ianyn breed. His horns were straight and keen as twin swords; his hoofs were honed obsidian, his coat a black fire. His great flaw was Mirain's own. He was not tall for one of his kind. But he was tall enough, and he was wonderful to see. Wonderful and deadly.

He halted a scant handspan from the fence and wheeled snorting. His eye rolled, red as blood, red as madness. It fixed upon the one who stood by the open door. His lean ears flattened. His head lowered, horns armed for battle. He charged.

One moment Mirain stood full in his path. The next, the prince was gone, the senel eluding the wall with speed more of cat than of herd-creature. Mirain's laughter was sharp and wild. The Mad One spun toward it. The prince advanced slowly, with no sign of fear. He was smiling; grinning, daring the stallion to touch him. The horns missed him by a hair's breadth. The sharp cloven hoofs slashed only air.

The Mad One stood still. His nostrils flared, scarlet as his eyes. He tossed his head and stamped, as if to demand, *How dare you be unafraid of me?*

"How dare I indeed?" Mirain shot back. "You are no madder than I, and far less royal. For you are the son of the dawn wind, but I am the son of the Sun."

Black lightning struck where he stood. He was not there. He stood with hand on hip, breathing easily, unshaken. "Do you threaten me, sir? Are you so bold? Come now, be sensible. You may have been stolen away from your old kingdom, but that was only to set you in a greater one. Would you not be my king of stallions?"

A stamp; a snort; a feint.

Mirain did not move, save that his head came up. *"I* should come to *you* with a hundred mares behind me? Does an emperor bear tribute to a vassal king?" He stepped forward well within reach of hoof and horn. The Mad One had only to rear and strike, to cut him down. "I should not trouble myself with you. There are seneldi in the barns yonder who would give their souls to bear me on their backs. But you are a king. Royalty, even in exile, demands its share of respect."

The Mad One surveyed him in something close to bafflement. He touched the velvet muzzle. The stallion quivered, but neither nipped nor pulled away. His hand traveled upward to the roots of the horns, resting lightly upon the whorl of hair between them. "Well, my lord? Shall we be kings together?"

Slowly the proud head bowed, sniffed at the golden hand, blew upon it.

Mirain drew closer still. Suddenly he was astride. The Mad One stood frozen, then reared, belling. The prince laughed. He was still laughing as the senel came down running, leaped the high fence, and hurtled through the stableyard. Men and animals scattered before them.

"The Mad One!" a deep voice bellowed. "The Mad One is loose!"

"Which one?" muttered Vadin. Sourly; but with a touch—a very reluctant touch—of admiration.

They met the king coming down from the hall, while behind them eddied a turbulent crowd. The Mad One came to a dancing halt; Mirain bowed to his grandsire. "I've found a friend, my lord," he said.

Vadin was as close as anyone dared to go: just out of reach of the stallion's heels. He would almost rather have been closer still than face the king's cold accusing eye. But that was fixed on Mirain, and on the senel who, untaught, bore his rider with ease and grace; whose mien had lost not a whit of either its pride or its wildness.

The coldness warmed. The thin lips twitched just perceptibly. "A friend indeed, grandson, and a great lord of seneldi. But I fear you will have to look after him yourself. No man will come near him."

"No longer," Mirain said, "if only none ventures to ride him. For after all, he is a king."

"After all," the king agreed with a touch of irony, "he is."

"We go now into the Vale. Will you come with us, sire?"

The king's smile won free, startling as the sun at midnight, and more miraculous. "Certainly I shall. Hian, saddle my charger. I ride forth with the prince."

From a tower of the castle Moranden saw them: the boy on the black stallion without bridle or saddle, and the old king on the red destrier, and a tangle of lords and servants and hangers-on. His knuckles greyed as he gripped the window ledge. "Priestess' bastard," he gritted through clenched teeth.

"That is most unkind."

He whirled upon Ymin. "Unkind? *Unkind?* You have all you can ask for. All your prophecies fulfilled, new songs to sing, and a pretty lad to pleasure your eye. But I—I have had a kingdom snatched from my hands."

"You never had it," she pointed out serenely, sitting cross-legged on his bed.

"I did when that whelp bewitched my father."

"Your father never named you his heir."

"And who else would there have been?"

She spread her hands. "Who knows? But Mirain has come. He is the god's son, Moranden. Of that I am certain."

"So you've come to gloat over me."

"No. To make you see sense. That boy can tame the Mad One. What could he not do to you?"

"No beggar's by-blow can snare me with spells."

"Moranden," she said with sudden, passionate urgency, "he is the one. The king foretold. Accept him. Yield to him."

He stood over her and seized her roughly, shaking her. "I yield to no one. Not to you, and not ever to a bastard boy."

"He is your sister's son."

"My sister!" he spat. "Sanelin, Sanelin, always Sanelin. Look, Moranden, look at your sister, how proud, how queenly, how very, very holy. Come, lad, be strong; when your sister comes back, would you have her be ashamed of you? Ah, Sanelin, dear lady, where has she gone? So long, so far, and never a true word." He spat again, as if to rid his tongue of a foulness. "Who ever took any notice of me? I was only Moranden, the afterthought, begotten on a captive. She was the loved one. She was the heir. She—woman and half-breed and priestess that she was—*she* would have Ianon. And for me, nothing. No throne, no kingdom. Nothing at all."

"Except honor and lordship and all the wealth you could wish for."

"*Nothing,*" he repeated with vicious softness.

Ymin was silent. He laughed, a hideous, strangled sound. "Then she died. I heard the news; I went away in secret and danced the fiercest joy-dance I knew; I dreamed of my kingdom. And now he comes, that puny child, claiming all she had. All. With such utter, absolute, unshakable certainty that he has the right—" Moranden broke off, flinging up his head. "Shall I bow to that interloper? Shall I endure what I have endured for all the years of my manhood? By all the gods and the powers below, I will not!"

"You are a fool." Ymin's voice was soft, edged with contempt. "Your mother on the other hand, whose words you parrot so faithfully—she is mad. In Han-Ianon even we women cut our leading-strings when our breasts begin to bud. No doubt it is different in the Marches." She broke free and rose. "I go to serve my prince. If you assail him, expect no mery from me. He is my lord as you have never been, nor ever will be."

Five

IN HAN-GILEN AND IN THE LANDS OF THE SOUTH ruled but one high god, the Lord of Light. But in the north the old ways held firm, the cult not of the One but of the Two, the Light coeval and coequal with his sister the Dark: Avaryan and Uveryen, Sun and Shadow, bound and battling for all eternity. Each had his priests and each his sacrifices. For Avaryan, the holy fire and the chants of praise; but for his sister, darkness and silence and the blood of chosen victims.

Avaryan's worship centered in his temples about his gold-torqued priesthood. Uveryen suffered no walls or images. Her realm was the realm of air and darkness, her priests chosen and consecrated in secret, masked and cowled and eternally nameless. In her holy groves and in the deep places of the earth they practiced her mysteries; nor ever did they suffer a stranger's presence.

Vadin crouched behind a stone, willing even his heart to be silent. It was a long cruel way from the castle to the place of the goddess, the wood upon the mountain spur where no axe had ever fallen. A long way, the last and worst of it on foot with all the stealth of his hunter's training, and before him one who was a better hunter than he. But Prince Moranden had not been looking for pursuit. He had ridden out quietly with a hawk on his wrist, as if for a solitary hunt; none but Vadin had seen him go, or dared to follow.

Whatever Moranden's thoughts of the one who had supplanted him, before men's faces he smiled and did proper obeisance. And stayed away as often as he might on one pretext or another. Hunting most often, or hawking, or governing his domains, for he was Lord of the Western Marches. Vadin had neither right nor duty to creep after him like a spy or an assassin. But Mirain had gone where Vadin could not follow, into Avaryan's temple. It was a day of fasting for the Sun's priests, the dark of Brightmoon, when the god's power grew weak before the might of the Dark; they would chant and pray from sunrise to sunrise, bolstering their god's strength with their own. Mirain, who had gone on his second day in the castle to chant the sunset hymn, had found himself more welcome there than anywhere else in Ianon, except perhaps in his grandfather's presence; thereafter he had sought the temple as often as he might. And he had made it clear that Vadin was not to dog his heels there, even in the outer chambers which were open to any who came.

Thus Vadin was at liberty, and by hell's own contriving he could take no joy in it. Mirain was already gone when he woke in the dawn; woke from a nightmare that haunted him long past waking. He rose, pulled on what garments came to hand, eyed with utterly unwonted disfavor the breakfast that Mirain's servants had left for him. He abandoned it untouched, wandering he cared not where, until he found himself in the stables; and saw Moranden saddling the black-barred dun.

Without thought for what he did, Vadin flung bridle and saddle on Rami and sent her in pursuit. If he had been thinking, he might have acknowledged some deep urge to accost this prince who had been kind to him. To be kind in return, somehow. To explain a betrayal that, doubtless, Moranden had never noticed among so many others.

Moranden had ridden easily but swiftly, without undue stealth, almost straight to the wood. No one hunted there if he valued his life and his soul, nor did anyone ride for pleasure beneath those dim trees. The prince had not loosed his falcon, and he had not turned back even from the guardians of the goddess' grove, and black birds which seemed to infest every branch. The air was full of their cries, the ground of their foul droppings.

Vadin shuddered in his place of concealment. Whether Moranden's intrusion had obscured his own, or whether he had moved more skillfully than he knew, the birds paid him no heed. Yet the wood itself seemed to tremble in outrage. Outlander that he was, bound by the king's command to the son of the Sun, still he dared to trespass in the domain of the Dark. The sky was black with thunder, casting deep twilight under the trees, where one by one the goddess' birds had settled to their rest.

Moranden stood a short spearcast from him, near the edge of a clearing. Open though it was, the darkness seemed no less there. The ground was bare, without grass or flower, save in the center where lay a slab of stone. Rough, hewn by no man's hands, it rose out of the barren earth; a great mound of flowers lay upon it, deep red like heart's blood. A mockery, it may have been, of the blossoms which adorned Avaryan's temple at this season of his waxing power.

Or was Avaryan's altar the mockery?

Again Vadin shivered. This was no place and no worship of his. Northern born, he feared the goddess and accorded her due respect, but he had never been able to love her. Love before Uveryen was a weakness. She fed on fear and on the bitterness of hate.

Moranden stood as if frozen, his falcon motionless upon his wrist, his stallion tethered at the wood's edge far from swift escape. Vadin could not see his face. His shoulders were braced, the muscles taut between them; his free hand was a fist.

The dim air stirred and thickened. Vadin swallowed a cry. Where had been only emptiness stood a half circle of figures. Black robes, black cowls, no face, no hand, no glimpse of brightness. Nor did they speak, these priests of the goddess. Or priestesses? There was no way to tell.

One glided forward. Moranden trembled, a sudden spasm, but held his ground. Perhaps he could not do otherwise.

Wings clapped. The falcon erupted from his hand, jesses broken. Blackness swept over it. A single feather fell, wintry gold, spiraling to Moranden's feet.

The birds of the goddess withdrew. Neither blood nor bone remained of the hawk, not even the bells upon its jesses.

"A pleasant morsel."

The voice was harsh and toneless. Vadin, glancing startled at the robed figure, saw upon its shoulder a black bird. Its beak opened. "A sufficient sacrifice," it said, "for the moment. What do you look for in return?"

Moranden's hand was raised as if the falcon perched even yet upon it. Very slowly he lowered it. "What—" His speech was thick; he shook his head hard and lifted it, drawing a long breath. "I look for nothing. I came as I was summoned. Is there to be no rite? Have I lost my best falcon for nothing?"

"There will be a rite." A mortal voice, this one, and not born within the circle. One stood beyond it, beyond the altar itself, robed as the rest. But her cowl was cast back from a face neither young nor gentle, beautiful and terrible as the flowers on the stone. "There will be a rite," she repeated, comming forward, "and you shall be the Young God once more. But only once. Hereafter we will have done with pretense, and with the blood of mere mute beasts."

The black bird left its perch to settle upon her shoulder. She smoothed its feathers with a finger, crooning to it.

Moranden stood taut, but it was a different tautness, with less of fear, less of awe, and more of impatience. "Pretense? What do you mean, pretense? That *is* the rite: the dance, the coupling. The sacrifice."

"The sacrifice," she said, "yes."

His breath hissed between his teeth. "You don't—" Her hand raised infinitesimally, sketching a flick of assent. "That is forbidden."

"By whom?" She stood full before him now, the bird motionless, eyes glittering. "By whom, Moranden? By the priests of burning Avaryan, and by the king who is their puppet. He gave his daughter to the Sun, who by long custom should have gone to the Dark. But in the end the goddess had her blood."

"Then the goddess should be content."

"Gods are never content."

Moranden's back was stiff. "So then. Once more I act the Young God; but it will be no act. I would have preferred that you had warned me."

Surely this woman was the Lady Odiya, and she was more terribly splendid even than rumor made her. She seemed torn between rage and bitter laughter. "You are a fine figure of a man, my child, and much to the Lady's taste. But you are also a fool. Once more, I have said, you act the god's part. Then do you abdicate in another's favor. Another will undergo the full and ancient rite."

"And die in it," Moranden said harshly. "I don't like it, Mother. Time was when every ninth year a young man died for the good of the tribe; and maybe the tribe was the better for it. Myself, I doubt it. Waste is waste, even in the gods' name."

"Fool," said the Lady Odiya. Once again the black bird shifted. Its talons gripped Moranden's shoulder. Its beak clacked beside his ear as he stood frozen, robbed of breath and arrogance alike. "Sacrifice is never wasted. Not when it can purchase the goddess' favor."

"It is murder."

"Murder," echoed the bird, mocking him. "Man," it said, "would you be king?"

"I would be king," Moranden answered; and that was not the least courageous thing he had ever done, to speak in a steady voice with such a horror on his shoulder. "But what does that have to do with—"

The bird pecked him very, very lightly a hair's breadth from his eye. His head jerked; his hand flew up. "Man," said the bird, arresting the hand in midflight, "you would be king. What would you give to gain the throne?"

"Anything," gritted Moranden. "Anything at all. Except—"

The beak poised like a dagger. *"Except,* man?"

"Except my honor. My soul," he said, "you may have. My life even, if you must."

"The goddess asks none of these. Yet. She asks only this. Give her your sister's son."

Moranden must have known what the creature would ask. Yet he stood as if stunned, bereft of speech.

His mother spoke softly, almost gently. "Give her the boy. Give her the being you hate most in this world, the one who has snatched your throne and your kingdom and given you naught but his scorn. Let him usurp your place but once more; let him die for you. Then you shall be king."

Moranden's eyes clenched shut; his mouth opened, half gasp, half cry. "No!"

The bird tightened its claws until blood welled, vivid upon the bare shoulder. He paid no heed to the pain. "I will have the throne, and very likely I'll have to kill the little bastard to get it. But not this way. Not creeping about in the dark."

Odiya had drawn herself to her full height. "Creeping, Moranden? Is it so you see me? Is it so you have looked on all your life of worship? Have I borne an apostate to destroy us all?"

"I'm a warrior, not a woman or a priest. I do my killing in the daylight where men can see it."

"He is a priest!" cried the queen who was not. "He is a sorcerer, a mage born. While you prate of honor and of war, he will witch you into the shadows you despise, and destroy you."

But Moranden was not to be swayed. "So be it. At least I'll die with my honor intact."

"Honor, Moranden? Is it honor to bow to him? Will you die his slave, you who are the only son of Ianon's king? Will you let him set his foot upon your neck?"

"I cannot—" Moranden's breath caught, almost a sob. "It's infamy. To sell—even—that—to betray my own blood."

"Even," the bird said, "to be king?"

"I was meant to be king! I was born—"

"So too was he."

Moranden's lips clamped upon wrath.

"He is mightier than you," said the bird. "He is the one foretold: the Sunborn, the god-king who shall bring all the world beneath his sway and turn all men to the worship of Avaryan. Beside him you are but a shadow, an empty posturer who dares to fancy himself worthy of a throne."

"He is a bastard child," Moranden spat with sudden venom.

"He is the son of the Sun."

Moranden ground his teeth.

"Foreigner and interloper though he is, all Ianon pays him homage. Its people are learning to love him; its beasts fawn before him; its very stones bow beneath his feet. *Lord,* they call him; *king* and *emperor,* godbegotten, prince of the morning."

"I hate him," grated Moranden. "I—hate—"

The bird's beak clashed; its wings stretched. "When we have him," it said, "you shall be king."

Moranden raised his fists. "No. You want him, you fetch him yourself. But be quick, or I'll have him. My way. None other. Or die. And be damned to all your treacheries!"

Sharply, viciously, the bird stabbed his cheek, driving deep through flesh into bone. Moranden's head snapped back. The bird sprang into the air. "Damned!" it shrieked. "Lost and damned!"

The wood was a tumult of wings and voices, sharp talons and cold mocking eyes. And beneath it, a sound as beautiful as it was horrible: the ripple of a woman's laughter.

Vadin staggered erect. Vast shapes loomed about him, trees both immense and ancient, cloaked in the presence of the goddess. Branches clawed at him, roots surged up against his feet; twigs thrust into his face, beating him back. He struck against them, wildly yet with a fixed, half-mad purpose.

His arms flailed at nothing. He stumbled painfully against stone. Flower-sweetness filled his brain, stronger than wine, stronger than dreamsmoke. He flung himself away.

By slow degrees his mind cleared. The space about the altar was empty of birds, of robed priests, of the goddess embodied in the mortal woman. Close by him, almost at his feet, lay what they had discarded. Its face was a mask of blood.

He dropped to his knees beside Moranden. With the hem of his cloak he wiped away the blood. Moranden neither moved nor uttered a sound. One eye stared blindly at the sky; the other was lost in a rush of scarlet.

Vadin might have wept had there been time, or had this been the place for it. Setting his jaw, he stooped and drew the slack arm around his shoulders. With all his half-grown strength, with curses and prayers, he dragged Moranden up. Grimly, step by step, he began to walk.

The wood was deathly silent. The only sound was the rasp of his breath and the hiss of Moranden's in his ear; the shuffling of their feet in the mould; and the hammering of his heart. There were eyes upon him. They watched; they waited. He could taste their hatred, cold and cruel, like blood and iron.

He shut it out with all his will, flooding the levels of his mind with every frivolity he could remember. Love songs, lovemaking, wine and mirth and bawdy jests. And he walked, dragging his senseless burden. Slowly, carefully, to the tune of a drunkard's dirge, while the wood closed in about him. In stillness was death, in surrender destruction; in terror, damnation.

Light glimmered. Surely it was illusion. This wood had no end. He was trapped within it until he went mad or died.

The light grew. And suddenly it was all about him, the clear light of day upon a long slope, and Rami tethered at a safe distance from Moranden's stallion, and the Vale below him. With a long sigh he let Moranden slide to the ground. His own body followed, suddenly boneless. A red mist thickened about him.

A shadow loomed in it, darkness edged with fire. It stooped over him, spreading vast wings, crying out in words of power and terror. He cried back and fought, drawing strength from the depths of his will. The shadow gripped him. A hand lifted, all dark, but in its center a sun.

Vadin gasped and went slack. The shadow was Mirain with the Mad One behind him, the hands Mirain's, holding Vadin up with ease that belied his body's smallness. There was blood on his face, on his kilt.

"Not mine," he said in his own familiar voice. "It covers you." He shifted Vadin's weight to his shoulder, raised his hand again. Involuntarily Vadin flinched. The god's brand flamed even yet, like molten gold.

It was warm, not hot; flesh-warm. It eased him down, drew forth a cloth from he knew not where, began gently to cleanse his face. He struck it aside. "Let me be. I need nothing. Help me look after the prince."

Mirain's expression had been grave, intent. Now it darkened. "You should have left him where he lay."

Vadin was as weak as a child, yet he dragged himself up, away from

Mirain, toward Moranden. The elder prince lay slack and somehow shrunken, as if the goddess had taken life with his blood, draining away his soul. As he had done by the altar, Vadin strove to stanch the flood. He could not see Moranden's eye. It was all blood. If it was pierced—
"It is no more than he deserves."
Vadin whirled in a white rage. Mirain, even proud Mirain, fell back a step. But he came forward again and looked down at his mother's brother and said in that calm, young, royal voice, "He plots treason. He deserves to lose much more than an eye."
"He is your kin."
"He is my enemy."
Vadin struck him. But the blow was feeble. Worse were the words he flung without measure or mercy. "Who are you to judge this man? You, you haughty prince, so firm in your righteousness, with the god's blood in your veins and your empire in front of you, what do you know of right or of power or of deserving?" His wrath had brought him to his feet; it held him there, towering over Mirain. "From the moment of your birth you were destined to be king. So you say. So the songs say. So even I was beginning to believe, in spite of all I could do.
"But now." His voice lowered almost to a whisper. "Now I see you for what you are. Go back to your grandfather and leave me to remember who is truly my lord!"
He was far beyond any care for his own safety. But when his voice had stilled, his heart beat hard, and not only with anger. All expression had vanished from Mirain's face, but the black eyes were blazing. He could strike Vadin down with the merest flick of his hand, blind him as he had blinded his mother's betrayer, turn all his high words to the croaking of carrion birds.
Vadin raised his chin and made himself meet that unmeetable gaze. "Or," he said quite calmly, "you can help me. He needs a healer, and quickly. Will your lordship deign to fetch one?"
Mirain's fist clenched. Vadin waited for him to strike. He said, "It would take too long to bring anyone from the castle."
Vadin turned his back on him. Moranden had changed even while they spoke. His face was grey beneath the lurid scarlet of the wound; his eyes were glazed, his breath rattling in his throat. "But," Vadin said to the heedless air, "his hurt is so small, and he so strong."
"The goddess is stronger than he."
Mirain knelt on the other side of Moranden's body. Vadin regarded him with a flat, empty stare. He was neither prince nor enemy now,

only a weary annoyance. "Yes," Vadin said without inflection, "she is strong. Will you kill him now? He's at your mercy."

Mirain looked at Vadin in something close to horror. Later, maybe, he would find some small comfort in that. "You are strong," Vadin went on. He cradled Moranden's head in his lap. "Now, god's son. Destroy this priest of the Dark."

Mirain tossed his head from side to side as if in pain. "I cannot. Not this way. Not . . ."

"Then," Vadin said, "heal him."

Mirain stared. He had never looked younger or less royal. "Heal him," Vadin repeated without compunction. "You're a mage, you told me yourself. You're full to bursting with your father's power. It can destroy this man, or it can save him. Choose!"

"And if I choose neither?" Mirain could hardly speak; his voice cracked on the final word, to his bitter and visible shame.

"If you won't choose, you're no king. Now or ever."

Mirain moved convulsively, flinging up his hand: defense, protest, royal outrage. Vadin held fast, although he averted his eyes from the flame of gold. "Choose," he said again.

Mirain's hand lowered. Slowly it settled upon Moranden's cheek. The elder prince trembled under it, and twisted as if in pain.

Death, Vadin thought dully. *He chooses death.* As in his own way Moranden had chosen, for the sake of the kingship. They were kin indeed, these two, closer than either could bear to know.

Mirain's eyes closed. His face tightened with strain; his breath came harsh. Someone cried out—Moranden, Mirain, Vadin, perhaps all three.

Mirain sank back upon his heels. Vadin looked down; his eyes stretched wide. Moranden lay still, eyes closed as if in sleep, breathing easily. Where the wound had been, on the high arch of cheekbone at the very edge of his eye, was a scar in the shape of a spearhead. It faded even as Vadin watched, and greyed as if with age.

A stir drew his glance upward again. Mirain stood erect, cradling his golden hand. "I am mad," he said. "Someday I may be king. But I am not a murderer. Not even when I can see—" A shudder racked him. "May the god preserve us all."

Six

VADIN STOOD ONCE MORE IN THE SHADOWS. CLEAN shadows, fire-cast, dancing about the edges of the king's chamber, seeming to keep time to the music of Ymin's harp. She played no melody that he could discern, simply a pattern of single notes, random and beautiful as rain upon a pool.

The king sat at a table near the fire. A lamp shed a steady yellow glow upon the book before him. He was a great rarity in a Ianyn lord: he could read. And did so as often as he could, and savored it enough to want to learn the intricate letters of Han-Gilen. Or maybe that was only an excuse to keep his grandson near him, standing as he stood now with his arm about the old man's shoulders, reading in a low clear voice. By all accounts the king had never been a man for touching, walking apart in the armor of his royalty; but Mirain had pierced those strong defenses. Strangely enough, the king seemed to accept that, even to take pleasure in it, although any other who dared such familiarity would have paid in pain.

They laughed, the old man and the young one, at a sudden turn of wit. So close together in the lamp's light, their faces were strikingly alike: proud, high-nosed, deep-eyed. When Mirain was old he would look just so, like a carven king.

Vadin shivered in a sudden chill. Mirain's face, gaining years in his mind's eye, blurred suddenly and faded. As if Mirain would never grow old. As if—

The squire shook himself hard. This whole hideous day had bereft him of his wits. Moondark fancies to begin it, and the horror in the wood, and the rest lost in a fog. When he tried to think he could not, or else saw nightmare visions. And Mirain had said no word to him since they left Moranden to recover his senses in the sunlight with words of guard upon him; since they rode back to the castle together, the prince half a length ahead and the squire behind as was eminently proper. With each of Rami's long smooth strides, Vadin had sunk deeper into silence. But Mirain had conducted himself as if nothing had happened, except that he made no effort to pierce his servant's new-forged armor.

The book was rolled and bound, the music stilled. Mirain sat at the king's feet with his arm across the scarred and age-hardened knees. "Yes," he said with the hint of a smile, "I walked up from Han-Gilen. At first because I would have been too conspicuous astride, with the prince scouring the land for me; and afterward because I found it pleasant. Outside of Han-Gilen, no one knew my face, and I kept my hand out of sight. I was only a vagabond like any other." His smile widened. "Sometimes I was wet or cold or hungry; but I was free, and it was splendid. I could go where I chose, stop where I pleased. I tarried a whole cycle of Greatmoon in a village that had lost its priest."

"A village?" The king's voice was a low rumble. "Among common folk?"

"Farmfolk and hunters," Mirain answered him. "They were good people, on the whole. And not one knew who or what I was. No one called me king or prince. No one bowed to me for my father's sake. One"—he laughed a little—"one even brawled with me. One of the girls had taken to following me about, and she was promised to a wealthy man as folk are reckoned there. His house had a door of wood, and his father had a bull and nine cows. He would not suffer such a rival as I, a spindling lad with a braid like a woman's. He challenged me. I accepted, of course; the lady was watching."

"And you promptly struck the peasant down for his insolence."

Mirain laughed again, freely. "I was trying to be careful, because I was war-trained by masters and he was but a plowboy. And he came round with a great sweeping blow and flattened me."

The king bridled. But Mirain was grinning. He smiled at last, wryly. "What said the lady to that?"

"She shrieked and ran to my aid, which was rather gratifying. But in the end she decided she would rather have a bull and nine cows and a wooden door, than a lover whose body was vowed to the god. I said the marriage-words for them the day I left. By then their new priestess had come, but both of them insisted: None but I must see them wedded. I foretold for them a dozen children and a lifetime of prosperity, and they were well content."

"Were you?" Ymin asked, abandoning her harp for the fire's warmth. Mirain turned to her, half grave, half smiling. "I was free again. I understand now why the law enjoins a Journey upon the young initiate, though mine perforce was shortened. But I made a year do for seven."

"You may yet have your full Journey," said the king.

Mirain clasped the gaunt gnarled hand in his young strong one. "No, my lord. My mother Journeyed for both of us while you waited with no word of her. You will not have to wait again."

The king's free hand passed over Mirain's thick waving hair, a rare caress. "I would wait for you though it were a hundred years."

"One and twenty are quite enough." Mirain raised his head. "Grandfather. Do I trouble you too much? Would you rather I had never come?"

Ymin drew her breath in sharply, but the king smiled. "You know I would not."

"Yes," Mirain admitted, "I do know. Nor would I be aught but here."

"Even to be free upon the world's road?"

"Even so," he said.

When Mirain left the king he did not go directly to bed, but remained for a time at his window. This had become a custom of his, a moment of silence with the garden's night scents rising to sweeten his chamber. It had been early spring when first he came, the passes but newly opened after winter's snows. Now it was full spring. Brightmoon was dark, but Greatmoon was rising, waxing to the full. The battlements glowed blue-white before him. "Father," Mirain said, "when you begot me, did you bethink yourself that I might not be equal to your task?"

The silence was absolute. Mirain sighed a little; when he spoke again it might have been Vadin he addressed, however obliquely. "Ah well. It's not as if he were a mortal man, or one of the thousand tamed gods of the west, to come at any creature's bidding. Even his own son." He rested his cheek against the edge of the window. The stone was luminous with somewhat more than moonlight, although it was far yet from dawn. It knew him, the king had said more than once. Where he was, the castle responded as to the sun's coming.

He turned, his right hand a fist at his side. It could not clench as tightly as it might, stiffened by gold where gold had no right to be. "It hurts," he said, soft yet taut. "It burns. It fills my hand like a great golden coin, a coin heated in fire, that I can never let go. Sometimes it's greater, sometimes less; sometimes it seems no worse than metal warmed too much by the sun, sometimes it takes all my poor strength to endure in silence. I'm proud of that, Vadin. I've never wept or cried out, or even spoken of it, since I was a young child. No one ever knew what pain was mine, except my mother, and the Prince of Han-Gilen. And certainly—certainly his sister." He paused; his brows knit, eased. He almost smiled. "Odd that I should think of her tonight. It must be my mood. Rampant self-pity. Little good it does, either, to put a name to it. Shall I conjure it away? Look."

Vadin had no choice, no time to choose. Mirain's eyes had seized him, enspelled him, sucked him in. He was within them. He *was* Mirain. A body of no great beauty or consequence, centered about a white agony. But the agony retreated, held at bay by a will as strong as forged iron. He saw a face: a child's thin solemn countenance with skin the color of amber and hair as red as new copper. From the time she could walk she had appointed herself Mirain's shadow; which often made the wits laugh, for he was the dark one, all blackwood and raven, and she was honey and fire. But she was unshakable, even for ridicule, even for outright cruelty.

"You shame me!" he had cried once. She had escaped her nurse and scorned the placid mount deemed proper for a maidchild of barely seven summers, and stolen his own outgrown pony, and set out after him as he rode upon a hunt. She had mastered the black devil of a pony, which surprised him not at all; but her intrusion on the chase, among a round dozen of the prince's squires, put him out of all charity.

"You shame me," he repeated in his coldest voice. "You drag at me like shackles. I don't want you here, I don't want you dangling at my tail, I don't—"

She looked at him. The pony was too large for her, the saddlecloth awry, her hair tangled with twigs and straggling over her eyes, but her stare set all the rest at naught. It was not the stare of a young child. "You're not ashamed," she said. "You don't hate me either."

He opened his mouth and shut it again. The hunt was long gone, hot on a scent and unmindful of his absence. He could hear the baying of the hounds growing faint even as he tarried.

The pony tossed its wicked head and threatened his stallion with its horns. It was all she could do to hold it back, but she did it without any lessening of her intensity. "I let you alone when you really need it. You know that."

"I must need it very seldom indeed, then."

"When you wanted to play with Kieri in the hayloft—"

His cheeks flamed; his head throbbed. He flung himself at her. They tumbled to the ground together, their mounts shying over and past them; he beneath, she flailing on top of him. She was a negligible weight, but her elbows were wickedly sharp.

He lay winded, trying to curse her. She sat on him and laughed. "Hal says you have to play all you can now before you win your torque, because after that—"

He clapped his marked hand over her mouth. The sight of it alone was enough for most, but Elian feared neither god nor man. She sank her teeth into it.

By design or by fortune, she bypassed the brand and bit flesh. Pain on top of spiraling pain emptied him of all wrath or shame and cast him howling on the edge of darkness.

The lesser pain faded. The greater swelled without cause, without end, beyond all hope of bearing. Yet he bore it, fully and horribly aware of it, even as the pit gaped before his feet. It would not swallow him into merciful oblivion. It would—not—

The pain was gone.

Not wholly. It had shrunk to its least dimensions, the closest to painlessness he could ever know, but after that blinding agony it was relief so perfect that he could have wept. His eyes, clearing, saw Elian kneeling by him, clutching his hand to her heart. Her face was grey-green, her voice a croak. "Mirain. Oh, Mirain!"

He had no strength to pull his hand away. He could barely speak. "What—what did you—"

"I took it away." Her face twisted. "It hurt. How can anything hurt so much?"

"You took it away," he repeated stupidly. "You . . . took it . . . Elian. Witch-baby. Do you know what you've done?"

"It *hurt.*" She cradled it as tenderly as if it had been her own. "It always hurts. Why, Mirain?"

"You can heal it. Elian, little firemane, you have your father's magic."

She disregarded that. Of course she had the power; she had always had it; and being what he was, he should have known. "Why does it hurt, Mirain?"

"Because my father makes it hurt."

Her brows met. Her jaw thrust forward. "Tell him to stop."

Even in his weakness he could laugh. "But, infant, he's the god. No one can tell him what to do."

"*I* can. He hurts you. He shouldn't. Especially there, where it hurts most. It's not right."

"It makes me remember who I am; what I'm for. It keeps me from growing too proud."

She scowled, stubborn. "There's no need for it."

"No?" he asked. "I was being cruel to you. You see how I paid."

"I have good strong teeth. Even if half of them aren't grown in yet." She patted his hand, which showed no marks of her passing. "You won't hurt again while I have anything to say about it."

"Nor did I," said Mirain. "Much. But I left her, to follow where my father led. No one here can cool the fire."

Vadin had no voice to speak. It was all lost in horror. Sorcery—soul-slavery—

"My father wrought me," Mirain said. "He shaped me for his purposes. The Sword of the Sun, his mightiest weapon against the Dark. But he made me in mortal likeness, flesh and blood and bone, and worst of all, a mind that can think and be afraid. I may not be strong enough. I may fail him. And if I fail—"

"Stop it!" Vadin's shout was raw with the twofold effort. Of speaking; of keeping his hands from that gold-circled throat. "My body is yours to do with as you will. My service is yours for as long as my body lasts. But if you touch my mind again, by all the gods that ever were, I'll kill you."

"I didn't touch your mind," Mirain said, low and still.

"You didn't, did you? No. You raped it."

For all the heed Mirain paid him, he might never have spoken. "I didn't touch you. I opened my own mind, and you plunged headlong into it."

"Wizard's logic. You led me into a trap. You violated me."

"I showed you the truth."

"Yes. That under the upstart prince is a trembling coward."

Mirain laughed. It sounded like honest mirth, with no great measure of mockery. But priests were good liars, and princes better, and royal pretenders best of all. "I'll lay you a wager, Vadin. Before this year is out, you'll call me friend. You'll do it willingly, and you'll do it gladly, and you'll do it without the least regret."

"I'll see you in hell first."

"That's possible," Mirain said, lightly but not in jest. "What will you lay on it?"

"My soul."

Mirain's breath hissed sharply. His teeth were sharper still, bared in a grin. "I warn you, Vadin. I can take it."

"I know you can." This was blackly wonderful, like racing the lightning, or dancing on blades. "And you? What stakes can you offer?"

"A place at my right hand, and the highest lordship, save only mine alone, in my empire that will be."

"I can claim that, Mirain of Han-Gilen."

"I know you can," said Mirain. His hand cast darts of light into Vadin's eyes. Its clasp that sealed the wager was startling for more than mere strength: it did not sear Vadin's own hand to ash. All the fire burned within.

They drew apart in the same instant, with the same feral wariness. Half of one another, half of the one who had come into the room behind them. Someone large, with a long stride, but light on his feet. They turned slowly, as if at ease, but their bodies tensed.

Prince Moranden stood in his accustomed stance, legs well apart, shoulders back. The goddess' brand had done nothing to mar his beauty, and he held his head as if he knew it. His eyes flicked from one to the other. With a quiver of the lids he dismissed the squire, focusing full and burning-cold upon his sister's son.

Mirain let the silence stretch until it broke. "Uncle," he said lightly, coolly, "you honor me. How may I serve you?"

The southern formality curled Moranden's lip. He sat without asking leave, stretching out at his ease. Vadin thought of the black lion of the mountains, that was most deadly when it seemed most quiet. "You, my lord?" asked the elder prince. "Serve me? That's an honor too great for this humble mortal to claim."

Mirain left the window and approached another chair, but he did not sit in it. While he stood, he was a little taller than his unwelcome guest. He leaned against the carven back. "We are inundated with honor tonight. I honor you with my service, you honor me with your presence. It is courtesy that brings you here at last? Or need? Or simple goodwill?"

Moranden laughed sincerely, but with an edge of bitterness. "Your manners are prettier than mine, prince. Shall we leave off playing? Courtesy's a word I don't know the meaning of, northern savage that I am. Need . . . the day I need the likes of you, my young kinsman, you can be sure I'm in dire straits."

"Then," said Mirain levelly, "it must be goodwill."

The elder prince hooked a knee over the arm of his chair. "Very good, sister-son! So good I'll even tell you a truth. I'd give my soul to be rid of you. I think I already have."

"Given your soul," Mirain asked, "or got rid of me?"

"Both." Moranden rubbed his cheek as if the scar pained him. But he smiled a white wolf-smile. "O beloved of my father, if you were given the chance and an ample reward, would you go back where you came from?"

"What sort of reward?"

"Why, anything. Anything at all, short of the throne."

"Which you would take for yourself."

"Of course. I've waited long enough for it. Considerably longer than you, and at considerably closer quarters."

"My mother," Mirain said softly, "was the king's heir."

"Much it meant to her, that she never bothered to come and prove it. But she was half a foreigner herself. I've heard the tales of her mother, the yellow woman; the Asanian emperor, having got her on a slave, thought it a fine jest to toss her to an outsize barbarian. Who fancied he was getting a princess, and strutted with it. She proved a poor bargain. One daughter as undersized as herself: that was all she could give to her lord and master."

"But the daughter had a child, who if equally undersized, at least was comfortably male."

Moranden looked him up and down. "Are you?"

"Shall I strip and let you see?"

Moranden laughed. He was laughing too much and too freely. Yes, Vadin thought; there was a scent of wine on him, and something else, sharp, acrid. Hate? Fear? He laughed, and his eyes glittered beneath the lowered lids. "Yes, by the gods! Strip and show me."

Mirain's own eyes were bitter-bright. With a swift movement he stripped off his kilt. "Well, sir?"

Moranden took his time about it. He rose for it, walking completely around the motionless prince like a buyer in a slave market. When he faced Mirain again, he set his hands on his hips and his head to one side. "Maybe," he said. One hand flashed out to Mirain's cheek, catching on the soft young stubble. "You don't try overly hard to prove it. Why do you make yourself like a eunuch? Are you someone's fancy-boy?"

Mirain sat where Moranden had sat, lolling where Moranden had lolled, smiling through set teeth. "Even if I were so bent, my vows would forbid it."

"Convenient, those vows of yours."

"They bind me. Until I come to the throne; then I'm free of them."

"No doubt you can hardly wait."

"I can wait as long as I must."

Again Moranden's hand went to his face. He brought it down sharply and clasped it behind him, scowling down the proud arch of his nose. Abruptly he said, "I remember. What you did."

"Under compulsion."

"You did it." Moranden's shoulders flexed. They did not take well to humility, even such haughty humility as this. "I owe you for that. My life, maybe. I was close to the edge when you brought me back."

"In my father's name. That should comfort you; for if the Dark One had your soul, you could not have answered that call."

"I owe you," Moranden repeated. The words were coming hard, as if around bile. "I'll give you this in return. Go now, and take what I offered you. Take all you can carry. You can conquer the world better from the Hundred Realms than you ever could from the wilds of the north."

"But Ianon is mine by blood-right and heir-right. What better place to begin?"

"If we let you."

It was a lion's growl. Mirain laughed at it. He looked feverish; his words came as if of their own accord, demonwords, light and mocking. "Let, say you? Let? When it took half a cask of wine to bring you here tonight?" He leaned back in his chair, foot swinging idly; but he cradled his hand as if it had been a wounded creature. "If your gratitude comes so hard, need I fear your enmity?"

Moranden seemed to swell in the firelight. With no memory of movement, Vadin found himself beside his liege lord, sword drawn and on guard. Above its glitter he met Moranden's eyes and found there a black and naked hate. "Child," said the elder prince deep in his throat. "Kingling. I won't offer again. Thanks or reward. Or anything else."

"That is well. You spare me the effort of refusal."

"You think yourself clever. Think on, little fool. But don't expect me to lick your feet."

"That," said Mirain, "I would not dream of." He yawned. "It grows late, and no doubt you are weary. You may go to your bed."

Moranden stood speechless. Abruptly he spun away.

For a long while prince and squire stared at the empty air, the closed door. Moranden had shut it with softness more potent than any violence.

Mirain raised his burning hand, turned it, clenched it: defying him, denying him, rejecting him utterly. "He cannot touch me. He has not the power. For he is a mortal man, and I am the king who will be. I . . . will . . . be king."

Seven

"**T**HERE SLINKS THE FOREIGNER'S DOG."

Vadin had been offending no one. He was free for the first time since Moranden's wounding, standing in the market contemplating a bit of frippery and the girl to whom he would give it, with Kav's comfortable bulk and still more comfortable silence for companions. It was Kav who kept him from lunging blindly toward the voice, who wrapped a broad hand around his narrow arm and simply stood, firm as the earth beneath their feet.

The voice was young and lordly and pitched to madden, sneering just behind Vadin's right ear. "Ah, look! He buys bangles and beads for his dainty master. How do they serve one another, do you think? Does the boy become a man when the lamps are out?"

"Let me go!" Vadin snarled at his captor.

Kav did not shift his grip. The clear eyes in the heavy sullen face flicked once toward the voice, and then away.

Again it pricked, with laughter in it. "They go well together, long-shanks and shortshanks, cowards of a feather. Did you hear what his highness will do when the throne comes to him? He'll dress all the lords in trousers, command them to shave their beards, and make them swear to serve him as slaves serve their masters."

Kav moved steadily and inexorably away from the voice and toward the wineshop. One or two squires were there already and well in their cups. Vadin fought; he could as easily have fought the castle wall. His hand fell to his dagger.

"Don't," Kav said in his deep growl of a voice.

Vadin cursed him. He grunted, which was his way of laughing. They were under the awning; he set Vadin firmly on the bench between Olvan and Ayan and thrust a cup into the clenching fist. Vadin gulped the sour ale, crying through it, "He spoke treason! He said—he said I—"

"Words," said Kav.

"Words breed blows, damn you!"

"Did he say anything you haven't thought yourself?"

"I don't *say* it." Vadin stopped, straightened. All three were looking at him. His mouth tasted of sickness. He lashed out. "Yes. Stare. You worship the ground he walks on. You'd kiss his foot if he asked."

"Except that he wouldn't," Ayan said, refilling Vadin's cup, "and that's why we worship him. Doesn't he take weapons practice with the rest of us? And didn't he insist on it, and dare the king's displeasure? And he a knight in Han-Gilen and ten times as good as most of us will ever be."

"Five times," Vadin judged sourly. "You know what people say about that. He won't take on anyone who'll come close to him; he knows he'll lose. So he makes fools of us, and witches us into loving him for it."

Olvan snorted. "Jealous nonsense. He learns from Adjan, who's the best teacher in Ianon. He teaches us when we insist. He likes us."

"Gods don't learn or like. They rule."

"Prince Mirain is only half a god," Ayan pointed out. But his tongue caressed the name, and he sighed; then he frowned. "We know that. We know him. But it's true, people are saying things, and not in whispers anymore, either. I was on watch last night; I broke up a fight, and people on both sides were howling that they were loyal to the true prince. They were breaking heads over it."

"Who won?" Kav inquired.

"No one," said Vadin before Ayan could speak. "No one at all." His cup was empty again. He could not remember draining it. He poured another, and another. He was going to have someone's neck. He was not certain whose. But lovely Ledi was there to divert him, even without the bauble he had meant to buy her. And another cup of ale, and a song or two, and a warm tangle in Ledi's bed, all four and she, and when he was done he would remember rage.

"Because," he said once or a dozen times, "no one—no one—calls Vadin alVadin a coward."

* * *

With the sun's coming, Ledi left the tangle to sort itself: Olvan and Ayan coiled about one another, and Kav solid and sufficient unto himself, and Vadin hunting blindly for the soft woman-body. He found something, and its skin was velvet, but steel-hard beneath; and it was much too narrow and supple to be Ledi. His eyes dragged themselves open. He had his arm crooked lovingly about Mirain's waist; the prince regarded him with wry amusement. He recoiled.

The wryness deepened. Vadin opened his mouth; Mirain's hand covered it. His other, golden, beckoned.

Out in the courtyard, with the sun beating down on his tortured skull, Vadin let it free. "What in the thrice nine hells are you doing here?"

Mirain's glance was pointed. Vadin fumbled into kilt and belt and cloak, and plunged his head into the vat of rainwater beside the gate. He came up a little clearer of mind, if in no less pain. "I thought I had the whole night to myself."

"You did." Mirain tilted his head. "Your Ledi is a woman of great wit and wisdom."

Vadin fought down his rising temper. "My lord," he said with great care, "I would thank you not to—"

"I'm not mocking her. She served me new bread and honey, and she talked with me. She wasn't afraid of me."

"And why should she be?"

Mirain looked at him. Down at him. With all the pride of a crowned king and all the puissance of a god. Then he was Mirain again, shoulder-high to Vadin, saying, "I see. I'm small, and therefore harmless. Who in Ianon can say differently?"

"All the king's squires, and one of your own, and a certain prince." Vadin shook himself before he turned into a poet. "Why are you here? Is something wrong?"

Mirain shrugged. He was looking very young and very guileless and therefore, to Vadin's mind, very suspicious. "I missed your presence."

"You had Pathan. Pathan the prince, who's heir to two fiefs and a princedom, and who's fought his way to captain of squires, and who'll make knight this High Summer. More than that; he'll be Younger Champion, and in a year or two he'll give the elder good reason to fear for his title. He should have been your squire from the first. *He's* worthy of you."

"Do you think that, Vadin?"

Vadin was not to be trapped, even by his own runaway tongue. "The king should think so. You're the light of his fading eyes."

"Pathan is pleasant enough," Mirain said. "Handsome. Brilliant. Not remarkably larger than I, and undisturbed by it. He plays a wicked game of kings-and-cities."

Vadin, who was none of those things, smote his hands together. *"So!* Ask your grandfather for him. He'd be hugely honored."

"Unfortunately," Mirain went on undeterred, "he bores me to tears. All that relentless perfection. And such utterly unshakable loyalty to his king's chosen heir. When he woke me—impeccably attired at the ungodly hour a Sun-priest has to wake, and awaiting on me with flawless effacement—it was all I could do not to scream. I did order him out. I think I was acceptably polite."

Vadin could see it. Pathan, the epitome of the squire, the vision toward which Adjan struggled ceaselessly to drive all the rest, waking Mirain with the exact courteous touch, bathing and dressing and serving him without the slightest slip of mind or body, and being dismissed with Mirain's inimitable, acid, southern-bred politeness. After, no doubt, a strong dose of that prince's resistance to any service which he preferred to perform himself.

Vadin's lips kept twitching. He bit them; they escaped. The laughter burst out of him all at once.

Mirain's grin was utterly wicked. Vadin fought for a scowl, managed only a dying gasp. "You—Pathan—you're as mad as I am."

"One could say I have deplorable taste. In seneldi, in causes, and in friends."

The last word drove Vadin back into himself. "I'm your servant. My lord."

The black eyes narrowed a fraction. The proud head bowed once, conceding nothing. "Ledi will feed you. Then I require your service."

Which was to trail behind him through every square and alley of the town in the market-day crowd, testing the currents of speech and, no doubt, of mind; tarrying to overhear a round of gossip, to down a cup of wine, to watch a sword-dancer. Like any proper wizard, Mirain could make himself invisible when he chose. Else surely people would not have been so free with their scandal-mongering, and they had much to say of the two princes, the new and the old.

"I'm for the man I know," said a buyer at the senel fair. "And what do we know about this Mirain? He comes all unlooked for, he wears a torque and a braid like a Sun-priest, he claims to be the gods know what. He could be out to slaughter us all."

"Prince Moranden is a hard man," opined a coppersmith's wife as she sat on her doorstep spinning wool into thread. "He looks fine and fair; he has a smile or a word for everyone; but he has a cold eye. I saw it happen when I was a girl in Shaios. Sweet as honey, Lord Keian was, till the day his father died; and people said afterward that maybe the old man had had help on his way. And when the heir came to the high seat, he went stark bitter. Killed all his kin, even to the women and babes, and taxed us till we starved, and went to war against Suveien. And won, thank the gods, but he died winning, and his lady ruled us well till the little lord Tien was old enough to take his place."

The elders sighed over their gaming in the sun, and the eldest said, "It's an ill day when there are two high princes and only one throne to be had, and the elder's not likely to step down for the upstart younger, chosen heir or not. They've drawn their lines; and mark my words, they won't take long now to come to blows."

"I hear they have already," the youngest of them observed, casting dice for his move in kings-and-cities. "I hear the young one came at the elder with a catsclaw dagger and laid his face open, and called on magic to heal it up again."

"For regret?" an onlooker wondered.

"For contempt. And the elder prince has a scar to remind him of the insult."

"Foreigners," muttered the eldest. "Both of them. Now if the king had had the sense to take a wife at home—"

The onlooker leaned across the board. "I hear they're neither of them his kin. The young one's an enchanter from the Nine Cities, painted up like one of us and enspelled to look like the princess who's dead; the elder belongs to one of the Marcher rebels. I remember when the king brought that woman here, and I remember how soon he got the whelp on her. Who's to say she wasn't carrying it when he took her?"

Mirain pulled Vadin away, and none too soon. He himself seemed no more than amused. "An enchanter," he said. "From the Nine Cities." He laughed. "O that I were! What would I do to this poor kingdom, do you think?"

"Turn it into a land of the walking dead."

Mirain sobered abruptly. "Don't say such things!" Vadin stared, startled at the change in him. His lips were touched with grey, his eyes wide and wild.

Little by little he calmed. Very quietly he said, "Never speak of what could be. Would you be heard and heeded?"

"Would you do what I said you would?"

"The goddess is my father's sister. She would give all her power to have me for her own, for that would wound him to the heart. And it would be—not impossible—perhaps not even difficult. Perhaps . . . perhaps . . . almost easy. To let her—to be—"

Vadin hauled Mirain up by the shoulders and shook him hard. And when he could walk, after a fashion, saw him into a stall and plied him with wine until the darkness began to fade. He caught at the cup and drank deep enough to drown, and came up gasping; but his eyes were clear. "My thanks," he said at last.

Vadin lifted his hand, let it fall. One did one's duty.

Mirain sighed and drained the wine. If he might have spoken again, another voice forestalled him, a clear trained voice embarked upon a tale.

"Indeed, sirs, it was a prodigy: a woman white as a bone, with eyes the color of blood." It was a talespinner in the motley rags of his calling, with a cup in one hand and a girl on his knee. Fine dark wine and a fine dark girl. He paused to savor both. She giggled; he kissed her soundly and drank deep. "Aye, white she was, which was a wonder and a horror. She belonged to the goddess, people said. Her kinsmen kept her in a cage built like a temple and fed her with sacrifices—taking the best portions for themselves, of course. She would writhe and babble; they would call it prophecy, and interpret it for whatever price the market would bear. Whole suns of gold, even, when the local chieftains came to ask about their wars. They were always pleased, because they were always promised victory."

"And did they get it?"

The man turned to Mirain with no hint of surprise to find him there. "Some did, prince. Some didn't; but they never came back to gainsay her. Till one fine day a young man came striding into the shrine. He gave her his sacrifice: a bit of journey-bread and a handful of berries. Her keepers would have whipped him out then, but they were curious to see what he would do. Very little, in fact. He sat down in front of the cage, and the sibyl ate what he had brought, untidily enough to be sure, with her unholy eyes upon him all the while. He stared straight back; he even smiled.

"He was mad, the keepers decided. He looked like a poor wayfarer, but they thought they glimpsed gold on him under the rags. Maybe, after all, he was a prince in disguise. 'Put your question,' they commanded him at length when he showed no sign of beginning.

"He paid them no heed at all. By then the sibyl had come to the bars of her cage, reaching through it. Her hands were as thin and sharp-taloned as a white eagle's. She was filthy; she stank. Yet our young hero took her hand and smiled and said, 'I shall set you free.'

"Her kinsmen reached for their daggers. But they found that they could not move. They were caged as securely as their prisoner, bound with chains no eye could see.

" 'Only name my name,' the stranger said, 'and you shall be free.'

"They had proclaimed themselves the mouthpieces of prophecy; yet not one could utter a word. But the madwoman, the idiot, the wordless seeress, bowed as low as the stranger would let her, and said clearly, 'Avaryan. Your name is Avaryan.' " The talespinner paused. The silence had spread from the wineseller's stall to the street without. His hearers waited, hardly breathing. He struck his hands together with a sound like a thunderclap. "And behold! Fire fell from heaven and shattered the cage, and smote to the ground all that false and venal priesthood; and their victim stood forth free and sane. But she wept. For the stranger who was the god—the stranger had vanished away."

The stall erupted into applause; a shower of coins fell into the girl's cupped hands. Mirain added his own, a silver solidus of Han-Gilen. For every patron the girl had a kiss or a curtsey, but he won the talespinner's own low bow. "My tale was pleasing to my prince?"

"It was well told," said Mirain, "though I pity the poor sibyl. Does she live yet?"

"Ah, my lord, that is another story."

Mirain smiled. "And you, of course, will tell it if we beg you."

"If my prince commands," said the talespinner.

"Well?" Mirain asked of the others. "Shall I?"

"Aye!" they called back.

Mirain turned to the talespinner. "Tell on then, with this bit of copper to sweeten your labor."

"Well now, that's bliss, to have time to spare for market tales."

Vadin had seen him come. Mirain must have sensed it; he turned slowly, with perfect calm. Moranden stood directly behind him. He smiled with a very slight edge. "What, uncle! Back already from the hunt?"

If that struck the mark, Moranden showed no sign of it. "No hunting for me today. But then, you wouldn't know, would you? Our troubles haven't yet come into the talespinners' repertoires."

People were watching and listening, distracted from the tale by the prospect of a royal quarrel. But Moranden blocked the only clear path of escape. "There's more to be had in the market than old legends," Mirain said. "Is it true, uncle, that the mountain folk have been raiding on the Western Marches?"

"A tribe or three," replied Moranden.

"And others have taken advantage of the opportunity, have they not? Have settled the tribes to be sure, but finding themselves armed and armored, have declared themselves free of their lord. A dire thing, that, and worse yet when the lord is royal and my uncle. Surely people lie when they accuse you of over-harshness."

Moranden's eyes narrowed and began to glitter. The scar was livid beneath them; his face twisted a little as if he knew pain. But wrath was stronger, tempered with hate. "Not all of us can rule under the sun of loving kindness, or take our ease among the rabble. Some must fight to keep that rabble in hand."

"As you will be doing, my lord?"

"As I must do. I leave at dawn to settle your borders, Throne Prince of Ianon. Do I merit your highness' blessing?"

Mirain was silent, tight-lipped. Moranden smiled. "Remember, my prince, as you sleep safe within these walls. No enemy has ever walked here, or so they say; nor shall he while I live to defend you."

Mirain's head came up. "You need not trouble yourself to protect me."

"Indeed?" Moranden looked down at him, measuring him with unveiled scorn. "Then who will?"

"I guard myself," gritted Mirain. "I am no ill warrior."

"You are not," his uncle conceded. "Certainly you hold your own among the younger lads."

Vadin should have moved then. He should have moved long since. But even breath was frozen out of him, or enspelled into stillness. He could only stand and watch, and know what this mad master of his would say. Said with great care, with the precision of icy rage. "I am a knight of Han-Gilen and a man in any reckoning; and I fight my own battles. Look for me at dawn, mine uncle. I ride at your right hand."

"You are insane." They had all said it, Vadin loudest and longest and to no effect at all. Ymin said it now, facing Mirain without fear although he rode still on a red tide of wrath. "You are quite mad. Moranden is a danger to you even in the castle under the king's protection. If you ride to war with him, he will have what he longs for."

"I can protect myself."

"Can you?" She thrust back her sleeves, gripping her forearms until the long nails, hardened from years of plucking the strings of her harp, seemed to pierce through flesh and muscle into bone. But her voice betrayed only impatience with his folly. "You are behaving like a spoiled child. And well he knows it. He sought you for just this purpose, to set you precisely where he wants you: in his hands, and too wild with rage and rivalry to care what befalls you."

He rounded upon her. "He has challenged me openly. If I refuse him, I have no right or power to claim kingship."

"If you refuse him, you prove that you are man enough, and king enough, to ignore an insult."

His face was closed, his will implacable. "I ride at dawn."

She reached for him. "Mirain," she said, not quite pleading. "If not for your own sake, for your grandsire's. Forsake this folly."

"No." He eluded her hands, and left them there in his chamber, the singer alone and hopeless, Vadin forgotten by the wall. The door thudded shut behind him.

Eight

VADIN SHIVERED, STRUGGLING TO STAY AWAKE. IT was an unholy hour to be out of bed: the black watch of the night when men most often died, and demons walked, and Uveryen defied her bright brother to overcome her power. He was ghastly cold, sitting in the king's antechamber, waiting on the royal pleasure. With the sublime illogic of the half-asleep, he did not fear for life or limb. He fretted over his baggage. Should he have packed one more warm cloak? Or one less? Had he forgotten something vital? Mirain's armor—was it—

"My lord will see you now."

The quiet words brought him lurching to his feet. They tangled. He sorted them with vicious patience, under the servant's cool eye. In some semblance of good order, he entered the lion's den.

The king was as the king always was, broad awake, fully clad, and somehow not quite human. Like a man in armor, warded against the world; but this one's armor was his own flesh and bone. Vadin, bowing at his feet, wondered if he had always been like that. An iron king, ruling with an iron will, loving nothing that lived.

Except Mirain. Vadin rose at the king's command, roused at last, beginning to be afraid. Princes did not often pay for their insanities. Their servants often did, bitterly.

The king stood close enough to touch. Vadin swallowed. Part of him was surprised. He did not have to look up by much. Two fingers' breadth. Three. He had never been so close before. He could see a scar on the king's cheek, a knife scar it must have been, thin and all but invisible, running into the braided beard. There were few lines on the king's face. It was all pared clean, skin stretched taut over haughty bones. Mirain's bones.

But not Mirain's eyes. These were hooded, deep but not bottomless, studying Vadin as he studied the king. No god flamed in them. No madness, either. But of magecraft, something. A flicker, low yet steady, strong enough to see a man's soul, too weak to walk in his mind.

"Sit," the king said.

Vadin obeyed without thinking. The chair was the king's own, high and ornate. The king would not let him find another. His tired body made the best of its cushions; his mind waited, alert for escape.

The king revived the dying fire, squatting on his haunches, tending the fragile new flames with great care. Vadin counted scars on the bare and corded back. Every man had scars; they were his pride, the badge of his manhood. The king had a royal throng of them.

The old man's voice seemed to come out of the fire, his words born in Vadin's own thoughts. "I fought many battles. To gain the eye of the king my father. To earn the name of prince. To become prince-heir, and to become king, and to hold my kingship. By the god's mercy, I had no need to wrest it from my father. A seneldi stallion killed him for me: a stallion and his own arrogance, that would suffer no creature to be greater than he. Of that beast's line I bred the Mad One. It was revenge, of a sort. The sons of the regicide would serve the sons of the king. The stallion himself I took and tamed and rode into every battle, until he died under me. Shot, I think. I do not remember. There have been so many. It has been so long."

He sounded ineffably old, ineffably weary. Vadin said nothing. It seemed to be his curse that kings confided in him. Or else and more likely, he was not going to live long enough for his knowledge to matter.

The king sat on his heels with ease that belied both voice and words. "It perturbs you, does it not? To know that I was young once. That I was born and not cast up armed and crowned from the earth; that I was a child and a youth and a young man. And yet I was all of them. I even had a mother. She died while I was still among the women. She had enemies; they said she had lovers. 'And why not?' she cried when they came for her. 'One night a year my lord and master grants me of his charity. All the rest belong to his wives and his concubines. He casts his seed where he pleases. Am I not a queen? May I not do the same?' She paid the price of her presumption. My father made me watch as they flayed her alive and bathed her in salt and hanged her from the battlements. I was royal. I must know how kings disposed of their betrayers. I was not seven summers old.

"I learned my father's lesson. A king must endure no threat to his rule. Not even where he loves, if that love turns against him. The throne is a dead thing, but its power is all-encompassing. It knows no human tenderness. It suffers no compassion.

"And on that day of my mother's death, with the screams of her dying ringing in my brain, I swore that I would be king; because for me to take the throne, my father must die. I know now that he was a hard man, cold and often cruel, but he was not evil. He was merely king. Then and for a long time after, I knew only that he had murdered my mother."

Vadin choked back a yawn. He kept waiting for the blow to fall. It was all very sad, and it explained a little of the king's madness, but Vadin could not see what it had to do with Mirain. Or with dragging Mirain's squire out of his warm blankets in the deeps of the night.

"Alas for me," said the king, "I learned to hate my father; I learned to cast aside mercy, to be most royally implacable. But I never learned not to love. For the kingdom's sake I took an Asanian queen. She would hold back the Golden Empire; she would enrich us with her splendid dowry. Herself I did not consider, save as a price to be paid: a pallid dwarfish creature, bred like a beast to ornament a western palace. And when she came, indeed she was small, as small as a maid of ten summers, but her heart was mighty; and in the arts of the bedchamber she had no equal.

"They say this land was too harsh for her. Yet she was learning to endure it, even perhaps to love it. She was growing strong; she was beginning to accept our ways. And I killed her. I set my child in her, knowing what I did, knowing what I must do, although she was too small by far to bear an heir of Ianyn kings. She kindled, and for a little while I dared to hope. The child was not large; she was bearing well, without pain. Yet when her time came, all went awry. The child was twisted in the womb, fighting its birth. Fighting with the strength of the mageborn, which taxed the full power of priests and birthing-women and, in desperation, of the shamans whom even then I had in mind to banish from my kingdom. They prevailed. My queen did not. She lingered a little. She saw her daughter. She heard me give the little one the name of heir. Then, content, she died.

"I mourned her. I still mourn her. But she had left my Sanelin, who had all her mother's valor and all her sweetness, but who was strong with the strength of our people.

"Yes," the king said, meeting Vadin's eyes with a shock like two blades clashing, "I loved my daughter too much. I loved her for herself, and I loved her for her mother who was lost. But I did not love her blindly. Nor was it merely the grieving lover who made his lady's child his heir. I knew what we had made together, my queen and I. In the body of a maidchild, slender and Asanian-small, dwelt the soul of an emperor."

"It was unfortunate," Vadin ventured, "that she was a woman."

The king rose. For all his age and his height and the weight of his bones, he moved like Mirain: like a panther springing. Vadin steeled himself for the killing stroke.

It never came. "Aye and aye," the king said heavily, "it was unfortunate. More unfortunate still that I had no sons. She was my only child, and she was pure gold; and the Sun took her. It was no choice of mine. From her infancy she knew who must be her lord and her lover. He had made her for himself. At last he took her from me. Rightly, after all; a daughter passes from her lord father to her lord husband, and she was Avaryan's bride. But she was also Ianon's heir."

Sometimes one gambled. Vadin made a reckless cast. "The Prince Moranden—"

The panther roused, snarling. It was laughter, harsh with disuse, ragged with pain. "You love him, do you not? Many love him. He is lordly; he is proud; he has his mother's beauty. But she is goddess-wise. He is not even clever."

"Why do you hate him?" Vadin asked. "What has he done to you?"

"He was born." The king said it quietly, without rancor. "Of all the errors of my life, the greatest was my taking captive the daughter of Umijan. She was suckled on hate; she came to me in hate. But her beauty struck me to the heart. I thought that I could tame her; I dreamed that she would come, if not to love me, at least to esteem me as her consort. I was a fool. The lynx does not lie down on the hunter's hearth."

"You should have killed her before she got her claws into your son."

"He was hers from the moment of his conception."

"Did you try to change it? You never let him forget who was your favorite. You made it obvious who would have the throne. Sanelin, or no one. It's a wonder he didn't slit your throat as soon as he knew how."

"He tried. Several times. I forgave him. I love him. I will not give my throne to him."

"What if Mirain had never come?"

"I knew that he would. Not only was it foretold. Not only had the god promised me in dreams that the great one would come. I knew that my daughter would be no more willing than I, to let her heritage fall into the hands of Odiya of Umijan."

Vadin marveled that he was here, sitting while the king stood, talking to him as if he were—why, as if he were Mirain. "I don't understand. I've known men who were never properly weaned. Prince Moranden is nothing like them. He's strong. He's Ianon's champion. He has no equal on the field, and few enough off it."

"There is more to the world than the wielding of a sword." The king turned his hands, much calloused with it, and half smiled. "Moranden is his mother's creature. When she commands, he obeys. Where she hates, he detests. She is the shape and he the shadow. Were he king on the throne of Ianon, she would rule. She rules already wherever he is lord."

"But—" Vadin began. He stopped. What use? The king knew what he knew. No Imeheni yokel could teach him otherwise.

If there was anything to teach him. Vadin shifted uncomfortably. Moranden was no monster. He had been kind to a lad from the outlands who was no threat to his power. He could be charming if it suited his purposes. But he was honorable even when it did not serve him. He was a mortal man; of course he was flawed. Even Mirain was far from perfect.

The servants fought to wait on Mirain. Moranden's name met with a shrug, a sigh, an acceptance of one's duty. Sometimes, they conceded, it was pleasant to serve him. Sometimes it was perilous. He was a lord. What could one expect?

He was not cruel. He was no more capricious than any other prince. Mirain was infinitely less predictable.

Mirain was Mirain. Even Vadin could not envision him as anything but what he was; nor was it conceivable that he would let anyone command him, let alone do his ruling for him. Moranden—yes, Moranden was a bit of a weathercock. Everyone knew it. A man could win his favor, not with copper, nothing so venal, but his friends were often the ones who flattered him most cleverly. He had no patience with the drudgeries of kingship: councils, audiences, endless and innumerable ceremonies. He had sunk low in the market, when he accused Mirain of shirking those duties, and let people think that he himself had been laboring long hours over them. Probably he had been dicing with his lordlings until the king called him to defend the Marches.

Vadin snorted softly to himself. Next he would be exonerating Mirain for idling in the market while the kingdom went to war. Mirain had not been idling, after all. Not exactly. He had been acquainting himself with his people.

"If Moranden is Odiya's puppet," Vadin said at last, "why did you give him a princedom?"

"I gave his mother a princedom, for a price. She would not set her son on me; I would leave them free to govern as they chose. Within the limits of the law."

"Which you had made."

"Just so," said the king.

Vadin sat back. "What are you telling me, my lord? What am I supposed to do?"

"Keep them from killing one another."

"Keep—" Vadin laughed. His voice came within a hair of cracking. "My lord, I don't know what Adjan told you about me, but I'm only human. I can't come between the thunder and the lightning."

The king seized him as if he had been a weanling pup, dragging him to his feet, shaking him until his eyes blurred. "You will do it. You will stand between them. You will not let them die at one another's hands."

"This time."

The king wound his fingers in Vadin's braids, wrenching his head back. "Never while I live. Swear it, Vadin alVadin."

"I can't," Vadin gasped. "Moranden—maybe—but Mirain—" The king's grip tightened to agony. He was mad. Stark mad. "My lord, I—"

The old man let him go. He fell to all fours. His head throbbed; he choked on bile. Trembling, hating himself for it, he peered up. The king knelt beside him. Not madness, he saw with bitter clarity. Love. The king gave tears to them; both of them. His voice was thick, but it yielded nothing. Even his pleading was proud. "You must try. You are all I have. The only one whom both are fond of. The only one whom I can trust."

It was too much. Mirain, and the king too. Vadin crouched and shook. The king touched him. He started like a deer. "It is the price you pay," the king said, "for your quality."

Little by little Vadin stilled. He drew himself up. Half his braids were down, the rest working loose. He shook them out of his eyes, and looked at the king. "My lord, I will do all I can, even if it kills me."

"It may kill us all." The king raised him, holding him with only a shadow of strength. "Go. Defend your lord. From himself, if need be."

* * *

The cold light of dawn found Mirain's temper calmed but his will un-shaken. Vadin looked at him and did not know whether to rage or to despair. "By the gods," he muttered under his breath, "if the king breaks his heart for that lunatic's sake, I'll—I'll—" Rami shifted under him, troubled. He bit back the hot swift tears and glared at the mad-man. Mirain bore no mark of his royalty, went armed like all the rest with sword and spear and shield, light plain armor and plain tunic beneath it and plain helmet on his head. And yet he was impossible to mistake, riding his wild black demon without bit or bridle, laughing as the beast lashed out at a soldier's gelding.

A tall figure approached him on foot. The Mad One stood suddenly still, ears pricked, eyes gleaming emberbright in the torchlight. Mirain bowed in the saddle. "Good morning, Grandfather."

"You will go," the king said. It was not a question. A little of the old, cold madness had returned to his face. "Fight well for me, your Mirain. But not so well that you die of it."

"I do not intend to die," said Mirain. He leaned out of his saddle and kissed the king's brow. "Look for me when Brightmoon waxes again."

"And every day until then." Abruptly the king turned away from him to confront Moranden. The elder prince, intent upon the mustering of his troops, had not yet mounted; a groom held the bridle of his charger. He met his father's stare with one as level, and as cold, and as unreadable. "Come back to me," the king said. "Both of you. Alive and whole."

Moranden said no word, but bowed and sprang astride. The gates swung back; a horn sounded, fierce and high. With a shout the com-pany leaped forth.

They passed the Towers of the Dawn in the full morning, riding steadily from the Vale to the height of the pass, winding down the steep ways into the outer fiefdoms of Ianon. The long riding lulled Vadin into a sort of peace. The king had been fiercely alive when they left him, and Mirain was far from dead, and Vadin knew certainly that at least a tithe of the men about him were the king's own. This might even prove to be no more than it seemed: a quelling of rebellion, a first testing of Ianon's heir in battle. Moranden was an honorable man; he would not do a murder that was certain to kill his father.

Vadin would let grief come when it came. Meanwhile he tried to be wise; he opened himself to the clean bright air and the company of men about him and the strong beast-body beneath him. Green Arkhan unfurled beneath Rami's feet; Avaryan wheeled to his zenith and sank westward behind the mountain walls.

Mirain was an exemplary soldier. He kept his place in the line beside Vadin, just ahead of the squires with the remounts; he held his Mad One to a quiet pace with no outbursts of stallion temper; when the company was silent he was silent, and when they sang he always seemed to know the songs. His accent, Vadin began to notice, had changed. His Ianyn was as good as Vadin's own, if not better: he had no Imeheni burr but the lilt of a lord of Han-Ianon, clear and melodious yet pitched to carry through field or hall. And he was working the magic of his presence. The men near him had fallen under his spell; Vadin watched it spread. They were not falling at his feet. Not yet. But they were warming to him. They were forgetting to hate him; as for shunning him, that battle was long lost.

Moranden knew it. He did not show it, but Vadin could sense a growing darkness in him. A set to his shoulders; a sharpening of the dun stallion's temper.

"It can't work, you know."

They were camped on the borders of Medras, sacrificing comfort in a lord's hall for the sake of speed and sobriety. Fine clear night that it was, Mirain had elected to bivouac with his mount, with a small fire and a warm blanket and the Mad One for wall and guard. The stallion admitted Vadin on sufferance, as much for Rami's sake as for Mirain's; he had taken an interest in the mare, chaste enough for it was not her season, and she was not inclined to discourage him. But no one else ventured near, or appeared to wish to.

"It can't work," Vadin repeated. "You can bedazzle people when they're near you, but when their eyes clear they turn straight back to your uncle."

Mirain fed the fire with deadwood from the thicket in which they camped. The flames, leaping, made his face strange: sharpened the curve of his nose, carved deep hollows beneath his cheekbones, glittered in his eyes. "Bedazzle people, Vadin? How am I doing that?"

Impatience flung Vadin's hand up and out, made him snap, "Don't play the innocent with me. You're subverting my lord's men under his very nose. And he can see it as well as I can."

"I am not—" Mirain rose abruptly. The Mad One snorted and threw up his head; the prince gentled him, centering himself on it, shutting Vadin out.

Vadin hammered at his gates. "Sure you aren't. You talk to them like a northerner born. Me you lisp at as sweetly and southernly as you ever did. Who's being played for a fool?"

Mirain's back was obdurately silent. One ruby eye glowed beyond and just above it, beneath a fire-honed blade of horn. Rami grazed peacefully on the edge of the firelight, oblivious to two-legged troubles. Not for the first time, Vadin cursed all mages and their intransigence. How could a mere man beat sense into the likes of them?

Mirain spun. "Sense? What sense? You accuse me of machinations I never meant. You fault me for trying my tongue in good Ianyn, and again to easing it with you who know and occasionally forget to despise me. What should I do, refuse to have anything to do with these men I have to fight beside?"

"Pack up and ride straight back to Han-Ianon where you belong."

"Ah no," said Mirain. "You won't turn me back now. It was too late for that when I faced Moranden in the market."

"You two should be brothers. You hate each other too absolutely to be anything less."

"I don't hate him." Mirain said it as if he believed it. Perhaps he did. Perhaps even Vadin did. "He lusts after what is mine. He'll never have it. Maybe one day I can teach him, if not to love me, at least to accept the truth."

"Are you really as arrogant as that, or are you simple? Men like him don't back down."

"They can be persuaded to step sidewise."

Vadin spat into the fire. "And the moons will dance the sword-dance, and the sun will shine all night."

To his great surprise, except that he was learning to be amazed by nothing Mirain said or did, the prince dropped down beside him and grinned. "Another wager, O doubter?"

"I won't rob you this time, O madman."

Mirain laughed. His teeth were very white. He lay with his head pillowed on his saddle, wrapping his blanket about him, eyes bright upon Vadin. "I won't kill him. That's too easy. I'll win him instead. Of his own free will, without magery."

"What am I, then? Your practice stroke?"

"My friend." Mirain was a shadow on shadow, even his eyes briefly hooded. They flashed open, silencing the snap of protest. "I'll do it, Vadin."

Vadin could understand how Mirain looked on Moranden. One could not hate a man afflicted with insanity. One pitied him; one had a hopeless compulsion to cure him. They were both mad, these princes. They were going to die for it. Then what would Ianon do for a king? Mirain was asleep. He could do that: will himself into oblivion between breath and breath, and leave the fretting to lesser mortals. Vadin inched toward him. He did not move. Nor did the Mad One, which was more to the point. The squire peered down at him. The fire, dying, only deepened the shadow of him, but his face was clear enough to memory. A face one could not forget. Someone had said that—Ymin, the king. It was in a song. Mirain had laughed when he heard it. Aye, he said, he was ugly enough to be remarkable.

He was stone blind and stark mad. With a sound between a growl and a groan, Vadin rolled himself into his own blanket. The gods looked after the afflicted, said all the priests. Let them do it, then, and give this poor mortal peace.

Perhaps, after all, the gods did their duty. No one tried to slip poison into Mirain's field rations or a dagger into his back. Moranden paid him no more heed than he paid any other trooper, and no less; and Vadin heard no such words as he had heard in Han-Ianon's market. The elder prince was ruling himself and he was ruling his men.

On the third day the bright weather faded. The dawn was dim, the sunrise scarlet and grey; by noon the rain fell in torrents. The company wrapped their weapons in oiled leather and themselves in heavy hooded cloaks and pressed on without pausing.

Early summer though it was, the rain was northern rain, mountain bred; it chilled to the bone. Men grumbled under their breaths, laying wagers on whether the prince would command them to harden themselves yet further by camping in the storm. Mirain took up one such. "He won't," he said. "We'll lodge warm and dry tonight."

He won a silver-hafted dagger. For as the grey light dimmed to dark, Moranden led his company up a long twisting track to a castle. It was smaller even than Asan-Geitan, and poorer, but it had a roof to keep out the rain. The men cheered as its gate creaked open to admit them.

Mirain would have been content to lodge in the guardroom with the rest. But as he moved toward the corner Vadin had claimed for him, Moranden's voice brought them both about. "Lord prince!"

Moranden was easy, affable, even smiling. The lord of the castle, a thin elderly man, looked ready to faint. As Vadin made his way behind Mirain through the crowding of men, he strangled laughter. The poor man was terrified enough to be playing host to the greatest lord in Ianon; now that lord presented him with the throne prince himself.

Who looked like a child, drenched and shivering; who raised his head and stood suddenly towering, full of the god; who spoke to the baron in his own rough patois and won his soul.

Vadin trailed the three of them in a sort of stupor. Much of it was wet and misery; some was fascination. He had never seen Mirain's magic worked so near, or to such devastating effect. Except that it was not magic, not exactly; not a thing of spells and cantrips. It was his whole self. His face, his bearing, his presence. His infallible knowledge of what to say, and when, and how. And his incomparable eyes.

They had the best the lord could offer, Moranden the room given over to guests, Mirain the lord's own chamber. The lord's own slaves built up the fire in the hearth, which smoked, but which was warm; even the squire had a warm robe, almost clean, and a cup of wine heated to scalding, and the slaves would not let him wait on his lord. He was a lord himself here. They were pitiably inept, but less so with him than with Mirain, who awed them into immobility. Until the prince loosed a smile and a word; then they fell over one another to please him.

Warm and dry and with the wine rising from his stomach to his brain, Vadin woke somewhat from his bemusement. After Han-Ianon this castle was shabby and unkempt and not remarkably clean, but it had an air of comfort; it felt like home. The slaves were ill-washed but well enough fed; the wine was good; the coverlet of the bed was beautiful. He remarked on the last, and Mirain smiled. "Your lady's weaving?" he asked the man who tended the fire, persuading it by degrees to smoke upward and not outward.

The slave bowed too low and too often, but he answered clearly enough. "Oh, yes, my lord, the Lady Gitani did it. It's poor stuff, I fear, as you great ones reckon it, but it's warm; the wool came from our own flocks."

"It's not poor at all; it's splendid. Look, Vadin, how pure a blue, like the sky in winter. Where ever did the lady find the dyes?"

"You must speak to her, great lord," the slave said, bowing. "She can tell you. It's a woman's art, my lord, but you a prince—she can tell you." He bowed yet again and took flight.

Mirain stood stroking the coverlet, smiling a little still, with the familiar wry twist. "How differently they look on a prince. When I was only a priest, I lodged in the stable or, if the family were pious, with the servants; no one ever stammered when I spoke to him. But I was Mirain then as I am now. Why should it matter?"

"You didn't have power then. You couldn't order one of them put to death, and be obeyed."

Mirain turned his eyes on Vadin. "Is that what makes a prince? The power to kill without penalty?"

"That's one way of putting it."

"No," Mirain said. "It has to be more than that."

"Not if you're a scullion in a hill fort."

The prince folded himself onto the splendid weaving, brows knit, chin on fist. Without the slaves to interfere, Vadin busied himself with their belongings, spreading wet garments to dry, inspecting the arms and armor in their wrappings. When he looked up again Mirain said, "I will be more than an exalted executioner. I will teach folk to see what a king can be. A guide, a guard. A protector of the weak against the strong."

Vadin rolled his eyes heavenward and squinted at Mirain's sword. The blade was beginning to dull. He reached for the whetstone.

"You scoff," Mirain said more in sorrow than in anger. "Is that all you know? Fear and force, and all power to the strongest?"

"What else is there?"

"Peace. Fearlessness. Law that rules every man, from the lowest to the highest."

"What odd dreams you have, my lord. Are they a southern sickness?"

"Now you're laughing at me." Mirain sighed deeply. "I know. If a king hopes to rule, he has to rule by force or he'll be struck from his throne. But if the force could be tempered with mercy—if he could teach another way, a gentler way, to those who were able to learn; if he could keep to his resolve and not surrender to the seductions of power —imagine it, Vadin. Imagine what he could do."

"He wouldn't last long in Ianon, my lord. We're howling barbarians here."

Mirain snorted. "You're no more a barbarian than the Prince of Han-Gilen."

"Not likely," said Vadin. "You won't catch me dead in trousers."

"Prince Orsan would shudder at the thought of a kilt. How ghastly to ride in. How utterly immodest."

"He must be as soft as a woman."

"No more than I."

Vadin eyed Mirain askance. "Have you been walking a shade gingerly for the past day or two?" He dodged the headrest from the bed, flung with alarming force. "What were you saying about mercy, my lord?"

"I had mercy. I took care to miss."

"See?" said Vadin. "Superior force. That's what makes you the prince and me the squire."

"Dear heaven, a philosopher. One of the new logicians, yet. I'll teach you to read, and you'll be a great master in the Nine Cities."

"Gods forbid," said Vadin with feeling.

Vadin dined in hall, seated perforce with the princes while the lesser folk took their ease below. At least he was allowed to set himself beside Mirain; no one had the wits or the courage to forbid him. He kept a wary eye on Moranden and a warier one on his own wild charge, who was enrapturing the lord's family as utterly as he had their kinsman. The women in particular were falling in love with him, although one doe-eyed youth—the youngest son, Vadin supposed—was long lost already. He waited on Mirain with something approaching grace, melting at a word or a glance, trembling if chance or duty brought him close enough to touch.

"Pretty," Vadin observed when the boy had retreated to fill the wine jar.

Mirain lifted a brow. "He's going to beg me to take him when I go. Shall I?"

"Why not? He looks as if he might be trainable."

The brow lifted another degree, but Mirain turned to answer a question, and did not turn back again.

Left to himself, Vadin watched the boy out of the corner of his eye. His amusement was going sour. Mirain did not mean it, of course. He already had more servants than he could bear. But the lad was extraordinarily pretty. Beautiful, in truth. Slender, graceful, with those great liquid eyes; his beard was only a sheen of down on his soft skin, and although his hair had grown long from the shaven head of childhood, he had not yet confined it in the braids of a man. Wrapped in soft wool and hung with jewels, he would make an exquisite girl. He was acting like one, swooning over Mirain.

Vadin's forehead ached. He realized that he was scowling. And who was he to disapprove? He had had a fling or two himself, though he much preferred to bed a woman.

Mirain smiled at the boy. What was his name? Ithan, Istan, something of the sort. It was one of Mirain's courtesan-smiles, not quite warm enough to burn. The boy swayed toward him. Caught himself, drew back in charming confusion. His glance crossed Vadin's; he flinched visibly and all but fled.

Amid all the sighing and swooning, Vadin could still observe that

Mirain left the hall sober and without incident, and moreover without lingering overmuch. Maybe he had grown as heartily sick of young love as Vadin had.

He slept at once and deeply, as always. Vadin, sharing the overlarge bed, lay awake as always. Not thinking of much; aware of the warm body near him, wishing it were Ledi's. One or two of the slaves had cast him glances; maybe, if he could slip out . . .

Mirain turned in his sleep. He came to Vadin as a pup to its dam, burrowed into the long bony body, sighed once and was still. Vadin's sigh was much deeper. Mirain did not feel anything like a woman, except for his skin. And his hair; it put Ithan's—Istan's—to shame. He had shaken it out of its braid; by morning it would be a hideous tangle. Without thinking, Vadin smoothed the mass of it. And kept smoothing it, stroking, keeping his hand light lest he wake Mirain. It was soothing, like petting a favorite hound.

Ianon would rise up in arms if it knew he thought such a thing. Mirain would laugh. He loved to look splendid and he knew when he did, but he was convinced of his own ugliness. Not that he was handsome, and he was anything but pretty. But beautiful, maybe. An odd, striking, inescapable beauty.

Vadin's hand stilled. He listened to the slow strong breathing, contemplated the arm that had settled itself across his chest. Suddenly he wanted to break free and bolt. Just as suddenly, he wanted to clutch at Mirain and babble an endless stream of nonsense. Waking him thereby and chancing his new-roused temper. Vadin lay very still and very quiet and made himself remember how to breathe. In, out. In, out. So. Out. In—

He had not lost his wager yet. That turned on friendship. There was nothing in it about falling in love.

Damn him, thought Vadin, still counting breaths. *Damn him, damn him, damn him.*

Nine

ISTAN BEGGED AS MIRAIN HAD FORETOLD, AND Mirain was kind to him, but firm. "I ride to battle; and I have a squire of the king's own choosing. Stay, grow strong, learn well all that your masters can teach. And when your hair is braided, if you can and will, come to Han-Ianon and I will welcome you."

The boy's great eyes swam with tears, but he held them back. He looked less like a boy then, and not at all like a girl. When Mirain rode away he was on the tower over the gate, watching. Vadin knew he would not move until they were long out of sight.

Mirain had not forgotten him; that was not his way. But he was focused ahead upon the loom of peaks that was the Marches, and the blue coverlet, given him as a gift, was folded away among the baggage.

Vadin was calm, riding beside him. Waking had been agony, not least for that he had lain immobile and sleepless for most of the night; and it was Mirain's rousing that had startled him into consciousness. The prince disentangled himself with no sign of shame, cross-grained as he always was on first waking but trying to train himself out of it, and oblivious to the wave of heat that laid Vadin low. Vadin looked at him and remembered, and considered hating himself, and froze in sudden horror. Mirain of all people, mage and god's son, walker in minds, could never be deceived. Vadin could feign the most perfect indifference, or be wise and conduct himself exactly as he always had, and Mirain would know. Would see. And if he cared, Vadin knew he would die of it; but he did not, that would be infinitely worse.

He had brought wine to Vadin still helpless under the coverlet, and he was the same as always. The god did not flame out of his eyes; they were clouded with sleep, but clearing, seeing nothing untoward. Vadin gulped the warm sweet wine, and it steadied him. Maybe, after all, he had nothing to fear. He did not have the kind of eyes that swooned, and Mirain would not invade a mind that resisted; and Avaryan's child or no, he was at his worst in the morning. By the time Mirain's wits were fully gathered, Vadin had himself well in hand.

With the wind in his face, fresh and cold with unmelted snows, he knew that he could master this. He was not like Istan. It was not Mirain's body he wanted; or not so much that he was weak with it. He would have something else. Maybe something unheard of.

"Look!" cried Mirain, flinging up his arm. Great wings boomed; an eagle dropped from the sky to settle like a falcon trained to jesses: a white eagle of the mountains, the royal bird of Ianon, companion of kings. Eye met eye, sun-fire to Sun-fire. With a high fierce cry the eagle cast itself sunward. It carried Mirain's soul with it, the body riding empty, easy in the tall war-saddle.

Vadin bent his stinging eyes upon Rami's ears. Gods and demons, he was lost indeed; jealous of a bird. And all for a wanderwit sorcerer who wanted to be a king. Who would probably die for wanting it. His eyes brimmed and overflowed; he swore at the whip of the wind.

The Marches came on slowly, in hills that swelled and rose and broke into mountains; in a spreading bleakness, green overwhelmed by the power of stone, trees stunted and twisted in the merciless wind. Summer had gained no foothold here. Where green could go, it was spring still, the snows but lately gone; the peaks were white with it, daring the sun to conquer them. But far away below was green and warmth and quiet, and as they rose higher Vadin could see the walls of Ianon's Vale across the rolling land, though not either Towers or castle. The former looked away from him toward the sunrise; the latter lay too well protected within its circling mountains.

They rode more cautiously now in a net of scouts and spies, feeling out this country that had risen against its lord. Yet they did not creep about like thieves. Moranden would have it known that he was in the Marches, but never precisely where. He would ride openly through a village, a cluster of huts beneath a crag; wind swiftly along hidden paths to a hold far distant; and take his rest there for a day, a night, or perhaps but an hour.

"Confusion," Mirain said to Vadin. "It makes the rebels uneasy. They're not as powerful here as they'd like to be; and the waverers are being reminded, often by their lord's own presence, that they swore oaths of fealty unto death."

A pretty chieftain remembered, and tried to appease both sides. He housed and feasted a ringleader, arrested him in his bed and sent word of the capture to the Prince Moranden. Moranden came, smiled, saw the rebel executed. And as the executioner brought him the head gaping and bleeding, raised his hand. His men seized the chieftain; the executioner, under Moranden's cold eye, did his duty yet again.

Vadin was no stranger to summary justice. He had grown up with it. But it was Mirain, raised in the gentle south, who watched unflinching, and Vadin who needed his head held afterward while he was thoroughly and shamefully sick. "I can kill," he gasped. "I can kill in battle. I know I can. But I can't—can't ever—Gods, his eyes when they took him. His *eyes.*"

Mirain did not insult him with either pity or sympathy. "He knew what he risked, but he refused to believe it. Traitors never do."

They had the garderobe to themselves, for a little while. Vadin turned in the doorway, his back to the curtain of leather that opened on the stair. "Would you have done what your uncle did?"

Mirain took time to relieve himself. It was dim, the cresset flickering above his bent head, but Vadin saw the thinning of his lips. At last he said, "I don't know. I . . . don't know." He straightened his kilt. "I've never been betrayed."

Yet. The word, unspoken, hung in the heavy air.

Moranden had made his point. His vassals sent him numerous protestations of loyalty. But the leaders, the begetters of the uprising, knew that they could expect no mercy. Gathering what forces they could, they fled in search of safety.

"Umijan," said the chief of Moranden's scouts, who had foundered a senel to reach his lord on the road between Shuan and Kerath. Vadin heard; Mirain, driven perhaps by prescience, had worked his way to the head of the line, and the elder prince's guards had made no effort to stop him.

"Yes," the scout repeated between gasps, accepting Moranden's own flask, drinking deep. "They hid a man in Kerath, nigh dead with fever, but not nigh enough. He babbled before he died. Umijan will shelter the rebels if they get there soon enough, and if they swear the proper oaths."

Moranden's face was rigid. Umijan was the heart of the Marches, its lord his close kinsman. Half-brother, whispered some who whispered also that he was no son of Raban the king. Save only for the giant-builded keep of Han-Ianon, it was the strongest holding in the kingdom, nor had it ever been taken. Once barricaded within, the fugitives could hold fast for as long as they chose. Or as Baron Ustaren chose, and he would not yield lightly; for he came of a long line of rebels against any lordship but their own.

"What if we come there first?" Mirain's voice brought them all about; at least one blade bared against him. He stared it down. "What if we come to Umijan before them?" he repeated. "What will Ustaren do then?"

"Impossible," rasped the captain nearest Moranden. "If they passed Kerath a full day and more ago, riding as fast as they should have been, they'll be inside the walls by tomorrow's sunset. We'll never catch them, let alone pass them."

"If we do," Mirain persisted, "will the lord hold to his treason? Or is he only playing a game he was bred to play? A race; to the winner his aid, to the loser his enmity."

The scout grinned. "That's it, my prince; there you have it. The Great Game, and he's a master of it, is my lord of Umijan. But the lead's too great. We can't close it in the time we have."

Moranden's charger fretted, ears flat, eye rolling at the Mad One. The elder prince forestalled a lunge, staining the foam with blood beneath the bit, but his mind was not on it. His eyes lay on Mirain. Vadin could not read them. They hated, yes, always, but not to blindness; they measured the mount and the rider, and narrowed. "Well, sister-son," he said, and that was a great concession before the army, "since your lordship chooses not to keep the place you were assigned to, tell us what you know that we're still ignorant of."

"I know nothing, lord commander," Mirain said without perceptible mockery, "but I don't believe we've lost the race. Give me ten men on the swiftest seneldi we have; provision us with what we can consume in the saddle; and I'll greet the traitors in your name from Umijan's gate."

"Why you? Why risk the throne prince on a venture that could kill him?"

"Because," Mirain answered, "the Mad One is the swiftest senel in Ianon, and he will suffer no rider but myself. He can win the race if no other can."

They watched, all the men who were close enough, and passed the tale in a murmur through the ranks. Mirain was challenging Moranden, whose commands hitherto he had not questioned; and Moranden was all too well aware of it. But there was no enmity in the challenge, on either side. Not this time, not with a common enemy before them.

"If I send you," said Moranden, "and you fall afoul of the enemy, or fail to convince Ustaren that you're a king and not a pawn in this game of his, I'll have more than Umijan raised against me."

"No. By my father I swear it. This venture is on my head alone. If you give me leave, my lord commander."

"And if I don't, my lord soldier?"

"I submit to your will. And," said Mirain, "we lose Umijan."

The dun stallion lowered its horns, snorting in outrage. Moranden's fist hammered it into submission. Suddenly he laughed, a deep free sound untainted with bitterness. "You have gall, boy. You may even have a chance. Pick your men, if you haven't already; Rakan, see to their provisioning."

Vadin did not ask to go. He assumed it. Rami could outrun anything on feet, perhaps even the Mad One himself. When he went to fill his saddlebags with journey-bread and presscakes and a double ration of water, Rakan the quartermaster gave him hardly a glance. He was part of Mirain, like the Mad One. He added all unnecessary burdens to the pile at Rakan's feet, even to shield and armor, even to his helmet, so light would they have to travel; but he kept sword and dagger, for no nobleman would go abroad without them. He regretted the sacrifice of his armor, although he would get it back when the army came to Umijan. Kilt and cloak were poor protection against edged bronze.

But they were not riding to a fight; they were riding to win a Marcher lord to Moranden's side in the game.

Mirain chose his men quickly enough to prove his uncle right. He chose well, Vadin judged and Moranden conceded. They were all young, but seasoned and strong; lightly built, most of them, long and light like Vadin or small and light like Mirain, and superbly mounted. They gathered ahead of the company, their seneldi fretting with eagerness, while Mirain faced Moranden once more and said, "Wish us well, my lord."

Moranden bowed his head. His eyes held Mirain's for a long moment. He did not smile, nor did he frown. Only Vadin was close enough to hear what he said. "For the king, priestess' bastard. For the kingdom one of us will rule. Ride hard and ride straight, and may the gods bring you there before the enemy."

Mirain smiled. "I'll see you in Umijan, my uncle." The Mad One wheeled on his haunches, belling. With a flash of his golden hand, Mirain flung them all into a gallop.

Afterward, when Vadin tried to remember that wild ride, he could call up most clearly the blur of wind and thunder, and Rami's mane whipping his hands, her long ears now flat with speed, now pricked as the riders slowed to breathe and eat and, far too briefly, to rest. They kept to the rhythm of the Great Race, grueling but not quite killing if senel and rider both were of the best. Rami was; Vadin was determined to be. She strode forth tirelessly, matching the Mad One pace for pace, even showing him her heels when once he faltered. A stone had caught him in a moment of carelessness; he surged up beside her on the narrow track, aimed a nip at her shoulder for her presumption. She scorned to notice him. Behind his flattened ears shone Mirain's sudden grin. Vadin bared his own teeth in reply, less grin than grimace.

They lost a man on the ridge called the Blade, sliding down its sheer side into a long level valley. His tall roan mare, taking the descent too suddenly, overbalanced; scrambled; hung suspended, and somersaulted screaming into air. The snap of her neck breaking was abrupt and hideous, but more hideous yet was the stillness of her rider. The three men behind could not stop, could only swerve and pray; of those ahead, one nearly died himself as his mount shied away from the plummeting bodies.

The last man slid to a halt on grass, trembling, the senel gasping, the soldier cursing in a steady drone. Mirain's voice cut across both. "The gods have taken their tribute. The army will tend the bodies when it passes. On now, for the love of Ianon. On!"

They lost the second man on a road of stones and scree. The spotted gelding stumbled and fell and came up lame; although his young rider wept on his neck, they left both to limp on as best they could. Avaryan was sinking and the country worsening, and they had lost their first bright edge of speed. And two gone already, with the night before them and the worst still far away.

But at last it seemed that the gods of this cruel country were sated. The company settled into a steady ground-devouring pace, close but not crowding, shifting as one or another dropped back to rest a little. Only the Mad One never relinquished his place; he ran before them all, untiring, with only the merest sheen of sweat to brighten his flanks.

Avaryan set in a torrent of fire. The stars bloomed one by one. Brightmoon would rise late and half full; Greatmoon climbed the sky at their backs, huge and ghostly pale. The Mad One ran as one with the shadows, but Mirain kept about him a last shimmer of sunset. It crowned him, faint yet clear; it glowed in the scarlet of his cloak. "Sunborn," someone said, far back behind Vadin. "Avaryan-lord. An-Sh'Endor." He had a fine voice; he made a chant of it, though no one else could spare breath for aught but living. Vadin found it echoing in his brain, set to the beat of Rami's hoofs. It was strong; there was power in it, the magic of true names. It bound them all to the one who led them, who found the way for them through the crowding dark. *Sunborn, Avaryan-lord, An-Sh'Endor.*

Just before the first glimmer of dawn, Mirain bade them halt. He had found a stream among the stones, and a patch or two of winter-blasted grass. They cooled their gasping mounts, watered and fed them, rubbed them down and dropped, falling into a sleep like death.

Vadin fought it. He had to see—he had to be sure—Mirain—

He opened his eyes on sunlight. They were strewn over the slope like the aftermath of battle, save only that no carrion birds had come to torment them. Those were circling, hopeful but not yet bold.

Mirain stood near him, face turned toward the sun as if he drank its sustenance. Vadin remembered part of his dream that might have been real: a dark sweet voice singing Avaryan into the sky. The prince turned, smiling slightly. Although Vadin knew beyond questioning that he had not slept, no weariness scarred him. His smile widened a fraction. "Priesthood," he said. "It thrives on long vigils." He bent, set something near Vadin's hand. "Eat. Drink. It's growing late."

Vadin groaned, but he obeyed. Mirain went round from man to man with a word and a touch for each, a cake, a bit of fruit, a gesture toward the stream. No one else voiced a complaint. In very little time by the sun, they were up and saddled and astride. Their water bottles were full, their mounts refreshed, although they rode with care at first to limber stiffened muscles. The sun warmed them; the wind was clean and keen. They stretched into racing pace.

The Black Peaks rose before them, curved about the high vale of Umijan. Somewhere in that tumble of ridge and valley, crag and tarn, ran the enemy. Sunset would find him at Umijan's gates. Sunset must find them within, with Baron Ustaren their sworn ally.

"Pray gods we get to the Gullet before the traitors," said Jeran, who was Marcher born, "or they'll swallow us while Ustaren watches."

The Gullet: the last stretch of the race, the long narrow way between walls of stone, rising slowly and then more steeply to the crag of the castle. Eight troopers and a prince, armed only with swords, mounted on spent seneldi, could find neither cover nor defense there.

Vadin was not afraid. He was far too intent on keeping the pace. Thus when they started up yet another of a thousand nameless slopes, he stopped without thinking, and only wondered when he saw the Mad One's saddle empty. Mirain running low to the crest. Still unthinking, he half fell to the ground, pursuing as stealthily as his exhausted body would allow, coming up beside the prince. The ridge looked down on a river meadow walled with crags and swarming with an army. Mounted men, men afoot, even a few chariots, advancing as the tide advances, steady and inexorable.

"The Gullet?" Vadin whispered, although he could see nothing that resembled a castle.

"Not yet," answered Mirain. "But this is the way, and there is no other, only a tangle of blind valleys."

Vadin peered at the walls. They were not precisely sheer to his hillman's eye, but a senel could not climb or traverse them. And the valley was full of rebels. With no wood or copse to conceal a passing company, only grass and stones and the bright path of the stream.

Jeran was beside them, greatly daring, whistling softly when he saw what there was to see. "They're slower than I thought: still an hour's gallop from the Gullet." He was haggard, caked with dust as they all were, trembling with weariness, but he grinned. "We'll make it yet, Sunborn."

Mirain did not react to his new title. He was intent on the army. "Arrogant," he muttered. "No scouts. No vanguard. Rearguard— No. They're all in the valley. We've come at them sidewise, that's luck, but not luck enough. Unless . . ." He paused, eyes narrowing. "Look; they're in good order, but not as good as they should be. They don't expect trouble."

"Will we give them some, my lord?" Jeran asked quickly, with a ghost of eagerness.

Mirain's eye glinted upon him. If Vadin had not known better, he would have sworn that Mirain was as fresh as a lordling newly risen from his bed. But his steadiness had to be an act of will: the strong face of a king before his people. Better that than the other choice, that he was much less human than he liked to appear. He touched the Marcher's shoulder, and the man glowed, waking to new vigor. "Tell the men to rest a little. If any dares not trust his mount or himself, let him be truthful. We must reach Umijan before yonder army."

No one would admit to weakness. No one flinched under Mirain's stare, although he did not spare the power of it, searching each hollowed face. At last his head bowed. He breathed deep, as if he had come to a decision. Slowly he raised his hands. "We are all at the edge of our endurance. But we must ride as we have never ridden before, and we must ride straight through the enemy. Else we are all lost." The unmarked hand spread toward the seneldi. Even the Mad One's proud neck drooped, although he tried to arch it under his lord's eye; his sides were matted with sweat and foam, his breath coming with effort. And he was the best of them all. Mirain turned his golden palm to catch the sun. "I have no strength to give you all, but what I have, I would give to our seneldi. Have I your leave?"

They stared at him, dulled minds struggling to understand. Vadin had an advantage: he had seen what Mirain could do. "Magic," he said sharply, to wake them. "God-power. He's asking leave to put a spell of endurance on your beasts."

One by one, raggedly together, they assented. They were Mirain's now, heart and soul. They watched him with awe and—yes—love, as he laid his hand on each broad brow beneath the horns of the lone gelding, between the eyes of the mares. And life flowed back into the spent bodies. Light kindled in dimmed eyes; nostrils flared, testing the wind. Last of all Mirain came to the Mad One. That one hardly needed his touch to swell and preen and stamp, but Mirain stood long by the strengthened shoulder, both hands on it, cheek against the tangled mane. With a sudden, almost convulsive movement he turned. Not Vadin alone caught his breath. In so little time, Mirain's face had aged years. But he sprang into the saddle, straight as ever, and the Mad One moved forward. "Come," Mirain commanded. "Follow me."

They rode openly over the crest, down the long slope toward the mass of the army. Whether by some trick of Mirain's power, or because they had not looked to be overtaken, the rebels made no move against them. Perhaps, with the sun in their eyes and the dust rising to cloud their advance, men judged the swift newcomers to be stragglers of their own force. No banner taught them otherwise, and no armor glinted warning. Filthy, worn to rags, mounted on lathered and gasping seneldi, the strangers might as easily have been fugitives in search of sanctuary.

There was space to skirt the left flank, a stretch like a road between army and cliff, and Mirain claimed it, with his men pounding after. Vadin heard a voice, a call that sounded like a question, growing peremptory. He crouched over Rami's neck. "Run," he prayed. "Longears, Rack-of-bones, love of my life, *run.*" His right eye was full of the glitter of weapons. His back crawled, yearning for its lost armor.

He fixed his whole being on the flying tassel of the Mad One's tail. It would carry him out of this. It would bring him safely home.

The voice begot echoes, not all born of air and mountainside. "Hold, I say! In whose name do you ride?"

"My own!" Mirain bellowed back. "Behind you—Moranden of the Vale—a day's ride—"

The Mad One veered. Mirain's arm swept the rest onward, but he sat his stallion well within bowshot of the captain who had hailed him. Vadin was bone-weary but he was not yet dead; he knew what Mirain was trying to do, and he had strength left to be appalled. He caught at the reins. But Rami with her velvet mouth, Rami whose obedience had never been less than perfect, Rami had the bit in her teeth and would not turn aside. He heard Mirain's voice, indistinct with distance. The lunatic was telling them where Moranden was, and how many men he had, and what his spies had said; but not what Mirain himself had said. And the army had slowed to hear him. The ranks behind were straggling. Some were cheering.

"But you," called a captain with a voice of brass. "How do you know this? Why are your men—" He broke off. He spurred his senel closer to the Mad One, who danced away, horns lowered. "Who are you?"

Mirain laughed and bared the torque at his throat and spun the stallion about. "Mirain," he called over his shoulder. "Mirain Prince of Ianon!"

The Mad One seemed to take wing, so swift was his escape. Behind him the army milled in disorder. But some of its men were quick of wit. Something sang, sweet and high and deadly. The Mad One came level with Rami.

A senel shrieked. Down—one was down before them with an arrow in its heart. Rami swerved; the Mad One leaped over the struggling body.

The rebels were beginning to move. It struck Vadin then, purest truth. If Mirain could hold them with his voice, could not one man hold them with his sword, tangle them further, gain more precious moments? Rami was free again, light in his hands. He gathered the reins to turn her about.

A band of unseen steel imprisoned his wrists. The mare strained forward. The Mad One's eye burned briefly upon Vadin's. Mad himself and raging, helpless as a man in chains, Vadin craned over his shoulder. Six. They were only six. Knots of men and beasts marked the fallen.

One of the six was free, or set free, stealing the glory Vadin had chosen. Riding in that swooping arc, singing a wicked satire, whirling his bright sword. Arrows could not touch him. Spears fell spent about him. Singing, he plunged into the foremost rank, and men howled and died. "Mirain!" Vadin stormed at a rider of stone. *"Mirain!"*

The vale narrowed before them. There at last beyond doubting was the black gorge and the loom of Umijan against the setting sun. Behind them the army had loosed its most deadly weapon: a company of mounted archers.

"Ride!" cried Mirain. "Trust to the god and ride! Umijan is before us."

Aye, like the very keep of hell, black Gullet, black crag, black castle. And the last of the Gullet was the Tongue, and that was a path against one sheer wall, for the other dropped away to a precipice and far below a cold gleam of water; and this eagles' track reared steeply to the frown of the gate. Truly Umijan could never be taken, for there was not even space for three men abreast to assail its walls, and the cliff that edged the path melted into the very crag of the castle.

If Vadin had had a grain of strength left, he would have laughed. He knew the gods did. Of all that terrible race, this must be the worst, with arrows raining and life pouring away and one misstep the road to certain death. With every stride he knew Rami's great heart would burst. The air beckoned, the emptiness beyond the narrow polished path, singing of rest. He clung to the pale mane, straining as Rami strained, willing her to run swift, run straight, run steady. "Only a little way now. Only a little. Up, my love. Up to the gate. Up!"

She heard him. The archers or the road had taken Vian. There was only Jeran behind him, and little Tuan, and Mirain—Mirain mad to the last, herding them, defying death to take him. Tuan's staggering roan went down, barring the narrow way. The Mad One swayed on the very edge of the precipice. Tuan shouted, shrill as a child, and howled as Mirain swept him headfirst across the saddle. The stallion gathered and hurtled over the dying mare. The foremost archer spurred upon his heels. The mare, thrashing, caught the foreleg of the rebel's mount. It screamed and toppled and spun slowly over the rim.

The Mad One hurled himself up the steep ledge. Jeran lagged, his lovely golden mare dying as she ran, he weeping and cursing and beseeching her forgiveness as he lashed her on. But it was the Mad One who gave her strength, who gored her flank with cruel horns, driving her upward.

Vadin burst into quiet, and for an eternal instant he knew that it was death. Until he saw walls and a paved court and people thronging, and the Mad One plunging through the gates with Jeran's mare before him, and the gates swinging shut. Slowly, slowly, the golden mare crumpled to the stones. Jeran lay beside her and wept.

The race was won. They had come to Umijan.

Ten

VADIN WAS ON THE GROUND. IT WAS COLD, AND HE did not remember falling. He dragged himself up, inch by tortured inch, knowing all the while that when he was on his feet he would go mad. He must tend Rami, or she would die; he must tend Mirain, or his honor as a squire would die.

They had Rami, people who insisted that they knew how to care for her. More gathered about Jeran's mare, and a valiant few tended the Mad One. Mirain—

Mirain stood in a circle of giants, eye to eye with the tallest of them all, who stood to Vadin as Vadin stood to Mirain. Even in his fog of exhaustion Vadin knew who this must be; the likeness to Moranden was uncanny.

Mirain's voice came clear and proud and indomitable. "Good day, lord baron, and greetings in the name of the Prince Moranden. He bids you make ready for his coming; he requests that his resting place be free of vermin."

Vadin sucked in his breath. The people about looked as shocked as he felt, and some were stiff with outrage. But Baron Ustaren looked at his kinsman's ambassador and laughed. "What! Shall I leave no rats for my cousin to hunt at his leisure?"

"Only if you are prepared to be counted among the quarry."

Vadin edged toward Mirain. Not that he had much hope of being useful; some of the onlookers had throwing spears and some had strung bows. And men in Umijan were large even for northerners. He was the merest stripling here, with barely strength to stand, let alone to fight. They let him stand at his lord's back, which proved the sublimity of their contempt. Mirain was oblivious to him. The prince was staring the baron down, and succeeding in it. Ustaren had less pride than Moranden had, or more guile; he yielded with all appearance of goodwill. "The rats shall be disposed of. How may I name the bearer of his lordship's command?"

"As Prince Moranden himself names me," Mirain answered. "Messenger."

"So then, sir messenger, shall I house you among the warriors? Or would I be wiser to treat you as my guest? or as a priest? or perhaps as the heir of Ianon?"

"Wherever I am placed, I remain myself." Mirain's chin lifted a degree. "Lord baron, you have vermin to hunt, and my companions stand in sore need of tending. Have I your leave?"

Ustaren bowed low and shaped a sign that Vadin almost knew. Others repeated it as he said, "All shall be done as the Sun's son commands." His voice raised to a roar. "Ho, Umijan! We ride to fight."

Vadin lay in a bed that should have been celestially soft, and ached in each separate muscle and bone. He had slept as much as he was going to, but his body could not heal itself as quickly as that. Even his ears throbbed dully. Someone was snoring, or more likely some two, Jeran and Tuan abed in the guard's niche of Umijan's great chamber. Mirain, who never snored, held the other half of that vast bed, long enough and broad enough to dwarf even the Lord of Umijan.

Someone must have laid them all in their places, undressed them and cleaned them. Vadin remembered coming here, and knowing whose chamber it was, but no more than that. The two soldiers had been carried unconscious. Vadin had walked, and been inordinately proud of it. Mirain had not only walked, he had been giving orders. He would have put himself to bed, simply to prove that he could do it.

With some effort and no little pain, Vadin raised himself on his elbow. Mirain slept like a child, lying on his stomach with his face turned toward Vadin and his hand fisted beside it. Maybe, had he been younger, his thumb would have been in his mouth. But the face was no child's. Even in sleep it was furrowed with exhaustion.

Vadin's teeth clicked together. Mirain did not sleep on his face. He slept sprawled on his back or curled neatly on his side. And not weariness alone had graven that deep line between his brows.

Very carefully Vadin folded back the blankets. Mirain's back was
clear, smooth, unhurt. No arrow had found its way there. He was wearing a kilt, clearly not his own; it was overlong and wrapped twice about
him. As if that could have deceived Vadin, who knew that Mirain slept
as bare as any other man in Ianon.

The kilt, pathetic subterfuge that it was, had slipped upward as he
slept, baring what it was meant to hide. Vadin wanted to howl like a
beast. Soft, Mirain was not, he had proven it beyond all questioning, but
he had not ridden all his life in the poor protection of kilt or battle
tunic. And he had ridden the greatest of all Great Races, half a day and
a night and nigh a full day again, and never once, never for an instant,
had he let slip that he was being flayed alive.

Vadin should have known. He should have thought. He should
have—

"Nonsense." Mirain was awake. He looked no less haggard, but his
eyes were clear. "You will say no word of this."

Vadin understood. Not that anyone would think the less of Mirain for
it, but that damnable pride of his—

"That has nothing to do with it!" Mirain snapped. "Can't you taste
the danger here? If it's known that I'm hurt, they'll hover over us day
and night, not merely keep a watch on the door."

The part about danger was true enough. Vadin started to unwind the
kilt; Mirain glared but did not try to stop him.

It was not as bad as he had feared. The wounds were clean, though
not pleasant to see. They had not festered. Vadin covered them with
care, and rose. Not till he reached the door did he realize that he had
forgotten how much he hurt. He drew the bolt and called out, "Redroot
salve and the softest bandages you can find, and something to eat. Be
quick!" He was slow in closing the door, and he was careful to move
stiffly.

The salve came in a covered jar, and it was redroot indeed; its pungency made his eyes water. The bandages were fine and soft, the food
substantial and steaming, and there was a pitcher of ale. They were
sparing no trouble here. For Mirain's sake, Vadin wondered briefly, or
for Moranden's? He bolted the door in curious faces and advanced on
Mirain.

The prince was sitting up, which was admirable for appearances but
appalling for his hurts. "Lie down," Vadin ordered him.

For a miracle he obeyed. Once he was flat again, he loosed a faint sigh
and closed his eyes. Vadin's own were wide and burning dry. He remembered his mother the day the brindled stallion had gored his father;

she had looked the way he felt now. Stiff and quiet, and very, very angry. The anger tainted his voice, made the words cruel. "Brace yourself. This will sting."

Vadin's hands were gentler than his tongue. Mirain was quiet, all but unflinching. But of course; he lived with a fire in his hand to which this was a mere flush of warmth. Not that the pain itself was any less, or the shame. Vadin said, "You're an initiate now. You've blooded your saddle; you've been anointed with redroot."

"What makes you think I need the reassurance?"

"So you don't," said Vadin, beginning the slow task of covering salved flesh with bandages. "So you're snapping at me because it amuses you. How do you think I got this leathered hide? Days in the saddle and nights on my face with redroot burning me to the bone, and half a dozen stints of wearing bandages wrapped like trousers."

"You should wear trousers to start with, and spare yourself suffering."

"That would be too easy. Or you'd have done it yourself."

Mirain stood for Vadin to finish, moving with care, looking as grim as his grandfather. "Easy. That's the heart of it. Trousers reek of ease and comfort and southern effeminacy. I can't wear them here and be looked on as either a man or a prince. Whereas my shaven face, now that is scandalous, but it's endurable: it's difficult, it's troublesome, it often draws blood. Men in Ianon will sacrifice their beards gladly for a fashion or a flattery, but they'll die before they wrap their legs in trousers."

"I'll die before I do either." Vadin bound off the last bandage, but he remained on his knees. It was strange to look up at Mirain and to know that it had nothing to do with wizardry. He sat on his heels. "I've earned my comfort in a kilt; I'm not about to atone for it with a razor."

"You *are* a philosopher." Mirain grinned so suddenly that Vadin blinked, and ran a finger down the squire's cheek. It was a gesture just short of insult, and just short of a caress. "Also much handsomer than I, and charmingly blind to the fact. It's not only your fine character that endears you to Ledi."

"Of course not. She loves my fine copper, and my occasional silver."

"Not to mention your splendid smile. And that cleft in your chin . . . ah!"

Vadin locked his hands together before they hit something. "You had better dress," he said, "my lord. Before the others wake and see."

"They won't." But Mirain went in search of clothing and found a tunic that made him a rather handsome robe, and Vadin found his temper again. As the prince approached the food, he was able to follow suit, even to keep from glowering. Even, in time, to muster a smile, albeit with a touch of a snarl.

When Moranden rode in at last, Mirain was there in his own kilt and cloak, now clean and mended. The elder prince had for escort his kinsman of Umijan; and every Umijeni behind them carried on his spear the head of a rebel. So too did a number of Ianyn, and they were singing as they came.

The women of Umijan raised their own shrill paean, the chant that was half of exultation for the victory, half of grief for the fallen. Amid the tumult Mirain stood alone with the three who were left of his companions, and there was a circle of stillness about them, a flicker of fingers in the sign Vadin had seen before. Again its familiarity pricked, again he had no time to remember. They were all coming toward Mirain, Moranden leading, handing the reins to one who reached for them, facing his sister's son. He was full of victory, magnanimous with it; he embraced his rival, and Mirain grinned at him as if they had never been aught but friends. Vadin could not understand why he was so little minded to join in the cheer that went up. It was not a feeble cheer. The army clashed spear on shield, roaring their names. *Mirain! Moranden! Moranden! Mirain!*

When some semblance of quiet had fallen, Moranden said, "Well done, kinsman. Splendidly done. If you weren't a knight of Han-Gilen, I'd make you one of Ianon."

Mirain smiled up into the glad and lordly face, so amiable to see, and responded with all sweetness, "I take your words as they are meant, my uncle."

Moranden laughed and clapped him on the back, staggering him, and turned to the baron. "I trust you've housed and looked after my kinsman as he deserves. He's no less than Ianon's heir."

"I've set him in my own chamber," Ustaren said, "and given him my own slaves to command as he wills."

"With which," said Mirain, "I am well content."

Such a love-feast. It was making Vadin ill. Mercifully they cut it short; there were wounded to see to, and trophies to hang, and women to be bedded in the rites of triumph. Mirain was encouraged to rest, with much solicitude for the toll his ride must have taken. Not that they knew the truth of it, or could guess; he refused to walk lame, and two days out of the saddle had smoothed the furrows of exhaustion from his face. He was being pampered like a royal maiden, nor could he help but know it, yet he left the courtyard with good grace.

Jeran went to see his mare, who was expected to live; Mirain had had something to do with that. Tuan followed with an eye on the hayloft and one of the serving maids. Mirain trailed at some distance.

They had had to set the Mad One apart in a stable of his own. He endured strange hands upon him, provided that they presumed only to tend him, but he would not suffer the stallion who ruled as king here. The beast, a splendid young bay, would bear the scars until he died, although the Mad One had forborne to slay him. For scorn, Vadin suspected. The black demon seemed content in his exile, with Rami near him and Jeran's mare coming slowly back to life within his sight. He accepted the delicacies Mirain had saved for him, submitted to the prince's scrutiny, snorted when Vadin observed, "Not a mark on him. You'd think he'd done nothing more strenuous than march on parade."

Mirain fondled Rami's head. The gap in the wall through which it had appeared had not been there before the Mad One came. "This beauty too," he said; "already she frets to be idle."

"You can talk to her," Vadin said more sullenly than he had meant.

"Seneldi don't use words." Mirain inspected the Mad One's hoof, bending with care, speaking as to it. "To Rami I'm a great one who shines in the night, a master of magic. I can speak clearly to her and know what she wishes me to know, and maybe she thinks well of me. But you are the one she loves."

Vadin barely heard. The words were only words, sound obscuring the thoughts behind, and memory had smitten him with such force that he nearly fell. Men in Han-Ianon, Marcher born, and secret signs, and a flicker of fingers wherever Mirain was. "The sign," he said. "The sign they all make where you can't quite see. It's a Great Sign. It's the sign against a prince of demons."

"I know," said Mirain calmly, releasing the hoof, smoothing a tangle in the black mane.

"You know?" Vadin shook with the effort of shouting in a whisper. "You know what it means? This is the goddess' country. What she is in Han-Gilen, and what the king would make her in Ianon, Avaryan is here. Enemy. Adversary. Burning devil. And they know that you're his son. Any man in Umijan could cut you down and be counted a saint for doing it."

"None has tried yet. None tried when we were all helpless. And now Moranden is here, and his army comes from the Vale."

"How do you know Moranden won't egg the murderer on? He goaded you into coming here. This may be his very own trap, all nicely baited."

"Have you turned so completely against him?"

Bile stung Vadin's throat. He choked it down. "No. No, I haven't. I only know what I would do if I were Moranden and this were my fief. I'd challenge you and kill you, and see that the truth never found its way eastward."

"And yet," Mirain said, "you forget. The army has learned to wish me well."

"That's too easily unlearned." Vadin gripped his arm, pulling him about. "Let's run for it. Now."

Mirain looked from Vadin's hand to his face, and raised a cool brow. "Have you suddenly turned coward?"

"I don't linger in closing traps."

Slowly Mirain's free hand raised in denial. "No, Vadin. I know what my pride has brought me to, but I can't flee now. The game is too well begun. I have to play it out."

"Even to your death?"

"Or Moranden's."

"Or both." Vadin let him go. "Why am I arguing with you? Ymin herself couldn't talk sense into you; and that was before you even started. Go ahead then. Kill yourself. You'll be comfortably dead, and you won't have to face what comes after."

That stung Mirain, but not enough. "If the god wills it, so be it. But I'll do all I can to forestall it. Can that content you?"

It would have to. Mirain would yield no further than that.

Baron Ustaren kept princely state in his hall. His knights dined on white wood, his captains on copper; for himself and his highborn guests there were plates and goblets of chased silver.

Here as elsewhere in the Marches, women did not eat with their men; but maids served the high table, robed and modestly veiled, with downcast eyes. One or two, Vadin thought, might have been lovely. The one who hovered about Mirain certainly was, if a soft dark eye and a lissome figure were any guide; though she was taller than Vadin, and beside Mirain she was a giantess. Unobtrusively Vadin tried to penetrate her veil, to see whether her face matched her eyes.

Mirain watched her likewise with an intensity that came close to insult. Close, but not, it seemed, on the mark. Ustaren laid a heavy hand on his shoulder and grinned. "My sister's daughter," he said, cocking his head toward the girl. "Do you like her?"

Mirain shaped his words with visible care. "She is very beautiful; she serves me well. She honors your house."

"Would she honor yours, Prince of Ianon?"

She had frozen like a hunted doe. Her fear was palpable. Of the baron; of Moranden, who watched and listened and said no word; of Mirain. Of Mirain most of all, a fear mingled with fascination and a strange, reluctant, piercing pity.

"I am young," he said, "to think of such things."

Ustaren laughed, a great bellow of mirth. "Too young for that, prince? Your stature may be a child's, but all the tales grant you a man's years. Do they lie after all?"

The hall, Vadin noticed abruptly, was very still. Neither Tuan nor Jeran sat close by, nor any other of the men who had shown themselves loyal to Mirain. Indeed he could not find them at all. Every man whose face Vadin knew, was Moranden's, watching Mirain steadily, with palpable hostility.

Old tactics, and effective. Separate the enemy from his allies; surround him and conquer.

Mirain's cup was full of strong sweet wine. He raised it and drank, saluting Ustaren. "A man is a man, whatever his size."

"Or maybe," said Ustaren, "he's half a god. Tell me, did he come to your mother as a man comes? Or as a spirit, or a shower of gold, or a warm rain? How would a god take his bride?"

Mirain's eyes glittered, but his voice was level. "That was, and remains, between herself and the god."

"However he came," Ustaren said unruffled, "he left his mark on you. Or so they say."

Mirain's fist clenched upon it. "He was so gracious as to leave me proof of my parentage."

"Are mere mortals permitted to look upon it?"

The tension in the hall had risen until it was all but visible. Vadin's brain throbbed with it. He struggled to speak.

"The mark!" a man cried. "Let us see the mark!"

Mirain rose suddenly, nearly oversetting his chair. One or two men laughed, thinking he had drunk his fair share. He flung up his fist. "Yes, my father marked me. Branded me for all to see. Here; look at it!"

Gold caught fire in his palm. Someone cried aloud.

Behind Vadin danger crouched. He tensed to leap. Too late. Strong arms locked about him, dragging him back.

Where Mirain's heart had been, a black blade clove the air. The maidservant spun, eyes wide and fixed.

Moranden surged to his feet. Men of Umijan were all about him. Two had Vadin, who fought with all the strength he had. But Mirain was

free. People in the hall had drawn back, taking the tables with them. A
wide space lay open around the central fire, and there was order in the
folk who rimmed it, the order of ritual. Men outside, veiled women in a
circle within, and in the center, Mirain with the baron's kinswoman.
She had cast aside her veil; she was even more lovely than Vadin had
suspected. And far more deadly. In each hand she held a dagger; one
was black and straight, one bronze-brown and curved. She moved
slowly, fluidly, as in a dance, closing in upon her prey.

Vadin bit a careless hand. Its owner struck him half senseless but did
not let him go. As he gathered to renew his struggle, Moranden shouted
with the roughness of rage, "No! I forbid this!"

It was Mirain who answered him, Mirain casting aside his robe of
honor, never losing a step in the dance of death. His voice was frighteningly gentle. "Let be, kinsman. I'll die and give you what you long for,
or I'll live to face you on the field of honor. How can you fail?" He
flashed his white smile. "*I* don't intend to."

The black knife licked out. He danced away. The girl smiled. "O
valiant," she said almost tenderly. "O brave boy, brought here to fight
in the war we made for you. It is a pity you must die. You are so
young."

"The black blade," Moranden said harshly over the fading echo of
her words. "The black blade is poisoned. The other is for your heart
when she has you. After it has taken your manhood."

"Gentle poison," she said. "It makes its victim long to lie down and
love me. Will you come to it? You are the goddess' own, so fair to see."

"So beloved of her enemy." Mirain saluted Moranden, who could not
or would not aid him, but who had given him what honor demanded.
He matched the woman step for step, mirroring her, keeping a distance
which she could not close. She was no swifter than he, but she was no
slower.

At first Vadin thought his ears tricked him. The hall was as silent as
any hall could be with half a thousand people in it, and a fire blazing,
and two mad creatures stalking one another around the hearth. But
under the silence and about it and through it wove a slow sweet music.
Darkness shot with gold. A voice at once deep and clear. Mirain had
begun to sing.

The woman—no, she was a priestess, a votary of the goddess; she
could be no other—the priestess sprang, clawed with bronze and black
iron. The chant broke. Resumed. It was clearly audible now, but the
words were strange. They seemed to have no meaning, or a meaning
beyond mere human words.

A massive form lunged into the circle. Ustaren, still-faced, still-eyed, enchanted. Mirain was gone like a shadow. The priestess wheeled, her daggers a blur in her hands. Black slashed foremost. The force of the baron's advance drove him full upon the poisoned blade. Slowly, with no more sound than a sigh, he sank down. The priestess laughed high and wild. "Blood! Blood for the goddess!"

Mirain was on her, cat-quick, cat-fluid. The black dagger lodged deep in Ustaren's body, stilling as the heart stilled. The bronze flashed so close to Mirain's cheek that surely it was shaven anew. He laughed sharp and fierce. His golden hand closed upon the woman's wrist; she wailed in agony.

The knife fell, she after it. He let her fall. The dagger he caught, wheeling about. The fire roared to the roof and collapsed into embers. He walked over it. Through it. The circle broke, shrinking from the terror of his eyes. They swept the greying faces. The god filled them, flamed in them, consumed them. "You fools," he said with terrible softness. "You brave, blind, treacherous fools."

"Hell-spawn!" howled one bolder, or madder, than the rest. It might have been a woman. It might have been a man shrill with fear.

Mirain did not answer. He faced his mother's brother and said, "I will remember that you spoke for me. Do you remember that I brought about the death of the chief of your rebels, the raiser of the Marches, the master of the tribes. He would have trapped us both, me to my death, you to be his puppet in the king's hall. I leave you his holding and his people." He hurled the dagger to the floor at Moranden's feet. It clattered in the silence. "Do with them as you will, my lord of the Western Marches. My father calls me elsewhere."

Eleven

SINCE MIRAIN LEFT, THE KING HAD TAKEN TO THE battlements again, gazing not southward now but westward. Ymin was with him through much of his vigil, still and silent, her eyes as often upon him as upon the horizon. He was old, she thought. He had always been old; yet he had been strong, like an ancient tree. Now he was brittle and like to break. When the wind blew chill from the mountains, he shivered, huddling in his cloak; when the sun beat down, he bowed under it.

On the fourth day of Brightmoon's waning, the twentieth since Mirain's leaving, the sun rose beyond a heavy curtain of cloud. A thin grey rain darkened the castle; yet the king kept his watch. Even Ymin had striven in vain to dissuade him. He stood unheeding under the canopy his servants had erected for him, with the rain in his face and the wind in his hair. Now and then a shiver would rack his body, despite a rich cloak of embroidered leather lined with fleece.

Those who came and went on the kingdom's business—for the king ruled as firmly from his battlements as from his throne—looked at one another and made signs which they thought he could not see. Surely, and at long last, he had fallen into his dotage.

He did not deign to notice them. Ymin suffered them, for having failed to entice him from his post she held her peace. Sometimes she sang to herself, old songs and new ones, rain-songs and hymns to the Sun.

Suddenly she faltered. He had stiffened and stepped forward into the full force of the wind.

The Vale of Ianon was hidden in a thin mist. Shapes moved within it, now all but invisible, now clear to see: farmfolk on errands that could not wait for a clear sky, a traveler or two trudging toward warmth and dry feet. Once there had been a post-rider, and once a lady's carriage.

This was a mounted company, drab in the rain. There were four of them. No banner floated over them; whatever badges they bore lay hidden under dark cloaks. Their mounts moved swiftly enough, but the beasts' necks were low with weariness.

The foremost was glistening black in the rain, and it alone seemed to run easily. It wore no bridle.

The king had already reached the stair to the gate.

The riders clattered under the carven arch. One by one, wearily, they dismounted to give reverence to the king. He ignored them. Mirain was slowest to leave his senel's back, yet he seemed less worn than the rest. He even smiled a little as he came to his grandfather's embrace, standing back when the king would let him and saying, "Why, you are as wet as I! Grandfather, have you been waiting for me?"

"Yes." The king held him at arm's length. "Where is Moranden?"

Mirain's face did not change. "Behind me. He had matters to settle."

"Such as the war?"

"The war is over." Mirain shivered and sneezed. "Grandfather, by your leave, may I dismiss my escort?"

If the king recognized the evasion, he saw the truth in it. "You also. I shall speak with you when you are dry and rested."

There was a fire on the hearth in the king's chamber and spiced wine warming over it, and in front of it the king, with Ymin on the stool beside him. Mirain sat by them without a word, accepting the cup the singer handed him. He had bathed; his hair was clean and loose and beginning to dry, and he had on a long soft robe. His face in firelight was still, almost a mask, his mouth set in a grimmer line than perhaps he knew of.

The king stirred. "Tell me," he said simply.

For a long moment Mirain was silent, staring down at his untouched wine. At length he said, "The war is over. Not that it was much of one, in the end. It was all a trick. Ustaren of Umijan played a large part in it. He is dead. I am here. Moranden will follow when he has settled his fief."

Again there was a silence. When Mirain showed no sign of continuing, the king said, "You left him early and all but alone. Why?"

"There was nothing for me to do."

"You could have remained to rule in my name. You are my heir, and will be king."

"Moranden is Lord of the Western Marches."

The king regarded him long and deeply. "Perhaps," he said, "you fled."

Mirain flung up his head. "Are you accusing me of cowardice?"

"I am saying what others will say. Are you prepared to defend yourself?"

"In that part of Ianon," Mirain said, "my parentage is not a thing to boast of. Lacking a war to fight in, I judged it best to return here."

"How did Ustaren die?"

If the question had been meant to take Mirain off guard, it failed. "He fell at the hands of one of his kin, a priestess of the goddess. She was quite mad. She was aiming," he added, "at me."

The king's face drew taut. "No one moved to defend you?"

"My uncle tried, as did my squire. They were prevented. Ustaren died. I did not."

"And you left."

"Before any others could die for me. It is not time yet to teach the Marches the error of their religion."

The king bowed his head as if suddenly it had grown too heavy to lift. In his eyes was a horror, a vision of Mirain dead with a black dagger in his heart.

Mirain knelt in front of him and laid his hands on the gnarled knees. "Grandfather," he said with an undertone of urgency, "I am safe. See; I am here, and alive, and unhurt. I will not die and leave you alone. By my father's hand I swear it."

"Your father's hand." The king lifted Mirain's own, touching with a fingertip the sun of gold. Briefly, painfully, he smiled. "Go to bed, child. You look to be in need of it."

Mirain hesitated, then rose and kissed his brow. "Good night, Grandfather."

"Good night," the king said, almost too softly to be heard.

Ymin eased the door shut behind her. The chamber was dim, the nightlamp burning with its shaded flame, flickering in a waft of air. The lad from Imehen surged up in his niche, eyes glittering, his body a shadow of alarm. She sang a Word; he subsided slowly.

Mirain was in bed but not asleep. He did not move as Ymin came to stand beside him. Nor did he glance at her, although he brought one arm up, bending it, pillowing his head on it. He was not wearing his torque. He looked odd without it, younger, strangely defenseless. That, she knew, was an illusion. Even at his lowest ebb, Mirain never lacked for defenses. He had only to raise his hand.

He spoke softly, coolly, without greeting. "You have great skill with the Voice."

"If I did not, I would not be the king's singer."

He turned his eyes upon her then. Perhaps he was amused. Certainly he was holding something at bay. "I cannot be so enchanted. Even," he said, "when I yearn to be."

She sat on the bed beside him. "Have you proven that?"

"My initiation into the priesthood was . . . hampered. One of the priests was young and strong and impatient. He tried force." Mirain paused for a heartbeat. The thing in his eyes, the surging darkness, the sudden light, came almost near enough to name. "He lived. He healed, after a fashion."

"You won your torque."

"Avaryan's priests would not refuse it to Avaryan's son. Even though he could not submit that last fraction of his will. Even though he had come within a breath of murder. Even though he could not master the power which was a deadly danger to them all."

"Perhaps," she said, "the power has its own laws, and your soul knows them but your mind does not. The rite of the torque was made for simple mortal folk, to teach them submission, to waken them to the might of the god. As his son you have need of neither."

"I have more need than any." He was quiet still, but she was beginning to understand. The darkness was wrath, and grief, and hatred of himself. The light was Sun-fire crying to be set free.

"Tell me," she bade him gently, yet with a tang of iron. "Tell me what you are hiding from the king."

His eyes hooded. "What is there to hide?"

Suddenly she had no patience at all. "Must we play at truth-and-falsehood like a pair of children? The king suffers it; he longs to spare you pain. I have no such scruples. You left Umijan because Moranden tried to kill you. Did you not?"

"Not Moranden. Ustaren, through a kinswoman of his, a priestess of the Dark One. Moranden gave me what aid he could."

"It was not enough."

"It was more than he needed to give."

"And that galls you."

Abruptly he rolled onto his face. The coverlet slipped; he made no effort to regain it. She looked with pleasure at his smooth-skinned compact body; saw the healing scars and knew them for what they were; yielded to temptation, running a light hand down his back. He shivered under it, but his voice was clear and unshaken. "It gladdens me. Moranden may have meant betrayal; he may have meant to challenge me. But in extremity he came to my aid. He may yet become my ally."

"Why then did you abandon him? Why did you not remain to press your advantage? Now he is in the Marches among his own people; he will forget alliance and remember only enmity, until he raises the folk against you. Why did you set him free to betray you?"

He moved all at once with blurring speed, half rising, seizing her hand in a grip she could not break. She met his wide dark stare. His nostrils flared; his lips drew back. "*I* did not set him free. I had no say in the matter. For I was threatened, and the power came, and it did as it chose. It lured Ustaren to his death. It laid the priestess low. It flung the Marches in Moranden's face and drove me back to this my kennel, where I may be safe and warm and protected from all harm." As suddenly as he had seized her he let her go, drawing into a knot of rage and misery. "The power did all these things, and now it sleeps. And I wake to face what I have done. Murder, madness, cowardice—"

"Wisdom." She had silenced him. "Yes, wisdom. I spoke ill before; I did not think. You were best away once your power had revealed itself, and Moranden will not turn against you yet. Not he. He will challenge you in the open before all Ianon. So much your power knew when it sent you back to us."

"My power did more than defend me. It killed. And I—I exulted. I gave blood to the goddess, and the god flamed in me, and it was sweeter than wine, sweeter than honey, sweeter even than desire." His voice broke on the last word; he coiled tighter, rocking, face hidden in his heavy hair. "I wonder, singer. Are these vows of mine a dire mistake? Perhaps if—I—" He laughed with a catch in it. "Maybe it's all perfectly simple. I only need do what any man does when the need is on him, and the power will see how sweet it is and forget the delights of slaughter."

Her foolish brain wondered if he had had more wine than was good for him. But her nose caught no scent but his own faint, distinct, male musk; and her eyes saw that his own were clear, if troubled; and her heart knew that he was only being himself. Begotten of a god, branded with it, laden with a destiny and compelled to pursue it, yet he was also a man, a very young one, a boy half grown given powers and burdens that would stagger a man in full prime.

She felt him in her mind, drawn into it, walking the paths of her thoughts. His face was set hard against pity. She felt none, which shocked him into himself. She watched him begin to be angry, realize how ridiculous it was, try to swallow mirth. He looked his proper age then. Before he could laugh she silenced him, laying her hand upon his lips. They were very warm.

She drew back carefully. His eyes were his own again. Grief and guilt would linger, anger would return, but the great storm had passed. Now he was regarding her, and for a Sun-priest raised in Han-Gilen he was astoundingly free of shame; he did not try to hide his body's tribute. "You had better go," he said steadily, with only the faintest hint of breathlessness.

Ymin did not move. "Would you like me to sing you to sleep?"

He stiffened, stung. "Do I seem so very much a child?"

"You seem very much a man. Who has sworn oaths that only death or a throne may break; who has done deeds to sing of, and suffered for them, and begun to find peace. You are the king who will be, and I am the king's singer. Shall I sing for you?"

The moment was gone, the danger faded. He lay on his side and drew up the coverlet, not quickly, not as if he would hide anything, but with a certain finality. The he smiled with all the sweetness in the world, and she could have killed him, for now that he had mastered himself he had robbed her of all her lofty detachment. And he did not even know what he had done. "Sing for me," he said, simple as a child.

She drew a long breath and obeyed.

Twelve

WHEN VADIN WOKE FROM A DREAM OF SONGS AND magic, he could have sung himself. Mirain was up and bathing and trying not to growl at the servants, and when Vadin came into the bathing-room he greeted his squire with a mixture of glare and grin that was almost painful, so long had he been locked away with his wrath and his god. "Come in here," he said, "and give these busybodies an excuse to flutter about elsewhere."

They were not even insulted, let alone deterred. They were bursting with joy to have their wild young lord back again; to have him waging his daily battle with them, which always had the same ending. He bathed and dressed and fed himself, but they drew his water and set the cleansing-foam where he could reach it, held the towels for him, laid out his clothing and served him at table. In Vadin's mind, they won the war by a hair.

As usual, Mirain shared bath and breakfast with Vadin. As usual, Vadin protested to the last. It was all perfectly as usual. After days in the saddle and nights in a tent and never a word except for the most dire necessity, it was an honest miracle.

And yet, when the old fey look came back, Vadin was not surprised. It was less staring-mad than it had been, and it did not last long. Only long enough for Mirain to look Vadin up and down, purse his lips, and say, "Put on your earrings. All of them. And the copper collar, I think. And your armlets, and the belt you keep for festivals."

Vadin's brows went up. "Where am I going? Whoring?"

A smile touched the corner of Mirain's mouth. "In a manner of speaking. I want you to look like the lord you are."

"Then I'd better take off your livery, my lord."

"No." The refusal was absolute. "Jayan, Ashirai, I give this victim to you. He is my squire. He is also the heir of Geitan. Make him the epitome of both."

The young servant and the old one, free Asanian and captive easterner, fell upon him with undisguised pleasure. He suffered it somewhat more graciously than Mirain ever did, which he took time to be proud of. It crowded out anxiety. Mirain's expression boded ill for someone, he dared not think whom.

The servants took Vadin's hair out of its squire's braids, combed it, braided it anew as befit the heir of a lord. They trimmed the ragged edges of his beard and plaited it with copper, and arranged his livery to perfection, and decked him as Mirain had commanded. They even did what he never troubled to do except for the very highest festivals: painted the sigil of his house between his brows, the red lion crouched to spring upon a crescent moon. And at the last they set him in front of the tall mirror, and a stranger stared back at him. Rather a handsome young fellow if truth be told, and lordly enough in his finery.

Royalty came to stand beside him, and it did not diminish him. It made him look more than ever the Ianyn nobleman; never Mirain's equal, but lofty enough in his own right. He could hold his head the higher for knowing that there was one to whom he would gladly bow it.

Mirain's reflection grinned at his own. "You, my friend, are frankly beautiful. Beautiful enough to call on a lady."

Vadin turned to face his prince. The anxiety was gathering into a knot in his middle. Mirain was a sworn priest; he could not send a go-between to one he fancied as a bride. Still less could he contemplate an alliance of plain pleasure. Which left—

"I have a gift," Mirain said, "for a great lady. I cannot, of course, insult her by presenting it with my own hands. Nor can I demean her by sending a servant. Will you bear it for me?"

Vadin's eyes narrowed. The request was so simple, so devoid of compulsion, that it was ominous. "Who is this lady? Or shouldn't I ask?"

"You should," Mirain said willingly. "It is the Lady Odiya. Will you go to her, Vadin?"

Dread mounted. Outrage drove it back. "Damn it, you don't have to play the courtesan with me! Why not give me my orders and have done with it?"

Mirain's head tilted. "I don't want to command you. Will you go of your own will?"

"Didn't I just tell you I would?" Now Mirain was laughing, and that was maddening, but it was better than anything that had come before. "You want—whatever it is—given from my hand to hers?"

"Yes." Mirain set it in his hand: a small box much longer than it was wide, carved of some fragrant southern wood and inlaid with gold. "You are to entrust it to no one else, and to see that no one hinders you."

That would not be easy, if the rumors were true. Vadin traced a curve of the inlay. "Do I linger for a response?"

"See that she opens the box. Say that I am returning what belongs to her." Mirain's teeth bared. It was not a smile. "You'll be in no danger. I assure you of that."

Vadin could think of any number of replies. None of them was wise with Mirain in this mood. He chose silence and a very low bow and a swift departure.

Imeheni women were raised to be modest, but they were not cloistered, and they certainly were not guarded by eunuchs. That was an affectation for barbarians and for Marchers. Vadin, face to face with Odiya's unmanned guard, found himself briefly bereft of words. The creature was as tall as himself and even more elongated, and his face was too smooth and his hair was too rich and his eyes were too deadly flat. They took in the young lord in his festival clothes and his vaunting maleness, and gave nothing back.

Vadin drove his voice at that mask of a face. "I come in the name of the throne prince. I would speak with the Lady Odiya. Let me pass."

The eyes shifted minutely. Vadin gathered himself for a second assault. The guard raised his lowered spear and stepped aside.

Vadin's spine crawled. He was admitted. So easily. As if he were expected.

This was an alien world, this eunuch-warded fastness, full of strange scents, amurmur with high voices. Not only Odiya dwelt here. Others of the king's ladies held each a room or a suite or a whole court, and most of those were free to come and go; Vadin had seen them sometimes in hall or about the castle, elderly ladies as a rule, mingling with kindred and courtiers. There were nine of them altogether, highborn and low, beautiful and not, chosen by custom and by the king's favor, that in his union with them he should make the kingdom strong. But the tenth was First Lady of the Palace. However exalted the others might be, however noble their lineage and their titles, it was she who ruled here, and she ruled absolutely.

Vadin, let into her domain, might have wandered for a long while without guidance. But he was a hunter, and hunters learned wisdom: to stop when lost, and to wait. In a little while one came, another eunuch, very old and withered, with eyes as bright as the other's had been dull. "Come," he said, and his voice was almost deep enough to be a man's.

Vadin went. He felt as if he were caught in a dream, and yet he was intensely alert, aware of every flicker of sound or movement. The box, light in his hand, held the weight of worlds.

People passed him, coming and going. Servants, a lady or two, once a pretty page who stopped to stare. In envy, maybe. This was no place for a male, even for a child of seven summers, even one with the almond eyes and the red-brown skin of the southlands. His owner, whoever she was, was kind, or fastidious; she had replaced the iron slave-collar with a necklet of copper.

The eunuch led Vadin past the child, up a long stair. At its summit stood another guard, a monster, a great hairless slug of a creature. But the worst of it was not its size or its smoothness; it was white, as white as the woman the talespinner had told of, but its eyes were grey as iron. Vadin shuddered in his own, warm, dusk-and-velvet hide, and took great care in passing, as if the eunuch could infect him with that maggot-pallor.

His guide was smiling with an edge of malice. "What, my young lord, do you not approve of Kashi? He is very rare and very wonderful, a son of the uttermost west, where folk are the color of snow. My lady paid a great fortune for him."

Vadin did not deign to respond. Bad enough that those bitter eyes had seen his revulsion; he would not give them more to mock at. Was he not the heir of Geitan? Was he not the throne prince's envoy?

His haughtiness carried him almost to the end. The Lady Odiya sat in a chamber of broad windows, and those open to wind and sun; and after all the guards and the tales and the seclusion, she was not even wearing a veil. Her long hair was braided like a man's, its raven sheen touched only lightly with silver, and her body was clad in a gown as plain as a servant's, and she wore no jewel; and her beauty was as piercing as it had been in the Wood of the Goddess. There was no softness in it, nothing gentle, nothing he had ever thought of as womanly, yet she was woman to the core of her. Woman as the goddess was woman, female incarnate, sister to the she-wolf and the tigress, daughter of moons and tides and darkness, relentless as the earth itself.

Pain startled Vadin out of his stupor, the edges of the box sharp as blades under his clenched fingers. A spell—she was casting a spell. He looked at her, and he made himself see an aging woman in a dark gown, her body thin under it, almost sexless. Her hair was dulled, her face carved to the bone by the bitter years. But she was still beautiful.

His body, trained, had brought him to one knee and bowed his head the precise degree due a royal concubine. His limbs felt even more ungainly than usual, his ribs more prominent, his beard more ragged. How dared he inflict his unlovely self upon this great queen?

Spells. The voice in his head sounded exactly like Mirain's. *Give her the box, Vadin.*

He was doing it. He was saying the words which Mirain had given him to say. "The throne prince sends this gift, great lady; what you have lost, he has found and now returns to you."

She took the box. Her face betrayed nothing. In that, it was like Mirain's, or like the king's. Royal.

"I am to see you open it, great lady," Vadin said.

Her eyes lifted. He could not have moved if he had wished to. She took in every line of his face from brow to chin. She said, "You are . . . almost . . . beautiful. You will be fair indeed when your body grows into itself. If," she said, "you live so long."

"Open the box," said Vadin. Or Mirain wielding Vadin's tongue, or terror leaving no wits and almost no words. His mind saw a dark chamber far from help, a knife raised and glittering, a new guard at the door. A young one who could remember what it was to be a man.

The lady's eyes released him so abruptly that he swayed. Her long fingers found the catch, raised the lid. She gazed down without surprise, but her calm had broken. That was rage which glittered beneath her brows, which bared her teeth. Two were missing, unlovely gaps, breaking the last of her spell.

With sudden violence she flung the box away. Its contents gleamed dully in her hand: the black dagger of Umijan's priestess. Vadin gaped at it. He had last seen it buried to the hilt in Ustaren's heart.

"Tell your master," said Odiya, and her voice was as harsh as that of a carrion bird, "tell your mighty prince that I have received his gift. I will keep it until the time comes for it to drink his blood. For my servants have been weak, but they will grow strong; and the goddess hungers."

"I hear," said Vadin's throat and tongue and lips. "I am not afraid.

Let the goddess lust after Sun-blood, but let her be warned. Its fire consumes all that comes of darkness."

"But in the end, it is the fire which is consumed."

"Who can know what the true end will be?" Vadin bowed again, again with precision. "Good day, my lady Odiya."

Thirteen

MORANDEN RODE INTO HAN-IANON IN THE LIGHT OF a blazing noon, with his men in their ranks behind him and his banners flying.

"Bold as brass," someone said as they clattered through the market.

"Hush!" another warned her fiercely. "Ears can hear."

"And so they should! Why, I've heard tell—"

Ymin edged her way through the press. She knew what the woman had heard. Everyone was hearing it.

"Tried to murder the heir, he did, or so they say."

"When they're not saying that he saved the prince's life."

"Saved it! Why, he lured the young lord away and tied him to an altar, and actually offered him up to the—"

"Be a good thing if he had. Mincing little foreigner. At least the other's proper Ianyn."

The singer pressed her lips together. That refrain would not die for all her singing and the king's proclaiming and Mirain's own great magic. With Moranden gone it had faded somewhat; now it would grow strong again, and the lines would draw themselves more firmly than ever. She shivered in the sun's heat, and cursed that clarity of her mind which could come so close to prophecy.

A sudden tumult drowned out all but itself. Ymin, crushed in the crowd, saw Moranden's company pause. A second troop was riding down from the keep, no banner over it and no great order to it: a company of the king's squires on holiday with hawks on wrists and hounds on leads. One of the hounds had escaped and was wreaking havoc among the stalls; two or three of the young hellions had spurred after it, baying like hounds on a scent.

Yet in the center of pandemonium was stillness, in the summer heat an island of cold. Mirain faced his mother's brother, he and his Mad One motionless but for the glitter of eyes. Moranden's weary charger fretted and stamped and fought to lower its horns.

A whoop and a yelp heralded the hound's capture. It was loud in the spreading silence. Ears strained; breathing quieted. The squires had drawn themselves into a line at Mirain's back, and their eyes were bright and hard.

"Greetings, uncle." Mirain's voice was clear and cool and proud, distinct in the stillness. "How goes the war?"

Moranden grinned, a baring of white teeth. "Well, prince. Well indeed." He leaned upon his high pommel, the image of lordly ease. "Better by far than it was going when you left it."

One or two of the squires, the lad from Geitan foremost, started forward. Mirain raised a hand; they stopped short. He smiled. "When I left," he said, "there was no war at all. Only"—he hesitated, as if he did not wish to say the word—"only treachery. I am glad to see that you are free of it."

Ymin's breath caught. The eyes about her were avid.

Moranden bowed over his charger's neck. "I have always been loyal to my rightful ruler."

"I do not doubt it," Mirain said. The Mad One danced around Moranden's dun, the point of a spear that clove a path through the company. Moranden's men followed it with their eyes. With a bark of command the elder prince brought them about, spurring his stallion up the road to the castle.

A sigh ran through the crowd. Of relief, it might have been, that the rivals had not come to blows. Or, more likely, of disappointment.

There was little enough time for anyone to feel himself cheated. Moranden had returned a few scant days before the greater of Ianon's two highest festivals, the feast of High Summer that was consecrated to Avaryan. And this one would be more splendid than any before it; for the central and holiest day of the festival was also Mirain's birth-feast, his first in the castle and his sixteenth in the world. Every lord and chieftain in Ianon, and many a commoner, had come to look on the heir to the kingdom; most bore gifts, as rich as each could afford.

Mirain woke early on the day itself, the solstice day, first of the new year, well before dawn. Yet Vadin was up before him, and more remarkable still, the king. When his eyes opened they fell first upon his grandfather's face, that bent over him, regarding him with a steady, patient stare. He sat up, scowling slightly, shaking his hair out of his eyes. "My lord, what—"

"Gifts," the king said. All his sternness melted; he loosed his rare and splendid smile. "Gifts for the Throne Prince of Ianon."

Gifts indeed. Vadin brought them one by one, an honor he had fought for; he fought less successfully to keep the grin from his face. Full panoply, made to Mirain's measure but with room for him to grow in: armor wrought as only smiths in Asanion could make it, light and strong and washed with gold, the breastplate graven with the rayed sun of his father; a tunic of well-padded leather to wear beneath, its skirt cut for ease and comfort and strengthened with gilded bronze; and a helmet of bright and burnished gold graven with flame-patterns and surmounted with a scarlet plume. And with these, baldric and scabbard likewise of scarlet and gold, and a sword of precious Asanian steel, its blade keen enough to draw blood from the air; and a cloak of scarlet clasped with gold, and a round Sun-shield, and a spear, and a saddle of scarlet leather inlaid with gold.

Mirain stroked the soft tooled leather and looked up at the king. Vadin had never seen him so close to speechlessness. "My lord," he said. "Grandfather. This gift is beyond price."

"Should the Sun's son defend his realm in less?" The king beckoned to the one servant Vadin had not managed to dispose of. "But that is for the time to come. This I give you for your festival."

It was a robe of honor, a royal robe of cloth of gold. The servant dressed Mirain in it, braided his hair with gold, weighted him with the treasure of the mountain kings. Mirain stood erect under it, meeting the old man's smile with one of his own.

"A fine prince you make," the king said.

"Cloth of gold," Mirain answered, "and a coronet. And," he added with a wicked glint, "a fine air of arrogance."

The king laughed aloud, so rare a thing that even Mirain stared astonished. He held out his hand. "Come, young king. Sing the sun into the sky for me."

Mirain sang the sunrise rite from the altar of Han-Ianon, chief among the priests, shining with more than gold and new sunlight. Vadin was there for once, with everyone else who could crowd into the temple, and he gasped with the rest of them when Avaryan, rising, struck the crystal upon the temple's summit and cast a spear of white fire upon the altar. That was not magic but art, a wonder of the yearly festival, familiar as the dancing fires at harvest time. But Mirain stood before the shining altar, and he raised his hand, and Avaryan himself came down to fill it. For a searing instant Vadin knew that he would be blind. Then he realized that he could see. He stood in the heart of the sun, in a world of pure light, and for all its blazing brilliance it lay cool and clean upon him. It was singing, chanting in a voice he knew, in words he had heard every High Summer since he was old enough to stand in the temple. He blinked; the brilliance faded, or melded itself into the world. Mirain went on with the rite in a cloud of priests and incense. The moment of the god's coming might never have been.

Maybe it never had. No one else remembered it. Kav stared at him when he asked, following the crowd to the hall and the morning feast there; Olvan laughed and said something about sorcerers' apprentices. At first Vadin could not get close enough to Mirain to ask, and when he pushed and cursed his way to his proper place behind the prince's chair, Mirain had taken it into his head to leave the lords to their glory and break his fast among the common folk in the market. The king smiled and let him go, and many of the high ones went with him, and Vadin's question lost itself in the tumult.

In the third hour of the morning, all but the most determined feasters streamed down from castle and city to the fields about it, gathering for the Summer Games: games of strength and skill, war-games and peace-games, footraces and mounted races and contests between lords in their war chariots.

This day was Mirain's, and he sat as ruler of the games, even the king set beside but slightly below him. He had stopped when he saw how it was to be, had looked as if he would protest, but the king met his eye and held it. Slowly he took the seat ordained for him. Slowly his frown lightened. When Vadin left to take his place among the squires, Mirain's unease seemed to have melted, to have turned all to joy.

The lord of the games could not compete in them. But the Lord of the Western Marches set himself to take every lordly prize. He heaped his winnings like the spoils of war, drawing the younger knights to him with the fascination of his victories.

"My lord is magnificent today."

Mirain looked down from the high seat, favoring Ymin with a slow smile. "But," he said, "he has to take his prizes from my hands."

She settled at his feet, which was the singer's privilege. On the field Moranden waited with a dozen princes and barons, the ragged line of chariots shifting as the teams fretted. His own beasts were quiet under his strong hand: matched mares, striped gold and umber. Their manes were clipped into stiff crests; their hoofs were sharpened and pointed with bronze.

Light and whippy though the racing chariot was, Moranden stood in it with easy grace. Like the rest he wore only a loinguard and a broad studded belt; the muscles rippled across his chest and shoulders. A garland of scarlet flowers lay upon them, a lady's favor.

"He is splendid to see," Mirain observed without perceptible envy.

"My lord is magnanimous today."

Mirain met her bright mirthful gaze and laughed. "My lady is full of compliments."

"The air is bursting with them. All Ianon is in love with you, for this day at least. Does that please you?"

Mirain drew a deep, joyous breath. "It sings in me." He spread his arms, which, by more than chance, was the signal for the race to begin. The seneldi sprang forward. The crowd roared. Mirain laughed.

He was smiling still when Moranden brought his foaming team round before the dais and leaped, running along the yoke-tree, springing lightly to the ground. His body gleamed with sweat; his nostrils flared; his eyes glittered.

Mirain rose with the prize, a harness of gold. Before Moranden could ascend the dais, he came down. Younger prince faced elder, Mirain on the second step, Moranden upon the grass.

"Well won again, kinsman," Mirain said. "You do our house great honor."

"That is its due." Moranden accepted the gold trappings with a deep bow. "After all, sister-son, I'm its only defender on this field."

"Every king should have such a champion."

"Is that a southern custom?" Moranden asked. "In the north, every king is his own champion."

Mirain's eyes narrowed, but he laughed. "Why, uncle! You have almost a southern wit." He bowed, a king's bow, catching the sun's fire in all his ornaments. "May you win often again for the honor of the mountain kings."

He returned to his throne, Moranden to his chariot. Ymin, watching them, sighed a very little.

The king marked her. Leaning toward her, he said very low, "Come, child. Stallions will fight and men will strike sparks from one another, and strong men the more strongly."

"These," she said, "are altogether too strong for my heart's ease."

"Strong, and young. Age will calm them."

"If either suffers the other to live so long." She shook herself, and smiled at the king. Hope was so rare in him, and so precious. "Ah, sire," she said almost lightly, "I seem determined to cast a shadow on your sun."

He gestured negation. "You cannot. For see, my son is the greatest of the victors, and my heir"—his voice softened—"my heir is the greatest of my princes. And Ianon knows it and him."

"So," she added too softly even for him to hear, "do both my lords. Both equally, and both all too well."

Vadin was no Moranden, but he was holding his own. He won the mounted race; he took a good second at swordplay among the young men. Then he won again twice, footrace and spearcast, and as he came for the latter prize he met Mirain's broad grin and realized with a shock that he had done it: he had put himself in the running for Younger Champion. So had Pathan the prince and quiet methodical Kav and a haughty lordling from Suveien. He thought briefly, ignobly, of running away to hide. Then Mirain said, "Win it for me, Vadin."

Vadin glared. "No tricks, Sunborn."

"No tricks," Mirain conceded, but his eyes danced. Vadin left him with a bow and a glance of deep distrust.

The Younger Champion won his crown in mounted combat, full-armed, with unblunted weapons. It was the same deadly rite as that which made a man, but easier, Vadin thought as his friends saw to his arming. He did not have to fight these battles after running the Great Race. Rami was fresh and eager, and his mood was rising to match hers. He knew he was good; he had been reckoned one of the best in Imehen. "We'll see if I'm one of the best in Ianon," he said to the mare. She rolled a molten eye and snorted, scenting battle. Lightly he vaulted onto her back. Hands passed up his weapons. Sword on its baldric, dagger at his belt, two throwing spears, the round shield with its Geitani blazon. The heralds were singing out his name. He was matched with the Suveieni. He touched heel to Rami's side; she danced forward, head up.

One mercy: the Suveieni charger was a mare likewise, a fine tall roan. No need to fear a goring from this one. Nor, on trial, was the rider so very much to be afraid of. He was good enough and he was fast, but he lost his temper easily, and with it much of his skill. Vadin let him flail and curse himself into exhaustion, and when his temper had robbed him of defenses, struck him down neatly, almost regretfully, with a flat-bladed blow.

On the other side of the field, Kav had put up a valiant fight, but Pathan had not only skill, he had brilliance. It was Pathan who remained to face Vadin when the vanquished left the battleground, Kav on his own feet and the Suveieni on his shield. As Vadin paused to breathe his mount, to lave his streaming face, to swallow a mouthful of water, he stared at the paragon of squires. The king would knight him tonight, that was an open secret. And here was Vadin alVadin, raw recruit two years at least from knighthood, daring to challenge him.

Pathan did not look as if he feared the outcome. He even smiled and saluted when he sensed Vadin's eye upon him. Hard though Kav had fought him, his armor shone unmarred, his handsome face unbloodied, his plume unruffled. His cream-pale stallion looked newly groomed; he sat the saddle as if he had been born there, light, easy, breathing without effort.

Rami was still fresh enough, but Vadin was dusty and his shield had a dent in it and he knew he reeked royally. He drew a deep breath. Mirain was a flame of gold on the field's edge; Vadin could have sworn he felt those eyes upon him, daring him to turn tail. As if Rami would have allowed it. He tightened his grip on spears and shield, bowed his head to the herald's glance. He was as ready as he would ever be.

The horn sang. Rami was already moving. A spear left his hand, aimed for the center of the prince's shield. Wind gusted, struck it awry. A blow like a hammer sent Vadin reeling back. He wrenched the spear from his own shield, flung the second—fool, fool, Adjan would have raged at him, he had not aimed before he loosed. But neither had Pathan, or perhaps the wind was doubly traitor. Vadin swept out his sword. At which Pathan had defeated him before. But not mounted, not with Rami fighting with him. The stallion was trained and he was swift and he had his wicked ivory horns; but Rami had learned about stallions and their weapons.

So too had Vadin. And these were sharpened, he could see. It was allowed. His folly that he had given his heart to a bare-browed mare, his loss that he would not burden her with horns of bronze set in her headstall.

They were playing, Pathan and the stallion. Teasing, feinting, pretending that neither could land a blow. Vadin astounded himself; he landed one, and it rocked Pathan in the saddle. How could the perfect swordsman have failed to see it coming?

Maybe he was not perfect. His mount shied infinitesimally from the clash of the blade on shield or helm or blade; he did not always seem to know it, and when he did, the touch of his heel brought the senel in too close, or not close enough. Vadin could not match his speed, could not quite match his skill, but maybe—

It had to be soon. Vadin's strength was waning, his skill failing even in defense. He held Rami steady between his knees, raised his aching shield arm a degree, parried a wicked slashing blow. Pathan's blade flicked back, flicked aside in a feint, darted into the gap in Vadin's parry. By a miracle Vadin was there, and the force of the meeting nearly felled him. Nearly. The stallion veered just visibly. Pathan kicked him inward. He skittered a fraction of a step. Pathan's new assault left an opening, a breath's pause, the thickness of a good bronze blade. Vadin filled it. Evaded the shield, turned the point of his sword, and disarmed and dismounted Pathan in the same swift serpentine movement.

There was a stunned silence. Pathan lay on his back, eyes open and glazed, and for an instant Vadin knew that he was dead. Then he stirred and groaned and sat up cradling a hand that stung without mercy. Vadin knew; he had learned his trick the hard way from the arms master in Geitan. He sprang from Rami's back, reaching to help Pathan to his feet, babbling like a fool. "I'm sorry, I didn't mean to, it was only—"

"You idiot of a child," growled Pathan, striking away the hand that stretched to him, rising stiffly but without visible pain.

Vadin opened his mouth and shut it again. Gods help him, he had made a fool of this proud prince before all Ianon, ruined the day of his knighthood, turned his lofty goodwill to bitter enmity.

Pathan's laughter stopped Vadin short. "Idiot child," the prince repeated, and this time his wry amusement was clear to see, "don't you ever know when you've won?"

Vadin blinked. One of those last fierce blows must have addled his brain. He turned slowly. Rami was cropping grass like the veriest plowbeast. Beyond her the folk of Ianon were going wild.

Pathan struck him, not gently. "Mount up, infant. Go and get your prize."

The heralds were there and saying much the same, and one had Rami's reins, and now that Vadin was aware of it the roar of the crowd was deafening. He took a moment to gather himself; as lightly as he could, he mounted, gathering the reins as Rami began to dance. *She* knew what was expected to her. He straightened his weary shoulders, raised his chin, and set his eyes firmly forward.

Mirain was not on the dais. The Mad One was coming, Mirain astride bearing the crown of gold and copper that a quick eye and a clever trick had won Vadin. Rami champed the bit and bucked lightly. "*Just* so," Vadin replied, and let her go.

They met at a gallop, black senel and silver, and wheeled about one another, manes flying, and halted in the same breath. Mirain said nothing, but his eyes said everything. Vadin's cheek were hot, and only partly with exertion; he ducked his head like a child praised too lavishly. A cool weight settled on his brows. He looked up in mild startlement as Mirain's hands lowered, empty. "Go on," the prince said. And when he hesitated: "Rami, of your courtesy, salvage your lord's honor."

She tossed her head, clamped the bit in her teeth, and began the victor's circuit of the field. The Mad One did not follow, and for this splendidly mortifying moment no one was even aware of him or of the one who rode him. Vadin looked back once. Mirain did not mind at all. "Sweet modesty," his voice said soft and clear in Vadin's ear, with laughter in it, and pride, and deep affection.

Damn it, why did they all have to be so indulgent? Was he a braidless boy to be smiled at and clucked over and made allowances for? Demons take them, he was a man grown; and he had proven it.

Anger did what nothing yet had been able to do. Awakened him to the truth. He had won. He was Younger Champion. He was the best of the squires in Ianon. He flung his sword up and caught it to a roar of approval, and wheeled Rami full about, and sent her plunging madly round that wide and glorious field.

Fourteen

A S THE SUN BEGAN TO SINK, THE GAMES ENDED IN splendor. Moranden had won the crown that was elder brother to Vadin's, as he had done at every High Summer since he won his knighthood. By custom the two champions met upon the field in a dance of war, a crossing of blades and a matching of their mounts' paces; rode side by side to the throne and bowed; and clasped hands in the amity of brothers and warriors. Moranden was not gentle, and his dance was swift enough to strain Vadin's lesser strength and speed, and his handclasp was painfully tight; but that was the custom: amicable as the Elder Champion might be, he neither forgot nor let the other forget that one day they would contest for his title. "You fought well," Moranden said as if he meant it, and he smiled his famous smile. "That last stroke —I don't suppose you'd teach it to me? Unless"—his smile widened to a grin—"you're planning to use it on me next High Summer."

"Not next year," Vadin said, "or for a good count of years after, I don't think, my lord. I'll need more than a trick and a stroke of luck to overcome the best fighting man in Ianon."

Moranden's brows raised. "Don't be so certain, sir. The mount lacked something in training, but the rider lacked somewhat in skill; and you had the eyes to see it. That's a rare gift." He clasped Vadin's hand again. "We ride to the castle together. I for one won't be ashamed of my company."

Nor was Vadin, but he was not at ease. He could not revel in the adulation that beat upon him. His eyes were on Mirain, who rode just ahead of him with the king. The younger prince had his share of the glory back again, and he rode on it, shining with it, borne as on wings. For that hour at least his people loved him utterly; even the fear of the Mad One had no power to hold them back. They reached for him, slowing him, doing battle for the touch of his hand or the glimmer of his smile.

The king's guards thrust forward, armed for his defense. The king stopped them with a glance. See, it said; Mirain could take no hurt. Not here, not now. All Han-Ianon lay in the hollow of his hand.

The great hall lay open to the long summer dusk, ablaze with torches, filled to bursting with the people of Ianon. Those who could not crowd themselves into the hall itself filled the court without and spread into the side courts, even the lowest of them feasting like lords on the bounty of the king.

Mirain sat upon the dais under a canopy of white silk edged with gold. His hall robe was startling in its simplicity, all white but for the torque of his priesthood; his head was bare, his hair in its single braid, and no jewel glittered at brow or throat or finger. Yet he shone, as brilliant in himself as any of the gold-decked princes of Ianon.

Moranden had taken the Elder Champion's place down the table on the king's right, flanked by glittering princelings, himself in black and vivid scarlet with a ruby like a drop of blood between his brows. His companions paid Mirain little heed, drinking more than they ate, waxing hilarious as the light died from the sky. They quieted but little for the dancers or the players, little more for Pathan's solemn knighting at the king's hands, and not at all for the singers led by Ymin and chanting the praises of the god. Although Moranden roistered with them, even from his own place of honor on the king's left Vadin could perceive that the prince's cup was seldom refilled; that he watched Mirain without seeming to watch: a steady, sidelong, unreadable stare.

But Mirain was far beyond notice of aught but his own elation. He was young, he was beloved, he would be king. His mood left no room for either hate or fear, let alone for simple caution. And Vadin, trapped among his own exuberant admirers, could not get close enough to beat him to his senses.

A very young singer came forth, a child with a voice like a flute, who sang of Mirain's birth at sunrise in the center of the god's great rite. The princelings paused in their revelry, caught in spite of themselves by the unnerving purity of that voice. Save one; tone-deaf or deaf with drink, he drawled, "Sunborn indeed. Prophecies, forsooth. How they do make up these tales!"

Every word was distinct, loud and dissonant against the chanting. Vadin tensed to surge up, subsided slowly. He could do nothing but make matters worse.

Mirain stirred. His eyes, that had been shining, lost in contemplation of wonders, focused slowly. Yet he was still half in his dream.

"Who knows what really happened?" growled another young lord. "He walks in here, he tells a pretty tale, he gets it all: throne, castle, and kingdom. Good work, says I, and mortal fast."

The singer did not falter, but he looked toward Ymin with frightened eyes. She did not move, perhaps could not. Mirain had roused all at once. The king's hand gripped his arm, thin and iron-hard yet trembling visibly. The prince spared him not even a glance. "Guards," he said softly and clearly, "remove these men."

A third lordling leaped up, sending his winecup flying. "Yes! Remove them, he says, before they betray too much of the truth."

He spoke to the hall, but his eyes rested on Moranden. The elder prince sat at his ease, lifting no hand as the guards seized his followers, although they strained toward him and shouted his name. He was watching Mirain.

The song ended unnoticed. The singer fled behind Ymin's skirts, too terrified for tears.

The third man fought against his captors, crying out, "Liar! He lies! He is no son of the god. His mother lay with the Prince of Han-Gilen; the high priestess of the temple would have put her to death for it; her lover cast down the priestess and set up the stranger in her place. But the priestess had her just revenge. She killed the liar with her own hand. I know it. My kinsman was there; he saw, he heard. This is no son of Avaryan. You give your worship to a lie."

A guard raised his fist as if to club the man into silence.

"No," Mirain said. His eyes were very wide and very bright. "Let him say what he has been taught to say."

For an instant the young man was nonplussed. Even his fellows were still, staring. He filled his lungs to shout, "No one taught me. This is an adventurer, a no-man's-son, sent up from the south to seize a kingdom. When he has it, the Prince of Han-Gilen will claim it and him."

Mirain laughed in genuine amusement. "There, sir, you betray yourself. What could Prince Orsan possibly want with a kingdom as remote, as barbaric, and as isolated as Ianon? Already he rules the richest of the Hundred Realms."

"No realm is too rich!" the man cried. "Tell the truth now, priestess' bastard. Your mother lied to save her lover and herself. But you betrayed her. For bearing you she died. You were her death."

Mirain was on his feet. The lordling struck again, struck deep. "You are accursed, matricide, destroyer of all you touch. 'Go to Ianon,' they begged you in Han-Gilen. 'Go, take your curse with you. The king is old; he is mad; soon he will die. Ianon is yours for the taking.' " He raised his arms in a grand gesture. "One thing they forgot. Ianon is not only an aged king and a pack of coward lords. One man is strong. One man remembers his honor and the honor of the kingdom. While the Prince Moranden lives, you shall not rule in Ianon."

Mirain's head tilted. "I suppose you have consulted him." He turned his eyes upon Moranden. "Mine uncle? Does this mockingbird belong to you?"

"He speaks out of turn," Moranden replied coolly, "but as for the truth of what he says, you know better than I."

"We all know it." Ymin's trained voice cut across the growing uproar, stilling it. "I have seen it and I have sung it. This is the one foretold. This is the king who comes from the Sun. Ill befall you, Moranden of Ianon, if you dare to oppose him. For he is gentle and he is merciful, but I have no such virtues; and I will wield against you all the power of my office."

Moranden laughed. "Such power, too, milady singer! You've always been his loyal lapdog. A gleam of gold, a well-told tale, and he had your heart in his hand. Look at him now! Gasping like a fish, with all his plots laid bare."

"What could he say to such monstrous words as yours?"

"What's monstrous in the truth? He knows it. He gags at it. And hides behind the skirts of whoever has the gall to defend him." Moranden's lip curled. "Some king he'll be, who needs a woman to fight his battles for him."

"Better that than a king who needs a woman to think his thoughts for him." Moranden surged up. Mirain faced him, icy calm. "Be silent henceforth, kinsman, and perhaps I shall forgive you for what your puppet has said of my mother. But I shall never forget it."

"Liar. Foreigner. Priestess' bastard. Because my father loved you and because you have a look of my sister, whom I also loved, I suffered you. But too much is too much. Before my father and my sister, there was Ianon; and Ianon groans at the thought of such a king."

"Ianon," said Mirain, "no. Only Moranden, whose soul gnaws itself in rage that he cannot have a throne." The hall was deathly silent.

Mirain met the black and burning eyes of his mother's brother. "And if you won it, my lord—if you won it, could you hope to hold it?"

"Child." Moranden's voice was different, softer, more deadly. "Not you alone are beloved of the high ones. Nor is this Han-Gilen, that casts out all gods but one and rears up in its pride and fancies itself blessed of Avaryan. The gods are shut out, but the gods remain. She remains, who alone is Avaryan's equal. *Is,* child. Is, was, and will be."

Mirain spoke as through a choking fog. Proud words, but muffled, bereft of their force. "I will chain her."

His kinsman laughed. "Will you, little man? Try it then. Try it now, Sunborn, child of the morning."

"I am—not—" Mirain reeled. His hand flew up, but its fire was dim. The laughter did not falter. Mirain cried out against it. "Moranden! Can you not see? You too are a puppet. You are being used, you are being wielded. Another voice is speaking through you."

"I am no man's toy!"

"No man's indeed, but a goddess' and a woman's."

Moranden fell upon him, mad-enraged, possessed, it did not matter. Vadin saw Mirain go down, and a wall of bodies between, and no weapon in all that hall of festival; and it was a nightmare, Umijan come again, with Mirain beaten before he began.

Darkness swept between scarlet and fallen white, severing them, hurling the scarlet against the wall. A deep voice spoke with softness more devastating than any bellow of rage. "Get out."

Moranden staggered, face slack with shock, and crumpled to his knees. The king looked down at him. Old and strong and terrible, he met his son's eyes; the younger man flinched visibly. "Get out," he said again.

Moranden's mouth worked. Words rent themselves from him. "Father! I—"

Hands like iron smote him to the ground. Stronger than they and more cruel, the harsh voice held him pinioned where he lay. "If the sun's rising finds you within reach of my castle, I will hunt you like a beast. Exile, accursed, let no man raise a hand to aid you. Let no woman take you into her house. Let no dweller in Ianon feed you or clothe you or give you to drink, lest by so doing he share your fate." The king turned away from him. "Moranden of Ianon is dead. Begone, nameless one, or die like the hound you are."

Moranden looked about. Every back was turned to him. Even his boldest followers had turned with the rest, sealing his exile.

Laughter escaped him. It was sharp, wild, edged like blades. "Such is the justice of Ianon. So am I condemned, without defense, without recourse. Alas for our kingdom!"

No one turned. The king stood most still and most implacable. Mirain and Moranden between them had forced him to choose. He had chosen. It was bitter, bitter. But Moranden saw only the motionless back, knew only what he had always known: that he was not the one his father loved.

A black rage swept over him, mastered him. He whirled to his feet. "A curse!" he cried. "A curse upon you all!"

Mirain stood once more, disarrayed but uncowed; he alone would meet Moranden's eyes. The light the elder prince saw there was bitter. "You," he said, almost purring. "You have Ianon now. I wish you joy of it." He bowed deeply, mockingly, and spun in a flare of scarlet. Past the king, past Mirain, past the lords and commons of Ianon he strode ever more swiftly. A torch caught a last blood-red gleam, and he was gone, into the outer darkness.

"Grandfather." Mirain's voice was loud in the silence. "Grandfather, call him back."

The king wheeled upon him. He gasped. The old lord's face was like a skull. Yet, "Call him back," Mirain repeated.

"He sought your throne and your life."

Mirain did what he had never done to anyone but his father: knelt at the king's feet and bowed his head. "Sire, I beg you."

Within the skull, puzzlement mingled with wrath. "Why?"

"It is not finished. It must be finished, or Ianon will be rent asunder."

"No," the king said, flat and hard.

Mirain's eyes glittered. "He must come back. We must fight now, while the battle is new, and the god must choose between us."

"I choose," grated the king. "You shall not fight."

"That is not for you to ordain, my lord of Ianon."

The king was immovable even before the enormity of that insolence. "I will not call him back."

Mirain looked up at the great and royal height of him. "Then I too must leave you."

A tremor racked the king's body. "Leave?" he repeated, as if the word had no meaning.

"It is war now between my kinsman and myself. A war which you, my lord, have made certain. Whatever befalls, whether battle or, by some mighty chance, reconcilement, I will not shatter this kingdom with the force of our enmity." Mirain's chin lifted still higher. "Since Moranden has gone into exile, so too must I."

In the hall and in the courtyards beyond, no one breathed. The king had the look of a man who has suffered a mortal blow. His daughter was dead. His son had turned openly upon his chosen heir. His daughter's son stood before him and cast his kingdom in his face.

"But," he demanded harshly, "when I am dead, who will rule in Ianon?"

"There are lords and princes enough. And every one knows his father." Mirain bowed low, even to the floor. "Farewell, my lord. May the god keep you."

He turned as Moranden had, white to the other's scarlet. Yet as he strode forth, the king seized his arm. He halted, eyes blazing. "Mirain," the king said. His fingers tightened. "Sunborn. By your father's hand—"

Mirain tensed to pull free, and froze. The king swayed. Mirain caught at a body turned all to bone and thin skin, yet massive still, overwhelming his slightness. Slowly he sank beneath the weight of it.

Death unfolded in the king's face, death held at bay and now let in for the kill. "No!" Mirain cried, clutching his grandfather's body as if his hands alone could hold it to life. "Not now. Not for me!"

"For you," the king whispered, "no." All his life and strength gathered in his eyes, that opened wide, fixed upon Mirain's face. "Summon my servants. I will not lie on the floor of my hall like one of the hounds."

Lamps guttered in the king's chamber, casting long shadows upon the great bed. The healers' chants had faded; the priests were silent. Alone in a corner, Ymin sat with her harp. Her fingers had fallen from the strings, her voice sunk to a murmur and died. Tears glistened upon her cheeks.

Mirain knelt beside the bed. He had not moved since the king was laid there, not for Vadin, not for the healers or the priests, not even for those high lords whose rank had won them past the guards. One hand gripped the king's; the other, the right, lay upon the still brow.

The king had slid from waking into a dim dream, and into light again. Even closed, his eyes turned toward Mirain.

Far away a cock crowed, calling forth the dawn. The king stirred. His eyes opened; his fingers tightened. His lips softened, almost a smile. "Yes," he said very low. "Curse me. Curse the oath you swore me."

"I swore not to die and leave you alone."

"You cannot abandon me now."

"No," Mirain said, yet wearily, without anger. "You have seen to it that I cannot."

"I? Not entirely, child. I had aid. Call it fate. Call it—"

"Poison. Subtle, sorcerous, and beyond my power to heal." The weariness was gone, the wrath returned. Although no spoken word had passed between them since they left the hall, it seemed that this battle of wills had been waging for long hours. Mirain bent forward. "She will pay for it."

"She will not." This too had an air of use, of resistance that would not be shaken.

"She has always been your weakness. She has been your death."

"That has been my great gift. To choose my death, and to choose its instrument; and to know that she was beautiful. But she has won no victory. My heir and not hers shall hold my throne." A breath, a cough: all the laughter he could muster. "Admit it, Sunborn. Beneath all the seemly and filial grief, you are glad of it."

"No. Never."

"Liar," the king said, amused still, almost tender. "I leave you no sage advice; even if your courtesy would bid you listen, you would not heed it. This only I command you: Rule in joy."

Mirain's eyes were hot and dry, his voice rough. "I shall see you to your pyre. What then if I simply walk away?"

"You will not."

"I can call Moranden back."

"Will you?" With the last of his strength the king drew Mirain's hand to his heart. "From the moment I saw you, I knew you. Avaryan's son . . . you are worthy of your father."

"You believe that?"

"I know." The king's eyelids drooped; his heart labored. With a deep sigh he loosed his will's hold upon it. Beat by beat it slowed. Mirain snatched at it with a cry, calling forth all the power he had from his father. The king's heart throbbed, briefly strong; slipped free; quivered; stilled.

Ianon's king was dead.

Ianon's king rose and settled the still hands upon the still breast, and turned. At the sight of his face, lords and healers and priests sank down, bowing to the floor.

"He willed this," Mirain said to them in a tight still voice. "Even unto death, to bind me here. He willed it!"

"Hail, king." Ymin's voice, silencing him; and Vadin's hoarse with weeping, and the rest in ragged chorus: "Hail, Mirain, king in Ianon."

Vadin, watching him even through the tears, saw the change begin in his eyes. Grief, anger, reluctance, none grew less. Yet at the name of king a light kindled. There was nothing of triumph in it. Only, and purely, acceptance.

And yet, accepting, at last he could weep.

Fifteen

"*P*RECIPITOUS FOOL." ODIYA HAD NO PATIENCE TO spare for the son she had borne. "If you had curbed your hounds, if you had seen fit to rest upon your victories—"

Moranden whirled upon her. "Curb my hounds? They were not mine!"

"They followed you. You made no effort to silence them."

"And who encouraged them to speak?" He stood over her. "No masks now, Mother. No pretenses. I know whose mind conceived that web of deception in Umijan. I know who stands behind tonight's madness. And so, madam, does the king."

"So did the king."

His hand gripped her throat. "What have you done? What have you done to him?"

"I," she said, "nothing. He wished to die. That gift was given him. When she chooses, the goddess can be merciful."

"The goddess!" He spat. "And who asked her? Who danced the spells? Who brewed the poison? It was poison, wasn't it? My lordlings, my anger, my exile—diversions, no more. The little bastard was right. You were using me!"

"Of course I used you," she said coolly. "You are an apt tool. Attractive, malleable, only intermittently clever. Yon interloper is a hundredfold the king that you will ever be."

"You are no mother to me, you daughter of tigers."

"I am giving you the throne you lust after."

His eyes narrowed. His grief was deep and rending, but his mind was clear, doing its cold duty. In that much he was his mother's son; and perhaps his father's. "The throne," he muttered. "It's empty now. And the boy—I heard him plead for me. He'll revoke my sentence. I'll challenge him; he'll fall. By tomorrow's dawn I'll be king."

"By tomorrow's dawn you will be riding to the Marches."

"Are you mad? I should leave now that you've thrown all Ianon in my face?"

"You shall go into exile as the lord your father has commanded. You grieve, you are justly angered, but you are a man of honor; you do as your king has bidden. If the new king calls you back, why then, is he any king of yours? You have sworn no oaths to him, nor will you, slayer of your father that he is."

"*You* slew my—"

She slapped him. He stood with his mouth open, staring. "Fool," she said to him. "Idiot child. It is no man you face. It is a mage, the son of a god. All Ianon's Vale lies under his spell. Every man he meets learns swiftly to worship him. Remember the ride to the west; remember how he was, effacing himself among your men, subverting them with a look or a smile, winning their souls with his magic. And he was the great victor in the war that never was. He conceived the race to Umijan, he ran it and won it while you tarried for dull duty. You were but the lord commander; he was the great hero.

"And you would stand up in hall before the king's body and dare to contend with him for the throne." Her lip curled. "Think! You were loved by some, respected by all, looked on as king to be. Outside of the Vale in great measure you are still. Go there; show yourself; keep yourself before the people while the foreigner learns that a throne can bind its claimant to it as with chains. And when at last he has gained the strength to break them, when he comes forth from the Vale to claim the whole of his kingdom, let him find that he is king only of the inmost lands. The rest shall be yours, an army at your back, sworn to you as rightful king. Then may you challenge the usurper. Then shall you rule in Ianon."

Moranden had stilled as she spoke, had gathered his wits, had mastered his temper. He heard her out almost calmly, toying with the copper-woven braids of his beard. When she ended, he paced from end to end of the long bare chamber, paused, turned to face her. "Wait—I can wait. I've waited a score of years already. But even my poor wit can see the flaw in your plotting. If the little bastard is a mage—and I don't doubt it's possible; I saw him in Umijan—if he's a master of magic, how can I ever challenge him? I'm a warrior, not a sorcerer."

"He fancies himself a man of war. Challenged as he will be challenged if you heed me, he will lay aside his power to come against you. And I can see to it that he holds to his vow."

"You. Always you."

"And where would you be if it were not for me?" She held out her hand. "Bid me farewell, my son. Your mount and your baggage are ready; your escort waits. Be swift, or the dawn will catch you."

He came as if he could not help it, but his bow was stiff and his lips did not touch her palm. "You'll stay here? After what you've done?"

"I will see my old enemy laid upon his pyre." She gestured imperiously. "Go. I will send word to you in the Marches."

With a last sharp inclination of the head, he turned on his heel and left her.

She was still there as the sun rose, alone by the eastward window, her mantle wrapped about her and her veil drawn over her head.

The light step upon her threshold, the presence at her back, did not at once bring her about. "Strangers do not often come here," she said to the flaming sky.

"I do not think," said a dark soft voice, "that we are strangers to one another."

She turned then. For all her wisdom and all her spies, he surprised her a little. He was so small, and yet he stood so far above her. And he looked so very much like his mother's father.

With a swift gesture she averted his spell. He dwindled. Somewhat. He was still in his white robe, rumpled now and stained, and his face was drawn with exhaustion. But he was calm; she could find no anger in him. "The king is dead," he said.

She astounded herself. She sank down under the weight of those simple words; she lay on her face, and she wept like a woman whose dearest love has been slain. And the pain was real. It tore at her vitals.

"Hate," Mirain said, "is womb-kin to love. Uveryen and Avaryan were born at one birthing."

She raised herself upon her hands. He knelt by her, not touching her, watching her as one would watch a beast engaged in some strange rite of its kind. But it was not a cold regard. It burned with subtle fire.

He shifted slightly, sitting on his heels, setting his fists upon his thighs. The right hand could not close fully; the tension in it was the tautness of pain. "You belong to me now," he said, "you and all my grandfather's chattels. Did you consider that when you dared to linger here?"

She came erect all in a motion, like the lynx she was named for. "I belong to no one. His death loosed my bonds; I am free."

His gesture of denial flashed sudden gold. "If you had been a slave, that would have been so; so likewise if you had been but a concubine. But he took you in clan-marriage, and clan-wives pass to the heir. To be used by him, or bestowed by him, as he sees fit."

"No," she said, "He never—"

"It is written in the book of his reign. It is recorded in the annals of his singer. Surely you knew."

Odiya's arms locked about her throbbing middle. Her grief was gone. Her hate was a crimson fire. Lies, black lies. She knew the form of clan-marriage, which in the west they called the mating of the sword. She had never undergone it. She had been taken from her chamber, she had been thrown down in her father's hall before his high seat, she had been—

"He never raped you in front of his men, nor ever in your father's blood." The voice was neither young nor gentle. It smote her with its likeness to the old king's. "He passed the sword over you. He spoke the words that mated you. He gave his name to the child you carried."

"Moranden is his son!" So far had she fallen; she fought her way back to the heart of this battle. "We were not sword-mated. We were *not.*"

"Because you would not say the words? That matters nothing under the blade." Mirain stood, head tilted back, regarding her down the long curve of his nose. It was a feat, that; she should have laughed at him, to break his spell again, to restore her strength. But she could only stare, raging within, and know that he was stronger than ever she had dreamed of.

She knew now. She would not underrate him again. She let her head bow, her body droop as if in defeat. "What will you do with me?"

"What should I do?" He said it so lightly that she nearly betrayed herself. "I don't want you for my bed. I don't trust you in my castle, and I don't trust you outside of it. I'm not even sure I trust you dead."

Her dread ran only as deep as her face. "Would you slay a helpless woman?"

He laughed in purest mirth. "Why, lady! Have you forgotten your daily hour with the sword? Or the potion you distilled yourself, which so sweetened my grandsire's wine?" His laughter vanished; he went cold. "Enough. You tempt me; you lure me into your darkness. Living or dead you are my enemy, living or dead you will strive to cast me down."

She waited in grim patience. She was not so strong in power, perhaps, but she was older and her hate was purer, unalloyed by childish fancies of compassion. For he was dreaming of that, even through his cruel words. If he had meant to kill her, he would not have tarried so long.

He spread his hands, the dark and the golden. "You may see the king to his pyre. But if you do that, be aware that you have chosen, that you must follow him into the fire. If you would live, depart this day from the castle and swear never again to raise your hand against the throne or its lord. Though if it is life you choose, I do not think your goddess will be long in taking it."

"That is a choice?"

"It is all you will have."

She was silent. Not debating her choice; that was not worth so much. Considering him. Letting her hate run cold and clear. "I could wish," she said through it, "that you had been my child."

"You can thank all your gods that I am not."

She smiled. "I choose life. As you knew I would. That is the great beauty in being a woman: one need not stand on honor, nor fear the shame of cowardice."

He bowed low as to a queen, and returned her smile without strain. "Ah, lady," he said, "well I know it, who am a king and the son of a god. Honor binds me, and shame, and my given word. But what they all mean . . . why, that is the great beauty in what I am. I can make them in my own image."

She went down lower still, even to the floor, and only half of it was mockery. When she rose again, he had gone. Even with the sunlight blazing through the broad window, the chamber seemed dark and dull, drained of the splendor that was his presence.

Sixteen

THEY BUILT THE PYRE OF RABAN, KING IN IANON, IN the great court of his castle, and raised it high up to heaven: all of rare woods, well seasoned and steeped in oil, scented with the god's own incense. At his feet they laid his best-loved hound to guard and guide his way into the god-country; his head lay upon the flank of his red charger, his mount upon the road. He himself was clad in a plain hooded mantle to deceive the demons who might lie in wait for a king but not for a simple wayfarer, yet lest he be so mistaken before the gods' gate, beneath the cloak he wore all the jeweled splendor of his kingship.

Mirain stood alone before the pyre. His kilt was plain to starkness, belted with a strap of leather and dyed the dull ocher of mourning; he had neither bound nor braided his hair nor put on any jewel. Barefoot and bareheaded, with no kin to stand at his back, he looked far too frail for the burden the old king had left him.

The rite of death was long, the sun seeming to hang motionless in a sky like hammered brass. More than one of Ianon's gathered people gave way to Avaryan's power, or retreated into what shade there was, or did as Vadin did: made their own shade with their ocher mantles. Yet Mirain, in the courtyard's center, sought no relief and received none. His voice in the responses was as firm at the end as when he began.

At last a priestess of Avaryan came forth with the vessel of the sacred fire. All bowed before it. Reverently she laid it upon the altar which stood between Mirain and the pyre. An acolyte, following her, knelt in front of her with an unlit torch. She blessed it; he turned to Mirain.

The young king did not move. The acolyte blinked and began to frown, not daring to prompt him but all too well aware of the waiting priestess.

Slowly Mirain reached for the torch. His fingers closed upon the wooden haft, raised it. The fire flickered in its basin; the pyre loomed above him. *Kindle it,* the watchers willed him. *For the gods' love, kindle the fire!*

Somewhere within the too-still body, strangeness stirred. Mirain flung the torch spinning up and up into the sun. His arms, freed, spread wide; his head fell back, his eyes opened wide to the sun's fire. It flooded into him, filled him. Out of the towering flame that had been his mortal body, a single dart sprang forth. Straight into the heart of the pyre it flew, and the oiled wood roared into flame.

The priests fled from that great eruption of light and heat. But Mirain stood full in front of it, oblivious to his peril. His body was his own again; he sang a hymn of grief and triumph mingled, sacred to the Sun.

The earth was dull and cold, a dark rain falling with the evening, quenching the fire. Mirain shivered, blinking, staring without comprehension at the charred and smoldering heap which had been his grandfather's pyre.

How often Vadin had spoken to him since his song faded, the squire himself did not know. Yet Vadin tried again, and it desperation he settled an arm around the damp chilled shoulders, tugging lightly, "Come," he said, rough with cold. And Mirain heard. He began to move. Swaying, staggering, but stubbornly, afoot, he let his squire lead him away.

Vadin took him not to the King's chamber which was his now by right, but to his own familiar room. A fire was lit there, dispelling the rain's chill; a bath waited, and dry clothes, and wine and bread to break the death-fast. He seemed hardly to see who ministered to him, although he let himself be tended, fed, cajoled into bed.

When he lay wrapped in blankets, his eyes focused at last. He saw who bent over him. Vadin he regarded without surprise, but the other made him start, half rising. Ymin pushed him firmly back again and held him there. "What is this?" he demanded. "Why are you here?"

She greeted his return to awareness with perfect calm. "Tonight at least," she said, "you are entitled to your solitude. I am seeing that you get it."

Vadin grimaced. "It hasn't been easy, either. And tomorrow it won't be possible. The king can't belong to himself; he belongs to Ianon."

Mirain tried again to rise from his bed; they allied to hold him down. He glared at them, struggling, but not with any great force. "I have to go to the hall. The feast—"

"No one looks for you tonight," Ymin said.

"But—"

"There is no need for the young king to drink the old one into the god-country. Not when the god's own fire has set the dead man upon his road."

"Is that what people are saying?"

"It happened," Vadin said. After a moment he added, "Sire."

Marain sat up, propping himself with shaking arms. "It happened," he echoed. "You see how it's left me. I'm hardly the god everyone must be thinking me."

"No; merely his son and our king." Calmly, matter-of-factly, Ymin supported him. "If anyone has needed proof of either, you have given it. Magnificently."

He tensed, drawing in upon himself. "I can never help myself. Wherever I turn, whatever I do, the god is there, waiting. Sometimes he takes me and wields me like a sword; and when he lets me go I'm like a newborn child. Strengthless, witless, and all but useless."

"Even gods have their limits."

"In Han-Gilen," he said, "they would call that a heresy."

"There are gods, and there is the High God. My doctrine is sound enough, my lord."

"In Ianon. Maybe." He glanced beyond her at Vadin. "I'm not a god. I'm scarcely yet a king. I don't know that I'll ever be one."

"Tomorrow you will be," Vadin said.

"In name. What if my grandfather was deceived? He was a great king. He thought he had found another like him. He paid for it with his life. What if he died for nothing?"

"He didn't," snapped Vadin with all the force he could muster, close as he was to tears. "And he knew it. Do you think Raban of Ianon would have let go the way he did if he wasn't leaving his kingdom in good hands?" Between them, he and Ymin eased Mirain down. "There now. Rest. You've a long day ahead of you."

"A long life." Mirain's burst of strength had faded; he labored even to speak. "I was so certain. That I had the right; that I was strong enough. That I could be king. I was an utter fool."

They said nothing. But Ymin smiled and gestured slightly, a flicker of dissent. He turned his face away from them both.

Vadin's eyes had overflowed again. They kept doing that; he had stopped trying to master them. But he was not weeping now for the king. The old man had gone in glory. It was the young one who made him want to lie down and howl.

A warm hand touched his arm. He met Ymin's gaze. "He has the strength," she said gently.

"Of course he does!" Vadin flared at her. "But—damn it, it's so soon!"

"It is never the proper time for a king to die." She sighed; her own eyes were suspiciously bright. "You too should rest, young lord. Have you even lain down since the Games?"

Vadin could not remember, and he did not care. "I'm not tired. I don't need to—"

Before he knew it he was in his cubicle, his pallet spread, her hand on his belt loosening the clasp. He slapped her away. She laughed, light and sweet as a girl, and stripped him with consummate neatness. Even as he snatched at his kilt, she caught him off balance and tripped him into his bed. She was amazingly strong. "Sleep." she commanded.

"Or?"

"Or I sit on you until you do."

It was not an idle threat, nor entirely an unpleasant one. For an older woman she had a fine figure. Thin, but fine.

Her kiss was as chaste as his mother's, a brush of lips upon his brow. Her tone was utterly maternal. "Sleep, child. Dream well."

He growled, but he did not rise. With the last flicker of a smile she left him.

Vadin could have slept the moon-cycle through and hardly noticed it, but Mirain woke renewed from his brief night's sleep. He even smiled, rarity of rarities, until darkness touched him. Memory, perhaps, of the king's death; of his own kingship.

He rose and stretched and found his smile again, turning it on Vadin. It swelled into a grin; it swept away, left him cold and shaking. "Avaryan," he said very low. "Oh, Father. I don't think I can—"

"Sire."

They both whipped about. A servant faced them: an elderly man of great dignity, dressed in the king's—in Mirain's—scarlet livery. If he was in any way perturbed to see his new lord reduced to a trembling child, he concealed it well. "Sire," he said, "your bath awaits you."

In the bedchamber Ianon's king was served by men of years and standing among their kind; in hall and about his kingdom by pages and esquires, the sons of great houses; and in the bath, which was a high service and much honored, by the daughters of Ianon's highest lords. Every one was a maiden, young and well-favored and clad practically, if none too sufficiently, in a wisp of white tunic.

Vadin went in with Mirain. He did not know that it was allowed, but no one told him it was forbidden, or tried to stop him.

He had fancied himself a man of the world. He was certainly no virgin. But he stopped short two paces past the door, ears afire, and could not move another step.

They did not even see him. They were waiting for Mirain. Modestly, with the dignity of their breeding, but their eyes were bright, their glances quick and eager. God or half-god or mortal man, he was young and well shaped and not at all ill to look on. After the aged Raban he must have been a delight.

Mirain too had stopped as if struck, but he was made of sterner stuff; he managed to drive himself forward. He even mustered something like nonchalance, although his back was stiff. His head turned, scanning downcast faces, pausing once or twice. One of the maidens had a marvelous tumble of curls. One had eyes like a doe's, melting upon him. And one was even smaller than himself, as delicate as a flower, with eyes as soft as sleep. She had Asanian blood: she was honey golden, with a hint of rose that deepened under his stare. But she smiled shyly. Mirain must have smiled back; her face lit like a lamp. Lightly then, with royal grace, Mirain gave himself into their hands.

When he was scoured clean, they did not dress him. There was nothing to dress him in. They shaved him; they combed his free hair and tamed it as much as they might; they anointed him with sweet oils, touching his brow, his lips, his heart and his hands, his genitals, his feet. Then they bowed one by one from least to greatest, and the greatest was the golden princess, and she kissed his torque and his golden palm.

The throne of Ianon stood no longer in the hall. Strong men had taken it in the night, brought it down through the Chain of Courts to the Court of the Gate, and there set it upon a high dais before the people. Spearmen in scarlet kept free a long aisle from the gate to the throne; lords and princes stood about it, surrounded by the king's own knights in all their panoply.

Between the royal bath and the outer court lay only empty halls. Mirain must pass them naked and alone, abandoned even by his squire.

Who barely had time to bolt by side ways into the sun and the crowds and the place kept for him beside the high seat.

Yet it seemed a long wait, those slow moments under Avaryan. Vadin's breath eased; he settled himself into some semblance of calm, and tried not to think of assassins' knives, and ambushes, and one lone unarmed unclad not-quite-king. The clamor of gathered people stilled slowly. All eyes turned with his own toward the gate. It was open, empty.

A bell rang, far and sweet. Many glanced toward the sound of it. When they glanced back, he stood under the arch of the gate. Only a shadow from this distance, a shape that said *man* in the breadth of its shoulders and the narrowness of its hips. Then it began to move, and it became Mirain. No one else had quite that panther-stride, or that straightness of the shoulders, or that tilt of the head. Or ever that way of cutting the world to his measure. He walked Ianyn-tall among them, a man grown, wise beyond any count of years, and royally proud; yet he was also a youth just out of boyhood, alone and afraid, without even a rag to cover him. They could see everything in the pitiless light: the long seamed scar in his side where a boar had tusked him long ago and almost killed him; the thin grey lines of sword-scars and the pitted hollow where an arrow had taken him in battle; the raw new flesh on buttocks and thighs, mark of his wild ride to Umijan. They could see that he was mortal and that he was imperfect, smaller than any man of them, not remarkably fair of face; but he was male, whole and strong, without mark or blemish save what branded him a man and a warrior. No woman in disguise, no eunuch living a lie, no soft coward laying claim to the throne of fighting kings.

Pacing slowly, face set and stern, eyes fixed upon the throne, he drew near to the dais. The circle of knights closed. Before them stood the eldest priestess of Avaryan in Ianon, ancient yet vigorous, robed all in sun-gold. As Mirain approached, she spread her arms wide to bar his way. He halted; she raised her thin old voice, that was strong still, and penetrating. "Who approaches Ianon's throne?"

Mirain paused an eyeblink, as if he could not trust his voice. But when it came it was clear, steady, blessedly deep, the voice of a man who had never known doubt. "I," it said. "Ianon's king."

"King, say you? By what right?"

"By right of the king who is dead, may the gods rest his soul, who chose me to be his successor; and by that of my mother, who was his daughter and who once was heir of Ianon. In the gods' name, reverend priestess, and in the name of Avaryan my father, let me pass."

"So I would," she said, "but that power remains with the lords and the people of Ianon. It is they who must grant you leave, not I."

Mirain lifted his hands, turning slowly. "My lords. My people. Will you have me for your king?"

They let him turn full circle. When he faced the throne again, the high ones knelt. Behind and about him the people loosed their voices in the single word: "Aye!"

The priestess bowed low and stepped aside. The circle opened, letting pass a small company of squires. Vadin led them, trying for dignity, hoping for grace. He knelt with only the merest hint of wobble and signaled to the rest. Mirain stood still for a wonder, suffering them to adorn him like the image of a god. Kilt of white leather cured to the softness of velvet, and broad belt of gold set with plates of amber, and great golden pectoral, and rings and armlets and earrings all of the sun-metal, and ropes of golden beads worked into the intricacy of the royal braids—Vadin's task, that last, and he kept his curses to himself, only thanking the gods for once that Mirain had no beard to battle with. Even as he bound off the last rebellious plait, the others weighted Mirain's shoulders with the great cloak of leather dyed scarlet and lined with priceless fur, white, but each hair tipped with a golden glint.

Last of all Vadin bound white sandals on Mirain's feet, the thongs edged with gold. He looked up, still on one knee, to find Mirain's eyes upon him. They were warm, almost laughing, but distant too, with the light of the god waiting to fill them. Without thinking, Vadin caught the hand that was closer to his face and kissed the flaming palm. That was not part of the rite, but his words were. "Lord king, your throne is waiting. Will it please you to take it?"

The way was clear to it now. Mirain's eyes lifted, and the god came, turning him all royal. Slowly, in swelling tumult, he mounted the dais and turned to face his people. Their shouting rose to a crescendo. They cried his name, proclaiming him lord, king, Sunborn, god-begotten. Again he raised his hands. The roaring died. The people waited, willing him to take his throne.

In the almost-silence, a horn brayed. Hoofs clattered on stone. Mounted men burst through the open gate. People scattered before them, crying out in anger and in pain. The seneldi, war-trained, attacked with horns and teeth and sharpened hoofs; the riders broadened Mirain's erstwhile path with the flats of their swords.

The cries rose to shrieks. A chariot plunged through the riders: a scythed war-car, and in it a glittering figure, a warrior in full armor.

The charioteer brought his team to a foaming halt at the foot of the dais. Even the knights of Ianon dared not venture against the deadly blades. He laughed at them, hollow and booming within his helmet. "Cowards and children! Indeed you have the king you deserve. There he stands, exulting in his power, who murdered the king before him. Poisoned, was he not, your majesty? And quickly too, once he had disposed of your only rival."

A rumble ran through the crowd, a name they had forbidden themselves to speak. Moranden. *Moranden.* "Moranden!"

Mirain's voice lashed them into silence. "It is not he!" He addressed the armored man more quietly, but still with the crack of command. "Take off your helmet."

He obeyed willingly enough. He was a big man, and young, and a Marcher by his accent. He looked at Mirain with well-cultivated contempt. "I have a message for you, boy." Mirain waited. The warrior scowled but could not hold his gaze. "I come to you from Ianon's true king, who although he has been cast out unjustly, nevertheless bows to the will of the king who is gone. He bids me say to you: 'Not all in Ianon have been led astray by your sorceries. Those who know the truth will come to me; many indeed have come already and bowed before me. Acknowledge your lies, priestess' bastard, and surrender now while yet you may hope to find mercy.' "

"If my uncle accepts his exile, which was perpetual," Mirain said with no hint of anger, "how may he hope to hold Ianon's throne? How does he even dare to claim it?"

"He is the true king. When all Ianon bids him, he shall return."

"And if all Ianon does not?"

"The kingdom is blinded by its grief for its old king, whom in turn you blinded with your sorceries. Southerner, wizard's brat, not all fall into your snares. When the people pause to think, then where will you be?"

"On the throne which my grandfather left me." Mirain sat in it with dignity but without ceremony. His eyes never left the messenger's face. "My uncle said and did much that could be construed as bitter enmity, and somewhat that came close to treason. In my predecessor's mind he richly deserved his exile. And yet," he said, sitting straight, and although he did not raise his voice it penetrated to the edges of the wide court, "I am willing to recall him."

The man's lip curled. "At what price?"

"This," said Mirain. "That he present himself in true repentance; that he beg forgiveness of all Ianon for what has been done in his name; and that he swear fealty to me as his lord and king."

The envoy laughed. "Should he crawl at your feet, who are not worthy to stand in his shadow?" He spat in the dust. "You are no king of his or of ours."

As the echoes of his words died, the throng began to mutter. It was a low sound, barely audible, yet blood-chilling. Still no one dared the scythes, but the press of bodies had tightened about the mounted men, hampering the seneldi.

Mirain raised his hand. Instinctively the messenger flinched from it, hauling at the reins. The chariot backed half a length and stopped short. A solid wall of people barred his escape. His mares trembled and sweated with eyes rolling white.

Gently Mirain said, "Give my message to my uncle."

"He will destroy you."

"Tell him." Mirain's voice rose a very little, speaking now to his people. "It was my will that these men should come here unmolested, else the Towers of the Dawn would have forbidden them. Let them go now as they came, unharmed."

The mutter turned to a rumble. Anger hung thick in the air, gathering like a storm. A senel screamed, rearing. A hundred hands pulled it down before its rider could free his sword from its scabbard.

"Let them go." Mirain had not risen, nor had he shouted. Yet he was heard. The rumble faltered. For an eternal moment the envoys' fate hung in the balance.

Mirain lowered his hands and sat back as if at his ease. Slowly, with reluctance as palpable as their outrage, the crowd freed their prisoners. Equally slowly, the invaders backed away from them. The messenger turned his chariot, gentling his frightened mares. With a sudden shout he lashed them forward. His escort spurred behind him.

Even beyond the gate they could hear the full-throated roar, the acclamation of the king enthroned.

Seventeen

MIRAIN WOULD GLADLY HAVE FEASTED UNTIL dawn, and his lords and his commons were minded to do just that, but it was hardly past sunset when Ymin gave the signal Vadin had been warned to expect. Although Mirain had been drinking considerably more than he ate, he was far from drunk; warm was the word, and joyous, and more prodigal than ever with the magic of his presence. His cloak was cast over the back of the high seat; he leaned across the table, watching a ring of fire-dancers and parrying the lethal wit of a lord who sat near the dais. Even as Vadin moved to touch his shoulder, he saluted a bold stroke and drank deep. He turned, laughing and glittering, and the simple nearness of him was enough to weaken Vadin's knees. "M— my lord," stammered Vadin, who had not stammered since he was weaned. "Sire, you must—"

The brilliance did not dim, but Mirain's eyes focused, touched with concern. "Trouble, Vadin?"

He laughed at that, shakily. "Gods, no! But it's time to go, my lord."

"Go!" Mirain frowned. "Am I a child, to be put to bed with the sun?"

Vadin had his self-possession back at last, and he grinned. "Of course not, my lord. You're the king, and there's one more thing you have to do to put the seal on it, and it's best you do it soon, before anyone catches on. Here, leave your cloak; they'll think you've just gone out to the privy."

For a moment Vadin knew Mirain would resist. But surely he knew what he was going to; he was the Sunborn, he knew everything. Except that he did not act as if he knew anything at all. Was it possible . . . ?

He came slowly, but he came. Maybe he used magic; no one seemed to care that he was leaving. Vadin led him down the passage behind the throne, up to the hidden door and the chambers that were now Mirain's. Some of his belongings had appeared there, but the touch of his hand was very faint yet, hardly perceptible over the deep imprint of the one who was gone.

But Vadin had not brought Mirain here to brood on the dead. He turned toward the bedchamber, opened the door, and stood back. "My lord," he said.

If Mirain was beginning to understand, he was far enough gone in wine not to hesitate. He entered the great room, its austerity soft-lit now with lamps, scented with flowers.

Others were there before him. Nine, Vadin counted from the door. Ten with Ymin. Ten women sitting or standing or kneeling, waiting in a shimmer of jewels. One or two were familiar, maidens of the king's bath now adorned as befit their rank; Vadin recognized several more from court and castle, and one at least of the guests who had come for High Summer and lingered for a funeral and a kingmaking. There was even one in the collar of a slave, but she had a fine bold eye, and she was one of the fairest, a daughter of velvet night.

Mirain stood stock-still under their eyes, almost as he had stood in the gateway before he claimed his throne. Vadin heard the sharp intake of his breath, saw the tensing of his back.

Ymin smiled at him. "Yes, my lord. One last test remains in the making of the king. As sacred singer I have been given authority to free you from the vow that binds you; as the king's singer I am sworn to accept the testimony of the lady you choose. Or ladies," she added with a touch of wickedness.

Mirain's voice was flat. "I do not wish to partake of this rite."

"You must, my lord. It is prescribed. Ianon knows that you are a man and that you bear no blemish which will weaken the land. Now you must prove your strength. Time was when you would have done so in the fields under the stars, for any to watch who wished to; and you would have kept a share of your seed for the earth itself."

"And now?"

"You need only satisfy your chosen one. Who will satisfy me that you are fit, and I will bear witness before your people."

"And . . . if I fail?"

"You will not." She spoke with assurance, coming forward and bowing low and holding out her hands. "If you please, my lord. Your torque."

His hand went to it. "I may not—" He stopped; he stripped off all his jewels, flinging them at her feet. But not his robe, and almost not his torque. At last, with visible reluctance, he unclasped it, held it up on his flattened palms. The words he spoke were in a tongue Vadin did not know, chanted softly and swiftly, almost angrily.

Ymin raised her own hands, responding in the same mode, in the same sonorous tongue. With all reverence she took the torque, kissed it, bowed over it, and set it again upon him.

As simple as that? Vadin wondered.

It would seem so. Mirain drew a long breath, and the way he stood spoke of a little regret, and a great deal of fear, but a worldful of relief; though he would die before he acknowledged any but the first. When he spoke again he sounded more like himself. "Must I be given so difficult a set of choices? Nine ladies of such beauty—how can I choose?"

"A king must always choose," Ymin said with the barest hint of iron beneath the softness.

He was delaying, that was obvious. Nervous as a virgin, and probably he was not far from one; and now he had to prove himself for such a cause, after so long an abstinence, with bitter consequences if his body played him false. Vadin wished desperately that there were something he could do. Anything.

He was not even supposed to be here. He bit his tongue and knotted his fists and made himself stay out of it. Mirain was Mirain, after all. And Ianon needed a strong king.

Mirain gathered himself all at once, and laughed almost freely. "I shall choose, then; and may the god guide my hand." He made a slow circuit, pausing before each lady, taking her hand, saying a word or two. He lingered longest for his golden princess of the bath, whose hands he even kissed, and she looked at him with her heart in her eyes. But he did not say the word that would seal the choosing. He drew back, and they all waited, hardly breathing. He faced Ymin, held out his hand. "Come," he said.

There was a stunned silence. Even she had not looked for this. Surely he was mocking her, taking his revenge for the ordeal which she had forced upon him.

She said what they were all thinking. "I am more than twice your age."

"And a head taller than I," he agreed willingly, "and no tender maid, and my chosen. It is permitted that I choose as I will." Again he held out his hand. "Come, singer."

If she shaped protests, she let them die before she uttered them. Coolly and quietly she dismissed the ladies who had been chosen with such care and to so little effect, setting Vadin the task of looking after them. The last he saw as he shut the door, they were facing one another, king and singer, and it looked more like war than love.

"Why?" Ymin asked when the rest were gone. She was still calm, but the mask was cracking.

Mirain's seemed the firmer for the weakness of hers. He shrugged and smiled. "I want you."

"Not the Princess Shirani?"

"She's very lovely. She's also terrified of me, although she calls it love. And tonight I'm not up to a maiden's holy awe." His face darkened. "Is it that I repel you? I know I have no beauty, and I'm too young to be a good lover, and too small to look well beside you."

"*No!*" Her hands took it on themselves to seize his, to hold them fast. "Never say such things. Never even think them."

"I was taught to speak the truth."

"The truth, aye and well. But that is a lie. Mirain my dearest lord, do you not know that you are beautiful? You have that which makes even the lovely Shirani seem commonplace beside you. A brilliance; a splendor. A magic. And a very fine pair of eyes in a very striking face, and a body with which I can find no fault."

"What, none at all?"

"Perhaps," she mused, "if I might see the whole of it . . ."

"Have you not already?"

"Ah, but that was the kingmaking, and I was blinded by the god in your eyes. I should like to see the man, since he has persisted in choosing me."

He freed himself easily, dropped his robe, stood for her to look at. She looked long, and she looked with great pleasure, and she smiled, for he was rousing to her presence. "No flaw at all, my lord. Not one."

"Sweet-tongued singer." He unbound the cincture of her robe. His hands were not quite steady. "I hope, my lady, that your modesty is only for the world."

"My lord, I am a famous wanton." She cast aside the heavy garment, growing reckless now that she had no retreat, and shook down the masses of her hair. It tumbled from its woven braids, pouring like water to her feet; his gasp of wonder made her laugh. But when he touched her she gasped herself, and their eyes met, and she sank down in the pool of her hair. His arms closed about her; she trembled within them. "My lord, you should not have done this to me."

He stroked her hair with gentle hands. "My name is Mirain."

She raised her head in a flare of sudden heat. "My lord!"

"Mirain." Gentle, implacable. "The kingdom commands that I do this, and the god commands that you be my chosen, but I will not be *my lord*. Unless you honestly wish me to fail."

Her heart went cold. He had let slip the truth at last. The god had commanded it. Not his will. Not his desire, nor ever his love. That his body responded to her beauty, that was mere fleshly desire; it meant nothing.

She knew her face was calm, but he did not read faces. He stared stricken, and he cried, "No, Ymin. No! Oh, damn my tripping tongue! The god guided me, I admit it, but only because I would never have dared it alone. How much easier to take one of yon eager worshipful maids, to do my duty, to send her away. You came harder. Because you outshone them all, body and soul. Because—because with you I would have more than duty and ritual. With you I would have love."

She raised her hand, let it come to rest upon his cheek. "Curse you," she said very softly, "for a mage and a seer."

He kissed her palm.

"Child," she said. He smiled. "Insolent boy. I have a daughter only a little younger than you. I would spank her if she looked at me as you are looking now."

"It would be appalling if she did." His hand found her breast; he paid it the homage of a kiss. "How beautiful you are."

"How ancient."

"And how young I am, and how little it matters." He kissed her other breast, and the warm secret space between them, and the curve of her belly beneath. Her body sang where he touched it; keened when he withdrew; began to sing again as he led her to the bed. Her mind, letting go its resistance, took up the descant. Its refrain was perfect in its purity: simply and endlessly his name, with no *lord* or *king* to taint it. He saw; he knew. His fire flooded over her and drowned her.

Vadin yawned and stretched, and grinned at the ceiling of his new chamber. Bold-eyed Jayida had gone back to her mistress, who had been one of the old king's ladies; but she had promised to visit him again. Nor had she seemed to find him a poor second to the king. After all, she had said, the king was half a god and all a priest, and that did not bode well for him as a lover. Whereas the king's squire . . .

Still grinning, he sat up, tossing back his loosened hair. No sound reached him from the king's bedchamber. He opened the door with great care and peered within. And jumped like a startled thief. Mirain stood in the opening and laughed, as bare and tousled as himself but somewhat wider awake. "Good morning, Vadin," he said. "Did she serve you well?"

Vadin flinched. It had occurred to him that he was usurping a woman chosen for the king. She had scoffed when he said it. But there were places where he would have paid in blood for his night's pleasure.

Mirain embraced him with unfeigned exuberance, dragged him to the bath that was blessedly empty of its maidens, pushed him in and leaped after him in a cloud of spray. Vadin came up spluttering, not ready yet to join in the game. "My lord, I—"

"My lord, you are forgiven, she is yours, you may have your joy of her. Shall I free her for you? I can do that."

Mirain was alight with it, knowing that he was king, that he was free, that he could do whatever he pleased. Vadin blinked water out of his eyes. "I don't think—she was just for a night. If I were asking for anyone I'd ask for Ledi. But—"

"But." Mirain had sobered. "You don't want gifts. When I hold Great Audience today I'll take the liege-oaths of all the lords who are here, and of the fighting men, and of the pages and the servants. And of the squires who served my grandfather. Would you like to go back to them? You no longer need look after me all alone; you can be a squire among the squires again, only taking your turn with me when it suits you. If it suits you at all."

Vadin stood very still in the warm ever-flowing water. Mirain waited without expression. Hoping, maybe, that Vadin would accept. Looking for an escape from his most reluctant servant.

Except that the reluctance had got itself lost somewhere, and the resistance had dwindled to a ritual, a saving of face. And the thought of going back to the barracks, of being plain Vadin the squire again, held no sweetness at all. Seeing someone else at Mirain's back—knowing that someone else would stand here dripping, enduring Mirain's gentle chaffing, sharing bath and breakfast—

Vadin swallowed hard, half choking. "Do you want me to go, my lord?"

"I don't want you to stay in a place that you dislike."

"What—" Vadin swallowed hard. "What if I don't dislike it?"

"Even though people call you my dog and my catamite?"

Vadin thought of the names they had called Mirain. Which, if he could but hear them—

"I have."

"You're walking in my mind again. After all I've said. You used my body when you sent me to that unspeakable woman. Who knows what you'll do to me next? But I'm getting used to you and your wizard's tricks. Life in the barracks would bore me silly."

"It would win your wager for you."

"Sure it would. And who'd nursemaid you when you got into one of your moods? No, my lord, you won't get rid of me now. I said I'd stay with you, and I'm a man of my word."

"Beware, Vadin; you'll be admitting to friendship next."

"Not likely," Vadin said, scooping up a handful of cleansing-foam. "Turn around and I'll wash your back."

Mirain did as he was told, but first he said, "I know exactly what I'm going to do with your soul when I win it. I'll house it in crystal and net it in gold and hang it over my bed."

"Fine sights it will see there," said Vadin unperturbed, "now that you're allowed to live like a man."

Mirain laughed, and that was answer and to spare.

Eighteen

IN THE GREY LIGHT BEFORE SUNRISE, A LONE RIDER
sent his mount through its paces. He rode superbly well, wrapped
with his stallion in a half-trance of leap and curvet and sudden swift
gallop, challenging the targets set here and there on the practice ground
of the castle: that art of princes called riding at the rings. Three circlets
of copper glinted on his spearpoint; as Ymin watched, he turned his
mount on its haunches, striking for a fourth.

"Well done!" she applauded him as he lowered his lance. Three rings
rolled from it; the fourth spun through the air into her hand. She smiled
and sank down in a low curtsey. "All thanks, my knight, for your
tribute."

"It is given where it is due." Mirain doffed his helmet, shaking his
braid free from its protective coil about his head. His face was damp; his
eyes glittered. He slid smoothly from the Mad One's back and ran his
hand down the sleek sweat-sheened neck; and turned more quickly than
her eye could follow, and drew her head down, and kissed her.

"My lord," she protested, as she must. And when he glared: "Mirain,
this is no fit place—"

"I have decreed that it is." But he stood a little apart, decorous, with
glinting eyes. "Walk with me," he said.

They walked for a time in silence, he at the Mad One's shoulder, she
at a cool and proper distance. At length she asked, "Would you ride to
war as you do now, without a saddle?"

"That would be foolish even for a child king."

She glanced at him. "So bitter, my lord?"

He brushed a fly from the Mad One's ear, caressing the tender place beneath it. "In one thing," he said, "Moranden's man spoke the truth. The sheen has worn away. Ianon has the king it asked for, but now it has paused to think upon the asking."

"Wisely, for the most part. No one in town or castle seems to regret the choice."

"Ah," he said, "but Ianon is much more than a single city, or even a single mountain-guarded vale."

"True, my dear lord. But have you heard none of the old songs? Time was when a king had to fight his way to the throne, and fight to sit in it, and leave as soon as he had taken it to put down a dozen risings. The day after your grandsire claimed his kingship, the whole of eastern Ianon rose against him, led by two of his own brothers."

"And I should hold my peace, should I not? Central Ianon is firmly sworn to me, and I have no more to fear than a rumbling in the Marches. With, of course, enough slighting rumors to set my teeth on edge; but no open threat, as yet, of cold iron." He sighed. "I've waited so long to be king. Now I am, and the end is the merest beginning. I find myself wishing that I could live my life like a hero in a song, striding from peak to peak, paying no heed to the dull stretches between."

"Surely it would grow wearisome, always to be at the summit of one's attainments."

"You think so?" he asked. "How much simpler it would be if I didn't have to endure all this waiting, if I could pass from my enthronement straight to the heart of war and there find an end. Whether my enemy's or my own."

"That will come soon enough," she said levelly.

"None too soon for me. My nerves are raw, and people are whispering. Do you know that I'm supposed to have been the Red Prince's boy?"

"Were you?"

He stopped as if struck.

She laid a hand on his arm. "My lord. Mirain. They are only words."

"So are your songs."

"Certainly. And I sing the truth. What are all the lies and foul tales to that?"

"Moranden cursed us all." He began to walk again along the wall which bordered the field. "I can think of a worse curse than his. That he actually gain what he longs for."

"To be king?"

"It would be fitting. A throne, a title, a kingdom full of subjects all eager to serve him—those are only trappings. The truth is a wall and a cage and fetters of gold. My people are my jailers. They bind me; I can't escape them. Courts and councils and the cares of a kingdom . . . even in my bed I'm not free of them."

"Am I so much a burden?"

"You," he cried with sudden force, "no!"

"Ah," she said sagely. "Prince Mehtar's daughter."

He scowled; suddenly he laughed. "Just so. And Lord Anden's niece. And Baron Ushin's ward. Not to mention half my maidens of the bath. Young I may be, undersized and no beauty, certainly foreign born and arguably a bastard, but I have one asset that far outweighs the rest: Ianon's throne."

"I thought I had taught you not to underrate yourself."

Mirain smiled his swift smile. "Prince Mehtar was quite blunt," he said. "I'm no great marvel of manhood, or so he informed me, but I am royal. More than royal if my claims be true. House Mehtar would be quite pleased to ally itself with me. The girl, they tell me, is well worth the trouble."

"She is a beauty," Ymin agreed. "They call her the Jewel of the Hills." She paused, regarding him. "Will you consider the offer?"

"Should I?"

"Beauty, wealth, and breeding—she has all of those. And a father who can sway most of the eastern fiefdoms to his will."

"He would be pleased to add the whole of Ianon." Their glances caught; his was bright and faintly mocking. "I pleaded extreme youth and the need to establish myself in my kingdom—and promised to have a look at the lady if I should happen to be in her vicinity."

Ymin laughed. "Spoken like a true king!"

"Or like a southerner born." He turned with his hand upon the Mad One's withers. "The sun is rising. Shall we sing him up together?"

The sun was fierce in the Court of Judgment. Although the high seat rested in the shade of a canopy, there was no escape from the heat; even Vadin's light kilt weighed upon him. Yet Mirain sat apparently at his ease, cheek resting on palm, cool and unruffled and thoroughly alert.

"A dry spring," whined the man in front of him, "and a burning summer. My herd has overgrazed its pasture; my crops are withering in the heat. And now, sire—and now this young ingrate tells me he has bid for a girl in the next village, and I must give him the groom-price, and not a moment's thought to spare for the hardship."

The young ingrate was not so very young. Thirty, Vadin judged, and looking older with hard work and poor feeding. He scowled at his feet and knotted his heavy hands, drawing up his shoulders as if against a blow. " 'S my right," he mumbled. "I waited. Every season I waited. 'S always too soon, or the weather's too bad, or the harvest's due in. No more, she said. Long enough is long enough. Bid for me like you've been promising to, or somebody else will get there first."

His father sputtered with fury.

"Are you the only son?" Mirain asked.

The young man looked up, a flash of sullen eyes that saw a throne and a blur of gold upon it, no more. "No," he said. "Sir. Got two brothers, sir."

"Older?"

"Yes, sir."

"Married?"

Again the eyes, more sullen still. "No, sir. Too soon, the weather's too bad, the harvest's due in . . ."

"So," Mirain said in his most neutral tone, but Vadin saw the glint in his eye. The son's hands twisted fiercely. "Go. Take your bride. Bid the groom-price, but see that your father adds to it another of equal worth, to begin your marriage properly." Mirain gestured to the scribe. "It is written. It shall be done."

There was no love in the young man's stare, and scarcely any gratitude. He bowed ungracefully, looked about for an exit, and departed, pursued by his father's howls of rage.

The next complainant had already begun. That was the king's justice: swift, thankless, and not to be opposed. Mirain shifted minutely in his seat. Vadin gestured where his eye could catch it, raising a cup of wine cooled with snow. He took the goblet and drank, a sip only, sighing just visibly. But his face was as calm as ever, intent. A perfect mask.

Vadin studied it and tried not to think of sleep. One of the older councillors was snoring on his feet. The voices droned on. So many matters of great moment to the people in the midst of them; so many tangled details flung down at the king's feet as if he and he alone could unravel them. "My lord," a scribe was saying in a bored monotone, "the titles to the property in question—"

Vadin did not know what roused him. Maybe it was only a precious whisper of breeze wandering lost in this sun-tortured place. Or maybe it was instinct honed by a season of serving a mage. But he was full awake and taut as a strung bow, his eyes sweeping the assembled faces. None rang the alarm in his brain. Good solid Ianyn faces with a sprinkling of foreigners: Asanian gold, southern brown, traders or sightseers; and there was the scholar from Anshan-i-Ormal, a wizened earth-colored creature with the merriest eyes Vadin had ever seen. They were almost quiet now, watching Mirain in tireless fascination. He was going to write a history, he had told Vadin only last night; he had been looking all his life for a fit subject, and now he thought he had found it in a young barbarian king. Mirain liked him, because he had no talent for flattery. He had a wicked tongue, which he tempered with laughter, and in his Ormalen custom he called even the king by his given name.

Something caught Vadin's eye beyond the turbaned head. A movement almost too quick to follow. A glint of light on metal. A guard on the wall, surely, saluting the king with his spear.

Spear. Vadin lunged, hurling Mirain away from the throne. The world spun; fire pierced it, transfixed it. Winds roared in Vadin's ears. The fire was pain, and it pinned him. He could not move. "The wall," he tried to cry out. "Damn you, the wall!"

The whirling stopped; the world came closer. Mirain filled it. Vadin hit him. "Get down, you fool. Get—"

Mirain's hand descended like the night, vast and inescapable. But his face looked strange and small. Except for the eyes. Such brilliant, bitter, ice-cold rage—

"Are you going to kill me?" Vadin's voice was faint, weak as a child's. It seemed very far away. He was losing his body. And yet how odd; how clear it all was. The court; the people in their shock or their outrage or their terror; the armed men hunting an assassin and finding him dead upon the parapet with his own knife in his throat. And the king on his knees in front of his throne, gripping the haft of a spear that pierced a sprawled ungainly body. Poor creature, he was done for, speared just below the heart, beginning to struggle with blind bodily panic. But he was brave; he was not screaming.

"No good," someone said. "The head's barbed. Poisoned too, I'll wager. Those are Marcher clan-marks on the haft; and they don't take chances."

Someone else responded with doleful relish, "Poison or not, they've won a life. That wound is mortal."

Gods rest him, Vadin thought. Whoever he was. Not that it mattered. He was going away, winged like a bird. Court and castle shrank beneath him. There was Ianon dwindling swiftly, a green jewel set in a ring of mountains, glimmering in the center of an orb like a child's ball, painted all in green and white and blue and brown. Why, it was just like the world as it was painted over the altar in Avaryan's temple. He traced the lands, naming them as the priests had taught him years ago in Geitan. From western Asanion to the isles of the east that looked upon the open sea; from the great desert that bordered on the southern principates, across the Hundred Realms to Ianon again, and its mountains, and Death's Fells beyond, and the wastes of ice—all lay under his wondering eyes, perfect as a jewel on a lady's finger. And such a lady: deep-breasted Night herself in her robe of stars. She smiled; she drew him to her; she kissed him with a mother's gentleness but with a lover's warmth.

"Vadin." The voice was vaguely familiar. It was a beautiful voice for a man's, both sweet and deep. But it sounded impatient, even angry. "Vadin alVadin, for the love of Avaryan, listen to me!"

But it was so pleasant here. Dark and warm, and a beautiful lady smiling, and maybe later there would be loving.

"Vadin!"

Yes, he was angry. What was his name? Vadin had done nothing to earn his displeasure. Did he want the lady? There was enough of her for both.

"I want no lady. Come, Vadin."

Mirain. That was his name. It was very flattering that he wanted Vadin and not so lovely a lady, but alas, Vadin was not in the mood. Maybe later, if he should still be inclined . . .

"Vadin alVadin of Asan-Geitan, by Avaryan and Uveryen, by life and death, by the Light and by the Dark that embraces it, I summon you before me."

The lady's arms opened. Vadin was slipping away. He clutched, desperate. She was gone. It was dark. Wind howled, thin and bitter. It tore at him with teeth of iron. The voice rang through it. "By the oath of fealty you have sworn me, by the kingship I hold, come. Come or be forever lost."

The voice was warm, laden with power. Vadin yearned toward it. But the wind beat him back. It was dark still, darker than dark, yet he could see with more than eyes. He stood on a road in a country of night, and the road ran but one way, and that was onward, away from that far sweet calling.

It swelled in strength and sweetness. It sang like a harp, it throbbed like drums. All words had forsaken it; it was pure power. The night quailed before it. The wind faltered. Inch by tortured inch, Vadin dragged himself about. There was no road behind. Only madness. Madness and Mirain. Vadin stretched out his hands. He could not reach—he could not—

He stretched impossibly, with every ounce of will and pride and strength. He touched. Slipped. Mirain's fingers clawed. Vadin clutched. They held.

The darkness burst in a storm of fire.

Vadin gasped as the pain struck him, gasped again as it vanished beneath a warmth like the sun. He had his body back again, and his wits, and a faint blur of sight. He knew where he was: still in the Court of Judgment, lying now on the dais in front of the throne, cradled in Mirain's arms. The spear was gone. He could not see the wound, and he did not want to. He knew that he was dying. He had died already, and Mirain's power had called him back. But it was not strong enough. It could not hold him.

"No," Mirain said fiercely. His cheeks were wet. Weeping in front of his people—fool of a foreigner, did he know what he was doing? "I know. I know to the last breath. I'll hold you. I'll heal you. I won't let you die for me."

As the old king had. And Mirain did not easily suffer defeat. Vadin looked at the vivid furious eyes and thought of reason and of sanity, but Mirain had never fallen prey to either. The warmth that had been pain was rising into heat. Sun's fire. Sun's child. It was something to be loved by a mage of that rank, a master of power whose father was a god. Maybe after all he could face death. Maybe, with the god behind him, he could win.

"Help me," Mirain's face turned to the sun, his eyes open to it, unblinded, unseeing. "Father, help me!" He did not bargain, Vadin noticed. He simply pleaded, in a tone very close to command.

It was very quiet. People stood all about, staring, mute. Some had drawn close. White robes or kilts, golden torques. One or two in grey and silver. Ymin's eyes were fixed on Mirain, almost blazing. She was giving him what power she had, prodigal of the cost. Blessed madwoman.

The heat mounted. It was like agony, but it was exquisitely pleasant, like a scalding bath after the Great Race. Healing anguish, flooding his body, setting his bones afire. He felt it focus at his center. He *felt* the outraged flesh begin to knit, the great ragged wound to close from its depths to its topmost reaches. He saw the fire of power working in him,

and he knew it, and he knew what it did, wise with the wisdom of the
one who healed him, endowed with more than mortal sight.

Mirain drew a long shuddering breath. His face was drawn as it had
been on the road to Umijan, but his eyes were clear and quiet, and he
smiled. Without a sound he crumpled.

Vadin caught him before he struck the stone, moving without
thought, without pain. Mirain was still conscious; he raised his hand to
touch the deep scar beneath Vadin's breast. "I healed you," he whispered. "I promised."

Vadin rose. Mirain was a light weight and an indomitable will, giving
his people a flash of golden hand before the darkness took him. Gently
Vadin carried him down the steps through the murmurs of awe, the
bodies crowding back to give him room, the eyes lowered and the heads
bowed as before a god.

When this was over, Vadin was going to be amused. Whoever the
assassin had been, whoever had sent him—whether Moranden or that
unnatural mother of his—he had not only failed to fell his target. He
had shown Ianon what in truth it had accepted as its king. Avaryan's
temple would be full by evening, nor would it be Avaryan alone to
whom the folk addressed their prayers. Mirain's legend would be all the
stronger hereafter.

Vadin had expected people to look on Mirain with greater reverence
now that he had shown them what power was in him. But the squire
had not reckoned on the consequences to himself. He was a wonder and
a strangeness, a man brought back from the dead. Even his friends
walked shy of him, even Kav who had been known to doubt the gods.
When he walked in the town, folk tried to touch him, to coax a blessing
from him, or made signs of awe and would not look him in the face.

Ledi was the crowning blow. She who had shared her bed with him,
called him by his love-name, faced him as an equal and slapped him
when he got above himself—when he came into the alehouse she did
not come running to wait on him, and when he called for her she bowed
low and called him *lord,* and when he tried to embrace her she fled.
And everyone in the drab familiar room was silent, staring, knowing
who he was. The Reborn. The king's miracle.

He was on his feet. He had meant to go after Ledi, to beat her into
her senses if need be. He turned slowly, with all the dignity he could
muster, and began to walk. Swifter and swifter through the whispering
streets in the hiss of the rain, running through the castle gate, winding
among the courts and passages, coming up short in Mirain's chamber.

The king was there, alone for once, prowling like a caged panther. He had been in council with Ianon's elders; he was dressed for it still in a dazzle of gold and royal white, although his mantle lay on the floor where he had flung it. When Vadin halted, panting and almost sobbing, Mirain whipped about in a blind flare of temper. "Wait, they tell me. Wait, and wait, and wait. So wise, they are. So very wise." His lip curled; he began to pace again, hurling the words over his shoulder. "It will grow easier, they tell me. My people are testing me; they are proving my fitness. It is all a great testing. The judgments and the petitions; the lords with all their retinues, appearing unannounced with disputes which only the king can settle. The embassies from my royal and princely neighbors, demanding hospitality and courtesy, reminding me of alliances made and unmade and remade. The hordes of traders and mountebanks, each of whom must attract my august eye or spread abroad the tale of my niggardliness. And always—always that fire smoldering in the Marches. Wait, they tell me. Hold fast. Let my loyal lords and my own actions hold off the threat." He stopped, spun. "Actions! What actions? I've not even left his castle since I took the throne. And when I flung that in their faces, they bowed and scraped and prayed my majesty's pardon, but if an assassin could come to me here in my own stronghold, how much more perilous it would be for me to ride abroad. No, no, I am young, of course I chafe under the restraints of my rule, but only let me be patient and soon I will be strong upon my throne. Then I may do as I will. Yes, then, when Moranden is king of all but this castle."

Vadin started to turn away, sighed and stayed. Mirain still prowled, still muttered, still saw him only as a target for heated words. "Ah no, the exile will never come so far. Lord Yrian, Lord Cassin, Prince Kirlian, all the lords whose lands border on the Marches—they have sworn to bring him to me. Limb by limb. Surely I can trust them who always served King Raban well. Maybe I can even trust Moranden. But his mother—now there is an enemy to be afraid of. *She* would never have sent anyone as conspicuous as an assassin with a spear. She will have my life while I tarry, and never count the cost. And, *Wait,* my elders intone. *Wait, sire. Wait and see.*"

Vadin said nothing. What were his little troubles to this great matter of war and rebellion? One silly fool of a girl was afraid of him because he had been killed and had come to life again and had walked away with only a fading scar. Ianon was about to tear itself apart, and he cried over a tuppenny whore.

Mirain had come to his senses a little. He saw Vadin and knew him;

his glare lightened to a scowl. "Your pardon, Vadin. I never meant to rage at you. But if I erupt in council, they all look gravely at one another and sigh, their wisdom sorely tried by my impetuous youth. I have to be cool, I have to be quiet, I have to try to reason with minds set in stone. They know, surely and absolutely, that I must not risk my precious neck in a war. Not even in a parley. Not even, gods forbid, in a royal progress. I must stay mewed up here while others do it all for me."

"Isn't that what it is to be a king?"

"Not you too." But Mirain's rage had passed; he rubbed his eyes with tired fingers. "I'm getting so I can't even think. I need to do something. Would you—" He broke off. "Aren't you supposed to be at liberty?"

"I . . . decided not to bother." Vadin picked up Mirain's mantle and folded it, laying it carefully in its chest. "Shall I fetch Ymin? Or would you prefer—"

Mirain stood in front of him, hands on his shoulders. "Do I have to take the answer out of your mind?"

Vadin wrenched away. "Don't you—don't you ever—Damn you, why didn't you let me die?"

"I couldn't." Mirain spoke very softly. "I *couldn't*, Vadin."

The squire choked on bile. Mirain's eyes were wide and full of pain, and he could see into them. He could hear the thoughts behind them. Love and grief, fear of loss, regret that it had led to this. *"Regret!"* Vadin cried. "Oh gods, you've even infected me with your magery. They can all see it. They're terrified of me. I died. I died and I came back, and I'm not Vadin anymore. Demons take you, King of Ianon. May the goddess' birds peck your bones."

There was a long throbbing silence. Vadin looked up at last, and Mirain stood still. His hands were fists at his sides. The god's brand rent him with its agony. Vadin knew. He could feel it himself if he willed to.

"We are bound," Mirain said with perfect calm. "I went very far to call you back. I cannot loose you, nor can I alter what my people saw. But time can heal you somewhat. You died, you were healed, you have changed, but you are still Vadin. Those who love you will learn to see it, once their awe passes."

"You sound exactly like your council. *Wait. Wait and see.*"

Mirain laughed, short and bitter. "Don't I? Unfortunately it's true."

"And what do I do while I wait? Study sorcery? It's all I seem to be fit for."

"You can go and show Ledi that you're still her favorite lover."

King or no king, Vadin would have struck him for that if he had been a shade less quick. "She hates me."

"She's crying now because she let herself listen to all the tales, and because she let them frighten her, and because you went away. Go to her, Vadin. She needs you."

"So do you, damn it."

"Not now. Go on."

"Come with me." Vadin's tongue had said that. Not his brain.

Mirain frowned, searching his mind, a touch like light fingers, or a warm breath, or a moth's wing in the dark. He thought of outrage, but he could not find it. Memory came between: the world floating in night, and a strong voice calling.

Between them they extricated Mirain from his state dress, unwound the king-braids and plaited his hair into the simplicity of priesthood, found a plain kilt and a plain dark mantle. Vadin wrapped himself in a dry cloak, swallowed the last of his regrets, and set his face toward the town.

This time no one seemed even to see Vadin, much less his companion. Ledi was not serving in the alehouse; the boy who waited on them did not know where she was, or care. They drank the ale he brought, Vadin tarrying out of fear, Mirain simply reveling in walls that were not the walls of his castle and in voices that were not the voices of his council. The taut line of his face had begun to ease. He looked younger, less hagridden. Dear gods, Vadin thought, he could not remember when last he had seen Mirain smile.

He looked down into his dwindling ale, flushing a little with shame. He had been thinking that all this worship did not trouble Mirain; the Sunborn had been used to it from his birth. Maybe that made it worse. Vadin could go back in time to plain humanity, and he could hope that it would be soon. Mirain could never go back at all.

Vadin tossed a coin on the table and stood. Mirain followed him through the crowd to the curtain with its painted lovers. The old harridan who stood guard took Vadin's silver, tested it with her one remaining tooth, grinned and let them by.

It was not easy, climbing those steep fetid steps with the King of Ianon behind him and Ledi somewhere ahead. Maybe she had taken a man to console her. Or two; she liked two, especially if they were Kav and Vadin. The other girls were busy, raw night that it was, providing warmth and comfort for a handful of copper.

Ledi had one of the better rooms, the one at the top with a window which she kept open even in winter. It made the air sweet, she said. As if she needed anything but her own warm scent and the herbs she sprinkled on her pillow. Her door was shut, but no length of green ribbon hung from the latch; she was in but alone. Vadin's heart hammered. She was going to be afraid, and she was going to submit as any woman must to a great lord, and he was an idiot for tormenting himself like this. He turned to face the shadow that was Mirain. "You can have her," he said roughly. "I don't want her."

Mirain did not say it aloud, but the word hung in the air. *Coward.*

With a low growl Vadin spun back to the door. He raised his trembling fist, struck once and then twice and then once again.

Nothing moved within. She would be huddled in her bed, praying that he would go away. He stepped back, braced for flight.

The latch grated. The door eased open. Lamplight brightened the stair and its landing; Ledi's face peered out, all puffed with crying, and her hair was a tangle and she had on her worst rag of a dress, and she had never been less pretty or more beloved. "Ledi," he said stupidly. "Ledi, I—"

She drew herself up. "My lord."

"And what have I done," he snapped with desperate temper, "to deserve that? Cold shoulder down below and cold words up here, and if it's that I haven't been coming so often lately, will you please remember that we've lost an old king and got a new one, and I've been caught in the middle?"

"That's not all you've been caught in," she said, unbending. She stood as straight and cold and haughty as a queen, and she would never bend now, since he had forced her to remember her pride.

"And can I help any of it?" he cried in a fine fire of rage. "Damn it, woman, don't you turn on me too!"

She looked at him with great care, squinting a little for her eyes were not of the best, frowning as if he were a stranger whose face she must remember. He was almost in tears, which was a great shame, but he did not care.

All at once she began to laugh, half weeping herself. She flung her arms about his neck and kissed him till he knew he would drown, and drew him through her door.

Then she saw who stood with him. She stiffened again. Only a little at first, with surprise. "You didn't say you'd brought a friend."

"He didn't," Mirain said. "I was only seeing to it that he didn't turn tail before he saw you."

"Then I owe you thanks," she said, letting Vadin go. It was a kiss she had in mind, with joy in it, and Mirain had both before she saw the light on his face and the sheen of his torque. She recoiled, dropping to her knees. "Majesty!"

Mirain did not raise her. "Madam." His voice was cold. "Since you know me, I trust that you will do as I command."

She bowed to the floor. "Yes, majesty."

"Very well. Get up and look at me, and do not bow to me again, nor ever call me by that unlovely title." She rose; she made herself look into his stern face. "Now, madam. Look after my squire, who stands in sore need of it, and consider well. When I was a prince you would speak to me without fear or fawning. Now that I am a king, I need that more than ever." The sternness softened; he held out his hands. "Can you forgive me, Ledi? I never meant to take your man away from you."

"Didn't you?" But she took his hands a little gingerly and mustered a smile. "Very well. I forgive you."

He bowed low, to her consternation and delight, and set a kiss in each palm as if she had been a great lady. "Look after my friend," he said.

Nineteen

VADIN ATE THORNFRUIT AND CREAM WITH NEW
bread and honey and a mug of ale, and Ledi to sweeten it, combing and braiding his hair while he ate. Through the window he could
hear the morning sounds of the town, feel the air cool on his face, bask
in the fitful sunlight. It would rain again later, he suspected. The sky
had that odd watery clarity it always had between storms, as if it had
paused to rest before its new onslaught.

Ledi clasped her arms about his middle, resting warm and bare
against his back. He half turned. She claimed a kiss that tasted of cream
and honey, and said, "You should be going. Your king will be needing
you."

He sighed a little. "Half a thousand people who live to wait on him,
and I'm the one he always seems to be needing."

"You're his friend."

"I think I was born under a curse." He reached for his kilt but did
not move to put it on. "I'm not his friend. I'm something fated. Like a
shadow, or a second self, or a brother of the same birth. I used to think
I hated him, till I realized that I didn't; I resented him. How dare he
come out of nowhere and change the world?"

"Your world," she said. Very lightly, and for the first time, she
touched the mark of the spear. "You're different. You're more like him.
Like . . . someone who knows what the gods are."

"I don't know anything."

His sullenness made her smile. "Go on. He's waiting for you."

Let him wait! he would have cried if he had had any sense. He dressed instead, kissed her again, and then again for good measure, and went lightly enough down the stair.

There were one or two people in the common room drinking their breakfast, and one who neither ate nor drank but sat in a corner, unseen and unremarked by any but Vadin, to whom his presence was like a fire on the skin. "Have you been here all night?" Vadin demanded.

"No." Mirain rose. Under his cloak he was dressed for riding: a short leather kilt over boots almost tall enough to pass for leggings. "Rami is outside."

"Where are we going?"

Mirain did not answer. He walked ahead of Vadin into the puddled courtyard. The Mad One was there, unsaddled, and Rami in saddle and bridle nibbling a bit of weed. When Vadin had seen to her girth and mounted, Mirain was already at the gate.

They rode in silence except for the thudding of hoofs and the creaking of Vadin's saddle, winding through the streets to the east gate, the Fieldgate that led to the open Vale. It was open, its guard snapping to attention as he recognized his king. Mirain laid him low with a smile and clapped heels to the Mad One's sides. The stallion bucked and belled and sprang into a gallop.

When at last they slowed, town and castle lay well behind them. The Vale rolled ahead of them, its green grass parched to gold with summer's heat, lapping at the foot of the mountain wall.

The Mad One snorted and shied at a stone; Rami bent a scornful ear at them both. She had no time to spare for nonsense. Piqued but subdued, the stallion settled into a swinging walk. His rider stroked his neck in wry sympathy. "Poor king. Neither of us has seen a sky without walls about it in an eon and an age."

"You're not a prisoner, you know," Vadin said.

"Aren't I?"

"Only if you think you are. Yon old vultures of your council would have you locked in a single room, with servants to wipe your nose for you, and no sharp edges to threaten your priceless hide."

"And no common labor to sully my royal hands."

Vadin tried not to grin. "Went to fetch the seneldi yourself, did you?"

"I did," said Mirain, sharp with annoyance. "You'd have thought I was proposing to turn Avaryan's temple into a brothel. What, his majesty of Ianon in the muck of the stable, touching brush and bridle with his sacred fingers?"

"Appalling." Vadin breathed deep, letting his head fall back, opening his eyes to the tumbled sky. A gust of laughter escaped him, not at Mirain, simply for gladness that he was alive and whole and riding in the wind.

Rami halted and dropped her head to graze. After a moment the Mad One followed suit. "When your beauty comes into season," Mirain said, "I should like to see a mating. Would you be willing?"

"With the Mad One?" Vadin had been going to ask. To beg if need be. But he kept his voice cool and his eye critical. "He's close to perfect to look at, if a little smaller than he should be; but she's got height to spare. And the bloodlines on both sides are good. But aren't you concerned that he'll pass on his madness?"

"He is not mad. He is a king who demands his due."

"Same thing," Vadin said.

"So then, we pray the gods for a foal with Rami's good sense. And a little fire, Vadin. Surely you'll allow that."

Vadin met Mirain's mockery with a long stony stare; then he loosed a grin. "A *little* fire, my lord," he conceded. "Meanwhile you'd better settle your kingdom before winter."

Mirain's brow went up.

"Because," Vadin explained, "I won't ride Rami once she's in foal, and she'll die before she'll let anybody else carry me into battle."

"For Rami's sake, then, we must surely move soon." Mirain was not laughing, not entirely. "This morning I sent out the hornsmen. I'm calling up my levies."

"You're joking." Mirain's gaze was unwavering. Vadin drew his breath in sharply. "All of them?"

"All within three days' ride."

"Your vul— Your elders will have a thing or two to say."

"Indeed."

Somewhere behind the royal mask was a wide and wicked smile. Vadin snorted at it. "When is the weapontake?"

"When Brightmoon comes to the full."

Vadin whooped, startling Rami into raising her head. Mirain's smile broke free, bloomed into a grin. The Mad One bucked and spun and danced, tossing his head like a half-broken colt. Rami observed him in queenly disdain; gathered herself together; bound him in a circle of flawless curvets and caracoles, and leaped from the last into flight, swift and weightless and breathless-beautiful as none but a seneldi mare could be. With a cry half of joy and half of royal outrage, the Mad One sprang in pursuit.

* * *

They came in late and wet with rain, their bellies full of a farmwife's good solid provender. She had been generous with it, and bursting with pride that the king himself had chosen her house to shelter in.

Mirain left the farmstead even lighter of heart than he had entered it. Yet as he drew near to the castle his mood darkened. His face grew still, the youth frozen out of it, his eyes filling with strangeness. Vadin did not try to meet them.

The rain had driven the market under cover and confined the less hardy souls of the court to the hall. There should have been wine and dicing and a smuggled girl or two, and from behind the ladies' screens a whisper of harpsong. In its place was a low and steady murmur. People gathered in clusters in the corners of the hall as under the market awnings; the ladies' music was silent, their voices rippling high over the rumble of the men.

Under Mirain's darkly brilliant gaze the murmur faltered. Eyes dropped or shifted toward the door behind the throne. He strode past them, swift enough to swirl his sodden cloak behind him. No one ventured to stand in his way.

In the small solar behind the hall, the Council of Elders sat or stood in a rough circle. Vultures indeed, Vadin thought, hunched in their black robes, surrounding their prey: a thin and ragged figure spattered with mud, its hair a wild tangle. With a small shock Vadin realized that, although it wore armor and bore an empty scabbard at its side, the shape was a woman's.

She raised her head to the newcomers. A deep wound, half healed, scored her cheek from temple to chin. "More of us?" she muttered hoarsely. "They come in better state than I."

"Watch your tongue, woman!" snapped the steward of the council.

"Be silent," Mirain said mildly. He knelt in front of the woman and took her cold hands.

She stared at him, dull-witted with exhaustion. "Give it up, young sir. Whether the king be god or demon, his council is a pack of mumbling fools. There is no help here for the likes of us."

"Have you despaired then?" he asked her.

She laughed short and harsh. "You are young. You look highborn. I was both once. A ruling lady, I was, mistress of Asan-Abaidan, that I held in fief to the Lord Yrian. That was before the old king died. We had a new one, they told me, no more than a boy but a legend already: half a god or half a demon, and bred in the south. Well for him, we thought in Abaidan; if he left us alone, what cared we for his name or his pedigree?

"Abaidan is a small fief, but prosperous enough, close to the eastern edge of Lord Yrian's lands but not so close as to tempt his neighbors, and a hard day's ride from the Marches. We heard of raiding in the north and west, a common enough thing, no cause for alarm. For comfort more than for safety, we armed our farmfolk and doubled the guard on our castle, but we did not look for undue trouble.

"When last Brightmoon waned, the raiders grew bolder. People began to appear on the roads, fleeing eastward. We took in such of those as asked for sanctuary. Our castle is fortunate; its wells are deep and never run dry, and we had laid in a good store of provisions. We had no need to turn suppliants away."

She stopped. She no longer saw Mirain, or anything about her. After a time she began again, speaking steadily, her tale worn smooth with much telling. "In the dark of Brightmoon, with Greatmoon three days from the full, a rider brought me my lord's summons. There was word that the raiding had ended. Many of our guests were glad, and made ready to return to their houses. But my lord Yrian was uneasy. He suspected that this was only a lull. He bade all his vassals gather to him, armed for battle.

"That was in the morning. By evening of the next day we were ready: myself; my son, who would not be left behind; my husband's old master-at-arms, and as many men as we could muster without leaving Abaidan defenseless.

"The eastward trickle had slowed. Yet as we marched toward the setting sun we met a great mass of folk, all in flight, all too wild with terror to heed us. Even as our lord's messengers set forth to summon the levies, an army had crossed the border. It was immense: all the tribes of the Marches had come together, laying aside their feuds and their quarrels. The border lords who ventured to resist had been overrun, yet those were terrifyingly few. The rest—all of them—had come to the enemy's heel.

"Some of my people would have turned back then and run with the tide. I lashed them forward with my tongue, and when that failed, with my scabbarded sword. Now more than ever our lord had need of us. Should we turn craven and betray him?"

Vadin set a cup in her hand. She drank blindly, without thought, tasting none of the honeyed wine. "We marched," she said. "Even after dark, with Greatmoon like a great swollen eye above us, we marched. I lost nine men out of my thirty. Maybe one or two of them indeed were too weak to keep the pace I set. By midnight five more were gone, lost in the dark, and we were close to the husting field. The roads had emptied. We were alone.

"And yet when we came in sight of the field we raised a shout. It was aglow with the fires of the army, and in its center they had raised our lord's standard. Surely all of Yrian's liege men had rallied to their lord.

"The closer we came, the greater grew our joy. For we saw other banners beside that of our lord. Lord Cassin was there, and Prince Kirlian, and more others than I could count. Looking to join a small but valiant company, we had come into a mighty army. Surely, I said to myself, however many the enemy might be, they could not hope to defeat such a force as this.

"Weary though I was, I held my head high. Perhaps even the king would come now and sweep his enemies away." She bent her head over the cup that lay half forgotten in her hand. "I instructed my sergeant to find a camping place for our men, and taking my son set off at once for my lord's tent. Late though it was, I knew he would wish to know that I had come. Lord Yrian pays heed to small things.

"As I had expected, he was awake still, and his tent was full to bursting with my fellow vassals. I saw Lord Cassin, and Prince Kirlian in his famous golden armor. And—" Her throat closed. She wrestled it open. "I saw the Prince Moranden."

The air rang into stillness as after the striking of a great bell. That was the tale that had struck to the heart both market and hall.

The woman tossed back her hair. "I saw the Prince Moranden. He sat as a king, and he wore a king's crowned helmet, and my lord Yrian bowed low at his feet.

"My eyes went blind. I had come to do battle with the rebel. Now, all too clearly, I was to follow him. Had not all the west already laid itself in his hand?

"I should have effaced myself, collected my men, and slipped away. But I have never been noted for my prudence. 'My lord,' I said to the one who held my oath, 'have we lost another king then?'

"Even then I might have escaped. I was close still to the opening of the tent. But my son had gone to greet a friend, a very young lord whose father, as fondly foolish as I, had brought him to the war. Close by them was an old enemy of mine. As soon as he heard my words, he seized my son and held him, and thus held me.

"Lord Yrian had turned when I spoke. Strange, I thought, he did not look like a traitor. 'Ah, Lady Alidan!' he called. 'You come in a good hour. Behold, the king himself is here to lead us.'

"It struck my heart to hear my words so twisted against me, little though he knew it who did it. 'I had heard that the king was a youth and a stranger,' I said. 'Is he dead? Have we a new lord?'

" 'This is your only true king,' said my lord Yrian as reverently as if he had never sworn his oath to the boy in Han-Ianon.

"I looked at the one he bowed to. I knew the prince; we all did. I had even sighed after him once, when I was a new widow and he stood beside Yrian to hear my oath of fealty. Yet now he was exiled by a king whose justice had been famous, and he rebelled against the king's chosen successor; and there was that in his eyes which I did not like, even though he smiled at me. 'The true king,' I said, to feel it on my tongue. 'Maybe. I have not seen the other. Nor has he raised war against his own people.'

" 'Not war,' he said still smiling. Oh, he was a handsome man, and well he knew it. 'The claiming of my right. You are beautiful, Lady Alidan. Will you ride beside me to take what is mine?'

"Now, mark you, even at my best, when I was a maid adorned for my bridal, I was never more than passable to look at. And that night I was clad as you see me now, and glowering besides. I was anything but beautiful.

"Thinking on this and looking into his face, I knew that he lied—if in this, then perhaps in everything. 'I think,' I said, 'that I will pass by your offer. Surely there are handsomer women to be found. Women who do not object to treason.' I did not bow. 'Good night, Lord Yrian, my lords. I wish you well of what you have chosen.'

"I turned to leave. But my way was barred. Even hemmed in as I was, I tried to draw my sword. And I saw my enemy—may all the gods damn him to deepest hell!—I saw him draw his dagger across my son's throat.

"My blade was out. I think I made a mark or two before it was wrenched from my hand. A knife slashed my face; even as the blood began to flow, I grappled for the weapon. Perhaps I would have won it, or perhaps I would have died, had not the prince's bellow driven my assailants back. They were reluctant but obedient, as hounds must always be. 'Let her go,' he commanded them. And when they protested, he sneered at them. 'Do you fear her so much? She is but a woman. What can she do? Disarm her and let her go.'

"My sword of course was gone. They took my dagger from me. They would not let me near my son, nor would they suffer me to find my men or my mount. Alone and afoot, I turned my face eastward.

"I walked. Sometimes I slept. I drew level with the fugitives; I kept to their pace; I passed them. I took shelter where I might, when I must, speaking to no one. My only thought was to find the king.

"Once I found food and a bed in a barn. There was a senel there, old but sturdy. I stole her. She kept me ahead of pursuit and brought me here. At Han-Ianon's gate I remembered how to speak.

" 'Moranden has crossed the borders,' I said to the guards. 'All the west has risen to follow him,' I cried in the market. 'Soon he will advance into the east,' I said in the hall. 'Arm yourselves and fight, if you love your king!' " She turned her head from side to side, eyes glittering in the ruined face. "And here in the king's own council I hear naught but weaseling words stained with disbelief. Surely, I am told, my wits have deserted me. There is no army in the west. The lords have not turned against their king. I am deluded; I am lying; I am most presumptuous, and a scandal besides: a woman dressed as a man, riding a stolen senel with no more harness than a bit of rope. Only let me go and cease my ravings, that are not fit for royal ears to hear."

"Are they not?" asked Mirain softly. The elders, opening their mouths to protest this outrage, choked upon their words.

Her hands gripped his arm. "Maybe," she said with sudden fierce hope, "maybe they will listen to you. You are a man; you look sane. Make them listen, or all Ianon is lost!"

"I have no need to compel them." He met her eyes. "I am the king."

For a long moment her hands held. She had hardly seen him yet, had seen only her grief and her wrath and her terrible urgency. She strained to focus her weary eyes, to make him real, not only her listener and her source of strength, but the king for whom she had lost all she possessed. "I sought you. I sought you all across your kingdom. To see . . . if . . ." Her voice died.

"To see if I was worth the life of your son."

Her eyes closed in pain. Exhaustion held them so; she forced them to open. To her own dismay she began to laugh. Grimly she mastered herself. "Your majesty. I should have known." She would have knelt at his feet; he held her to her chair. His strength surprised her. "My lord—"

"You are my guest; you owe me no homage. Come. You need food, and healing, and sleep."

She braced her will against him. "I cannot. Until I know— Do you believe me?"

"I have called up my levies. When Brightmoon is full, we go to war."

The elders gasped. Neither Mirain nor Alidan heeded them. She clasped his hands and kissed them one by one, and slowly, very slowly, let her body give way to its weariness. "You are my king," she said, or thought, or wished to think.

Her last memory was of Mirain's face, and of his hand warm almost to burning on her torn cheek.

Twenty

*E*VEN BEFORE THE FULL OF BRIGHTMOON, THE LEVIES of Ianon began to fill the castle and the town. "Three thousands," Mirain reckoned them, standing at his grandfather's old post upon the battlements. Brightmoon hung above the eastern mountains, its orb as yet two days from the full. There was a tang of frost in the air, harbinger of the long northern winter. He shivered slightly and drew his mantle about him.

Ymin sat on the parapet, shaping an odd winding melody upon her harp. Beyond her Vadin paced, restless with waiting. "Three thousands," he said, echoing the king. "A fine brave number to look at. But there should have been twice as many."

"Rumor gives Moranden more still," said Mirain, "and has him marching slowly eastward, pillaging and burning as he advances. I can't ask any lord to leave his lands unprotected."

Vadin laughed sharp and hard. "Can't you? They're holding back. Moranden they know; not everyone loves him, but he's famous for his strength. You may be the rightful king, but you're untried, and you weren't born here. This way, if you win, every petty baron can say he helped you; if you lose he can declare that you forced him, and point to all the men he kept home, and use them for a threat if anyone argues."

"I will force no one to follow me."

"When you use that tone," murmured Ymin, "I know you long to be contradicted."

Mirain laughed, but his words were somber. "I will not lead unwilling men to this battle. Better three thousand who are loyal than twenty who will turn against me at a word."

"You're a dreamer," growled Vadin.

"Surely. But I'm a mage; I dream true."

"A king can't rule a country full of friends."

"He can try. He can even be truly outrageous and dream of ruling a world of them."

"Can any man do that?" Ymin asked, soft beneath the ripple of harpsong.

Mirain's face was lost in shadow, but the moon caught the glitter of his eyes. "When I was begotten, my father laid a foretelling upon me. When I had won the throne ordained for me, I would come to a parting of my fate. Either I would die in early manhood and pass my throne to my slayer and be forgotten, or I would triumph over him and hold all the world in my hand."

"You are doing what you can to choose the first."

"I am doing what I can to be true to both my people and myself."

"Mostly the latter." She shrugged. "You are the king. You do as you will. The rest of us must live with it, or die trying."

"You sound like my council. They're horrified not simply that I should contemplate riding to war, but that I've called up my forces without consulting them. To silence them I had to invoke my kingship. Now they're convinced that I'm a tyrant in the making, and quite mad."

"I would not call you a tyrant. Nor would I call you mad. Not precisely."

"My thanks," he said dryly.

A fourth figure joined them. The moon limned the long pale scar upon one cheek.

"Alidan," said Mirain.

She bowed to him and moved toward the parapet, letting her cloak blow free about her. Given to choose, she had put on a woman's gown but belted it with sword and dagger. Both lords and commons looked askance at her; she had yet to acknowledge their existence, or indeed that of any but the three who stood with her now. "Look," she said, "Greatmoon is rising."

The Towers of the Dawn shimmered blue-pale as if through clear water; above them curved the great arc of the moon, a bow of ghostly blue, dimming the stars about it. At the full it was glorious; so close to its death it seemed a huge cancerous eye, glaring westward over the Vale of Ianon.

Alidan turned her back on it and her face to the wind. Mirain was close beside her. Without her willing it, her hand went to her cheek. "They say," she said slowly, "they say, my lord, that you have powers. A power. That you know all that is hidden. That you can bring down fire from heaven. Why do you not simply blast all your enemies now and have done?"

A gleam drew her eyes downward. Greatmoon shone in his palm, the Sun turned to blue-white fire. Darkness covered it: his fingers, closing into a fist. His voice came soft out of the night. Soft and strange, as if he were not truly there at all, but spoke from a great and dreaming distance. "What power I have, I have from my father, through his gift. Knowing and making and healing; ruling, perhaps. The fire is his own."

She hardly heard him. "If you smote them now, you would preserve your kingdom and the lives of your people. Ianon would be free again."

"Ianon would not be free. Ten thousand men would be dead, and I would still have lost."

Alidan strained to see his face. For all her efforts she gained only a blur of darker darkness, a suggestion of his profile. "It is a waste, all this war. You need not even destroy the enemy's army, only the leaders. Surely you would shed more blood than that if you rode into battle against them."

"I cannot use my power for destruction."

"Cannot or will not?"

For a long while he was silent. Surely he remembered Umijan, and a man who had died, lured into the blade that had been meant for himself. At last he said, "It is an ancient war, this between my father and his sister. His victory is life. Hers is destruction. Were I to use his gifts to sweep away all my enemies, I would but serve his great enemy."

"Death by fire, death by the sword: what difference is there? It is all death."

"No," Mirain said. "Against the fire nothing mortal can stand. And I am half mortal. I would vanquish my enemies, but I myself would fall, crumbling into ash, and my soul would belong to the goddess." His voice turned wry, though still oddly remote. "So you see, beyond all the rest I think of my own safety. It's my father's law. For the works of light I may do whatever my will and my strength allow. But if I turn to the dark, I myself will be destroyed."

"And if that befalls—"

"If that befalls, the Sunborn will be no more, and the goddess will have won this battle in the long war. For I am not only the god's son whom he has made a king. I am also his weapon. The Sword of Avaryan, forged against the Dark."

She shivered. Quiet though his voice was, the voice of a young man, a boy scarcely older than the son she had lost, its very quietness was terrible. Her hand found his arm. Under the mantle it was rigid. "My lord. My poor king."

"Poor?" It came from the depths of his throat, yet it comforted her. For the growl in it was wholly human, drawn back entirely from whatever cold distances had held him. *"Poor,* say you? Dare you pity me?"

"It is not pity. It is compassion. To bear such a burden: so much fate, so much divinity. And for what? Why must it be you? Let your father fight his own battles."

She uttered heresy and certain blasphemy; and he was a priest. But the shadow of his head bent; his response was softer even than his words before. "I have asked him. Often. Too often. If he ever answers, it is in truth no answer at all: that it is his will, and that this is my world. And that even gods must obey the laws which they have made."

"As must kings," said Ymin. It was not quite a question.

"As must kings." A sound escaped him. It might have been laughter; it might have been a sob. "And the first law of all is: Let nothing come easily. Let every man strive for what is his. Without transgressing any other of the laws."

"Which of course," she said, "by making the striving more difficult, strengthens the first law."

"The universe is perfect even in its imperfections." Mirain wrapped himself more tightly in his cloak. "It's cold on the heights."

"Even for you?" asked Alidan.

"Especially for me." He turned away from the battlements. "Shall we go down?"

Ten of the king's squires would ride to war with him, and Adjan at their head to see that they did not disgrace their training. The chosen few, still reeling with the honor and the terror of it, had won a night's escape. "Get out," Adjan had snarled at the pack of them, "and leave the others in peace. But mind you well, we ride at the stroke of sunup. Any man who comes late gets left behind."

They saw Vadin as he came to the alehouse in search of Ledi, and they were far enough gone in ale to forget that they were in awe of him. "Share a cup," begged Olvan, thrusting his own into Vadin's hand without heed for the great gout that leaped onto the table. "Just one. It's good for you. Warms up your blood." He winked broadly.

Vadin started to demur, but Ayan had his other hand and they were all crying for him to stay; and he could not see Ledi anywhere in the thronged and boisterous room. Someone pulled him down; he yielded to the inevitable and drained what little remained in the cup. They cheered. He found that he was grinning. He had Ledi back again, and in a little while he would go to her, and now his friends had remembered their friendship.

And yet it was not the same. With Ledi, it was better. Deeper, sweeter. Sometimes at the peak of loving he thought he could see her soul, and it was like a glass filled with light, inexpressibly beautiful. But crushed in with all these raucous young men, reeling in the fumes of wine and ale and dreamsmoke, he could think only of escape. Not that he disliked any of his companions. Some maybe he came close to loving. It was only . . . they seemed so foolish, like children playing at being men. Did it never occur to them that they would be utterly wretched when morning came?

He smiled and nursed a cup and waited for Ledi to find him. The others were growing uproarious. Nuran had begun a wardance on the table to a drumming of hilts and fists.

Suddenly Olvan loosed a shout. Nuran lost the rhythm and toppled laughing into half a dozen laps. Olvan sprang into his place. "Men!" he proclaimed. He had a strong voice and a gift for speechmaking; he won silence not only among the squires but for a fair distance round about. "Are we the king's men?"

"Yes!" they shouted back.

"Are we going to fight for him? Are we going to kill the traitor for him? Are we going to set him firm upon his throne?"

"Yes!"

"So then." He dropped to one knee and lowered his voice. "Listen to me. I say we should show him how loyal we are. Let's do something that brands us his in front of all Ianon."

Fists rocked the heavy table on its legs. *"All* Ianon!" the squires chorused joyfully.

But Ayan drew his brows together. "What should we do? We wear his colors. He's given us his new blazon, the Sun-badge that we all wear on our cloaks. We'll ride with him and we'll wait on him and we'll take care of his weapons. What else is there to do?"

"What else?" cried Olvan. "Why, my love, a thousand things. But one will do. Let's show him how we love him. Let's sacrifice our beards for him."

Jaws dropped. "Sacrifice our—" Ayan stopped. He caressed the wisps of down that he had struggled so long and so hard to grow. "Olvan, you're mad."

"I'm my king's man. Who's got courage? Who's with me?"

"All the girls will laugh at us," said Suvin.

"They don't laugh at the king." Nuran struck his hands together. "I'm with you! Here, whose knife is sharpest?"

Once one had fallen, the rest tumbled after, Ayan last and dubious and yielding only for love of Olvan. Vadin said nothing, and no one asked him to; when they poured into the courtyard to draw water, yelling for lamps and towels and cleansing-foam, he followed in silence, surrounded by clamorous onlookers.

Olvan went first, Ayan next with the air of a prisoner approaching the block. Kav whose hands were steadiest wielded the knife, transforming the lovers into strangers. Ayan was as pretty as a girl. Olvan, square and solid and bearded to the eyes, had a strong fine face beneath. Ayan looked at him and saw no one he knew, and fell promptly and utterly in love.

The rest crowded past them to the sacrifice. Kav yielded the blade to Nuran and gave himself up to water and foam. His beard was a man's already, full and thick and braided with copper; they roared as it fell away. He roared back. Nuran had nicked him. "Blood for the gods!" someone shrilled.

Vadin shuddered. They were turning toward him. "Ho, king's man! Come and join our brotherhood."

Others were doing it now, turning it into a high sacrifice, a hundred victims laid upon an altar none could see. Drunk as they were, it would be a miracle if the morning found no man dead with his throat slit.

Vadin stiffened against the hands that closed upon his arms. "No," he said. "Enough is enough. He knows my mind. I don't need to—"

They laughed, but their eyes glittered. They were many and they were strong; the ale was working in them, making them cruel. "Down with you, my lad. You'll be our captain. Aren't you the one he wept for? Aren't you the one he loves?"

He fought. They laughed. He cursed them. They pulled him down and sat on him. Kav had the knife again, newly honed, gleaming. Vadin lay still. "Kav," he said. "Don't."

His old friend looked at him out of an alien face. Kav had not profited from his sacrifice; without the beautiful beard he was even less lovely than before, a great brute of a man with a jaw like an outcropping of granite. He bent. He laid his blade against Vadin's cheek, and it was so cold that it burned. Vadin set his jaw against it.

With a bark of laughter Kav thrust the knife into his belt. "Let him go," he said. And kept saying it until they growled and obeyed. Vadin got up stiffly, favoring a bruised knee. The squires had drawn back. Now they knew what he had known since he sat down with them. He was no longer one of them. They had chosen to be the king's men; he was Mirain's utterly, against his will and to his very soul. He dipped his head to Kav, even smiled a little, and walked away. They did not try to hold him back.

The old woman at the curtain took Vadin's coin, but she did not move to let him pass. She peered at him as if he had been a stranger. "Who'll it be?"

He scowled. Of all nights for Kondyi to turn senile, of course it had to be this one. "Who do you think? Ledi, of course."

"Can't have her."

"What do you mean, I can't have her? She promised me. Tonight she'd save for me."

"Can't have her," Kondyi repeated. "She went. Man came and bought her. Paid a gold sun for her."

Vadin could have howled aloud. He dragged the hag up by the neck, shaking her till she squealed in fear. "Who? *Who?* By the gods, I'll kill him!"

She would not tell him. Or could not. If she had been feigning witlessness before, his rage drove her within a whisper of the truth; she could only crouch and whimper and beg him to go away. At last the tavernkeeper came, and he had his man with him, and Vadin still had a few wits left. He spun away with a bitter curse and flung himself into the night.

Mirain's outer door was shut, his inner door barred. Happy man. He had his woman; she loved him and she belonged to him, and no one could buy her away from him. Vadin stalked from the mute mocking barrier into the dark of his own chamber, stripping off his finery as he went. He had put it on so joyfully only a little while ago, thinking of Ledi, of how she would look long at him and smile and declare him the handsomest of her lovers; and then they would make a game of taking it all off.

He stumbled. A sharp word escaped him. He had forgotten the baggage heaped by the door, awaiting the morning. He kicked it, and cursed again as his knee cried protest. He was perilously close to tears.

Something rustled in the dark. He froze, hand dropping to hilt, mind and body suddenly still. His sword hissed from its sheath.

A spark grew to a flame, settled into the lamp by his bed. Ledi blinked at the spectacle of him in a glittering trail of ornaments, sword in hand. She was as bare as she was born except for a string of beads as blue as heaven-flowers. She rose and came to him and embraced him, sword and all. "Poor love, were you looking for me? I tried to send you a message, but first there wasn't time, and then you were gone and they wouldn't let me go after you."

He buried his face in the sweetness of her hair. "Kondyi, damn her—Kondyi said you were sold."

"I was." He thrust free; she smiled, luminous with joy. "Yes, Vadin. A man came, and he had gold; Kondyi and Hodan dickered but they took it, though I fought and I damned them and I even cried. What say did I have in it, after all? I was only a slave. Then," she said, "then the man took me away, and he was very kind, and he didn't go far. Only to the castle. I was beginning to be afraid. The man handed me over to a roomful of very disdainful women; they all carried themselves like queens, though they said they were servants. They made me wash all over, and they searched me for vermin and for worse things, and I began to be angry."

Vadin let his sword slip into its scabbard, dropped blade and belt atop his baggage, let Ledi draw him to the bed and settle herself in his lap. She kissed his breast over his heart and sighed. "Of course I knew what they took me for. A common whore." Her hand on his lips silenced the protest. "So I was, love, though I tried to be a clean one and I wouldn't take every man who asked for me. Now, the women said, I was to learn new ways. I'd not been bought to ply my trade in the castle."

She was silent for a while. At last Vadin could not bear it. "What were you bought for?"

"They wouldn't tell me," she said. "Not for a long time. They showed me things. How to dress; and they gave me fine clothes to learn in. How to do my hair. How to use scents and paints. As if I didn't know all of that; but this was different. They were showing me how to be a lady. Or how to serve one. A very high one, Vadin. Do you know the Princess Shirani?"

"Of course," he said. "She's one of the king's maidens."

"I know that. She loves him to distraction. Poor lady, her father the Prince Kirlian is one of the rebels, and she lives for a glance from the king, and she's sure she'll die for being a traitor's daughter. I told her not to be afraid. The king knows who's true and who's false."

"But how did Shirani happen to buy you? A man I could understand; you're famous. But a maiden princess—"

Ledi laughed. "Of course she didn't buy me. I'm a gift. That's what happened afterward, you see. A woman came and asked the princess if I'd do, and she, sweet child, said I was perfect. The woman wasn't amused. She told me I was wanted elsewhere, and mind my manners. I wanted sorely to act the way she was sure I would, perfectly vulgar, but I wouldn't do that in front of my lady. I put on my best new face and let the woman lead me out." She laughed again. "Oh, it was wonderful, and I was terrified. She took me to a man, and the man took me to a boy, and the boy took me to the king. And he stood up in front of a dozen lords, and he hugged me as if I'd been his kin, and asked me if I was pleased with my new place. Then he told me—Vadin, he told me I was free. I could serve the princess if I liked, but if I'd rather go else-where I could, and he would give me whatever I needed. 'I mean that,' he said. 'Whatever you need.' So I said . . . I said I was happy, if only he would let me see you. He said I could see you whenever I wanted. Then he kissed me and sent me away."

Vadin could not breathe. Mirain had bought her. She was free. King's freedom, that could raise a woman from slave to queen. Not that Mirain had raised Ledi so high, but she could not have borne it; and Vadin was no prince. Only a king's servant, as she was servant to a princess.

His silence troubled her. She raised her head from his breast, and her face was still, braced for the worst. "You aren't glad. You have your women here. I was for your nights in the town, when you wanted a fresh face and a paid love: someone you could leave when you liked and forget when it suited you. I'll go away if you ask, my lord. I won't haunt you."

He tightened his grip on her and glared down into her eyes. They were wide, steady, steeled against tears. "Is that what you want? To go away?"

"I won't stay where I'm not wanted."

"He bought you for me, you know," Vadin said. "He knew I'd never take a gift from him. So he set you free and put you in Shirani's service and left it to you to decide if you wanted me. Sly little bastard."

"He is the king."

A queen could have said it with no more coolness and no more certainty. "He is that," Vadin agreed. "He's also a born conniver. And he thinks the world of you." That cast her into confusion; Vadin kissed her. "Ledi love, we'd best be careful, or he won't just see us bedded; he'll make sure we're wedded."

"Oh, no. We can't do that. You're a lord and a champion and a king's friend. While I—"

"While you are a lady and a wisewoman and a king's friend. Don't you see how he thinks? If I'd finally got together enough silver to buy your liberty, you'd only be a freedwoman. Since he bought you, you're of whatever rank the king decrees. And of free women, only the highest born may wait on a princess."

"Why," she said in wonder, "he is downright wicked." Her own smile was not a jot less. "Tell me, my lord. May a noblewoman disport herself with a man not her husband?"

"It's not widely approved, but it's done."

"I'm not widely approved, either. And I don't intend to be. That's fair warning, Vadin."

"Very fair." His eye was on her body, and half his mind with it. She pushed him down. He smiled; she played with the beard he had so nearly lost. "I suppose," he said, "I'll have to beggar myself to keep your favor."

"Maybe," she said, fitting her body to his. "Maybe not. I was not a good whore. I picked more favorites for love than for money, and many nights I wouldn't work at all."

"But when you did," he said, "ah!" His gasp drew itself out, catching as she did something exquisitely wanton. "Witch."

"Lovely boy," said she who was all of a season older than he. He bared his teeth; she laughed and wove another spell to tangle him in.

"Mirain!"

It kept them all warm in the chill of the dawn: the army drawing up on the Vale in an endless tangle of men and beasts and wagons and chariots; the people come to watch them go, women and children and old men, servants and caretakers and the elders who would ward the kingdom at Mirain's back. "Mirain!" they cried, now in snatches, now all together. And as chaos became an army, a new shout went up, rolling like a drumbeat. "An-Sh'Endor! An-Sh'Endor!"

From within the walls it was like the roaring of the sea. Vadin, dragged cold and surly from his warm bed, took a last unwarranted tug at Rami's girth. Her look of reproach made him feel like a monster. He mounted as gently as he could and looked about. Foolish; Ledi had not come to see him off. She had a princess to wait on, and she hated farewells. She would not even admit that he might not come back. But she had dressed him and armed him and braided his hair for war, and she had given him something to remember her by: a kiss ages long and far too short. His lips were still burning with it.

Grimly he turned his mind from her before he bolted back into her arms. The Mad One was being a fine hellion, taunting Adjan's sternly bitted charger with his own bridleless freedom. He had already kicked a groom for presuming to come after him with a halter.

At long last Mirain appeared, coming bright and exalted from solitary prayer in the temple. He was all scarlet and gold, aflame in the rising dawn; at the sight of him a shout went up among his escort and among the few townsfolk who had lingered inside the walls, dim echo of the crowds and clamor without. He flashed them a grin, striding swiftly to his waiting senel, catching himself in front of his squires. A poor hangdog few they looked, much the worse for their night's debauch, with every face scraped naked for the world to see. Vadin had heard the end of Adjan's peroration on their folly, and it had been scathing.

But under Mirain's eye they straightened. Their chins came up. Their eyes lifted and firmed and began to shine. When he saluted them, with a touch of irony it was true, but with more than a touch of respect, they looked as if they would burst with love and pride.

Mirain moved again in a flare of scarlet, springing into the Mad One's saddle. The gate rolled open; the morning wind cried through it, made potent with the roaring of the crowd. He rode down into it, and Vadin raised his new banner, Sun of gold on a blood-red field. The shouting rose to a fever pitch.

Where the ground leveled from the steep slope of the castle's rock, Mirain wheeled the Mad One on his haunches and swept out his sword, whirling it about his head. Along the column sparks leaped: swords and spears flung up in answer. A horn rang. With a clatter of hoofs and a rumbling of wagons and chariots, the army began to move.

"Now he is in his element," Ymin said. She rode in the van with Vadin and Alidan and the scholar from Anshan, with her harp upon her back and no weapon at her side. Her eyes were on Mirain, who was riding now far back among the footsoldiers. He had hung his helmet from his saddlebow; as she watched, his teeth flashed white in laughter at some jest.

"He's a born leader," said Vadin. "Whether he's a general too, we've yet to see."

"He will be." Alidan shifted in the saddle. Her stallion champed his bit; she let him dance a little until he settled again into his long-legged walk. "He can be anything he chooses to be."

"Remember," said Obri the chronicler, "he had his training in Han-Gilen. Soft the Hundred Realms may be in the reckoning of the north, but they breed famous commanders. A southern general, I've always thought, and an army from the north: the two together would be invincible."

"He is not a southerner!" Alidan cried.

"He is Sanelin's child and our king." Alidan's face did not soften; Ymin smiled at it. "And you, lady, are his most loyal worshipper."

Vadin's brows met. "It's talk like that, that he's desperate to get away from. Push him hard enough with it and he'll get himself killed, just to prove he's mortal."

"Or that he is not." Alidan left them, forging ahead upon the open road.

Twenty-one

THE ARMY ADVANCED AT A STEADY PACE PAST fields ripe with the harvest. Those who labored there were women and children, the old and the lame and a few—a very few—men of fighting strength who kept their weapons close to hand. They paused to watch the column pass, bowing low to the vivid figure of the king.

Yet even in Ianon's heart the poison had spread. Once from amid a field of bowing farmfolk a shout thrust forth like a spear: "Upstart! Priestess' bastard!"

With a snarl a full company burst from the line. Mirain clapped heels to the Mad One's sides, hurling him across their path, driving them back. He sat his stallion before them, eyes blazing. "Do we ride against farmers or fighters? The enemy lies yonder. Save your wrath for him." The Mad One bounded forward. "To the Marches!"

"To the Marches!" they thundered back.

The Towers of the Dawn rose before them, rose and loomed and passed. Some of them had come this way with Moranden as their commander, riding to a war that had been a lie; as this one was not. Beyond them rolled the green hills of Arkhan, and Medras fief, and the cold snow-waters of Ilien with its outstretched arms: Amilien that ran through the cleft of Sun's Pass into the eastern mountains, and Umilien flowing dark and deep into the labyrinths of Night's Pass in the south and east of Ianon. But Mirain turned west past the branching of the waters and crossed the fords, entering into Yrios.

Here at last, terribly and inescapably, was the mark of the enemy. The fields were black and charred, the farmsteads crumbling in ruins. The villages were villages of the dead. It was as if a long line of fire had swept across the hills, sparing nothing made by man, stopping short where the level land began. Neither man nor beast remained, and of birds only the carrion creatures that feasted upon the fires' leavings.

"Days old," said Vadin through the bile of sickness, standing by a mound of ash that had been a byre. The stench of smoke was strong, catching at his throat, but stale; the ashes were cold.

Mirain trod through the ruins, heedless of the soot that blackened his cloak. His eyes were strange, blind. "Four days," he said. His foot brushed a grey-white shape: the arch of ribs, a small human skull. He lifted it tenderly, but it crumbled in his fingers. With a sound like a sob he let it fall. He wheeled. There were tears on his cheeks, white fury in his eyes. "All this land lies under a shadow. I find no sign in it of my enemy. But she is here. By her absence I shall find her."

"She?" wondered Kav who kept near to him, exchanging glances with Vadin.

Mirain heard. "The goddess," he said like a curse. "Come, up. Up, before more of my people die to feed her!"

Beyond the place of the skull he led his army north and west, following the wide swath of destruction. There seemed no end to it. The marauders had not always burned what they had taken; fields of grain lay low as if borne down by trampling feet, and amid them stood broken villages, and orchards hacked and hewn, the fruits taken or trodden into the ground.

"This is not the passage of a king coming to claim his throne," said Alidan, her voice harsh with horror. "What can he hope to rule if he destroys all he passes? He must be mad."

It was evening, the sun new set; they had camped on the east bank of Ilien, well outside of a village of corpses. Although Mirain had not summoned them, Alidan had come with Ymin and Obri to his tent, to find Vadin there as always, with Adjan and one or two other captains, and the burly form of that Prince Mehtar who had offered Mirain his daughter. Mirain himself sat well back among them, eyes closed, as if he would have preferred to be alone.

It was Prince Mehtar who responded to Alidan's words. "Not mad," he said. "Taunting. He tells us, 'Come, out, follow me; see what I'll do to you when I let you catch me.' "

"But to slaughter innocent people—his own people—"

"Now, lady," said Mehtar, "of course you find this hard to bear. War is no place for a woman."

She half rose; with an effort she controlled herself, but she could not keep her hand from her swordhilt. "A mountain bandit will take what he can and despoil the rest. A man who would be king would preserve all that he may and save his armed strength for his enemy."

Mirain stirred, drawing their eyes to him. "Moranden would be king. But you forget his mother and the one she serves. They have no care for common folk save as sacrifices. It is not he who commands this, but they."

"How do you know?" Mehtar demanded.

Mirain regarded him. He was a large man and overbearing, and though respectful of Mirain's rank and parentage, inclined to let the youth's body blind him to the king. Under that steady stare he subsided rapidly. "I know," Mirain said. "I think . . ." He spoke with care, as if the words tasted ill upon his tongue, yet he could not help but speak them. "I hate him for what he has done. Yet I think I pity him. To be condemned to this, to see his country laid waste and to have no power to prevent it—that is a suffering I would not wish on any man."

Soft, Mehtar's eyes said clearly, although his tongue was silent.

"Would it help any of us if I raged before you and howled for his blood?"

Still Mehtar said nothing.

Crowded though the tent was, Mirain rose and began to prowl. He circled the silent staring company and left them. After a moment Ymin followed.

He stood close by the tent, but the air was free upon his face. She could see his guards, two of his proud shaven squires, but they stood apart in shadow. Mirain was almost alone.

He drew a deep breath. His tent stood on a low hill; all about it flickered the fires of the camp. The air was keen with frost, Brightmoon waning but strong still. Greatmoon would not rise until dawn, close as he was to his dark, when was the goddess' greatest power. That was her holy day, as Brightmoon's full marked Avaryan's rite.

He shivered. It was not a physical cold; his cloak was lined with fleece and he was well clad beneath. Ymin moved toward him, close but not touching, her face turned to the stars. She was keenly aware of his eyes upon her; she let him look his fill, knowing that he took comfort in it.

He choked on laughter. She turned to him, thinking a question. After a moment he answered it. "I stand here, stark with the terror of my destiny, and lose all my fear in a woman's face. It seems that I may be a man after all."

"Have you ever doubted it?"

"No," he said. "No. But it betrays a talent for distraction."

"Since you need it," she said, "shall we find a fire? Then you may gaze to your heart's content, and I can return the compliment."

"*I* am nothing to stare at." His finger brushed her cheek. "They weave a cloth in Asanion, rich and soft, fit for kings. Velvet, they call it. Your skin is dark velvet."

"And yours. You are far from ugly, my dear lord."

"But far from beautiful."

"Moranden has beauty. Has it saved him?"

"It may yet." The cold had come back into his voice. "He's out there. I can't find him. But I feel him. Shadow guards him."

"The goddess branded him. You healed the brand. You are a part of him also, a little, although he has no knowledge of it."

"Not enough to help him. Far too much for my own peace."

"I think we had better look for that fire."

It was faint and feeble, but it was laughter. He took her hand and kissed it and held it a moment, head bowed. Before she could speak he was gone, back to the tent and the great ones huddled together like children afraid of the dark.

It was Vadin who haled them out, prince and all, and ordered the guards to see that no one else came to trouble the king's sleep.

"Sleep?" Mirain inquired with lifted brow.

"Sleep," said Vadin firmly. "You think I don't know how you've been spending your nights? Brooding doesn't make you any fitter for battle, and magic's not working, and you can't plot strategy till you know where your enemy is."

Mirain submitted to the stripping of his kilt and the freeing of his braid, but his brain was not so easily subdued. "We're being lured and we're being mocked. Odiya's revenge, long and deadly sweet. When it pleases her she'll slip her son's leash, and we'll lie neatly in the trap."

"For a mage whose enemy's spells are too strong to break, you know a great deal about her mind."

"She's no stronger than I. She's merely hiding. And I can use my wits as easily as anyone. I know what I would do if I were she."

"You wouldn't wreck your kingdom behind you."

"No?" Mirain lay where Vadin set him, on his stomach on the narrow cot, hands laced under his chin. As Vadin began to knead the tensed muscles of his shoulders, he sighed with the pure and unselfconscious pleasure of a cat. "I think," he mused, "if I were as bitter as she, and nursed so ancient a grudge, I might find no price too high to pay for my vengeance."

"That's your trouble. You persist in seeing all sides."

"So do you."

Vadin attacked a knot with such force that Mirain grunted. "I see them. I don't condone them. And I don't pity the man in whose name whole villages are burned to the ground. He's a man and a prince. He shouldn't suffer it."

"Ah well, you were raised a lord in Ianon. We foreign bastards are less implacable."

"Foreign," Vadin muttered. "Bastard." He glared at the smooth well-muscled back. Not a scar on it. Those were all in front, or below where a lord carried the brands of his life in the saddle. "You didn't lose your breakfast in the first village we came to."

"So then, Ianon breeds strong minds, the south strong stomachs. I saw as bad or worse in the war against the Nine Cities. They don't simply kill and burn the innocent. They make an art of torment."

"Did you pity them too?"

"I learned to. It was a hard lesson. I was very young then."

And what was he now?

Ageless, Vadin answered himself. And the more so the longer this march went on, with no enemy and no fighting and only a dead land before and behind. The army was losing its edge. Horror and outrage could only sustain them for so long; Mirain was holding them with his magic, spending himself with no certain hope of return.

Vadin's fingers lightened on the easing muscles, more caress now than compulsion. Mirain's eyes had fallen shut although his mind was still awake; his breathing eased, deepened. "Listen," he murmured. "Listen, Vadin."

Silence underlaid with the sounds of an army asleep. Far away a direwolf hymned the moon. Mirain's voice came soft and slow. "No, my brother. Listen within."

Nothing at all. Utter stillness.

"Yes. A fullness of silence. It will be soon now. Mark you. Mark . . ."

He was asleep, his last words surely part of a dream. Vadin drew up the rough blanket Mirain insisted on, no better than a common soldier's, and snuffed all the lamps but the one by the cot. In the dim flickering light he spread his own blanket and lay down. A grim smile had found its way to his face. He was fast going as mad as his master. Bidden to work magic, he had obeyed and not even thought to resist, let alone to be afraid.

When at last Vadin's mind let go, his dreams were of darkness and of silence and of nameless fear. But it was not he who was frightened. He lay cradled in Avaryan's hand upon the breast of his Lady Night.

Twenty-two

A MIST CAME WITH THE DAWN. THE SUN TURNED IT to gold and rolled it away, baring twin ranks of hills that marched from north to south. In the distance they curved together; here they bounded a level plain, all but treeless, with Ilien running narrow and swift down its center.

Across the western hills and spilling onto the level lay a darkness which did not lift. There were sparks in it. Swords' points, spearpoints, and the eyes of the enemy. Vadin's dream had taken shape in the living daylight.

Mirain stepped from his tent into the sun's warmth. He had taken time to dress, to plait his hair, to don his armor. At the sight of him a ragged cheer went up. But most eyes strained westward. "It's vast," someone whispered near Vadin. "Thousands—ten thousands—gods preserve us! They carry their own night."

"But we," said Mirain in a voice that carried, "bear light." He swept up his sword. "Avaryan is with us. No darkness shall conquer us. Swift now, to arms!"

His trumpeters took up the call. The enemy's spell broke; the army began to seethe.

"Well done, my lord," Adjan said, dry and cool. "Once they're armed, you'd best feed them and set the scouts to their work. Yonder horde doesn't have a feel of early battle."

"It does not," Mirain agreed. "Vadin, see to the feeding. The scouts, Captain, are yours to command."

Armed, fed, and drawn up in battle array on the western slope of the ridge, the king's men settled to wait. The enemy seemed motionless beneath their shroud. As the sun mounted and the stillness reigned unbroken, a horror crept through the ranks. Raid or skirmish, siege or open battle, all of those they could face. This half-seen enemy who had grown out of the night, who now showed no sign of attack or even of life, made them forget their courage. More and more their eyes sought the king.

At first he settled by his tent to break his fast and to speak with his commanders. Even from the edges of the camp his scarlet cloak was clear to see. As the morning advanced with no word from his scouts and no move from the enemy, he beckoned to Vadin, leaving the captains to debate battle now, battle later, battle never. The Mad One, whom no tether or hobble could hold, had freed Rami from her picket and led her up the hill. The grooms had brushed them both until they shone, and plaited their manes scarlet battle-streamers.

King and squire descended to meet them. The Mad One lowered his head to blow into his comrade's hands, and pawed the ground. In an instant Mirain was on his back.

Adjan found the king among the cavalry of Arkhan, admiring the points of a trooper's dappled mare. His eyes flashed at once to the captain, but he brought his colloquy to a graceful and unhurried end, withdrawing easily, taking with him the men's goodwill. But once behind the lines, he loosed his hold on his patience. "Well? What news?"

"One scout has come back," Adjan answered. "The others he knows of are dead. He's not well off himself."

"Is he badly hurt?"

"Arrow in the shoulder. A flesh wound, no more; the doctors are taking care of it. But his mind . . ."

The Mad One was stretching already from canter into gallop.

It was as Adjan had said. The scout sat in the healers' tent, hale enough in body, while an apprentice bound his shoulder. But his eyes were too wide; a thin film of sweat gleamed on his brow. As Mirain approached he thrust himself to his feet, sending the healer sprawling. "Sire! Thank all the gods!" Under the terror he was a goodly enough man, square and solid though smaller than most men in Ianon, hardly taller than Mirain himself. He was no novice, nor was he the sort of man who was given to night terrors. Yet he fell at Mirain's feet, clutching them, weeping like a child.

Mirain dragged him erect. "Surian," he said sharply. At the sound of his name, the man quieted a little. "Surian, control yourself." With a visible effort the man obeyed. Mirain kept a grip on his good shoulder. "Soldier, you have a report to make."

He drew a shuddering breath. Under Mirain's hand and eye he found the words he needed. "I set out as commanded, to reconnoiter the southeastern edge of the enemy's army. There were six men with me. We kept to our places, each of us signaling his safety at intervals. We met no opposition. If the enemy had sent out scouts, they were better at their work than we.

"We advanced with all caution. A bowshot from the enemy we stopped. No; *were* stopped. It was an act of will to move forward. The enemy was still a shape in shadow; when I tried to reckon numbers my mind spun and went dark. I never called myself a coward, sire, but I swear, at that moment I could have bolted, honor and duty be damned.

"One of my men broke, left his cover and ran. An arrow caught him in the throat. An arrow out of the air, with no bowman to be seen behind it.

"That must have been a signal. Arrows swarmed over us. No matter where we were or what we did, we were hit. My lord, I swear by Avaryan's hand, I saw one *bend* around a rock and bury itself in a man's eye."

"Yes," Mirain said with flat and calming acceptance. "They all died, I was told. But you live."

Surian swallowed hard, trembling with shock and pain and remembered horror. "I . . . I live. I think, sire, I was meant to. No, I know it. I'm meant for a message and a mockery."

"She knows us wholly," Mirain muttered, "and we grope for knowledge of her." Surian stared at him, afraid to understand him. He smiled faintly but truly. "You've done well. Rest now. While I live, no darkness shall harm you."

The sun passed its zenith and began to sink into the spell-wrought shadow. Still the enemy had not moved. Mirain's army, drawn taut too long, began to slacken.

"Imagine days of this," Vadin said.

"Our enemy is well capable of it." Mirain had bidden his men be fed again, for diversion as well as for strength, although Vadin had not been able to make him break his own fast. He paced instead with a bit of fruit forgotten in his hand. "But if we attack, we attack blind. Literally, maybe. I'm not yet as desperate as that."

"What do you counsel then?" demanded Prince Mehtar, doffing his helmet and handing it to his squire, biting into a half-loaf spread thick with softened cheese. "We can sit here until we starve, and then the enemy can roll over us."

"With all of us begging to be trampled." Alidan drained a cup of ale as handily as any man-at-arms. "My lord, we have to do better than that."

Mirain glared at the ground where already he had paced out a path in the sparse grass of the hilltop. "Yes, we must. But I dare not give in to my instincts and lead a full charge against the enemy. What they did to a dozen scouts, mountain tribesmen and hunters of Ianon, they can do to three thousand of my warriors."

"Die swift or die slow," Mehtar said, "die we will, if this army is as large as it looks."

"Ah, but is it?" Mirain ceased his pacing at the farthest extent of his path, eyes turned westward under his shading hand. "Think now. The Marchers have men in plenty, and my turncoat lords likewise. But not enough to fill yonder hills, or to stretch back as far as these seem to stretch."

"Yes," said Vadin, "and it's been making me wonder. These are men we know, men like us, some probably forced to fight at their lords' command, others following Moranden in good faith. If we can hardly endure the shadow at this distance, how can they march under it?"

"Illusion," Mirain answered him, "and delusion: the black heart of magic. They see no shadow: they think the sun is free and their minds likewise, even as they think only the thoughts the mages permit them to think. They dream that they have come to rid the throne of an impostor and the kingdom of a threat; commanded to slay and burn, they see in front of them not villages of women and children but camps of my soldiers. And the witch whose spells rule them—the witch laughs. Her laughter shudders in my bones."

He spun on his heel. They were all silent. Some of them thought he might be mad. "No," he said, "only god-ridden. My lords, my ladies, our enemy dares us to fight or fly. I've never had much skill in running. Shall we fight?"

"That will be a swift death," Mehtar said, approving.

"Maybe not, my lord. The witch taunts us with her strength. Let us prove to her that strength can matter little. The tactics of the wolf: strike, slash, leap away."

Adjan's eyes narrowed as he calculated. "We can do that. Wear down the enemy's men, who can't be so very many more than we are, and keep our own happy. But we can't stretch out our necks too far, or we'll lose too many and the other side not enough."

"Ten captains," said Mirain. "Ten men of proven courage with hand-picked troops. Adjan, my lord prince, will you command two of the companies?"

"Aye," Mehtar said for both. "Eight more to find, then. Shall I do it, sire?"

"Seven," Mirain corrected him. "I shall take a company. You may choose the rest as you will. We ride out within the hour. Choose well and choose swiftly."

Mehtar opened his mouth, shut it again carefully. With equal care he bowed. "As my king commands."

Each captain of the sortie led twice nine men. Mirain commanded nine men and five of his own guard, and Vadin, and Jeran and Tuan of the race to Umijan; and Alidan. They formed ranks quietly but without undue stealth behind the main line of forces, mounted on seneldi chosen for speed and courage.

Vadin glanced from side to side. Alidan was close on his right hand, anonymous in armor and helmet, wearing the scarlet cloak of the king's guard. She looked both capable and deadly, and she sat her fiery stallion better than most men. At his left rode Mirain, aglitter in his golden armor. Beyond them on either side he saw the other companies drawn up, mounted and ready.

It was like a melee at the Summer Games; and yet how unlike. This was real. Men would die here for the king who sat lightly in his tall saddle, toying with a wayward battle-streamer. By his word they stood; by his word they would fall.

Vadin's heart hammered. His nostrils twitched with the faint sharp tang of his own fear. Death he was not afraid of; he had lain in its arms. But he could fear pain, fear overlaid and underlaid and shot through with something light and fierce and salty-sweet. Something like gaiety, something like passion: the inimitable scent and sense of battle. Everything was sharper, clearer, more wonderful and more terrible. He laughed, and because people stared, laughed again in pure mirth. In the midst of it his eye caught a flame of gold. Mirain had raised his hand.

The lines opened, here, there. Rami gathered her haunches beneath her. The companies darted forth, no two at once, no two in the same direction. Mirain's force thundered straight to the center, over the plain, through the swift tumble of Ilien, up the slight slope beyond. There was no cover there; they were naked to the sky and to the waiting shadow.

Vadin settled himself more firmly in the saddle. Rami's gallop was smooth, effortless. The silver mane floated over his hand. One blood-red streamer whipped back to strike his wrist.

The enemy waited. He could see as one sees at dusk: shapes, eyes, but no features. The eyes wore no more expression than the weapons bent against him.

He drew his sword. It was light in his hand, although the blade was strangely dark, its polished sheen lost in dimness.

The company rode together still, close at Mirain's back. But some did not ride easily; their mounts fretted, veering and shying. One man flogged his senel on with his scabbard, the face within the open helmet like a demon-mask, teeth bared, eyes white-rimmed. The horror touched Vadin as a wind will, brushing and chilling but going no deeper than the skin. Looking down, he saw with mild surprise that his body was clothed in a faint golden shimmer, a pale echo of the shining splendor that was Mirain.

Close now. No arrows hummed out of the massed ranks; no spear flew. There was a taste in his mouth as strong as fear. *Trap.* He set his teeth against it. Rami leaped the last yards, braced for battle. Vadin swung up his sword.

The enemy wavered like a mirage, melted and faded and vanished away. Vadin heard cries of anger or of terror. Seneldi screamed. The arrows began to fall.

The Mad One trumpeted, a great stallion-blast of rage and challenge. "On!" Mirain cried to him and to all who could hear. *"On!"*

Shadows, all shadows. Vadin's blade clove air again and again. Yet still he struck, still he pressed on. Bolts sang past him; one pierced his flying cloak. He laughed at them.

With a shock so powerful that it nearly flung him to the ground, his sword struck flesh. Blood fountained, red as Rami's streamers.

As if a spell had been broken, suddenly he could see. Though dim and shadowed still, an army spread before and about him, drawn up under banners he knew. They had few cavalry: the Marches were not known for their herds. Most of the seneldi drew chariots.

Those he could not face, even wild with battle as he was. Mirain had given them a wide berth, striking against knights and infantry; Vadin sent Rami after him. The enemy fought well and fiercely enough, but there was a strangeness in their eyes, as if they did not truly see him.

They struck only when struck first; they did not attack. All along their lines, knots of combat alternated with unnatural stillness. Even the chariots did not roll forth to hew the attackers into bloody fragments, but stood where they were set, the charioteers' eyes fixed straight before them.

In Geitan they had told Vadin that he was rarely blessed, a warrior who could sing as he fought. But that was against men who were free to sing in turn, fight in turn, slay in turn. This was a travesty, a sorcerous horror. His lips drew back from his teeth in sudden, deadly rage. "Fight damn you!" he howled. "Turn on us! Hammer us down!"

The eyes did not change. His sword turned in his hand; he began to lay about him with the flat of it, stunning but not wounding. He sensed Mirain close by him: a gathering of power, stronger, stronger, until surely he would burst with it.

Mirain let it go. The light upon him mounted to a blaze. Eyes woke to life, to fear, to battle-madness. With a shrill cry a charioteer lashed his team against the attackers.

Darkness roared down. Rami wheeled uncommanded, running as she had never run before, flat to the ground, ears pinned to her head. She burst from the shadow like a demon out of hell, eyes and nostrils fire-red. The stream flashed silver about her feet. Beyond it she slowed, became a seneldi mare again, breathing hard, with foam white upon her neck.

Vadin blinked in the bright sunlight. His fingers were clamped about the hilt of his sword; painfully he loosed them, wiping his blade on his cloak. Blood faded into royal scarlet. With a convulsive movement he thrust the sword into its sheath.

Mirain's sortie had done what it intended. The enemy was in turmoil, too intent upon the spell's breaking to muster an assault. But the cost had been frighteningly high. Mirain's men milled here and there on the hither side of the water, with riderless seneldi running among them. They moved with order in their confusion, a swift and steady retreat with an eye constantly upon the enemy, and there were far fewer in the retreat than had ridden to the attack.

Mirain's own company gathered to him. Vadin counted and groaned aloud. Of eighteen, twelve were gone. The six who remained rode like wounded men, several on wounded beasts.

Alidan reached king and squire first, Alidan without her helmet, her hair escaped from its braids, her sword hand bloody to the wrist. But there was no wound on her. Mounted as they both were, Mirain pulled her into a tight embrace.

For each of the others he had the same. They all had the look of men who had passed through one of the thrice nine hells: grey and stunned, staring without comprehension at the plain daylight.

"We tried to follow you, my lords," Alidan said for them all. "The shadows turned into men and fought us; we fought back. But you were too fast for us. My lords, you shone like gods. You went deeper and deeper, and at last we could not force our mounts forward. We tried to hold the line behind you. It broke. Our seneldi carried us out. My lord king, any punishment you name—"

"Punishment?" Mirain laughed painfully. "I did exactly the same as you, and abandoned you to boot. No, my friends. You did what few other mortal men could have done." His eyes caught Alidan's; he laughed again with less pain and more mirth. "Mortal men, and one woman."

They rode back slowly. They were barely half of the way from the stream to the battle-lines—those lines bending outward against all discipline to receive their king—when a horn rang. The Mad One whipped about, Mirain's sword flashing from its scabbard.

The enemy's lines opened. Out of them came a single rider, a man on a smoke-grey senel, all in grey himself with a torque of grey iron about his neck. That and the grey banner without device proclaimed him a herald, sacred before men and gods, owing allegiance to one chosen lord. His eyes rested neutrally upon the army, but when they touched Mirain they narrowed and darkened.

"Men of Ianon," he said. He had a superb voice, rich and deep, trained to carry without effort over a great distance. "Followers of the usurper, the one who calls himself Mirain, bastard child of a priestess and false claimant of the throne of the mountain kings, I bring you word from your true lord. Lay down your arms, he bids you. Yield up the boy and you shall go free."

"Never!" shouted Alidan, fierce and shrill. Deeper voices echoed her.

The herald waited patiently for silence. When he had it he spoke again. "You are loyal, if not wise. But your rightful king remembers what you choose to forget: that you are his people. He would not willingly send his army against you for a battle that would end only, and inevitably, in your destruction."

"What about the villages?" bawled a man with a voice of brass. "What about the children cut down and burned in their houses?"

The herald continued coolly, undismayed. "The king proposes a different course, one both ancient and honorable. Two men claim a throne which only one may hold. Let them contend for it, body to body and life to life: a single combat, with all spoils to the victor. Thus will none die but one man, and the division of Ianon be healed, and the throne secured. What say you, men of Ianon? Will you accept my lord's proposal?"

Mirain rode forward a senel-length. The movement silenced his army. He faced the herald, taking off his helmet and setting it on his pommel. "Will Moranden swear to that? That the victor take all, with no treachery and no further slaughter?"

The herald's nostrils flared. "Have I not said so?" *Upstart,* his eyes said. He was a man who believed in his commander.

Even from behind, Vadin heard the smile in Mirain's voice. "Will you condescend to take him my answer?"

"He gives you until sunset to make your choice."

"He is generous." The Mad One advanced another length. Mirain's words came bright and strong. "Tell him yes. Yes, I will do it."

The herald bowed: barest courtesy, no more. "It is the privilege of the challenger to choose time and place, of the challenged to choose the weapons and the mode of battle, whether single or seconded. My lord bids you to meet him here between the armies, tomorrow, at sunrise."

Mirain's bow was deeper, rebuking bare courtesy with true courtliness. "So shall I do. We shall fight singly, overseen by one judge and one witness of each side. As for weapons . . ." He paused. His army waited, drawn thin with tension. "Tell your commander that I choose *no* weapons. Bare hands and bare body: the most ancient way of all." He bowed again. "Tomorrow at sunrise. May the gods favor the truth."

Twenty-three

"**U**NARMED!"

Even Adjan had taken up the cry, shocked out of all dignity. Mirain turned a deaf ear to him as to the rest, laboring first among the healers and then, and only then, returning to his tent. The protests had followed him; they continued as his squires disarmed him. Blood had soaked even to his undertunic, and dried there; there was a long breathless pause until his pursuers saw that none of it was his own. With sudden fierce revulsion he tore at the garment, stripping it off, flinging it as far from him as he might.

Which was, by design or chance, into Adjan's hands. "My lord," the arms master said with some remnant of his usual control, "single combat is an old and honored way of resolving conflicts. But unarmed combat—no weapon, no armor, no defense at all—"

Mirain looked at him. Simply looked, as a stranger might, a stranger who was a king. "If it would soothe your outraged modesty, I could wear a loinguard."

"The dark," someone muttered. "He rode into it and fought it. It's driven him mad."

Vadin stared the man down until he fled. That began an exodus. Vadin remained; and Adjan, and Obri the chronicler who was like a shadow on the wall, and Ymin with Alidan. Olvan and Ayan, moving with great care, began to prepare the king's bath. They filled the broad copper basin; Mirain let them wheedle him into the water, a letting that had no passivity in it. His eyes were still upon Adjan. "Well, Captain, would a loinguard content you?"

"Full armor would be no more than adequate. And sword and spear and shield with it."

"And the body of one of your northern giants." Mirain glanced down at himself. He had grown since he came to Han-Ianon; he would not, after all, be so very small. Middle height in the south, perhaps, but in Ianon, small still; smoothly and compactly made, with the lithe strength of a rider or a swordsman.

And ensorceled surely, to have bound himself to a contest without weapons against the most formidable fighting man in Ianon.

"No," Mirain said with tight-reined impatience. *"No.* Unbind your brains, my friends, and think. I'm skilled in arms, I know it well enough; with the sword I may even become a master. My charger has no peer in this kingdom. *But."* He stepped out of the bath, neither flaunting his body nor belittling it. "Moranden is a man grown, in his full prime, trained from earliest youth in the arts of war. He can wield a larger sword, a longer spear; if he can't out-ride me, he can hold his own against my Mad One. While I flail uselessly at him, he can smite me at his leisure, like a man beset by a little child."

"He can do the same without weapons," snapped Adjan. "His arms are half again as long as yours; he stands head and shoulders above you. And he's strong. The Python, his enemies used to call him: he strikes like a snake, fast and deadly, with all the force of his size."

"In the west," said Mirain, "there is a creature. She is small, no larger than my two hands can hold, with a long supple tail, and great soft eyes like a lovely woman's. She sheathes her claws in velvet. They call her Dancer in the Grasses, and Night Singer, and most often *Issanulin,* Slayer of Serpents. There is no creature swifter or fiercer or more cunning than she. Even the great serpent-lord, the crested king, whose poison is most deadly of all—even he falls prey to this small hunter."

"She has claws and teeth," Adjan said, immovable. "What have you?"

"Hands," he answered, "and wits. Come, sir. You're a famous fighter; I've heard you called the best master-at-arms in the north of the world. See if you can strike me."

The old soldier looked hard at him. He stood loose, easy, smiling. But a keen eye could detect the tension in him.

Adjan was noted for his swift hand, whether or not it held a weapon. As the others drew back to the walls, he shifted slightly, almost invisibly; feinted right; lashed out with his left hand, too swift for the eye to follow.

Mirain seemed not to have moved. But Adjan's fist had struck only air.

Adjan's brows knit. He advanced a step or two. Mirain did not retreat. "Seriously now," he said, "strike me."

This time Mirain's movement was clearly visible, an effortless, sidewise bending. He laughed. "Seize me, Adjan. Surely you can do that. I'm in your arms already."

He was; he was not.

Adjan lowered his hands. His face was a study; he composed it. "So. You're uncatchable. What use is that in a duel, unless you can land a blow where it matters?"

Mirain stepped back with the supple grace of a cat. "You're angry. I've made you look like a fool. Attack me, Captain. Wrestle me down and teach me to listen to your wisdom."

There was nothing Adjan would have liked better. But he was wary, and well he might be. He had said it before when he faced Mirain at practice in front of the squires: In all his years of fighting and of training fighters, he had only once seen speed to equal Mirain's. In Moranden when the prince came into his manhood. Three years, four, five—let the king get his growth and hone his skill, and he would be a warrior to make songs of.

If he lived past the next sunrise.

Adjan attacked. Mirain let him come, shifting a little, poising upon the balls of his feet. Suddenly Adjan was in the air, whirling head over heels, sprawling amid the coverlets of Mirain's bed. And Mirain was kneeling by him, holding his reeling head, saying in a tone of deep contrition, "Adjan! Your pardon, I beg you. I never meant to throw you so far."

Adjan shut his mouth with a snap. A sound burst out of him, a harsh bark of laughter. "Throw me, boy? Throw me? I weigh enough for two of you!"

Mirain bit his lip. His eyes hovered between laughter and apology. "You do. And I used a good part of it against you. A little more and I could have killed you."

The arms master staggered to his feet. "Of course you could have. The more fool I. I should have known you'd have the western art."

"The gentle killing. Yes, I have it. I learned it of a master, by my mother's will. She knew I'd grow to be like her: western stature, northern face. And people in the west, being so small beside the rest of mankind, have learned to turn their smallness to advantage. Since they can't conquer by brute strength, they conquer by art. I've seen a child from Asanion, a maidchild mind you, younger and smaller than I, cast down a man nigh as big as Moranden, and kill him when he refused to yield."

"I've seen something like it. It's enough to make me believe the stories that Asanians have interbred with devils."

"Precisely the tale they tell of me." Mirain rose. "Now do you understand? With weapons I have no skill that Moranden cannot either equal or surpass. Without them I may be able to even the balance. He's a big man; he relies on his strength. So too shall I."

"I still think you're mad. If you would see sense, find another champion—" Adjan broke off. Abruptly and deeply he bowed, the full obeisance of a warrior to his king. "However it ends, my lord, it will be a battle to make songs of. There's no power of mine that will keep you from it."

Mirain bowed his head. Suddenly he seemed immeasurably weary. "Please go," he said. "All of you."

They obeyed, none willingly. Ymin hung back, but found no yielding in him. Slowly she retreated, letting the tent flap fall behind her.

But Vadin did not go. He made himself invisible, withdrawing into the darkest corner, thinking not-thoughts. It had its effect. Mirain did not glance at him; did not order him out.

The tent seemed larger for the people who had left it, lit by a single lamp, warm and quiet in the heart of the night. The squires had taken the bath with them; Mirain sat where it had been, on carpets flattened by the weight of water and basin, and set himself to a task they had not come to: loosing and combing his hair. It was even less straight above the root of his braid than below; cut short, it would have sprung into a riot of curls.

A shield hung from the central pole, polished to mirror sheen. He met his reflected stare. Vadin, invisible, unable to help himself, slipped inch by inch into Mirain's mind, following his thoughts as if he had spoken them aloud. Quiet thoughts, a little wry, like the tilt of his head as he contemplated his face. Westerners had smooth oval faces and sleek rounded bodies and hair that curled with abandon; they were light-skinned, gold and sometimes ivory, and often their hair was straw-pale. Mirain had inherited none of that but the curling of his hair. He was all dark, indubitably of Ianon: high cheekbones, arched nose, proud thin-lipped mouth. "Imagine the alternative," he said aloud. "Western face, northern body. The strength to stand against Moranden as warrior to armed warrior, without art or trickery." He sighed. "And I would still be a boy half grown, with size and skill yet to gain."

He tied his hair back with a bit of cord and clasped his knees. There was the heart of it. Moranden was strong and skilled and implacable in his enmity; and he had strong sorcery behind him. What was to prevent his mother and her goddess from giving him art to equal Mirain's?

"Father," he whispered. "Father, I am afraid."

When he was very young, sometimes he had wept because his hand burned him so terribly, and because he had no father he could touch, or run to, or cry on. There was his mother, who was all the mother a child could wish for, and Prince Orsan whom he called foster-father, and the princess; and Halenan, and later Elian, brother and sister in love if not in blood. But for father he had only pain, and the distant fire of the sun, and the rites in the temple.

When he was older, he taught himself not to weep. But he faced his mother and demanded of her, "How can it be true? I know how children are made; Hal told me. How can my father be a spirit of fire?"

"He is a god," she had answered. "For a god, all things are possible."

He set his chin, stubborn. "It takes a man, Mother. He comes to a woman, and he—"

She laughed and laid a finger on his lips, silencing him. "I know how it is done. But a god is not like a man. He has no need to be. He can simply will a thing, and it is so."

Mirain scowled. "That's horrible. To give you all the pain and trouble of bearing me, without any pleasure at all."

"Oh," she said, a breath of wonder and delight, "oh, no. There was pleasure. More than pleasure. Ecstasy. He was there, all about me; and I was his love, his bride, his chosen one. I knew the very moment you began in me, a joy so sweet that I wept. Oh, no, Mirain. How could I wish for the feeble pleasures of the flesh when I have known a god?"

"*I* don't know him," Mirain said sullenly, setting his will against the strength of her joy.

She gathered him up, great lad that he was, seven summers old and already making his mark among the boys in training for war. "Of course you know him. This very morning I saw him in you and you in him, riding your pony down by the river."

"That was no god. That was—was—" Words failed him. "I was happy, that's all."

"That was your father. Light and joy and a bright strong presence. Did you not feel as if the world loved you, and you loved it in return?

As if there were someone with you, taking joy in your joy, bearing you up when you faltered?"

"I'd rather have someone I can see."

"You have me. You have Prince Orsan, and Hal, and—"

"I don't want them. I want a father."

She laughed. She was full of laughter, was the Priestess of Han-Gilen. Some people frowned at her, thinking that the god's own bride should be grave and austere and visibly saintly; but Sanelin was a creature of light. And he, being her child, found to his dismay that he could not be sullen in front of her. Already the laughter was bubbling up in him. How absurd to cry for a father, when of course he had one already, more than anyone else had, present always in him and with him. And when he needed a physical presence he had no less than the Prince of Han-Gilen, that tall man with his stern face and his merry eyes and his hair like the sun's own fire.

Sanelin was dead, Prince Orsan long leagues away. But the god was there when Mirain looked for him, in the core of his own soul: a presence too intimate to bear either name or face. Nor did he offer comfort in words. It went far deeper than that.

Deeper still went the fear. "Father, I could die tomorrow. I probably will die. This is an enemy I am ill-equipped to face."

Should he be afraid of death? It was but a passage; and after it, joy unspeakable.

"But to die now with my destiny all unfilfilled—to know that by my death I leave my kingdom open to the servants of our Enemy—how can I endure it?"

Ah, then it was not death he feared. He feared that he would not live to hold back the goddess. He had a fine sense of his own worth.

"And who set it in me?"

To make him strong. Not to make him arrogant.

"It makes no difference, then. If Moranden kills me, the throne is safe; his mother will not rule through him with her wizards and her priests, turning all Ianon to the worship of the goddess."

It would make a difference. Perhaps, once Moranden had his throne, he could hold against his mother; perhaps he would prove too feeble for her purposes. Or perhaps, and most likely, what Mirain foresaw would come to pass.

"Perhaps is an alarming word for a god to use."

A god might choose to think as a man, for his own ends. As he might choose to lend aid where aid was needed, if it were sought in the proper fashion.

"Father! You will be with me?"

The god was always with his son.

"You comfort me," said Mirain with a touch of irony.

But not completely.

"Of course not. I know what this battle is to you. Another stroke against your sister." Mirain tossed back his heavy mane, quivering with sudden, passionate anger. "But why? Why? You are a god. She is a goddess. Fight your own battles in your own realm. Let us be!"

The god's presence seemed to smile, a smile full of sadness; his thought took shape clearly as words in a voice soft and deep, like and yet unlike his son's. *Again I tell you, again I bid you remember: When we shaped your world, we swore a truce. War between us would destroy all we made together. Rather than chance that, we bound ourselves to this, that all our battles henceforth be waged through the creatures we had made.*

Mirain's lip curled. "Ah, Father, you are cruel. Say it clearly. Say that you toy with us as a cat toys with its prey."

No. We do not.

"If you do not, what of the other? It is annihilation she craves. Why should she not break the truce and conquer?"

She does not crave annihilation. No more than do I. She would destroy what is pleasing to me and cloak the world in the night she made, and rule it, sole queen and sole goddess.

"And you?"

I would have balance. Light and dark divided, each in its proper place.

"With you as sole king and sole god."

You say it. Not I.

"Yes," Mirain said bitterly. "It is always I who say it. I love you, I cannot help it. But, Father, I am mortal and I am young, and I do not have your wisdom to see always what I must do."

Win your battle. The rest will follow in its own time.

"Win my battle," Mirain repeated. "Win it." He flung himself on his bed. "Oh, dear god, I am afraid!"

The lamp flickered; a thin cold wind skittered about the tent and fled. Vadin found himself standing over Mirain, and he could not stop shaking, and he could not name what shook him, whether it was terror of the god who burned and blazed in him, or terror of the king who huddled and trembled on the cot. A god without face or living voice, a king with the semblance of a frightened boy. Paradoxes. Vadin was a simple man, a mountain warrior. He was not made for this.

He had walked through death into the living light. He was marked with Mirain's power, that came from the god.

He lowered himself to one knee. Mirain's trembling had eased; he had drawn into a knot, almost pitifully small. Very lightly Vadin touched his shoulder.

"Get out," he said. His voice was still and cold.

Vadin did not move. The moment stretched, counted in slow breaths. Mirain drew tighter still.

Without warning he burst outward and upward, hurling Vadin onto his back, "Get out, damn you. Get out!"

Vadin found his wind where it had fled, blinked away the sparks of shock and mild pain. "Why?" he asked reasonably.

Mirain hauled him up. The king was stronger than he had any right to be, and fully as dangerous as a startled leopard; but Vadin could not remember to be afraid, even when the strong small hands shook him like a bundle of straw. He kept his body limp and his teeth together, and waited for the storm to pass.

Mirain let him go. He swayed, steadied. "Why should I get out?" he asked again. "Because I saw you acting human for once?"

"Have I no right to my solitude?"

Vadin drew a breath. His ribs ached, from the sortie, from Mirain's violence. He considered the vivid furious face. "Do you really want to be alone?"

"I—" It was a rarity indeed: Mirain at a loss for words. "You were in my mind."

"Wasn't I?" And whose fault was it that Vadin could be?

Mirain heard all of it, spoken and unspoken. "You had no right," he said.

"Not even the right of a friend?"

The silence sang on a high strange note. Vadin had spoken without thought, through the fading brilliance of the god. Mirain had heard at first only through the crackle of his anger. As the crackle died, his eyes widened; Vadin felt his own do the same. His heart began to hammer. His fists clenched into pain.

Mirain spoke softly, with great care. "Say it again, Vadin. Say it yourself, without my father to drive you."

Vadin's throat closed. He thought of cursing the god and all his madness. He said, "A friend. A friend, may your own father damn you, and if you're half the mage you claim to be you'll know I lost my wager cycles ago. And doesn't a friend have a right to stay where he's needed?

Especially," he added grimly, "when it's a god who's possessed him to
do it."

"I need no one."

Haughty words and most unwise, and a staring lie. Vadin did not
dignify them with his notice. "Friend," he said. And more awkwardly:
"Brother. I don't think less of you because you're afraid. Only fools and
infants, and maybe gods, have never known fear."

"Gods—gods can be afraid." Mirain pricked his temper anew, reared
up his pride and made a weapon of it. "Do you think you can do
anything to help me? You who cannot even shape the letters of your
name?"

Vadin burst out laughing. Mirain in the depths of terror was still
worthy of all respect, because his fear was the valiant fear of a strong
man and a mage. But that he, so wise, should insult Vadin for what any
Ianyn lord was more proud of than not . . . "What, my lord, have I
had it all wrong? Are you going to duel with pens and tablets? It's true I
can't write a word, but I can sharpen your pen for you; shall I fletch it
too and show you how to make a dart of it?"

Mirain's chin came up. In spite of his reckless mood Vadin knew a
moment's chill, a flicker of doubt lest he had gone too far. "You mock
me," the king said, still and cold again.

"Listen to me," said Vadin in a flare of temper. "You have to go out
there tomorrow and fight all alone, and no one's holding out much hope
for you, and maybe you'll die; and you're so scared you can hardly see,
but you'll do it because you have to. Because you can't do anything else.
And you'd rather be eaten by demons than let anyone guess how close
your bowels are to turning to water."

"They aren't," snapped Mirain. "They already have."

Vadin paused for a heartbeat. He was not sure he dared to smile. "So
of course you wanted to be alone with your shame. You can't have the
world finding out that you're a man and not the hero of a song." He
struck his hands together. "Idiot! How do you think you'll be by morning if you spend the night brooding and shaking and hating yourself for
being afraid? Do you *want* to lose this fight?"

"Vadin," Mirain said with elaborate patience, "Vadin my reluctant
brother, I know as well as anyone what chance I have against Ianon's
great champion. I also know how much brooding is good for me; and I
have arts that will assure my rest. If," he added acidly, "you will let me
practice them."

"You're playing with the truth again." Vadin eluded a blow without
much force behind it, and seized Mirain. The king stiffened, but he did

not struggle. "You've got my soul, Mirain. It's yours to do whatever you like with. Even to throw away, if that's your pleasure."

"That would be a dire waste." At half an arm's length Mirain had to tilt his head well back to see Vadin's face. The king did not smile, nor did his expression soften, but his eyes were clearer and steadier than they had been in a long while. "You called me by my name."

"I'm sorry, my lord."

"Sure you are." Vadin's own way of speaking, his very tone. A thin line grew between Mirain's brows, counter to the vanishingly faint upcurve of his lips. "You'll not 'my lord' me in private again, sir. It's bad enough that I have to suffer it from everyone else."

"You should have thought of that before you got yourself born a royal heir."

"Sweet hindsight." Mirain smiled at last, if somewhat thinly. "You're good for me, I think. Like one of Ivrin Healer's more potent doses."

"Gods! Am I that bad?"

"Worse." But Mirain's mood had shifted, turning from the old black madness to something almost light. "Bitter I would say, but bracing. Will you be my witness tomorrow?"

"Is it politic? Prince Mehtar—"

"Damn Prince Mehtar," Mirain said in a voice so mild it was alarming. He took Vadin's hands, held them in a grip the other could not break. "If I live I'll be strong enough to deal with him. If I die, it won't matter. And," he said, "I'd much rather have you under my eye than trying to creep behind."

Vadin's ears were hot. "I wouldn't—"

"Now who's telling lies?" Mirain let go Vadin's hands. He moved closer yet, catching the squire in a sudden tight embrace. "Brother, I humble myself; I admit it. I need you. Will you be my witness?"

Yes, thought Vadin, knowing Mirain would hear. A little stiffly, a little shyly, he closed the embrace. He did not know why he thought of Ledi. She was his woman. Mirain was—was—

"Brother," Mirain said. He drew back, smiling a little. "Shall I bring her to you?"

Vadin did not doubt that Mirain could do it. But his hand rose in refusal. "Thank you, no. There's no need to tire yourself working magic. I'll be well enough for a little self-denial."

Mirain shrugged slightly, as if he would disagree, but he let Vadin go. "Good night, brother," he said.

"Good night," answered Vadin. "Brother."

* * *

Ymin sat on the ground outside of Mirain's tent, a grey shadow on the edge of firelight. But Vadin, coming out under the sky, saw her as easily as she saw him. Their eyes met. His, she thought, were not the eyes of a boy, still less of a simple Ianyn warrior. She had to firm her will to face them.

He bowed his head a very little. Acknowledgment, encouragement, a sudden white smile. She rose. Her heart, foolish creature, was beating hard. When she glanced back, the squire had taken her place and her post.

Mirain lay on his bed, arms behind his head, eyes upon the lamp above him. She dropped her robe and lay beside him, folded about him, head pillowed on his breast. His arms came down to circle her; he kissed the smooth parting of her hair. His pulse had quickened, but he was cool yet, unready. She lay quietly, saying nothing, thinking of little but peace.

His voice came soft and deep yet very young. "Ladylove, do you know how alarmingly beautiful you are?"

"Alarming, my dear lord?"

"Terrifying. I'm an utter coward, my lady. Everything frightens me."

"Even battle?"

"That most of all. I have no courage, only its seeming. An instinct, blind and quite mad, which drives me full upon whatever I fear most."

"I think," she said, "that that is true courage. To know what horror one faces, and to dread it, yet to confront it with no appearance of flinching."

"Then is all bravery but cowardice turned upon itself?"

"Even so." She raised her head to look into his face. "I would not call you a coward, Mirain An-Sh'Endor."

"But I am!" He bit his lip. "I am," he said again. "I am also a madman, a fool, and all the rest of it. I know it all too well. And I want to forget it. For a while. Until I have to remember."

"In Ianon," she said, "in the old time before our people turned to the ways of the west and the soft south, when the king kept vigil before battle, there was a ritual. It gave strength to the king, and through him to his kingdom; often it brought him victory."

He sat motionless, his eyes wide, full of lamplight and of her face.

She continued softly, calmly. "After the sun had set, while his army kept the night watch, the king would sit in his tent, alone or perhaps with one other who was as close to him as a brother. There he would fight his secret battle against what fears he might have, for himself, for his people. But that battle is never wisely fought if fought too long. Near to its end, another would come, not only to fight beside him but to make him forget. This one was always a woman, neither maiden nor matron but one who by her vows and her will had chosen to set herself apart from the common lot of her sex, to be a thing far greater. The holy one, the king's strength."

"And his singer?"

"That too. Sometimes."

"Then it seems," he said, "that I chose wisely on the night of my kingmaking. One woman for all I might desire." His voice roughened. "But there's no need tonight to invent titles and rituals. Only say it. Say it plainly. You think I need a woman."

"Do you not?" she asked unruffled, even though she knew it maddened him.

Maddened, he struck to wound. "What makes you think it's you I need? Maybe it's time I chose one closer to my own size. One who is not old enough to be my mother."

She laughed on her inimitable, rippling scale, with no pain in it that she would let him perceive. "Perhaps it is time and perhaps it is wise, but I am here and I am quite comfortable; and you are much too fastidious to make do with a camp follower."

He gulped air and outrage. "How dare you—" It came as a half-shriek, so utterly disgraceful that it shattered all his anger. Laughter rose to fill the void: breathless, helpless laughter that loosened all his bones and left him hiccoughing in her arms.

Her own laughter died with his, but a smile lingered; her eyes danced. "There truly was a ritual," she said.

"And I truly . . . seem to . . . need . . . Damn you, Ymin!" He was burning under her hands. Abruptly he pulled away, leaping to his feet. "Why do you keep coming back to me? What can you gain from it? Do you do it only because it is your office—your duty? Or . . . do you . . ."

"You have beauty. It is not a common beauty; it is stronger, stranger. It sings in the blood. You have strength, the strength of youth which will ripen into splendid manhood. You have that indefinable air which is royal. And," she said, taking both his hands and drawing them to her heart, "you have that which makes me love you."

He looked down at her. His face was cold, all at once, and very still.

"I am not your life's love," she said. "I do not ask to be. But what I can give you, what I have always given you, on this night of all nights I do give."

Almost he wept. Almost he laughed. In this she had succeeded magnificently: he had forgotten all his black dread. Yet he had given her a trouble of her own, albeit one as sweet as it was painful. She kept her face serene, her smile undimmed, her thoughts bright and strong and fearless. She did not think of what they both knew. They might never lie together again.

But he was too much the mage and too much the Sunborn. He saw; he knew. She had released his hands; he lifted one to stroke her cheek. "I would not give you grief," he said very gently.

"Then give me joy."

It flowered in him for all that he could do. Even without power she sensed it. Her arms enfolded him; she drew him down.

Twenty-four

WITH THE SUN'S SINKING, THE SHADOW ABOUT THE enemy's camp seemed to melt away. By full dark the sentries upon the hilltops could discern a camp but little different from their own, an ordered pattern of watchfires gleaming in the night.

The level between the camps was dark even for one with night-eyes, the stream whispering in its passage. Alidan crept down the bank with a hunter's caution; she was clad in her own midnight skin, her hair braided and coiled tight about her head, a dagger bound to her thigh, hilt and sheath wrapped in black to hide the gleam of metal. So she had passed Mirain's sentries, as softly as a wind in the grass.

On Ilien's edge she paused. Briefly she looked back. Mirain's tent was invisible among the rest; he slept within it, safe in his singer's arms, his Geitani squire keeping watch without. She smiled, thinking of them, and sighed a little. She wished that she had been able to say farewell to the king at least; but he would have forbidden her, and this was a thing which she must do.

Ilien sang before her. The enemy's camp stretched beyond. Still she could detect no shadow but that of the night, no hint of vigilance other than the pacing of the guards. They moved easily in armor that glinted in the scattered firelight, some accoutered in the fashion of the Marches, some clad as knights of western Ianon. One, close to the stream, wore on his cloak the badge of the Lord Cassin.

Alidan released her breath slowly and lowered herself into the water.

It was bitter cold on her bare skin. She set her teeth and glided forward, shaping her movements to the rhythm of the stream upon its stones. More than once she froze, crouching, but no eyes turned toward her.

At last she lay upon the western bank. The sentries paced oblivious. They had the air of men who kept watch out of duty, but who feared no assault.

She gathered herself muscle by muscle. Silently but swiftly she ran up the slope. A guard paused, peering; she halted. He resumed his pacing.

The fires flickered before her; the sentries passed behind. She moved with somewhat less care, but cautious still, keeping to the shadows, edging toward the pavilion that stood in the center of the camp. A standard fluttered before it: Moranden's sign of the wolf's head, wearing now a crown.

Lamplight blazed within, catching in the eyes of the two who confronted one another. Moranden stood as if drawn taut by a hidden hand. His mother sat enthroned upon a carven chair, clad with her perennial simplicity, starker still beside the prince's splendor. But her face was calm and unwearied, and his was worn to the bone as with a long and hopeless struggle.

"I let you play, child," she said, "I let your men call you king, while they shun me and call me witch and worse. I will let you finish your game of kings and warriors with yonder upstart. But I do not intend to give him the smallest chance of victory."

"How can he win? He's half my size. I can take him apart while he's still struggling to get close."

"The Sunchild is a fool, but he is not entirely mad. He sees some advantage in the mode of battle he has chosen. Very likely that advantage will partake of sorcery."

"I'll see that he swears to use none, and you can see that he holds to the oath. But no more. None of your poisons and none of your spells. I'll kill him in fair fight."

"No," she said, flat and final. "You will know when I—"

He bent over her. So grim was his face that even she knew a moment's apprehension. He spoke very softly, very distinctly, with every vestige of his hoarded strength. "Woman, I have had enough. You thought you had my eyes well clouded, but I know what this army has been doing to my country. *My* country, woman. Ravaging it. Destroying it. Taking your revenge on an enemy cycles dead, who never did more to you than put down your viper of a father and set you as high as any traitor's spawn could be set. And love you, in his way. That was the unforgivable sin. He never condescended to hate you."

She struck him. Her long nails left weals above his beard; he made no move to touch them, although one begot a thin stream of blood. It seemed to spring from no new wound but from the old scar beneath his eye, remembrance of another battle in this same endless war. "Yes," he said, "when words fail, you always strike; and the truth drives you mad."

"Truth!" She laughed. "What do you know of truth? You whose claim to kingship is a lie. You were never a king's son, Moranden."

He drew back a step. The bile was thick in his throat, gnawing at his words. "That is vicious slander. He was my father. He acknowledged me."

She smiled, sure now that she had won, as she always had. "That was the bargain I struck. He could have me if he would give his name to my child. He was weak and I was very beautiful. He did as I bade him."

"Lies," gritted Moranden. "Or if they are the truth . . ." His teeth bared in a dire grin. "You've made a mistake, mother whore. By your testimony I have no legal claim to the throne of Ianon. I'll give it up; I'll go now, abandon this travesty of a war, and find my fortune somewhere far and safe. I'll no longer be your puppet."

He was stronger than she had thought, and saner. She saw it; and she said, "Certainly that must prove your parentage. Sanity does not run in the royal line."

"Neither does murder, which is unfortunate for me. My father should have strangled you the day he met you."

"No father of yours."

"He was all the father you ever let me have!" Moranden drew himself up, gathering both temper and courage. "I will fight my battle in my own way. The honorable way. If you make the slightest move toward my enemy, I will kill you with my own hands." His voice lashed her with sudden force. "Now get out!"

She rose, but she did not flee. "When he has his knee upon your throat, remember what you have said to me."

"When I cast him down and set my foot on him, take care, mother mine, that I don't throw you to his dogs. And the kingdom after it—the kingdom to which you tell me I have no right."

"You have the right of the king's acknowledged son." She drew her veil over her head above the glitter of her eyes. "I will rule Ianon with you or in spite of you. Perhaps after all it is time this land knew a ruling queen."

"You still need me to dispose of the ruling king."

"No," she said, "I need you not at all. But I too am weak. I suffer your folly because you are the child of my body. Because," she said with such raw outrage that he could not help but believe her, "because I love you."

Alidan crouched in deepest shadow a palm's width from the tent wall, hardly breathing. But her dizziness came not only from the shortness of her breath, nor even from the terror of discovery. She had stopped thinking of revenge. There was only necessity; but what was that? The traitor prince would destroy Mirain's body. The sorceress would strike at his soul. And there would be no time to smite them both.

Which?

In the dark behind her eyes, she saw her son fall. And she saw Moranden's face in the moment after Shian died. It was stiff, stunned. She heard words through the roaring in her ears. "Have we fallen to the murder of children? Guards! Take that man!"

A king did as he must. Even the murder of children. And Ilien's course was one long bleak road of the dead.

And he had cried out against it.

But he would kill Mirain.

But the woman would steal the king's will, ensorcel his soul.

If she could.

If Moranden could—

Alidan crept through darkness. One hand closed about the hilt of the long thin dagger which she had meant for Moranden's heart. To save Mirain; to save his empire that would be.

Light flared. Alidan flattened herself into shadow. A tall dark shape held up the tent flap. Light from within struck fire in the silver at her throat.

Alidan's brain reeled. Betrayal upon betrayal. Treason upon treason. Hatred—

The flap fell. Ymin stood in the tent, facing mother and son. They were astonished. She was cool, as if she had nothing to fear. "I give you greeting," she said. They did not speak. Perhaps they could not. She smiled and sat on a cushioned stool, arranging her robe with care, folding her hands in her lap.

Moranden broke the silence abruptly. "How did you get here? What do you want with us?"

"I walked," she answered. "Perhaps I sang a word or two. I wish to speak with you."

"Why? Can't he keep you satisfied?"

She smiled, rich with remembrance. "He is the king in all respects."

"So. You're making the best of it."

"I am more than content." She considered him. "You do not look well, my lord."

"War is hard on a man."

"Yes," she said. "And rebellion is cruel, is it not? One must destroy so much that one yearns to preserve."

He stiffened at the blow. His eyes flicked to his mother, hating, pleading. She watched without a word. Her startlement had given way to something less easily read; but it was not dismay. Not at all. Almost she might have been smiling.

She looked like Ymin. Serene, superior, secure in the certainty that the world was hers to shape as she willed.

Ymin met her gaze. "You know that if your son fails, you have no hope."

"My son will not fail."

"That is no child whom he faces. It is the son of a god. He is stronger by far than he seems; he is the fated king."

"My son shall be king in Ianon."

"So he may be," said Ymin. She turned back to Moranden. "So you can be. Do you think that Mirain will linger here? This is only his beginning. And when he rides to take his full inheritance, Ianon will need a man to rule her. What better man than his own kinsman?"

"His dear kinsman." Moranden bared his teeth. "I'm no sage and I'm no god's get, but I'm not an utter idiot. I know how much love I can expect from Mirain the priestess' bastard. He'd see me dead before he'd let me near his throne."

"Would he? You have begun all amiss, I grant you, but he has grown since he took the kingship. He can forgive you, if you will allow him. He can give you all you ever longed for."

Moranden's face contorted with sudden passion. He flung his hand toward his mother. "Even her head on a pike?"

"Even that," said Ymin steadily.

Odiya laughed, free and startlingly sweet. "Why, this is better than a troupe of mountebanks! Singer, have you lost your wits? Or is it merely the madness of desperation? Your lover has no hope in combat, you know as well as we. But you will not buy his life with empty promises."

"They are not empty," Ymin said.

Odiya merely smiled.

Ymin rose. She raised her chin; she pitched her voice to throb in Moranden's heart. "You are no fool, my lord; no woman's plaything. And yet your mother rules you. Without you she is nothing. Without her you are a man of strength and wisdom. Cast off your shackles. See the truth. Know that you can be king, if only you have patience."

He wavered. She tempted him. She lured him with a vision of splendors that would be. Freedom, joy, a throne at last. And no Odiya to make his life a misery.

He shook himself heavily, hands to head, breathing rough and hard. "No." His fingers clawed. He tore them away. The pain was less than the marks of his mother's hand, than the burning cold of her stare. "No. Too late. It was too late the day my father named Sanelin Amalin his heir. This is only the last movement of the long dance. I must finish it. I will be king."

"My lord," Ymin began.

"Madam," said Odiya, "the king has spoken."

"He has sealed his destruction." But Ymin's strength had faded into mere defiance. She was trapped here; her back knew that guards waited beyond the tent, armed and braced to take her. Moranden might have let her go. Odiya would never surrender so precious a captive. She glanced about, swift, desperate. She drew breath, mustering what magery she had, focusing it in her voice.

"Spare yourself," said Odiya. She spoke a Word. Ymin was mute, without even will to struggle. Odiya took her slack hand. "Come, child."

Ymin could not speak, nor could she resist, but she could smile. It was not the smile of one who had surrendered, nor was there any fear in it, although she saw her death in Odiya's eyes. She met them levelly. She made them fall. Her smile grew and steadied.

Alidan drew herself together. Horror, having darkened her mind, now swept it clear. She knew what she would do, and what she must. Captor and captive emerged from the tent. In their moment of blindness between light and night, Alidan sprang.

Demons and serpents, a body too sinuous-strong to be human, a gleam of deadly eyes. The knife pierced flesh, caught on bone, tore free. Breath broke off sharp in Alidan's ear. Iron fingers wrenched the hilt from her hand and locked about her throat. Too many fingers, too many hands beating her back and down. Firelight blinded her.

"By the gods!" a man burst out. "A woman."

"Ho there! The queen's hurt. Quick, you, fetch a blood-stancher!"

"Enough!" rapped the voice Alidan knew too well now, too strong by far for a woman sorely wounded. "She has but scratched me. Move back; let me see her."

The circle of shadows widened and fell away, but their eyes lingered on Alidan like burning hands. She thought of covering her nakedness; she thought of laughing, and she thought of weeping. She had failed. She had slain herself for nothing, not even for a savorless vengeance. They would die together, she and the mute motionless singer.

A new shadow loomed over her. A suggestion of great beauty, an aura of great terror, a tang of blood. "Goddess," whispered Alidan. "Goddess-bearer."

"Who are you?" The words boomed in her mind.

"Woman." She smiled. "Only woman."

"Who?" pressed the queen who was not. "Who are you?"

"Lost." Alidan's smile faded. The sorceress bent low, eyes alarmed to cleave her soul. The goddess dwelt in them, all dark. "But," protested Alidan, "she is not—she is not all—" No use; the sorceress could not know, would not. No more than she would know who, or why, or whence. There was blood bright and lurid upon her black gown, pain in the set of her face, wrath and power in her eyes. Great wrath, for with blood she lost strength, with strength the power to work her sorceries. Yet her power was great enough still to deal with this frail madwoman; and it promised torment.

Terror gibbered on the edges of Alidan's mind. Madness coiled at the center. Ymin's eyes burned between. Words flamed in them. *Run. Run now.* Wise fool. There was no escape for either of them.

The singer stumbled. Her body lurched against Odiya's, striking the wounded side. The woman reeled, blind with pain. Ymin's eyes, Alidan's feet, met and clashed and chose. Alidan bolted into the night.

As the stars wheeled toward midnight, Vadin eased himself into Mirain's tent. Ymin was gone. Mirain lay alone, sprawled like a child, smiling faintly in his sleep. Vadin settled beside him. It was not a thing of conscious thought. Mirain was warm and sated, fitting himself into the hollows of Vadin's body, sighing even deeper into sleep. But Vadin woke nightlong, guarding his dreams.

Mirain passed without transition from sleep into waking. One moment he was deep asleep; the next, he met Vadin's stare and smiled. That was unwonted enough to freeze Vadin where he lay. The king looked bright and clear-witted and almost happy, freed for once from his morning temper. Today, his eyes said, might be his death day; it might mark the first great victory of his kingship. Whatever the end, now that he came to it, he welcomed it.

Although it was barely dawn, most of the camp was up and about. None of them seemed to have had any more sleep than Vadin had. And all of them, soldiers, squires, lords and captains, were grim-faced, hollow-eyed, as if they and not Mirain would be dead by evening.

He was light and calm. He ate with good appetite; he smiled, he jested, he wrung laughter from them all. But it died as soon as he turned away.

Nuran and Kav took him in hand, bathed him and shaved him, plaited his hair and bound it about his head. While they were occupied, someone hissed from the door. Adjan caught Vadin's eye. The arms master's face was set in stone. Moving without haste but without tarrying, Vadin emerged into the cold dawn. "What—"

He stopped. Adjan supported a second figure, one to which, even cloaked and staggering, Vadin could set a name. "Alidan!" It was all he could do to keep his voice low. She was naked under the mantle, her hair straggling, matted with mud and blood. But her eyes were the worst of it. They were quiet, they were sane, and they had lost all hope.

He tried to be gentle. "Alidan, what's happened?"

"I left my mark on the western witch," she answered him, soft and calm. "She will have no power to betray my king."

Vadin's anxiety went cold. He could not even take refuge in incomprehension. He was too far gone in magecraft. He knew what she was saying; he had begun to suspect what she had left unsaid. She rejoiced in what she had done: black treachery, betrayal of all honor, and perhaps the one hope of Mirain's salvation. But her joy was turned all to darkness.

Adjan said it, short and brutal. "They have the singer. If she's lucky, they'll have killed her quickly."

Vadin's feet carried him toward the ashes of the fire. He stood over them. There was no life in them.

Adjan and Alidan were warm and painful presences at his back. His stomach wanted to empty itself. He exerted his will upon it; with dragging reluctance it yielded. "Why?" he demanded of Alidan. "Why did you do it?"

The woman closed her eyes. It was too dark to see her face; her shape in the gloom was stiff, her voice level. "We were not together. I was going to rid us of the rebel. I wounded his mother instead. The singer was going to persuade him to surrender. His mother overcame her. She was mad," said Alidan who for revenge had walked naked into the enemy's camp and blooded her blade in a witch's body. "She trusted in her singer's power, and in a few nights' loving long ago. He was her daughter's father, did you know that? He never did. Now he never will."

"Damn her," whispered Vadin. "Of all the people in Ianon—she knew what it would do to Mirain. She knew!"

"If she had succeeded—" Alidan began.

"If she had succeeded, she would have shamed him beyond retrieving: she would have proven that even his lover had no hope for his victory."

"It would have prevented bloodshed, and won him a mighty ally."

Vadin tossed his aching head. Women's logic. Damn honor, damn glory, damn manhood—nothing mattered but the winning. He flung up his fists. Alidan did not flinch. She said, "It was a sacrifice. Now the woman of Umijan must die. Now the old king shall be avenged. You speak of shame; what do you call my lord's folly in suffering his assassin to walk free?"

"She may not only walk free. She may rule us." Vadin knotted his hands behind his back, lest he strike the madwoman down. "Get out of sight and stay out of sight. I'll keep this from Mirain for as long as I can." He groaned aloud. *"Gods!* She was supposed to be one of his judges. Adjan, can we rescue her before the sun comes?"

"No." Adjan was quieter than Vadin, and much more deadly. "There's a solid wall of sentries around the camp. They let one woman go; they're keeping the other. She's their best weapon, and they know it."

"It may turn in their hands." Obri the chronicler stood at Vadin's elbow as if he had always been there, no more perturbed than ever by Ianyn size or Ianyn temper. "May I offer a thought?" Vadin snarled at him; he took it for assent. "The king has prepared his mind, no? It is all on the battle before him. Let it stay so. I will go in the judge's cloak, if someone will cut it in half for me." His teeth gleamed as he smiled. "After all, I need to see it to write of it. The singer is indisposed. Poor lady, she loves too much. She has broken, her friend is with her, they will not weaken the king's courage with their tears."

"Mirain will never believe it," Vadin said. "Another woman, maybe. Not Ymin. She's royal born; her heart is Ianyn iron."

"But," Obri persisted, "the king was born in the south, where both men and women are gentler. While he has the battle to think of, he will have less leisure for questions; I will see that he asks none." And when

Vadin would not soften: "Trust me, young lord. I was hoodwinking princess when your father was in swaddling bands."

"What in all the hells are—" But Vadin was conquered. Obri grinned, bowed his mocking bow, and melted into the night. In his wake he left a flicker of amusement, and an image of an infant wrapped from head to foot like a spider's prey. Vadin shuddered. "Go on," he snapped to Alidan. "Vanish. And you, Captain: stay as far from the king as you can. And pray that we carry it off, or we're all done for."

They obeyed him. He was rather surprised. He paused, steeling himself, and went to face Mirain.

He seemed not even to have noticed Vadin's absence. His squires were arranging the last fold of his scarlet cloak. Almost before they were done, he turned with that unmistakable grace of his, and paused. His armor lay all in its place, cleaned and burnished. He ran his finger along the edge of his shield, toyed for a moment with his helmet's scarlet plume.

Abruptly he turned away. They watched him, all of them. He lifted his chin and smiled at them, bright and strong. They parted to let him pass.

Upon the easternmost hill of the camp an altar had risen in the night: a hewn stone banked with earth and green turf. The sacred fire burned upon it, warded by the priests of the army, Avaryan's warriors armed and mantled in Sun-gold. Already before Mirain came to them they had begun the Rite of Battle. Ancient, half-pagan, its rhythms throbbed in the blood: blood and iron, earth and fire, interwoven with drums and the high eerie wailing of pipes. They set Mirain upon their altar, anointed him with earth and blood, hedged him with iron tempered in the god's fire.

Standing there on the height, with the rite weaving above him and his mind struggling to weave itself into Mirain's, Vadin gazed through the other's eyes across the dawn-dim hills. The enemy's fires flickered, growing pale as Avaryan drew nearer, but in the center near the great scarlet pavilion of the commander a torrent of flame roared up to heaven. Men massed about it. Nearest to it a lone shape, encircled by cowled figures, moved in what looked to be a strange wild dance. It was terrible to see, black patched with scarlet, and its movements were jerky, a parody of grace, like the dance of a cripple. Vadin did not know it. Would not know it. Prayed with all his soul that it was not what he feared.

Even as he watched, the flames leaped higher still. The dancer whirled; music shrilled, high and maddening. The fire writhed like hands clawing at the sky: hands of flame, blood red, wine red, the black-red of flesh flayed from bone. They reached. They enfolded the dancer. They drew it keening into the fire's heart.

Sun's fire seared his face. Mirain's face. The priest lowered the vessel of the sacred fire and turned the king eastward toward the waxing flame of Avaryan. Mirain raised his hands to it. The words of the rite flowed over him and through him, and mingled there, shaping into a single soul-deep cry of welcome, of panic-pleading, and at the last, of acceptance.

"So be it," sang the priest. And in Mirain's heart, and in Vadin's caught willy-nilly within: *So be it.*

By the Law of Battle the champion must ride alone to the place of combat, accompanied only by his judge and his witness. They rode at Mirain's back, Obri's brown robe and Vadin's lordly finery hidden beneath mantles of white and ocher. White for victory, ocher for death. In one hand Obri bore the staff of his office: a plain wooden rod tipped at one end with ivory, at the other with amber.

They did not speak. Obri had been as good as his word. Mirain accepted the chronicler's presence; he was not fretting over the absence of his singer. All his mind fixed firmly upon the battle before him.

The army had taken its ranks behind them, the foremost marking the edge of the camp: near enough to see, too far to help. The space between grew wider with each stride, the sky brighter, the enemy closer.

Moranden's lines were free still of shadow or of illusion, as if the sorcery had failed or been abandoned. But his following was very large for all that, the full strength of western Ianon and the Marches. If Mirain had had a second army, he could have overrun their lands behind them.

If he won this battle, he would rule them all unchallenged.

A small company left the ranks, approaching Ilien from the west. Vadin urged Rami forward between Mirain and the river, although what he could do without even a dagger, he did not know. Die again for Mirain, he supposed.

But he saw no weapons among the riders. The herald rode first, mantled in white and ocher, carrying the judge's wand. Directly behind him came Moranden on his blackbarred stallion, riding straight and proud, cloaked as was Mirain in the scarlet of the king at war. And at Moranden's back rode his second witness, the Lady Odiya unmistak-

able even huddled and shrunken behind a swathing of veils; and her
ancient eunuch leading a laden senel.

Vadin and the herald reached the water together, but neither ventured into it. "What is this?" Vadin called across the rush of Ilien.
"Why do so many come to the field of combat?"

"We come who must," responded the herald, "and we bring your
king what he appears to have mislaid."

The eunuch rode forward, dragging the reluctant packbeast down the
bank and across the stream. Vadin knew the shape of the black-wrapped
burden: long and narrow, stiff yet supple, with the shadow of death
upon it. But he was like a man in a dream. He could do nothing but
what he did: give the rider space to come up but none to approach
Mirain, and wait for what inevitably must come. Without word or
glance the eunuch tossed the leadrein into Vadin's hand, turned,
spurred back toward his mistress.

Very slowly Vadin slid from Rami's saddle. He had not planned for
this. He had not been thinking at all since he woke. He knew only that
Mirain must not see. He had to fight. He could not be grieving for his
lover. Or raging for the loss of her.

For a wild instant Vadin knew that he must bolt, he and this silent
dead thing. Bolt far away and bury it deep, and Mirain would never
know.

Someone moved past him, someone in royal scarlet, small enough to
slip under his arm, swift enough to elude his snatching hand. Mirain
reached for the bindings. Vadin tried again and desperately to pull him
back. He was as immovable as a stone, his face set in stone. The cords
gave way all at once, tumbling their contents into Mirain's arms.

She had not died easily, or prettily, or swiftly. Vadin knew. He had
seen her die, driven into the goddess' fire. It had left only enough of her
body that one could tell her sex, and one could tell that she had suffered
before she died, beaten and flayed and perhaps worse still. But neither
fire nor torturers had touched her face, save only her eyes. Beneath that
twofold ruin her features were serene, free of either horror or pain.

"How she must have maddened them," Mirain said, "dying in peace
in spite of them." His voice was mad, because it was so perfectly sane.
Calm. Unmoved. He lowered her with all gentleness, drawing the black
wrappings over her, as if she could wake and know pain. His hand
lingered on her cheek. Vadin could not read his face; his mind was a
fortress. Vadin's strongest assault could not break down its gate.

The herald's voice rang over the water. "So do we recompense all
spies and assassins. Think well upon it, O king who would send a

woman to slay his enemy. You see that she failed. You shall not escape this duel of honor."

Mirain stooped as if he had not heard, and kissed Ymin upon the lips. He said nothing to her that anyone could hear. He straightened, turned. Although he spoke softly, they heard him as if he had shouted every word. "You were not wise to do this, my lady Odiya. For even if I could forgive you the murder of my singer, you have shown Ianon once more what you would do to it and to its people. Ianon may endure your son hereafter, but you have lost all claim to its mercy."

She answered him with deadly quiet. Wounded though her body was, her voice was strong. "You are not the prophet your mother purported to be, nor the king you like to pretend. You are not even a lover. So much she confessed while still she had tongue to speak."

Mirain raised his head. He laughed, and it was terrible to hear, for even as he mocked her, he wept. "You are a poor liar, O servant of the Lie. I see your shame; I taste your thwarted wrath. She would not break. She died as she had lived, strong and valiant." His voice deepened. It had beauty still, but all its velvet had worn away. Iron lay beneath: iron and adamant. "I swear to you and to all the gods, she will have her vengeance."

Odiya would not be cowed. There was death between them; it bore witness to her power. It laid bare the truth: that he could not protect even where he loved. She met his mockery with bitter mockery. "Will you come to battle now, Mirain who had no father? Dare you?"

"I dare, O queen of vipers. And when I have done with your puppet, look well to yourself."

He turned the fire of his hand toward Obri. The chronicler urged his grey mare shying past the pool of black and scarlet, cloak and blood, into the swift bright water, halting in the center. "Here is the midpoint between our forces." He spoke evenly, with more strength than anyone might have believed possible, small and withered as he was. "But since no custom dictates that the champions engage in the midst of a river, and since the choice of ground rests with the challenger, let him choose where he will fight."

"My lord," answered the herald, "bids you engage upon the western bank."

"So shall we do," said Obri, riding forward.

Together with the herald in a barbed amity of duty, Obri dismounted and marked with his rod upon the ground the half of a circle: twenty paces from edge to edge, joined at its twin extremities to the half-circle of the other. When the battleground was made they left it. Moranden

prepared to dismount; the herald took his bridle. Vadin stood at the
Mad One's head.

Mirain sprang down lightly. His head did not even come to Vadin's
shoulder. The squire's eyes pricked with tears; he blinked them away.
By the gods' fortune Mirain had not seen. Eyes and mind bent upon the
fastening of his cloak. Firmly, almost roughly, Vadin set his hands aside
and loosed the clasp. Mirain smiled a very little. Vadin flung the cloak
over the stallion's saddle; Mirain unwrapped his kilt, setting it atop the
sweep of scarlet, running a hand down the Mad One's neck.

Moranden waited within the circle, arms folded. But Mirain paused.
He caught Obri in a swift embrace, startling the scholar for once into
speechlessness. And he reached for Vadin before the squire could escape, pulled his head down with effortless strength, and kissed him on
the lips. The king's touch was like the lightning, swift and potent and
burning-fierce.

Vadin drew a sharp and hurting breath. "Mirain," he said. "Mirain,
try to hold on to your temper. You know what happens when you lose
it."

"Be at ease, brother," Mirain said, light and calm: a royal calm. "I
will mourn her when it is time to mourn. But now I have a battle to
fight." He smiled his sudden smile, with a touch of wryness, a touch of
something very like comfort. "May the god keep you," he said to them
both.

He stepped into the circle. The herald stood in its center with rod
uplifted. Obri raised his own rod and strode forward.

"Hold!"

Obri stopped.

Odiya would not enter the circle, but she stood at the witness' post on
the western edge, leaning on her eunuch's shoulder. "One matter," she
said, clear and cold, "is not yet settled. Yonder stands no simple warrior
but a priest of demon Avaryan, mage-trained by masters. Shall he be
left free to wield his power against one who cannot match it?"

"I will not," Mirain said with equal clarity, equal coldness.

"Swear," she commanded.

He raised his branded hand. For all her pride and power, she
flinched. A small grim smile touched his mouth. He took off his torque
and laid the golden weight of it in Vadin's unwilling hands, standing a
little straighter for its passing, saying levelly, "I swear by the hand of
my father, whose image I bear, whose torque I lay aside in token of my
oath: This battle shall be a battle of bodies alone, without magecraft or

deceit. Swear now in your turn, priestess of the goddess, mage-trained by masters. Swear as I have sworn."

"What need?" she countered haughtily. "It is not I whom you must fight."

"Swear." Moranden's voice, his face implacable. "Swear, my lady mother, or leave this field. Bound and gagged and sealed with my enemy's sorceries."

"Has he such strength?" *Have you?* her eyes demanded. But she yielded with all appearance of submission. She swore the solemn oath, lowering herself to the earth that was the breast of the goddess. "And may she cast me into her nethermost hell if I break this oath which I have sworn."

Before her servant had helped her to her feet, they had forgotten her. The judges stood back to back, each facing the other's champion, waiting. With infinite slowness Avaryan climbed above the eastern margin of the world. At last he poised upon the hills, his great disk swollen, the color of blood. As one, the rods swept down.

Twenty-five

THE JUDGES WITHDREW FROM THE CENTER OF THE circle to its edge; the champions advanced from edge to center. From both armies a shout went up. That of the west held a note of triumph; that of the east, of defiance. For Moranden stood as tall as the mountains of his birth, massive yet graceful, with a glitter of gold in his hair and in the braids of his beard. Mirain beside him was no larger than a child, slight and smooth-skinned, with weight and inches yet to gain; and he would never equal his enemy in either. And he had sacrificed his one advantage: the sword and armor of his power. He had not even his torque to defend his throat.

Vadin had slid from the verge of tears to the verge of howling aloud. There was Mirain staring at his adversary like a small cornered animal, but managing the shadow of a smile. There was Moranden staring back and forbearing to sneer. And yet how alike they were; how damnably alike, two kinsmen matched in their pride, bristling and baring their teeth and granting one another no quarter. And for what? A word and a name and a piece of carven wood.

They were slow to move, as if this battle must be one of eyes alone. But after a while that stretched long and long, Mirain said, "Greetings again at last, my uncle."

Moranden looked him up and down as he had on the first day of Mirain's coming. If he knew any regret, he did not betray it. "Are you ready to die, boy?"

Mirain shrugged slightly. "I'm not afraid of it." His head tilted. "And you?"

"I'm not the one who'll fall here. Won't you reconsider, child? Take what I offered you once. Go back to your southlands and leave me what is mine."

"Bargains?" asked Mirian, amused. "Well then, let me cast my own counters into the cup. Recant and surrender your army. Swear fealty to me as your king. And when the time comes, if you prove yourself worthy, you will be king after all. King in Ianon as you always longed to be, subject only to me as emperor."

"There's the rub," Moranden said. "Under you. How have you managed on the throne of the mountain kings? Do you perch yourself on cushions like a child allowed to sit at table? With a footstool, of course, to keep your feet from dangling. I trust no one dares to laugh."

"Oh, no," said Mirain. "No one laughs at me."

As they spoke they crouched, circling slowly. Mirain wore a small tight smile. Moranden wore no expression at all. He was light on his feet for a big man, and fast; when he struck, he struck with the suddenness of a snake.

Mirain escaped the stroke, but only just. His smile slipped, shifted. Barred from Mirain's mind by the oath which the king had sworn—and dear gods, after all this time and in spite of all his resistance it had become second nature, so that its loss was cruel to endure—still Vadin could read Mirain's face and eyes and body as easily as that young scholar-king could read a book. His mind had narrowed and focused, doubt and grief and terror blurred into distance. There was no fear in him, only fierceness and the beginnings of delight. He was strong and he was swift, and ah, how he loved a battle.

Mirain poised, waiting. Moranden's hand came round: a long, lazy, contemptuous blow, as a man will cuff his hound. Mirain eluded it with a flicker of laughter.

He won no smile in return but a grin like a snarl. "Aha! They pit me against a dancing boy. Dance for me now, little priest. Awe me with your art."

"Better yet, uncle, let us dance together." Mirain moved close, tantalizing; and when Moranden made no move to strike or seize, closer still, deathly close, as if his daring had overwhelmed his prudence.

Moranden struck.

Mirain stood just out of his reach, hand on hip. "Adjan is faster than you," he said.

"Adjan stoops to dance with slaves and children. You can run, priestess' bastard. Can you fight?"

"If you like," said Mirain with the air of a king granting his vassal a favor.

Moranden straightened from his wrestler's crouch and stepped back. Mirain waited. The prince flexed his wide shoulders, filled his lungs, emptied them. Easily, fluidly, he settled into a stance that made Obri, close by Vadin, catch his breath. Vadin saw only that it was lethally graceful, like a cat before it springs. It had a look of—

"The gentle killing," Obri said. He was losing the coolness he was so proud of, the detachment of the scholar. He was like everyone but Moranden and the witch of Umijan. He had fallen in love with Mirain. "The rebel has it. Of course he has it. He is a Marcher and a westerner."

Mirain neither wavered nor retreated. If he saw that he faced a master of his own art, he was too much the warrior to show it. His body shifted toward its center and steadied, taking the posture of his defense.

"*Issan-ulin,*" Obri murmured. "The Serpent-slayer. Pray your gods, Vadin alVadin, that the tale your lord told Adjan was more than a vaunt. Pray your gods that it can save him."

Vadin's prayer was wordless, nor had he eye or mind for naming the movements of this subtle dance, but his will matched the foreigner's. Let Mirain be wise, let him be strong. Let him put up a good fight before he died.

Moranden stalked his prey in silence the more deadly for all his words before; Mirain watched him as the *issan-ulin* watches the serpent, both fierce and wary, striking no blow.

Moranden's hand lashed out and round; his foot followed it in a smooth concerted motion, as graceful as it was deadly. Mirain caught the hand upon his forearm, deflected it, swayed beneath and away from the striking foot.

There was a measured and measuring pause. Moranden feinted. Mirain slid away.

Moranden sprang. Mirain grasped his shoulder, then his surging thigh, and guided them up, back, headlong to the ground, whipping about even as Moranden left his hands.

The prince had spun in the air, coming to earth on one knee, bounding erect. Even as Mirain turned, Moranden seized him. One arm caught his middle in a grip of iron. One hand clamped upon his throat. Moranden laughed, little more than a gasp, and raised him higher, the better to break his body.

Mirain writhed, kicking, mouth gaping for air, eyes wide and blind. With all his failing strength, he drove his head into Moranden's jaw.

Moranden staggered. Mirain dropped. For a long count of breaths he lay utterly helpless.

His enemy loomed above him, foot raised and pointed for a bitter blow. Mirain snatched wildly at it. Held. Thrust it upward. Moranden went down like a mountain falling.

Mirain set his knee upon his kinsman's chest and closed his hands about the heavy neck, setting his thumbs over the windpipe. Moranden made no effort to cast him off. "Uncle," Mirain said, his voice a croak, coming hard from his bruised throat, "yield and I will pardon you."

Moranden's eyes opened wide. Mirain met them. He gasped and froze like a man under a spell, or like a boy who cannot make his kill. Vadin wanted to howl Ymin's name. But his throat had locked, and Mirain was lost. With a faint wordless protest, he hurled himself away.

His body struck the ground. Moranden's full weight plunged down upon it. Desperately Mirain scrambled sidewise. A hammer-blow smote him, driving his arm and shoulder deep into the yielding earth, wringing from him a short sharp cry. Moranden's hands tore cruelly at his hair, freeing the braid from its coil, twisting it, dragging him to his feet. He looked into Moranden's face. With brutal strength the prince wrenched his head back.

Mirain stood as one who waits to die. His left arm hung useless; his body shook with tremors. He smiled.

Moranden thrust him away. He staggered and fell. Yet he rose, although he bled from the stones that had stabbed his cheek, although at first he could not stand. With excruciating slowness he raised himself to his knees. More slowly still, he stood. His lips were grey with pain.

Moranden watched him from a few strides' distance, arms folded, lip curled. For yet a while longer he would toy with his prey. Tease it; torment it; teach it all the myriad degrees of pain. Then—only then—he would slay it.

Mirain's head came up. His eyes glittered. He seemed to grow, to swell with newborn strength. He raised his hands, the left but little less easily than the right, and glided forward. *Issan-ulin* once more, but *issan-ulin* pricked to fury, closing in upon the Lord of Serpents.

Moranden's contempt wavered.

"Yes," Mirain said softly. "Yes, uncle. The game is past. Now the battle begins in earnest."

Moranden spat at him. "Fool and braggart! God's son or very god, you stand in a body reckoned puny even in the south that bred you; and you have given up your magic. You can do no more than your flesh allows. And I," he said, spreading his arms wide, "am the Champion of Ianon."

"Are you indeed?" Mirain beckoned. "Come, O champion. Conquer me."

Once and once again they circled. As smoothly as dancers in a king's hall, they closed. Moranden was strong, but Mirain was swift to strike, swift to spring away. Moranden's blow swung wide as he reeled.

Mirain struck again. Moranden staggered, flailing. One fist brushed Mirain's brow, rocking but not felling him. "Uncle, uncle," he chided, "where is your strength?"

Moranden hissed and began to sway, serpent-supple. It was beautiful, it was horrible, to see that great-muscled body turned suddenly boneless. The lips drew back; the eyes glittered, flat and cold. Death coiled within them.

For a bare instant Mirain faltered. His face twisted, as if all his hurts had burst free at once from their bonds. Moranden lashed out.

Mirain parried. Moranden advanced, hands a deadly blur, feet flying. This too had its name in the west: the Direwolf. Moranden was the great wolf-chieftain, Mirain the tender prey, fleeing round the circle of battle past the silent judges, the silent and helpless witnesses. Moranden passed his mother, who had let her veil fall. Her face was grey and old, furrowed deep with the pain of her wound. She smiled. He did not or would not see her. Full before her, Mirain turned at bay; the combatants closed, grappling near the circle's edge, almost upon it.

Metal flashed in Odiya's hand. She held that weapon which had dogged them all from Umijan: the black dagger of the goddess. It licked toward the struggling figures, hesitated. They were twined like lovers, flesh woven with flesh, no clear target for the blade. And the herald watched, making no move to prevent her.

"Foul!" cried Vadin. "Treason! Stop her!" He flung himself forward.

The dagger sang to its zenith. And fell. No will and no hand guided it. Odiya's eyes were very wide, very surprised, and very, very angry. Her eunuch stood beside her, still bearing her up with a hand on her arm. In his other hand, a blade ran red. "Treason indeed," he said with perfect calm, in part to Vadin, in part to her. "It is time the world was free of it."

Her lips drew back from her teeth. Her hands came up. Black fire filled them. She spoke a word; the fire leaped forth, caught the withered body, transfixed it. But the eunuch laughed. "See, mistress! I win the cast; revenge is mine. Do you not even know that you are dead?"

The fire leaped for his open mouth. Voice and laughter died. But even as he fell, Odiya convulsed. She reared up, and her face was the face of death, her power bleeding like black blood from her hands, hopeless, helpless, unstoppable. She clawed at the blind uncaring sky. She raged at it. She cursed it and its deadly sun and the goddess whose realm lay beneath it. Her power poured away. The poison filled her body. Her life flamed and flared, guttered, rallied, and went out.

The eunuch was dead when he struck the ground. But Odiya was dead before she began to fall.

Mirain and Moranden were up, apart, staring appalled. Vadin, coming too late, dared the black mist of sorcery which hung even yet over the dead; he knelt beside them and closed the staring eyes of slayer and slain, each of whom was both. The woman's face raged even in death. The eunuch smiled with terrible sweetness.

Moranden stooped over them. One eye was swelling shut, but he bore no other wound. "Beautiful, treacherous bitch." He spat upon her, and he bent to kiss her brow. With a strangled roar he whirled.

Mirain, the madman, held out his hands. "Uncle." He might never have been wounded, never have come within a breath of dying with the goddess' blade in his back. "Uncle, it's over. The one who would have besmirched our honor is dead. Come. Swear peace. Rule with me."

Moranden's head sank between his shoulders. His fists clenched and unclenched. A shudder racked him; he nearly fell.

"Uncle," Mirain said, "it was she who drove you, she who made a bitter pawn of you. You yourself, you alone, I can forgive. Will you not share this kingdom with me?"

"Share! *Forgive!*" It was hardly human, that voice. Less human still was the laughter that came behind it. "I hated her, little bastard. I hated her and I loved her, and because of you she is dead. What have you left me but revenge?"

Moranden leaped. He took Mirain off guard. But not wholly. His assault drove the king back but not down. And Mirain, having offered peace at the utmost extremity, having shown Moranden the forbearance of a very saint, now had no mercy left. He had fought with passion and even with anger, in a red heat of battle. Now he advanced in white-cold rage.

Moranden looked into the other's eyes and saw his death waiting there, as Mirain's waited in his own. He laughed at the paradox of it and made a hammer of his fist. Mirain caught it, set his weight against it, swung all that massive body about. Unbalancing it; wrenching the captive arm up and back. Moranden howled and flailed left-handed.

Mirain rocked with the blows; his lip split and bled. He tightened his grip. His jaw set beneath dirt and blood. He twisted.

The bone snapped. Moranden bellowed like a bull. The force of his struggle flung Mirain's light weight away. But his arm was still prisoner, his pain a white agony. He hurled himself through it; his good hand clawed, raking breast and face, groping for eyes. He found the thick hair working free of its plait. With a snarl of triumph he wound his fingers into it.

Mirain let go the useless wrist. His face was a terrible thing, stretched out of all humanity by the grip on his hair, the bones thrusting fierce and sharp through the skin. Suddenly he went limp. Moranden loosened his hold a fraction, shifting to peer into the slack face. Two hands joined shot upward, smote his jaw with an audible crack. His head snapped back. His body arched.

Once more Mirain bestrode his chest. He struggled beneath as a fish struggles when hurled from water into the deadly air, and as vainly, and as mindlessly.

Mirain's cheeks were wet with more than blood, his breath sobbing with more than pain. Again he raised the club of his knotted hands. With all his strength he brought it down, full between the eyes.

There was a long silence. Ages long. Mirain stumbled up, away from the body that had stilled at last. His hands hung limp at his sides. His hair straggled about his face. He was crying like a child.

Vadin damned the circle, damned the Law of Battle. He crossed the line and reached for the trembling shoulders.

Mirain wheeled, poised to kill. But his strength was gone. He wavered; his hands dropped. Sanity dawned in his eyes. "Vadin?" He could hardly speak. "Vadin, I—"

"It's all right," Vadin said, rough with the effort of keeping back his own tears. "It's all right. You're alive. You've won."

Mirain's head tossed from side to side. Vadin laid an arm about his shoulders, pulling him close, stroking away the dirt and blood and tears with a corner of the parti-colored cloak. Mirain neither resisted nor acknowledged his squire's ministrations. "I killed him. I didn't—I wanted—I killed him. Vadin, I killed him!"

His voice was shrill. Vadin nerved himself, and hit him.

Mirain gasped. His head rose. He opened his eyes to the sky, to Avaryan clear and strong and unsullied in a field of cloudless blue. "I killed him." But now he said it calmly, with sane and seemly grief. "He must go to his pyre with all honor. So must they all. Even—even she. She was my bitter enemy; she slew my grandfather, she destroyed my beloved, she would have shattered my kingdom. But she was a great queen."

Vadin could not speak. He was no godborn king. He had no power to forgive what was beyond forgiving.

Mirain's head bowed, raised again. He straightened. Vadin let him go. He faced his judges, standing erect and royal although the tears ran unchecked down his face. "Do your office," he commanded.

They woke as from a trance. The herald turned toward the west with his rod uplifted, its tip of amber catching the bitter light. But Obri faced the east, and ivory glowed with his own springing joy, proclaiming Mirain's victory.

They turned back to Mirain. Obri knelt and kissed his hand: homage as rare as it was heartfelt. Mirain found a smile for him, although it did not live long.

The herald stood stiff, fist clenched grey-knuckled upon his rod. Half of his anger was fear, and an awe for which he despised himself. He forced words through his clenched teeth. "You have won. You must put me to death. It is the law. I knew of the weapon which my lady turned against you."

Vadin could have struck the creature. Could he not see how utterly exhausted Mirain was? The king had spent all his strength; he had none left even for joy in his triumph. And he had so much yet to do. Ten thousand men wavered on the brink of battle, their commanders reeling still with the shock of Moranden's defeat. Only that, and the herald's stillness, held them back from a charge.

Mirain regarded the herald with eyes in which the god's fire burned ashen low. "You and all your people are bound to me now until death or I shall free you. That is a penalty more fitting than swift death, and perhaps more terrible."

For a long moment the herald did not stir. Then he bent down and down, even to the ground. His voice boomed forth as if from the earth itself. "Hail, Mirain, king in Ianon!"

Mirain's own men echoed him, clashing spear upon shield, shaking the sky with their jubilation.

The west was silent. Ominously silent.

Somewhere amid the ranks a great voice rang out. "Mirain!" Another joined it. Another. Another. Five, ten, a hundred, a thousand. It rose like a wave, and crested, and crashed down upon him. "Mirain! King in Ianon! Mirain!"

He moved away from his judges and his witness. The army of the west advanced with weapons reversed, chanting his name. But his eyes lifted, fixing beyond it where Ianon's mountains marched against the sky. Shadow lay coiled among them. He raised his golden hand. "Some-day," he said, "I will chain you."

The Mad One burst free at last from the bonds of his will and plunged into the circle. Herald and squire and scholar parted before him. A hair's breadth from Mirain's body, the flying hoofs settled into stillness. The horned head bent, nostrils flaring at the scent of blood and battle. Softly Obri laid the scarlet cloak about Mirain's shoulders; Vadin set the torque about his throat. The Mad One knelt. Mirain settled in the saddle; smoothly the senel rose.

East and west and all about them, the armies came together, clashed, and mingled. One army, one kingdom. And above them all one banner: The Sun-standard of Ianon's king.

Mirain bowed under the weight of them all: grief and joy and king-ship, and triumph wrested from black defeat. But somewhere in the depths of his soul, he found a seed of strength. His eyes kindled. He drew himself erect, squared his shoulders, flung back his hair. The ar-mies roared his name. He rode forth from the circle to claim his own.

THE LADY
OF HAN-GILEN

To my agent, Jane Butler
For performance above and beyond
the call of duty

Endros Ap Shipdor
The Realms of the Sunborn

One

"**E**LIAN! OH, LADY! ELIAN!"

The Hawkmaster paused in mending a hood and raised an inquiring brow. Elian laid a finger on her lips.

The voice drew nearer, a high sweet voice like a bird's. "Lady? Lady, where *have* you got to? Your lady mother—"

Elian sighed deeply. It was always her lady mother. She bound off her last stitch and smoothed the crest of feathers thus attached to the hood: feathers the color of fire or of new copper, rising above soft leather dyed a deep and luminous green. Flame and green for the ruling house of Han-Gilen: green to match her much-patched coat, flame no brighter than her hair.

She laid the hood in the box with the others she had made, and rose. The Hawkmaster watched her. Although he was not mute, he seldom spoke save to address his falcons in their own wild tongue. He did not speak now, nor did she. But his eyes held a smile for her.

In the mews beyond the workroom, the hooded falcons rested on their perches. The small russet hunters for the ladies and the servants; the knights' grey beauties, each with its heraldic hood; her brother's red hawk shifting restlessly in its bonds, for it was young and but newly proven; and in solitary splendor, the white eagle which came to no hand but that of the prince her father.

Her own falcon drowsed near her brother's. Though smaller, it was swifter, and rarer even than the eagle: a golden falcon from the north.

Her father's gift for her birth-feast, a season past. It had been new-caught then; soon it would be ready for proving, that first, free hunt, when the bird must choose to come back to its tamer's hand or to escape into freedom.

She paused to stroke the shimmering back with a feather. The falcon roused slightly from its dream, a tightening of talons on the perch, an infinitesimal turning of the blinded head.

"Lady!"

The mews erupted in a flurry of wings and fierce hawk-screams. Only the eagle held still. The eagle, and Elian's falcon, that opened its beak in a contemptuous hiss and was silent.

The Hawkmaster emerged from his workroom, followed by his two lads. Wordlessly they set about soothing their charges.

The cause of the uproar paid it no heed at all. She fit her voice admirably well, plump and pretty, wrinkling her delicate nose at the scents of the mews and holding her skirts well away from the floor. "Lady, *look* at you! What her highness will say—"

Elian had already thrust past her, nearly oversetting her into the mud of the yard.

The Princess of Han-Gilen sat among her ladies in a bower of living green, her gown all green and gold, and a circlet of gold binding her brows. A delicate embroidery lay half finished in her lap; one of her ladies plucked a soft melody upon a lute.

She contemplated her daughter for a long while in silence. Elian kept her back straight and her chin up, but she was all too painfully aware of the figure she cut. Her coat had been her brother's; it was ancient, threadbare, and much too large. Her shirt and breeches and boots fit well enough, but they stood in sore need of cleaning. She bore with her a faint but distinct odor of the stables, overlaid with the pungency of the mews. She was, in short, a disgrace.

The princess released Elian from her gaze to stitch a perfect blossom. Once the most beautiful woman in her father's princedom of Sarios, she remained the fairest lady in Han-Gilen. Her smooth skin was the color of honey; her eyes were long and dark and enchantingly tilted, with fined arching brows; her hair beneath its drift of veil was deep bronze with golden lights. Her one flaw, the chin which was a shade too pronounced, a shade too obstinate, only strengthened her beauty. Without it she would have been lovely; with it, she was breathtaking.

At last she spoke. "We have been searching for you since the morning."

"I was riding." In spite of all her efforts, Elian knew she sounded sullen. "Then I had an hour with the Hawkmaster. Will you be keeping me long, Mother? The embassy from Asanion will be arriving today, and Father has a council just before. He bade me—"

"At your insistence." The princess' voice was soft but unyielding. "He is the most indulgent of fathers. Yet even he would not be pleased to see you as you are now."

Elian battled an impulse to straighten her coat. "I would not attend council in this state, my lady."

"Let us hope that you would not," said the princess. "I have heard that you have done so in garb but little more proper. Breeched and booted, and at your side a dagger." The princess continued her embroidery, each word she spoke as careful and as minutely calculated as the movements of her needle. "When you were still a child, I suffered it, since your father seemed inclined to encourage it. There were some who even found it charming: Han-Gilen's willful Lady trailing after her brothers, insisting that she be taught as they were taught. You learned fighting and hawking and wild riding; you can read, you can write, you can speak half a dozen tongues. You have all the arts of a Gileni prince."

"And those of a princess as well!" Elian burst out. "I can sew a fine stitch. I can dance a pretty dance. I can play the small harp and the greater harp and the lute. I have a full repertoire of songs, all charming, all suitable for a lady's bower."

"And some scarcely fit for a guardroom." The princess set down her work and folded her hands over it. "My daughter, you have been a woman for three full years. When I was as old as you, I had been two years a wife and nigh three seasons a mother."

"And always," muttered Elian, "a perfect lady."

The princess smiled, startling her a little. "Nay, daughter, I had been a famous hoyden. But I had not so doting a father, nor so lax a mother. With the coming of my woman's courses, I had perforce to put on a gown and bind up my hair and accept the husband my family had found for me. I was fortunate. He was scarce a decade older than I; he was comely; and he was kind to me. The man chosen for my sister had been none of those things."

Elian's hands were fists. She kept her voice level with an effort of will, so level that it was flat. "I have another suitor."

"Indeed," said the princess with unruffled patience. "One whom you would do well to treat with something resembling courtesy."

"Have I ever done any less?"

The princess drew a slow breath: her first sign of temper. "You have been . . . polite. With utmost politeness you rode with Lord Uzian the Hunter, and brought back two stags for his every one, and slew the boar which would have destroyed him. You saved his life; he remembered an earlier betrothal and departed. When the two barons Insh'ai would have dueled for your hand, you offered most politely to engage each one and to accept the one who bested you. You defeated them both, and thus they lost you with the match. Then I call to mind your courtesy to the Prince Komorion. Lover of scholarly dabate that he was, you engaged him in dispute, demolishing him so utterly that he retreated to a house of the Grey Monks and forsook all claim to his princedom."

"He was more than half a monk already," Elian said sharply. "I had no desire to wed a saint."

"Apparently you have no desire to wed at all." Elian opened her mouth to speak, but the princess said, "You are the daughter of the Red Prince, the Lady of Han-Gilen. Hitherto you have been permitted to run wild, not only because your father loves you to the point of folly; I too can understand how sweet is freedom. But you are no longer a child. It is time you became a woman in more than body."

"I will wed," said Elian, speaking with great care, "when I find a man who can stand beside me. Who will not stalk away in a temper when I best him; who will be able, on occasion, to best me. An equal, Mother. A king."

"Then it were best that you find him soon." The velvet had fallen aside at last, baring steel. "Today with the embassy of Asanion comes the High Prince Ziad-Ilarios himself, heir to the throne of the Golden Empire. He has sent word that he comes not only to propose a new and strong alliance with Han-Gilen; it would be his great pleasure to seal that alliance by a union with the Flower of the South."

Elian had never felt less like a flower, unless it were the flameflower, that consumed itself with its own fire. "And if it is not *my* pleasure?"

"I encourage you to consider it." The princess raised a slender hand. "Kieri. Escort my lady to her chamber. She will prepare herself to meet with the high prince."

Elian stood stiff and still in a flutter of ladies. They had bathed her and scented her. Now they arrayed her in the elaborate gown of a Gileni princess. A tall mirror cast back her image, mocking her. She had not been a comely child: awkward, gangling, all arms and legs and eyes. But suddenly, as she grew into a woman, she had changed. Her awkwardness turned to a startling grace, her thinness to slenderness, her angles to curves that caught many a man's eye. And her face—her strong-jawed, big-eyed face, with her mother's honey skin and her father's fire-bright hair—had shaped itself into something much too unusual for prettiness. People looked and called it interesting; looked again, much longer, and declared it beautiful.

She glowered at it. Her gown dragged at her; a maid weighted her with gold and jewels, while another arrayed her hair in the fashion of a maiden, falling loose and fiery to her knees. Gently, with skillful hands, a third lady began to paint her face. Rose-honey for her lips, honey-rose for her cheeks, and a shimmer of gilt about her eyes.

A low whistle brought her about sharply, winning a hiss of temper from the maid with the brushes. Elian's glare turned to laughter and back to a glare again as her brother fell to his knees before her. "Ah, fairest of ladies!" he cried extravagantly. "How my heart longs for you!"

She cuffed him; he swayed aside, laughing, and leaped to his feet. He was tall and lithe, and as like to her in face and form as any man could be. Unlike most men of the Hundred Realms, who reckoned their beards a deformity and shaved or plucked them into smoothness, he had let his own grow to frame his face. It made him look striking, rakish, and more outrageously handsome than ever.

"And all too well you know it," said Elian, tugging at it.

"*Ai,* woman! You have a hard hand. And you so fair the god himself would sigh after you. Are you setting yourself to melt the hearts of Father's whole council?"

"If Mother has her way," Elian said grimly, "I'll win a better prize than that. Prince Ziad-Ilarios is coming to have a look at the merchandise."

Halenan's laughter retreated to his eyes. "So I've heard. Is that why your anger is fierce enough to set me burning even in my lady's chamber?"

"Little help you need there," she said.

He grinned. "I find marriage more than congenial. Even after five years of it."

"Don't you?" She thought of his two sons, and of his lady in her bower awaiting in milky calm the advent of their sister. A love match, that had been, and it had startled most of Han-Gilen; for his bride was neither a great lady nor a great beauty, but the broad-hipped, sweet-faced, eminently sensible daughter of a very minor baron. That good sense had taken her quite placidly from her father's minute holding to the palace of the Red Prince's heir, and kept her there through all the murmurings of the court, as the high ones waited in vain for her handsome husband to tire of her.

With a sharp gesture Elian dismissed her ladies. As the last silken skirt vanished behind the door, she faced her brother. "You know why I can't do as Mother is asking."

"I know why you think you can't."

"I gave my word," she said.

"The word of a child."

"The word of the Lady of Han-Gilen."

He raised his hands, not quite as if he wanted to shake her. "Lia, you were eight years old."

"And he was fifteen," she finished for him, with very little patience. "And he was my brother in all but blood, and people were plenty who said he was that too, because no man could be the son of a god, least of all the son of the Sun. And whether he was half a god or all a man, he was heir by right to a barbarian kingdom, and when the time came, he went to claim his own. He had to go. I had to stay. But I promised him: My time would come. I would go to fight with him. Because his mother left him a kingdom, but his father begot him to rule the world."

Halenan opened his mouth, closed it. Once he would not have been so kind. Once he would have said what he could not keep from thinking. The thinking was cruel enough between them who were mageborn and magebred. To Mirain their foster brother, son of a priestess and a god, great mage and warrior even in his youth, Elian had been the merest infant: his sister, his shadow, trailing after him like a worshipful hound. Wherever he was, she was sure to be. It was certain proof of his parentage, a wag had said once. Who but a god's son could endure such constant adoration?

And now he was a man grown, king in distant Ianon and raising legends about his name. If he even remembered her, it would not be as a woman who kept her word; it would be as a child who had wept to lose her brother, and sworn a child's heedless oath, more threat than promise.

"What will you do?" Halenan pricked at her. "Join his harem in Han-Ianon?"

"He has slaves enough," she snapped, the sharper for that her cheeks had caught fire. "I will fight for him, and wield my magery for him, and be free."

"And if he has changed? What then, Lia? What if he has gone barbarian? Or worse, gone all strange with the god's power that is in him?"

"Then," she said with steadiness she had fought for, "I will make him remember what he was."

Halenan set his hands on her shoulders. She came perilously close to laughing. Even in the utmost of exasperation, he took care not to rumple her gown. That much, husbandhood had done for him.

He glared at her, but half of it was mirth. "Little sister, tell me the truth. You do all of this simply to drive the rest of us mad."

"I do it because I can do nothing else."

"Exactly." He let her go and sighed. "Maybe after all you should go to Mirain. He could make you see sense when no one else could."

"I will go when it is time to go."

"And meanwhile, you turn away suitor after suitor, and refuse adamantly to tell even Father why you do it."

"You don't, either."

"I keep my promises." Their eyes met; his wavered the merest fraction. He rallied with a flare of Gilen temper. "Maybe I should. Mother would see the perfect resolution: a match between you and your oldest love. With the Hundred Realms for a dowry, and Avaryan's Throne for a marriage couch, and—"

She struck him with a lash of power. It stopped his mouth. It did not stop his mind. He was laughing at her. He always laughed at her, even when she pricked him to a rage.

"It's love," he said, "and absurdity. And maybe desperation."

"You never were a match for me."

He bowed to the stroke, utterly unoffended. "Come now, O my conqueror. We're late for council."

Two

THE HIGH PRINCE ZIAD-ILARIOS BOWED LOW BEFORE the Lady of Han-Gilen. When he straightened, he stood still, his eyes steady upon her, a long measuring look that warmed into approval. She returned it with no expression at all. He was fair even for a westerner, his hair like hot gold, his eyes as golden as a falcon's, his skin the color of fine ivory; though no taller than she, he was deep-chested and strong, and very good to look on.

Her stare should have disconcerted him; it made him smile, a remarkably sweet smile, like a child's. But no child ever had a voice so rich or so deep. "My lady, you are fairer even than I looked for, with but songs and painted likenesses to guide me."

She had a weakness for a fine voice. Grimly she suppressed it. "Indeed, highness, you flatter me."

He would not err so far as to bow again. Nor would he oblige her by speaking as most men did to a lovely woman, as to an idiot child. "I have an unfortunate flaw, my lady. I tend to speak my mind. You must forgive me. Should I abase myself at your surpassingly comely feet?"

Before she knew it, she was laughing. Some people said that her merriment was like bells; others, that it was much too free for a maiden's. They stared now, discreetly enough, to be sure: all her father's court, even her father enthroned under his golden canopy with his princess beside him. He smiled, a softening of his dark stern face;

she looked away, back to her companion. Oh yes, he was a pleasing young man. She could do far worse than he.

He was smiling again and inviting her, not quite touching her hand, walking slowly through the glittering throng. She matched his pace. No one impeded them, although everyone watched them. "Already they have us wedded," she said.

He eluded the trap as neatly as if it had never been laid. "That is the sport of lesser mortals: to make legends of their rulers. Your legend is fascinating, my lady. In Asanion, we cannot decide whether it is a wonder or a scandal. A princess, yet you have mastered all the arts of princehood; you challenge your suitors to defeat you in their own chosen skills, and send them away when you find them wanting."

"And what is your skill?" she demanded of him.

He shrugged, a minute gesture, barely visible within his golden robes. "None. Except, perhaps, that of ruling. 'Kinging it,' the common folk would say. I do it rather well."

"You speak our tongue very well indeed."

"That is part of it. So much of ruling is in the tongue. Too much, some might add."

"Especially here in the Hundred Realms."

"In the Golden Empire, fully as much. You are eloquent, I am told, and have the gift of tongues."

"I like to talk."

"Why, so do I. But wit is hard to come by, and one cannot always converse with oneself."

"I talked a philosopher into the ground once. He sought to wed me; he wedded with solitude instead."

"He made a poor choice."

"Did he? I am thinking of taking a vow, my lord. To take lovers by the dozen, but never a husband."

"Surely you would grow weary of constant variety."

"Do you think I would?" She halted in the midst of the court and fixed her eyes upon him. "Have you?"

His laughter was as sweet as his smile. "Oh, long since! Twice nine-score concubines: that is the number allotted to the heir of Asanion. One for each day of the sun's year. Alas, I am cursed with a constant nature; where I take pleasure, there do I most prefer to love. So you see, if I follow my nature, some few of my ladies are content; the rest either dissolve in tears or succumb to murderous envy. But if I strive to please them all, I fail utterly to content myself."

"So you seek a wife."

"So I seek a wife. A married man, you see, may free his concubines."

"Ah," she said in something close to delight. "Your motives are hardly pure at all. I had begun to fear that there would be no flaw in you."

"But surely perfection is most unutterably dull?"

"You are not tall. That is a flaw, but one I cannot in conscience condemn; for you are also beautiful."

"In Asanion I am reckoned a tall man."

"And fair?"

"That is not a word we like to use in speaking of men. But yes, they call me comely. We breed for it."

"My mother has Asanian blood." Elian changed tacks abruptly, fixing him with her most disconcerting stare. "Some said that you would not come to us; that your borders are beset, and that your father has need of you there."

Ilarios was not disconcerted at all. He shifted as rapidly and as smoothly as she. "He has greater need of Han-Gilen and the Hundred Realms." His eyes leveled. They were all gold, like an animal's, but the light in them was godly bright. "You know what concerns us."

"The barbarians in the north."

"Even so. We have never exerted ourselves to conquer them, reckoning them little better than savages, too deeply embroiled in their own petty feuds to unite against us. So they should have remained. But they have spawned a monster, it seems. A chieftain—he calls himself a king —who seized the throne of one of the northern provinces—"

"Ianon," she murmured.

"Ianon," he agreed, with a swift glance. "He usurped its throne, gathered its clans, and proceeded to do the same to its neighbors. It was easier than it might have been. He rode—rides still, for the matter of that—under the banner of the Sun-god; his father, so he claims, is the god himself, his mother—"

He broke off. For once, Elian could see, his ready tongue had led him farther than he liked to go.

She led him to the end of it. "His mother was a priestess, born in Ianon but raised to the greatest eminence of her order: high priestess of the Temple of Avaryan in Han-Gilen. In addition to which, she was prophet of the realm, and bound in close friendship with its prince." She smiled, closing in for the kill. "Tell me more of her son."

"But surely—" He stopped. His eyes knew what she did, and dared to guess why. They flickered as a hawk's will, veiling just perceptibly. Calmly he said, "Her son appeared in Ianon some few summers past.

He was little more than a child then; he is, so they say, very young still. But he is a skilled general, for a barbarian, and he has a knack of gathering men to himself. Hindered not at all by the parentage he claims and the destiny he has revealed to any who will listen. The world is his, he proclaims. He was born to rule it."

"Simply to rule it?" asked Elian.

"Ah," said Ilarios, "he says that it is not simple at all. He is the trueborn heir of Avaryan, the emperor foretold, the Sword of the Sun; he will bring all the world under his sway, and cast down the darkness and bind it in chains, and found an imperishable empire."

"He says? Have you spoken with him?"

"Would the son of the Sun deign to speak with a mere high prince of Asanion?"

She regarded him sidelong. "If he were anywhere within reach of you, he might."

"Soon he may be. However mad his ambitions may be, his generalship is entirely sane. With an army no larger than the vanguard of our own, he has set all the north under his heel. Since winter loosed its hold, he has begun to threaten our northern satrapies. We suspect that, should he fail there, he will move east and south into the Hundred Realms."

"We in turn suspect that he will move first against us, thinking to forge an alliance, and with our strength to advance upon Asanion."

"So he might," Ilarios said. "And so I am here, rather than in the north of the empire. We have much more to fear from a barbarian allied with you than from a barbarian alone."

"That would be a deadly joining, would it not? A hundred realms, a hundred quarrels, we say here, but at need we can band together. Not easily, not for long, but long enough to drive back any enemy. The Nine Cities, the last time. I was very young, but I remember. Have you ever fought in a war?"

He seemed no more disturbed by this latest barb than by anything else she had said. "There has been no war since I was a child."

"But if there had been?"

"I would have fought in it. The heir of the empire commands its armies."

"The Sunborn has been a warrior since his childhood. He rides always in the van, with scarlet cloak and plume lest anyone fail to know him. And under him a demon in the shape of a black charger, fully as terrible in battle as its master."

For the first time, Prince Ilarios frowned. "He is a demon himself, they say, a mighty sorcerer, a shapeshifter who may choose to be seen as a giant among his northern giants, or as a dwarf no taller than a nine-days' infant. But in his own flesh he is nothing to look at, little larger than a child, with no beauty at all."

"What, none?"

"So I have heard."

Elian looked at him, head tilted. "You would be delighted if he were hideous, would you not?"

"Women sigh at the thought of him. Young, barbarian, and half a god —how wonderful. How enchanting."

"How utterly exasperating. You, after all, were born to be emperor; if you become a great conqueror, you but do as your fathers have done before you. Whereas this upstart has but to gather a handful of mountain tribes and he becomes a mighty hero."

"Who is blasphemous enough to name Avaryan his father. They call him An-Sh'Endor: God-begotten, Son of the Morning." Ilarios sighed and let his ill temper fade. "He vaunts; but more to the point, he conquers. Much to our distaste. We prefer our world as it is, and not as some young madman would have it."

"Oh, yes, he is mad. God-mad." She smiled, but not at Ilarios. "His birthname is Mirain. He was my foster brother. One morning before dawn he left us. I saw him go. I like to think I helped him, though what could a small girlchild do when her brother would leave and her father would have him stay? except follow him and get in his way and try not to cry. The last thing he did was cuff me and tell me to stop my sniffling, and promise to come back." And the last thing she had done was to swear her great oath. But that was no matter for this stranger's pondering.

This stranger had clearer eyes than any outlander should have, and he no mage nor seer, only a mortal man. They rested level upon her, and they granted no quarter. "Ah," he said, soft and deep. "You were in love with him"

She met stroke with stroke. "Of course I was. He was all that was wonderful, and I was eight summers old."

"Yet now you are a woman. I can make you an empress."

Her throat had dried. She defied it with mockery. "What, prince! A barbarian queen over the Golden Empire? Could your people endure the enormity of it?"

"They will endure whatever I bid them endure." He was all iron, saying it. Then he was all gold as he smiled at her. "Your high heart would not be content with the place of a lesser wife, however honored, however exalted. Nor would I set you so low."

"Nor would Mirain," she said, reckless. "I knew him once. You, I do not know at all."

"That can be remedied," he said.

She looked at him. She was shaking. She stiffened, angrily, and made herself toss her head. "Ah! Now I see. You are jealous of him."

He smiled with all the sweetness in the world. It was deadly, because there was no malice in it. "Perhaps. He is a dream and a memory. I am here and real and quite royal, though no god sired me. And I know that I could love you."

"I think," she said slowly, "that I could . . . very easily . . ." He waited, not daring to move. But hope shone in his eyes. Splendid eyes, all gold. He was beautiful; he was all that a woman could wish for, even a princess.

Except. *Except.* She curtsied, hardly knowing what she did, and fled blindly.

The nightlamp was lit in her chamber. Her ladies flocked about her; she tore herself free and bolted her door against them all.

She flung off her robes and her ornaments, scoured the paint from her face. It stared from her mirror, all eyes, with the wildness of a trapped beast.

A trap, yes. This one was most exquisitely baited. So fair a young man; he spoke to her as an equal, and looked at her with those splendid eyes, and promised her a throne.

And why not? asked a small demon-voice, deep in her mind. *Only a fool or a child would refuse it.*

"Then I am both." She met her mirrored glare. Either she would accept this prince and ride off with him to Asanion, splendid in the robes of an empress-to-be. Or—

Or.

Mirain.

Her throat ached with the effort of keeping back a cry. It had all been so simple, all her life mapped and ordained. A childhood of training and strengthening; and when she became a woman, she would ride to take her place at Mirain's right hand. Her suitors had been a nuisance, but easy enough to dispose of: not one was her equal. Not one could make her forget her oath.

Until this one. It was not only a fair face and a sweet voice. It was the whole of him. He was perfection. He was made to be her lover.

"No," she gritted to the air. "No. I must not. I have sworn."

You have sworn. Do you intend ever to fulfill it? Behold, here you stand, a legend in your own right, acknowledged a master of the arts of princes: why have you never gone as you vowed to go?

"It was not time."

It was no vow. You will never go. It would be folly, and well you know it. Better far to take this man who offers himself so freely, and to submit as every woman must submit to the bonds of her body.

"No," she said. It was a whisper, lest she scream it. Not that Ilarios would bind her. That he could, so easily; and that her word had bound her long ago. If she lingered, she was forsworn, surely and irrevocably. If she left, she lost Ilarios. And for what? A child's dream. A man who by now had become a stranger.

Her eyes darted about. At her familiar chamber; at her gown flung upon the floor; at her mirror. At her reflection in its shift of fine linen, boy-slim but for the high small breasts. Her hair was a wild tangle, bright as fire. She gathered it in her hands, pulling it back from her face. Her features were fine but strong, like Halenan's when he was a boy. Prettiness, never. But beauty all too certainly. And wit. And royal pride. She cursed them all.

Prince Ilarios would remain for all of Brightmoon's cycle. A scant hour with him had all but overcome her. A month . . .

Her dagger lay upon the table, strange among the bottles of scent and paint, the little coffers of jewels, the brushes and combs and ointments. A man's dagger, deadly sharp, Hal's gift for her birth-feast. Freeing one hand from her hair, she drew the blade.

For the honor of her oath.

The bright bronze flashed toward her throat, and veered. One deft stroke, two, three. Her hair pooled like flame about her feet. A stranger stood in it, a boy with a wild bright mane hacked off above his shoulders.

A boy with a definite curve of breast.

She bound it tight and flat, and hid it beneath her leather riding tunic. Breeched and booted, with sword and dagger at her belt and a hunter's cap over her hair, she was the image of her brother in his youth, even to the fierce white grin and the hint of a swagger.

She swallowed sudden, wild laughter. If her mother knew what she did now, woman grown or no, she would win a royal whipping.

Han-Gilen's palace was large, ancient, and labyrinthine. When she was very young, she had managed with her brothers to find passages no one else knew of. One such opened behind an arras in her own chamber. She had used it once before, for it led almost directly to the postern gate, and near it a long-forgotten bolt-hole: when Mirain eluded the prince's guardianship to vanish into the north.

Now she followed him, lightless as he had been then, cold and shaking as she had been when she crept in his wake. In places the way was narrow, so that she had to crawl sidewise; elsewhere the ceiling dipped low, driving her to hands and knees. Dust choked her; small live things fled her advance. More than once she paused. She could not do this. It was too early. It was too late.

She must. She said it aloud, startling the echoes into flight. "I *must.*"

Her shorn hair brushed her cheek. She tossed it back, set her jaw, and went on.

With Asanion's prince in the city, even the postern gate was guarded. Elian crouched in shadow, watching the lone armed man. From where he stood with a cresset over his head, he commanded the gate and a goodly portion of the approach to it, and the hidden entrance to the bolt-hole. Despite the obscurity of his post, he was zealous. He kept himself alert, pacing up and down in the circle of light, rattling his sword in its scabbard.

Elian caught her lower lip between her teeth. What she had to do was forbidden. More than forbidden. Banned.

So was all she did on this mad night.

She drew a cautious breath. The man did not hear. Carefully she cleared her mind of all but the need to pass the gate. More carefully still, she lowered her inner shields one by one. Not so much as to lie open to any power that passed; but not so little as to bind her strength within, enclosed and useless.

Thoughts murmured on the edge of consciousness, a babel of minds, indistinguishable. But one was close, brighter than the rest. Little by little she enfolded it. *Rest,* she willed it. *Rest and see. No one will pass. All is quiet; all remains so. All danger sleeps.*

The man paused in his pacing, hand on hilt, immobile beneath the torch. His eyes scanned the circle of its light. They saw nothing. Not even the figure which left the shadows and passed him, walking softly but without stealth. Shadow took it; his mind, freed, held no memory of captivity.

At the end of darkness lay starlight and free air. But a shape barred the way.

So near to escape, and yet so far. Elian's teeth bared; she snatched her dagger.

Long strong fingers closed about her wrist, forcing the weapon back to its sheath. "Sister," said Halenan, "there's no need to murder me."

Fight him though she would, he was stronger; and he had had the same teachers as she. At length she was still.

He let her go. She made no attempt to bolt. Her eyes caught his, held. He would weaken. He would let her pass. He would—

She cried out in pain.

His voice was soft in the gloom. "You forget, Lia. Mind-tricks succeed only with the mind-blind. Which I am not."

"I won't go back," she said, low and harsh.

He drew her out of the tunnel into the starlight. Brightmoon had risen; though waning, it was bright enough for such eyes as theirs. He ran a hand over her cropped hair. "So. This time you mean it. Did the Asanian repel you as strongly as that?"

"No. He drew me." Her teeth rattled; she clenched her jaw. "I won't go back, Hal. I can't." He lifted a brow. She pressed on before he could begin anew the old battle. "Mirain is riding southward. I'll catch him before he enters the Hundred Realms. If he means us ill, I'll stop him. I won't let him bring war on our people."

"What makes you think you can sway him?"

"What makes you think I can't?"

He paused, drew a sharp breath, let it go. "Mother will be more than displeased with you. Father will grieve. Prince Ilarios—"

"Prince Ilarios will press for the alliance, because he stands in dire need of it. Let me go, Hal."

"I'm not holding you." He stepped aside. Beyond him a shadow stirred, moving into the moonlight. Warm breath caressed Elian's cheek; her own red mare whickered in her ear. She was bridled, saddled. On the saddle Elian found a familiar shape: bow and laden quiver.

Tears pricked. Fiercely she blinked them away. Halenan stood waiting; she thought of battering him down. For knowing, damn him. For helping her. She flung her arms about him.

"Give Mirain my greetings," he said, not as lightly as he would perhaps have liked. "And tell him—" His voice roughened. "Tell the damned fool that if he sets foot in my lands, it had better be as a friend; or god's son though he be, I'll have his head on my spear."

"I'll tell him," she said.

"Do that." He laced his fingers; she set her foot in them and vaulted lightly into the saddle. Even as she gathered the reins, her brother was gone, lost in the shadows of the tunnel.

Three

ONCE ELIAN HAD BEGUN, SHE DID NOT LOOK BACK. With Brightmoon on her right hand, she turned her face toward the north.

She kept to the road, riding swiftly, trusting to the dark and to her mare's sure feet. Lone riders were common enough in peaceful Han-Gilen: travelers, messengers, postriders of the prince. Nor yet did she look for pursuit. Halenan would see to that.

The first light of dawn found her in the wooded hills, looking down from afar upon her father's city. The nightflame burned low upon the topmost tower of the temple of the Sun. She fancied that she could hear the dawn bells, and the high pure voices of the priestesses calling to the god.

She swallowed hard. Suddenly the world was very wide, and the road was very narrow, and there was only captivity at either end of it. East, west, south—any of them would take her, set her free.

The mare fretted against a sudden tightening of the reins. Abruptly Elian wheeled her about, startling her into a canter. Northward, away from the Asanian. Northward to her oath's fulfilling.

By sunrise the mare had slowed to a walk. Hill and wood lay between Elian's eyes and the city; she drowsed in the saddle.

The mare stumbled. Elian jolted into wakefulness. For an instant, memory failed her; she looked about wildly. The senel had halted in a glade, and finding no resistance, begun to graze.

Elian slid to the ground. A great rock reared above her, with a stream leaping down the face of it and a pool at its foot. The mare stepped delicately into the water, ruffled it with her breath, and drank. After a moment Elian followed her. First she took off the mare's bit and bridle, then the saddle; then she lay on her face by the pool, drinking deep.

The mare nibbled her hair. She batted the dripping muzzle aside, and laughed as water ran down her neck. With sudden recklessness she plunged her head into the pool, rising in an icy spray. All thought of sleep had fled; hunger filled its place.

Her saddle pouches were full, every one. She found wine, cheese, new bread and journeybread, fruit and meat and a packet of honey sweets. At the last she laughed, but with a catch at the end of it. Who but Hal would have remembered that gluttonous passion of hers?

"He knows me better than I know myself." The mare, rolling in the ferns, took no notice of her. She ate sparingly and drank a little of the wine. The sun was warm upon her damp head. She lay back in the sweet-scented grass and closed her eyes.

The dream at first was sunlit, harmless. A woman walked in a garden under the sun. She wore the plain white robe of a priestess in the temple of Han-Gilen, her hair braided down her back, a torque gleaming golden at her throat. There was a flower in her hair, white upon raven.

She turned, bending with rare grace to pluck a second blossom, and Elian saw her face. It was a striking, foreign face, eagle-keen and very dark, the face of a woman from the north. On her breast lay the golden disk of the High Priestess of Avaryan.

A child ran down the path, a boy in shirt and breeches that sorely needed a washing, his hair a riot of unshorn curls. "Mother, come and see! Fleetfoot had her colt, and he's all white, and his eyes are blue, and Herdmaster says he's demon-gotten but Foster-father says nonsense. I say nonsense too. There's no dark in him, only colt-thoughts. Herdmaster wants to give him to the temple. Come and see him!"

The priestess laughed and smoothed his tangled hair. He was as dark as she, with the same striking face and the same great black eyes set level in it. "Come and claim him, you mean to say. Is it a white war-stallion you're wanting, then?"

"Not for me," he said. "For you. For the best rider in the world."

"Flatterer." Still laughing, she let him pull her to the garden's gate.

It flew open. Mother and son halted. A man flung himself at the priestess' feet. In face, garb, and bearing he was a commoner, a farmholder of Han-Gilen with the earth of his steading upon his feet.

"Lady," he gasped. "Lady, great sickness—my woman, my sons—all at once, out of blue heaven—"

All laughter fled from the priestess' face. She drew taut, as one who listens to a voice on the edge of hearing. Her face twisted, smoothed. Its calm, where a moment before it had been so mobile, was terrible to see. She looked down. "Do you command me, freeman?"

The man clutched her knees. "Lady, they say you are a healer. They say—"

She raised her hand. He stiffened. For a moment he was different, a subtle difference, gone before it won a name. The priestess bowed her head. "Lead me," she said.

He leaped up. "Oh, lady! Thank all the gods I found you here with none to keep me from you. Come now, come quickly!"

But her son held her back with all his young strength. She turned in his grip. For a moment she was herself, brows meeting, warning. "Mirain—"

He held her more tightly, his eyes wide and wild. "Don't go, Mother."

"Lady," the man said. "For the gods' sake."

She stood between them, her eyes steady upon her son. "I must go."

"No." He strove to drag her back. "It's dark. All dark."

Gently but firmly she freed herself. "You will stay here, Mirain. I am called; I cannot refuse. You will see me again. I promise you." She held out her hand to the man. "Show me where I must go."

For a long while after she was gone, Mirain stood frozen. Only his eyes could move, and they blazed.

But the priestess summoned her bay stallion and a mount for the messenger, and rode from the temple. No one took undue notice of her leaving. The lady of the temple often rode out so to work her healing about the princedom, led or followed by a desperate wife or husband, kinsman or kinswoman, village priest or headman. Her miracles were famous, and justly so, gifts of the god who had taken her as his bride.

At last her son broke free from the binding. Running with unwonted awkwardness, stumbling, seeing nothing and no one, he passed the door of the prince's stable. The prince himself was there, that dark man with his bright hair, intent still upon Fleetfoot's foal. Mirain nearly fell against him; stared at him with eyes that saw him not at all; fumbled with the latch of a stall door. A black muzzle thrust through the opening; a body followed it, a wicked, dagger-horned, swift-heeled demon of a pony.

The prince braved hoofs and horns to catch Mirain's shoulders. "Mirain!" The name took shape in more than voice. "Mirain, what haunts you?"

Mirain stood very still. "Mother," he said distinctly. "Treachery. She knows it. She rides to it. They will kill her."

Prince Orsan let him go. He mounted and clapped heels to the sleek sides. Even as he burst into the sunlight, a red stallion thundered after, likewise bridleless and saddleless; but his rider bore a drawn sword.

The farmer's holding lay at a great distance from the city; so he told the priestess, disjointedly, driving his borrowed mount with brutal urgency. Her own stallion, better bred and more lightly ridden, kept a steady pace up from the level land into the hills. They followed the wide North Road; those who passed upon it gave way swiftly before them. Some, knowing the priestess, bowed in her wake.

The road lost itself in trees. The man slowed not at all. He rode well and skillfully for one who could not often have spared time or coin for the art. She let her stallion fall back a little, for the trees were thick, raising root and branch to catch the unwary.

Her guide veered from the track up a steep narrow path treacherous with stones. His mount slid, stumbled, recovered; the priestess heard its laboring breath. "Wait!" she cried. "Will you slay your poor beast?"

His only answer was to lash it with the reins, sending it plunging up the slope. There was light beyond; he vanished into it.

Just short of the summit, the priestess checked her senel. There was fear in her eyes, here where none could see.

None but the god, and Elian dreaming. The god would not speak. Elian could not.

Need not. All this, long ago, the priestess had foreseen. She had chosen it. She must not turn back, now that it had come upon her. Her lips firmed; her eyes kindled. Lightly she touched heel to the bay's side.

The trees opened upon a greensward, a stream and a pool, a loom of stone. By the pool her guide waited. She rode toward him.

Something hissed. Her stallion reared, suddenly wild, stretched to his full height, and toppled, convulsed upon the grass. A black arrow pierced his throat.

The priestess had sprung free and fallen, rolling. Swift though she was, warrior-trained, her long robe hampered her; before she could rise fully, the weight of many bodies bore her down.

After the first instinctive struggle, she lay still. Hard hands dragged her to her feet. Gauntleted hands; masks of woodland green and brown, with eyes glittering behind them.

Her guide had dismounted. Now that his part was ended, he carried himself not at all like a farmholder; his lip curled as he looked at her, and he swaggered, a broad dun-clad figure among the band of forest folk. She met his stare and smiled faintly. His eyes held but a moment before they slid away. "If one of your folk has need of healing," she said, "I will tend him freely, without betrayal."

"Without betrayal, say you?" This was a new voice. It raised a ripple among the reivers: a clear, cold, contemptuous voice with an accent which could only be heard in the very highest houses of Han-Gilen. Its owner advanced through the circle of armed men to stand beside the pool. A body once slender had grown gaunt with time and suffering; hair once red-gold was ashen grey, strained back from a face which even yet was beautiful, like an image cast in bronze. The eyes in it were lovely still, though terrible, black and burning cold.

The priestess regarded her in neither surprise nor fear. "My lady," she said, giving high birth its due, "you are well within the borders of Han-Gilen. It is death for you to walk here."

"Death?" The woman laughed with no hint of mirth. "What is death to the dead?" She moved closer, a tall sexless figure in mottled green, and gazed down from immeasurable heights, too high even for hatred. "Dead indeed, dead and rotted, with a curse upon my grave; for I dared the unthinkable. High priestess of Avaryan in Han-Gilen, face to face with a wandering initiate from the north, I accepted her into my temple. She swore by all the holy things, by the god's own hand she swore that she had kept her vows. To serve the god with all her being; to Journey as he bade her, seven years of wandering, cleaving to his laws; to know no man.

"Aye, she served him well indeed in whatever task we set her, even servants' work, slaves' work, though she boasted that she was the daughter of a king. There were some who thought she might become a saint.

"But saints do not grow big with child. Nor do even common priestesses, unless they hunger after death: the sun-death, chained atop the tower of the temple, with an altar of iron beneath them and Avaryan's crystal above.

"I was slow to see. I was high lady of the temple, and she did her service in the kitchens; and a priestess' robe can hide much. But not the belly of a woman within a Brightmoon-waning of her time, as she bends over a washtub scouring a cauldron. And every priestess in the kitchens moving to conceal her, conspiring against their lady, defying the law of their order.

"I dared observe it. I held the trial. No answer did it gain me, no defense save one, that the miscreant had broken no vows. Her guilt was as clear as her body's shape, stripped now to its shift that strained to cover her. I condemned her. I commanded what by law I must command. 'I have broken no vows,' she said to me, unshakable.

"And who should come upon us but the Prince of Han-Gilen? He defied me, son of my brother though he was, lay votary of the order, bound to obedience within the walls of my temple. His men-at-arms loosed the prisoner, and my priests stood aside with sheathed swords, for she had bewitched them also. I cursed them all. In the law's name I snatched a sword to do execution. And they seized me, my own priests, and my kinsman held me to trial. I had dared to lay hands upon the god's chosen bride, and through her his true-begotten son, heir of Avaryan and emperor that would be. My law had no defense for me; the prince had what he called mercy. Forbearing to put me to death, instead he stripped me of my torque and my office, unbound and cut away my braid, and cast me into exile. And all the while his woman watched me with his bastard in her belly."

The words were like hammer blows, weighted with long years of bitterness. The priestess bore them in silence. When the exile ended at last, the younger woman spoke. "You chose your punishment. You could have kept your office and accepted the truth; or you could have stepped aside in honor, setting me in your place and retiring to the cloister."

"Honor, say you?" The exile's contempt was absolute. "You, who would found an empire on a lie?"

"On the god's own truth."

The exile's face was a mask. "You have found the truth here, O betrayer of your vows. All Han-Gilen lies under your spell. But I have escaped it. I have wielded my freedom in its guise of banishment, to gather such men as will not succumb to sorcery, to restore the shattered law. It remains. It waits to take you."

The priestess smiled. "Not the law; the god. Can you not hear how he calls me?"

"The god has turned his face from you."

"No. Nor has he abandoned you, greatly though you fear it, greatly enough to turn all against him and bow at the feet of his dark sister. When first I came to you, when you saw me and hated me for the love you knew he bore me, how terribly I pitied you; for you had no knowledge at all of his love for you. Rank you had, and power, but where you looked for him you could not find him. You despaired; yet you had but sought him where he was not. He waited still, calling to your deaf ears, waiting for your eyes to turn to him. Even now he cries to you. Will you not listen? Will you not see?"

There were tears in the priestess' eyes, tears of compassion. The exile's hands came up to her face; she thrust them down. Her voice lashed out. "Silence her!"

Blades flashed. The priestess smiled. If she knew pain, it could not touch the heart of her joy.

Hoofs rang upon stone. A deep voice cried out: "Sanelin!" A lighter one rose above it, close to a shriek: *"Mother!"* Black pony and red charger plunged into the glade.

The priestess lay where her captors had flung her, on her back by the water. Bright blood stained the grass. Men howled, trampled under sharpened hoofs, cloven by the prince's sword. She neither heard nor saw. Above her loomed her enemy. The exile's hand rose high, with a dagger glittering in it; yet even as the blade poised to fall, the woman looked up. Hoofs struck at her, both dainty and deadly; a narrow wicked head tossed, slashing sidewise with its horns. She writhed away, about, beneath. Her knife flashed upward, past the pony, toward its rider.

Sanelin cried out. Mirain flung up his hand. Lightnings leaped from it.

The knife found flesh. But its force was feeble. Its wielder cried aloud and reeled, clawing at her eyes, and fled.

The pony stood still, snorting. Mirain wavered half stunned, his hand dangling, burning. The fire flickered in it, burning low now, a golden ember. Sanelin could not draw his gaze, could not speak. A great fist smote him to the ground.

The silence was absolute. No living enemy stood in the glade. The man who had struck Mirain had turned and found himself alone and undefended, with the black pony rearing over him; he had bolted without a sound.

Here and there on the grass huddled shapes clad in mottled green. A red stallion stood over one in green as dark as evening, with a bloodied sword clutched in the lifeless hand. The senel nuzzled the bright tumble of hair, snorting at the scent of blood upon it.

Sanelin's legs would not yield to her will. Slowly, with many pauses, she dragged herself toward her son. He had fallen in a heap, his hand outflung, a long shallow cut stretching red from elbow to wrist. The

palm flamed as if it cupped molten gold. She fell beside it and pressed
her lips to it. It was searing hot, molten indeed, brand and sigil of the
god, with which he had marked his son. And with which he had struck
down the exile. Her anguish shuddered in the earth.

Elian shuddered with it, and gasped. Wind whispered through the
grass. The red senel had dropped its head to graze; no proud stallion
horns crowned its brow, no sorely wounded prince lay at its feet. No
slain men, no boy and no pony, and no dying priestess. Elian was alone
and awake in the place where the holy one had died; where her father
had come close to death, and lived only through Mirain, who coming to
his senses had given the prince what healing the god vouchsafed, and
brought him back to the city.

That was Elian's earliest clear memory: the prince bloodied and unconscious upon the stallion, and the boy riding behind him to steady
him, and the pony following like a hound. And bound to the pony's
back with strips of mottled green, the body of Avaryan's bride.

Elian sat up, shaking. The vision fled; yet in its place grew one that
made her cry out. The face of the slayer, terrible in its beauty, like a
skull of bronze and silver. Its eyes were human no longer, great blind
demon-eyes, pale as flawed pearls. Even in their blindness they hunted,
seeking the one who had destroyed them.

"No," Elian whispered. She hardly knew what she denied. The hate,
yes; the threat to Mirain, and through him to Han-Gilen and its prince.
And perhaps most of all, the dream itself. Such dreams were from the
god, his gift to the princes of Han-Gilen, shaped for the protection of
the realm. But she had forsaken it. She could not be its prophet.

Her mouth was dust-dry. She knelt to drink from the pool, and recoiled with a gasp. Visions seethed in the clear water. Powers, prophecies; fates and fortunes and the deeds of kings. They drew her, eye and
soul, down and down into depths unfathomable save by the trueborn
seer. So much—so much—

Through the spell's glamour pierced a dart of rage. Gods and demons
—how dared they torment her? She bent, and with her eyes tightly shut,
drank long and deeply. Almost she had expected the water to taste of
blood and iron, but it was pure and icy cold; it quenched her terrible
thirst.

Cautiously she opened her eyes. No visions beset them. There was
only the glint of sun on water, and through its ripples the pattern of
stones upon the bottom of the pool.

She sat on her heels. The sun was high in a clear sky, the air warm and richly scented. Her mare grazed calmly, pausing as Elian watched, nipping a fly upon her flank. Whatever power of light or darkness had led her to this hidden meadow, it had left her unperturbed.

A small portion of Elian's mind gibbered at her to mount, to ride, to escape. But cold sanity held her still. Even at this distance from the city, any Gileni peasant would know both mare and rider for royal, and any pursuit would mark them. They were well hidden here where no one ever came; when darkness fell, they could ride.

Elian prowled the glade. Its beauty now seemed a mockery, its shelter a trap. Like Han-Gilen itself, enclosed and beset; like herself.

She made herself sit down, crouching on the grass well away from the pool. The sun crawled across the sky. "I cannot go back," she said over and over. "Let Father see visions, or Hal. I cannot go back!"

The water laughed at her. *Prophet,* it said. *Prince's prophet. You have the gift. You cannot refuse it.*

"I can!" She scrambled to her feet, fumbling for bridle and saddle.

Han-Gilen has had no prophet since the priestess died. Her mantle lies upon the Altar of Seeing over the living water. Go back. Forsake this child's folly. Take what is yours.

The mare skittered away from Elian's hands, eyeing the bridle in mock alarm. It was an old game; but Elian had no patience to spare for it. She snapped a thought like the lash of a whip. The mare stopped as if struck.

So too must you. The soft voice was a water-voice no longer. Deep, quiet, hauntingly familiar. *You play at duty. Yet what is it but flight from the path ordained for you?*

Elian slipped the bridle over the mare's ears, smoothing the long forelock. Her hands were trembling, but her smile mocked them all. "It is not," she said. "It is anything but that."

Is it?

She knew that voice. Oh, yes, she knew it. She hated it.

Hated? Or loved?

She flung pad and saddle over the mare's back, and after them the bags of her belongings, and last of all herself.

Elian.

The voice crept through all her barriers, throbbing to the heart of her.

Elian.

She struck at it. "*You* sent the vision. You tried to trap me. But I won't be held. Not by a lie."

It is no lie, and well you know it. The god has stretched out his hand to you and laid you open to me.

Hands reached for her. She kicked her senel into a jolting trot. The shadows were black under the trees, the sky blood-red beyond the branches.

Elian, come. Come back. Behind her eyelids a figure stood, tall, dark, crowned with fire. *Daughter, it is madness, this that you do. Come back to us.*

"To my oath's betrayal."

To those who love you.

"I cannot."

His thought had borne a hint of sorrow and a promise of forgiveness. Now it hardened. Whatever her mother might say, Prince Orsan of Han-Gilen was far from besotted with his daughter. He had raised her as she wished, as a boy, not only in the freedom but in the punishments, meted out to her precisely as to her brothers. *Elian.* She trembled in the saddle, but urged her mare onward. *This is no child's game. Will you come back, or must I compel you?*

Walls closed in upon her mind. There was but one escape, and her father filled it. Even yet, his eyes held more sorrow than wrath. He held out his hands. *Daughter. Come home.*

With a soft wordless cry she backed away. Her body rode at break-neck pace through a darkening wood. But in her mind she huddled within a fortress made of defiance, and her father towered over her, clothed in the red-golden fire of his magery. He was far stronger than she. *You are of Han-Gilen, blood and bone. This venture is a bitter mockery of both your lineage and your power. So might a child do, or a coward. Not the Lady of Han-Gilen.*

"No." There was no force in the word. Yet somewhere deep within her, a spark kindled. "No. I have sworn an oath. I will keep it, or die in the trying."

You will come home.

His will was as strong as a chain, its links of tempered steel, drawing her to him. In a madness of resistance she clung to the stronghold of her mind. Earth; three walls of will; her father. But above her the open sky. She hurled herself into it.

The mare shied. Elian clutched blindly at the saddle. Her body ached; her fingers could barely unclench from the pommel to take up the reins, to guide her mount. She could not see. For an instant she wavered on the edge of panic; but her eyes, straining, found the shadowy shapes of trees, and through the woven branches a twilit sky.

The mare had settled into a running walk, smooth and swift as water. The footing was good, soft leafmold upon the level surface of a road. Without guidance, the mare had found the northward way through the wood.

Elian tensed to quicken the senel's pace, but did not complete the movement. Her father knew surely where she was and where she went. The forest should have been alive with searchers, the realm with pursuit. But none followed her. Han-Gilen was quiescent about her.

As if, she thought when at last she took time to think, as if, after all, her father was minded to let her go.

She had a brief, striking vision: a hawk, freed to hunt for its master or to escape his will. And far beneath it in its flight, her father, watching, waiting for it to return to his hand.

Anger blurred the image and scattered it. He was so certain; so splendidly, utterly confident that in the end she would yield.

"I'll die first!" she cried.

Four

THE NORTHERN BORDER OF HAN-GILEN WAS CALLED the Rampart of the North, its pass the Eye of the Realm. There the hills rose to lofty ridge and fell sheer, down and down to the rolling green levels of Iban.

Because Iban's lord was tributary and kinsman to the Prince of Han-Gilen, the fortress that guarded the Eye was lightly manned, watchful but not suspicious even of one who rode alone by night. Although Elian's neck prickled and her heart thudded, certain that her father had laid his trap here where she had no escape, no challenge rang from the gate; no armed company barred her way. She was free to go or to stay.

In the high center of the Eye, she halted the mare. Han-Gilen lay behind her. Iban was a shadow ahead, moonlit and starlit, deep in its midnight sleep. Above her loomed the tower, dark and silent. If she called out, named herself, demanded lodging, she would have it, and in the morning an armed escort to bring her to her father.

Her back stiffened. Had she come so far, to turn back now? With high head and set face, she sent her mare down into Iban.

When Elian was young, she had learned by rote the names of all the Hundred Realms. Some were tiny, little more than a walled town and its fields; some were kingdom-wide. Most owed friendship or tribute to the Red Prince of Han-Gilen.

As she rode across sleeping Iban, she called to mind the realms between Han-Gilen and the wild north. Green Iban; Kurion with its singing forests; Sarios where ruled her mother's father; Baian, Emari; Halion and Irion whose princes were always blood brothers; Ebros and Poros and stony Ashan. And beyond the fortress walls of Ashan, the wild lands and the wilder tribes that called Mirain king.

So close to mighty Han-Gilen and so far still from the outlands, her father's peace held firm. But there was a strangeness in the air. Mirain An-Sh'Endor: men dreaded the rumor of him with his barbarian hordes. Had not imperial Asanion itself begun to arm against him?

No, she thought, pausing before dawn to lever a stone from her mare's hoof. It was not all fear. Some of it was anticipation, some even joy at the coming of the Sun-king.

No hiding place offered itself to her with the dawn, only the open fields and a village clustered about an ancient shrine. Elian might have pressed on past, but the mare, unused to steady traveling, was stumbling with weariness. And no temple, however small, would deny a traveler shelter, whoever that traveler might be.

This shrine was small indeed, made of stone but shaped like the villagers' huts, round and peak-roofed with a door-curtain of leather. Its altar stood where the hearth should be, with the Sun's fire on it in a battered bowl, and a clutter of holy things.

Behind the shrine stood the priesthouse, a simple wattle hut with a pen for an odd assortment of animals: a lame woolbeast, a white hind, a one-eyed hound. The woolbeast blatted at mare and rider, the hound yawned, the hind watched from a far corner with eyes like blood rubies.

Elian dismounted stiffly. The village seemed asleep or deserted, but she felt the pressure of eyes upon her. Her hand went unconsciously to her head, to the cap that hid her hair, drawing it down over the bright sweep of her brows.

Someone moved within the hut. Tired though she was, the senel lifted her head, ears pricked.

This village had a priestess, a woman in late middle years, square and solid, red-brown as the earth her fathers had sprung from. Her robe was shabby but clean, her torque of red gold dimmed with age, as if it had passed through many hands, over many years, to this latest bearer. Over her shoulders she bore a yoke and a pair of buckets.

She regarded Elian with a calm unquestioning stare. "Your senel may share the pen," she said, "but you will have to cut her fodder yourself."

For an instant Elian stood stiff, outraged. That was servants' work. And she—

She was a rankless vagabond, by her own free choice. She made herself bow her head and say the proper words. "For the hospitality of your house, my thanks."

The priestess bowed in return, as courteous as any lady in hall. "The house is open to you. Take what you will and be welcome."

First Elian saw to the mare. There was grass not far away, and her knife was sharp; she cut an ample armful. As she brought it back to the pen, she found she had companions: a handful of children, some too young for breeches, others almost old enough to be men or women. There were one or two in the enclosure itself, coaxing the mare with bits of grass. At Elian's coming they scattered, but not far, less afraid of her in her strange splendid gear than fascinated by her mount. One was even bold enough to speak to her. The priestess' dialect had been thick but clear enough, but this was like an alien tongue.

"He asks, 'Is this a real battle charger?' "

Elian started. The priestess stepped past her to dip water into the beasts' trough, saying to the children in her deep soft voice, "Yes, it is a war-mare, and a fine one too; and isn't that your father calling you to the fields?"

The children fled, with many glances over their shoulders. The priestess laid down her yoke and straightened. "Very fine indeed," she repeated, "and worn to a rag, from the look of her. Will you rest in the temple or in my house?"

"Wherever you like," Elian answered her, suddenly weary beyond telling.

"In my house then," said the woman. "Come."

This sleep was deep, untouched by visions. Elian woke from it to firelit darkness, and a scent of herbs, and a deep sense of peace. Slowly she realized that she lay on a hard pallet; that there was a blanket over her; and that she wore only her shirt beneath it.

She sat up in alarm. The firelight fell upon metal and cloth: her clothing, her weapons, all together, all laid neatly at the foot of her bed. Beyond them knelt the priestess, tending a pot that simmered over the hearth. She looked up calmly. "Good evening," she said.

Elian clutched the blanket to her breast. "Why did you—how dared you—"

The priestess' gaze silenced her. "My name is Ani. Yours I need not know unless you choose. Here, eat."

Elian took the fragrant bowl but did not move to eat, although her stomach knotted with sudden fierce hunger. "My name is Elian," she said almost defiantly.

Ani gestured assent. Her mind was dark and impenetrable, like deep water. "Eat," she repeated. And when Elian had obeyed: "Sleep."

Power, Elian thought, even as she sank back. *This is power. A witch . . . I must . . .*

". . . go." Elian's own voice startled her. The hut was deserted, the fire quenched. Sunlight slanted through the open door-curtain. Her clothes lay as she remembered, her weapons beside them, and close to her hand a covered bowl. In it lay bread, still faintly warm from the baking, and a bit of hard yellow cheese.

She found that she was hungry. She ate; found a bucket filled with clean water to wash in; dressed and combed her hair and pulled on her cap, and ventured into the light. She felt better than she had since she left Han-Gilen; and the day matched it, a clear day of early summer, warm and bright and wild with birdsong.

The mare seemed to have sworn friendship with her odd penmates, sharing with them a mound of fresh-cut grass. For her mistress she had a glance and a flick of one ear, but no more. She was clean and well brushed, her mane and the tassel of her tail combed like silk. After a moment Elian left her, seeking the shrine.

Ani was there, sweeping the worn stone floor, brisk as any goodwife in her house. Like the mare, she greeted Elian with a glance, but she added, "Wait a bit for me."

The temple was oddly peaceful even in the midst of its cleaning. Elian sat on the altar step and watched the priestess, remembering the great temple in Han-Gilen. This place could barely have encompassed one of its lesser altars, let alone the high one with its armies of priests and priestesses devoted entirely to its tending.

Someone had brought a garland of flowers to lay beside the Sun-fire. It was fresh still, with a sweet scent: a lovers' garland, seeking the god's favor for two who were soon to wed.

Elian set her teeth. Let them have each other. She had her oath and her flight.

"Maybe I should become a priestess."

She did not know that she had spoken aloud until Ani said, "No. That, you were never made to be."

"How can you know?" demanded Elian.

The woman set her broom tidily in its niche behind the altar. "If the god had wanted you, he would have called you."

"Maybe he has."

Ani filled the nightlamp with oil from a jar, and trimmed its wick carefully, without haste. "Not to that, Lady of Han-Gilen." Elian was silent, struck dumb. "No; he has another task for you. Are you strong enough to bear his burden?"

"I am not returning to my father. I am riding north. A geas binds me. You cannot stop me."

"Should I want to?" The priestess seemed honestly surprised.

"You *are* a witch."

Ani considered that. "Maybe," she conceded, "I am. When I was a novice they said I might make a saint, if I didn't go over to the darkness first. I know I'm far from saintly, but I like to think I've evaded the other as well. So too should you." Her eyes changed. Though no less calm, they were harder, sterner. "It lays its snares for you. Walk carefully, child."

"I try to." Elian made no effort to keep the sullenness out of her voice.

"And well you might. There is more than the Sun's son waiting across your path."

In spite of herself Elian shivered. "The—the goddess?"

The priestess brushed the altar with her fingertips, as if to gain its protection. "Not she. Not yet. But one who serves her and grows strong in her service. One who hates in love's name, and calls envy obedience, and binds her soul to an outworn law. Guard yourself against her."

Against her will, Elian saw again what she had seen in the glade by the pool: the exile who was of her own blood. But what danger could dwell in the woman, outlaw that she was, without eyes to see?

"Much," Ani said, "with the goddess beside her, and maybe other, more earthly allies."

"But who—"

"Asanion. Any prince in the Hundred Realms. The north."

"Not Mirain. Mirain would never—"

"People aren't likely to know that. And the goddess is strong among the tribes."

"No. He would never allow it. But Asanion—Asanion serves itself. If it could conquer us all . . ." Ziad-Ilarios' face gleamed ivory-pale behind her eyes. She had dealt his pride a crippling blow. If another alliance offered itself, a means to defeat Mirain, even if by treachery, would he not take it? Or if not he, then surely his father, the one they called the Spider Emperor, who spun his webs to trap all not yet bound to his empire.

Her father's peace was hard won through a long and bitter war. Mirain had fought in it, been knighted in it, he and Halenan together. Would he remember that? Or would his hordes roll over the Hundred

Realms to clash with those of Asanion, crushing the princedoms between them?

She covered her face with her hands. But that only strengthened the vision. Han-Gilen's banner, flameflower burning on shadow green; Asanion's imperial gold; and one both strange and familiar, scarlet field, golden sun. With the ease of a dream they shimmered and melted, revealing faces. Hal and her father side by side, more alike than she had ever thought they could be, and Ziad-Ilarios with an old man who held a mask of gold before his face, and the exile with her terrible blind eyes. But the sun remained and seemed to kindle, to blaze up like Avaryan itself, surrounding her, overwhelming her, bringing blessed blindness.

Ani's voice was strong and quiet in her ear. "Go where you will to go. The god will guide you."

Away from it all. *Away.*

She lowered her hands. They were shaking; she made them be still. Ani looked down at her without either awe or pity. "I . . . I will go," she said. "For your welcome, for your help—"

"Give your thanks to the god. I'll saddle the mare for you."

Ani left her there alone and shaking. When she rose, she was steady; the sick fear had faded. She could make the proper obeisance, and walk away with her chin up and her feet firm.

Ani held the mare's bridle. On impulse Elian embraced her. She was strong, calm and calming, but warm with a human warmth; she returned the clasp freely. Neither spoke. Elian mounted. She raised her hand in farewell, and rode out upon the northward road.

Five

SENT OUT FROM IBAN BY DAYLIGHT, ELIAN RODE UNder the sun, one of many passers through the north of the Hundred Realms. By night she sheltered in wayside shrines or in farmholders' byres, or, once and boldly, in an inn in Ebros. Darkness and rain and the rumor of highwaymen had driven her there, with some touch of wildness that tempted her to test her disguise in close company. None but Ani seemed to have divined the truth; to all she met, she was the youth she looked to be, with her cap pulled rakishly low over her eyes.

There was a goodly crowd in the inn. A party of pilgrims journeying south to Han-Gilen; a merchant with his armed company coming back from Asanion; sundry folk from the town, high and low, some with painted, bare-breasted women. Elian kept to herself in a corner, nursing a mug of ale. In the steaming heat she had yielded at last to discomfort and taken off her cap. The coppery gleam of her hair, even in the dimness, drew not a few eyes; but there were men in the merchant's party with manes scarcely less remarkable, tawny or straw-pale. The eyes slid away, intent on the drink or the women or the flow of speech about the common room.

An-Sh'Endor. His name was everywhere. He was riding south, they said. He had taken Cuvien without a struggle, received the homage of its chieftains and held a festival for his army. Now he looked toward Ashan. But no, tribes to the west were rising; he would deal with them first, and turn then upon Asanion.

"Now there is one fine fighter," said a man almost dark enough to be a northerner, a pilgrim's robe straining across his massive chest. "Have you heard how he took the castle of Ordian? It was impregnable, everyone said. Food and water enough for two years' siege, and no way up to it but under its gate, with the whole tribe defending it from above. So what does he do? Lines up his army just out of the gate's reach, makes all the motions of settling in for a siege—and sends a company round the back up a road a mountain goat would shrink from, with himself in the lead. So here's the tribe, laughing at the army and daring it to come closer, and shooting offal at a man in the king's armor; then the joke turns on them. A round hundred bows aimed at them from behind, and a cocky young fellow telling them they'd better surrender before he feeds them to his army."

One of the merchant's guards laughed, short and scornful. "Tribesmen's tales," he said in a thick western accent. "He has never met a proper army, nor faced Asanian steel."

"That lad is afraid of nothing," the first man said. "He'll go where no one else will go, and take his army with him."

"So?" someone asked. "Have you seen him?"

"Seen him? I've fought with him. That was before I saw the light: he was a fosterling in Han-Gilen and I was one of the prince's hired swords. Fourteen summers old, he was, and the prince knighted him in battle, with the whole army yelling his name."

The Asanian curled his lip. "If he ever knew the ways of civilized man, he has left them far behind him. He is a mountain bandit, and he will die one."

"Not so!" cried a new voice. It was a very young one, almost painfully sweet. Elian, seeking its source, found a thin dark boy in the grey robe of a sacred singer, with his harp at his back and his eyes burning in his narrow Ashani face. "Oh, not so! He is the holy one, the god-king. He comes to claim his inheritance."

"What inheritance?" demanded a bejeweled young fellow, a local lordling by his accent, which strove to be cultivated. "He had some claim to Ianon, or so they say: his mother was its king's bastard. He murdered the king, by poison I hear, and killed the king's son in an ambush."

The pilgrim's voice boomed from end to end of the crowded room. "Begging your pardon, young sir, but that's a barefaced lie. The Sunborn's mother was heir of Ianon in her own right, being the king's daughter by his queen, who was an Asanian princess." His eye lingered for a moment on the westerner. "The old king died, true enough, and maybe poison speeded it, but it wasn't my lord who sweetened his wine. He had a son who really was a bastard, who had a hand in his killing, and who tried to claim the throne. The Sunborn fought the pretender man to man, barehanded. That was a fight to sing songs of! My lord is a great warrior and a great king, but he's not what you'd call a big man; and he was still only half grown. His uncle was a giant even for a Ianyn, and the greatest champion in the north of the world. But they fought, and my lord won, full and fair."

"And the king came forth and took his throne, and the gods bowed down before him." The singer's eyes shone; his voice thrummed like the strings of his own harp.

"If he is so divine a wonder," inquired the Asanian, "why does he march armed across the north? He need but raise his hand to bring the world to his feet." He yawned with feline delicacy. "The boy is mad. Power-mad. He will seize what he may seize, destroy what he may destroy, and set his foot upon the necks of kings. Until Asanion rises to crush him."

The singer, if dream-mad, was obstinate. "He brings Avaryan's peace to the world. But men cling to their old darknesses. Them he must conquer by force of arms, since no other force do they understand. In the end they shall all be his. Even Asanion, with its thousand demons. Its emperor shall bow down to the Lord of the Sun."

"Moonshine," drawled the westerner.

The boy looked ready to do battle for his dreams. But the pilgrim laughed, quelling them both. "Me, I walk down the middle. Yon's the best general this old world's seen in a long age. If he chases after a god and a dream, what's that to me? The fighting's good, the loot's better, and the man's well worth the service."

There was a brief silence, the pause due a subject well interred. Thereafter the talk shredded and scattered, blurring in a haze of wine.

Elian yawned and thought of bed. But a chance word froze her where she sat. "—the Exile." She could not see who spoke, but it was a new voice, and close. "Yes, Kiyali, *the Exile:* that's what they're calling her. Half the bandits on the roads are holding up travelers in her name."

"And the other half swear by the Sunborn," put in another man. "If you ask me, they're one and the same, and that's nobody at all, just a good way to shake gold out of locked purses. You know what they do in outland villages? Name a name, Outcast or Sunborn, and tell the folk to pay up and the local bandits will protect them."

"Or flatten them if they refuse. But the Sunborn exists. Maybe the other does too. I've heard tell she's a great sorceress; she rules in the woods, no one knows where, and she's as rich as an emperor. She lives on blood and fear, and she sleeps on gold."

The second man laughed. "What is she then? A dragon?"

"A woman. That's monster enough, all the gods know. My youngest wife, now—"

They spoke no more of exiles or of Sunborn kings, although Elian strained all her senses to hear them. At last she rose. She was weary and her mood had darkened; the sour ale sat ill beneath her breastbone. She made her way through the crowd, seeking the stair to the sleepingroom and a night of formless dreams.

Beyond Ebros the land turned wild, towns and villages growing fewer, hill and forest rising toward the northern mountains. The rumors here were dark, tales of marauders upon the roads, villages sacked and burned, forces moving under captains who swore allegiance to no lord, but perhaps to a young barbarian king. There was even that wild tale, that Mirain had sworn alliance with the reivers of the roads, to open the way before him into the Hundred Realms.

Elian began to meet with people fleeing south like birds before a storm. Pilgrims, most called themselves, or travelers, but none faced northward. Those who went north went for need, and they went armed.

She rode with care, but none molested her. Outlaws sought fat merchants in their caravans, where the booty might be well worth the battle; lone riders, armed and well mounted, they let be.

Perhaps her long safety lulled her into folly; perhaps she thought too much on her journey's end, which was close now, close enough to sense with the barest flicker of power. She even fancied that she had found Mirain: a rioting golden fire, center and focus of all his army.

Herself focused upon it, she rode down from the hills into a wooded valley. The sun was setting behind a veil of cloud; the wind promised rain before dawn. She was weary and hungry, beginning to think of a camp and a fire and a haunch of the wildbuck which she had shot in the morning. On the edge of thought, she took note of the silence in these woods that should have been alive with birds and beasts. The only sound was the soft thud of hoofs upon the track, the creak of leather, the jingle of the bit. Even the wind had stilled with the sun's sinking.

Uneasiness grew, rousing her from her half-dream. She looked back. Already the trees had closed in upon the path. She could see no more than a few lengths behind, a few lengths ahead.

She was not, yet, afraid. The road was clear enough even in the gloom. Mirain's army was no more than two days distant, perhaps less, camped on the fells beyond the border of Ashan.

Her mare snorted and shied. She gentled the beast and halted, stroking the bright mane, every sense alert. There was no sound at all.

Softly Elian slid from the saddle. The mare stood braced, head high, eyes and nostrils wide. At the passing of weight from her back, she shuddered once and was still.

Something rustled in the undergrowth. A small beast—a bird.

Another. The wood was coming alive. Somewhere a bird called. Elian eased her sword from its scabbard.

An insect buzzed. The mare bucked and reared. Blood stained her haunches. A second arrow sang between her ears.

Elian wheeled. "Cowards! Cravens! Come out and fight like men!"

They came at her call, more than she could count, figures swathed in green and brown, with masked faces and strung bows. The mare whirled into attack. Blades flashed through the sharp slashing hoofs; she fell kicking.

Elian hardly saw. She had her back to a tree, sword and dagger a bright blur before her.

A shadow fell from above: a net, trapping her, drawing tighter as she struggled. Steel pricked, her own sword, more deadly now to her than to her enemies. She loosed her grip upon it; it fell through the net. Hard hands tore the dagger from her fingers.

Two of her captors heaved her to their shoulders. As they began to walk, she saw her mare rigid in death, and faceless men stripping the body of its trappings. There was no room in her for grief. Only for rage.

Twilight turned to darkness. It began to rain, a light drizzle, warm and not unpleasant. One of her bearers cursed it in a tongue she knew, a dialect of northern Sarios. "Go out, she says, lay an ambush, she says, take what comes, she says. So what comes? One futtering boy on a futtering mare, and now this futtering rain, and not enough futtering loot to keep a mouse happy."

"Shut your flapping mouth," snarled the man behind him, "or she'll nail it shut."

Elian shivered, and not with the rain. *She.* Only one woman that she knew of commanded outlaws, masked men in woodland colors. After all the warnings and all the foreseeings and all of Elian's own fears, the Exile had taken her.

The men mounted a slope with much hard breathing and not a few curses. From the height of it Elian looked down into a wide clearing. Fires flickered there in despite of the rain; men moved about them.

Most had shed their masks. She glimpsed a face or two: Ebran, Gileni, a dark hawk-nosed northerner.

Her captors bore her through them all in silence full of eyes, to the central and greatest fire. A shelter rose behind it, made of stripped boughs and overlaid with oiled leather. The leather was dark, perhaps black, perhaps deep blue or violet, the standard set in the ground before it dark likewise, without device.

Elian tumbled to the ground, rolled about without mercy as her bearers freed her from the net. Dizzy, all but stunned, she let them haul her to her feet. A hand struck between her shoulders, thrusting her into the shelter.

After the bright firelight, this was nearly total darkness, the only light the ember-glow of a lamp. Slowly Elian's eyes cleared. She discerned the dim shapes of furnishings, few as they were, and simple to starkness. And in the lone chair, a woman.

She was alone. She seemed oblivious. Thin and frail, her hair white, pulled back from her face and knotted at her nape. Her eyes were lowered as if to contemplate the creature nestled in her lap. It was of cat-kind, silken-furred, purring as she stroked it.

The purring stilled. The cat's eyes opened. Elian shivered. They were white as silver, pupils slitted even in the dimness, fixing her with intensity that spoke of no dim beast-mind. It knew her; and it laughed, knowing that she knew.

"So," her tongue said for her. "You turned to the Mageguild."

The Exile raised her head. She had aged little since she slew the god's bride; her beauty had deepened, the ravages of bitterness smoothed, fined, transmuted. As if she had yielded. As if she had come through cruel battle to acceptance of her suffering. "I am mageborn," she said. Her accent was Elian's own.

"Mageborn," said Elian, "and Guild-trained. I know that robe. But why do you require a familiar? Did Mirain take more from you than your eyes?"

"He gave more than he took," the Exile said with something very like serenity.

Elian looked about. Her fear had faded not at all: she was stiff with it. But scorn was a potent weapon. She wielded it with reckless extravagance. "What have you gained? I see a bandit queen with a demon in her lap. She is blind; she is old; she has no name and no country. To her kin she is as if she had never been. Even her Guild—why are you here? Did they too grow weary of your arrogance, and drive you out of the Nine Cities?"

"I cannot fault you," the Exile said without anger. "You are too young to have known the truth of it."

"I know all I need to know."

The Exile smiled. She was not gentle—she could not be that. But she could indulge a child's innocence. "Do you, O Lady of Han-Gilen? You dream that you ride in fulfillment of an oath. Yet what was that oath? What was it truly? Was it to fight beside the priestess' son? Or was it to be his queen?"

Elian bit her tongue, hard. The Exile wanted her to cry out, to deny the twisted truth. Yes, she had sworn that she would marry none but Mirain. But not at the last. Only when she was very young, hardly more than an infant. Never when she knew what vow she was taking.

"Wise," said the Exile. "Most wise. Perhaps after all you knew. In Asanion they mate brother and sister. In Han-Gilen they shrink from it."

Still Elian held her tongue. It was a bitter battle, and it was no victory. The Exile knew what she struggled not to say. Knew everything; and toyed with her, for amusement, before the headiness of the kill.

"No," the woman said. "It need not be so. We are kin, you and I. As you are now, so was I once: the beauty and the high heart, and the reckless bravery. For them I fell. Had I held back, waited, seemed to submit to my brother's son and his northern paramour, I would have spared myself much suffering. I could have slain not only the mother but the monster which she bore."

"Mirain is no—"

Elian bit off the rest. The Exile forbore to smile. "He is comely enough, they tell me. In body. It is the spirit I speak of. I am not the seer that you will be, kinswoman, but a little of the gift is mine. I have seen what he would make of the world. No greater danger has ever beset it."

"He will save it. He will bring it to the worship of Avaryan."

"He will cast it into the Sun's fires." The Exile rose. Her familiar wove about her feet, tail high, gaze never shifting from Elian's face. The woman held up her hands, not pleading, not precisely. Her blind eyes seemed to look deep into Elian's own, with such a shimmer on them as lies in the pearlbeast's heart. This, Mirain had made. This, he had done, scarcely knowing what he did.

"He is not evil," the Exile said. "I grant him that. Perhaps truly he believes his mother's lies. But he is deadly dangerous. Mageborn as he is, bred to be king, with the soul of a conqueror, he cannot do aught but what he does. Nor in turn can I. He threatens the chains that bind the world. So I saw before ever he was born."

"You saw a threat to your own power."

"That also," the Exile admitted without shame, "and for my sin I fell. Now I am given grace to redeem myself. I live, and I am strong. I have conquered hate. I have learned to serve justice alone."

"And in the name of justice you command the reivers of the roads."

"It is necessary."

"Of course," said Elian with a curl of her lip. "How else can you buy traitors, unless you steal the wherewithal?"

"I do as I must."

Elian stilled. That was madness, that calm fixity. It turned upon her. It seized her.

"Kinswoman," the Exile said. "I have waited for you. I have prayed that you would see what for so long I have seen. If my men have handled you ill, I cry your pardon. They are men; they do not know subtlety. Come now, sit, be at ease. Grant your sufferance at least to my words."

Elian would not obey her. Could not. Must not. Not though that face spoke ever more to her of her own; though that voice entreated her ears with the accents of her own kin. "You weave me about in lies," she said tightly. "You think to seduce me. You know how strong Mirain will be, if he has me to stand beside him and fight for him and be his prophet. You dream that I can sway your enemies, even my father. Especially my father. But much though he loves me, he loves his realm more. He would never destroy it for my sake."

"You would be its salvation. Think you that his intent can be secret? He has forged alliances throughout the Hundred Realms. He toys with Asanion, to ease its suspicions. Yet his purpose is clear to any who can see. When the Hundred Realms are firm in his grasp, he will give them as a gift to the conqueror."

"If the conqueror proves worthy of them."

"By his existence he is worthy. He was bred to rule under your father's hand."

"Old lies," said Elian, "and old spite. How can I credit a word of it? You who were high priestess of Avaryan—you wear the robes of a black mage. You stink of darkness."

"It is all one," the Exile said. "Light and dark, all one. That is truth, kinswoman. To that, your father is blind; and with him the one whom he wrought for empire."

"So then must I be. I am no slave of the goddess. I will not yield to you."

"I did not speak of yielding. I spoke of taking arms for the truth." The Exile sighed as if weariness had overcome her. "Time will be your teacher. Time, and your clear sight, which in the end you cannot deny."

Torment, Elian could have borne. There was no ambiguity in it. This was subtler. She had a tent to herself. She was bound, but lightly, with a tether long enough that she could move about. Food and drink waited for her to deign to notice them.

She refused. It would be a yielding; and she must not yield. She crouched by the tentpole and shivered, weeping a little, child-fashion, less for fear than for humiliation.

Something watched her. She froze. The Exile's familiar sat before her where had been empty air, washing its forepaw with perfect and oblivious innocence.

Her eyes narrowed. The beast nibbled a claw. No stink of the hells lay on it. It seemed but a lady's pet, harmless, absorbed in itself. Yet it was here, and it had not come through the sealed door.

Mageborn, she had studied little of the sorcerer's art. She needed neither spell nor familiar. Her power ran deeper, closer to instinct. But her father had taught her enough, or tried to teach her, if she could but remember.

It came to her in a flicker of vision: three magelings before the master, and two were red Gileni and one was Ianyn-dark, and the youngest was small enough to sit on the master's knee as he spoke, and set her ear against his chest, and fill her head with the drum-deep cadences of his voice. "A familiar," he said, speaking as much to her as to her brothers, "like a staff or a grimoire, is a vessel of power. It need have none in itself. It can be eyes and ears and feet, and it can guard what the mage wishes it to guard."

"Useful," said Halenan. His voice, which was breaking, wavered even on the single word; Elian was too interested to laugh at him.

"Useful," Mirain agreed, "but cumbersome, and maybe dangerous. What if the familiar is captured by another mage? Or killed? What happens to its master then?"

"That depends upon the depth of the bond," answered the Red Prince. He stroked Elian's hair, idly. It was pleasant; she let him do it, slitting her eyes to make the world go strange. Mirain's face blurred into a shadow.

"I would never so divide my power," he said.

"You need not," said the Red Prince. "It is born in you. But if you were a simple man, and you had come to magic through spells and long art, a familiar would not lessen your power: it would focus it, and nurture it, and make it strong."

"But I would always be vulnerable," said Mirain.

Elian drew a slow breath. The familiar coiled bonelessly upon itself, scouring the base of its tail. She tugged at the thongs that bound her wrists. The creature raised its head, turned its eyes upon her. She set teeth to her tether.

White pain flung her back. Her cheek burned and throbbed. Blood spattered her coat.

The cat sat erect, vigilant. She bared her teeth. It yawned. Its fangs were white needles. She crouched, and would not think of pain. Surely those claws had raked her to the bone. The bleeding would not stop, even for her hands pressed to it, an awkward knot of leather and flesh.

She struggled to gather her power. It kept scattering, eluding her grasp, mocking her with a spit of feline laughter. Grimly she kept her temper. Rage would fell her. Despair would cast her into her enemy's hands.

She had it. Not all of it, but perhaps, by the god's will, enough. It writhed and fought as if it were no part of her at all but an alien thing. She set upon it the full force of her will.

Her hands were free. The tent's door was open, a guard blank-eyed before it. She stepped toward him.

The cat yowled. She whirled. Claws raked her tender breast; teeth snapped at her throat. She tore the thing away, flung it with all her trained strength.

Silence. Stillness. She backed away. Nothing. She spun, leaped past the motionless guard.

Her power was quiet in her center, obedient at last. She let it lead her round the edge of the camp. No one saw her. No one would see her. The forest waited beyond with its promise of safety.

It came without warning, springing out of the night, swift and silent and terrible. Its claws stretched to seize her, to rend her. She flung up all her shields.

The shadows rippled with cold cat-mirth. For she stood full in the light of a watchfire, clear for any mortal eyes to see.

Someone shouted.

Left was night, and the green gleam of eyes. She darted right, round the flames. Voices cried out. Fire seared her face. With the strength of desperation she dropped her mind-shield, thrusting all her power into the fire. Her body sprang after it. Flames roared high, engulfing her. The shadow-beast veered away.

In the instant of confusion, she reached from the very core of her.

The fire vanished. Darkness swathed her, the darkness of earthly night, with a shimmer of stars and a whisper of wind in leaves.

Later she would begin to shake. She had gone—otherwhere. But where or how far, she could not tell, although the air tasted still of the woodlands of Ashan. Her power, unguided, had served her far better than she had any right to expect. Or perhaps it was luck, or fate. Or the god.

Her knees buckled. Power, strength, she had none. All gone. All spent. If men or sorcery found her now, she had no defense. "Avaryan," she breathed as if he could hear, or would. "Help—protect—"

The night opened its arms. She let it take her.

Six

*L*IGHT WOKE HER FIRST. SHE TURNED HER HEAD away from it, waking pain. With a groan she burrowed into her bed.

And sneezed. Her bed was no bed at all, but deep leafmold; her face was pillowed in it. She levered herself up on her hands. Trees loomed all about her, evergreens with but little growth between them. Their sharp fine needles matted in her hair, pricked her skin. She worked her knees beneath her and brushed at the clinging fragments.

At the sight of herself she made a small sound, part pain, part disgust. She was filthy, spattered with blood, with her garments hanging open like a harlot's. Cheek and breast were raked with thin deep scratches, bleeding no longer, but burning fiercely. She managed with some fumbling to fasten her coat; enough remained of buttons and lacings for that. She was ravenously hungry and parched with thirst. And no water within sight or scent, nor enough of power left to find any.

The sun slanted through branches almost full before her. Left and perhaps north the ground sloped downward, broken with stones and hollows. Downward, her masters had taught her, water runs downward always, and many a hillside boasts a stream at its foot.

She was safe, uncaught, unbound. She would not think of the rest: that she was alone, afoot, and wounded, without water or food or weapon, and sorely worn from her battle of power; and that she had no knowledge of this place into which her waning witchery had cast her. For all she knew, she was but returning the way she had come. It was enough now that she set one foot before the other, and that if she stumbled she did not often fall.

Once she fell badly. The slope was steep; she rolled, bruising herself on root and stone, stopped at last by the solid strength of a tree. For a long while she could not move at all, nor even breathe.

Little by little she gathered herself together. Nothing had broken. But ah, she hurt. She made herself stand, take one limping step, then another.

She scented it before she heard it, an awareness far below the conscious, a blind turning of the body toward its greatest need. Water, a trickle over moss and stone, pausing in a pool little bigger than her hand. She collapsed beside it, to drink until she could drink no more. Every muscle cried then for rest, but she took off her garments one by one, slowly, like a very old woman, and washed herself a hand's breadth at a time. Only when she was clean would she lie back with the sun's warmth seeping into her bones.

Food. That, she needed still, and sorely. But the sun lay like a healer's hand upon her skin. She let it lull her into a doze.

Wake! It was not a voice, not precisely. *Wake and move. Sleep after power—sleep is deadly. Wake!*

Feebly she tried to close it out, to sink back into her stupor. Yet her body stirred and rose and fumbled into its filthy coverings. They were stiff; they itched and they stank. Her clean skin shrank from them.

Food. Here, green, and a white root, crisp and succulent. There in an open space, a tangle of brambles with fruit nestled within their thorns. Beyond, a widening of the stream; a small silver fish, now leaping in her hand, now cold and sweet upon her tongue.

She gagged, but the fish had found her stomach, and she was herself again, weak and still hungry but clear enough in mind. She found a further handful of thornfruit, and a clump of greens, root and top. Time enough later to fashion a snare for the meat she needed.

She drank from the stream and knelt for a time beside it, laving her face. Her father had warned her often and often. All power had its price. Used lightly, it asked no more of the body than any other exercise. Expended to its limit, it drained all the body's strength, could even kill unless its wielder moved to master it. And even with mastery one needed long sleep after, and ample food and drink, and a day or more of rest. She had never gone so far, but she had seen her father after some great feat of wizardry, building or healing or calling of the wind, borne away like an invalid, bereft of all strength.

But she had done so little. Unlocking; illusion; shielding; swift travel from place to unknown place. Yet she had come as close to dissolution as she ever cared to come.

It was still too soon to remember. She stood wavering. Only a little farther. Then she would seek shelter and set her traps. She began to walk beside the water. She felt hale enough but very weary. A little farther—a little. Where the stream, wider now, descended between steep banks and bent out of sight, she stopped. Her knees folded beneath her. Shelter—her snares—

A shadow crossed the sun. She regarded it without alarm. A voice spoke above her, strange words, yet she ought to have known them.

The shadow cast a shape. A man in kilt and cloak of shadow green, a very dark man, black indeed, with a proud arch of nose over a richly braided beard.

Fear erupted within her, and beneath it despair. She was caught again. There would be no second escape.

Another man appeared beside the other, dark likewise, and taller, and perhaps younger; his face was clean-shaven. From where she lay they seemed very giants. The newcomer stooped, reaching for her.

She fought. But her blows were feeble; the men laughed. They were handsome men, with very white teeth, and rings of copper in their ears and about their necks and upon their arms. The taller one said something; she thought it might have been, "Now, brave warrior, be still. We'll not be killing you right this moment."

No. She would die slowly, at the Exile's hands. She renewed her struggle, striking with all the strength that was left her.

"Aiee!" yelped the man who held her arms. "He's a regular wildcat. Tangled with one too, from the look of him." Her elbow caught him in the ribs; he grunted. *"Now* then, you. No more of that!"

It was less a blow than a cuff, but it half stunned her. She sagged in his grip. He slung her over his shoulder and strode forth, with his companion following.

Belatedly, and numbly, she realized that they had been speaking the tongue of Ianon.

With no more transition than a thinning of trees and a leveling of the hillside, the forest ended. Elian had come by then to herself, but she rode quiescent on the broad shoulder, only lifting her head to see what she might see. She marked the opening of land and sky, and the changing of the ground from leafmold to long grass and stones; and she heard and scented and felt the camp upon the field. Here were the voices of men and beasts; the pungency of a cookfire; an ingathering of folk to inspect the arrivals, with much curiosity and some amusement. "Hoi, Cuthan!" they called. "What luck in the hunt?"

"Better than I looked for," her bearer called back.

In the center of the gathering he halted and set Elian down. Tall though she was for a Gileni woman, as tall as many men, he stood head and shoulders above her. Yet she faced him bristling, eyes snapping, hands fisted at her sides. He grinned. "See," he said, "a wildcat."

There were not, after all, so very many people about. A dozen, maybe. And despite their amusement, they had watchful eyes; their fire was well shielded, with little scent and no smoke, their seneldi tethered near the trees. Binding each cloak or glinting on the collar of each coat was a brooch of gold in the shape of a rayed sun.

Although no one held her, she was surrounded. Several of the men held bows, loose in their hands but strung, with arrows ready to fit to the string.

"Well, little redhead," said the man called Cuthan, "suppose you tell us who you are."

"You are Mirain's men," she said. Few of them were northerners. She marked trousered southerners, red and brown, and one Asanian clad incongruously in northern finery. "Where is he, then? Is he close by? For if he is, he trespasses. This land belongs to Ashan's prince."

"Does it now?" Cuthan gestured, no more than a flicker of the eyes. The scouts began with seeming casualness to disperse, but several stayed close by. He laid a hand on Elian's shoulder, guiding her toward the fire, seating her there.

His knife glittered as he drew it. She tensed. He barely glanced at her, cutting a collop from the haunch that roasted over the flames, bringing it to her. He did not lend her the knife to cut it. She held it gingerly, for it was searing hot, and nibbled with care.

Cuthan waited, patient. When the meat was gone, he held out a cup. She sniffed it. Water. Gratefully she drank.

A second man sat on his heels beside Cuthan: the Asanian. In that company he seemed almost a dwarf, a smooth sleek ageless man with bitter eyes. They took in Elian with neither favor nor trust. "Gileni," he said in thickly accented Ianyn. "Born liar."

"Maybe not," said Cuthan.

"Maybe so," the Asanian said. "Test it. He spoke clearly enough. This is Ashan; its prince is no more a fool than our king. He would have engaged spies."

"Redheaded Gileni spies?"

"Why not? Red mane, witch-power, they say in the south."

Cuthan frowned. "I'll question him. That's fair enough. But I'm not sure—"

"If I were spying," said Elian, "you would never have caught me. I was looking for your army. I want to fight for your king."

"Why?"

"Why not?" Elian bit her tongue. Cuthan was amused, but not entirely. She met his eyes. "Your . . . friend sees this much of the truth. I am from Han-Gilen. I heard of the Sunborn. I wanted to be free. I wanted to fight. I thought that if I joined with him I would have both. I ran away from home." Cuthan's grin came back. He believed that. She found an answering grin. "My mother would never have let me go. At night I ran away."

"You came alone? Unarmed? Afoot?"

"Alone, yes. The rest I—I lost. Back yonder. Have you heard of the woman called the Exile?"

The men within hearing tensed. Cuthan leaned forward. The Asanian's look was almost a look of triumph.

Her fist clenched at her belt where her sword had hung. "She camps a day's journey south, maybe more. She has men with her. They caught me and killed my mare and took all I had."

The Asanian's full lip curled. "They let you go."

She bared her teeth at him. "No. Not the likes of me. Red mane, witch-power. She knows that as well as you. But not well enough."

"No one escapes from that demon incarnate."

"One does if she happens to turn her mind elsewhere. She is not, yet, omniscient."

"Southern lies."

"Plain truth." Elian faced Cuthan. "Take me to the king and let him judge."

The Asanian leaped to his feet. "The Exile is Gileni. Red Gileni, witch and sorceress. What better weapon against my lord than one of her kin? Young and innocent to look at, but shaped for murder, as she murdered the god's bride."

"She is traitor and outcast, abhorred by all her kin." Elian flung back her tangled hair. "Your king will know. Take me to him."

Cuthan shifted. Shamelessly she followed his thoughts. He was commander here, but he was young, and a better judge of land than of men. An obvious spy, a grown man prowling where he ought not to be, that was easy enough to judge. But this lordly youth, pretty as a girl, found fainting by the waterside: was he truly what he seemed to be, or was he indeed a servant of the enemy?

"The king," said Elian. "He can judge."

"He can," Cuthan said slowly. "Maybe he'd better. But first we'll see to those scratches. They look nasty."

"They should. The witch's familiar gave them to me." Elian held out her hands. "Take me now. The sooner I see the king, the better."

"Not with your face like that," said Cuthan, stubborn. "Even if I could allow it, the king would have my hide."

She sighed and submitted. He himself cleaned her cheek and salved it with numbroot, clicking his tongue the while, mourning her poor marred beauty. His hands were light and skilled. Elian found herself smiling at him, crookedly, all numbed as she was.

"Bind him," snapped the Asanian, who had never taken his eyes from them. "Or should I? You're half in love with him already."

Cuthan seemed unoffended. "No need of that. I'm taking him where he wants to go."

"And if he knifes you in the back?"

"I'll chance it." Beneath Cuthan's lightness lay steel. The Asanian subsided with the swiftness of wisdom.

Elian was honored with trust. She had a senel to herself, no cord to bind her and no leadrein to bind her mount, and Cuthan's guardianship was light to invisibility. He rode beside her or ahead of her, sometimes silent, more often singing. His voice was very pleasant to hear.

In one of his silences she asked him, "Is it common for a captain of scouts to proclaim his presence to the whole realm?"

"If the realm is his king's own," answered Cuthan, "yes."

Elian's breath shortened. She had kept herself from thinking. That she was almost there. In front of Mirain. Telling him why she had come.

I told you that I would.

I keep my promises.

I want to fight for you.

Or most shameful, and closest to the truth: *There was a man, I was as much as commanded to marry him, I could have done it in all gladness, and for the sheer terror of it I ran away.*

As far as she could, as far into her childhood as she might. Running to Mirain as she had then, to be held and rocked and maybe chided a little, maybe more than a little, but always granted his indulgence.

Truth. It burned. *I promised. My first promise. I would marry you, or I would marry no one at all.*

And *no one* could so easily, so appallingly easily, have become *someone,* a face carved in ivory, lamplight in golden eyes.

She fixed her stare on Cuthan, for distraction, for exorcism. He was singing again. She made herself think of nothing but his song.

In spite of all the tales, the army of the Sunborn was no barbarian horde. Each nation and tribe and mercenary company had its place in the encampment, even to the camp followers: merchants and artisans, women and boys, singers and dancers and talespinners. It was like a city set on the moor, a city with order and discipline under the rule of a strong king.

Elian almost turned at the edge of it and bolted southward. It was not good sense that held her. Far from it. Good sense would have kept her in Han-Gilen and wedded her to the Asanian prince.

Pride brought her into the camp, and temper steadied her within. The king would not oblige her by waiting docilely in his tent. Everyone knew where he was, and everyone named a different place. Cuthan seemed content, even pleased, to play the hunter; and why not? He was a captain of scouts.

"Is this common?" Elian demanded after the fourth guide had led them to a space full of men and arms and seneldi, but empty of the king.

Cuthan had the effrontery to laugh. "He's not easy to keep up with, is my lord." He said it lightly, but the respect behind it came very close to worship. "Come now. I know where he may be."

This city, like any other, had its market: wide enough and varied enough to rouse even Elian's respect. She found herself loitering by a stall spilling over with gaudy silks, stretched into a trot to catch Cuthan. She had matched his grin before she thought. She flushed; her grin twisted into a scowl. He laughed and led her deeper into the maze of tents and stalls and booths.

Its heart was not its center. A stall with a reek of wine about it; a clamor of men and the odd shriek of a woman's laughter; someone singing, the clatter of a drum, the sudden sweetness of a flute. The faces were all northern faces, like a gathering of black eagles. Elian saw more gold on one man than a whole band of women would flaunt in Han-Gilen. And beneath it, more bare skin than she had ever seen in one place. One of the women wore nothing but ornaments. Her nipples were gilded. Elian blushed and looked away.

At, it chanced, one of the more bedizened of the men. He was tall and he was handsome even among these tall handsome people, beautiful indeed, so that Elian's eye caught and lingered. He lounged on the bench like some long-limbed hunting cat, awkwardness transmuted into grace, and although he wore the full, barbaric, copper-clashing finery of his people, he wore it as easily as he wore his skin; one could not envision him without it.

He met her gaze with no expression that she could read, not staring as others did at her bright hair and her torn face, simply returning look for look. He was young, perhaps. Under the beard and the baubles it was hard to tell. His skin was smooth, his face unlined; but his eyes were ancient. Or newborn.

He was not a mage. He was not born to magic, nor trained to it. Yet there was power in him, on him, part of him. He would wield it as he breathed, because he could do no other. Elian had never seen anything like him.

She looked away from him. Clamor burst upon her. Only he had eyes for her. Everyone else was fixed on someone whom she could not see, a shadow in shadow, with a voice that came suddenly clear. A black-velvet voice, sweet as the honey of the southlands, saying words that mattered too little for remembrance. A question. The answer was shrill beside it, and harsh, and thick with outland consonants.

Elian's feet took her out of the sunlight. New eyes found her, widened. She took no notice. The dark sweet voice rippled into laughter. Its bearer rose out of the tall man's shadow, leaning on the glittering shoulder, glittering himself, white teeth flashing in the face she knew best of any in the world.

He had always called it ugly. It had never sunk to prettiness; it was too irregular to be handsome. All Ianon was in that bladed curve of nose, in those cheekbones carved fierce and high, in those brows set level over the deep eyes.

Why, she thought. He had hardly changed at all.

But ah, he had.

He was neither the dwarf nor the giant of his legend. He stood a little taller than she, middling for a man in Han-Gilen. His hair submitted no more tamely than ever to its priestly braid; his body was slender still, a swordsman's body or a dancer's, graceful even at rest.

The difference was not in his eyes. God's eyes; no one had ever found it easy to meet them. Nor was it his face. All northern faces were made for arrogance. Nor was it even that he had forsaken the good plain clothes of the south for the gaudy near-nakedness of the north, so that the torque of his father's priesthood seemed lost amid the extravagance of copper and gold. No; the change ran deeper than that. She had bidden farewell to a boy, her brother. This was a man and a king.

He drained his cup, still leaning lightly on his companion. Their eyes met for an instant as he lowered the cup; a spark leaped in the meeting. It was nothing as feeble as passion, nothing as shallow as love. As one's self would meet one's self; as brother to soul's brother.

Elian knew then who the tall man must be. Vadin alVadin, Lord of Asan-Geitan in the kingdom of Ianon. He, next to Mirain himself, was the heart of the legend that was An-Sh'Endor. Commanded by the old King of Ianon to serve an upstart, southern-born prince, he had obeyed with utmost reluctance. Reluctantly he had seen the prince raised to king, and continued as squire and unwilling confidant; and he had died for his master, taking the assassin's spear that had been meant for Mirain. But Mirain had brought him back, and he had discovered that his reluctance was lost, and that he loved his outland king. They had sworn the oath of brothers-in-blood; and more, people said, but that, no one had ever proven. No one needed to prove it. To the eyes of power they were like the halves of a single shining creature.

Elian did not understand why her heart constricted. It was not fear of the visible and palpable power that dwelt in the man. She was mageborn herself, and stronger than he would ever be. And if they were sworn brothers, if somewhere among the long campaigns they had been lovers, what could it matter to her?

It could matter. He stood where she had sworn to stand. He had what she had come to take.

Mirain was laughing again, refusing a new cup of wine. "No, no, I've had my fill already, and I've a pack of lords clamoring for their king. What will they say if I reel in like a drunken soldier?"

"You?" someone called out. "Drunken? Never!"

"Ah," he said, wicked. "I'll tell you a secret, Bredan: I can't hold my wine at all. I slip it to my brother."

They roared at that, but they let him go. He seemed not to see the hands that reached as he passed, touching him as by accident, or falling short; loving him.

Elian knew the precise instant when he saw her. He checked, the merest hesitation. His face betrayed nothing. He passed her without a glance, striding into the sunlight.

Someone touched her. She wheeled, hand to hilt. Cuthan beckoned. And when she did not move, set his hand on her shoulder, light but inescapable.

Beyond the winestall was a space like an alleyway, a joining of blank walls, deserted. Mirain stood there, alone. In the glare of the Sun his father, he was no one she knew. God's son, conqueror, Ianyn king. His eyes were level upon her, and cold, and still.

His hand rose, gestured. Sun-gold blinded her. Cuthan was gone. Where he had been was the coldness of absence, and curiosity rigidly restrained, and a flicker of fear for her, melting like a mist in the sun.

She stood mute, with her chin at its most defiant angle. Let this stranger cast her out. Let him even kill her. She had gone too far to care.

Mirain's head tilted. His lips quirked, the old not-quite-smile. "Well?" he asked her. The Gileni word. In a tone she knew so well that the hearing of it was like pain.

"Well?" she countered, angry at nothing and at everything. "Now you can dispose of me. Majesty."

"So I might," he agreed. Damn him. He folded his arms, looked her up and down. "I've been waiting for you."

She clenched her jaw before it could drop. "How in the hells—"

He seemed not to have heard. "You took your time about it. I was beginning to wonder if you'd forgotten. You were very young when you swore on my hand that you would follow me to Ianon."

"I thought *you* had forgotten," she said. "With so much to think of— a world to conquer—"

His hand silenced her. She stood, awkward, on the edge between anger and flight. His eyes had stilled again.

He held out his hands. She stared at them. He smiled. His eyes were dancing. She leaped, laughing, and spun with him in a long, breathless, delighted embrace.

At length and as one they stepped apart. Again Mirain looked at her, and now he was not cold at all. "You've grown," he said.

"So have you."

"The whole half of a handspan," he said a little wryly. He ran a lock of her hair between his fingers. "Redder than ever. And your temper?"

"Worse than ever."

"Impossible." She bared her teeth at him; he grinned, looking for a moment no older than she. "How is Fosterfather? And Hal? And—"

"All well and all prospering. Hal has two strapping sons, and another child coming: a daughter, he says. He takes his dynastic duties very seriously."

Her tone must have betrayed something. His glance sharpened. "And you? You look a little the worse for wear. Were you beset upon the road?"

"I was beset," she answered steadily, and as calmly as she could. "I ran afoul of your old enemy." He frowned slightly. Of course he would have forgotten; it had been so long ago. "The one who lost her name and her eyes for denying you. My kinswoman, whom my father drove out. She caught me, but I escaped her. She hates you, Mirain."

"So," Mirain said softly, as if to himself. "It begins." He looked up, sudden enough to make her gasp. "And you have cast in your lot with me. Your father might forgive me for allowing it. Would your mother?"

Elian swallowed hard. Her mind was empty. It made her words as light as she could ever have wished them to be. "Mother is preeminently practical. Better you, she'll judge, than some of the alternatives. At least you'll see that my virtue remains intact."

"Will I?"

Her face was hot. She tried to laugh. "You had better, if you want to be forgiven."

He bent to pluck a sprig of heather, sweet and startling in this trampled place. "Then I must try, mustn't I?" He turned the blossom in his fingers. "My regents in Ianon are waiting for you. Both are great ladies, and Alidan bears arms. You'd like one another, I think."

"No!" Her vehemence brought him about. She tried to speak more softly. "I don't want to be packed off like—like baggage. I came to see you. To fight for you. I came to be free."

"You are free." Her chin was set, stubborn; he faced her with stubbornness no less. "You vowed to come to Ianon."

"I vowed to fight for you."

"Elian," he said with mighty patience, "I can't assign you to one of my companies. Even if your disguise would outlast the first river crossing, you make far too handsome a boy to thrust among an army."

"I thought you would understand. But you're like all the rest." She thrust her hands in his face. "Tie me up then. Send me back to Han-Gilen. See me wrapped in silks till I can't move at all, and auctioned off to the highest bidder."

"Elian." He spoke quietly, but his tone was like a slap. "I do not send either women or fair-faced boys to eat and sleep and fight with my veterans, unless they are well prepared to contend with the consequences. Which you, my lady of Han-Gilen, are not." She was silent, eyes blazing; he continued implacably, "There is a place for you in Ianon; I can provide an escort to take you there, or to return you to your family, as you choose."

She could have railed at him; she could have burst into tears. She struck him with all her trained strength.

He rocked under the blow but did not fall. She stood still, shaking, beginning to be appalled. She had raised her hand against a king.

Suddenly he laughed.

She hit him again. Still laughing, he caught her hand; then the other. She hurled her weight against him.

They rolled in the trampled grass, he laughing like a madman, she kicking and spitting and cursing him in every tongue she knew. A stone caught her. She lay gasping, hating him. There were tears on his cheeks, tears of laughter. But his face had sobered; his eyes met hers, dark and bottomless. Abruptly he was gone.

She rose shakily. He stood a little apart, watching her. His face was cold and still. Either he had grown or the world had shrunk. He towered over her, lofty, unreachable, royal. "By the laws of war you are my captive, to do with as I will. I can send you back to your father as one lord returns a strayed herdbeast to another. I can dismiss you to Ianon to await my return and my pleasure. I can keep you with me, take you and use you and discard you when I tire of you."

"Not you," she said without thinking. "Not that."

The mask cracked a very little. He stood no longer quite so high. "No. I confess I have no taste for rape. What else can I do? I won't inflict you on one of my captains."

"Then," she cried recklessly, "let me do something else. Let me be your guard, your servant, anything!"

He looked at her, measuring her as if she were a stranger. She could not meet his stare. "It happens," he said at last, "that I stand in need of a squire."

She opened her mouth and closed it again. His face had softened not at all. And yet he offered her this. Esquire. Armor-bearer. Guard and servant both, yet higher than either; to ride at his right hand, sleep at his bed's foot, and serve him with life and loyalty until death or knighthood freed her.

And this lord of all lords—he had his legend. He had no squire of his body. Not since the one who had died for him, whom he had raised again, whom he had made a knight and a prince and a sworn brother. That he judged her worthy of that one's place, was a gift beyond price.

"Surely," she said, "surely there are princes vying for the honor."

"You are a princess."

She could not speak.

His lips thinned. "Yes, you do well to hesitate. Any woman who speaks to me is soon called my lover. One sleeping in my very tent, close by me always, would lose all pretense to good name."

Her voice flooded back, as strong as it had ever been. "What of a boy?"

"If that is your choice," he said, "I'll do nothing to betray you. But in the end the truth will out."

"Let that be as it will be." She knelt at his feet. "I will serve you, my lord, in all that you ask of me; even to death, if so the god wills it."

He laid his hands upon her head. "I accept your oath and your service, your heart and your hand, to hold and to guard while my life lasts. In Avaryan's name, so let it be."

She swallowed hard. She had said only what came to her; but this was ritual, the binding of the vassal to his lord, complete and irrevocable.

It was what she had come for. Perhaps. She sprang lightly up and found a grin for him. "Well, my lord? How shall I begin?"

"By walking back to my tent with me."

But as she came to his side, he paused. His eyes were fixed upon her. She looked down. The bindings of her garments had weakened in the struggle; they parted even as she moved, baring her breast and the long deep weals there.

His hand went out, but did not touch her; his breath hissed between his teeth. "You didn't tell me of that."

"It's nothing." She pulled the broken laces free, angrily. *"Damn!* Now everyone in the world will be able to see—"

Gently but firmly he set her hands aside and eased back coat and shirt. She did not resist him, at first for defiance, and after because there was nothing shameful in either his look or his touch. The wounds were red, inflamed, a steady pain which she schooled herself to ignore. Yet where his hand passed, even where she was most tender and most cruelly torn, the pain lessened, faded and shrank and was gone; the scarlet weals paled to scars and vanished.

His hand rose to her cheek. She caught it. "No," she said. He blinked, caught between power and its refusal. "Let me have my own pain."

"It will scar," he said.

"I've earned it with my foolishness."

For yet a moment he was still. Then he bowed his head. "Here," he said in the most ordinary of tones, holding out a bit of leather from his belt, "see if this will hold."

It would, admirably. With her shirt well and tightly laced and her coat belted against the world, she strode with Mirain into the clamor of the camp.

Seven

MIRAIN'S LORDS GATHERED ABOUT HIS TENT, AND their clamor sounded for all the world like the lowing of cattle. When he plunged into the midst of them with Elian at his heels, their silence was abrupt and absolute. Elian admired it; even Prince Orsan had not mastered that art as Mirain had. He stood in the center of them under the Sun-standard, and settled his arm easily, lightly, over Elian's shoulders. "See," he said, with no more greeting than that. "I have a new squire. Galan, my lords and captains."

Later she would match the faces to the names out of Mirain's legend. Now they were a blur: curiosity, hostility, haughty indifference. One or two were envious. One or two, perhaps, wished her well.

One gave her nothing at all. He stood a little aloof, glittering in his finery, meeting her gaze as he had in the winestall. "Ho, Vadin!" Mirain called out in pure and hateful exuberance, "I've found us a new recruit; or your brother has, with a little help from his scouts. What do you think of him?"

The Lord of Geitan made his way through the clustered captains. Elian, looking up and up, knew that he would hate her.

He looked down and down. He was cool, proud, running those splendid eyes over her disheveled and travelworn figure. Pausing. Raising a brow the merest suggestion of a degree. Her probe met a wall. It was high, it was broad, and it was impenetrable. His face betrayed nothing but consummate northern arrogance. His voice was neither warm nor cold, although she knew he had a temper, a hot one; it was in all the tales. He could be as cruel as any mountain bandit, as gentle as any sheltered maiden. "So this is a red Gileni," he said. "Red indeed! I've seen fire that was paler."

"So this," said Elian, "is a Ianyn of the old breed. I've seen eagles who were humbler."

Vadin startled her speechless: he grinned, wide and white and irrepressible. He looked exactly like Cuthan his brother, no older and not a whit wiser. "By the gods, you've got a tongue on you. A temper too. What do you do for sport? Trade insults with dragons?"

"Only if they insult me first."

He laughed, undismayed. "I wasn't insulting, I was admiring. We love copper, we savages. What a wonder to grow one's own."

"Pretty, no?" Mirain's eyes glinted upon them both, and flickered round the circle of faces. "My lords, I am at your disposal." And as they bowed, he returned to the two who still faced one another, and said, "Vadin, for charity, take my squire in hand. He's had good training, but he's a stranger here; there's much that you can teach him."

The Ianyn bowed his high head. Mirain smiled his swift splendid smile and left them, striding swiftly, with his lords in a gaggle behind.

Elian watched him go, and considered hating him. He had abandoned her. She was alone, a stranger to all that was here, where everyone had his duties and his place. She had nothing but the clothes she stood in and the throbbing weals upon her cheek.

Slowly she turned to face her guide. Vadin was expressionless again, and no doubt seething. He was the right hand of An-Sh'Endor, chief of the lords and generals; for a certainty he had duties far higher and more pressing than the nursemaiding of one young foreigner.

His lips twitched. "I've done it before," he said, driving her behind her strongest shields. "Come, youngling. We'll make you one of us."

At the beginning of their progress Vadin acquired a servant, a great hulk of a man who bore with ease the weight of clothing and weapons and the odd necessity. "No kilt for you, I think," Vadin said as she contemplated one in utter dismay. "My lord likes to see his people in their own proper dress. Even," he added with a curl of his lip, "in trousers."

She kept her temper in hand. It was not easy. "Don't you sometimes find a kilt rather uncomfortable? In the saddle, for example? In the dead of winter?"

"In winter we lace our boots high and pin our cloaks tightly and laugh at the wind. In the saddle," said Vadin, and now he was certainly laughing, "which is where all of us are born, we're perfectly comfortable."

"I'll wager you cheat and wear breeches underneath."

"Would you like me to show you?" He laid a hand on his belt; his eyes danced, utterly wicked.

Elian closed her mouth and set it tight. Yes, she hated Mirain. Of all the men in all his horde, why had he thrown her on the mercy of this one?

"Southern kit," Vadin said to the quartermaster, blissfully ignorant of her fury, "in the king's colors. Dress and campaign issue both, and be quick. My lord will be waiting for it."

The quartermaster all but licked the Ianyn's feet. Likewise the armorer, who measured Elian with much commentary on her fine boyish figure, and how much growing room was the lad likely to need?

"Not overmuch," replied her insufferable guide. "We'll take a knife now, and a sword. The three longswords you forged for my lord before he found one that satisfied him—bring them out."

"But, lord, they—"

Vadin's voice did not rise, but the man stopped as if struck. "The king's body-squire must be armed as well as the king himself. Bring out the blades."

They were plain, yet perfect in their plainness: pure, unadorned, deadly beauty, forged not of bronze but of priceless steel. In the Hundred Realms, few even of princes had such weapons. Prince Orsan had two; they were the greatest treasures of his armory. Neither was as fine as these.

She tested each with the reverence it deserved. Each fit well into her hand. But one, lifted, settled as if it had grown there. "This—this one," she said unsteadily, tearing her eyes from that wondrous, shimmering edge.

When she left the armorer's tent, the sword hung scabbarded from her belt, and she walked a little the straighter for it. Even Vadin's presence seemed less of a burden; as he led her toward the cavalry lines, it slipped from her mind altogether.

The north was famous for its seneldi, and Ianon above all; and these were the cream therefrom. Even the draybeasts were fine strong creatures; the war-seneldi, horned battle-stallions and tall fierce mares, were magnificent. Elian walked down the long lines, among the penned wagonbeasts and the remounts, pausing here and there to return a whickered greeting.

Alone of them all, one son of the night wind was free to run where he would. He was as black as polished obsidian, without mark or blemish; his horns were as long as swords, his eyes as red as heart's blood. He trotted through his domain with such splendid, royal arrogance that even the stallions made no move to challenge him.

"There goes a creature worth a kingdom," Elian said.

"If any king could master him," said Vadin. "No one but Mirain has ever sat on the Mad One's back."

The senel came closer. Grooms and idlers were quick to clear his path. Even Vadin stepped aside, without fear but with considerable respect.

Elian stood her ground. She was no less royal than the stallion; while she had no hope of becoming his master, she was certainly his equal.

She was full in his path. On either side stretched a long line of tethered mounts. He snorted and flattened his ears. "Courteously, sir," she said.

His teeth bared. He pawed the ground.

"If you harm me, my lord may not be pleased."

He seemed to ponder that, lean ears flicking forward, back. As if in sudden decision, they pricked. He stepped forward. With utmost delicacy he lowered his head and blew sweet breath upon her palm. She ran a hand over his ears, along the splendid arch of his neck. "Indeed, lord king, now you may pass. But if it would please you, is there one of your herd who would consent to carry me?"

He himself would, and gladly, but he had but one lord. Yet there were some . . . He turned, stepping softly. She laced her fingers in his mane.

As the Mad One permitted no man but Mirain on his back, likewise he suffered no other beast to do that service. Even so, Ianon's king traveled with his own stable: the nine royal mounts decreed by custom, and the mounts and remounts of his household. These held to their own guarded lines, watched over by grooms in scarlet kilts.

The Mad One paid no heed to the lesser beasts, the least of them as fine as Elian's poor lost mare. He passed them in cool disdain, seeking out the center of the line and the King's Nine tethered there. Two were stallions, a black and a grey, sleek with light work and good feeding. The rest were mares, one of each color: brown, bay, roan, grey, striped dun, and gold. The ninth, a mare likewise, grazed apart. She had been tethered; Elian saw a halter empty upon the ground.

The Mad One loosed a high, imperious cry. The mare raised her head, and Elian caught her breath. Line for line, the young senel was the Mad One's image. Save only in color: that was the precise, fiery red-gold of Elian's hair.

The stallion arched his neck. His daughter, this was: Ilhari, Firemane. She was young; she was very foolish; she had never yet been ridden. But she would carry the lady, if the lady wished it.

Ilhari flattened her ears. And what right had he to say what she would or would not do?

The same right, he responded with a toss of his head, that the Sunborn had to bring a useless filly to war. One who, moreover, could not even keep her place in the line, but would slip free at every opportunity and run wild on the grass.

Precisely like her sire.

Elian laughed, approaching the mare slowly. Indeed Ilhari was the Mad One's daughter. She had the same wild ruby eye, the same wicked temper. Yet she also had his deep and well-concealed core of perfect sanity. She watched, but she did not threaten, merely lifted a hind foot in warning.

"Princess," asked Elian, "would you consent to carry me?"

Ilhari's back quivered as if to cast off a fly. It would certainly please yon great black bully. For herself . . .

Elian touched the quivering muzzle. The mare was finer than her sire, smaller, more delicate. Elian stroked aside the long silken forelock and smoothed the star upon her forehead. "I would not bridle you, nor tether you. A saddle I would need, for battle if for naught else."

No one had ever sat upon Ilhari's back. The Sunborn had not allowed it. She was the free one, the king's ninth mount, the Mad One's daughter.

"I am royal. The Sunborn calls me his kin. The Mad One has consented to accept me."

Ilhari snorted. Ah, the Mad One! He did as he pleased.

"And might not we? Come, stand, so. Yes. Yes!" Lightly Elian swung onto her back. For a long moment Ilhari stood rigid. Cautiously she essayed a step. She felt strange, unbalanced.

"That passes," said Elian.

She reared. Elian's knees tightened; her body shifted forward; her fingers knotted in the long mane. Ilhari bucked and twisted. Elian only clung the tighter. The mare reared again, wheeling as she came down, flinging herself forward, plowing to a halt.

Elian laughed.

Ilhari snorted. Rider, nothing. This was a leech.

Elian stroked the sleek neck. "You're not angry with me. You only pretend to be."

Ilhari extended a forefoot to rub an itch from her cheek. It was not so very unpleasant. Perhaps. Once she learned the way of it.

"Well," said Elian, "shall we begin?"

Caught up in the beginnings of subtle and intricate art, with the Mad One both mocking and teaching beside them, neither noticed until very late that they had gathered an audience. Elian had her first hint of it when, glancing sidewise, she met Mirain's white smile. He had come up unseen, smooth as a partner in a dance, and found his way onto the stallion's back.

She tensed. Ilhari had halted, immobile as a carven senel. "My lord, she's yours, I know it, but—"

"Mine," he said, "she never has been. If her sire sees fit to bring you two together, should I interfere?"

"But—"

"She has made her own choice." He saluted them both with a flourish. "The singers will have a new song tonight."

"Singers? Song?" Elian looked beyond him. She had completely forgotten Vadin. He stood near the lines, foremost of a mob of watchers. Even at that distance she could see his smile and the hand he raised in salute. All about him, a cheer went up, high and exuberant.

She acknowledged them without conscious thought, a bow and a smile they could see, and words they could not hear. "Sun and stars! How long have they been there?"

"A good hour, I should think."

Elian dismounted hastily and ran her hands over Ilhari's flanks. The mare was sweating lightly but otherwise unharmed, and scarcely weary. She danced a little, nuzzling Elian's hair. That had been delightful. When could they do it again?

"Tomorrow," Elian promised her.

The king's council was less an affair of state than a gathering of friends. Splendid as the evening was, warm and clear, with a sunset like a storm of fire, they sat as they pleased before his tent, eating and drinking and conversing at first of small things.

Elian did squire's duty for the king until the wine went round, when he drew her down beside him. One or two kilted chieftains looked askance. The others, Geitan's lord conspicuous among them, took no notice.

She settled herself as comfortably as she might in her stiff new livery, and toyed with a cup of wine, resting its coolness against her torn cheek. The flow of speech had shifted. Hawks and hounds and women, fine mounts and old battles, passed and were forgotten.

"We have a choice," said a man who had once called himself a king. He decked himself still with a circlet of gold, although he was lavish in his homage to his conqueror. "We can strike south into the Hundred Realms. Or we can turn west. There's a wide land between here and Asanion, full of tribes ripe, and rich, for conquest."

"West, say I." The accent was Ianyn, and proud with it. "Then south, with whole force of the north behind us."

Another man of Ianon spoke from across the fire. "Why not head south now? We're in Ashan already, or as close as makes no matter. There's easy pickings here by all accounts, and easier the farther you go: fat rich southerners gone lazy with peace."

"Not that lazy," said one with the twang of Ebros and the garb of a mercenary captain. "They can fight when they're roused. They drove back all the armies of the Nine Cities not so long ago, and kept them back."

"Talked them back, I hear," a northerner drawled. "Southerners and westerners, they talk. We fight."

Someone came up round the edge of the council. With a small start, Elian recognized Cuthan. He flashed her a glance that took in her place and her livery, and saluted her with a smile, even as he bent to murmur in Mirain's ear. She opened mind and ears to overhear.

"Nothing, sire," Cuthan was saying. "We found evidence of a fair-sized camp, and not an old one either, but it was completely deserted, with nothing to show where the reivers had gone."

"Might they have scattered?" Mirain asked.

"Maybe. If so, they went to all the dozen winds, and covered their tracks behind them."

"How many might there have been?"

"Hard to tell, my lord. Say, half a hundred. Maybe less, not likely more, or they'd have left some traces."

Mirain bowed his head. "You've done well. Go out again for me, and search further. If you find even the smallest thing, see that I hear of it."

"Aye, my lord. The god keep you."

Cuthan grinned at his brother, and again at Elian. With a scout's skill, he merged himself with the twilight and was gone. Mirain reclined as before, propped up on his elbow, eyes hooded as the council continued about him. Elian knew better than to think that he had missed a word of it.

Voices raised, cutting across one another. "And I say the north is enough! What do we want with a pack of barbarians, southern, western, whatever they may be?"

"What do we want? Damn you, we want to rule them! What else are barbarians good for?"

"Yes." Mirain spoke softly, but he won sudden silence. "What are we good for? For I was born in the south."

"Your mother was heir of Ianon," said the man who had spoken last, with a touch of belligerence.

"Her mother was a princess of Asanion." Mirain rose. He could use his height exactly as he chose, to tower over the seated captains, yet to make clear to them that he lacked much of the stature of Ianon. "My lords, you speak of choices. South or west; east no one seems to think of, but that's only wild lands and the sea. Well then. West are our kinsmen, tribes who serve the god as we serve him, and past these the marches of the Golden Empire. South lie the Hundred Realms. Another empire, one might say, though none of the people there would choose to call it that."

"Well, so are we," said Vadin, speaking for the first time. "The empire of the north. And hasn't your father given you the world to rule?"

Mirain's smile was wry. *"Given* is hardly the word, brother, and well you know it. Offered for my winning, rather." His eyes flashed round them. "What next, then? South or west? Who will choose?"

"You, of course," said Vadin. "Who has a better right?"

"Someone may. Galan!"

She started. Mirain faced her, suddenly a stranger, fierce and fey. "Galan, where would you have me go?"

She spoke her thought, unsoftened and unadorned. "When you're done with your jesting, you will do exactly as you always meant to do: pass the border your scouts have already pierced, and march upon the south. Halenan knew. He gave me a message for you. He called you a damned fool; he said, 'If he sets foot in my lands, it had better be as a friend, or god's son or no, I'll have his head on my spear.' "

Anger flared within the circle. But Mirain laughed, light and wild. "Did he say that? He can say it again when we meet. For southward indeed I will go, with the god before me. What of you, Red Prince's kin? Will you ride at my right hand?"

He wanted a bold brave answer. Elian gave him one; though not perhaps the one he had expected. "I will ride at your right hand," she said. "And see to it that it is indeed friendship in which you come. Or—"

"Or?" He was bright, laughing, dangerous.

She grinned back. "Or you will answer not simply to me, or to Halenan. You will answer to the Red Prince himself."

"I think I need not fear that."

"You should," she said, surprising herself: because she believed it. "But as for me, I have given you my oath. While I live I will keep it. I will ride south with you, Mirain An-Sh'Endor."

Eight

THE SON OF THE SUN TOOK ASHAN WITHOUT A BLOW struck. For as his army passed the forest that was the northern march of the princedom and entered upon its maze of stony valleys, riders came to him under the yellow banner of the prince. They laid themselves at Mirain's feet, sued for peace, and called him king, beseeching him to receive their lord's homage in his own walled city. Themselves they offered as hostages, and with them an open-faced young fellow who, but for the distinct red-brown cast of his skin, might have been Ianyn; he was, he said, close kin to the prince.

Not the heir, Elian took note, but close enough. Old Luian, who might have waged a long and deadly war among his crags, had cast in his lot with the conqueror.

And, having made his choice, he stinted nothing. His castles lay open to the army; his folk hailed them as victors; his vassals came forth with gifts and homage. It was no invasion but a royal progress that brought Mirain to Han-Ashan where waited the prince.

He was old. Too old, his messengers said, to venture his bones upon the mountain tracks. He received Mirain at the gate of his own hall, leaning on the arms of two stalwart young men, the most favored of his twoscore sons; yet he left his living props to perform the full obeisance of a vassal before his king.

Mirain received it as he had received all else in Ashan, with gracious words, royal mien, and the expressionless face of a god carved in stone.

His king-face, Elian called it. His mind yielded nothing at all to her, blank and impenetrable as the walls of Luian's castle.

She served him at the feast in Prince Luian's hall, squire service much eased by the courtesy of the host; there was in fact little for her to do but stand behind Mirain's seat and see that the servants kept both his cup and his plate filled. He ate little, she noticed, and only pretended to drink.

She thought she knew why. Ashani women lived like women of the west, veiled and set apart from men, but the highborn dined in hall at festivals. Luian's chief wife shared his throne, a woman of great bulk and yet also of great and imposing beauty; many of his lords and commons kept company with wives or mistresses. Of unwedded women there were few, and those only the highest: a tall lithe woman with a priestess' torque who was the prince's daughter, and the daughters of one or two of his sons.

One of whom, child of the heir himself, had been set between Mirain and her father. This, Elian well knew, was somewhat out of the proper order. Most of the royal ladies tended to favor their grandsire: Ianyn-tall, nearly Ianyn-dark, and strikingly handsome. This one was smaller, slight and shapely, her delicate hands and her smooth brow unmarred by any taint of southern bronze, her eyes huge, round, and darkly liquid as the eyes of a doe. The rest of her face was clear enough to see beneath the veil, a delicate oval, a suggestion of perfect teeth. If she had a flaw, it was her voice: high and, though she took pains to soften it, rather sharp.

Mirain seemed captivated, leaning close to hear her murmured speech, smiling at a jest. He was splendid to see, clad in the full finery of a Ianyn king, all white and gold; his skin gleamed against it like ebony. Elian herself had braided the ropes of gold into his hair. He had turned as she struggled to tame the unruly mass of it, and ruffled her own newly subdued mane, and laughed at her flash of temper.

Her lips twisted wryly. Well; was that not what she had wanted? She walked abroad as a man, and he regarded her as one; although she shared his tent, he had never once touched her save as a brother or a friend, nor looked at her as a man might look at a woman. Even when he had seen her naked breast, he had seen only wounds that cried for healing.

The lady held his hands in hers, giggling on a high and piercing note. The god's mark fascinated her: the Sun of gold set in the flesh, fused with it, part of it.

"You can touch it," he said, warm and indulgent. "It won't hurt you."

She giggled. "No. Oh, no! I couldn't. That would be sacrilege!" But she did not let go his hand.

Elian's glance crossed Vadin's. The Ianyn lord had evaded the bonds of princely protocol by the simple expedient of commanding his brother to take his name and his place, and putting on the garb and the bearing of a guard, and setting himself to watch over Mirain. Elian had learned, not easily, that it did no good to resent him. He went where he would, did as he pleased, and answered only to his king. Elian he treated with unfailing courtesy, which some might even have taken for friendliness: the friendliness of a man toward his brother's favorite hound.

He leaned against the wall, cool and easy, smiling a little. "My lord is well entertained tonight," he observed. "They make a handsome pair, don't you think?"

Elian kept her face quiet, but her eyes glittered. "How can he endure her?"

"How does any man endure a beautiful woman?"

"She has a voice like a tortured cat."

"She has a rich dowry."

Elian drew a sharp breath.

"After all," said Vadin, "he's been king these seven years. It's time he got himself an heir."

"Strong throne, strong succession." Elian bit off the words. "I know that. Who doesn't? But this—"

"Can you offer a better candidate?"

Elian would not answer. Dared not. And Vadin did not press her. He was, inexplicably and maddeningly, amused. Yet he did not know. He could not.

Elian put on her best, boyish scowl. Vadin only grinned and wandered off on some whim of his own.

Mirain came up very late from the feasting. Later than Elian, who had left as soon as was proper, after the second passing of the wine; but the women had retired before the first.

He greeted her with his quick smile. He had been drinking deep: his eyes were bright and his breath wine-scented. Yet he was steady on his feet. As she rose from her pallet, he motioned her down again. "No, be at ease; I can undress myself."

She came in despite of him to catch his cloak and his jewels as they fell. He always turned his back on her to doff his kilt, more for her

modesty's sake than for his own; in Ianon, Cuthan had told her, all the
servants of his bath were women, maiden daughters of noble houses.
She smiled in spite of herself as she unbound the intricate plaits of his
hair, remembering the tale, a young priest from Han-Gilen forced for
the first time to strip naked before a roomful of fine ladies. And knowing full well the root of the custom: the strengthening of noble lines
with the blood royal, perhaps even the choosing of one favored lady to
share the throne.

Mirain yawned and stretched, supple as a cat. "Hold still," Elian
bade him, half annoyed, half preoccupied. He obeyed docilely enough.
She continued her patient unraveling, letting each freed strand fall to
his shoulders. He had battle scars in plenty, but all were on his front;
his back was smooth, unmarred. Once, as by accident, she let her fingertips brush his skin. It was soft like a child's, but the muscles were steel-
hard beneath.

He yawned again. "These Ashani," he said. "They seem to practice
half their statecraft in a haze of wine."

"They have a maxim: Wine to begin a thought, sleep and morning
light to end it. And another: Soften your opponent with wine, and mold
him when he wakes from it."

"They do the same in Ianon. But not so blatantly. Once he had the
company down to the serious drinkers, Prince Luian launched his attack. He would become my true and loyal liege man, faithful servant of
the god's son, if only I would grant a small favor in return."

"Of course. How small?"

"Minuscule. The merest trifle. It seems that he can't agree with the
Prince of Ebros as to the lordship of a certain valley. The Prince of
Ebros has garrisoned it very recently with his own troops. Will I lend
my army to restore the vale to its rightful master?"

"Will you?"

"I've been considering it. There's been a great deal of tumult over this
bit of green with a river running through it: embassies and counter-
embassies, threats and counterthreats. I've a mind to see if I can uncover the rights of the matter."

His hair was free. She coiled its golden bindings in their box; when
she turned back, Mirain was upright in the bed, the coverlet drawn up.
wielding a comb with no patience at all. Deftly she won the comb and
began to repair the damage. "Ebros and Ashan have never been fond of
one another. If you march on this valley, even if you only intend to
determine its possession, Ebros' prince will say you've come to start a
war."

"In that event, I'll make sure I come out the victor."

"You want Ebros, don't you? However you get it."

He looked up. He was still, quiet. But the mask had gone up between his heart and the world. "Will you stop me?"

She considered it with no little care. He watched her. She scowled at him. "You're playing with me again. Pretending that what I say can matter."

"But," he said, "it can."

Her scowl blackened. "Because I'm myself, or because I have a father who can raise the south against you?"

"Or," he continued for her, "because the High Prince of Asanion wants you for his harem?"

Her heart stilled. Her throat locked, all but strangling her voice. "I— I never—how did you—"

"Spies," he answered. He was not laughing. She could not read him at all. "They have an ill name, these royal Asanians. They are trained from the cradle in the arts of the bedchamber; they keep women like cattle; they worship all gods and none. They have three great arts: love, and sophistry, and treachery. And their greatest pride lies in the weaving of all three."

"Ilarios is not like that at all." The silence was abrupt, and somehow frightening. Elian filled it with a rush of words. "He asked for me in all honor. He promised to make me his empress."

"And you came to me."

"I came because I promised."

Mirain said nothing for a long count of breaths. When he spoke, he spoke softly, and as if Ilarios had never been. "I will have Ebros. If I must take it by force, so be it. But I will rule it in peace." He shifted, body and mind; he lightened, turned wry. "A subtle man, my host. He sweetens his conditions with purest honey: the offer of his granddaughter's hand."

Elian's hand stopped. "Did you accept it?"

He laughed. "I have a policy," he said. "When a man offers to make a marriage for me, I thank him kindly. I promise to consider the matter. And I make no further mention of it."

"And if he insists?"

"I speak of something else."

She was silent, combing the wild mane into smoothness. Many a woman might have envied it, waist-long, thick and curling as it was. At length she said, "A king should marry for the sake of his dynasty." Her lip curled a little as she said it. Wise words. Her mother had said very nearly the same thing, in very nearly the same tone.

Mirain could not see her face; he said calmly, "So a king should. So shall I."

"When you've found a woman fit to be your queen?"

"I have found her."

Elian's eyes dimmed as if she had been struck a blow. But she was royal; she had learned discipline, seldom though she chose to exercise it. "How wise of you," she said lightly, "to let your allies believe that they are free to bind you with their kinswomen. What is she like, this lady of yours?"

"Very beautiful. Very witty. Rather wild, if the truth be told; but I have a weakness for wild things."

"Well dowered, I suppose."

"Very. She is a princess."

"Of course." Elian was done, but she toyed with his hair, lingering, like a woman who frets with an aching tooth, testing again and again the intensity of the pain. "Her kinsmen must be very pleased."

"Her kin know nothing of it. I've not yet offered for her. She's shy, you see, and elusive, and wary as a young lynx. She is no man's to give, nor ever mine to compel. She must come to me of her own will, however slowly, however long the coming."

"That's not wise. What if someone takes her while you are away on your wars?"

"I think I need have no fear of that."

Slowly, carefully, Elian set the comb aside. "You are fortunate."

He lay back. His smile was a cat's, drowsy, sated, with the merest hint of irony. "Yes," he said. "I am."

She turned her back on him and sought her pallet.

"Good night," he called softly.

"Good night, my lord," she said.

Nine

*E*LIAN FLEXED HER SHOULDERS. HER NEW PANOPLY
fit like a skin of bronze and gold, but its weight was strange, both
lighter and stronger than the Gileni armor she was used to.

Under her, Ilhari shifted. Strangeness? Maybe. Or maybe it was simple fear. She for one would be greatly pleased when her first battle lay
behind her.

Ilhari's logic was as usual impeccable. Elian smoothed the battle-
streamers woven into the mare's mane, green on red-gold. Mirain, she
noticed, was just completing the same gesture. The Mad One's streamers were scarlet, the color of blood.

He seemed unconcerned, even lighthearted, sitting at ease in the saddle, gazing down a long gentle slope at the enemy. His army massed
behind him, swelled now with Ashani troops. The field beneath it had
been golden with grain, but the grain was trampled, its gold dimmed.
The earth had sprouted another crop altogether, a harvest of flesh and
steel.

Elian watched him consider it calmly, without haste. His forces were
disposed on the ground he had chosen, a shoulder of Ashan's mountains that dwindled here to a low rolling hill, with wide lands behind
and his camp settled in them.

More than a garrison faced him. The whole army of Ebros had mustered to drive back the northerners; had refused all his embassies and
his offers of just and bloodless judgment; had forsaken the high-walled

town whose folk tilled these fields, and come forth to open combat. They had the town and its steep hill at their backs, but their own emplacements lay perforce below Mirain's; if they charged, it must be uphill against a rain of arrows. Yet they were strong, and they had a wing of that most terrible of weapons, the scythed battle-car. Even their own men kept well away from those deadly whirling wheels.

Their commander rode up and down before them in a lesser chariot, yet one very splendid, flashing gold and crimson. Matched mares drew it, their coats bright gold, their manes flowing like white water. He himself shone in golden armor, with a coronet on his high helmet.

"Indrion of Ebros," said Prince Luian's heir from his chariot beside Mirain, with a century of bitter feuding in his voice and in the glitter of his eyes. "Now we shall settle with that cattle thief."

It was an ill word, Elian thought, for that splendid royal vision. Mirain paid its speaker no heed. The enemy had begun to fret before the massed stillness of his army. Yet that stillness was his own, the immobility of the lion before it springs.

The Ebran line could bear it no longer. With a roar it surged forward. Still Mirain did not move.

Elian's heart thudded. The Ebrans were close, perilously close. She could pick out single men from among the mass: a mounted knight, a light-armed charioteer, a footsoldier in worn leather with a patch in his breeks. She saw the patch very clearly. It was ill-sewn, as if he had done it himself, and of a lighter leather than the rest, incongruously new and clean.

A hand touched her. She started and stiffened. Mirain's hand left her, but his eyes held. No man's eyes, those, but the eyes of a god: bright, cold, alien. "Remember," he said, soft but very clear. "No heroics. You cling to me like a burr; you look after my weapons; you leave the rest to my army."

She opened her mouth to speak, perhaps to protest. But he had turned from her, and his household was watching. Some smiled. The younger ones in particular; they thought they understood. "Cheer up, lad," said the one closest. "You'll get your chance."

"Aye and aye!" agreed another. "Here's luck, and glory enough for everybody." He grinned and clapped her on the shoulder, rocking her in the saddle. She grinned back through clenched teeth.

Ebros reached the hill's foot. Bows sang. Arrows arced upward. One fell spent at the Mad One's feet.

For a long moment Mirain regarded it. Elian longed to shriek at him, to beat him into motion.

His sword swept from its scabbard. With a fierce stallion-scream, the Mad One charged.

Ilhari pounded upon his heels. Elian clung to the saddle by blind instinct. All her anger, all her impatience, even the sickness of her fear, lost itsef in the thunder of the charge. There remained only startlement, and a growing exhilaration. The wind in her face; the splendid sword—when had she drawn it?—in her hand; the surge of seneldi strength beneath her. Behind her, the army; before her, always before her, the scarlet fire of the Sunborn. No target practice, this, no game of war upon a table. This was battle as the singers sang of it. She laughed and bent over the flying mane.

With a mighty shock, the armies clashed.

Alone, Elian might have run wild. But Ilhari would not leave the Mad One. That too was madness, of a sort; for there always was the press thickest, the battle hottest. Southern-trained Mirain might be, but he fought as a chieftain of the north, at the forefront of his army, guide and beacon for all the rest.

He was mad. God-mad; possessed. No arrow touched him. No blade pierced his flashing guard. His eyes shone; his body kindled with light that waxed as he advanced. Even when a cloud dimmed the sun, he blazed forth bright golden.

Elian, tossing in his wake, carrying his spears and the shield that, like a true madman, he scorned to use, felt the last of her temper drain away. Awe rose in its place.

She fought it as she fought the enemy who massed about her, fiercely. This was her brother. She had taken her first steps clinging to his hand, shaped her first letters under his teaching, learned first how to wield a sword with his hand over hers upon the hilt. He ate and slept like any man, dreamed both well and ill, and woke blear-eyed, tousled and boylike and faintly cross-grained. He laughed at soldiers' jests, wept unashamedly when his singer lamented the sorrows of old lovers, cast admiring eyes upon a good mount or a fine hound or a handsome woman. He was human. Living, breathing, warm and solid, human.

He rode in battle like a god.

A blade leaped at her. She parried, riposted, as her weapons master had taught her. The keen steel plunged through hardened leather into flesh and grated on bone. With a wrench she freed it. She never saw the man fall. Her first man. Ilhari slashed with hoofs and teeth at a smaller, broader senel, its rider fantastically armored, whirling a sword about his head.

Heroics, thought Elian. His bravado left bare the unarmored space between arm and side. Her sword's point found it, pierced it.

" *'Ware right!* "

She wheeled. Bronze sang past her arm. Another's blade cut down her attacker; a white grin flashed at her. Vadin in barbaric splendor, His Helm crowned with copper and plumed with gold, his gorget of copper set with Ianyn amber. His brother was with him, trying to echo his grin, but regarding Elian with eyes wide, level, and much too dark. Why, she thought, nettled, the boy had been terrified for her. Suddenly it all seemed wonderfully ridiculous. She laughed. "My thanks!" she called out to them both.

Vadin bowed and laughed with her and spun his mare away. Cuthan nudged his tall stallion to her side as if he meant to stay there. He refused to see her glare.

For a moment the tide of battle had ebbed. The vanguard could rest, catch breath, inspect one another for wounds. Mirain's standardbearer grounded the staff of the Sun-banner and gentled his restive mount. The king sat still, eyes running over the field.

It was a good vantage. They had passed the hill's foot and begun to mount the slope to the town. All over the wide field the battle raged; but the northerners had thrust deep, drivine Ebros against the walls. The prince's banner caught the wind before the gate. He kept to the custom of southern generals, ruling from behind, where he could see all that passed and escape danger to himself.

"It goes well," said Cuthan. "See, their right has fallen."

"Their left holds," another of the household pointed out, "and they've got walls to retreat to. We're not done yet."

"They're regrouping." Cuthan leaned forward, intent. The enemy was drawing back, gathering together, mustered by trumpets and by the shouts of captains. Mirain's forces pursued them hotly; they offered little resistance.

Mirain loosed an exclamation. His trumpeter glanced at him. His hand swept out in assent.

His army heard the sudden clear notes. *Retreat,* they sang. *Retreat and re-form.* The companies wavered. *Retreat!* the trumpet cried.

Slowly, then more swiftly, the army moved to obey. But one great company was not so minded. Deaf or obstinate, it pressed on, harrying its Ebran prey. Its captain rode behind it under the banner of Ashan.

Ebros massed now before the walls. As the last company fought its way forward, the ranks seethed. Horns rang. Cymbals clashed.

Mirain's voice lashed out at his household. *"Stay!"* But the Mad One was in motion, springing toward the Ashani forces.

Ilhari followed. Elian urged her on. Mirain's glance blazed upon them, his will like a physical blow. Cuthan's stallion, close and dogged upon their heels, staggered and bucked to a halt, and would not advance for all of Cuthan's spurring and cursing. Ilhari stumbled, shook her head, lengthened and steadied her stride.

Glittering, deadly, the scythed chariots rolled forth from the Ebran lines.

The Mad One stretched from a gallop to his full, winged speed. He closed in upon the Ashani rearguard, veered left.

Ilhari swayed toward the right. The wind whipped into Elian's eyes, blinding her; yet she knew where they passed. Round the racing army, footmen, cavalry, chariots. Chariots foremost, the light war-cars of nobles, unscythed, all but unarmored, their strength resting wholly in the arms of the warriors who rode them.

Ilhari hurled herself across their path. Seneldi veered. Reins and wheels tangled. Men rolled under sharp cloven hoofs. "Back!" cried Elian, high and piercing. "In Avaryan's name, back!"

Sun's fire blazed, dazzling her. A deep voice echoed her own. The Ashani ground to a halt.

"Back!" roared Mirain.

Step by step, then in a rush of hoofs and feet and a clashing of bronze, they obeyed him.

Thunder rumbled behind. Indrion had loosed the scythed chariots.

Ilhari tensed to bolt. The Mad One spun on his haunches. His nostrils were wide, blood-red, his neck whitened with foam, yet Mirain seemed as calm as ever, Enspelled, perhaps, by the whirling scythes.

"No," he said. Softly though he spoke, Elian heard him distinctly. "See. They hinder one another; they fear their own fellows." He might have been on the training field, instructing her in the arts of war. "Come now. We have our own work yet to do."

He did not return directly to his command, but angled right, riding swiftly yet easily. When Elian glanced over her shoulder, the chariots were closer. Yet, terrible though they were, still they were but a few. And Mirain's army was drawn up in a wide crescent. At its center, the charge's target, massed a phalanx of men on foot, shields linked into a wall. Before them waited mounted archers, and men in light armor on light swift mares, armed with long lances.

Ashan's men found their place in the right wing. Some companies might have continued their flight once it was begun, but if the Ashani were fools, they were brave fools. They turned again to fight at need.

As Mirain crossed the face of his army and circled the phalanx to find his banner, a shout ran with him, deep and jubilant. It had his name in it, and his titles, and—Elian stiffened a little, startled—her own usename. But she had done nothing. It was Ilhari who had refused to leave her sire.

And Galan who brought half a charging legion to a standstill. Stern though Mirain's face was, his mind-voice held more approval than not. He was almost proud of her. Almost. There was still the matter of his command and of her flagrant disobedience.

She would pay for it later. But as she returned to the household gathered behind the phalanx as behind a wall, she felt the warmth of their greeting. Even Cuthan met her with a wide white grin. Recklessly she returned it.

The chariots came on. Behind them advanced the Ebran army. The prince's banner rode in the center now, edging forward.

Mirain's mounted archers sprang into a gallop, fanning across the field. In the spaces between them spurred the lancers. Their spears swung down in a long glittering wave, and leveled, and held.

The air filled with arrows. So slow, they were, rising in lazy arcs yet dropping with blurring speed. Seneldi screamed. Men howled and fell. The lancers thrust in among the racing beasts, striking at them, veering away from the scythes. Arrows sought targets, men and seneldi both, harnessed beasts and unarmed charioteers.

A senel misstepped, stumbled, fell into the whirling blades. Its screams shrilled over the din of battle. Elian squeezed her eyes shut.

The screams faded; hoofs crashed upon metal. Her eyes flew open. The chariots had collided with the phalanx. It held. By Avaryan, it held.

Buckled. Swayed. Stiffened. Broke.

Mirain snatched the trumpet from its startled bearer, set it to his lips, blew a clear imperious call. A roar answered it. With a great clangor of bronze on bronze, the wings of his army closed upon the enemy.

Glory was a fine word in the morning when one was fresh and unscathed and rode at the Sunborn's back. But glory lost its luster in hour after hour of grueling labor, dust and sweat and screaming muscles, blood and entrails, shrieks of pain, curses and gasps and the ceaseless, numbing, smithy-clamor of battle.

Elian no longer knew or cared where she went, save only that the

Mad One remained in her sight, black demon spattered with bright blood. For a time she thought they might be falling back, driven before the chariots and the fierce defenders of Ebros. Then, as a wrestler musters all his strength and surges against his enemy, they thrust forward again. On, on, up the slope of the hill, under the walls.

No, she thought. *No.*

A deadly rain fell upon them: arrows, stones, sand heated in cauldrons and poured down from the walls, seeping beneath armor, searing through flesh into bone.

Mirain's voice cut across the shrieks of agony. The infantry, embattled, thrust together. Shields locked again into the moving fortress of the phalanx. Relentlessly it advanced. Ebros stood at bay with its back to the walls.

Heedless of the hail from the battlements, Mirain sent his stallion plunging against the Ebran line. "Indrion!" he cried, his voice rough with long shouting. "Indrion!"

The Prince of Ebros had long since forsaken either custom or prudence to fight in the first rank of his army. He turned now, hacking his way through Ashani troops, striving to reach Mirain. The young king, battle-wild, strained toward him.

Even as they came together, a chariot cut between them. A man in Ashani armor struck wildly at his old enemy.

Mirain's sword flashed round. The charioteer flailed at reins that held no longer. The flat of the king's blade caught the team across their rumps, sent them bucking and plunging into the heart of the Ashani forces.

Freed of the obstacle, they faced one another, king and prince. Indrion was a tall man, northern-tall, but not so dark; his eyes beneath the plumed helmet were almost golden, and feral as a cat's. With a single graceful movement he vaulted from his chariot and bowed in not-quite-mockery.

Mirain laughed and sprang from the Mad One's back. They stood a moment, poised, taking one another's measure. Without a word, they closed in combat.

Elian's breath came harsh in her throat. Oh, he was mad, mad, mad. He all but held the victory: his shieldwall battered at the gate; his cavalry drove that of Ebros in rout across the field. Yet he faced this giant, this warrior famous throughout the Hundred Realms, and he laughed, daring death to snatch away his triumph.

She clapped heels to Ilhari's sides. The mare set her ears back and braced her feet. Elian tensed to fling herself from the saddle, but iron hands held her fast. She glared into Vadin's eyes. "No," he said. "This is the kingfight. It's not for lesser folk to meddle in."

Elian cursed him, and her obstinate mare, and her madman of a king. Not one of them would yield.

All about them the fight had cooled. Enemies stood side by side, blades drawn and dripping, eyes upon their lords. Even the folk upon the battlements—women, Elian saw now; boys and old men and a mere handful of warriors—had ceased their barrage.

Mirain and Indrion fought alone, gold and gold, scarlet against crimson. Mirain was a warrior in ten thousand, but he had fought unstinting from the first; god's son or no, he was made of flesh, and he was weary. Indrion, newer to the battle, met his skill with skill no less, and with greater strength.

The king was weakening. His blows were less strong, his parries less firm. The two swords locked, guard to guard; his own trembled visibly.

A dead silence held the field. In it, his breathing was hoarse, labored.

With a mighty heave, Indrion flung him back. He stumbled, half fell, recovered without grace. All his guards were down. Even his proud head drooped.

He was beaten. Beaten and waiting to fall. Indrion laughed short and sharp, and closed in for the kill.

Steel whirled in a flashing arc. Up, around, down, full upon the prince's golden helmet. Indrion reeled, incredulous, and toppled.

Mirain stood over the prone body. He was breathing hard, but not as hard as he had pretended; his sword was steady in his hand. City and armies waited for the killing stroke.

He pulled off his helmet and tossed it into the nearest hands—an Ebran's, a youth in the prince's livery, his charioteer. As the boy gaped, Mirain said, "I claim my prisoner and all that is his. Who challenges me?"

No one moved.

Mirain's sword hissed into its sheath. "So." His eyes flashed across the field. "I claim my prisoner, and I set him free. You—you—you. A litter for the prince. Who commands now for him?"

"I command for myself." Prince Indrion could barely sit up. His face was grey, his eyes glazed; but his voice was clear enough. "I yield, my lord king. On this sole condition: that neither my men nor my town be destroyed."

"I had meant it to be so," Mirain said. His hand clasped the prince's; his smile illumined the air between them. With his own hands he saw Indrion settled in a litter and borne from the field.

Ten

*E*BROS WAS CONQUERED. MIRAIN'S ARMY HELD THE town; Prince Indrion's camped without, under the walls. In the grey evening, men with torches moved slowly over the battlefield, heaping the dead for burning, bearing the wounded to the healers' tents on the edge of the Ebran camp. Wherever they passed, the croaking of carrion birds followed them.

Elian could hear it even in the keep. Having seen to it that Mirain doffed his armor and washed away the stains of battle, she had been banished to her bed. She had not struggled overly hard against his will. He had only gone to break bread in hall with the captains of both sides, and she was bone-weary. She had bathed long and rapturously; she had put on a clean shirt, soft over her many bruises and her few, slight wounds; she had lain as Mirain commanded her across the foot of the great bed reserved for the lord of the keep. But sleep would not come.

Her bed was soft, her body no less comfortable than it had been after many a long hunt. She was numb with exhaustion. And she lay openeyed, hearing the harsh cries of the birds called heirs of battle, children of the goddess, eaters of the slain. Where men fought, they fed. They grew fat on slaughter.

She lay on her face deep in the feather bed. In the darkness behind her eyes, the battle unfolded itself, clearer by far in memory than it had been while she fought in it. She saw her bright sword swing up; she saw it fall and grow lurid with blood.

She was a warrior now. Her blade had been blooded. She had learned to kill.

None of the songs told of what came after the fierce joy of the charge: the blood upon the trampled grain, the scatter of limbs and entrails, the carrion stench. There was no splendor in it. Only a dull ache, a sickness in body and brain.

They called her valiant, the men of Mirain's household. After the battle they had given her their accolade, the armor of the Ebran lord whom she had slain, such a trophy as a squire could not claim save by the will of his lord's whole company. And seldom indeed could he win it in his first battle.

If they could see her now, they would despise her.

Or worse, they would know her for a woman. They would mock her, a girlchild who played at manhood, a hoyden princess who feigned the voice and manners of a boy. And there forever would be her fame: in the rude jests of soldiers, where it well deserved to be.

She rolled onto her side. Her stomach heaved; her body knotted about it. "No," she said aloud. "No!"

Abruptly she rose. She pulled on trousers and boots and snatched up the first warm garment that came to hand. Mirain's cloak; but she made no effort to exchange it for a coat of her own. It was warm; it covered her; it carried a faint, comforting scent of him.

The town was quiet, startlingly so. Mirain's army, forbidden either sack or rapine, had also found the stores of strong drink well and firmly guarded. Well fed and sparingly wined, they kept order as in camp, with discipline which many a southern general might have envied. And, Elian thought, remarkably little grumbling.

The gate-guards knew her; they let her pass unchallenged. She paused beyond them. The sky was dark, starless; a thin cold wind skittered over the field. Torches flickered there, moving to and fro like ghost-lights, rising and dipping and sometimes holding still for a long count of breaths. Among them she discerned humped shadows, mounds of the dead. There were three: Ebran, Ashani, Ianyn.

Round the curve of the wall spread the Ebran camp, a huddle of fires, a silent massing of tents. Neither voice nor song rose from them, nor the muted revelry of Mirain's men, nor even the keening of grief. Defeated, pardoned, they took no chances upon their new lord's mercy.

But one pavillion more than made up for the silence of the rest: the healers' tent between the outer wards and the battlefield. Here was clamor, such an uproar as might rise out of hell: moaning and shouting, cries and curses and shrieks of pain.

Close to it, the tumult was numbing, overlaid with a gagging stink and lit with a red demon-light. But worse than the assault upon the body's senses was that upon the mind, wave upon wave of mortal agony.

Elian staggered under it. The tent flaps gaped open; within, men lay in row upon row, lamplit, with somberclad healers bending over them. The wounded, the maimed and the dying, all mingled, friend and enemy, in a red fellowship of pain.

Someone jostled her, muttered a curse, pointed sharply toward a corner. "Walking wounded over there. We'll get to you when we get to you." Before she could speak, the man was gone, tight-drawn with the immensity of his labor.

She edged into the tent. Whatever had brought her here would not let her escape, although the manifold odors of suffering set her stomach in revolt. Battling to master it, she stumbled and fell to her knees.

A man stared at her. A northerner, dark and eagle-proud yet abject with pain. A great wound gaped in his side, roughly bound with strips torn from a cloak. He was dying; he knew it; and his terror tore at all her defenses.

She flung up both hands against it. One brushed the wound, waking agony. Her power swelled like a wave and broke.

Part of her stood aside and watched it and was grimly amused. Blessed, O blessed Lady of Han-Gilen! She who dealt wounds could also heal them; she who slew could bring new life to the dying.

No, not she. The power that dwelt in her, mark of her breeding as surely as the fire of her hair. For those were the three magics of Han-Gilen: to see what would be, to read and to master men's souls, and to heal the wounds of body and mind. Prophet, mage, and healer; by the god's will she was all three. Under her hand the flesh lay whole, marked only by a greying scar.

She looked up. Dark eyes met her own. Mirain bowed his head, equal to equal. This gift too he had, the legacy of his father.

He knelt beside a man in battered Ebran armor. She moved past him to another who waited with death at his shoulder.

Thunder woke Elian from a deep and dreamless sleep. For a long moment she lay bemused. She could remember in snatches: laboring far into the night, finding at last that nothing remained for her to do; every man was dead or healed or would heal of himself. And she who had been weary when she began, had passed beyond exhaustion. She had felt light, hollow, almost drunken. So wonderful, this healing was, the only

magic which left one more joyous than one began, that healed the
healer as well as the one she tended.

Mirain had appeared out of the shadow of the tent, smiling. She
swayed; he caught her, himself far from steady. Leaning on one another, they made their way to the keep.

They ate, she remembered that. The bread was warm, the first of the
new day's baking. The wine was rich with spices. There was fruit and
new cream and a handful of honey sweets. Mirain was as gluttonous for
them as she. They laughed, counting them out, half for each and one
over. "You take it," he said.

"No, you."

He grinned and bit off half of the confection and fed her the rest.
There remained only the wine, a whole flask of it, strong and heady.
Elian, warm with it, loosened the laces of her shirt and let it fall open as
it would.

He watched her, head tilted. "You should never do that where anyone can see you."

"Not even you?" she asked.

"Maybe." His finger brushed her cheek lightly, tracing the paling
scars. "It must be sorcery. When you stand in armor or in my livery, I
see a boy, a youth, Halenan when he was very young. But now, no one
with eyes could possibly take you for aught but a woman. Even your
face: it's too fine to be handsome. It's beautiful."

She snorted. "Some of the men say I'm too pretty for my own good,
scars and all. And much too well aware of it."

"No. That, you aren't. I remember when you used to lament. Your
eyes were too long and too wide; your chin was too stubborn; your body
was too thin and too awkward. For all that anyone can say, you still
believe it."

"That's the best part of this game. No one treats me the way people
treat a beautiful woman. A boy is different, even a pretty boy."

He reflected on that in the way he had; but the wine had lifted his
barriers. His eyes were as clear as water, with a brightness in the heart
of them.

"You are *not* ugly!" she said sharply.

He laughed. That had always been the end of her complaining. He
would say, "Ah, but I really am as unlovely as you think you are." And
she would cry out against him, and he would laugh, because he believed
himself, and she never would; and that was the way of their world.

She seized his face in her two hands and glared into his eyes. "There are plenty of handsome men in the world, brother my love. But there is only one of you."

"Thank Avaryan for that."

"Yes, for begetting you. Who else would have let me be what I want most to be?"

"But what is that?"

She let him go abruptly, filled his cup, thrust it into his hand. "Now's no time to go all cryptic and kingly. Here, drink up. To victory!"

He might have said more, but he paused. His brow lifted; he raised his cup and drank. "To victory," he agreed.

They had drunk, and drunk again. And then, what? Sleep, yes. There had been a very mild quarrel, that she would spread a pallet on the floor, with so wide a bed, and he needing so little of it.

She lay on celestial softness. He had won, then. Carefully she opened an eye. It had been good wine; the light was bearable. Mirain slept in utter and youthful abandon, with the whole long line of his side not a handspan from her own. Whatever his quarrel with his face, even he could not deny that the rest of him was well made. That was clear to see; for he slept as he always slept, as bare as he was born.

And so, this drunken night, had she.

Her breath caught. If anyone ever, ever heard of this, then there would be a scandal in truth. Who would believe that they had done nothing?

They had had wine enough and to spare, but they had not fallen to that. He had not even hinted at it. Had only looked at her long and long, smiled at last, and taken the far side of the bed, with an acre of blankets between.

Again, thunder. It had been rolling at intervals since first she woke.

This burst shook her fully out of her dreaming. Not thunder; a swordhilt upon the massive door. For an instant she froze. They knew —they all knew. They had come to denounce her. Liar, deceiver, harlot—

Idiot. She rolled out of bed, snatched the first garment that came to hand, pulled it on. Swiftly but quietly she slid back the bolt.

The man without was shaking with urgency: a big man, Ianyn, one of Mirain's household. Even as the door opened he cried, "My lord!" And stopped at the sight of her, seeing only the hair at first, and his own disappointment. Of course it would be the squire who opened the door. Face and manner shifted, and stilled again. His eyes widened.

She glanced down swiftly. She was covered. She had her shirt.

Her thin, unlaced, entirely undeceptive shirt.

It came as memory comes, swift, piercing: a vision not of what was past but of what was still to come. The man, his message delivered, returned to his companions, and he had a new and startling tale to tell. One that traveled as all such tales must, swifter than fire through a dry field.

Foresight passed. In its aftermath she knew only a weary irony. All her fears—she had shrugged them aside as folly. And they had been prescience.

Mirain's voice spoke close to her ear, shattering the impasse. "Bredan. You have news?"

The king's presence and his own training brought Bredan to attention. His eyes strove not to follow Elian as she gave Mirain the doorway. "Urgent news, sire. The Lord Cuthan sent me to wake you."

"Go on." Mirain was wide awake; and he was blocking Bredan's view of the chamber.

"Troops, sire," the man said, recalling his urgency. "South of here, across the river where Ebros and Poros meet. A whole army, thousands strong. They march under royal banners, princes' banners. The Hundred Realms have come to fight us."

Mirain did not flinch or falter. "All of them?" he asked.

"My lord counted upwards of five thousand men, and twenty-odd standards. Including . . ." Bredan paused, and swallowed. "Including Han-Gilen."

"Following? Or leading?"

Bredan swallowed again, very carefully not attempting to find the Gileni face behind his lord's back. "Leading, sire."

"Yes," Mirain said as calmly as ever, "Han-Gilen would lead. Go now, Bredan. See that my captains are told of this."

"Aye, my lord. Should we post guards?"

"See to it. And send a man to the lords of Ashan and of Ebros. I'll speak with them after I've broken my fast."

Mirain bathed almost leisurely, and ate with good appetite. Her half of the bath, Elian was more than glad of, but she could not eat. She tended Mirain's hair instead, cursing to herself when it proved more than usually intractable.

"Yes," he said as if she had addressed him, "your game is over. Even if you hadn't betrayed yourself, there would still be Han-Gilen's army to face."

"And my brother." She knew that, beneath thought, as she knew that her father had not come. She doubted that it was arrogance. She wondered if it was wisdom. "Are you going to make me fight?"

"Would you?"

She breathed deep, to steady herself. "I swore an oath."

"You did." His hair was half braided; he freed the plait from her fumbling fingers and finished it much more deftly than she had begun it, and surveyed her, a swift keen glance. She wore livery as always, with her sword girded over the scarlet surcoat. "Come," he said to her.

The keep's wide hall was full of men and thrumming with tension. Although some had come here on honest business with the king, most seemed merely to be hangers-on. Mirain's own men mingled freely enough, but there were two distinct camps set well apart and bristling at one another. Luian's heir led one. Over the other rose the tall form of Ebros' prince. He came forward as Mirain entered the hall, bowing regally, if somewhat painfully, as lord to high lord.

Mirain smiled his quick smile and clasped Indrion's hand. "You look well, lord prince. I trust that you are recovered?"

"I am well," the prince answered, smiling in return, his eyes warming to amber. "Apart from an aching head. That was a shrewd blow, my lord."

"A simple one, and an old trick."

"Ah, but it succeeded."

There was a bench nearby. Mirain sat on it. Elian, taking her place behind him, admired his art that turned the humble seat into a throne, and in the same instant invited his new vassal to share the seat but not, ever, the kingship.

Indrion hesitated no more than a heartbeat, and slowly sat. His smile was gone, but he looked on Mirain in deep respect. "My lord," he said, "I regret that I challenged your kingship. But I shall never regret the fight. It was a fine battle, and well won."

"As well lost." Mirain raised a hand. "Lord Omian."

Luian's heir left the ranks of his countrymen. To reach Mirain he had to cross before the Ebrans. He neither speeded nor slowed his progress for them, nor acknowledged that they existed. He bowed to Mirain, and without perceptible pause, to Indrion.

Mirain smiled warmly and beckoned. "Sit by me, sir."

There was space on the bench, but only beside Indrion. Ebros' prince had made certain of that. Omian sat with perfect ease, and with a smile, which was more than his enemy could muster.

Mirain seemed to see none of it, either hostility or forced amity.

When Omian was settled, the king said, "The Hundred Realms have risen, my lords, and come to meet us. They are close now to the ford of Isebros."

Neither of the princes would glance at the other. "Indeed, sire," Indrion said, "I had had word that Han-Gilen was rousing the princedoms. I had not thought they would arrive so swiftly."

"Had you not?" asked Omian. "Surely you were praying for them to overtake us and cut us down while we were still in disorder from fighting you."

Indrion shrugged slightly. "I was a fool, I grant you that. I should have held to my walls and waited and let you mount a siege, to be crushed by the advancing forces. But I thought I could stop you. I chose open battle, a day too soon. I am well paid for it."

"Aye, and now you think to catch us with your Ebran treachery."

At last Indrion's temper escaped its careful bonds. "And what of yours, dog's son? You could not but have known what Han-Gilen called for. Yet you and your hound of a father plotted to be first at the trough, to lick the king's feet and to win all his favor, and to steal my land into the bargain."

"Your land, cattle thief? You knew you claimed what was never yours; you knew the judgment would go against you. Thus you gambled. Either you would slay my king and win my valley, or he would defeat you in combat and offer you his famous clemency, which else you had no hope of."

Indrion half rose; Omian bared his teeth in a feral grin. Mirain's glance quelled them both. Ebros' prince hooded eyes gone hot gold. Ashan's heir sat still, with but the merest suggestion of a smile. Quietly the king said, "When I have done what needs doing here, I shall ride to meet the army."

"My forces are at your disposal," said Indrion a little tightly still.

"And mine," Omian said, "my lord."

"My thanks," said Mirain. "I shall take twoscore men; and you with them, sirs, if you are willing."

Omian laughed, incredulous. "Twoscore men against five thousand?"

"It will suffice." Mirain did not ask him where he had learned their number. "If you will pardon me, my lords, I have duties."

It seemed to Elian as she kept to the squire's place that every man in the hall watched her, and whispered, and wondered. Eyes flicked toward her, held, flicked away. They had always done that: bored, or intrigued by the brightness of her hair, or caught by the beauty of her face. Now they strained to see if it were true that the boy was indeed a woman; they peered at the slim erect form in the king's livery, searching for curves no boy could claim. Maybe they laid wagers. Surely they sniggered, recalling that she spent her every night with the king, and wondering if she would turn her eyes elsewhere. Bold as she was, how could she be aught but wanton?

In a pause between petitioners, Mirain touched her hand. "Go free," he murmured. "You'll know when it's time to ride."

Her brain blurred, shifting from her own troubles to the danger he faced. "You want me there?"

"At my right hand, you promised me." He smiled a little. "It's not a fight we go to."

No. No prince would attack a mere twoscore men, if they rode with care. Certainly Halenan would not. And he would talk to Mirain, if only for memory's sake. She bowed. "I'll ride with you, my lord."

Mirain's smile followed her from the hall. So too, and much less warmly, did the stares. She straightened her back and stalked away from them.

Eleven

*I*T WAS AN HOUR'S RIDE FROM THE TOWN TO THE FORD of Isebros. The road was wide and well kept, running past villages whose folk hid in their houses, and farmsteads barricaded against invading armies. The word had spread abroad that the Sunborn had swept out of the north, and that the Hundred Realms had massed against him. And when princes struggled for mastery, it was the land and its people who suffered most.

A goodly land, this vale on the marches of Ashan between Ebros and Poros. Its fields were rich; its villages seemed prosperous even in their fear.

Where the river swept wide round the last low outrider of Ashan's mountains, its ford offered passage from Ebros into Poros. No town had grown there on either side, but walled villages stood in sight of it; somewhat upstream of it on the Poros side, a bold soul had built a watermill.

Oddly, when Elian remembered after, the mill came first to her mind: the turning and the clacking of the wheel and the washing of water through it. How foolish, she thought. Any marauder could overrun the mill, and hold it or destroy it as he chose. Yet it was built of stone and well fortified, and folk from leagues about could bring their grain to it to enrich the miller.

Perhaps she focused upon it to avoid what could not be avoided. All the green land between the mill and the village was lost to sight, overspread with the camp of a great army. The banners were banners Elian knew, every one a royal standard, sigil of a prince from the north of the Hundred Realms; and beneath each one ranged a city of tents. Not since the war on the Nine Cities had so many princes come together into a single force.

Now as then, the center and command post, first among equals, was the flameflower of Han-Gilen. Elian sat very straight on Ilhari's back. She might yet have to draw blade against her own kin; but as she rode beside Mirain to the river's bank, she knew no shame of her lineage. Han-Gilen's princes had ruled in the south before ever king or emperor rose to challenge them; kings and emperors had fallen, and they remained, stronger than ever. And they would remain, she knew with sudden certainty. Whatever befell between this hour and the sun's setting, the Halenani would endure.

Mirain raised a hand. His escort halted. The Mad One stepped delicately down the bank into the swift shallow water. There he too was still.

Their riding had been marked. A line of men had formed on the camp's edge, arrows nocked to bows. Beyond them others crowded, a manifold glitter of eyes. Mirain's banner was clear for them to see, whipped wide as the wind swept down from the north. Ebros' and Ashan's unfurled on either side of it but slightly behind, in token of subjection.

Behind the archers a horn rang. As one the bows lowered. Elian loosed a faint and involuntary sigh of relief.

A company made its way from the camp's center, mounted and yet apparently unarmored. Every man was clad as for a procession, adorned with jewels that dazzled in the sunlight, but the only metal was the gold and silver and copper worked into the embroideries of coats and trousers, into the heels of the riders' boots, into the saddles and bridles of their seneldi. Elian saw no weapon anywhere.

No banner floated over them, but they needed none. The man who rode foremost, tall on a tall grey stallion, shone in green and flame-gold; his head was bare, his hair and beard red as fire.

Without Elian's urging, Ilhari advanced to the very edge of the water.

The Mad One had reached the middle of the ford. Like Halenan, Mirain wore no armor and no weapon; only a light kilt and his scarlet war-cloak and a glitter of ornaments, gold and ruby, and the heavy torque of his priesthood about his throat. Any man of the southern army could have shot him down as he waited there.

Free at last of the press of men, Halenan's senel stretched into a gallop. The prince's eyes were fixed on Mirain, his face as stern and still as ever his father's could be.

The grey left the escort behind, leaping down the long slope of the bank, plunging into the river. The Mad One stood his ground, horns lowered slightly, but his ears pricked. In a great shower of spray the grey stallion halted. Miraculously Halenan was dry, even to the high golden heels of his boots. His gaze never left Mirain's face, searching it keenly, suffering no secrets.

It seemed that Mirain yielded none. Abruptly Halenan said, "It has been a long while. Brother." He spoke the word as if in challenge, daring Mirain to remember.

"Long years, my brother," Mirain answered.

From the sudden light in Halenan's face, Elian knew that Mirain smiled. The air between them warmed and softened; Halenan essayed a smile in return. "Will it please my lord to enter into Poros with me?"

Mirain did not move. "What if I do not enter as a friend?"

"You are my enemy then?" asked Halenan amid a great stillness.

"That depends upon your own intent."

There was a pause. At length Halenan backed his stallion and turned, leaving the way open for Mirain to pass. "Let us judge that upon dry land, under my word of honor."

Mirain bowed his head very slightly. He raised his hand to his escort; the Mad One moved forward. One by one the company followed in his wake.

North and south faced one another on the riverbank, wary, forbearing to mingle. Elian, hanging well back, saw faces she knew, noblemen all, all intent upon the two who faced one another in their center. Neither had yet dismounted; neither had touched, or ventured it, despite the growing amity between them. Perhaps it was only that their stallions would not allow it.

Again it was Halenan who broke the lengthening silence. "I see that you have won Ebros."

"Yesterday," said Mirain without either gloating or humility.

"Some might say that you should no longer be called king. That you should name yourself emperor."

"Not yet."

"Perhaps. You have only lessened the Hundred Realms by two. It could be a very long conquest, brother."

"Or very short," said Mirain. "I count a score of banners yonder. If it is battle you look for, I may win the north of the Realms at a stroke."

Halenan laughed suddenly. "Ah, kinsman! Your arrogance is as splendid as ever."

"It is not arrogance. It is certainty."

Halenan's grin lingered, bright and fierce. "Test your foresight here, King of Ianon. We have read your intent in your conquest of the north; we have seen its proof in the taking of Ashan and Ebros. This is our answer. The Great Alliance: all the Hundred Realms gathered together before you under the command of Han-Gilen. Yonder sits its vanguard, the tithe of its full strength. Is it not a fine brave number?"

"I have more, honed in my wars. But yes, it is fair to see. Have you brought it here to challenge me?"

"To challenge you?" Halenan looked back at his men with such a sheen of joy and pride and sheer boyish mischief, that Elian dared at last to understand. He leaped from the saddle, kneeling in the road, eyes shining. "No, my lord An-Sh'Endor. To lay at your feet."

For a long moment Mirain sat still, gazing down. All his life he had waited for this. Yet now that it had come, he seemed stunned, shaken to the heart of him. There before him in the hands of this bright-maned prince lay the empire he had been born to rule.

Slowly he swung his leg over the pommel and slid to the ground. "Brother," he said. "Halenan. Do you know what you have done?"

"The god's will," Halenan answered promptly. "And my father's, if it comes to that. It was easier than we thought it might be. The Realms were ready for you."

Mirain tried to speak, but no words came. He drew Halenan up and embraced him long and hard, putting into it all his love and his wonder and his joy, and even his awe of these princes who, in the purity of their pride, would choose the king whom they wished to rule over them.

Halenan's awe was deeper, but tempered with mirth. "Just for once," he said laughing, "I've rendered you speechless. Who'll ever believe I did it?"

Mirain smiled, grinned, laughed aloud. "Who will believe you did any of this? Hal—Hal, you madman, without a blow struck or a drop of blood shed, you've changed the whole shape of the world."

Elian had seen Mirain exalted in battle, or before his men, or in the face of victory; but now, as he rode through this army that had come to follow him, he was more than exalted. He was touched with the high and shining splendor of a god.

Elian could be glad of his gladness, but she could not share in it. Anonymous in surcoat and helmet, well hidden between Cuthan and his silent and unreadable brother, she veiled herself from the mind as well as from the eye. But she felt Halenan's searching, passing and passing again.

His tent stood in an open circle kept clear by his guards. There were seats under a canopy, and servants with wine and ices, and grooms to tend the escort's seneldi. Halenan welcomed Mirain to it with a flourish; but still he hunted with eyes and power.

It was Vadin who betrayed her. As the two companies mingled in the tumult of dismounting, Ilhari jostled his mare. The tall grey laid back her ears. Ilhari skittered, bucked, threatened with heels and teeth.

Vadin laughed, sharp in a sudden pause. "What, little firemane! Menace your own mother, would you?"

Ilhari thought better of it. On her back, Elian sat stiff and still. Halenan had heard. He turned. His eyes met hers.

She left the saddle. All at once, her brother was there. "Elian," he said.

People were staring. Whispering. Someone laughed. *Damn them!* she thought.

And then: *Damn all of it!* For Halenan was holding her, shaking her, shouting at her; and she knew how deeply, terribly, endlessly he had feared for her. Damning himself more fiercely than she ever could, not only for letting her go, but for helping her to do it.

There were tears on her cheeks. She dashed them away. He held her, taking her in, helmet and livery and all. "Sister," he said roughly. "Little sister. I've had hell to pay in Han-Gilen."

"Were they fearfully angry?" She sounded plaintive; she scowled to make up for it.

"Not angry," he said. "Not after a while. You left Father to make some very difficult explanations."

She swallowed. "I—I thought—"

"You didn't think at all, infant. But you seem to be thriving."

That was a refuge. She snatched at it. "I am. I'm Mirain's squire. I have a new sword; it's steel. It's a marvel. You see my mare—Ilhari. Her sire is the Mad One. We've fought our first battle together. The household gave me a trophy. You'll see it—when—"

She broke off. He was no longer looking at her but beyond her, with an expression which she labored to decipher. Greeting; respect; apprehension. And a touch—the merest inexplicable touch—of compassion.

She turned in his hands. A man stood there. A man no taller than she, clad all in golden silk, regarding her with a steady golden stare.

If Halenan had not held her, she would have staggered. Of all the

people she had ever thought to see, this was the last. "But," she said
stupidly, "you were supposed to go back to Asanion."

"But," he answered her, "I chose to come here."

"For me?" She flushed, twisting out of her brother's grip. "No. Of
course not. You wanted to see the Sunborn. To know what, in the end,
cost you the alliance with my father. You were not very wise, my lord.
The High Prince of Asanion is a hostage of very great value indeed."

"Should you be the only one to gamble fate and fame and fortune on
the wind from the north?"

He was more handsome even than she remembered, more witty and
more gentle. She pulled off her helmet, shaking out the shorn bright
hair, turning her torn cheek to the sun.

He winced at the marred loveliness, yet he smiled, finding in her a
greater beauty still: that not of the hound chained in hall, but of the she-
wolf running wild in the wood.

"My lord," she said to him, "your father can be no more pleased with
your choice than is mine."

He shrugged. "So, lady, we pay. But the game is well worth the
price."

Her eyes found Mirain. He stood near the tent in a circle of taller
men, yet he stood taller than any of them. One of them was Halenan;
and she had not even seen him go.

"There," said Ziad-Ilarios, "is an emperor. I was bred to rule and not
to serve, but with that one . . . oh, indeed, I could be tempted."

"You mock him, surely."

"No. Not now. Not in his living presence."

"He is not a god," she said sharply.

"Only the son of one."

She turned to him. "You know what must be. The world will not
suffer two emperors. And Mirain will not yield what he has gained to
any mortal man."

"Then the gods be thanked that I am not my father."

Some demon made her catch at his hand. It was warm and strong,
and yet it trembled. Her own was little more steady, her voice breathless, pitched a shade too high. "Come. Come and speak to him."

They were much alike, the dark man and the golden. High lords
both, emperors born, each measuring the other with a long level stare.
Here could be great love, or a great and lasting hate.

For a long moment the balance hung suspended. The silence spread.
Even the seneldi stilled. Ilhari was watching. Thinking of stallions:

horns lowered, poised, choosing, whether to suffer one another or to kill.

They moved in the same instant, to a handclasp that was like a battle. Mirain was taller, but Ilarios was broader; they were well matched.

As they had begun, they ended, within a single moment. But Ilarios' smile showed his clenched teeth. Mirain's was freer, if no warmer. "Well met, my lord high prince. My esquire has told me of you."

"Of you, lord king," said Ilarios, "my lady of Han-Gilen has had much to say. It was she who first whetted my appetite for a sight of you, if only to see at first hand what sort of creature you were."

"And what am I?" asked Mirain with a glint in his eye.

"A barbarian," Ilarios answered, "and a king. But not now, and not ever, emperor in Asanion."

Elian sucked her breath in sharply. Some even of Halenan's men had reached for their swordhilts; Mirain's escort drew together, narrow-eyed.

Mirain laughed and pulled Ilarios into a swift half-embrace, as if he were delighted with the jest. And that, by every law and custom of the Golden Empire, was *lèse-majesté*. An upstart foreigner had dared to lay hands upon the sacred person of the high prince.

Ilarios stood rigid, outraged. Mirain grinned at him, white, fierce, and splendidly unrepentant. Ah, his eyes said, you are high prince, but I am Sunborn. Hate me if you please, but never dare to despise me.

Asanion's heir flashed back with all the pride of a thousand years of emperors. And laughed. Unwillingly, unable to help himself, caught up in the sheer absurdity of their rivalry. Laughing, he reached, completing the half-embrace, meeting the bright dark eyes. "And yet, Sunborn," he said, granting that much to Mirain's pride, "whatever comes hereafter, we are well met."

Twelve

BEFORE MIRAIN TURNED SOUTHWARD, HE RESTED his troops where they had won this last victory: where Ashan and Ebros and Poros met, an hour's ride from the ford. It was a great and splendid festival, and a wonder to all the lands about. People came three days' journey merely to look at the city of tents about Isebros' walled town, and at the high king over them all.

Both were well worth looking at. The mingled armies of north and south had put on their finery to enter into the revelry. And Mirain had a love of splendor and the flair to carry it off, whether it might be the kilt and the clashing ornaments of the north or the boots and trousers and richly embroidered coat of the south; or even and often the stark simplicity of his priesthood, the golden torque and the long white robe girdled with gold.

But then, thought Elian, he could put on his worn riding kilt and stroll through the camp, and still draw every eye to himself. It was the light of him; the splendor of his eyes and of his face, and the royalty of his bearing.

The army knew now who and what she was. An easy camaraderie had begun between the king's squire and his men, in particular the knights of his household. This was gone. No one denounced her; no one avoided her openly; but the ease had turned to a guarded courtesy. Even Mirain—even he was turned to a stranger.

No, she told herself when she was calmest. It was only that, all at once, he had become lord of a great empire. Kingship was not all silk and jewels and state processions; there was a great deal of drudgery in it, long hours buried in councils or in clerkery, and innumerable and interminable audiences. He seemed to thrive on it, but he had little leisure, and none it seemed for his squire. There were servants now in plenty to bathe him and dress him and tend to his needs. She slept at his bed's foot as before, and served him at table, but more of him she did not have.

Halenan could not help. From their first meeting at the ford, king and prince had settled together as if they had never been parted. Odd brothers they made, Halenan tall and graceful and dark golden, with his fiery hair, and Mirain Ianyn-dark, Asanian-small.

And there was a third, always a third. Halenan had faced Vadin much as Ilarios had faced Mirain, but the sparks had flown less fiercely and settled more swiftly. Vadin sneered at Halenan's trousers but applauded his beard; Halenan raised his brows at the barbarian's kilt and braids and superfluity of ornaments, and admired his long-legged grey mare. Out of scorn they had forged respect, and out of respect a strong bond of amity. Now they were inseperable, the right and left hands of the king, and where Vadin saw to the ordering of the army and its festival, Halenan scaled the mountain of scribework. He kept the king's seal, and wore it on a chain of gold about his neck. That was burden enough; Elian would not add her own to it.

And yet there was one who had time for her. Ziad-Ilarios was known as the king's friend, but he held himself somewhat aloof. He was a guest, and royal; there was little that he could do and less that he must. When Elian rode Ilhari as long and as far as they both could go, his golden stallion valiantly kept pace; when she hung about the castle or the camp, he found occasion to hang about with her, coaxing her into smiles and even into laughter. Even when she was as close to tears as she would ever let herself come, he knew precisely how to make her forget her troubles.

Somehow, somewhere between Han-Gilen and the marches of Ashan, she had lost all her fear of him. Yet she had more reason than ever to be afraid. It was clear in his eyes, indeed in everything he did and said: He had not come so far against his father's will and command, endangering himself and his empire, only to look on the Sunborn. He had come because he loved her.

She knew it. She did not try to stop it. Perhaps she had begun to love him, a little. She found herself looking for him when he was not immediately in evidence. Sometimes she even sought him out, for the pure pleasure of seeing his face, or of hearing his beautiful voice that could make a song of plain Gileni words.

"Why are you always guarded?" she asked him once as they rode in the sun. She glanced over her shoulder at the men who followed at a careful distance, unobtrusive as shadows, clad in shadow-black, who never spoke even when she spoke to them. She had never seen their faces: they went veiled, only their eyes visible, cold yellow falcon-eyes that saw everything and judged nothing. "Do they follow you even into the harem?"

For some little time she thought he would not answer. He did not glance at his twin shadows; he busied himself with a tangle in his stallion's mane. At last he said, "My guards are part of me. It is necessary."

"Who would dare to threaten you?"

He looked up, startled, almost laughing with it. "Why, lady, who would not? I am the heir of the Golden Throne."

She frowned. "No one would try to kill Mirain outside of battle. Or Hal; or Father."

"Some at least have ventured against the Sunborn."

"Years ago. People learn. The king is the king."

"The king is a mage. That matters, my lady. In Asanion we are confined to our own poor wits, and to our guards' loyalty."

"Your court is very decadent, Father says. Death is a game. The subtler the poison, the greater the prize. Lives are taken as easily as we would pluck a blossom, and one's own life is a counter like any other, to be cast away when the game commands."

"It is not as simple as that," said Ilarios. "I for one must live, or all my game will come to nothing."

"Are you a pawn, then?"

His eyes sparked, but he smiled. "I like to think that I have a little power in the play. I will, after all, be emperor."

"How grim," she said, musing, "to live so. And the poor women. Penned like cattle where no man can see them; veiled and bound and forbidden to walk under the sky. They must go mad with boredom."

"No more than do their lords. The emperor is kept as straitly as any concubine, for his life's safety and for the sanctity of his office. He must never leave his palace. He must never set foot on common earth. He must never speak to any save through his sacred Voice."

"What, not even his empress?"

"Perhaps," admitted Ilarios, "to her he might speak directly. And she may see his face. His people must not. They see him always enthroned, robed and masked in gold like a god."

"That is horrible," she said.

"No," he answered her. "It only sounds so. An emperor's body must be confined; it is holy, it is given to the gods. Yet he rules, and in ruling he is free. No man is freer than he."

"My father rules unmasked and unchained. Mirain is king incarnate, and his throne is the Mad One's saddle."

"Your father rules from Han-Gilen; he did not ride into the north. I would wager that he could not. And the Sunborn is the first of his line, a barbarian king, a soldier and a conqueror. The burden of empire has barely begun to fall upon him."

"How strange you look," she said, "when you speak of empires. As if it terrifies you; and yet you revel in it. You will welcome the mask when it comes to you."

"It is what I was born for." He looked at her. "You are like me. You flee the cage which your lineage has raised about you, and yet what you flee to is a captivity no less potent, and far less easily escaped. You can comprehend the mind of the Golden Emperor."

She touched him, because she wanted to, because she could not help herself. He quivered under her hand, but did not pull away. "Am I transgressing?" she asked him.

"I give you leave," he said. Light; a little breathless. Smiling a sudden luminous smile. "You may touch me whenever you choose."

It was great daring, that, in an Asanian high prince. "I am corrupting you," she said. "See, your shadows are uneasy. What will they tell your father?"

"That I have gone barbarian." He laughed, and met touch with touch: a brush of fingertips from her cheek to her chin, tracing the path of her scars. It was like cool fire. Swift, and startling, and all too quickly gone.

She would have caught his hand; but his golden stallion had danced away, impatient, and the moment escaped. She did not try to pursue it. Her folly that she had even let it begin.

It did not come back. She told herself that it had never been; she made herself stop regretting it. Ilarios' presence was enough, and his beauty, and his golden voice. She needed no more.

On a grey morning with too much in it of winter, Elian wandered down a passage of the keep. She had meant to ride in the hills, but a driving rain had sent even the Mad One into the shelter of the castle. Mirain was closeted with Halenan and Vadin and the captains. She, having no more to do with her freedom than squander it in prowling the corridors, heard her name. Her ears pricked; she stopped. The speakers were Ianyn by their accents, men of the king's household playing at chance in a guardroom.

"Elian?" one mused, rattling the dice in the cup, in no hurry to throw. "Now there's a fine piece of womanflesh."

"How can you know?" his companion demanded. "She doesn't show any of it."

"Sure she does. It just takes a good eye."

"I've got a good eye. And all it sees is angles. If it's boys you like, why not take a boy and have done with it?"

"*She's* no boy," the first man declared. "Dress her up proper now, a little paint and a gewgaw or two, and you'll have something worth looking at."

"Not for my money. I like mine plump and toothsome. Less sharp in the tongue, too. They say she can swear like a trooper."

"The king fancies her, for all of that. So do plenty of others. The boys down in the camp have got a wager on how long she'll last. I put a silver sun on it, with a side bet that he marries her before the year is out."

"You've lost your money, then. She's highborn, they say, sister to that southern general, the one who wears his beard like a man. Good in bed, too, if the king's kept her this long and this steady. But he won't make her queen. He can't. It's the law in Ianon, don't forget: No whore can share the throne." The soldier hawked and spat. "Here now. Are you going to throw those dice or hatch them?"

Elian stumbled away. Her feet felt huge, clumsy; she could not see.

She passed Ilarios without recognizing him. When he called to her, she stopped, losing the will to move. "Lady," he said. She could taste his concern. It was salt, like tears. "Lady, are you ill?"

"No," her voice replied. "No, I'm well."

His arm dared mightily. It circled her shoulders. She let him lead her; she did not care where. His own chamber, it turned out to be; he had been given one in the keep. There was no room in it for his guards, who perforce must stand without, with the door between, and solitude within, scented with flowers. Elian had found a tangle of briar roses, the last of summer, golden and flame red; they had brought back a bowlful at great cost to their fingers. But the heady scent was worth any pain.

It did not ease hers now. He made her sit in a nest of cushions, and set a cup in her hand, filled with the yellow wine of Asanion. "Drink," he bade her.

She obeyed him, hardly knowing what she did. The wine was sharp to her taste, almost sour, yet strong. It both dizzied and steadied her.

Her eyes cleared; she breathed deep. Lightly, calmly, she said, "It has finally happened. A man has said what they all think. I have no reputation left, my lord. Is that not amusing?"

"Who has dared it? Tell me!"

His intensity brought her eyes to him. His own were burning, blazing. Hating the one who had hurt her. Loving her with all that was in him.

For a long while she could only stare at him, stupid with shock. That it could matter so much to him. That she could care, and caring, wake to truth. "It does no good to run away," she said. "I have learned that. The world is a circle; one always comes back to one's beginnings. I went to Mirain to escape Han-Gilen; now he prepares to march there. I shall have to face my mother, with what I have done and what I am supposed to have done on the lips of every talespinner in this part of the world. And the worst of it—the very worst—is that I have not had the pleasure that goes with the tale. I doubt if Mirain even realizes that I am a woman."

He said nothing.

She laughed, not too badly, she thought, although he winced. "In truth I would not wish him to. He accepts me. He lets me be what I choose to be. The tragedy is this: His army is part of him also. And his army knows what I am. I betrayed myself, do you know? So careful, I was. So private, so well disguised. I even relieved myself where none could see, though that is nothing to brag of. Camp privies can be too utterly vile even for men. The hardest thing was to watch people swimming, and to have to pretend that I had duties; especially on the march, with the heat and the dust and the flies. A basin is a very poor substitute for a whole cool river, when even one's king is in it, fighting water battles like a half-grown boy."

"Tomorrow," he said carefully, "if the weather changes, you could go to the river, to one of the pools."

"What for?" she demanded, all contrary.

There was no banter in him; no mirth at all, and no comfort. He looked at her with wide eyes, all gold. "I see," he said. "One's king would not be in it."

She stared back at him. She was almost angry. Almost. That he could speak so: he too, of all who knew her.

His hair was as unruly a mane as Mirain's, and fully as splendid, left free in the custom of Asanian royalty though bound with a circlet about his brows. She stroked it. It was silken soft. "Gold should be cold to the touch," she said.

"And fire should burn." His hand ventured upon it, light, gentle, as if he feared to do her hurt. They were very close. She could feel the living warmth of him, and catch the scent he bore, faint yet distinct. Musk and saddle leather and briar roses. Their lips touched.

He was very beautiful and very strong, and his kiss was sweet. Warm and warming. He tasted of spices.

He drew back. His eyes had darkened to amber. "Lady," he said very softly. "Lady, you are a breaker of hearts."

She looked at him, not understanding, not wanting to understand.

He smiled as one in pain. "For every man who speaks ill of you, there are a thousand who would die for you. Remember that." He bowed low, as low as his royalty had ever permitted, and left her there.

With even Ilarios gone strange, she had thought that she had nothing left. But no blow ever falls alone. Toward evening Mirain summoned her, who had never had to do such a thing, close by him as she always was.

He was in the cell he used as a workroom. The clerks were gone; a brazier struggled to warm the chill air. Rolls and tablets heaped high about him, some sealed with his Sun-seal, some not. In his priest's robe, with a stylus in his hand, he looked like the boy who had taught her her letters. But he was frowning, if only slightly; his gaze was cool almost to coldness.

She stood in front of him with the worktable between them. Unconsciously she had drawn herself to attention. What sin had she committed, that he should look at her so? All her duties were done, and well done. She had given him nothing to complain of.

His eyes released her, but they had not softened. "In three days," he said, "we begin the march to Han-Gilen. It will be long, for I shall make of it a royal progress. I do not expect that we shall see the city very much before the opening of winter."

Her throat was locked. She swallowed to open a way for her voice. "The weather will be gentler as we go south. You will have no need to hasten because of it."

"Perhaps not." He turned the stylus in his hands. They were small for a man's, but the fingers were long and fine. A ring circled one, an intricate weaving of gold and ruby, flaming as it caught the light. She watched half-enspelled.

His soft voice lulled her, but his words shocked her fully awake. "As long as the riding will be, and with Han-Gilen at the end of it, I have given much thought to your place within it. My men know now who you are. They have accepted the knowledge well and without undue scandal, for you have proven yourself in the best of all ways, by your valor in battle. Yet there is scandal, and it will not grow less as we ride through the Hundred Realms. For your sake then and for that of your family, I have asked that your brother take you into his tent."

"And my oath?" she asked quietly. It sounded well, cool and steady, but she could muster nothing louder.

"I release you," he answered. "You have served me well. More than well. For that I would make you a knight, the first of my new empire."

Her lip curled. "So. It is no longer convenient for your majesty to keep his esquire, now that men know he is a she, and a princess of Han-Gilen at that. It is most unpolitic. And, no doubt, it does not suit you to have your chosen lady hear of it. Best and easiest then to be rid of me, with a rich bribe to keep me quiet. Unfortunately, my lord emperor, I am not to be bought."

He rose. Even in her anger she dreaded his wrath, but he was fully masked. "I had thought to honor you, to restore your good name. My own I have no care for; I am a man, it does not matter. But in the way of this world, yours is greatly endangered. I would not have it so. Halenan is more than willing to share his lodgings with you, and he has promised not to bind you, nor in any way to restrict your freedom. He will even let you keep to your boy's guise. You lose nothing by the change, and gain much. A knight of my household is truly free to do and to be what he chooses."

She shut her eyes against his logic. It was the core of it that mattered, that fanned her temper into a blaze. "Bribery. You rid yourself of a stain upon your majesty, a ribald jest in every tavern. What is an emperor's economy? A squire who can serve him as well at night as in the day. And what sort of squire is that? A squire who is also a woman."

"No one says such things," he said. His voice deepened and lost its clarity. "No one would dare."

"Not in your presence, sire. I have long ears. I can also read your mind, though you shield it with all your father's power. I did not leave Han-Gilen and all I had been and could be, to be sent into my brother's care like an unruly child."

"What would you have, then?"

"Things as they were before," she answered swiftly. She faced him. "Your good name does not matter, you say. Let me look after my own. Or are you afraid of what Mother will say to you?"

"I fear what she will say to you."

She could have hit him. "Damn you, I can take care of myself! What does it take for me to prove that? A man's body as well as a man's clothes?"

In spite of his control, his lips twitched. "I would never wish for that, my lady. It is only . . . words can wound deep, far deeper than they ought. And you suffer most from them. Someday you may wish to be truly free, even to marry. I would not have you fear that no man will take you."

"I'm not afraid of that!" she snapped. And she added, because a demon was on her tongue, "Ziad-Ilarios would take me now, as I am, muddied name and all."

She had meant only to quell his arguments. She had not looked to drive him behind all his walls, with the gates barred and the banner of his kingship raised above the keep. "Very well," he said, "remain in my service. But do not expect me to ease your way with my subjects or with your family." He returned to his seat and opened a scroll. She was dismissed.

And she had won. But the victory held no sweetness. Almost she could wish that she had not won at all.

Thirteen

THE DAY BEFORE MIRAIN BEGAN HIS PROGRESS INTO the south, a strong force departed under Vadin's command, turning back toward Ianon and the north. They would secure the tribes upon the borders of Asanion, and ascertain that all was well in Ianon.

"And I," said Vadin, "have a lady who objects to a cold bed."

Elian had gone to brood in solitude. The cavalry lines were quiet under the setting sun, the seneldi drowsing or grazing quietly, the grooms and the guards drawn off to a comfortable distance. She lay on her belly in the long grass, chewing a stem and watching Ilhari.

Voices startled her. Before she thought, she had flattened herself to invisibility. They nearly walked over her, too intent on one another to see her, striding together with a single woven shadow stretching long behind them. They stopped almost within her reach and stood side by side, not touching, not needing to touch.

Vadin swept his hand over the high plumes of grass, beheaded one, stripped it of its grains and offered it to the wind. Mirain turned his face to the setting sun. He frowned at it, but it was to Vadin that he spoke. His voice was sharp with impatience. "I have no skill in the wooing of women."

Vadin snorted. "You have more than anyone. You've seduced whole kingdoms."

"Ah," said Mirain with a flick of his hand. "Kingdoms. Women are infinitely more complex. And that one . . . whatever I do, she makes it clear that I should have done the opposite."

"Gods know what you see in her," Vadin said. Mirain glared; he grinned. "And I can guess. You like them difficult. Do you remember the little wildcat in Kurrikaz?"

Mirain grimaced. "My scars remember." He began to pace, a brief circuit. "She was dalliance. They all were."

"All three of them," Vadin muttered.

"Four." Mirain spun to face him. "This is truth, Vadin. This is the one who must be my queen: who always has been. And I know nothing of pursuit. All the rest have flung themselves at me, or been flung by fathers or brothers or procurers."

"Not that you've condescended to take any you didn't fancy."

"It's the curse of the mageborn. The body is never enough. Souls must meet; and so few even wish to. I tried once," said Mirain, "to take pleasure as a simple man would. It was like bathing in mire. She never saw me at all. Only my wealth and my title, and the use she could make of them."

"They're not all like that," said Vadin.

"I know it!" Mirain cried. "And the one I long for, the one I must have—she hardly knows I'm a man."

"Do you treat her like a woman?"

Mirain stopped short.

Vadin laid an arm about his shoulders, shaking him lightly. "I've seen how you are with her. Stiff and distant, and prim as a priestess. How is she to know you want her, if you persist in acting as if she were your youngest sister?"

"But she is—"

"She is royal and a beauty, and you want her so desperately you can hardly think. Let alone tell her the truth. She won't wait for you, Mirain; not unless she knows there's something to wait for."

"How can I tell her? She's as shy as a mountain lynx. She ran away from the last man who even began to court her."

"And he went after her, and now he's deathly close to winning her."

Mirain pulled free. His shoulders were knotted with tension. Suddenly he laughed, sharp and mirthless. "Here am I, new lord of the eastern world, fretting over a chit of a girl. An infant. A child who knows nothing of her own heart."

"Isn't it time you set about telling her?"

"I can't," Mirain said. "Call it pride. Call it stupidity."

"Cowardice," said Vadin.

Mirain bared his teeth. "That too. I can't conquer a woman as I would a city."

"Why not? Think of it as a siege. So you don't walk up to her and demand her hand in marriage. You can start hinting. Set up your siege engines: put on your best smile, give her a little of yourself, let her know she's beautiful." Mirain opened his mouth; Vadin overran him. "That's no more than the other man does. When she's warmed a little, then you can start beating down the gates. As," said Vadin, relentless, "he already has."

"Damn you, Vadin," growled Mirain. "I don't recall that you were so wise when you were the sufferer. Wasn't it I who made you start courting her? And didn't I have to give you a royal command before you'd marry her?"

"So," said Vadin, "I've learned how it's done. From you, O my brother."

"Did you, O my brother? Finish it, then. Win her for me."

"I can't," Vadin said. "I have to hold the north for you."

"Liar. It's your wife you have to hold."

"They're all one, aren't they? Beautiful, willful, and determined not to come second in their lords' eyes. Go on, brother. Win your lady. It ought to be easier without me to get in the way."

"She's fonder of you than she knows."

"Hah," said Vadin. "Here now, stop glaring. Start your wooing, before she runs off with his royal Asanian highness."

Mirain paused, but suddenly he grinned. He aimed a blow at Vadin, which caught only air; he laughed, and went almost lightly, like the boy he still was. Vadin lingered, pondering the grass about his feet.

Elian's fingers clawed in it. She did not want to understand. She did not dare. That Mirain—might—want—

It was someone else. He had said it.

Had he?

It was a child's folly, to dream that every colloquy concerned oneself. And he had never—

He had said—

She scrambled to her feet. She never saw Vadin move. One instant he was frozen, startled. The next, his dagger pricked her throat. She met his hot glare, her own heat gone all cold. "You were talking about me." she said.

The blade dropped away. The sting of it lingered. Vadin eased, muscle by muscle, and began to laugh.

She waited. At long last he stopped. His brows went up. "You heard us?"

"Every word."

"Gods." He was almost appalled. Almost. A grin broke free. "So I won. You've found out. What will you do about it? Run away?"

"Where would I run to?"

"Asanion."

She closed her eyes. She was feeling nothing yet. Or too much. "I came for this," she said. "Because I promised. That I would—"

"Did you come for the promise, or for him?"

Her eyes snapped open. "I promised! I—" She bit her tongue. "If Mirain had not been Mirain, I would never have sworn my oath."

"Prettily said," drawled Vadin. He flung his long body to the ground at her feet. He was not wearing breeches under the kilt. She tore her eyes away. He propped himself on his elbow and regarded her from under level brows. "Sit," he said.

She did, with little grace. His amusement stung like the edge of his dagger.

"You're not a fool," he said, "well though you pretend to be. You know what you can do to a man simply by being yourself. It's diverting, isn't it? It's all a splendid game. Setting Han-Gilen on its ear, hoodwinking the army of the Sunborn, playing two imperial lovers against one another. Whet the Asanian's appetite with a long and perilous chase into the Sunborn's arms; prick the Sunborn to madness by falling into the Asanian's embrace. If you play your game cleverly enough, you can balance the two until the stars fall. Or," said Vadin, "until one loses patience and demands an accounting. What then, princess? Which heart will you break? One or both?"

"I think," she said, measuring each word in ice, "that I hate you."

"You hate the truth."

"It is *not* the truth!" She was on her feet, shaking, choking on murder. "I never meant this to be. From the very first that I can remember, I knew what I wanted. Mirain. He belonged to me. No one else could ever have him. Then—then he went away. Father tried to hold him back until he was grown and could muster an army for the claiming of Ianon. He obeyed as long as he could, but he fretted; his father was in him, burning, and time was running ever faster.

"In the night, in the spring, when he had won his torque but not yet had his fifteenth birth-feast, he covered himself in magery and slipped away.

"But I knew. He could never hide anything from me. I followed. I caught him; he almost killed me before he knew me, and came close enough after. I begged to go with him, though I knew I couldn't. He had to go alone; his father wanted it, and he needed it. He thought it was his persuasion that won me over. It was my power, and a glimmering of prophecy. 'Go,' I said. 'Be king. And when you are king, I will come to you.'

"He kissed me and set his face toward the northward road. And I stayed. I had to grow; I had to learn all I could, that would help me when I fulfilled my promise. It was never a grim duty, but the pleasure grew with me.

"Then I was a woman, and it was time, and it was never quite time. There was always some new art to learn, some new suitor to dispose of, some new hawk or hound or senel to tame. And I had kin who, though they could madden me, loved me deeply, and I them. *Tomorrow,* I kept saying. *Tomorrow I'll go.*

"I never stopped wanting Mirain. None of the men who came panting after me was ever his equal. Few of them came close to being mine.

"Until," she said, "until I saw Ziad-Ilarios." She stopped, staring a little wildly at the man who lay in the grass. The sun had lost itself somewhere. Vadin was a long shadow, kilted in scarlet, hung with copper and gold. She did not know him at all. Outlander, barbarian, soulbound with Mirain whom she knew too deeply to know what she knew.

"Ziad-Ilarios," she said, like an incantation, or a curse. "I suppose to you he looks soft and small and daintily effeminate. To me he is all gold.

"Mirain is the other half of me," she said. "Ilarios is the man to my woman."

Vadin did not rise up to throttle her. Nor did he wither her with contempt. "I see," he said. "Mirain is too familiar to be interesting. The Asanian sets your body throbbing."

"The Asanian admits that he wants me."

Vadin sighed. "And you want both. A pity you're not a man, to keep two mates. Or a whore, to have as many as you please."

"That," she said levelly, "I have been called before."

His grin was white in the shadow of his face. "I married one, you know." Her silence troubled him not at all. He settled more comfortably and drew an easy breath, like a talespinner with his audience firm in his hand. "She was born to free farmfolk. One year when the crops failed, her father sold her to a procurer. She was good at her trade; she could have risen to a courtesan and bought her freedom, and no doubt set herself up in her own business. But I came along, and somehow I ended up being her favorite lover, which is no credit to my prowess: at that age I had none to speak of. I think she looked on me as a challenge; and Ledi loves challenges. Then Mirain set her free and gave her rank to match mine. Before I knew it we'd been maneuvered into the marriage bed."

Elian would not be shocked. He in his turn would not be disappointed. "So you see, I have to go and leave Mirain to his fate: or should I say, to you. Ledi has issued her ultimatum. I come home and inspect the tribe I've fathered, or they come after me. There are two I've hardly seen, the twins, they were beautiful when they were born but Mirain called me off to help him put down a nest of mages; and then, what with one thing and another, I never got back after. They're nigh a year old now."

"A tribe?" Elian asked, interested in spite of herself. "How many of them are there?"

"Two maids—that's the twins. And five lads. Seven in all." *Only* seven, his tone said; and there was no irony in it. "But then I've only the one lady, and somehow I've never had much of an eye for anyone else. She does her valiant best. She wants twins again this time, she says, and that will make nine, which is a good round number. She has a very strong will, does my Ledi-love."

"So," gritted Elian, "do I."

"Don't you? A pity it doesn't know what it wants."

She set her teeth until they ached, and was silent. His head tilted. "You don't like me, do you?"

"Am I supposed to answer that?"

He shrugged. It was fascinating to watch, for what it did to all his rings and necklaces and earrings. Three in one ear, copper and gold and one great carbuncle like a coal in the dusk. "Let me guess. You had Mirain first. Then he abandoned you. He attached himself to me, who didn't even have the good grace to appreciate the honor, and made me so much a part of him that now there's no dividing us. And you came and found us as we are, and Mirain persists in acting as if nothing has changed between you. And not only does that madden you; I don't even have the kindness to be jealous."

"That's not true."

"Give me credit for some intelligence." He sounded sharp but not angry. "I give you more than your fair share for not despising a gaudy barbarian. But you want me to hate you and to fight with Mirain over a love that's big enough for us all. Alas, I can't. I lost that degree of humanity when I took the lance in my vitals. It went both ways, that miracle. Mirain called me back, and I saw the full extent of what he was and is and always will be. He's mine, always, irrevocably. He's also Ianon's, and the north's, and the south's; he belongs to your father, he belongs to Hal, he belongs to you. It's no good to want to have all of him. Even Avaryan can't have that."

"What are you?" she cried through the tangle that was her mind.

"A prodigy," he answered, and his voice was bitter. "A monster. A dead man walking."

"No." She seized his hand. Its palm was hard with calluses, its back surprisingly silken, warm and strong and very much alive. "I didn't mean that. I'm not—you do surprise me. I'd hate you if you were I, sneaking little interloper that I am, and in trousers too."

That warmed him; his smile gleamed from the shadow of his face. "But," he said, "I never thought you were a boy."

Her jaw dropped. She picked it up with care. "You—"

"Oh yes, I would have resented a swaggering little cock-a-whoop who thought he could take my place. You only wanted your own back. You got it, and it was wonderfully amusing to watch you hoodwink the army. Stone blind, all of them. Even in a kilt you'd walk like a she-panther. And you've got breasts. Not much yet, and in all honesty you'll never match my lady, but breasts you've got. Didn't anyone ever tell you about strapping them flat?"

Her free hand flew to them, flew away. Her cheeks flamed. "I tried for a while. It was ghastly uncomfortable." Dark though it had grown, she glared at him. "You are presumptuous."

"Is that all?" Laughter rippled in his voice. "I'd say I was skirting the edge of the unforgivable. Or I would be, if I weren't so disgustingly close to being your kinsman. Has anyone told you lately that you're beautiful?"

"No!" she snapped. "Yes. I don't know."

She was still holding his hand. It gripped hers; it drew her to him. He was a shadow and a gleam, and a warmth as much of the mind as of the body. "Listen to me, Elian. I have to go away. There's no help for it; Mirain's god is leading him into the south, and someone has to keep the north strong behind him. I know we'll be part of one another wherever we go, and I know he'll never be alone while he has Hal to stand beside him. But he needs more. He doesn't know it; if he did, he wouldn't admit it. He's proud too, that one, and sometimes he's as blind as any ordinary idiot."

Elian was stiff in his grasp, breathing in the scent of him, the sheer foreignness of his presence. But his mind was not foreign at all; and that disturbed her more than any of the rest. One word, one flicker of the will, and they would be bound, brother, sister, kindred as he had named them: kindred in power.

"Look after him," said the outland voice in the outland tongue. "Take care of him. Don't let him be any more of a lunatic than you can help. And if you need me, send your power to me. I'll come. Because," he said, both solemn and wicked, "I also keep my promises."

Her eyes narrowed; her fists clenched. "After all you've said and done to me, you can ask me to take your place with him?"

"I'm asking you to choose as you have to choose, but not to break him in doing it. You love him enough for that, I think. Even if you bind your body to the Asanian."

She could not speak. He rose, drew her into a swift inescapable embrace, let her go. He towered against the stars.

"What—" she whispered. Her voice rose. "What do I tell Mirain?"

"If you're wise," he answered, "everything. Or nothing." He bowed and set a kiss in her hand. "Avaryan's luck with you, Lady of Han-Gilen. We'll meet again."

Fourteen

VADIN WAS GONE. WELL GONE, ELIAN WANTED TO think. He knew too damnably much, and understood it all, and refused—adamantly refused—to despise her for it.

Mirain without him was no less Mirain. It was Elian who found herself looking for him. Missing his eternal and exasperating presence, and his scathing wit, and his talent for saying what no one else dared to say. However much she had resented his presence, she resented his absence more deeply still. It had nothing to do with liking him. It had everything to do with needing him.

She did not see him off. Would not. She had lain awake nightlong, watching Mirain sleep, as if suddenly he would wake and cry, "Choose me!"

And if he had, she would have fled. It had been so simple when she did not know: when he seemed content to be her brother, and she was content to be his squire. Now she must lie, or she must tell him what she knew, and lose her brother, and gain the burden of a lover.

Familiar, Vadin had said. Mirain was that. Too familiar. She could as easily lust after Halenan as after Mirain. He had known her since she was born. He was part of her, blood and bone.

"Ziad-Ilarios," she whispered in the deeps of the night, and shivered. He was alien, and beautiful, and all desirable. She had seen all of Mirain that there was to see. Of Ilarios she had seen the face, and the hands, and a glimpse of comely feet. She could only guess what lay between. Beauty carved in ivory, with dust of gold.

Ebony slept oblivious, obstinate in its silence; and woke as if she had never been more to him than sister and servant. She was soul-glad; she hated him for it. She held her tongue and veiled her eyes and let him have his peace. In a blessedly little while, she had found a scrap of it for herself; she tended it, and schooled herself to think of naught beyond it.

When Mirain began his riding into the south, her joy in it could be almost as unalloyed as his own. The sun blazed upon him in all the splendor of autumn, the leaves of the woods as golden as the Sun on his banner; and he rode under both as light as a boy, with all his drudgeries packed away in the clerks' wagons far down the line. Men sang behind him, a marching song of the north that the southerners had taken a fancy to. The Mad One danced in time to it; and Mirain laughed with the simple joy of it, that he was alive, and king, and riding in the sun before the cream of his newborn empire.

His glance drew Elian into his delight. She could resist him, but not when all the earth seemed to conspire with him. She flashed him her brightest grin, and set Ilhari dancing likewise, matching the Mad One step for step.

They crossed Ilien and entered Poros with Prince Indrion in the van, guiding his emperor through his brother realm. It was indeed the royal progress Mirain had looked for; night found him in the heart of the princedom, feasting in its palace, surrounded by its people. Its women, Elian noticed, were enchanted with him. She noticed also that he betrayed no interest in any one in particular, although some were very beautiful, and some were very charming, and a few were both.

To her he had not changed at all. Not even when she surprised him with a glance or a smile, daring him to begin the siege. Not even when the demon in her sent her to Ilarios' side and kept her there, and made her bold and brazen, and brought her close to hating herself. Until Ilarios turned his golden eyes upon her and smiled, knowing what she did, forgiving her. She had kissed him before she knew it, there where everyone could see. She started back, blushing furiously. "I—" she began.

His finger silenced her, not quite touching her lips. "I know," he said. And began to speak of something else entirely.

When at last it struck her, it struck hard. Ilarios had won a victory. She had forgotten Mirain. She looked, and he was gone; and she had not seen him go.

He was in bed. Alone. Sleeping as a child sleeps, in blissful peace. She cursed him, but whispering, through gritted teeth. *"You* are no thwarted lover. He lied, that great lanky shadow of yours. Or I dreamed it all." He never stirred. She hissed at him. "Damn you, Mirain! How can I know if I want you, if you won't even ask?"

The king's progress continued in a splendor of sunlight. But the nights seemed doubly dark for the brightness between. Elian dreamed, and her dreams were fearful, but when she woke she could not remember them. She began to fight against sleep.

It was not her little tangle of lovers. This ran deeper, down to the heart of power, where prophecy had its lair. Fear was in it, and a darkness of the soul; and something terribly like yearning. Something wanted her. Something strove to draw her to it, if only she would lower her defenses, if only she would yield. Only a little. Only enough to know what summoned her.

She would not. And she dreamed; and there was a black and crooked comfort in it. Dreaming, dreading sleep, she had less leisure to fret over a man who would not admit that he wanted her, and over a man whom she wanted but not—quite yet—with all that was in her.

When autumn was well advanced but the trees wore still their scarlet and gold, Mirain paused near the border of Iban in the forests of Kurion. Having seen the army settled in a great field, almost a plain, within the wood, and his own household established in a forest manor of Kurion's prince, he rode out hunting. The air was like wine, the quarry both swift and crafty, the golden deer of the south. Elian, daring a long shot from Ilhari's saddle, brought down a splendid hart; its flesh made their supper, its hide she gave to Ilarios, who had lent her his bow for the shot. Its crown of ivory antlers she kept as a trophy.

The hunt had been good, but hers was the best kill; for that, as champion of the hunt, she had the place of honor at table. Mirain made her put aside his livery—"My scarlet does your hair no justice," he said —and he gave her a gift, a coat the color of an emerald, edged and embroidered and belted with gold. It was a man's coat, yet when she put it on over long fine tunic and silken trousers, there could be no doubt at all that she was a woman.

Her first instinct was to strip it all off and snatch for her livery. But he was watching, his eyes for a moment unguarded, and he said, "Sister, if I had only you to think of, I'd change my livery to green, and keep it so."

She waited. Her heart hammered. Now—now he would speak. But

he only set a casket in her hands and went to his own dressing. She opened the casket. It was a royal gift, but not of necessity a lover's. A thin circlet of gold to bind her brows, and emeralds set in gold for her ears, and a collar of gold set with emeralds. She put them on with hands that wanted desperately to shake. Mirain was gone already. She made herself follow him.

Strange as her mood was, her entrance into the hall won all the stares she could have wished for. It was almost like old times: the hungry eyes, the smitten faces, leavened now with a large portion of startlement. Few might have guessed that livery could hide so much.

Mirain's face betrayed nothing. He smiled as she sat by him, no more or less warmly than he ever did, and greeted her with empty words. His nearness was like a fire on her skin.

It must be that, for the first time since she came to him, she both looked and felt a woman. And he was close, and he was a man; she had never thought before how very much a man he was. It made him all a stranger. It made him almost frightening.

He brushed against her in reaching for his winecup. She shivered. He wore scarlet tonight, but its fashion was the fashion of the south, very close indeed to her own, ruby to her emerald. His northerners were learning, slowly, not to be appalled when he put on trousers.

She tried to distract herself. He was not going to speak, now or ever. And she could not. She could not say, *Be my lover.* No more could she say, *You will never be more to me than a brother.*

His profile fascinated her. The purity of it; the fierce foreignness that yet was utterly familiar. The ruby in his ear glowed against his darkness, begging her to touch it.

She tore her eyes from him. She was beginning to comprehend the common lot of males: the prick of passion, sudden, urgent, bitter to refuse. There was no logic in it, and very little sanity; it knew nothing of times and seasons. Save that this was her time and this her season, springtide of her womanhood, when blood sang to blood, and fire to banked and shielded fire.

She took refuge in Halenan's face. He was splendid to see, but his beauty only warmed her; it did not burn. He sat oblivious, deep in speech with the Kurionin prince, smiling suddenly at a turn of wit. Beyond them at the table's end sat Ilarios. It might have been chance that set him so far from her. It might have been calculation. His eyes lifted, warming as they caught hers. She could not hold them. Her glance slid aside, restless, uneasy, alighting on comfort. Of a sort.

Cuthan had been her friend, or so she had thought, before the truth of her womanhood built its wall between them. Sensing her gaze, he looked up. Without its white grin his face was as haughty as any in Ianon. His eyes were black, like his brother's, like Mirain's, and steady, taking her in as if she were a stranger. She could not tell what he thought of her.

Suddenly both eyes and face were transformed. He grinned and saluted her as he had in the battle, offering for this little while all that she had lost.

Her throat was tight. But she did as she had done then: she returned his grin. Cobbled courage, but it bore her up. And it distracted her most admirably.

This dream she would remember—must remember. Darkness and whirling, and a face, the face of the woman called Kiyali. Close, coming closer, drawn by her own desperate denial. The Exile's eyes in the dreamworld were not blind at all but terribly, bitterly keen, piercing Elian to the heart. Perceiving all her hidden places, her flaws and her secrets, her lies and her cruelties and her follies.

And understanding, and forgiving. *Kinswoman,* the low voice said. *Blood of my blood. Why do you fear me? Why do you flee?*

"No kin," Elian willed herself to say. It was a gasp. "Never. Enemy—"

I am not your enemy.

"You are Mirain's." Elian's voice was stronger, her resistance firmer. Because she must resist. Blood knew blood. Kin called to kin, however bitterly sundered.

I must oppose him. The law binds me, though its upholders sought to cast me out.

"What law? Temple law? It was never broken. The priestess never knew man. She bore a son to the god, as all the prophecies had foretold."

She lied. She was mageborn, and strong; and her lover was stronger yet.

"And the Sun in Mirain's hand? How do you deny that?"

Magery, the Exile said. Elian heard desperation in her simplicity. She shifted, coming closer yet. The furred collar about her shoulders opened eyes full of malice, and grinned a fanged grin. Elian's scars throbbed into pain.

It is the truth, said the Exile, here where no lie could be. *The Ianyn king is a monster of mages' making, a weapon of the light against the chains that bind the worlds. He will break them, and call it victory, and never know the true terror of what he has done. For the sun is splendid and much beloved, but its full force can blind and destroy. And your young king would loose it upon us all.*

"He will put down the dark."

Has it ever risen? It is necessary, kinswoman. It is the proper counter to the force of the light. Night after burning day; winter which bears the seeds of summer, as the summer begets the winter.

"No," said Elian.

The Exile stood silent. Her familiar had begun to purr.

"No," Elian said again. "Mirain is the god's son. I know it. My bones know it. Even—even if his body may not be—" Her tongue tangled in confusion. That was not what she had meant to say. "The god does as he wills. He is Mirain's father."

The Exile raised her chin. Age had gentled her manner, but never her pride. *You deny what you cannot accept. You toy with the thought of loving him. You cannot endure that he may be your father's son.*

The familiar hissed. It was laughing. It knew more than its mistress would tell. Brother and sister mated: what terror in that? Asanians were much given to it. In no way else could they have bred their emperors. Ziad-Ilarios himself . . .

Elian clapped her hands over her ears, little good as it did, crying out against it all. The lies which the outcast called truth, and the truth which was woven inextricably with lies.

Come, said the Exile. *Come to me. I can give you truth unalloyed. I can set you free of all your bonds. You need never marry, nor bow to kings, nor submit to the caprices of your father.*

Elian tossed, battling.

Free. Be free. Come with me to the world's aid. It must not fall to the sword of the light. Stand with me as your power bids you do. It is greater than you know, and wiser. Listen to it.

She could not hear it. The voice drowned it.

Come with me. Come.

Her hand stretched. Wanting—willing—

"*No!*"

She sprang awake, crying aloud. There were hands on her, arms about her, a voice in her ear. Not that voice. Not, by the god, that deadly voice. "Elian. Elian, wake; it was only a dream."

With agonizing slowness the dream retreated. She crouched trembling, gasping as if she had run long and far from a terror too great to bear, clutching at the warm strength that held her, only dimly aware that it was Mirain.

The awareness grew, calming her. He was the Sunborn. He would not let the darkness take her.

Her breathing quieted. Her head drooped upon his breast over the slow strong beating of his heart. He held her there without speaking, letting the silence heal her.

After a long while she said, "It was more than a dream. It was power."

He stroked her hair gently, saying nothing.

"Power," she repeated. "Prophecy. It has been haunting me; I have been fighting it. But power will not be denied. The enemy is arming against us. She is very, very strong. As she should be; for she is my kin, and trained in all the arts of power, both light and dark." She stiffened, straightening in his grasp. "We've been foolish, riding in the sunlight as if no cloud would ever come. She will make us pay."

"No," he said. "She will not. I have been on guard. She cannot enter my kingdom."

Elian looked long into his face. "She cannot, but she need not. She is in it already."

He did not deny it; and that frightened her as nothing else had. But he said, "She shall not touch you. By my father's hand I swear it."

It would be easy, so easy, to rest in the circle of his protection. Her body clung to him still, and found him strong. Yet her mind locked in resistance. "I'll fight my own battles, my lord."

"Is this your battle?"

She pulled away from him. "You can't protect me from prophecy. Only I can do that."

"By accepting it?"

"No!" she said quickly. But after a moment, very slowly, as if each word were dragged from her: "Yes. By—by letting it come. When we come to Han-Gilen . . . there are ways and rituals . . . O 'Varyan! Why did I have to be the one?"

He sat on his heels beside her pallet and reached again for her, this time to take her hands and hold them. "Elian, little sister, the god gives gifts where he chooses. You are rich in them, because in his reckoning you are strong enough to bear them. I'd bear them for you if I could, if either he or you would let me."

"We won't. I can't. Any more than I can be what you are."

He smiled faintly, painfully. "You wouldn't want that."

"Don't try to be me, then. And don't be so sure of yourself. Your enemy is mortal, but she is powerful, and she serves the dark. Are you strong enough to face her?"

His hands tightened upon hers. He could sense as strongly as she the current of seeing that ran through her, speaking in her voice. "Who knows?" he said. "Who can know, unless I try?"

"You can't. Not now. Not tonight."

"No," he agreed. "Not tonight." He raised her hands and kissed the palm of each. "Rest now. The vision is gone; it will let you have peace."

Whether he spoke the truth, or whether it was his own power that worked upon her, she slept almost at once, deeply, without dreams.

Fifteen

MIRAIN'S VANGUARD LOOKED DOWN FROM THE hills of Han-Gilen. Below them spread the plain and the river and the white city. The sun, riding low, cast long shadows behind it of wall and turret and thin wind-whipped banner. Upon the tower of the temple the Sun-crystal flamed, brighter in the evening than the sun itself.

The king gazed at it for a long still while. He had been born there in that temple in the chanting and the incense. He had grown to young manhood under the care of its prince. This, more than Ianon, more than any other province of his empire, was the place his heart longed for.

Elian beside him, raw with homecoming, could not tell which pangs were his and which were her own. His were sharp with years of absence, but hers were still new, edged with fear of what she would find. He could expect a royal welcome. She . . .

Ilarios leaned from his saddle to touch the hand that clenched upon her thigh. "It will be well," he said.

She tossed her hair out of her face, fiercely. Mirain was already moving. He would be inside the walls by night, with great ceremony, and up till dawn settling his people. She sent Ilhari after him.

All the road to the city was rimmed with people, the gates beyond them ablaze with light. Halenan and Mirain rode side by side, the prince in a splendor of green and gold, the king all in white that glowed in the dusk, with a great mantle of white fur pouring over the Mad One's flanks. Its scarlet lining shone in the flicker of torchlight, now blood-bright, now blood-black.

Elian would have ridden as she had ridden to the meeting at the ford, well back among the army. But Ilhari knew her proper place: beside her sire. With no bit or bridle to compel her, and neither the will nor the willingness to overbear her with power, Elian had perforce to go where she was taken.

The livery of the king was no shield here, where every man and woman and child knew her face. They cheered for Mirain, they cheered for Halenan, but they cried out also for her, their lady, their brightmaned princess. She greeted them with lifted hand and a fixed, brilliant smile. But her eyes saw none of them.

Under the arch of the White Gate a mounted man waited alone. His stallion was as white as milk, his coat resplendent with gold; gold crowned his fiery hair. Dark as his face was, black in the dusk, Elian could not discern his expression, only the gleam of his eyes. They were fixed upon the boy he had fostered, who had escaped his care one deep night to gain a northern kingdom, whom he had made an emperor. As the riders drew near, he dismounted and waited, tall beside his tall senel.

Elian saw the glint of Mirain's eyes, the swirl of his cloak as he left the saddle with the Mad One still advancing. He half strode, half ran up the last of the road; caught Prince Orsan in the act of bowing to the ground; drew him into a swift, jubilant embrace. "Foster-father," he said, clear in the sudden silence, "never bow to me, you or your princess or your children. You are my heart's kin; I owe you all that I have."

The prince's voice came deep and quiet, but touched with great joy. "Not all of it, my lord An-Sh'Endor."

"Enough." Mirain returned to the Mad One's back. When the prince also had mounted, the king held out his golden hand. "I shall never forget it; I, or all the sons of my sons."

Ceremony was a mighty protector of sinners. Caught up in the welcoming of the emperor to the heart of his empire, neither prince nor princess could so far trespass upon dignity as to take official notice of the face above the squire's surcoat. But they were aware of her. Painfully. Excruciatingly, as the grand entry gave way to the presentation in the temple, the rite and the praises of the god, and at last to the feast of welcome.

Elian stood close enough to her father to touch; her mother's perfume was sweet and subtle in her nostrils, the princess clear to see on Mirain's left side, a flawless profile, a serene dark eye. Elian could have escaped with utmost ease, with but a word, a plea to be excused. There was enough and more than enough to do outside in the growing camp. Hal, having had an hour alone with Anaki, was there now, seeing that everything was ordered as Mirain wished it. Cuthan had gone with him. Even Ilarios had chosen to escape this lordly duty. She had no allies here.

She had known that before she committed herself to it. As she had known what a squire's place was: here, standing behind her lord's chair for every Gileni noble and servant to stare at. Wild though she had always been, none of them had ever thought to see her there.

The end was merciful, wine and graceful words, the departure of hosts and guests to their beds or to their duties. Prince Orsan had repaired and refurbished a whole wing of the palace for Mirain, at what expense she could hardly guess. He had stinted nothing.

Mirain stood in the center of the Asanian carpet as she labored patiently to undo the fastenings of his coat. He was silent: absorbed, she thought, in contemplation of the long night's work before him.

She herself had little to say. She slipped the coat from his shoulders and laid it in the clothing chest, careful of its jeweled splendor. When she turned back, he was still in his trousers and his fine linen shirt, watching her. She took up his working garb, a kilt as plain as any trooper's. "You should take a cloak," she said. "The nights are cold this close to solstice."

He accepted the kilt, but made no move to don it. "Elian," he said. "Why have you said no word to either your father or your mother?"

She stood still. His gaze was steady. She knew that if she reached, his mind would be open to her touch. Her shields closed and firmed. "There has been no occasion," she said, speaking High Gileni, distant and formal, with no warmth in it.

He met her coldness with a flare of heat and the patois of the city. "You spent a whole turn of the watch within their arms' reach."

"They made no effort to speak to me."

"They waited for you."

"Did they?" She began to unbind his hair.

He pulled free. How strange, she thought within her barriers. He was aflare with temper, and she was utterly cool, utterly in control.

"You are not!" he snapped. "Your obstinacy lies within you like an egg, hard and round and heavy, shelled in ice. Come away from it and look at yourself."

There was a mirror near the bed, polished silver. Because he held her in front of it, she regarded the stranger there. Whoever it was, it was not the child who had fled Han-Gilen in the night, this bright-haired person of ambiguous gender, lean and hard with long riding, with four thin parallel scars seaming one cheek. Its eyes had seen much and grown dark with it; its mouth tightened upon—what? Grief? Pain? Anger? Crippling shyness?

His hands held hers in a fierce grip. "You see? How can they speak to this? Easier to reason with the sword's edge."

"What could they say? That my beauty is ruined? That my value on the market has dropped to nothing?"

"They could say that they love you; that they grieved for your absence; that they are glad beyond words to have you back again."

"Let them say it then."

"They will." His eyes met her mirrored stare, his face beside hers, dark and eager. "Go to them. Now. They wait for you."

She turned her back on him and on her own face. "If they wish to see me, they may summon me." She pulled off her surcoat and reached for a coat as plain as the kilt he had abandoned. "Will my lord dress himself, or would he prefer that I aid him?"

Walled in the perfection of her coldness, she could not sense either his thought or his temper. She changed from state dress into common garb, in silence he made no move to break. When she passed him in search of her boots, her heart speeded a little in spite of itself. But he did not seize her. His face had hardened to match her own. "I have no further need of your services tonight," he said, cool and precise. "If you choose not to do as I bid you, then you had best confine yourself to quarters. I shall speak with you later."

Sitting on her pallet with her boots hanging limp and forgotten in her hands, she stared at the wall. Her eyes were dry to burning. He had sent her to bed like a wayward child; and for what? Because she would not abase herself before anyone, not even her father. Nor would she face her mother and listen to the long, gentle-voiced, relentless catalogue of her sins and shortcomings. Foremost of which was the stain with which she had defiled the reputation of her house. Not only had she shorn her hair and taken on the seeming of a boy; she had traveled alone and unattended through the north of the Hundred Realms, and slain men in battle, and shared the bed of a man neither wedded nor betrothed to her. She was a scandal from western Asanion to the Eastern Isles, utterly, irredeemably.

And she would not go to them and weep with them and beg to be forgiven. She could not. She was too proud; or too utterly craven.

"They can come to me," she said aloud. "They know where I am."

In Mirain's bed?

She laughed bitterly. "If only I were!"

With sharp, vicious movements she stripped off her garments, letting them lie where they fell. The mirror gleamed in the outer chamber. She faced it again.

She was too thin; but not everywhere. There could be no doubt at all now that this sullen-faced person was a woman. A gown, a daub or three of paint, and she would outshine any harlot on Lantern Street. Her hair was long enough now to tie back, even to twist into a short braid: the exact length prescribed for a woman of ill repute.

A small knife lay on a table. Mirain's, for cutting meat at feasts. Its hilt shone frostily, set with diamonds. Yet for all its beauty it was no toy. Its blade was deadly sharp.

She took it up. Carefully, deliberately, she cut her hair, cropping it well above the shoulders.

She let the knife fall. Her hands were shaking. The face in the mirror was green-pale under its cap of coppery hair; and yet it bared its sharp white teeth. "Now let them see how I mean to go on. Han-Gilen may house me, but it cannot hold me. I have freed myself."

Ah, but from what?

Elian sat alone in the barren garden, staring at nothing, thinking of nothing.

"Lady." She started, waking as from sleep. Cuthan stood over her, tall as a tree and vivid as a sunbird in the grey cloudlight. His face and his eyes and his bearing were at once bold and shy; she thought he might be blushing under the black velvet of his skin. "Lady," he repeated, "it will rain soon."

Elian looked at him and thought of hating him. "I am no lady."

The Ianyn captain sat on a low flat stone, clasping his knees, boylike, with a frown between his fine arched brows. "You refuse the name, but you can't change the truth. You're still what blood and training have made you."

"I have cut myself off from it."

"Have you ever tried to cut a jet of blood with a sword?"

"I have cloven flesh and bone, and taken the life within."

"It's less easy to sever oneself from one's kin."

Elian's anger flared white-hot. "Who set you on me? Mirain?

Halenan? Or even"—her voice cracked, startling her, feeding her rage
—"or even my father?"

"Your father," said Cuthan calmly, "is a very great prince. In Ianon
we would call him a king. And he loves you."

"He let me go. I have come back, but not to his hand."

"I said love, not jesses and a lure."

Elian tensed to rise. She meant to strike with fierce words, and to flee
his unwelcome presence, this mingling of youthful shyness and borrowed wisdom that pricked her almost to madness. But she heard herself say in a voice she hardly knew as her own, "I went to the mews. I
thought it would be quiet there. Hawks and the Hawkmaster have no
care for the cut of one's hair. It was quiet, and the master did not care.
But she was gone, my golden falcon. After I left, when I did not come
back, they flew her, and she never returned. If I had been there, she
would have come."

"Would she?"

Elian did rise then, fists clenched. "Yes. Yes! She was mine. I tamed
her. I loved her. She would have come back."

"You," said Cuthan, "did not. Or will not."

"I am not a falcon!"

"But your father is a falconer?"

Elian willed herself to stalk away from this transparent subterfuge,
this parroting of words learned by rote from the whole tribe of her kin.
Of whom he seemed to count himself one, however tortuous the kinship: brother of her foster brother's oathbrother. Later she would laugh.
Now she could not even move. Her body seemed rooted here on the
winter grass, with the sky beginning to weep great cold tears. "You have
no right to sit in judgment upon me."

"None at all," Cuthan agreed willingly, "except that of friendship. I
thought we had that, you and I."

"Galan had it. Now you know he was a lie."

To her amazement, Cuthan laughed, light and free. "I knew all
along." He spread his hands as if to sweep away all lies and disguises. "I
only look like a brawn-brained fool; and I trained to be a singer for a
while, till my master told me I had a fine voice, a fine mind, and no
calling at all to the grey robe. But even with the little learning I had, I
knew that Orsan of Han-Gilen would never have gotten a bastard—
least of all a boy of exactly the same age, size, and looks as his famous
daughter. A good part of whose fame lay in her ability to outride,
outhunt, and outfight any man she met."

"Is there anyone who didn't know the truth?" Elian asked sourly.

His eyes were wide and dark and surprised. "Who else could have? Except Mirain, of course. And Vadin. Vadin always knows everything Mirain does. We didn't tell anyone. We didn't even tell each other till the secret got out."

"That explains a great deal. All your hanging about. Your fretting over me in the battle."

He had the grace to look sheepish and the gall to defend himself. "I wasn't hanging about. I was doing what any man would do for his friend. I never intended to humiliate you."

"No?" Her mouth twisted. "No, of course not. I'm a woman. Delicate. Fragile. Featherheaded. I can't be humiliated. Only protected to death."

"Lady," Cuthan said with heroic patience, "you wear defiance like a suit of armor. Won't you take off the helmet at least and look around you? The only one who's tormenting you is yourself."

Elian's hand lifted to strike him. With an effort of will she lowered it. "How much did my kinsmen pay you to say these things?"

The black eyes kindled, swift and terrible as a flame in a sunlit wood. "Barbarian I may be, and no king's son, but I'm no one's hireling. I saw pain in my king, and in his brother, and in a lord and a lady whom I've learned to admire. I saw it most of all in my friend, who simply happened to be a woman. Now I understand that I saw a friend where I had none. Unless that is friendship here in the south, to meet love with tooth and claw. In the north, even the lynx of the wood will not do that." He stood. His face was cold and hard. He bowed very slightly, very stiffly, as to a stranger. "I at least will go in out of the rain. Good day, lady."

The title was like a slap. Elian watched him go, unable to move, unable to speak, while the rain beat her with flails of ice.

She could have crawled into some dark corner and huddled there, and burned and shivered all alone. But deeper than rage or hate or even craven terror was the pride that had spawned them. Wet to the skin, steady by sheer force of will, she returned to Mirain's chamber.

He was there, as she had known he would be. He was alone, which she had not expected. A large and busy company she could have faced, effacing herself in it, but that solitary figure in a long robe lined with fur, seated by a brazier with a book in his lap, nearly undid her.

His eyes were lowered, but the book was closed, its spools bound together with golden cords. Deep in thought as he was, he did not hear her coming. She wavered in the door, dripping on the carpet, gathering herself to bolt. He looked like Cuthan. Damnably like. But the rain had washed her anger away, leaving only an echoing emptiness. Something roused him: perhaps the chattering of her teeth. The sudden light of his eyes nearly felled her. His hands were burning hot, drawing her into the room, setting her by the brazier, stripping her of her sopping clothes. He flung his own robe about her and fastened it high under her chin, and took her icy hands in his own and chafed them until the pain of life woke within them.

She should pull free. He was the king. It was not fitting that he should do squire service for his squire.

Gently he pressed her into his chair, drying her dripping hair with a cloth from his bath. She suffered it as she had suffered Cuthan's bitter words, with inward resistance, outward helplessness.

With the worst of the wet wiped away, he reached for the comb he had brought with the cloth. She blocked his hand. Her own had almost no strength, but he paused. "Say it," she gritted. "Say all of it."

"It has been said." He eluded her grasp and began to comb her cropped hair. He had more patience with its tangles than he ever had with his own.

"Of course," he said. "There's less of it." His palm rested against her cheek, warm now, but not to burning. Yet it was the right, which bore the god's fire, which had blinded his mother's murderer.

Elian swallowed round the knot in her throat. "Cuthan told the truth. The whole ugly truth. But I can't—can't—"

He was behind her; she could not see his face. His voice was soft. "Elian, my sister. Only the weak refuse to weep."

"I *won't!*" she cried, leaping up, facing him. "You have duties. We both do. And you in nothing but a loinguard. You could perish of a chill."

"Elian."

"No." She fumbled with the fastenings of the robe, pulling them free. "No. Not—not yet."

That minute concession was, in its way, as cruel as Cuthan's farewell. Yet Mirain accepted it with more grace than Elian could ever have mustered. Which in turn was its own, subtle, and well-deserved rebuke.

Sixteen

"HERE," SAID MIRAIN, "I SHALL BUILD MY CITY."
The wind was loud on the plain of the river, and knife-edged
with cold, but Mirain's words came soft and clear beneath it. He stood
with feet set well apart, head up and eyes alight, with his cloak whipping about him; his own fire warmed him, the fire of prophecy.

He spread his arms wide, taking in all the broad hilltop. Steep slopes
bastioned it in the north and east; in the west rushed the deep flood of
Suvien; southward it dipped gently into the levels of Han-Gilen, looking
across the windswept land to the prince's white city.

"Easy to defend," said Cuthan. "With a good rampart all around and
a good road up to your gate, you'll be as well served as any king alive."

"Better than most." Adjan paced off the edge of the hilltop. "There'll
be water in any wells you sink; and there's space here for whole farmsteads."

"And the river to ride on and trade on," Cuthan said.

Mirain laughed as sometimes he did, for simple joy. "It will be the
richest city in the world, and the greatest, and the most splendid. See:
white walls, white towers; Sun-gold upon the gates, and Sun's fire in its
people, under the rule of the god."

Elian moved apart from the company about the king, through a city
of shadows shaped out of power and sunlight for his servants to marvel
at. She needed no such mummeries, who could see in truth as well as

he. With a flicker of will she banished the image, leaving only the winter-dulled grass and the empty air and the fitful dazzle of sunlight.

Her feet had brought her to the bank of Suvien. The water ran black and cold, swirling about deep-rooted stones, eating away at the hillside. But the far bank rose sheer and implacable. There stood no wide welcoming hill, no seat of empire, but a jut of naked stone, black as the river, shunned even by the birds.

"Endros Avaryan," she said to herself. Avaryan's Throne. A curse lay on it. Curse, or fate, or prophecy. No man might walk there unless he be born of a god; and even he could not tarry lest he go mad and die.

No man but Mirain, who had been little more than a child when he ventured it: young and wild and armored in his lineage, and mad enough to dare even that great curse.

And Elian. He had not known that she was following him until he stood breathless on the summit. She, climbing to within a man-length of him, set her foot upon a stone which gave way beneath it, and fell with a sharp despairing cry.

She had not fallen far: another length down the sheer cliff to a sliver of ledge. But he, in rage that was half deadly fear, plunged down to catch her. Between her own fear and her own young, erratic magery, she shot out of his hands, up the last of the crag onto the bare cold stone. There she lay gasping until he dragged her up. "Fool!" he cried. "Idiot! Lunatic! You'll die here!"

His voice, which was breaking, cracked from a bellow into a shriek. She could not help it; she began to laugh. She roared with it, rolling on the top of Avaryan's throne, with the sun himself glaring down at her sacrilege.

Mirain snatched her up and shook her until at last she quieted. She looked up at him, blinking, hiccoughing. Somehow she managed to say, "I won't die."

"The curse—"

"I won't." She knew it as surely as she knew that the curse was real. It thrummed in the stone. "It can't touch me. I'm not a man."

Suddenly he was hardly taller than she, and changed: his free hair braided, his throat circled by the torque of his father's priesthood. She swayed for a moment in the throes of memory. So caught, timeless, she saw Mirain-then and Mirain-now, and beyond and about him a sweep of darkness shot with diamond light.

His hands gripped her, steadying her. "Look," she said. "The tower. But who would dare—"

"Tower?"

Was he blind? "Tower! There, on Endros. Someone's built a tower—on—" Her voice died. It was clear, so clear. Tall and terrible like the crag, black stone polished smooth as glass, wrought without door or window, and on its pinnacle a sun. Yet even as she gazed at it, it shimmered and shrank. There was only the rock and the wind and the empty sky.

Suddenly she was cold, bone-cold. Mirain said nothing, only spread his cloak about them both. Her will tensed to pull away; her body huddled into the warmth. Thoughts babbled about her, orderless and shieldless, bastard children of minds without power. Some were amused, and some were annoyed, and some were even envious, knowing only what mere eyes knew, dark head and bright one close together and one cloak between them.

"It's me they envy," said Mirain.

"And me they laugh at." Her shivering had stopped, her visions faded. Her body was her own again. Smoothly she slid away from him. He let her go; which, irrationally, roused her temper. She strode past him through the knot of guards and friends and hangers-on, daring them to stare. None did. They were all most carefully considering the city that would be.

Ilhari was grazing on the southern slope, eyed by a stallion or two: Ilarios' gold, Cuthan's tall blue dun. Halenan's grey, whom she rather favored, was not among them. With Anaki so close to her time, the prince did not like to ride far from her, nor would Mirain ask it.

Elian laid her cheek against the warm thick coat, breathing in the scent of wind and grass and senel-hide. "Oh, sister," she said, "you have all the blessings. No fates and prophecies, and no family to grieve you."

The mare raised her head, laying back her ears at the dun, who was venturing too close. Prudently he retreated. She returned to her grazing. Ah yes, seneldi had sense, though the stallions could be a nuisance. One came into heat, one mated, one carried a foal. One bore it, one nursed it, one weaned it, and that was that. No endless two-legged follies. But then, humans were cursed, were they not? Never fully weaned and always in heat.

Elian laughed unwillingly. "Straight to the mark, as always. And when you add power, it's worse than a curse. It's pure hell."

Ilhari snorted. Follies. A good gallop, that would cure them.

Or obscure them. Elian settled into the saddle; the mare sprang forward.

They ran abreast of the wind round the hill that would be the City of the Sunborn, out upon the open plain. Ilhari bucked; Elian whooped.

This was senel-wisdom, beast-wisdom: fate and folly be damned, cities and kings and the hope of dynasties. Whoever ruled, the earth remained, and the wind, and the sun riding above them. Elian began to sing.

When Ilhari brought Elian back to the hilltop, the escort was gathered in a hollow out of the wind, clearing away the last of the daymeal. Adjan, whose skill in such things came close to wizardry, had kindled a fire; the wine which Mirain passed to Elian in his own silver traveling-cup was steaming hot and pungent with spices.

As she sipped it, Ilarios set beside her a napkinful of bread and meat. This was an ill day for her mind-shields. She caught a guardsman's vision of her fortune: to be waited on by emperors, when by right, for abandoning her post, she should have had nothing but a reprimand.

She smiled a little wryly, a little wickedly. Ziad-Ilarios smiled back. Mirain did not see; he had turned to speak to Cuthan.

Elian's fingers tightened round the figured surface of the cup. Her mood was as treacherous as a wind in spring. Perhaps her courses—

She drank deep of the cooling wine. No, she could not lay the blame on her body. She had been so since the army turned toward Han-Gilen, and worse since she came there.

"Yes," Mirain was saying to Cuthan, "it has begun. He knew it would be today."

The young lord laughed. "One would think he was the one who was birthing the child."

"I think he would if he could. But Anaki knows her business. She bears well and easily, and as serenely as she does all else."

"A very great lady, that one."

"Greater than most people know. She could be a queen if she chose."

"An empress?"

Mirain tossed back his heavy braid and laughed. "Her lord might allow it, under duress. But she never would."

Carefully Elian set down the empty cup. She could sense what Mirain spoke of, that the birthing had begun. It would not go on long, as such things went. With Anaki it never did. By the time the riders reached the city, the banners would be flying, green for a royal daughter.

The wine's warmth had faded. Elian was suddenly, freezingly cold.

As the last light of Avaryan touched the turrets of the city, no banners flew there, either princess green or princely gold. Ah well, thought Elian, it was early yet. And she was a fool for thinking so much of it.

What did it matter to her how long Anaki lay in childbed? She was no part of it. She had sundered herself from her kin.

Neither prince nor princess took the nightmeal in hall. Mirain, alight still with the dream of his city, was inclined to tarry, spreading great rolls of parchment on a cleared table, bending over them with brush and stylus. When Elian withdrew, he was deep in colloquy with a small man in blue, her father's master builder.

"When he dreams," said Ilarios beside her, "he dreams to the purpose."

She walked with him down the lamplit corridor. "Mirain has no dreams. Only true visions. Even when he was a child, he never said *if.* He always said *when.*"

"Superb in his confidence, that one." The high prince clasped his hands behind him, studying her. "Lady, are you troubled?"

Her brows knit. "Why should I be?"

He shrugged slightly.

She turned with the sharpness of temper, striding down a side passage. After a moment's hesitation he followed her. She did not look at him, but she saw him too clearly, a golden presence on the edge of vision. "Why do you always wear gold? Is it a law?"

"I thought it suited me."

"It does," she said.

"Should I try another color, for variety? Green, maybe? Scarlet?"

"Black. That would be striking."

He bowed, amused. "Black it shall be, then. An incognito. Have you ever marked this? If a man wears always one color or fashion, he has but to change it and no one will know him."

"Everyone knows you."

"Yes? I venture a wager, lady. Any stakes you name."

She stopped. He was laughing, delighted with himself. "What would you venture, my lord?"

"I, my lady—I would wager the topaz in my coronet, against . . ." He paused, eyes dancing. "Against a kiss."

Her lip curled. "Then you are a fool. If I win, I gain a great jewel; if I lose, I lose nothing by it."

"Well, two kisses, and a lock of your hair."

"And this knife to cut it with."

"Done, my lady." He bowed over her hand, half courtly, half mocking. "Shall I escort you to your chamber?"

"My thanks," she said, "but no."

He knew her well, now. He did not try to press her. She watched him go, turning then, letting her feet lead her as they pleased. Where she wished to go, she did not know. Some of the palace ways teemed with people; she sought those less frequented, winding through the labyrinth, yet with no fear of losing herself. No child of the Halenani could do that, not in this place which the Red Princes had built.

At last she paused. The door before her was different from the others, richly carved with beasts and birds. It opened easily at the touch of her hand.

Within, all was dark, with the hollowness of disuse. She made a witchlight in the palm of her hand and advanced slowly. Nothing had changed. There was the bed with its green hangings; the carpet like a flowery meadow; the table and the great silver mirror; and her armor on its frame like a guardsman in the gloom. Over it lay a silken veil, flung there she could not remember when, and left so because it suited her whimsy.

Setting the light to hover above her head, she took up the veil. Its fineness caught and rasped upon her callused fingers. She draped it, drawing it across her cheek. The mirror reflected a paradox: a royal squire with the head of a maiden. She laughed, an abrupt, harsh sound.

Her gowns lay all in their presses, scented with sweet herbs. Green, gold, blue, white. No scarlet. Red gowns and red hair made an ill match.

She drew out a glow of deep green, splendid yet simple, velvet of Asanion sewn with a shimmer of tiny firestones. Prince Orsan had had it made for her, the princess and her ladies stitched the myriad jewels, a gift for Elian's birth-feast.

It fit still. She had grown no taller and certainly no broader, though the bodice was somewhat more snug than she remembered. Now the strangeness was reversed: boy's shorn mane, maiden's ripening body. Her face hung between, more maid indeed than boy, with a drawn and discontented look. "Life," she said to it, "seems not to agree with you."

She sank down. The full skirt pooled about her. Unconsciously she smoothed it, as a bird will preen even in a cage, gazing beyond it at the heap of scarlet which was her livery. Here, exactly here, she had begun it all. And here in the end she had returned. To sneer at what she had been; to exult over her victory; to huddle on the floor, too bleak to weep, too empty to rage.

This then was her oath's fulfillment. A closed door and a dark room, and no one to care where she went. No one to ask, no one to tell—

She flung herself to her feet. "Gods damn them all!"

* * *

The prince was not in his chamber nor the princess in her bower; the bed they shared was empty, their servants meeting Elian's fire with carefully bland faces. Having humbled herself so far, she could not bear to be so thwarted. "Where are they, then?" she snapped.

It was her father's body-servant who answered, perfect in his dignity; but when she was very small he had played at hunt-and-hide with her. His eyes upon her were warm and brimming, radiating welcome. "Surely my lady knows: they are with my lord Halenan."

Who was with his lady in his own great house, in a shell of silence. No royal child of Han-Gilen could be laid open at birth to the sorceries of an enemy; so was each born within the shield of its kinsfolk's power. In her preoccupation with her own troubles, she had forgotten.

She paused. Surely her errand could wait. Shame was creeping in, and shyness, and some of her old obstinacy. The morning would be a good time, a glad time, better and gladder than this. No one needed her now. She would only be in the way.

Somehow she had a mantle about her and a page before her with a lamp, and the gate-guards were letting her pass, bowing before her.

Halenan's house under the sun was high and fair, set in the lee of the temple, with gardens running down to the river. In this black night it loomed like the crag of Endros, its gate shut and barred, all within as silent to the mind as to the ear.

The guard was long in coming to her call, longer still in opening the gate. But he did not forbid her the entry, although he eyed her in what might have been suspicion.

There were shields within shields. This that caught her upon the threshold had a dark gleam, a hint of her father. She flared her own red-gold against it. Slowly it yielded. A moment only; firming behind her, on guard against any threat.

Even in her cloak of fur, she was cold. But was it not always so? She had never been outside it before, but in its heart, lending her own power to the rest. She gathered her skirts and pressed forward.

Twice more she was halted, twice more she proclaimed her right to pass. And a door was open before her with a woman on guard, and within, the birthing.

Her father sat on the ledge of a shuttered window, eyes closed, yet seeing all about him with the keenness of power. Her mother, lovely as always, elegant as always, rested beside him with a lamp above her and a bit of needlework in her hands. On the bed lay Anaki, Hal's bright head bent over her and the birthing-woman intent upon her. It was like a vision in water, silent but for the rasp of Anaki's breath; and in the mind, nothing.

The prince's eyes opened. The princess turned her head. Halenan looked up.

Elian stepped through the door, and staggered. Pain—there was always that. But this was worse—worse—

She never remembered crossing the room, but she was there, beside the bed. Anaki's sweet plain face was streaming wet, distorted with pain, yet she managed a smile, a word. "Sister. So glad—"

Halenan silenced her with a caress. His smile was less successful than hers, but his voice was stronger. "Yes, little sister, we are glad."

"What," Elian said. "What is—"

"Our daughter," he answered almost lightly, "takes after you. All contrary, and fighting us into the bargain."

Contrary indeed. Elian, unfolding a tendril of power, found the child head upward, feet braced. And being what she was, magebred, she fought not only with her body but with her infant power, struggling against this force that would compel her into the cruel light, striking at her mother in her blind and blinded terror. Anaki had power of her own, both strong and quiet, but this battle had sapped it; she could not both bear her body's pain and soothe her child.

"She needs greater healing than I can give," the Red Prince said. He had come to Elian's side and taken her hand, calmly, as if nothing had ever happened between them. She let her cold fingers rest in his warm strong ones. She felt dull, numbed, as if she had endured a long siege of weeping. Of course it would happen so. It must.

Unless—

"Mirain," she said. "He has the power. He can—"

Her brother looked at her. Simply looked, without either pleading or condemnation.

Her eyes slid away. Anaki strained under the midwife's hands, twisting, crying out with effort and with agony. The lash of power from within, untrained, uncontrolled, turned the cry to a shriek.

Elian's own power reached without her willing it, in pure instinct, clasping, bending, *thus.* There were words in it. *Ah no, child. Would you kill your mother? Come with me. Come, so . . .*

"Elian." She stared at what Hal set in her hands. Dark red, writhing feebly, and howling with all its strength. Above it hovered its father's broad white grin. "And Elian," he said in high glee. "What better name for your very image?"

"My very—" She drew her namesake close, and returned her brother's grin with one that wobbled before it steadied. "She is beautiful, isn't she?"

"Breathtakingly." Halenan reclaimed his offspring, to lay her in her mother's arms. Anaki was grey-pale and weary, but she smiled.

Elian's knees buckled. Hands caught her. Many. Her father's; her mother's. Mirain's. She blinked. "Where—how—"

"Rest first."

She fought free, glaring at Mirain. "You knew! You plotted this. You *made* me—"

"We did," Mirain agreed. "Later, if you like, you may continue in your cowardice. Today you will be civil. And that, madam, is a command."

His eyes flickered upon her. Half of it was laughter; half of it was not. She looked past him. She came of a proud family. They would never plead, would never even hint at it. Yet the eyes upon her were warm, offering, if only she would take. Only if she would take.

Her throat closed. She held out her hands. "Since," she choked out, "since my king commands . . . and since . . ."

They were there, all of them who could be, and Anaki in spirit, enfolding her. In that circle where she most longed to be strong, she broke and cried like a child.

Seventeen

*F*ROM THE SCREENED GALLERY, ONE COULD LOOK down into the hall and not be seen oneself. Which was why that narrow balcony was called the ladies' bower, and the sentry post.

Elian supposed that she was a little of both. Although she had returned to Mirain's livery, a gown or two had found its way among the coats and trousers in her clothing chest. Her mother had not even looked askance at her. The joy of reunion was still too fresh, and with it the fear of a new flight.

Not so long ago, she would have been glad to see her mother taking pains to voice no censure, to accept her as she was. But now that she had the upper hand, it did not matter. Victories were always so. Savorless, even a little shameful.

She shook herself hard. *That* victory deserved no sweetness. The best of it was the joy: that she had her family again; that her battle with them had been no battle at all, only her own craven stubbornness. Even now her father's mind brushed hers; she felt the warmth of his smile, although he seemed to be intent upon the petitioner before his throne. Her brother stood behind him. Mirain, though king and emperor, did not interfere in this business of the ruling prince, but effaced himself among the higher nobles. Or tried. Not a man there but knew where he was, he who without height or beauty or splendor of dress remained the Sunborn.

Elian peered down at the gathering. Today Ilarios meant to win his wager; restraining power, she left the search to her eyes. Who would have believed that there were so many fair-haired people in Han-Gilen? Or that so many of them would choose to wear dark colors on this day of all days?

Some of them were women. Some were too tall, some too broad or too narrow, most too dark of face: Gileni brown or bronze. One with a mane of the true bright gold—but no, it was a woman, and she wore deep blue.

There, at last. Near the somber-clad scribes, almost among them. That angle of the head was unmistakable. Somehow he had disposed of his shadows, or they had concealed themselves too perfectly even for her eyes' finding. He wore a scribe's fusty gown, and he carried a writing case; his hair was pulled back and knotted at the nape of his neck. Without that golden frame, his face seemed rounder, younger. Yet he still looked royal; imperial.

No one took the slightest notice of him.

A man approached him, a lord of the court. Knowing surely who he was, speaking to him. Ilarios bent his head in what he must have deemed to be humility. And the lord gestured, lordly-wise, and Asanion's high prince sat cross-legged at the end of the line of scribes and began to write to the nobleman's dictation.

Was that a smile in the corner of his mouth?

When Ilarios left the hall, Elian was waiting for him. He clutched his writing case to his breast and bowed, all servile; but when he straightened he was laughing for sheer delight.

She laughed with him, and kissed him. There was no thought in it. It was very sweet, and he was startled, which made it sweeter still.

He took her hand. "Lady," he said breathlessly. "Oh, lady." But though he looked and sounded even younger than she, he remained Ilarios. "There are better places than this to collect the rest of my wager."

A lady passed with all her retinue. Seeing the scribe and the squire together in the passage, she beckoned imperiously. "Here, penman! I have need of you."

Elian stiffened. But Ilario's eyes danced. Oh, people were blinder even than she had thought, if they reckoned him a meek commoner. "Yes, madam," he said. "At once, madam."

Elian caught his sleeve, slowing his retreat. "When you finish. The south tower."

His smile was his only response.

* * *

He was slow in coming to the tower. But it was a pleasant place, high up over the city, with her father's library at the bottom of it. Choosing a book at random, Elian mounted the long twisting stair.

The chamber at the top had been a schoolroom not so long ago, and would be again when Halenan's children were old enough to leave their nurse for a tutor. The furnishings were ancient and battered and exceedingly comfortable, laden with memories. The tallest chair had been hers, because she was the smallest, and because it had the only cushioned seat, though the cushion was stone-hard and full of lumps. Her behind, settling into it, remembered each hill and valley.

She leaned upon the heavy age-darkened table. Its top was much hacked and hewn, inscribed with the names of bored pupils. Royal names, most of them. *Halenan* was very common, carved in numerous hands. Nine, Hal had always insisted, although their firstfather could not possibly have learned his letters here, wild wanderer that he was, with nothing to his name when he came to Han-Gilen but a sword and a gift of wizardry. But Hal had carved the ancient name again, making it ten, and ruined his second-best dagger in doing it.

Her finger traced the letters, gliding from them across the ridged wood to the bright gleam of a wonder. It looked like a sunburst marvelously wrought of inlaid gold. But no goldsmith had set it there to gleam incongruously amid the childish scrawls. Mirain had done it by no will of his own, not long after his mother died, when power and temper roiled in him and made his grief a deadly thing. Pricked by some small slight—a sally from Halenan, or his tutor's reprimand—he had risen and braced himself, and his power had come roaring and flaming. Yet at the last instant he had mastered his rage; the power, thwarted, too potent to be contained, had left this mark of its passing.

With a swift movement Elian left chair and table. High narrow windows cleft the wall at intervals, letting in the cool sunlight. She knelt beside the hooded hearth, where a fire was laid neatly, as if there were daily need of it. Although flint and steel rested in their niche, she gathered a spark of power, held it a moment until its fierce heat began to sear her hand, and cast it upon the wood. Flames leaped up, red-gold like her hair, settling into their common red and yellow and burning blue.

Warmth laved her face. She had forgotten her book upon the table; she let it be, resting her eyes upon the dance of the fire. Shapes formed in it, images, past and present and to come. A corner of her mind struggled, protesting. The rest watched calmly. Peace-visions, these, with no taint of fear. Anaki and her si-Elian, small bright-downy head and smooth deep-brown one. Anaki was smiling a deep, secret smile, and her plainness was beautiful. Prince Orsan and his princess, all their royal dignity laid aside, laughing together, and after a time moving close, mirth forgotten, until body touched body. Ilhari with Hal's grey stallion in a green meadow, silver on fire gold.

Elian flushed with more than the heat of the fire. Seeing, this certainly was, but all her teaching had told her that the seer could shape what she saw. Even unwitting.

Sharply, almost angrily, she banished the senel-shapes. The flames were flames, no more. No visions. No longings.

And what do you long for? Her inner voice was mocking. The fire rose and shaped itself. Once, and once again. Dark, gold. Emperor and emperor to be.

True child of the Halenani, she. Beset with maiden moods, she settled only upon the very highest. The one, she could have if she but said the word. The other . . .

The other vanished. Ilarios knelt by the fire, still in his scribe's gown. His face was as white as bleached bone; his eyes were the burning sulfur-yellow of a cat's. With tight-controlled savagery he ripped the bindings from his hair. It poured down his back, tumbled into his face.

Her teeth unclamped from her lip. She tasted blood. "My lord," she said. "Has someone offended you?" And when he did not answer: "Your wager is well won. Too well, maybe. If anyone has spoken ill to you, you should forgive him. He cannot have known—"

He flung back his hair. For all his leashed fury, his voice was mild. Alarmingly so. "No one has slighted me. Though to be a scribe and not the high prince . . . it is interesting. One sees so much. And one is never noticed. Until—" His breath came ragged. "Until one is forced to reveal oneself."

She waited.

He contemplated his fists clenched upon his thighs. His breathing quieted, but the tension did not leave him. "We have had an embassy. So many, there have been, since the Sunborn came to Han-Gilen. This one was small, plain, and to the point. And from my father." He looked up, a flash of burning gold. "With all due respect to his divine majesty, the Lord An-Sh'Endor has followers in plenty. He does not need the heir of Asanion."

"When?" She could barely speak; even the single word took all her strength.

His smile was bitter. "Oh, I need not take flight at once. That would be unseemly. I am given three days to order my affairs."

"And if you do not go?"

"I am to be reminded that, although I have no legitimate brothers, I have fifteen who are sons of concubines. All grown, ambitious, and eager to serve my royal father."

She sat still. After a long moment she said, "You knew this would come."

"I knew it." He unclenched his fists, first the right, then the left. "There are my half brothers. There are also my full sisters. Four of them. Two, yet unwed, are priestesses of various of the thousand rapacious gods. Two are wed to princes. Ambitious princes. One is rich, but not fabulously rich; the other reckons himself poor. And Asanion's throne is wrought all of pure gold."

Her hand went out. Living gold stirred under it; then warm flesh. Panther-swift, panther-strong, he seized her. "Lady," he said. "Elian. Come with me."

Never in all her life had she been so close to a man. Body to body. Heart to thudding heart.

Her hands were crushed between. She worked them free, linked them behind his neck. "Come with me," he said again.

He was fire-warm, trembling, yet all his anger had left him. She looked into his eyes, sun-gold now, both burning and tender.

"By all the gods, by your own bright Avaryan: Elian, Lady of Han-Gilen, I love you. I have always loved you. Come with me and be my bride."

Her teeth set. Her body burned; there was an ache between her thighs. Every line of him was distinct against her.

"I will make you my empress," he said. "Or if you will not have that, if a throne of gold seems too high and cold for you, then I will abandon it." He laughed, brief and wild. "You yearn for freedom; so too do I. Let us disguise ourselves and flee, north or east or south, or even west where my face is a common thing; and we can make our way as we can, and live as we please, and love as the simple folk love, for no fate or pride or dynasty, but only for ourselves." His arms tightened. "Oh, lady! Will you? Will you love me?"

His passion was like wind and fire; his beauty pierced her heart. And yet the cold corner of her mind observed, *How young he looks!*

He was nineteen. But the cool, controlled high prince had seemed a man grown. As old as Mirain, as Halenan, as—as her father.

He was no more than a boy.

A lovely, fiery, desperate boy. Her voice would not obey her and speak. Her body would not be silent.

This kiss was ages long and burning sweet.

At last they parted. Elian blinked, startled. Her eyes were brimming; her cheeks were wet. "I—" she began, and foundered, and began again. "I love you. But not—I am not worth a throne."

His joy blazed forth; he laughed with it, and yet he trembled. "A throne is worth nothing unless you share it with me."

"I love you," she repeated doggedly. "But—I am not—I must think!"

There was no quenching this new fire, although he tried. He did quell his face and his voice; but his eyes flamed. "Yes," he said in the gentlest of tones, "it is hard. You were away so long, and your quarrels are all so newly mended. But if you depart as my princess, will not your kin be glad?"

"Mother would be rather more than glad." She stiffened slightly; he released her, watching her with those hurting-bright eyes. "I have to think. Might you—could you—"

His smile was the one she remembered, child-sweet yet not a child's at all. "I shall leave you to your thoughts. You need not hasten them. I have three days yet."

"Not so long. I can think— Tonight. After the night-bell."

He gestured assent. "Here?"

Her eyes flicked about, flinched, closed. "No. Somewhere else. Somewhere—" She paused. "Somewhere for solitude. The temple. No one will come there so late."

"The temple," he said, "after the night-bell." He rose and stooped, brushing her lips with his. "Until then, beloved. May your god guide you."

Elian laughed wildly into the empty space; and then she wept; and then she laughed again. And squire service still to do. She straightened her livery and smoothed her hair and went down to it.

There was little enough to do, and that little she did ill. Mirain, intent on some business for which she cared nothing, dismissed her early. Not in disgrace, to be sure. He hardly knew she was there, nor cared.

A bath calmed her a little. She performed her duties of the bedchamber: turned down the bed, filled the nightlamp, readied Mirain's bath. He liked a very little scent, for the freshness: leaves of the *ailith* tree mingled with sweet herbs. As she cast them into the steaming water, a darkness filled her mind; she began to shake.

"Fool," she cursed herself. "Idiot! A lovesick heifer has more grace."

Was it love, or was it fear? Of herself; of Ilarios; of—whatever one chose to name. Of falling after all into the trap which she had fled. She had kept her oath. She had come to Mirain; she had fought for him. The other, older vow . . . need she keep it? Did she even wish to? Voices sounded in the bedchamber. Mirain bidding goodnight to a lord or two, dismissing his servants.

She willed herself to rise, but her knees would not straighten. If she wedded Ilarios, she would not do this again. Servant's labor. Menial things: scenting Mirain's bath, braiding his hair, arranging his cloak. Cleaning his armor, grooming his senel, riding at his right hand. With Hal on his left and Ilhari under her and the wind in her face.

He stood in the doorway in his simple Ianyn kilt, with his cloak flung over his shoulder. How dark he was, how deceptively slight; how deadly bright his eyes.

They saw nothing. She stood. "Your bath is ready. Shall I wait on you?"

Most often he refused. Tonight he said, "Yes. My hair needs washing."

He grimaced as he said it; in spite of herself she smiled. "You could cut it," she said.

He laughed a little. "That would be too easy. And," he added with a wicked glint, "I wouldn't need you to tend it for me."

Her throat closed. He never noticed; he was stripping off his kilt, laying it with his cloak beside the great basin. With his back turned to her, he took up a loinguard and began to put it on.

"Leave that," she said harshly. And when he glanced over his shoulder: "Am I any more delicate than your bath-maids in Ianon? I know what a man looks like."

He paused. After a moment he shrugged, dropped the loinguard, turned.

The heat raced from her soles to her crown and back again, stumbling between. But she made herself look at him. All of him.

With the suggestion of a smile he stepped into the bath. She began to loose his braid. Her fingers fumbled; silently she cursed herself.

Mirain lay in the water, eyes shut, utterly at ease. He looked like a great indolent cat. A panther, with a velvet hide and an air of tight-leashed power.

Her eyes slitted. A wildness unfolded within her. Even her shirt, soft and brief as it was, grated against her burning skin. She shed it. Mirain waited with the perfect, oblivious calm of royalty, for her to serve him. She filled her hand with cleansing-foam. Still Mirain had not moved.

But he was not asleep. His awareness hovered, flawless as a globe of crystal. Great mage and great king, god's son, child of the morning, he was warm and drowsy, and he smiled, drifting in the scented water.

She bent. He tasted of wine, and of honeycakes, and of fire.

The crystal flamed. Strength like a storm of wind bore her up, back. The world reeled.

Yet did not fall. Black eyes opened wide. She gasped, drowning. *Elian!* It was silent; it filled her brain and washed it clean.

She lay on a heap of damp softness. Clothing, she realized; drying-cloths; a cloak lined with fur. And on her, all the length of her, a body as bare as her own: little taller, little broader save in the shoulder, and fully as male as she was female.

Mirain looked down at her. His eyes were veiled, and yet they glittered

Say it, she willed him. *Say that you want me.*

He moved, half rising, to lie beside her. His face was calm. He was not going to speak. He was going to let her go, or stay, or do nothing at all.

Her demon sat up, prick-eared. No strength of hers could quell it. It said, "It was never like this with Ilarios."

He was still, like a stone king.

"He's very sweet. He warms my body. But this—no wonder you have so few women!"

"Am I so revolting?"

She had pierced a wall or two. His voice came deep and almost harsh; his face was frightening. Yet she bit down hard on laughter. "Dear heaven, no! Never. But if your kiss can drive your own sister mad, what if you give more? There must be very few who can bear the full fire of you."

"There is none," he said, still in that half-growl.

"None at all?" The laughter escaped, although she caught it swiftly and strangled it. "Not your lady regents? Not your nine beauties of the bath? Not—"

His hand stopped her mouth. "None." Her eyes danced disbelief. He glared. "There have been women in my bed. How not? Priest's vows can't hold a king. But the fire . . . is something else." He released her, pushing back his hair. Half wet, half dry, it covered his shoulders like a tattered cloak. "Though I fancy, from milord's dazed look of late, that you are stronger than I. Or hotter."

Her temper reared up and began to burn. "I've given him no whit more than I've given you."

"Ah," he said, drawing it out until she could have struck him. Then he laughed, painfully. "Poor prince! He has no power to shield him. Take care, lady; mere mortals are no match for the likes of us."

"I'm no god's get!" She scrambled to her knees. "He wants me to marry him. To go with him when he goes, and be his empress."

"And will you?"

Iron. Iron and adamant, and royal refusal to say a word, even one word of aught but what befit a brother. "I don't know!" she shouted at him.

And sank down upon her heels. For that was not what she had meant to say at all.

"I love him," she said. The mask never stirred. The lids had lowered over the black eyes. "I do love him," she repeated. "It's impossible not to. He's so splendid, strong and gentle, merry and wise, all royal and all beautiful. There's nothing in him that isn't perfect of its kind. And he loves me to distraction."

She looked at herself and at Mirain, and laughed until a sob broke it. "Here I sit like a whore with her client, telling over old lovers. But I told him I'd chose tonight, and I don't know. I can't even think. But I should!"

"Know? Or think?"

"Both!" Her fists clenched over her eyes. She saw a red darkness shot with stars. "Every scrap of sense I have, and most of my body, cries out to me to take him. But something stops me. It isn't fear. I could live as Empress of Asanion. I could make an empire in my image: even that one, with all its thousand years of queens." He said nothing. She let the light in. It hurt. Blessed, cursed pain. "Damn it, Mirain," she said. "Why don't you say it and get it over?"

"What am I to say?"

Cold, that. Kingly. She knew the pride of it. That same pride had held her apart from her kin until death's own shadow drove her back to them.

"I heard you," she said, not too unsteadily, "before Vadin left for Ianon."

Mirain's jaw clenched, eased. She wished that he would rage, or laugh, or turn away in shame. Anything but this damnable stillness. "What made you believe that we spoke of you?"

"Vadin told me. And," she said, "I knew."

"And?"

"And." She wanted to touch him. Her hand would not obey her. "It wasn't too late. Then. Maybe even now—" She could not look at him.

She fixed her eyes on her feet. "The vow I meant to keep was to be your queen. If you would have me."

"Duty." His voice was soft. "Your given word. Your wildness is all illusion. You live by your princely honor. Else," he said, "else you would long since have fled us all, and gone to a place where none could bind you."

"I've . . . thought of it." She knotted her hands together until they began to hurt. "I would love you if you asked."

Her demon had said it. Mirain laughed with no mirth at all. "And if I refuse?"

"Damn you, Mirain. *Damn* you!" And herself, for asking that he ask.

He was as calm as ever, and as maddening in his stubbornness. "You want me to make your choice for you. I won't, Elian. Your heart is your own. Only you can follow it."

"Do you even have one?" He would not deign to answer that. "Yes, I went to you because I promised. And because I loved you. And because Ilarios could all too easily have taken your place; and that would have been a betrayal."

"Of what? Your leaden duty?"

Her eyes narrowed. Her lips drew back from her teeth. "They're right, your enemies. You suffer slaves and vassals. But never an equal."

"My equal would never demand that I do her thinking for her."

Proud, proud, proud. They were too well matched, he and she; too damnably alike. Ilarios' pride was subtler. Saner. More sweetly reasonable. He would never cast back love because it was less perfect than his whim demanded.

She rose. Mirain watched her, and there was no yielding in him. "Your bath grows cold, my lord," she said, meeting stone with stone. "And I have a promise to keep."

After all her tarrying, Elian was early. The night-bell rang even as she passed the gate of the temple.

Within, all was quiet. It was a very old temple, and very holy; shadows veiled the heavy pillars and lost themselves in the great vault of the dome. In its open center glittered a single, icy star.

Elian trod the worn stones, moving slowly. Patterns unfolded beneath her feet, broken and blurred with time: leaves and flowers, men and beasts, birds of the air and fishes of the sea. Some ran up the pillars, twining round them, glinting here and there with gold or a precious stone.

From all this faded splendor the altar stood apart, raised high upon a dais. It alone bore no ornament or jewel: a simple square of white stone, unadorned. But behind it upon the wall shone and flamed the only likeness of himself which the god would ever allow. Gold, pure and splendid, dazzling even in the light of the vigil lamp; yet in all but size, the image of the Sun in Mirain's hand.

Elian bowed low before it. There was no prayer in her. After a moment she turned from it.

Lesser altars stood in sheltered niches round the circle of pillars. Some were tombs of old princes. One held the body of the god's chosen, his bride, the priestess Sanelin. And one, very small, very ancient, drew her to itself. No high lord or lady rested there; no gold adorned it, no carving lightened it. Even its stone had not the pure beauty of the high altar: plain grey granite, rough-hewn and set into the floor. Its top was smoothed somewhat—that much one could see, and no more. For it was covered with darkness, cloth woven it seemed of the very shadows; yet that was no altar cloth but a hooded mantle. And beneath it, a hollow in the stone, and water that never fouled or shrank away, but remained ever the same, clear and pure as water fresh-drawn from a spring. The Water of Seeing, veiled in the mantle of the Prophet of Han-Gilen.

It knew her. It called to her. *Take my veil. Look at me. Master me. Prophet. Prophet of Han-Gilen.*

She had schooled herself to resist it. But power would never be denied. Had it bent her mind even in her father's palace, bidden her meet Ilarios here, to bring her to itself?

Look at me. You know not what course to choose. Look at me and see.

"I'll choose him," she whispered, "to escape from you."

Look at me, it chanted. *Master me.*

"No!"

She spun on her heel. She had put on a gown, for reasons she could not have explained even to herself; its heavy skirts swirled about her ankles. In the same movement, her cropped hair brushed her cheeks.

Would she ever be aught but a contradiction?

A shadow stirred among the shadows. Lamplight glimmered on gold. She leaped forward; stopped short; advanced more sedately, unsmiling.

Ilarios took her hands and kissed them. He wore his black robe still, with a dark cloak flung over it. But the hood lay on his shoulders, and his hair was free.

"My lord," she said very softly.

"My lady." It was not a question. Yet a question throbbed in it, an eagerness harshly curbed, a fear he dared not admit. He would be a courtier if she asked it, speak of small things, circle gracefully round his heart's desire.

She could not bear it. To play the courtier; to make her choice. His hands were warm and strong and trembling deep within. His face was pale. His gaze was level and very bright.

"My lord." She swallowed hard. "I—Forgive me. Oh, please forgive me."

She did not know what she meant. But the light drained from his eyes; his face lost its last glimmer of color.

And she cried, "I can't be what you need me to be! I can't be your empress or your wandering love. I can't love you that way. It isn't in me."

"It is," he said. His eyes were bitter. "But not for me."

She tossed her head, in protest, in pain. "Please understand. I want to accept you. I long to. But I can't. Han-Gilen holds me. My squire-oath binds me. I have to live out my fate here."

"I understand," he said. He was very calm. Too calm. "You are of your realm as I am of mine. And when the war comes, as it must come, for this world cannot sustain two empires—better for us both that we not be torn between the two enemies."

"There can still be an alliance. If—"

"There can be one. For a while. Perhaps for a long while: a year, a decade, a score of years. But in the end the conflict must come, and no union of ours may avert it. Empires take no account of lovers, even of lovers who are royal."

"No," she said. "No."

He smiled. It was sweet still, and sad, but there was nothing of innocence in it. There never had been, save in her foolish fancy. He was a royal Asanian, son of a thousand years of emperors. He said, "I can take you whether you give me yea or nay, whether it be wisdom or folly or plain blind insanity. Because you are my heart's love. Because without you I do not think that I can live."

He held her hands; she tensed to pull free, stilled. Shadows took shape: his guards in their eternal, unyielding black, cold-eyed, armed with Asanian steel. Her power could find no grip upon them.

"Yes," Ilarios said softly, "my bred warriors, my Olenyai. They are armed against magecraft. They are sworn to die for me, as you are sworn to die for your bandit king."

She stared at him. He was all new to her, his masks fallen, his gentleness no less for that it was not the simple whole of him. Mirain laughed as he slew, and wept for the wounded after. Ziad-Ilarios would weep in the slaying, and weep after, but his hand would be none the less implacable for that. As he would seize her, compel her, bear her away to be his bride.

She was not afraid. She was fascinated. How strange they grew, these royal males, in the face of a woman's intransigence. How wonderful to stand against them; how like the exhilaration of battle. She almost laughed. She was hemmed in, and she was free. She could choose one, both, neither. She could run away. She could die. She could do anything at all.

She looked at her hands held lightly in his, and up, into his pale taut face. Was this love, this sweet wildness? She wanted to kiss him. She wanted to strike him. She wanted to pull him down in the very temple, and have her will of him. She wanted to run far away, and cast aside all thought of him, and be as she had been before ever he came to beset her. Her mind cried out to him. *Yes! Yes, I will go. Damn my fates, damn my prophecies, damn my haughty king who will not, cannot speak.*

He could not hear her. He was no mage; only a mortal man. He would be emperor as he was born to be. He would age as all his kindred did, swiftly, cruelly, his gold all turned to grey, his beauty lost, his life burning to ash, as if flesh could not endure the fire of his spirit.

She could make him live. She could be his strength, her flame suffice for both. And she could do it willingly, gladly, exultantly. If only her demon would yield up her tongue.

His finger traced her rigid cheek. His voice was infinitely tender, infinitely regretful. "I cannot do it. I cannot compel you. My grief; my fatal weakness. I love you far too much. You are a creature of the free air. In the Golden Palace you would wither and die. As must I. But I was born to it, and I have learned to accept it; even, a little, to overcome it. That much you have given me. For that alone may I thank the gods that I have known you." He bowed low and low. "I depart at dawn. May your god keep you."

She reached to catch him, to pull him back, to cry her protests. But he was gone. The night had taken him.

And she, utterly cold, utterly bereft, could not even weep.

Eighteen

*E*LIAN WANDERED FOR A VERY LONG WHILE, NOT caring where she went, not caring where the hours fled. The tears would not come.

More than once she stopped short. She could still turn back. She could still run to him. Hold him. Tell him that she had lied, she had lost her wits, she had but tested him. Cruel, cruel testing. When had she ever been aught but cruel? Vadin had had the right of it. She had made it all a game. Played at love, played at loss. Held a man's heart as light as a pawn upon a board.

And she had dealt him a wound which might never heal.

She huddled in a cold and nameless corner, shivering, staring into the lightless dark. Now that she had lost him, she knew surely that she loved him. Her tongue and her cowardice had played her false. Her grief had reft her of will to do what she could do. Go back. Go with him. Be his empress. Raise strong children, bright-haired, with golden eyes. Bring him joy in the heart of his high cold empire.

Her head rose. There was a window before her; it looked out on darkness. The deep dark before dawn.

She was on her feet. She was running, blindly but with burning purpose. A door fell back before her. Chambers opened, rich, hung with Asanian silks, scented with Asanian unguents.

Empty.

Everywhere, empty. His guards, his servants, his belongings, gone.

His presence darkened into bitter absence. But in the mound of cushions that had been his bed, something glittered. A topaz, filling her palm, rent from his coronet. It had no look of a trifle flung down and forgotten. It held a memory of his eyes. They gazed into her own, level, golden, loving her. Words drifted through her mind. "Alas, I am cursed with a constant nature. Where I take pleasure, there do I most prefer to love. And where I love, I love eternally."

She lay on her face in the alien silks, the jewel clenched in her fist, its edges sharpening to pain. She gripped it tighter. Waves of weeping rose within her, crested, poised and would not, could not fall. Higher, higher, higher. She gasped with the force of them.

Someone stood behind her. Had stood for a long while, waiting, watching. She dragged herself about.

Mirain looked at her and said nothing.

Her tongue had not yet had its fill of havoc. "He left me," it cried. "He left me before I could go to him. I *wanted* him!"

Still, silence. Mirain was a shadow, a gleam of eyes, a glimmer of gold in his ear, at his throat. She hated him with sudden, passionate intensity. "I don't want you!" she spat at him.

He sat on a heap of cushions, tucking his feet under him, tilting his head. He had always done that when she gave herself up to her temper. Studying it. Contemplating refinements of his own rages. Even in that, Mirain did not take kindly to a rival.

She raised her will against the spell. He was not her elder brother. She was not his small exasperating sister. No more could he ever be her lover. He had refused to help her choose, and her choosing had gone all awry, and for that she had lost Ilarios.

"I am not yours," she said, soft and taut, "simply because I am not his. He has gone in despair, but I will follow him. You cannot stop me."

"I will not try."

"Then why are you here?"

His shoulder lifted. A shrug, northern-brief. But he was in trousers, his coat dark, plain, royal only in its quality. She was going mad, that she could notice it now, when all her mind was a roil of dark and gold, grief and rage and prophecy. "You need me," he said.

Arrogant; insufferable. "I need no one!"

"Not even your Asanian?"

"He needs me." She choked, gasped, tossed her throbbing head. Her hand hurt. She forced the fingers to open. The topaz glittered like gold and ice. "Let me go."

"Am I stopping you?"

She staggered up, fell against him. He caught her. She stood rigid. "I wish I had never been born."

"It might have spared us grief," he said.

She snapped erect. That was not even Mirain's art. That was her father's.

"But," he went on, "since you are here and all too much alive, you might consider that your choices are your own. You sent the high prince away. You, not I, not some nameless demon."

She tore free. His face was as calm as ever it could be. It was not even ugly. It was perfectly imperfect. Its cheek, unshaven, pricked her palm. She recoiled. He had not moved. "I hate you," she said.

His head bowed, came up again. Accepting. "If you ride swiftly," he said, "you may catch him before the sun rises."

Her breath caught in her throat. Her eyes darted. Her heart was beating like a bird's: swift, shallow, frightening. Mirain was like an image of himself. "Cruel," her tongue whispered. "O cruel."

He smiled.

Her knees gave way. She sank down shaking. He stood over her, and his smile had faded to a memory, a glimmer at the corner of his mouth. She surged, pulled them down. He came without resistance; but his strength was potent in her hands, yielding of its free will, setting them face to glaring face. He blinked once, calmly. "Time passes," he pointed out.

She could not rise. She could hardly speak. The words that came were nothing of her own. "Do you love me?"

"That," he said, "is not what matters. Do *you* love *me?*"

"I love Ilarios!" Her demon seized her throat again, closing it. She bit down on her fist, hard. Mirain watched her. His chin had raised a degree. His eyes had hooded.

"No," she said hoarsely. "Not you too. I can't bear it. I can't lose you too!"

"Do you love me?"

There, her demon said. There was Ilarios' failing. He could not make himself be cruel to her. He was weak. Gentle. Compassionate. All fire and all sweetness, and a lover to the core of him.

Weak, the demon repeated. He had lost all his strength in words. He spoke of seizing her, binding her, bearing her away. He had not been strong enough to do it.

Mirain had let her go.

Because he knew what she would do. She belonged to him. She had always belonged to him.

And he to her.

She rocked from side to side. She did not want this. She did not want any of it. She wanted to go away, be free, be anyone but Elian of Han-Gilen.

"Do you love me?" Mirain, again. Pressing her. Driving her mad.

He seized her with bruising force. *"Do you love me?"*

"Not," she gritted, "while you are doing your best to break my arms."

He eased a fraction. Waited.

She looked at him. He did not look like a lover. He looked like a conqueror at the gates of a city. Waiting for it to surrender; or to defy him.

She gasped with the force of revelation. He was afraid. Mirain iVaryan, afraid.

And did she love him?

From her mother's womb. But as a woman loves a man . . . She studied him, carefully, thoroughly. And calmly. She had gone so far in her madness; she could be calm, she could think, she could ponder all her choices. And Ilarios was riding, fleeing the sunrise, setting the long leagues between himself and the woman he could never have. He had always known it. He had never thought to have her. But because he was Ilarios, he had done all that he might to win her.

He had lost her. She was of Han-Gilen; she would never be of Asanion. But in this much he had won. He had taught her that her fate was not fixed, that she could love another man than Mirain. That she could be free, if so she chose.

If so she chose.

She raised her chin to match Mirain's. "I give you leave," she said in High Gileni, "to sue for my hand."

His breath hissed. She could not tell if it was anger, or relief, or plain astonishment.

"You may court me," she said. "I do not promise to accept you."

He swallowed. Gaining courage? Restraining rage? Struggling not to laugh? "And what," he asked, "if I manage to discourage any other who should presume to seek your hand?"

"I can live unwed," she said, "my lord. The prospect does not frighten me."

His head tilted. "No; I can see that it does not." He rose and bowed, king to her queen. "I shall court you, my lady, by your gracious leave."

She inclined her head. And spoiled it all by bursting into laughter, and the laughter dissolved into tears, and Mirain was holding her, rocking her, being for this last helpless moment her elder brother. She could not even hate him for it. He had taken all her hate, and shown her that it was only the other face of love.

"But not of a lover!" she cried, rebellious. "Only of a brother."

He said nothing. His silence was denial enough.

"It shouldn't matter so much," Elian said to Ilhari. "I have my family back again, with Mirain and Sieli added to it. I have you. I have the whole of Han-Gilen, if it comes to that."

The mare shifted slightly under the brush. Her neck itched. Ah, there. She leaned into the rubbing.

"I miss him," Elian said through gritted teeth. "I miss him with every bone in my body. He filled so many emptinesses. He was friend, brother, lover. He was all that a woman could wish for. And I let him go. For what? For a man who won't even begin to court me."

Ilhari swiveled an ear at her. That came of two-legged stupidity. If she had let one of them mount her, then it all would have been settled. Her ache would be gone and so would they, painlessly.

Elian laughed with a catch at the end of it. "There are plenty of men who are like that, and women too; but neither of them is so minded. Nor I." She set down the brush. Even in the heaviness of her winter coat, Ilhari shone like polished copper. "Sometimes I wonder if I'm made wrong. Or maybe I'm mad. There's a wild streak in our family, that goes with the power. That one has it—the nameless one. She never settled on a man, either; and the god rejected her for an outlander. No wonder she did what she did."

She was a crawling on the skin. Ilhari twitched it off and investigated her manger. A grain or two lingered there; she lipped them up.

"I can't ever condone what she did. But I begin to understand her. She's still out there, you know. Hiding herself in shadows. Watching and listening. Waiting for me to break and go to her."

How could she watch? She was blind.

"Her power can see." Elian shivered. She had been a fool to say so much, even to Ilhari. The Exile had not beset her dreams since she came to Han-Gilen: her father's doing. No power for ill could enter his princedom. And she had been all tangled in her muddle of lovers.

But the Exile waited. Elian knew it beyond knowing. She would wait until Elian came, or until she died; or perhaps she had the power to wait beyond death, to ensnare her prey in bonds no living creature could break.

"Midwinter," Elian said, too quickly and too loudly. "Tomorrow is

Midwinter. We'll sing the dark away this year with more power than we've ever had, with Mirain here to do the singing and dance the Dance. Do you know he won't be high priest? They've asked him three times, and the place has been empty this year and more, and they won't fill it, but no more will he. The world's throne is enough, he says. Let the temple choose someone more holy."

Thrones and temples meant nothing to the mare. She contemplated the heap of sweet hay which Elian spread for her, and began to nibble it.

"He'll take it in the end," Elian went on, mostly to herself. The Exile's presence was all but banished; but not quite. "It will be that, or leave the order without a leader. After all, they can't take a mere mortal, however wise and holy, with Avaryan's own son building his city half a day's ride away."

Cities were uncomfortable. So were stables. Open air was better, and an open plain.

"It's snowing."

The mare nudged her aside and trotted to the stable door. It swung open at a touch. Cold air swirled in, clothed in snow. Ilhari snorted at it and plunged into it, dancing and tossing her head.

Elian trudged in her wake, feeling irredeemably earthbound. The shouts of children rang in her ears. New though the storm was, they were all out in it, urchin and lordling alike. Nor were all of them so very small. She saw youths—men—in the garb of Mirain's army: southerners in particular, to whom a snowfall before Midwinter was a rare and precious thing, but great tall Ianyn soldiers too, fighting snow battles that began and ended in laughter.

White softness showered over her, blinding her. She gasped and wheeled. Mirain's grin was as wide and wicked as a child's. A bright-haired boychild clung to his legs and crowed at her: Halenan's eldest, Korhalion.

As she spluttered and glared, Mirain swung the child onto his shoulders and filled his hands with snow. "Throw it!" Korhalion cried. "Throw it!"

The last assault was melting into icy runnels down her back. With a smothered cry, half of wrath, half of mirth, she wheeled and bolted. She was as swift as a golden deer, darting through the great court. But Mirain was a panther, ridden by a laughing demon.

Everyone was cheering, some in Mirain's name, some in her own. Shapes flew past her: faces, bodies, a bright gleam of eyes. The cold and the race and the shouting came together like strong wine, filling her with a sweet wild delight. She eeled round a man like a tall pillar—

Cuthan's white grin atop it—and stopped short behind, and laughed in Mirain's startled face; and slid beneath his snatching hands. Snatching herself great glistening armfuls, and wheeling, and flinging them upon him. Revenge had a taste like wild honey. She danced about him, taunting, showering him with snow.

He lunged. Korhalion's weight overbalanced him; he slipped and fell, bearing her down in a tangle of limps, full into a drift of snow.

He lay winded, trying to laugh. Elian, whose fierce twist had brought her down between child and king, set Korhalion on his feet and brushed the snow from his face. His tongue quested after it; his eyes danced upon her. "Do it again?" he begged.

Mirain struggled up and cuffed him lightly. "Not quite yet, imp. Every racer needs a brief rest between courses."

Korhalion's face fell, but brightened again in an instant. "So then, I don't need you. I've got my new pony. Lia, did you see him? Mirain gave him to me. He's black, just like the Mad One."

"His grandsire was my first pony," Mirain added. "Do you remember him?"

"I should," said Elian. "I inherited him."

Mirain's hair was full of snow, his brows and his thick lashes starred with it. Swallowing new and perilous mirth, she brushed it away. He laughed unabashed and reached to serve her likewise. His hand was light and deft and fire-warm.

Korhalion danced between them, sparking with impatience. "Come and see!"

The pony occupied a stall in the corner of Halenan's stable. It was black indeed, clean-limbed as a stag beneath its heavy coat, with a mad green eye and a swift slash of horns.

"He's Demon's get," Elian said with assurance as the black head snaked over the stall door, lips rolled back, teeth gleaming. Deftly she evaded the snap of them to seize the woolly ear. "Nurse must be appalled."

"Nurse doesn't know about him yet," said Korhalion. "Mirain's going to teach me to ride. He said you'd help. He says you can ride anything he can. Can you, Lia?"

"Yes," she answered swiftly, with a glance at Mirain. He was all innocence, feeding a bit of fruit to Anaki's placid gelding. "I can do better than he can. Demon never bucked *me* off."

"I calmed him down before I passed him on to you," Mirain said.

"Calmed him? Passed him on? He was as wild as he ever was when I got away from Nurse and the grooms and put a saddle on him. But I taught him to mind me. He was like the Mad One. All bluster." She smiled at Mirain, sweetly. "As they say: Like master, like mount." He laughed aloud. "As they also say: Was never a woman born but yearned to rule her man. And all his chattels."

"*Her* man?" She tossed her head. Her heart was leaping strangely. "Not quite yet, brother."

"Perhaps not, little sister. And," added Mirain, "perhaps so." He cocked an eye at Korhalion. "Shall we give her her gift now? Or make her wait for it?"

"Now!" cried Korhalion.

They were bursting with a great secret, the man as much as the child. But neither would be his own betrayer. Elian let herself be led unresisting, with Korhalion tugging eagerly at her hand. In the quiet of her mind, she tested Mirain's mood. Strong though his shields always were, more than eagerness crept through: a thrumming tension, strong almost as fear.

They left Halenan's house, passing through the snow-clad streets to the palace. In the wing which Mirain had taken was a wide roofed court. He had filled the chambers about it with his own picked men. Already they called themselves the Chosen of An-Sh'Endor, the Company of the Sun. The open space served them as gathering hall and training ground, full always with men and voices and the clash of weapons.

But on this day of snow it was unwontedly quiet. The men of the company stood round the edges, drawn up in loose ranks, armed as for inspection. In the center by the winter-dry fountain, ten waited alone. Their cloaks were somber green; they bore no device. One was Cuthan, head up, wearing torque of greened bronze. Five were women. Tall or short, plump or reed-slender, every one looked strong and capable, and held herself like one trained to arms.

The scarlet company saluted their king with a great clash of spear on shield. But those in green stood erect and still.

Elian turned on Mirain. "I never knew there were warrior women in your army."

"I have a few," he answered her in the ringing silence, and smiled. "The whole company would have been of women, but I reckoned without my men. They protested vehemently; they came close to rioting. You see their ringleader yonder: the one I've punished with the captain's torque. For him I had to give way, and settle it with a mixed

company, half of each. For both of us I cry your pardon that there are
only ten to greet you; we've not had time to raise the full hundred."

"A thousand would vie for the honor, my lady," Cuthan said, clear
and proud. His eye was steady, laughing a little, but grave too. It
seemed that he had forgiven her for lacking the sense to come out of the
rain.

She looked at him and at his command. It was a careful scrutiny,
missing no small detail: the excellence of their arms and armor, the
pride in their faces. One of the women was as lovely as a flower of
bronze. Another must surely have been born of the red earth of Han-
Gilen, a broad, sturdy, strong-handed peasant woman. She had a level
eye and a touch of a smile, as if to mock all this display.

Last of all, Elian looked at the giver of the gift. Very quietly, very
carefully, she said, "My lord forgets. I am not to be pensioned off. If he
will dismiss me, then let him do so outright, without pretense."

Equally quietly he responded, "It is not a dismissal."

"Shall a squire boast her own Guard? And one of them a high nobleman?"

"A squire, no. But a queen well may."

It did not strike her all at once. Her tongue spoke of its own accord.
"I am no queen. I am but a princess."

"A queen is one who weds a king," he said as patiently as to a child.

"But the only king here is—" At last, mind and mouth met. Her
limbs went cold. Her voice went high and wild. "You *can't!*"

"Why not?" he asked reasonably.

How could he be reasonable? He had trapped her. No word at all but
what she had beaten out of him, and suddenly this, in front of his whole
household. Where she could not refuse. When she could not accept.

He reached. If he had not been Mirain, she might have said that he
moved with diffidence. But he was Mirain, and his eyes were steady,
black-brilliant. "You are my queen," he said.

Her hands rested cold and limp in his burning-strong ones. Her mind
was a hundredfold. It laughed, or wept, or howled in rage, or gibbered
in stark terror. How dared he trap her? How dared he be so sure of her?
She was no man's possession. She was herself. She did not want him.
She did. She did not. She *did.*

"My lady." He spoke to mind and ears alike, a murmur as soft as
sleep. "My queen. My heart's love."

She struggled in blind panic. It was not that he had said it. It was not
that he had said it here, for his army to hear. The worst of it, the very
worst, was her own inner singing. It mattered nothing that he was king

and emperor, that the god's blood flamed in his veins, that he had chosen her of all living women, that he had half the world to lay at her feet. It mattered only that he was himself. Mirain.

She had lost Ilarios for her tongue's slowness, and he was gone. Mirain would go nowhere until he had made her his own. As if she had no choice but that; as if she could have none. Fate. Prophecy. Inevitability.

She tore her hands from his. "My thanks to my lord king," she said with venomous softness, "but I am not the stuff of which queens are made."

He said nothing, made no move. She remembered with a stab of pain how he had looked when she spoke of loving Ilarios. Precisely the same. Cold and still and royal, offering nothing, taking nothing.

Her teeth bared. "This company I will take, because it is a free gift, theirs as much as yours. I think I can command a force of ten in my king's service. The rest"—she swallowed round bile—"O son of the Sun, do you keep for your proper empress."

"There can be none but you."

Had they been alone, she would have struck him. She bit down on her fist until her tongue tasted the iron sweetness of blood. "Oh, you men! Why do you always fix upon the worst?"

"That," he asked gently, "always being you?"

"Yes, damn you! You hound me, you haunt me. You moon after my so-called beauty, make allowances for my notorious wildness, and calculate my lineage and my dowry down to the last half-cousin and quarter-star. Can't you understand that I want none of you? None!"

His tension had turned to amusement. He even had the gall to smile. Worse—he dared to say nothing of all he might have said, of the true and of the cruel and of what was both together. It was the smile of a great king or of a carven god: calm, assured, and infinitely wise. And giving not a hair's breadth to her will.

She did the worst thing, the craven thing, the thing she always did. She ran away from him.

She did not run far. That great impulse which had sent her northward had long since faded. But she gathered her belongings upon the bed she still kept near Mirain's own: an untidy heap, surprisingly high. And there was her armor, and her trophies. She would need a servant to help her with it all.

Even in moving to summon one, she sank to the floor. Where could she go? Her old chambers—he knew all the ways to them, both open and secret. Nor would he hesitate to use them. She knew this mood of his. Mirain An-Sh'Endor would have what he meant to have.

Ilarios' topaz had found its way into her hand. She stared at it, only half seeing it. She stared for a very long time. Her mind was utterly empty.

A shadow crossed it. Her eyes turned slowly. Even yet they could widen.

The perfect lady was never to be seen afoot, only seated upon a throne or in her bower, or for the greatest festivals, in a curtained litter. If indeed she deigned to touch her delicate sole to the ground, it was to be cushioned with carpets and shod in the most elegant of sandals. Nor was she ever to be seen unattended.

The Lady Eleni was alone. Her gown was as practical as a servant's; there were boots on her feet. Boots of the finest leather, with inlaid heels, but boots. They looked as if they had been in snow, and even, wonder of wonders, in stable mire. The heavy coils of her hair were glistening with melting snow; if she had had a veil, she had lost it.

"Mother," said Elian. "Where are your maids? What are you doing here?"

The princess sat in the one chair the room afforded, and settled her skirts. "My maids are in their proper places. I have been searching for you."

"Anyone could have told you where I was."

"Anyone could not. Your father and your brother have other troubles."

"And the Sunborn would not."

"The Sunborn was occupied." The princess frowned slightly. "I made a vow that I would let you be. I intend still to keep it. But I will remind you that our guest is no longer merely our foster kin. He is the king."

"He's still Mirain."

"He is Mirain An-Sh'Endor."

The words, so close to Elian's own thoughts, cut at old wounds. "I know who he is! I wait on him day and night. Day," she repeated, "and night."

Her mother betrayed not the least disturbance. "I have not come to plead for your reputation. I do not even beg you to accept his suit, mighty though that match would be, the mightiest in our world. I only wish to know: Why?"

Elian would not answer.

"It may be the Asanian prince," Eleni mused. "I think not. Is it then some youth of low degree, a servant or a farmholder, or a soldier in

Mirain's army? You should not shrink from telling us. Halenani have wedded with outlanders before. They have even wedded with commoners. Though you have no look of one who loves without hope. Why then, Elian? Why do you do battle against every man who asks for you?"

Still, silence, with a hint of obduracy.

"Is it perhaps that you are afraid? You are fiercer than is maidens' wont, and you have always been free. You have never met a man as strong as yourself, or as sure in his strength. Unless it be Mirain." The princess folded her hands. "Yet in the end, however feeble the man, his lady must give of herself. Her body certainly, perhaps her heart if she is fortunate. The giving is frightening, and the more so the stronger one is. Is that your reason, daughter? Are you afraid to face your womanhood?"

"No!" It burst out of her with no grace at all. "I know what men do with women. I've seen it in the army." For all her bravado, Elian's cheeks flushed hotly; her tongue was thick, unwieldy. "It is not fear. Believe me, Mother, it is not. I've always expected that I would marry. One day. When it was time. I meant my husband to be Mirain. Because it had to be. Because there could never be another.

"Then I saw Ilarios. And nothing *had* to be; there was no such thing as destiny, and if there was, how dared it bind me? My world was rocking on its foundations. I fled in search of safety.

"To Mirain. Who acted as if I were no more than his sister. And I found that I was glad of it. I began to think that maybe, after all, my vows and my destinies had been mere childish fancies: the infatuation of a very young maid for her splendid elder brother.

"And Ilarios came after me. When at last Mirain admitted that he wanted me, he spoke too late and not to me; and my heart was shifting, turning toward its new freedom. My life was not foreordained. I could choose. To wed, or not. To wed with any man I fancied, or with none. Ilarios paid court to me, and I began to think that, yes, I could be his lover, and he mine. Mirain did nothing to stop us. Maybe I wanted him to do nothing. I think I wanted him to do something. Claim me. Tell me I belonged to him. And he would not. And now," said Elian, "he has, and I don't know what to do. He says he loves me. I know—I know—" Her voice broke. Incredulous. Frightened. "I know I love him. After all, I know . . . I love him. I turned Ilarios away because of him." Elian's fists clenched; her voice rose. "Mother, I *can't!* He's the king. The Sunborn. The god's son."

"He is still Mirain."

Again, her own words. She flung back her mother's. "He is An-Sh'Endor!" Her hair was in her eyes. She scraped it back. "He's not a tyrant to be afraid of. But he's king. Great king. Emperor. How in all the world did I ever hope to stand beside him?"

"It seems to me," said the princess, "that you have been doing just that. Do you know what the army has begun to call you? Kalirien. Lady who is swift and valiant. I note that, daughter. Lady, and valiant. When Mirain set out to choose a Guard for you, a thousand men, hearing but the rumor of it, clamored to be chosen; a thousand more thronged after them. He had to set a difficult test, and then another more difficult still, and then a third; and in the end, to ask that each one submit to the probing of his power. The five who were taken are now the envy of the army, ranked as high as princes."

"Oh aye, for having an easy path to my famous bed."

"Such thoughts demean yourself and your Guard. Where is the truth which we raised you to see? An-Sh'Endor's soldiers have chosen you for their lady. So too have the common folk."

"And the high ones?" Elian rose. "What of them?"

"The high ones know what they see. Some can even understand it."

"No," Elian said. That had been her second word.

The first had been spoken clearly and firmly to the center of her world. Not the name of mother or father, or even of the nurse who had raised her. No. From the very first, she had known who mattered most. Mirain.

"I'm afraid," she said. "I'm not valiant at all. I'm terrified. After all I've sworn and done and plotted—I can't be his queen."

Very gently the princess said, "You can be his lover. All the rest will follow."

It was even more shocking than that she should be here, alone, speaking freely and even knowing what soldiers thought: that she could say such a word to her maiden daughter. *Lover.* And with such tenderness.

Elian looked at her hands and at the bed. Both were empty. While she spoke, while her mind paid no heed, she had returned each possession to its place. Save the jewel. It lay in her hand and glittered, and the light of it was cruel. She thrust it into her coat.

She could have wept. She could have screamed. She huddled on the bed, knees to chin, eyes burning dry, and said, "I can't understand him. What if he only wants me for my face? And my dowry, and my father's goodwill. He never acted like a lover. He hardly seemed to notice me. Was he so sure of me? Or is it that he didn't care? He wasn't even jealous of Ilarios."

"Was he not?"

"No!" she snapped. With an effort she softened her voice. "Ilarios wanted me to go away with him. When I told Mirain, he wouldn't decide for me. He didn't try to make me stay."

"He did not counsel you to leave." The princess smiled. "Ah, child, if you saw nothing, still there were others who could see. He would watch you when you were together with the prince, watch you steadily and constantly. Or if you were gone, riding or walking, his mind would wander; he would snap for no reason. Ah, yes, he was jealous. Bitterly so."

"Then why didn't he—"

"He was too proud."

Of course he was too proud. A man had to be humble, to woo a woman properly. "He can't love *me!*" cried Elian.

Her mother laughed softly. "But, daughter, he always has." She sobered, though only a little. "I can understand your fear. He is dear to us all, and he is most human, but he remains Avaryan's son. And yet, being man as much as god, he is very easily hurt. Take care lest you wound him too deeply for any healing."

"I would never—" Elian broke off. "Oh, Mother, why does it have to be me?"

"If I knew," the princess answered, "I would be a goddess myself." She slid from her chair to her knees, unwonted as all she had done in the past hour, and circled her daughter with her arms. "When I bore you, I knew the god intended great things for you. He has given you many and wondrous blessings. Now he asks for his payment. You are strong enough to give it. Believe me, child," she said, measuring each word, "you are strong enough."

Nineteen

THE NIGHT BEFORE MIDWINTER WAS THE DARK OF the Year. In old days it had been the great festival of the goddess; when Avaryan rose to full and sole power in Han-Gilen, her rites were forbidden, her festival diminished before the feast of Sunreturn. But the old ways lingered. At the Dark of the Year, all fires were extinguished. The temple was dark, the priests silent. Folk huddled together and shivered, and thought on death and dying and on the cold of the grave.

The palace nourished warmth in its old bones; but as the sunless day passed, the chill crept closer. With music and song forbidden and laughter quenched, the halls seemed darker still.

Elian passed a warm delicious time with Anaki, who as a new mother need not endure the fireless cold. But both guilt and duty drove her forth. The sky had begun to loose its burden of snow.

She left its grey weight for the icy air of the palace. Mirain was in the workroom with his clerks; they, needing lamps for their work, warmed their hands at the small flames. They had no need of her; no more did he, although he smiled at her, a swift preoccupied smile. She went to polish his armor. It was a hideous task, but it warmed her blood wonderfully.

The gold-washed plates gleamed, splendid even in the gloom. As she rubbed at his helmet, pursing her lips over a dent which the smith had failed to smooth completely, soft darkness fell over her.

She struggled out of it. It was a cloak, a wonderful thing, deep green velvet lined with fur as fiery vivid as her hair, light and soft and warm as down, as beautiful to the touch as to the eye. Her fingers lost themselves in it; her breath caught in wonder. *"Hazia,"* she said. "This must be *hazia.*"

Mirain sat at her feet, smiling. "Yes, it is."

"But it's as precious as rubies. More precious."

He gestured assent. "The beast is little larger than a mouse, and elusive, and shy besides. It took, said the merchant, the better part of twenty years to gather enough for your cloak." He tilted his head. "Do you like it?"

"Don't be a fool!" The heat flooded to her face; she scowled. "You can't buy me, Mirain."

"May I not give you a Midwinter gift?"

"I have one already. My Guard."

"And this is another," he said. His finger stroked the fur lightly, almost absently. "I'm appallingly wealthy, you know. The tribes of the north are richer than you would ever believe; and their richest kings have paid me tribute, every one. After a while it begins to seem like sea-sand. Worthless with surfeit. Except to give away."

"Don't give it *all* away!" she cried, stung to practicality.

He laughed. "No fear of that, my lady. Even if I were so minded, my clerks would bring me to my senses. Armies have to be paid; and there's my city." His eyes kindled as they always did when he spoke of that. "When the spring comes, we'll begin the building. You'll help us with it. There are things you'll be wanting in the palace and in the city."

"How can it matter what I want?" she asked. She was cold in her splendid cloak.

"You matter," he said. And added very calmly, "I should like to be wedded after the snows pass. On your birth-feast, in the spring; or on mine if you would prefer, at High Summer. Or anywhere between."

She hated him. She hated his cool assurance; she hated his steady regard. She hated her own heart, that had turned traitor and begun to beat hard, and her voice, that was weak, half strangled. "What if I won't choose?"

He touched her hand, the merest brush of a fingertip, yet she felt it as a line of flame. "There's time yet for deciding. And"—he followed the burning touch with a white-fire kiss—"for loving."

She choked on bile. Treacherous, treacherous body. It sang with his nearness. It yearned to be nearer still.

But he moved a little away, and her anger was swift, fierce, and utterly reasonless. His voice had lost its softness, turned crisp: his brother-voice, with a hint of the king. "Meanwhile, there is the winter. After tomorrow's feast I'll send the bulk of my allies home to rule their lands for me. The summer will see us on the march again."

She shuddered.

He clasped her hand. No fire now, only warmth and strength. "Asanion, if not our ally, is not yet our enemy. For a time. That much Ziad-Ilarios won from me. But the east is rising. The Nine Cities encroach on the princedoms of the farthest south, at the desert's edge. I hear of horrors committed and of armies strengthened. The Syndics are testing my flanks for weaknesses."

The cold in her was sudden and soul-deep. "Sooner," she said very low. "Cold. North."

His grasp tightened. "The north is firm, and mine."

"The north holds the dark."

He frowned. "It's Midwinter, sister-love. It chills us all."

"No," she said with swift heat. "I can feel it."

She had touched his pride. "My realm is like my body to me. It lies at rest, deep in winter's grip. Save only for the uneasiness in the south. And," he added more slowly, "a little in the north. A very little. A raid or two. The tribes thrive on them; without them, all the young men would go mad and turn on one another."

"Tribes? In the Hundred Realms?"

"It is not—"

It was Ashan. The messenger came in late and chilled to the bone, his mare all but foundered. With wine in his belly and a warm robe about him, he told his tale. "Men of Asan-Eridan began it," he said. "A girl of theirs, a favorite of the lord's favorite bastard, caught the eye of a visitor. He was a man of little enough account, but he had kin in Asan-Sheian. He accosted the girl and raped her; her man caught him at it, and quite legally and rightly, if somewhat precipitously, saw to it that the outlander would never enjoy another woman. The culprit, turned loose, made his way back to Sheian; and his kin by then were weary of winter and eager for a diversion.

"That would have been little enough, sire, and easily dealt with. But my lord Omian is marriage-kin to Sheian's lady, and he was there when the wounded man returned. He bound his own men to Sheian's cause.

"Now Eridan lies near Ebros' border, and has close ties of alliance and of kinship with a handful of its Ebran neighbors. Faced with Luian's own troops, Eridan's lord called on his friends. And now we have the beginnings of a healthy war." He left his seat to kneel before Mirain.

"We would not trouble you, Sunborn. But my lord is old and his heir is not minded to make peace, and of the rest of the sons, most have arrayed themselves with the younger lord to rouse war against Ebros. Before the end, Ashan may well turn upon Ashan, and fight as fiercely within as without." The man clasped his hands in formal pleading. "Majesty, if this small fragment of your great empire is of any worth to you, we beg you, aid us in our trouble."

Mirain looked down at the messenger. Elian knew that look: dark, level, and utterly unreadable. She had seen high lords flinch before it.

This man was no lord, of blood or of spirit. He crouched upon the floor, shielding his head with his hands. But he had the strength to cry, "Sunborn! By your father's name, give us your aid."

The words rang in silence. In the heart of it a note sang, faint yet clear: the chiming of a bell. Mirain raised his head to it. "Avaryan sets," he said. "The temple waits for me."

The envoy clutched his knees; great daring and great desperation. *"Sire!"*

"After the rite," said Mirain, "you will have my answer." He seemed to do nothing, but he was free and striding through the hall, the messenger kneeling still, gripping air.

Though crowded with the folk of the city, Avaryan's temple held within it a black and ancient cold. The high ones felt it in their places near the altar, prince and princess seated side by side, their son and their daughter standing close behind them. Although no fire lightened the darkness, a glow clung to them, a faint red-golden shimmer: the mage-light, that was always strongest in the heart of Han-Gilen. It shone even through Elian's cloak.

She barely heeded it. The cold within her had deepened to burning. Her mind was brittle, clear and bright and fragile as ice. The thoughts of the gathered people rang upon it. But stronger than they was the call of the darkened altar, the mantle and the water of prophecy. All her will scarcely sufficed to hold her in her place. *It is time,* sang the water. *Time and time and time. Come, seer. Come and rule me.*

Her jaw set, aching-hard. There was no one to cling to, even if she could. Orsan and his lady were just out of her reach. Hal supported Anaki, who would come to this ritual, even though she came in a chair. Mated, all of them, and centered upon one another.

Light flared blinding-bright in the gloom. A child's voice, high and piercingly pure, rent the murmuring silence.

Every priest and priestess in Han-Gilen walked in that endless procession, a stream of white robes, golden torques, fine-honed voices. Before them trod the novices in saffron gold, bearing tall candles. Behind them came a great light.

The Halenani shone with power. But this was Avaryan's own child, in Avaryan's greatest temple: robe and torque like all the rest, voice as pure as a sacred singer's, yet all of it but a veil over light. Elian's eyes blurred and flinched before its brilliance.

If he will not be called high priest now, her cold self said, *then the name is nothing. He is only what he is. The god's son, greatest of the priests of the Sun.*

He mounted to the high altar and bowed as a flame will bow in a high wind. She never heard what words he sang, nor saw the movements of his dance, the dance of the binding of the goddess. For the darkness' binding loosed other powers, Elian's own far from the least of them. With no memory of movement, she stood no longer beside her brother, but shivered in deep shadow. Perilously close, close enough to touch, lay the Altar of Seeing. No mind but hers focused upon it, no eyes turned toward it. She was as much alone there as if the temple had been empty.

Her hand stretched out. The mantle was thick and startlingly soft, pouring over her hand like water. Black water, glistening in its hollow in the stone, stirring and kindling. She should fight—fight—

Come, it whispered. *Rule. Be strong and see.*

Strength lay in surrender. Strength was to open wide the mind, to let the water pour into it with all its burden of dreams and nightmares and true sight, to master the visions; to gather, and shape, and rule.

Rule. Her brain was a dazzle of images. Yet her eyes saw, her mind knew where she stood: by the altar of prophecy, with the black mantle cast over Mirain's gift of green velvet and *hazia*. She was no longer cold. All the temple flared with the Sun's fire: while she bound her visions, Mirain had kindled the light of Sunreturn. Priests and Sunborn sang the great antiphon, deep voices shot with the silver brilliance of the novices and the priestesses. *And the god came forth,* they sang, *and clove to his bride.* And he alone: *And the darkness was cast down, and the light rose up: sun in triumph, conqueror unconquered, king forever. . . .*

King forever, a single voice echoed him. With a shock she knew her own, though higher and purer and fiercer than she had ever known it could be. The ranks of priests wavered. The people turned, staring. Their eyes smote her. Yet the voice ran on of its own accord, like a bell that, once struck, continues to sound, untouched by any hand: "King forever or king never, son of the Sun! Look; even as you stand here binding the dark with chains of light and song, it moves against you. And you sing, and you dance the Dance, and you ponder this small trouble in the north. You are restless with winter—you will go yourself to settle it, to cow your rebellious people with your own mighty presence. Ill pondered and ill chosen, Sunborn. North waits the full power of ancient Night. North lies your death."

Mirain stood unmoving behind the high altar. His light had faded to a shimmer, barely perceptible in the splendor of the full-lit temple. He wore no mark of rank, only the vestments of a priest in the rite, white without adornment, and his torque. His face blurred through the flocking visions: Mirain the boy atop Endros; Mirain the youth on his throne in Ianon; Mirain but little older, locked in deadly combat with a giant of the north; Mirain come to manhood, riding to claim his empire. Mirain lying on cold stone, eyes open to the sky, all light fled from them; and over him a shape of shadow, mantled in night. It stretched forth a long gaunt hand, and bent, and reft his heart from his breast.

"Send another," Elian said quite calmly, quite clearly. "Send one who will be strong at need, ruthless at need; and tarry here. Then indeed shall you be king forever, you and all the heirs of your body. All the worlds shall bow before you."

It was strange how clear her mind was. She could see through Mirain as through a glass; the others, the lesser ones, were like bright water babbling unheeded on the edge of perception. But he was still, cleareyed, and completely unafraid. "How may I send another," he asked, "if I dare not send myself?"

"It is not a matter of daring or of cowardice. It is a matter of the world that hereafter shall be. You are the sword of Avaryan against the dark. If you are broken before the time appointed, what hope then has any child of the light?"

"You are the seer," he said. "See for your king. Is my death inescapable."

"If you go not into the north, you may escape it."

"And if I go? Is all hope lost?"

She shivered. But the sight knew neither mercy nor human fear. It spoke through her, cold and distinct. "Your death waits in Ashan. Yet on one thread of time's tapestry—one thread only, of all the myriads—there is hope. Hope for your life. What that life shall be, whether prisoned in deep dungeons or hounded into exile or even—pray the god it be so—set again upon your throne, I cannot see. A shadow lies upon my sight."

"But I shall live."

"You may. If you pursue that one course of the many, make the one proper choice, speak the word and make the gesture and face the danger as the seeing demands. But the word and the gesture I cannot see."

"No. You would not. My enemy is strong enough to darken even prophecy. Yet hope cannot be hidden." His voice rang out, clear and strong. "I shall venture it. I shall go forth and crush this serpent in the grass of my kingdom, and my father will defend me. No mortal can conquer me."

"But a goddess may," said Elian.

No one heard her. They were all crying his name. And he—he chose not to listen. He even smiled; and he turned back to the rite, singing more splendidly than ever, with all the power of the god in his voice and in his eyes.

Twenty

"WILL YOU GO?"

Mirain was clad for the feasting in full Ianyn splendor, but Elian wore still the gown and the cloak she had had in the temple, with the prophet's mantle cast haphazardly over them. No one had touched her or spoken to her. She was a figure of awe now, the seer of Han-Gilen.

She hardly heeded it, or the servants who moved about Mirain, settling his broad collar of gold, braiding gold and pearls into his hair, painting the sunburst of his father between his brows. "Will you go?" she demanded again.

He left his servants to approach her. He was not like the rest; he dared to slip black mantle and green from her shoulders, to touch the lacings of her dark plain gown. "I will go," he said. He beckoned. One of his dressers came forward with a cascade of gold and white, the robe of a princess, a queen.

They dressed her as if she had been a carven image, women who came from she knew not where, with faces she might have known. They suppressed sighs over her cropped hair, though that had grown out a little, binding it with a jeweled fillet, painting her eyes and her cheeks and her cold lips. When they were done they held up a silver mirror, but she did not need it. Her beauty shone in Mirain's still face. He bowed over her hands, and kissed the palms one by one. "You are the fairest lady in the world," he said.

She was empty of words. Over his royal finery, death lay like a cloak. Yet his touch was warm and living, his arm strong, his smile luminous. The small child in her wanted to cling to him and never let him go. The newborn prophet held herself aloof, suffering him to lead her, but offering nothing of speech or of gesture.

They walked from his chambers, maids and manservants falling in behind. Two guards stood at the door: one of his men in scarlet, one of her women in green. Mirain smiled at them. Elian could muster nothing but a bare inclination of the head.

Haughty lady, her mind mocked her. *How can they endure you?*

"Because they love you," Mirain said softly, for her alone to hear.

A deep shudder racked her. The coldness fled. She stopped short, tangling the retinue behind her. "You will go," she said. "So be it. But first you shall make me your queen."

He glanced at their followers, who were careful to be oblivious. His brow, raised, conceded the justice of her assault now, all unlooked for, in front of a full company of servants. But she had had no thought at all of revenge.

"Is that your seeing?" he asked her.

"It is my will."

He looked hard at her. She stared back. His lips tightened. "Why? Why now, after so much resistance?"

"Because," she said. Fire came and went in her face; her fists knotted. "Because—after all—I see—I love you."

"Because your power tells you I will die." That was brutal, but he struck harder still. "I will not marry for pity, Elian."

She stiffened at the blow, yet she answered calm with flawless calm. "Even for the sake of the dynasty that will be?"

His breath hissed between his teeth. "When I return from Ashan," he said with great precision, "then we shall be wedded. If that is still your will."

She tossed her head, her fear bursting forth in a flare of temper. "No! I want it now. Tonight. The feast is ready. We're both arrayed for it. And afterward . . ."

"Child," said Mirain with utmost gentleness, "whatever you wish for, you wish for with all that is in you."

"You want it as much as I."

"Not this way. When I take you, I shall take you as a queen, not as a battle-bride. Without haste, and without regret."

"I would never regret it."

"No?" He smiled and set her hand upon his, and began again to walk. "After Ashan," he promised her.

He was immovable. He would have her, but not until it suited his whim. She could not even touch his mind, let alone sway it to her will.

It was a wondrous feast, the most magnificent she could remember. Half the royalty of the Hundred Realms adorned the hall: princes and close kin of princes, high lords and their ladies, chieftains of the north in kilts and mountain copper, even the ambassador of Asanion with his perpetually pained expression, as if it irked him to be cast among all these savages.

Mirain sat not as lord but as high-honored guest, and she beside him, stared at and wondered at. That, she had been born to, and she had made herself a legend beyond her lineage. Many of the songs sung that night were of her, or spoke of her.

For the third time her cup was empty. A page came forward to fill it. But Mirain's hand stopped his. "Eat first," he said to her.

"Are you my nursemaid?" she flared at him.

He laughed, lifted a morsel from his plate, proffered it with a flourish. For all his merriment, he knew well what he did. Should she accept, she would accept his suit: the first movement of the formal betrothal. She considered it minutely, through a haze of wine. Considered him more minutely still. "Tonight?" she asked.

"After Ashan."

Her eyes narrowed. Slowly she took what he offered. A bit of honey-cake, heavy with sweetness. From her own plate she took another. He was not as slow as she.

When he had taken it, he rose. The singers faltered. Scattered voices cheered him. But he turned away from them to the prince and the princess, and bowed the bow of king to king. "My lord," he said clearly, "my lady. You have given me gifts beyond the desire of emperors. Yet in my great presumption I ask you for yet another. It shall be the last, I promise you."

The prince stood to face him. How young he looked, thought Elian. Scarcely older than Halenan, whose smile flashed white beyond him. Prince Orsan seldom smiled, and did not smile now, but his eyes upon Mirain were warm, his voice likewise. "You who are my lord and my foster son know that all I have to give is too paltry a gift for you. Only ask what you desire and it shall be yours."

Mirain's eyes glinted. "Take care, my lord! I may seek no less than the greatest jewel in all your princedom."

"It is yours," Orsan said unwaveringly, "with all else that is mine."

"Even your daughter?"

A murmur ran through the hall. Prince Orsan looked down from his great height at the man who was his king. "Even my daughter," he replied. "If she is willing."

"She is," said Elian. "She asks that you bless the union, now, tonight." She paused, and added with tight-leashed passion, "No, she does not ask. She begs."

Mirain turned, outflanked but unsurprised. It was not easy to surprise Mirain. Nor was it easy to face him as she faced him now, before the cream of the Hundred Realms. She smiled her sweetest smile and rose, only to sink down in a deep curtsey. Softly, demurely, she said, "The choice lies with the lady, my lords. And the lady, having tarried so long for her folly, would wed without delay. Will you say the words, Father?"

"*I* will not," gritted Mirain, but not for all to hear.

She met his glare and laughed. "I shall be your luck and your talisman. Am I not fair to see?"

"You are wondrous fair." His voice deepened with warning. "Elian—"

"Father," she said, pressing.

The prince regarded them for a long moment. One could never tell what moved him, whether mirth or grim anger.

Suddenly the mask cracked. He smiled, he grinned, he laughed aloud. His people gaped. His peers and his allies stared nonplussed. He stretched out his hands. "Come, my son, my daughter. Be wedded with my blessing."

The hall cleared for them, the joy of festival turned to something brighter and stronger. There could be no garlands in winter; for flower-clad maidens there were the women of Elian's Guard; and the feast was consumed, its remnants swept away to make room for the rite. It was never the wedding Elian had looked to have; yet she would have chosen no other.

She stood in the circle of her guards, and tried not to tremble. Not all was fear. Some was wine, and much was plain weariness.

Her mother's perfume sweetened the air; the firm gentle touch startled her. For a moment she rested upon it.

"Child," said the princess. "Ah, child, how would the singers live without you?"

Elian stood straight and lifted her chin. "This may be precipitous, Mother, but I think it is wise."

The Lady Eleni glanced across the hall, where a knot of young men marked Mirain's place. The king himself was not to be seen, but Halenan's hair was like a beacon; Cuthan towered over him, flashing with copper and gold. From the sound of it, they were more than pleased with the turn the feast had taken.

"It is wise," the lady said, "and utterly like you."

Elian laughed shakily. "Oh, no, I know what a fool I am. But this folly is so extreme that it can only be wisdom."

Her mother stroked her hair smooth, settling the fillet more becomingly over it. "You have always followed your heart, even when you seemed most to oppose it. Follow it now, and be strong. Has it not chosen the greatest of all kings to be its lord?"

"It has. I have." Elian drew a shuddering breath. "I don't know whether to be glad or terrified."

"Both," said the princess. She kissed Elian's brow and turned her about. "Come. The men are ready."

The tables were gone, the folk in the hall arrayed in twin ranks with a passage between. A single pure voice soared up in the silence, the song of the bride brought to her wedding. The circle of young men tightened to a wedge and began to advance. Elian's women faced outward.

Wedge met half-circle. By custom the maids should shriek and scatter and leave their lady undefended. But these were warriors, and Elian's warriors at that. Each laughing man found himself confronting a cold-eyed woman. The advance halted in confusion.

Halenan, at the point of the wedge, swept a deep bow. "Greetings, fair ladies," he said with perfect courtesy. "We come in search of your queen. Will you help us to bring her to our king?"

"I shall," said the princess, coming forward to take her son's hand. "Come, ladies. Let the king look on our queen."

Glances flickered round the circle. Smiles followed it. Hand met hand; men and maids linked in a ring.

Elian stood in its center, face to face with Mirain. He had his grim and royal look. A corner of her mouth curved upward. His eye answered it with a brief, reluctant spark. She sank down in a pool of shimmering skirts, bowing to the floor.

He raised her. Beyond that first glance he would give her nothing. His eyes fixed upon the dais and the prince; his mind walled against her.

Anger warred with amusement. The hunter hunted, the pursuer pursued. *It's a mercy for us all that you always win your battles,* she said to the fortress of his mind: *even this small loss is too much for you.*

He stiffened but did not turn or respond. Side by side, pace and pace, they approached the prince. Their followers spread behind them.

Drums joined the lone marvelous voice, beating in time to their hearts; harps and pipes wove through them. The lamps blazed sunbright, dazzling.

"Lady of Han-Gilen," intoned the prince beneath the complex melody, "son of the Sun. Elian and Mirain, child of my body and child of my heart, before Avaryan and before the people of this empire he has forged, I bring you together, body and body, soul and soul, matched and mated in the god's name. Is it your will that I speak the words of binding?"

"Yes," said Elian with only the slightest quaver, and that not for herself. Mirain could still refuse. Could still shame her. He was fully as proud as she, and he could be no less perfect an idiot.

"Yes," he said distinctly, without a moment's hesitation. "I so will it."

The tension fled from her body. Almost her knees buckled. She stiffened them; his hands clasped hers, holding fast. Her father's settled over them. "Hear then and take heed. On this night of the goddess' binding, between two who stand so high in the world's ways, we forge not only a bond of earthly marriage but one of mighty magic. As the goddess is bound below, let these two be bound above; as the god strides free through the heavens, so shall they be free within their loving: two who are one, greater together than ever alone." He raised his arms and his voice. "Sing now, people of the Sun. Sing the binding that is their freeing."

Mirain shut the door of his chamber upon the throng of revelers, and shot the bolts. Their shouts and laughter echoed dimly through the panel, punctuated with snatches of song and the drumming of fists and feet.

Elian sat where her attendants had left her, in a chair made into a wedding throne. Cloth of gold covered it; rare spices scented it, lingering in the air about her. She herself wore a white gown, simple to starkness, clasped at the throat with a single green jewel.

The king turned his back to the door and the tumult, and folded his arms. "Well, my lady? Shall we let them in?"

The shouts had come together into a song reckoned bawdy even in Prince Orsan's guardrooms. Elian, who had been known to sing it without a tremor, felt the blood rise to scald her face. Mirain seemed quite frankly amused, as if he had surrendered wholeheartedly to her will; but however complete her triumph might be, she had never known him to yield without a battle. And Mirain was one who laughed as he fought.

She swallowed. Her mouth was dry. "It is for my lord to choose," she said.

Since my lady has chosen all the rest of it? He smiled with a wry twist. "By custom we should let them look on you and sing to you, and in the end put you to bed with me. In Ianon a chosen pair, man and woman, would remain to see that the rite was performed in full."

Her blush fled.

"But," he added after a pause, "neither of us is a great follower of custom."

He left the door. Involuntarily she stiffened. He passed her with scarcely a glance, stripping off his ornaments, casting them into their casket. His cloak followed, flung over a chest. Again he passed her, again with eyes forward, striding toward the bathing-room. He loosened his braids as he went.

She hissed in sudden, furious comprehension, and sprang to bar his way, forgetting the peculiarity of the bridal robe. Its clasp gave way; the heavy fabric fell free. She wore nothing beneath it but a chain of gold and emeralds, riding just above the swell of her hips.

Mirain halted as if he had struck a wall. Had she been less angry, she might have laughed.

His face disciplined itself. His eyes hooded. "You may bathe first," he said, "and take my bed. I shall sleep well enough in your old one."

Elian did laugh then, sharp and high. "Oh, no, Mirain. You wanted me, now that you have me, you can't cast me off."

"I wanted you in the full and proper time."

"Don't be afraid," she said acidly. "My father has no intention of withholding my dowry."

"I don't *want* your damned—" He broke off and spun away from her, tearing at his plaits. A cord snapped; pearls flew wide.

"You're angry," she said. "You wanted me on your terms, and yours only. So then, I tricked you. I trapped you. I admit it. Can you forgive me? Or have you been king too long to remember how?"

He wheeled with blazing eyes. "You self-centered little fool! You see what will be; have you no comprehension of what is? I will go to Ashan. I will not be encumbered with a wife—one who is all too likely to be carrying my child."

"All the more reason for us to be wedded now. Then, if you—die—"

"If I die, the world is well rid of me. If I live, I swear by my father's power that I shall give you such a wedding night as never a woman knew before."

She approached him, stepping softly, to lay her hands upon his shoulders. "Give it to me now."

"A choice," he said, "and a bargain. I shall give you what you ask for. More: the full three days of the wedding festival. Afterward I shall go to Ashan. You will remain here in safety."

"Or?"

"Or I ride to Ashan in the morning, and you ride with me, wedded in name only."

"I would go with you no matter which you made me choose."

"Not if I laid a binding on you."

"Could you?"

Under her hands his shoulders flexed; he breathed deep. Power sang in her mind's ears.

She smiled. Like an eel, like a golden fish, she slipped through all his shields, deep into the bright waters of his mind. They roared; they seethed. She rode at her ease in the depths where no storms could come, in halls of pearl and fire, wrapped about in the protection of his inmost will. *Bind me,* she said. *I welcome it. For if you do it, you too will be bound; and that will keep you from Ashan.*

Nothing will keep me from Ashan. His voice was a distant booming, like waves upon stone.

And nothing will keep me apart from you, she said.

Not even this surety? Our union will bring forth an heir. And our enemies will know it. They will strike at you then, at the life new-kindled within you, and through you both they will destroy me.

Or be destroyed, said Elian.

No. I will not allow it.

I will do it whether you allow it or no. Elian drifted closer to his voice, swelling with her own strong power. *Listen to me, Sunborn. Alone you may defeat your mortal enemies, but never the dark that stands behind them. It is too strong, and too well aware of your strength. But with me you may have hope. More than hope. Victory.*

Waves of denial bore her back. She struggled against them, twisting, leaping, up and out.

His braids had unraveled, falling over his shoulder. There in the hollow where bone met bone lay a deep and pitted scar, mark of a northern dart. It had been poisoned; he had almost died. She set her lips to it.

"I know that I am mortal!" he cried.

Her hands slid between his hair and his skin, stroking, kneading the knotted muscles. They hardened against her. He stared stonily ahead, his nostrils pinched tight, his mouth a thin line.

"Is that what I've been looking like?" she asked, bemused. "No wonder I made everyone so angry."

He pulled free, leaving his kilt in her hands, and spun away. But she saw enough to blush hotly, and to smile in spite of herself. "You're not all in agreement, are you?"

He opened the inner door. She let the garment fall and came after him. The bathing-room was warm, walls and floor both, from the hypocaust beneath; water steamed in the great gilded basin. That too was custom. The viewing of the bride; the singing; the disrobing and the bathing. Men and maids would try to keep the lovers apart while taunting each with the other's manifold beauties. Sometimes the guardianship would fail and the marriage be consummated then and there.

Mirain halted on the far side of the basin and faced her across it. "Yes," he said, "I want you. But if you come to me, you must swear that you will remain in Han-Gilen."

"You know I won't."

"Then my body will school itself to wait. It's most skilled in that."

"I'm not, and I won't." She stepped into the water, wading through it, ready to leap if he moved. "I could swear your oath, take my three days, and do as I please. But I'm honorable; I tell you the truth. Whether you give me three nights or none, when you go to Ashan I go with you. I'm your hope, Mirain. Your hope and your queen."

Her voice quivered on the title. She cursed herself for it, for the doubt it betrayed. That the certainty of her knowledge might be not of the light but of the mocking dark.

Mirain stood motionless, face of a royal stranger, body of an eager lover. But the eagerness was fading, yielding to his will.

She closed her eyes. The hope that had borne her up, the power of prophecy that had moved within her, ebbed away, leaving behind an utter weariness. She let her knees yield, her body sink into the warm scented water.

Strong arms lifted her. She looked into Mirain's face. Seeking for no yielding, she found none.

All damp and dripping as she was, he laid her in his bed. His arms were very gentle; his expression was cold, almost angry. "Woman," he said, low and rough, "you would tax the patience of a god."

"I know." It was a sigh. "You've always said it: I don't think. I just am. I love you, Mirain."

"And I . . ." He stroked the hair from her brow, tender hand, grim mouth. "There's never been anyone for me but you. Women—lovers—friends, some of them; but only one of you. Though I never knew how very much I wanted you until I saw you there in the wineseller's stall, so obviously and exquisitely you that I wondered how anyone could possibly take you for a boy. Do you know what it cost me, then and after, to keep my distance?"

"No more than it costs you now. And that is remarkably little."

"No," he said. "Oh, no. It costs the world."

She clasped her arms about his neck. There was no calculation in it. He was stone-stiff, stone-hard. Her lips touched his. Cold, so cold, with no yielding in them. She opened lips and mind, both at once, offering all she had to give.

Fire burst from him. Light and heat and sudden, fierce, uncontrollable joy.

Twenty-one

*E*LIAN OPENED HER EYES. MORNING LIGHT MET them. She lay in it, warm, languid, every muscle loosed.

Warmth stirred against her, and memory flooded. She was a maid no longer. She was a woman and a queen.

Dark eyes caught hers. "Regrets?" Mirain asked softly.

She touched his cheek, following the line of it down his jaw to his neck to the plane of his chest. A slow smile rose and bloomed. But she said, "Yes." His eyes stretched wide; she laughed. "Yes, that it took me so long to know my own mind. And," she added with the beginnings of a blush, "your body."

He laughed, deep and joyous, and rose above her. "Would you know it better still, my lady?"

She kindled; but she held him back, palms flat upon his breast. "Are *you* sorry, Mirain? You could have had any woman in the world. There are many more beautiful, and some more witty, and a few of higher birth; and any one of them would be more sweetly submissive than I."

"How excruciatingly dull," he said.

"Am I interesting?" she asked, all wide eyes and astonishment.

He leaped. Her laughter broke into a gasp, half of startlement, half of piercing pleasure.

When it was past, Mirain was very quiet. Not sad; but his high delight had faded, his mind withdrawn into some realm of its own. She, seeking, met a wall. Not a high one nor very strong, but she respected it, turning her will to the suppression of a sudden and utterly ridiculous jealousy.

Her head rested on his breast; his arms circled her, one hand tangled in her hair. Its fire fascinated him. "And fire even . . . there," he had marveled in the night, laughing at her fierce blush and taking her by storm.

A memory flitted past. Ziad-Ilarios in the temple, all gold and all lost. She clung to Mirain with sudden fierceness, startling him out of his reverie. "I won't let them kill you!" she cried. "I won't!"

"Nor shall they," he said with royal confidence. He sat up, drawing her with him, and smiled as he smoothed her hair out of her face. "Now, ladylove. How shall we receive the waking party?"

It found them most decently clad, he in a white kilt and she robed in green, playing at kings-and-cities beside the glowing brazier. Even the most uproarious young lord stood still before their calm. But the women smiled, the maids in admiration mingled with envy, the wedded ladies with approval; and the eldest folded back the bed's coverlet. There was the maiden-chain, and the marriage stain.

With a roar of delight the young men fell upon the lovers. Two, the youngest, bore garlands of winter green; with these they crowned both, while others brought forth cloaks of fur to wrap them, and lifted them up, singing the morning song.

For that was the wedding of a great lady in the southlands: three evenings and three nights alone with her lord, but three mornings of festival. On the first, they must be carried in procession through the keep, and break their fast with their closest kin; on the second, all the palace would see them and feast with them; and on the third, they would be borne through the city and presented in the temple, and brought forth to bestow their blessing and their largesse upon their people.

Elian clung to every moment. Even in the depths of his mind Mirain betrayed no impatience, but she knew: the fourth morning would begin the ride to Ashan. With but a word or two, to Adjan the commander of his armies in Vadin's absence, to Halenan the general of the southern legions, he had seen to it that all would be ready. And having so settled his fate, he laid it aside, becoming wholly the young lover.

She tried. But she was a woman and a seer. She could not make herself forget.

The third day fled like the dove before the hawk. She had dreaded the ordeal in the temple, the long ritual so close to the Altar of Seeing. Yet the altar was silent, the water unclouded by visions; and soon she was spun away from it. The blessing, which she barely heard even as she uttered it; the feasting, of which she partook almost nothing, so that the old dames and the young bucks exchanged wicked, knowing looks; and she was alone again, the doors bolted, and Mirain sinking to the bed with a sigh.

She perched beside him, stiff in her jeweled skirts, and regarded him without speaking. His quick hand found the lacing of her bodice; it came free all at once and somewhat to his surprise. His hand closed over her bared breast.

She shivered convulsively. He found the fastenings of her skirts and loosed them one by one, letting them fall where they would, and wrapped her in a furred robe.

Even that could not take away the chill. He drew her close and held her. "I know," she said through chattering teeth. "I know what it is. It's seeing. It's—knowing, and trying not to know. Mirain, I hoped this would be the saving of you. I prayed it would be. But—I don't—know. It's so cold."

"And dark."

She clutched at him. "You know. You know too!"

"Yes." His lips brushed her hair; his fingers kneaded the knotted muscles of her back. "We have enemies who would rob us of all hope. And now there are two of us for them to strike."

"Three," she whispered.

His arms tightened until she gasped. But, "Three," he said steadily. "We may be deadly weak. Or—as the god is my father—we may be stronger than ever we were alone. The dark would never let us see that. But we can believe it. We must."

"I want to." Her voice was stronger; she was a little warmer. A very little. "I will. If only—" She pulled back to see his face. "You can't make me stay behind."

His brows knit. "Distance is nothing to power. You can aid me just as well from here. Better, maybe, with no hardships of travel to—"

She cut him off with a flare of anger. "Don't be an idiot! By your own logic, I can be killed as easily here as in Ashan. More easily, what with fretting for you and pacing in a cage."

"The child—"

"The child is the merest spark of life, but it won't go out for a little riding in the wind. On the contrary. We'll both thrive on it."

He laid a light hand on her belly. "You see why I wanted to wait for you. Now I'll be doubly afraid."

"And doubly dangerous to anyone you meet," she countered swiftly. "We'll make you strong, the little one and I. We'll make you conquer. Because if you won't, my dearest lord, we'll do it ourselves."

Suddenly he laughed. "Why, you've already done it! You believe now. You're warm again."

She was, to burning. She bore him back and down, and pinned him there. "Do you love me?" she demanded of him.

"Desperately. Madly. Eternally."

For all his lightness, his mind bore not a grain of mockery. She searched it, piercing deep through all his open barriers, knowing that he saw likewise into her own soul. No one else had ever gone down so far. It was like nakedness—worse than nakedness, for her body had nothing to hide. Even its womanhood; had he not possessed all of it already?

Gently, and in the same moment, they withdrew. Mirain brushed her lips with his fingertip. "Lady," he said, "you are as wondrous fair within as without."

"And you," she said, "are splendid. Within, and without."

For once he did not try to deny her.

Lamplight illumined serenity: the Prince of Han-Gilen stretched out upon a low couch, half in a dream. His princess sat beside him with a lute, playing softly, singing in her low sweet voice. His hand moved idly among the freed masses of her hair.

Elian hesitated in the curtained doorway. She had looked on this scene, or on scenes like it, more often than she could remember. It was a fact of the world's existence, like the rising of Avaryan or the running of Suvien, certain, immutable: that she was the child of two who were lovers. She knew how very rare it was, and how very precious.

But her own new joy made her the more keenly aware of it, an awareness close to pain. She had this, and oh, it was sweet. Yet would she have it when the child within her was grown? Would it even live to be born?

The prince stirred. The song ended; he turned his head a little, smiling, holding out his hand.

She came to it as a drowning man to a lifeline. There in the warmth between the two of them, for a little while she rested. They did not press her with speech. Her mother returned to the lute, a melody like spring rain, note by limpid note.

Elian stared at her father's fingers that held her own. A mage's fingers, a warrior's, long and fine but very strong. A thin scar ran across the knuckles, mark of one of his first battles.

Their family lived long and aged late. But he was no longer young. Odd uncomfortable thought to have when he was so strong and so sure in his power: no grey in the fire of his hair, no weakening of the long lean body, and his daughter newly wedded to the man whom he had made an emperor. He alone, by the working of his will upon the princes of the Hundred Realms.

Mortality preyed upon her mind. It saw Mirain as she had left him, asleep and smiling, looking hardly more than a boy. He was young by any reckoning; and before the moons waned again, he could be dead.

She did not even know why her eyes blurred, until her father brushed a tear from her cheek. "I love him so much," she said. "And I'm close —so close—to losing him."

The lutestrings stilled. "Sometimes," the princess said, "a prophecy is its own fulfillment."

"Which it need not be." The prince drew his daughter close. "Elian, if you despair, all that you fear may come to pass. But if you are strong —we are not gods, daughter. But we can oppose fate. Sometimes we can even defeat it."

Elian blinked the tears away, scowling. "I know that. You taught it to me in the cradle. It's only . . . he knows it too. Too well. He doesn't even care that he might die!"

"That is why he is what he is. The art of kings and of gods: to venture all on a glimmer of hope, and to waste no strength in anguish."

"Then a queen's art—a woman's, at least—must be to feel the anguish for him. Especially if she's cursed with the sight."

They gave her no pity, and less compassion than she had looked for. "Yes," her mother said, "there is balance in all things. The king dares; the queen bears. And stands ready to be his prop and his shield."

"An ill one I make," muttered Elian. "He still calls me *child* and *little sister*. And I am."

"And you are not," the prince said.

She took the lute from her mother's lap, plucked a formless tune. Her fingers were stiff, out of practice. "Everyone is so strong and so sure, so certain that he has the right to work his will on the world. I was; when I made Mirain take me in my good time, and not in his . . . I was. I'll never forget it. But I'm no longer—I don't know—" Her voice was breaking. She stopped, mended it. "Nothing will keep him here, short of the god's own bonds. Not when he knows the danger. It's a madness in him. Part of his pride. He's been challenged; he can't retreat. He won't. Not even for me."

Her fingers stumbled, steadied. She lowered her head over the lute, aware of their eyes, concentrating very hard upon the halting music. No longer quite so halting. She was remembering her skill.

A touch like wind brushed her hair. Her father's hand, her mother's kiss.

With a sudden, convulsive movement she flung the lute away. Her face was tight, her throat sore. "I'm going to be strong. I'll be his strength when all of his is gone. And I'll save him. I'll give him life. He'll never die while I live to defend him."

Twenty-two

THE DAYS OF THE WEDDING HAD SEEN A BREAK IN the cold, a melting of the snow, a baring of startlingly bright green. Here on winter's threshold, spring made a brief and precarious entry.

The air was soft even in the early morning, the sun rising in mist, casting a silvered light upon armor and spearpoints. A hundred of Mirain's best gathered in the paved square before the palace: the chosen of his Chosen; picked men of the Green Company of Han-Gilen, honor guard of the prince-heir and under his command; and the ten men and women of the Queen's Guard. They were a fine brave sight in the morning, raising a shout as their king came forth with his foster brother and his queen.

Others of the army who stood by, watched with envy. Those who had not already returned to guard their own realms, or who would not be returning in due time, would garrison Han-Gilen under the regency of the prince. It was a proud duty, but none so proud as this, to ride with that small striking-force into Ashan.

"Small," Mirain had said, "for speed, and for a message. I will ride swiftly, I will settle this quarrel, I will return. I will not dignify it with the full strength of my empire." To which he had added to the Halenani alone, "If a hundred picked troops cannot end this treachery, twenty thousand will not. And will cost me a kingdom's wealth besides in stores and in time."

He seemed fresh and joyous now in scarlet and gold. His Chosen laughed and whooped; one called out, "Aiee, Sunborn! Married life becomes you."

Elian swung into Ilhari's saddle in a shimmer of armor, a swirl of green cloak. "So it should," she called back, "when it's me he's married to."

They roared at that, all of them, and Ilhari reared and belled. *Yes,* thought Elian fiercely, *laugh. Laugh at death, and watch her shrivel!* She knew she was fey; it was blackly wonderful.

The Mad One whirled close to her. Mirain had something in his hands. Copper-gold helmet, proud green plume, and circling it a golden coronet. Her old bronze helmet he tossed away, setting the new and royal one on her head, smiling his brilliant smile. "Now we match," he said. He kissed her, to loud and prolonged applause, and spun his stallion away again, gathering the company.

They left the white city by the north road, as they had come in; as Elian had gone—was it only half a year past? The road was mud and melting snow, the air was luminous; the men sang as they rode. Elian's women sang the descant; one, burly and black-browed as many a man, had a voice like shaken silver. Elian raised her own to match it, and Ilhari danced, weaving through the ranks, out to the fore and the Mad One's side.

The weather held. And held, through Iban, through Kurion, through Sarios and Baian and Shaiar. Sun like spring, moons and stars in a merciful sky. They camped in comfort as often as they lodged with the highborn, finding the former to be wiser. A lord, faced with An-Sh'Endor himself, would flutter and scurry; assured that the army would take care of itself, still he would insist that the king and the queen accept his full hospitality. And inevitably, once morning came, he would beg the high ones to linger for the merest moment, an hour only; there was a case, a judgment, a quarrel which only the Sunborn's wisdom could resolve. And there would go a morning, a noon, a full day of marching time without a furlong's advance toward Ashan; and another night to endure his lordship's entertainment. By then the cream of the local talent would have gathered, and all the gentry who could crowd themselves into the hall, for a feast that would leave the countryside to face a lean and hungry winter.

The camps were best. A tent no bigger than a trooper's, with a cot in it and a stool and one small chest for two; field rations and firelight, and music better than anything in hall.

This was Mirain's element. Even as a boy he had fretted within walls; the man, who had learned to be a king, still took to the march and the camp like a hawk to the air. Elian had not even known how cramped he was until she saw him free. At first she dreaded the nights and the dreams they would bring. But the power, having wielded her, lay now at rest; and the Exile seemed to have given up the battle, or else to have drawn back beyond the edge of perception. For whole days Elian even forgot to what she rode. The forgetting turned the long advance into a wedding journey.

As for the nights . . .

"So it's true," she said in the midst of one, fitting her body to Mirain's on the narrow bed, "the best lovers are . . . small men."

"*Small?*" It came from the depths of his chest.

"Well, middling," she conceded wickedly, twining her legs with his. "How nicely we fit. If you were as big as Cuthan, or even Hal, we'd never get both of us into this bed."

"Have you been proving it?"

Her laughter lost itself in his hair.

Deftly, and with no effort at all, he tossed her out of bed. She grunted in surprise, and a little in pain. Even carpeted, the ground was hard.

He stood over her with fists on hips, brows knit over the arch of his nose. Her mirth flooded through the tent. "Oh, you *are* a fine figure of a man!"

"A small man."

"A very well endowed, just tall enough, perfect, wonderful—"

"Don't strain your ingenuity," he said dryly.

She hooked his ankles and overset him, perching on his chest. "—splendid, beautiful, royal husband," she finished triumphantly.

He raised a brow. After a moment the other went up to join it. He weighed her breast in his hand. "They're growing," he said. "You're growing all over."

She looked down at herself in real dismay. "I am not!" she cried. "I won't even start to show for—I wouldn't even know, if I weren't—" His eyes mocked her. She pulled his hair until he yelped; and they rolled on the carpets in battle that was all love.

The tent wall brought them up short. Elian tossed back her hair, breathing hard. "The whole camp can hear us," she said.

"And who began it?" He ran his fingers down her side. "In Ianon the kingdom lives by the manhood of its king. I caused my people no end of worry, so few lovers as I took, and so seldom. And not a single bastard to prove my strength."

"I should hope not!"

He laughed softly. "Lady, you have fire enough for three. For you, for me, and for him." His hand rested on her belly. It was as flat and firm as ever, the life within waxing invisibly yet surely. "When he grows big enough to see, he'll have to have a name."

"What if he's a she?"

"Is he?"

Elian looked at his hand, suddenly finding it fascinating. And a little, a very little, frightening: as any miracle can frighten, for its simple strangeness. She shook herself. "It's . . . he. Maybe. Or she. Does it matter?"

"It's ours. Our firstborn. My heir."

"Even if it's a daughter?"

He hesitated only a fraction. "Even then."

Her joy leaped, startling a grin out of him. She laughed and kissed the corner of his mouth. "It will be dark like you."

"And red-haired like you."

"With your Ianyn nose."

"Ah, poor child. And your Halenani height, and your beauty, and a Sun in his hand. Or hers."

"Imagine," she said softly. "We made this, you and I. Son or daughter, it will be a child even the god can be proud of."

"It will be." Mirain kissed the place where his hand had been lying. "Truly and certainly, it will be."

On the Marches of Ebros at last the weather broke, and with a vengeance. They waded into Ashan through torrents of icy rain, in a wind that howled straight out of the north. Even in armor, even in oiled leather, the riders were wet to the skin. Their mounts plodded with heads down, ears plastered back. The Mad One was vicious in misery; not even Ilhari dared to come within reach of his heels.

Where the rain turned to sleet, the hills turned to mountains: the steep cruel ridges of Ashan. There the northerners might have burst into song, for this was a shadow of their own country; but even they trudged and cursed, forced afoot by the icy paths.

The southerners were long since emptied of oaths. Elian, struggling up and down the line, heard little more than harsh breathing, and the clatter and slide of hoofs on ice, and the wailing of the wind. Wrapped in the leather coat of a trooper, with a scarf wound about her head, she was blessedly anonymous; men who would never accept aid from a woman, and least of all from their queen, availed themselves willingly enough of her steadying hand. Some, young Gileni dandies, suffered cruelly in their handsome boots, narrow and high of heel as those were, and never meant for walking, let alone for scrambling over mountain passes in the sleet.

Mirain's tribesmen sneered at them, making no secret of their scorn. "Fancy-boy have hurtings in his little feet?" they sang in mincing voices. "Oh, be careful, sweetling; don't tear your pretty trousers." One, with the aid of liberal swallows from his belt flask, mocked the Gileni's painful gait with much swaying of his hips and a comical display of not quite losing his balance.

Elian's temper flared. She sprang; and as he laughed, thinking her one of the sufferers, she kicked his feet from under him. He toppled like a tree. She set her foot upon his throat, with the merest hint of pressure. "One more move," she said, her voice hoarse with damp, "only one more, and I'll pitch you into the next valley."

He gasped and gaped. With a snort of disgust she hauled him up. "Here. You dance so lightly over these mountains; lend the rest of us a hand."

Ilhari appeared out of the storm to snap wicked teeth in his face. It went slack; he dropped to his knees and pressed his forehead to Elian's sodden boot. A moment later, with conspicuous enthusiasm if with little grace, he offered his shoulder to a stumbling Gileni.

A shout rang out ahead. Elian clawed the ice from her eyelids and strained to see. The mare nudged her. The way was not too hard for the Mad One's daughter, whatever the foolish two-legs might think.

Elian peeled away the saddle's covering and swung astride. Ilhari strode forth, sure-footed as a cat, and proud with it. Even half-frozen as she was, Elian managed to smile.

The vanguard had halted above, just below the summit of the pass. But its numbers had doubled; beside the dripping Sun-banner flapped one of water-darkened yellow, its staff wound with the grey streamers of a messenger.

Mirain was on the ground under a canopy of leather, a tent upheld by a handful of his Chosen. Halenan shared the shelter with him, and a stranger, a man of middle years with a cough that woke Elian's anger. What right had anyone, even a prince, to send a man so ill on an errand so grueling, in such a storm?

His glance caught her as she slid between the king and the prince, but he did not break off his speech. It was hoarse and painful, yet clear enough. "Yes, sire, my lord prince has left Han-Ashan, hoping by his living presence to restrain the combatants. He left word that, should you deign to come to his aid, I should ride to meet you, and direct you to him."

"Where is he now?" asked Halenan.

"He rode first to sojourn with his kin in Asan-Sheian, though I fear that by this time his son will have led the young bloods to attack Eridan. I am bidden to conduct you to Sheian, and thence, if my lord is gone, to Eridan."

The prince's glance met Elian's. *He's telling the truth,* she said in her mind. *Or the truth as he's been allowed to see it.* She addressed the messenger herself, a little sharply. "How far is Sheian from here?"

She watched his courteous efforts to place her, muffled as she was, her voice gone sexless with the cold. But, though dizzy with fever, he was no fool. He could guess who would be here between these two men, and speaking as freely as they. "Two day's ride in good weather," he answered her, "my lady. Longer in this; but there is a castle in the valley yonder, and its lord is loyal to my prince. He begs you to accept his hospitality."

Elian ran her tongue over her cracked lips. She did not like the feel of this. Yet the man was honest. Transparently so; and so feeble that, for all his strength of will, he could barely keep his feet.

Her eyes flicked to Mirain. He had his king-look: weighing, pondering. He could press on with those of his company who could manage, leaving the rest behind; and if there was a trap, spring it before it was well set. Or was that the trap itself, to separate him from the main body of his men? Or was there after all no trap and no treachery? The messenger had no falsehood in him. Conflict rumbled in the earth of Ashan: troops gathering, fear mounting. Mirain knew the taste of civil war. It burst upon Elian's tongue, hot and foul; she gagged on it.

The messenger swayed. She caught him, to his surprise, not least at her strength. But though he was tall, he had no more flesh than a bird. "I think," she said, "that we should try to sleep dry tonight at least. And the men need rest, and some will need healing. It's been a cruel march."

Yet, having spoken, she felt no better. There was a wrongness in it. But if Mirain tried to go on . . .

The king's chin lifted; his brows met. "It has been bitter," he said, "and I for one would welcome dry feet. Lord Casien, will yonder castle hold my full company?"

The man coughed, deep and racking, battling to master himself. Elian's power uncoiled. His voice, freed, came almost clear. "I fear not, majesty. But there is a place on the mountain's knees close to the pass, an arm of the vale and a great cavern. Your men would be at ease there, and out of the rain."

And neatly closed in like rats in a trap.

So would they be if they were shut up within a castle wall. Elian set her teeth. She was letting her fears master her.

Briskly Mirain gestured: assent, command. "Very well. Lead us, then; and send a man ahead to the lord of—?"

"Asan-Garin, sire."

"I shall accept his offer, with thanks. My men have food, but would be glad of fuel, and any other aid he may provide."

"It shall be done, majesty."

As Elian mounted to the top of the pass, the lashing of sleet eased. The clouds boiled and broke, laying bare a deep cleft of valley amid mountain walls. Beyond the pass it divided like a stream flowing past a stone, one arm thrusting deep into the east, the other, shorter and higher, slanting into a treeless upland and a steep loom of cliff. But the east way was the way to Asan-Garin, the Fortress of the Wolf: black trees and black stones, and at its head where the mountains met, a spur of the peaks. Men had built upon it, erecting walls and keep far above the floor of the vale.

"Impressive," Hal muttered beside her. "But what's the use of a castle there if there's none here, where anyone can come in?"

Elian worked her numb fingers within her gloves, and settled deeper into the saddle. "Maybe people are supposed to come in. Have you ever seen a spider's parlor?"

"Cheerful child." He grinned through the ice in his beard. "Race you down."

"In *this?*"

He laughed and sent his grey over the edge at a pace just short of lethal. After an instant's gathering pause, Ilhari launched herself after him.

Twenty-three

"THERE'S WHY HIS LORDSHIP DOESN'T NEED A CAStle here," Elian said when she had got her breath back. She had won the race, plunging ahead even of the Mad One, skidding to a halt at the edge of the western meadow. It was high, and sloped higher, almost to the level of the pass; there the mountains opened. Man's hand had touched it, or perhaps the hands of giants; for as she drew closer she was the vast stone gates open wide, seeming almost to be a part of the peak, save that no mountain wall boasted hinges of grey and rustless metal.

The cavern was both broad and deep, smooth-floored, with hearths built at intervals along its walls and its center; from the air's movement she thought there would be vents far above. There was ample room here for a hundred men, indeed for ten times as many.

Hoofs clattered behind her; voices woke echoes. "Magnificent," breathed Mirain, halting by her side, springing from the Mad One's back. "Look, there were lamps here once, set in the stone. And a stair—there. I wonder where—"

"Sire!"

He turned. Elian realized that the company could not see them. They were lost in the darkness beyond the cavern's center, seeing with witch-eyes where mortal sight was useless.

Light blazed. Mirain had stripped the glove from his right hand. The shadows fled from a mighty vault of smoothed stone, a hall of giants.

And giants there were, marching upon the far wall. An army, deep carven: men like the tribesmen of the north, tall and high-nosed and proud; chariots drawn by strange beasts, cats and broad-horned bulls and winged direwolves; women riding upon huge birds. Above them all rode a man in armor in a burning chariot, and drawing it yoked lions, their manes fanning like flames.

Mirain's mirth was light and free. "See! Even the giants of the old time knew my father."

Elian tilted her head back to study the carven god. His armor was strange, ornate, covering his whole body like a skin of jointed metal; over it he wore a long loose surcoat and a flowing cloak. But his head was bare, the hair blown into rays about it. "He has your face," she said to Mirain.

To the life; even to the slight curl at the corner of the mouth. Mirain had it now, examining this his portrait that had been made long ages before he was born. "What an eagle's beak I have!"

"You," she said severely, "are unspeakably vain."

"Isn't he, now?"

Elian almost laughed. As she leaped to set herself between Mirain and the voice, Mirain leaped to set himself before her. They ended shoulder to shoulder, swords drawn, points meeting at a throat some few handbreaths above their own. Their captive grinned white in a face as dark as any in Ianon, and lounged against the cavern's wall. Torches, kindled, struck fire in all his northern finery.

"Vadin!" Mirain's sword flashed into its sheath; his joy leaped with him into his oathbrother's embrace. And died, thrusting him back, chilling his voice. "I sent you to hold the north. I remember no word of your meeting me here."

Vadin glanced at Elian. She stared back, refusing to flinch. Mirain looked from one to the other. His brows drew together. "Elian," he said, soft and still.

She sheathed her sword, taking her time about it. She did not think either of them could see her hand shake. She inclined her head to Vadin. "My lord. I trust you had a pleasant journey."

"Pleasant enough," he answered, "considering. And you?"

"The same."

"I see he finally got up the nerve to declare himself to you."

She tossed her head. "Nerve! He had nerve. He did it in front of his whole household. And even then I had to trick him into marrying me."

"That's Mirain," Vadin said, sighing. "With armies and kingdoms he puts an Asanian courtesan to shame. With women he goes all tongue-tied."

"Only at the beginning," said Elian. "Once he had warmed to it . . ."

"Elian." Mirain's tone was ominous in its gentleness. "What have you done?"

She faced him. He was not angry. He was determined not to be. Because if he let go, even for a moment, he would flay her alive.

She lifted her chin to its most maddening angle. "What do you think I've done?"

There were words for it. One or two might have been acceptable outside of a guardroom. Vadin spared Mirain the trouble of uttering them. "I had a summons from my lady empress. It was concise. She had need of me. Would I meet her in Ashan?"

Mirain's breath left him in a hiss. His eyes glittered upon Elian. "You don't even like him."

"What does that have to do with it? My power says we need him. Therefore we have him. If nothing else," she said, "he can give us a proper burial."

"They burn Ianyn kings," Vadin informed her. And as they both glared: "Now see here, children. This is a very clever trap, very enticingly baited. I've had a day or two to sniff around it." He stepped aside. His shadow bred men: great bearded Ianyn warriors who poured out of the mountain to overwhelm their king, drowning what more Vadin would have said, sweeping them all toward the hall's hearth.

Mirain's own company was in and dismounted, settled well within where wind and sleet could not reach, tending their seneldi, freeing the packbeasts of their burdens. Adjan had found fuel, only he knew where or how, and kindled a fire in the central hearthpit. They all leaped up from it in the face of the invasion.

"Peace," said Mirain. "These are friends."

They settled slowly. Vadin's barbarians eyed the southerners in open contempt, and took care to crouch well away from them, but as close to their king as they might come.

Mirain's barbarians, Elian noticed, had taken umbrage. They mingled conspicuously with their trousered comrades; they glowered at their kinsmen.

She swallowed a smile as she sat between Mirain and Vadin. It boded well for the empire, that mingling and that outrage.

And now they were three tight circles: the warriors of Ianon, and the soldiers of the empire, and the followers of the Lord Casien. The last of them huddled apart, surrounding their lord. Here in the mountain, with a hundred king's men hemming them in, lounging about with hands never far from hilts, they had a taut and wary look. One, though shivering convulsively, tried to press a steaming cup on his master.

Mirain beckoned to Halenan and Cuthan and a captain or two. They withdrew somewhat from the rest, leaning forward as Vadin finished what he had begun. "Yes," he said, "this is a trap. The whole of Ashan is a trap, for the matter of that. The center of it is here."

"How do you know that?" Mirain asked. Curious; completely unafraid.

"I feel it in my bones." Vadin grinned, a baring of sharp teeth. "And I've been exploring. This cavern is only an antechamber. The mountain behind it is a maze of tunnels. Most of them lead to nothing but blank walls. Some are traps; I lost a man in learning it. One winds up to the Wolf's castle. Its side ways are . . . interesting. And rather well guarded.

"It's true what you've been told, that there's no room in Garin for you," Vadin said. "It's large enough to hold an army; and an army fills it."

"Ashani?" asked Halenan.

"Ashani," Vadin answered. "They're turned on you, Mirain."

Mirain smiled. It was not comfortable to see. "Have they?" he asked, almost purring. "Luian alone? Or do his sons have a part in it?"

"Luian and his heir. The rest run at their heels. I found them marching up from Han-Ashan; I tracked them here. I saw them send out their bait." Vadin glanced at Casien. The lord slumped against one of his escort: a kinsman, perhaps. His eyes were closed. If he was not unconscious, he was perilously close to it. "He's an innocent; they know that much of hoodwinking mages. And they rely on your famous clemency to keep you from inquiring too deeply into his memories and finding any hint that might betray their plotting."

"They think I'm soft." Mirain laughed at the sudden rash of denials. "Of course they do. Look at me. I'm young, I'm a priest, I'm famous for sparing my enemies. And I'm arrogant to idiocy. Even if I caught wind of Luian's ambush, I'd throw myself into it, because he sent a messenger near death from sickness, and because I am the god's son; I am not for any man's slaying."

They stared at him. "You wouldn't," Elian said.

"Why not? It's a pity to waste so lovely a trap."

Even Vadin was appalled. Unsurprised, but appalled. "That's insane even for you."

"What's mad about it? I know what Luian intends. I have my best men with me. And I have you, who know the hidden ways to the castle. I'll ambush the ambush."

"Ah," said Halenan. "An attack from the rear. For a moment I thought you were going to spring the trap."

"I am." Mirain was on his feet, beating down the outcry. "I must! Else they'll know that I suspect something."

Elian left the protesting to the men. They could as easily have moved the mountain as persuaded Mirain to see sense. More easily. Mere stone would yield to a mage's will.

When the flood had ebbed a little, she said, "There's always an alternative. A ruse. A soldier spelled to look like Mirain."

The king rounded on her. "I will not command a man of mine to die in my place."

"In your name, often. But never in your place." She stood, the better to bear the brunt of his anger. "If you go, I go."

"You will not."

"I will." She smiled sweetly. "By your hand I swear it."

For a mad instant she knew that he would strike her down with that same glittering hand. But it rose only as high as his breast, and fell, trembling. It could not clench. The white agony of it pierced her shields. She caught it, held it to her heart, taking the pain as she had taken it since she was a young child.

He drew himself up. He was as well aware as she of the life that sparked below his hand. "Take back your oath."

"You know I can't."

"I must go." He had forgotten the others; he was all centered on her, his hand shifting of itself, cupping the breast beneath the sodden leather of her coat. "No one else can do what I can do: blind Luian, convince him that I come in all ignorance, ensure that the castle lies open to my army."

"You could retreat. Luian will hang himself soon enough, or be hanged, when his allies turn against him. As they will if you come riding with all Ebros at your back."

"But," he said, "that would take time; and my enemies would call it flight, and proclaim that a clever man can betray me and live."

"When have you ever cared what your enemies say of you?"

"I care that an ally has betrayed me. I mean to win him back; or to have his head."

Vadin spoke behind her. He sounded both weary and furious. "A valiant effort, my lady. But useless. He's bent on killing himself, and on playing the just king while he goes about it."

"Have I died yet?" Mirain asked sharply.

"No," Vadin replied. "But I have. Who will call you back? I'm no god's son, to win battles with milady death."

"And therefore you need me." Elian met Mirain's hot stare. "Unless you have the wits to desist. We can take Garin from the tunnels; we've no need to risk our necks by riding in the front gate."

"Luian needs it," Mirain said, obstinate. "If I can win him, there will be no need to fight at all."

She sighed deeply. She was not afraid; she was too utterly exasperated. "Very well then. We'd best go, before our enemies become suspicious."

"Elian—"

Her eyes held his; her hand gripped his own. "I keep my promises, Mirain."

He pulled free, hand, eyes. He would yield. He must. She set all her will upon him.

He turned his back on her, raised his voice. "Lord Casien," he said, "I leave you here in the care of my Chosen." As the man moved to speak, Mirain held up a hand. "You should be abed and under a healer's care. My company can provide the beginnings of both."

"Sire, my prince has commanded me—I am to accompany you wherever—"

"You will not endanger your life by riding farther tonight. Surely your prince will understand that." Mirain crooked a finger at the man with the cup. "You, sir. See that your master has all he needs. My men will give you whatever you ask for."

The servant bowed, still shivering. Not all of it was cold. Elian marked the way his eyes kept sliding round the cavern to the carven wall, and back in a nervous skitter to Mirain's face.

If the king saw, he took no notice of it. His eyes ran over his company. Swiftly he named names: twenty altogether, gathering before him, grinning like the valiant idiots they were. None of them was Halenan.

The prince's face was dangerously still. "My lord king. It is my right as your general—"

"It is your duty as my general to command the army in my absence."

"The Lord of Geitan is perfectly capable of commanding your troops by himself. And," said Halenan, "he knows the secret ways to Garin."

"You will share the command." Mirain was immovable; but he held out his hand. "Brother, I need you here, with your wits and your power and a guard on the pass. Whom else may I trust so?"

Elian suppressed an urge out of childhood, to vanish into a corner. Halenan's hot eye flashed to her; Mirain's had no need. "My lady has sworn to come with me," he said with a touch of irony. "What power has any of us to prevent her?"

"That's idiocy!" snapped Halenan. "I have two sons and a daughter, all safe in my city. What have you?"

Elian started forward, but Mirain's hand caught her, steel-strong and unyielding. Quietly he said, "My brothers, you know what you must do. If by tomorrow's nooning I have sent you no signal, nor any word of my victory over Luian, mount the attack."

Halenan opened his mouth. Vadin silenced him with a firm hand. The Ianyn lord looked long at Mirain, and pulled him into a swift embrace. "Try to come out of this alive," he said.

Mirain grinned up at him. "I'll do more than try. I'll be victorious."

"Arrogant." Vadin let him go. He turned, facing Halenan. The prince was stiff, angry. Mirain tilted his head, brows up.

"Farewell," said Halenan coldly, "sire."

"Farewell," said Mirain, "brother."

Halenan unbent a very little. He suffered Mirain's embrace, and Elian's after it. He returned the latter somewhat more warmly than he might have, and stepped back, nursing his temper.

Elian faced Vadin. They did not speak, nor did they touch, save glance to glance. She groped for resentment, even for dislike. Neither would come to her hand. He was necessary. He was part of the world as it must be; part of Mirain. *Project him,* he willed her, *until I come.*

Always, she answered. And: *If your bones tell you to come, don't linger. Come quickly, and come with all your strength. Else . . . else we lose him.*

He bowed. It was a promise.

The last Elian saw of either of them, they stood in the arch of the great gate. Vadin stood still, arms folded, both haughty and patient. Halenan's head was bare in the bitter wind; his eyes burned even at the full length of the meadow.

She faced forward. If there was worse misery than riding from dawn to dusk in a storm of sleet, it was pausing by a fire; beginning to remember warmth and dry feet; and riding out again.

The escort was silent. Ten of Mirain's best in scarlet darkened by the wet to the color of drying blood; her own ten in moldy black that had begun as green. It was little mercy that the sleet had thinned almost to nothing: the wind had risen, knife-keen.

From the vale of the cavern the land fell down into the deep wooded coomb of Garin. The road was narrow, following a stony stream; where trees overhung the track, careful hands had cut back the branches to the height of a rider's head.

"That's not bandits' custom," Elian said. Her teeth were chattering; she bit down hard.

Mirain's knee brushed hers. With a startling-swift movement he swept her into his own saddle, settling on the crupper, wrapping his cloak about them both. The Mad One was steady beneath them, tolerant of their follies, even amused.

Warmth crept through Elian's body. She basked in it, although she knew that there were grins behind her. The army took an unholy delight in watching their lord and their lady at love-play, however innocent.

"Of course," Mirain said in her ear. "It proves we're actively pursuing our dynastic duty."

"Not in this saddle," she muttered.

He laughed and kissed the back of her neck. "Later, then. Shall we be scandalous? Bathe together, dispose of our supper and our enemies as quickly as we can, and go to bed sinfully early."

"And sin all night." She leaned back against the living warmth of him, hands laced with his at her waist. He was choosing to forgive her; accepting the inevitable. She was choosing to allow it. "Sometimes I think I'm too happy. Even here, even with what waits for us in Garin . . . it almost isn't fair."

"Of course it's fair. Eminently so. It's love, you see; and we're riding to a war."

She smiled a little. "The Grey Monks say that love is the worse of the two. A man can go his life long without once dreaming of battles, but even eunuchs dream of love."

"Do they?"

"I knew one once. He'd been a slave in Asanion. He said he never even thought of women; but I know he dreamed of men."

Mirain considered that in his inimitable fashion, both swiftly and thoroughly. She liked to watch the turning of his mind; to fit herself into it, turning with it, losing for a little while her shallow, flighty self.

She looked out of his eyes. Aware of the differences: the angles of his body, the joining of hip and shoulder, the fullness where she had none; and no need to balance the soft heaviness of breasts. And the sparking awareness of warm woman-body against him—desire as keen as a sword, and half-mirthful suppression, and a wonderfully gratifying rush of blood to his cheeks.

She was herself, odd-familiar, laughing softly. And he reached, and he was there, sharing her body, searching out its curves and crevices. How strange it was, how marvelous, with its secret places where he was all open to the world; it's softness where he was hard, and its deep-rooted strength.

Through her eyes he saw the road's sharp curve; through her ears he heard what made the Mad One pause, head up, nostrils flared. Metal on metal; hoofs on stone.

Ilhari ventured ahead alone. At the bend of the road, she halted. Mirain, enclosed within his own body once more, sent the stallion to join her.

From the curve the road ran almost straight into a grey light and the loom of mountain wall. A small company rode there: mounted men surrounding a laden wain, and foremost, the man whom Lord Casien had sent, spurring his weary mount forward, bowing over his pommel. "Lord Garin of Garin, your majesty—he comes himself to greet you."

The Wolf fit his name well. He was not an old man, but his hair was iron grey, cut thick and short like a wolf's mane. The face under it was narrow, long-nosed, and yellow-pale, with eyes narrow and tilted and the same amber-gold as a wolf's. They glinted, bright and mocking, taking in the man, and the woman in man's dress, and the small plain-clad escort. "Your majesty," he said, bowing low in the saddle, baring long yellow teeth. "My lady—Kalirien, is it not?"

Even with her back to it, Elian felt the cold brilliance of Mirain's smile. "Kalirien indeed; and Elian ilOrsan of Han-Gilen; and my queen."

"Majesty," said the Lord Garin, unruffled. "You honor us." He indicated the wagon with a flick of his hand. "Here I have fuel, and food and drink, and blankets against the cold. Your men will not suffer in your absence."

"My lord is generous," Mirain said.

"I am a loyal man, your majesty."

"You do seem so, my lord Garin," said Elian, sliding smoothly from the Mad One's saddle to Ilhari's. The mare stamped; Elian smiled a slight, edged smile. "Shall we go up to your castle?"

Twenty-four

THE ROAD, THOUGH STEEP, WAS SMOOTH, THE CASTLE much larger than distance had made it. As large within its grey walls as Han-Ashan itself; and that was no small stronghold.

But Han-Ashan pretended to grace: fine carvings, fine tapestries, and even the slaves well and often elegantly clad. Asan-Garin feigned nothing. It was a fortress, a strong holding. Its men walked in leather or in well-worn armor. Its women kept to their houses or flitted in shadows, heavily veiled. Its barefoot, bare-bodied children stared solemnly at the newcomers and made no sound.

The silence was eerie. Every other holding—every one—had rung with acclaim for the king. Grudging, some of it, but clearly audible. These people did not cheer, did not call out his name or his titles. They simply stood in the courtyards and in the corridors, and watched.

There were too few of them for an army. Elian, seeking with power, found none beyond them; and no love for Mirain, but no hate. He was nothing to them.

Had Vadin lied? Or had he been decieved? Perhaps he had tricked Mirain into a place of safety, so that he might dispose of his king's enemies without danger to his king. Perhaps Luian had repented and withdrawn to Sheian. Perhaps—

The grey walls closed in about her. Instinct struggled and shrieked. Brutally she beat it down. She had bound herself to this. She made herself walk coolly onward, now beside Mirain, now ahead or behind as the way narrowed, warded always by their escort. They were calm, these chosen of their king, eyes watchful, hands resting lightly on swordhilts.

Cuthan walked just behind Elian, close as her shadow, relaxed but wary. "Rather like home, this," he observed pleasantly.

Lord Garin did not choose to notice him. Nobleman or no, he was a mere guard, and speaking out of turn. But Mirain said, "It does have an air of the north. The stern walls; the stern faces. No southern fripperies here."

The lord paused before a guarded door. The sentry opened it crisply but without haste. "I hope this will be to your satisfaction, sire," Lord Garin said. His eyes were full of wolf-laughter.

In spite of her determination to be unmoved, Elian stared. It was as if all the luxury of the south and west had drained from the castle into this one tower. A broad chamber with the proportions of a guardroom and the furnishings of a seraglio; an inner room dominated by a huge bed hung and draped with velvet, lush with furs and Asanian carpets; and a bath of lapis and silver, deep enough and wide enough to swim in.

Mirain took it all in and laughed, the free and joyous laughter of a boy. "Why, my lord! You're a voluptuary in disguise."

"Not I, sire. My late father." Lord Garin showed his sharp teeth. "A reiver of repute, was my lord Garin the elder."

"Indeed," said Mirain unabashed, "that's clear to see. Not I myself could have done better."

That caught the Wolf off guard; for a moment his glance betrayed a hint of admiration. "You flatter my father, sire. No doubt his bones are warmed by it, cold as they have been all these years, naked under the gallows tree."

"Ah! Who hanged him?"

"Why, sire, I did. I am a respectable man, you see."

With the door shut and barred from within and his own men warding it, Mirain laughed again, long and deeply. He spun still laughing, and spread his arms. "Come now, my friends! This is no time for grim faces."

"Isn't it?" Elian muttered. But her lips twitched. "You're quite mad, you know."

"Oh, quite! Milord is more his father's son than ever he would wish us to dream; but I find I like him for it. He has wit; he has subtlety. And he has no fear of me at all."

"Neither do I," Elian pointed out.

"So. But you I do not like." His eyes danced. "You, I love." He swept her up, heedless of her struggles, and carried her past the grinning guards, and kicked open the door of the inner chamber, and dropped her onto the bed.

She struggled out of the tangle of bedclothes. He was stripped already and striding toward the bath.

She plunged in after him. The water was a wonder, a marvel, a long delight: warm, sweet-scented, and swirling gently, bearing all her travel stains away.

With a shock she realized that the doors were open, the guardroom clear to see. The women had arranged a curtain between themselves and the men, but both could look straight into the pool.

Mirain's white grin surfaced beside her. "Ho, guards!" he called. "There's room here for us all. Quick now, while the water's hot!"

The full score of them came in a mob, whooping. The men were shyer than the women; the Ianyn, too dark to show their blushes, looked everywhere but where their minds were. Elian laughed at them, and needled them until they laughed back. But Cuthan led them in a gloriously wet revenge.

Mirain was first off the field as he had been the first on it, leaping out of the battle and snatching the least sodden of the drying-cloths. " 'Varyan!" he said. "I'm dying of your foolishness. Go on then, drown yourselves in mere water. I'm for mine host's good wine."

As Elian watched him saunter away with his cloth flung over his shoulder, Cuthan spoke beside her, half amused, half somber. "He's always like that: looking for a better way to die." He bent, took up a cloth, wrapped it calmly and boldly and quite firmly about her. The others had quieted and begun to scatter, drying one another, sorting out the tangle of clothing.

Elian looked up. She had to crane her neck a little. Cuthan's face was unwontedly still; he looked more than ever like his brother. Quietly, rather slowly, he said, "I have no wizardry, but my nose is keen enough; and there's that in the air which I don't like. This trap is not as it should be."

Elian hugged the cloth to her, trying not to shiver. "I know. I can't find the army Vadin spoke of. If it's gone, I yearn to know where, and why. But if it is not . . . My power is strong, Cuthan. Any mage who can hide an army from me may prove too much even for Mirain."

"Maybe there is no army after all," Cuthan said. "Maybe Lord Garin is no more than he seems."

"Maybe." Elian sat on the pool's edge, running her fingers through her hair, wrestling out the tangles. "This is a very strange place. Every mind is clear enough to me, down to a certain point. Then nothing. Nothing at all. It's uncanny. Like looking at a crowd and realizing all at once that none of them is real; they're only masks set up on spears."

"Even the lord?"

"He's the worst of all. And yet he's no sorcerer. He has no power."

"A lord may be without magic but employ a mage. There are all too many such in the north: court wizards and tame enchanters, and shamans of the wilder tribes. Most are foreign-trained, mages from the Nine Cities or followers of one or several of Asanion's thousand gods."

The name of the Nine Cities rang in Elian's head like a gong, dizzying her, catching her breath in her throat. And it was in Ashan that the Exile had found her; into the wilds of Ashan that she had vanished. If she was here, if it was she who raised these walls of nothingness, then Elian had need of more than fear. She needed all the strength she had, and all the resistance.

She made herself face Cuthan steadily, speak coolly, calmly. "I've heard the songs," she said. "Mirain and the Insh'u Master; the Sunborn and the Mage of Arriman; the Ballad of An-Sh'Endor and the Thirty Sorcerers."

"There were only six," said Cuthan with a surprising touch of severity, "and four were apprentices." He grinned suddenly, and that was more surprising still. "But what's a song if it cleaves to the truth? I'm composing one now. A very good one, I'm so presumptuous as to think: the tale of the Sunborn and the Lady Kalirien."

But for once Elian could not return his lightness. Her power had been stretching itself, of itself, with no will to compel it. And her fear was mounting. "Cuthan," she said very low, "this strangeness has another face. It hems my power in. I can't mindspeak to anyone outside of these walls; I dare not force the barriers. Whoever, whatever wields power here"—*Not the Exile,* her inward self keened, *O Avaryan, may it not be she*—"must not know what our brothers will do. Which means—"

"Which means," he said, and she loved him for that quickness of wit, "that my lord cannot give the signal to attack. And morning may be too late."

"Morning will be too late," she whispered. It was dark behind her eyes. In the dark was light, grey-cold like a winter dawn; and Mirain fallen upon cold stone.

Cuthan's hands were warm, gripping her. She let them hold her to the world of life and love and hope of victory. "I'll go if I can," he said, "as soon as I can. I'll bring the army to you."

She smiled. It was not as hard as she had feared it would be. Cuthan was very easy to smile at. "To me, my captain? Not to your king?"

He looked down abashed, but he looked up again swiftly, with lordly pride. "I am *your* captain, my lady."

"Gallant knight." She rose. "Come. Let us gird ourselves for the slaughter."

With the wine, which was the sweet golden vintage of Anshan-i-Ormal, Lord Garin had sent robes of honor. White Asanian silk for Mirain; and for Elian a gown the color of flame, and a golden veil. The gown might have been made to her measure. The veil she almost cast away; but she paused. It was a lovely thing, cloud-soft, cloud-fragile. If it was meant for an insult to the notorious Lady Kalirien, why then, let it become a badge of honor.

She draped it carefully. Nimble hands aided her: Igani, the beauty of her Guard. The warrior woman was as deft as a lady's maid, but no maid ever wore such a wicked smile, or said as she settled the golden fillet, "Give 'em hell, my lady."

Elian met her own mirrored eyes and smiled slowly. Paint and perfumes she had none, and no jewels but the fillet, yet she was—fair. More than fair. She would not shame her king.

Nor did he put his own legend to shame. Despite his words, he had drunk but a sip of wine; the glitter in his eyes was his own, and the sheen that lay upon him, of danger and daring and of high royalty. She, meeting that splendid gaze, for a moment was blinded.

He bowed low and kissed her fingertips; her palms; her throbbing wrists. Whispering with each: "Lady. Queen. Beloved."

She looked down at his bent head, bent her own, and kissed it.

He straightened. Her eyes, freed, flicked round. The guards had drawn together about them, a living shieldwall. Beyond them the door stood open, with Lord Garin in it.

The ruler of Garin had put off his riding leathers for a plain brown coat. No jewels, no precious metals; only a belt with a simple clasp, and a knife hanging sheathed from it, both hilt and clasp of hammered bronze. Like his people, like all his castle save this tower, he affected no elegance.

That in itself, perhaps, was an affectation. He regarded the king and the queen with a careful scrutiny and a bow that conceded very little. And yet, veiled though his mind was, Elian sensed strong stirrings beneath. Tension, tight-reined fear, and—elation?

The gloating of the wolf before it pulls down its prey. Yet, Mirain said in her mind, *this victim is armed and ready. It will not fall as easily as he may hope.* He offered his hand. Elian laid hers upon it. With a smooth concerted movement, the wall of guards parted. King and queen paced forth. The guards followed them, save only those who warded the chambers behind them.

Whatever splendors the elder Garin had brought to his hall, his son had long since stripped away. The chamber was long, its grey stone bare, with no softening of trophy or tapestry. Torches illumined the walls, thrust into brackets of iron. Its center was a hearth where roared and smoked a great blaze.

Just within the cavernous door, Elian stopped. The folk of Asan-Garin stood along the walls, or sat on benches, or crouched upon the rushes. Faces, eyes—tens, hundreds. Men in brown, men in grey, men in yellow, men in mottled green.

With all her power she mastered her face. She could have cried aloud for purest relief, and for purest, most exhilarating terror. An army, after all. An enemy to face and, the god willing, to overcome.

As if some will had worked upon it, the hearthfire leaped up and died abruptly. Beyond it spread a dais and a high board. People sat there in state: men, a veiled woman or two. Elian's eyes, blurred with smoke and sudden dimness, would not come clear.

They had no need. She knew those handsome black-bronze faces, those affable smiles. They were all there as they should have been: Luiani of Ashan, the Prince-Heir Omian foremost and on his feet, and in the tall canopied chair of the lord, the Prince of Ashan himself.

But those faded and paled before the one who sat at Luian's right hand. Tall, gaunt, clad in black, with eyes like flawed pearls. Her familiar purred in her arms.

Four thin lines of fire seared Elian's cheek; but she hardly felt the pain. Prophecy was a keener fire, and cleaner. It burned away her fear, left her calm, almost content. *So,* her mind observed, *it has come at last.* And the sooner come, the sooner gone, for good or for ill.

Behind her the doors boomed shut. Shouts sounded dim beyond, the outrage of the guards, the mockery of Garin's men. One only had outrun the closing of the gates: Cuthan, swift to see and swift to move, and closest to his lady.

Mirain stood at his royal ease, almost smiling. As Cuthan halted behind him, he said to the man who had guided him here, "There is no need of that, my lord Garin. I shall not attempt to escape." Coolly he moved forward, Elian at his side, the Ianyn lord a bulwark behind, down the length of the hall, skirting the fire. His smile was quite visible and quite amused. "Prince Luian; Prince Omian. This is a pleasant meeting. Have you then settled the matter of Eridan?" The prince examined him minutely, as if he had been a stranger. Elian, watching him, for the moment unregarded, reeled with vertigo. He was not *there.* He could be seen, he could be heard; he could even be smelt, a faint musty odor like old rooms long untenanted. But to the mind there was nothing.

Her power unfolded. All her outward senses cried out to her of crowding bodies: Luian's men, Garin's people, the followers of the woman called Kiyali. Her mind met only void. Even Mirain—even he—

Wrath drove back her panic. The Exile sat as a queen of mages, smiling at Elian. Without a word of mind or tongue, she beckoned. She invited. She offered strength that was infinite beside Mirain's haughty weakness, and power that knew no bonds of light or dark. Elian raised all her barriers and huddled within them. Immovable, by the god; unassailable. Though bolts of seduction battered the gates, and temptation sang its sweet song, beckoning her into the deadly air.

Luian spoke, dry and cold. She took refuge in his insolence. "Eridan shall be dealt with in its proper time. Meanwhile I have other and more immediate concerns."

"Such as myself." Mirain tilted his head to one side, all bright interest. "You were rather clever, prince. I would have expected you to trap me in Sheian, or even to wait until we came to Eridan. But this is much more convenient. A spacious and isolated prison for my army; a strong castle to lock me in, with ample room for all your forces; a lord who is, by his own admission, a loyal man. You have even managed to tame a sorceress to oppose my famous wizardry; and that one of all sorceresses . . . has she ever told you why she is blind?"

The Exile's smile gained an edge. "I have told him, King of Ianon. All of it. You took me once by surprise; you can never do so again."

"No," said Mirain willingly, "I cannot. You have grown strong since you betrayed my mother."

"I executed her by the law of her order. The order you claim, priestess' child, no-man's-son. You have risen high on the strength of her lies. But every falsehood must be uncovered at last; and the greater the lie, the more terrible is its revealing."

Mirain looked about him. "They believe you, I see. Your skill in mind-twisting is impressive. But then, you build on strong foundations. My lord Garin, the loyal man; Prince Omian, whom I forced into close and constant commerce with his ancestral enemy; my royal lord of Ashan, displaced from first and greatest ally to scarce-regarded vassal. Men were content with their wars and their petty thieveries before I came to disturb them, I with my mad conviction that the world is mine to rule."

"By your own words are you condemned."

"And quite cheerfully, kinswoman; for some vices make excellent substitutes for virtue. You know that well, who slew the bride of Avaryan. I regret that I took such vengeance as I did. I should have killed you cleanly, or let you go wholly free."

"You had no such power. You were a child then, untaught, unrestrained. You are a child still. Else you would never be here before me."

"I might. I might have decided, kingly-wise, that it is time you were disposed of. You subvert my people; you disrupt my kingdom. You are, in short, a nuisance."

The Exile laughed softly. "Am I not? We are always troublesome, we defenders of the truth."

"Can you even tell what is truth and what is a lie?" Mirain mounted the dais, moving with that swift grace which made him so deadly in battle. The Ashani princes drew back from him, their smiles long gone. Luian, trapped by the proud bulk of the throne, held his ground, although Mirain leaned upon the table and fixed him with a steady, glittering stare. "So, prince. I have obliged you; I have fallen into your web. I admire art, even in treachery. But this I cannot forgive: your cruel misuse of your messenger. Kingslaying may have its excuses. The murder of an ill and innocent man has none."

The prince's eyes hooded; his face was unmoved. "Lord Casien is an utterly honest man and an utter fool. As for his illness, the songs give you great powers of healing. Are they lies then?"

"Prince," said Mirain softly, "you cannot have two truths. If the tales of me are true, then I am indeed the king, and you are a traitor. If the tales are false, you are something less foul, perhaps, but more despicable: a murderer of his own good servants." He leaned forward slightly, resting on his hands. "Whichever you are, Luian of Ashan, and whichever I am, mind you this: You have me. You do not have my empire. And it will avenge me."

"Will it, King of Ianon?" murmured the sorceress. "Are you so greatly beloved? With arms and songs you won the north. The Hundred Realms came to you by gift of the man who fostered you. Fathered you, it might be thought. But for his power, you could never have come so far; never, with all your pride and your vaunted wizardry, have laid claim to an empire. It is Orsan of Han-Gilen who rules in the world's heart, and who has always ruled there, whomever he raises as his figurehead."

Mirain stood straight, still at his ease, unruffled. "That may well be. You who were of the Halenani know well their greatest pride. Kings they are not and will not be. They are princes among the princes of the Hundred Realms; they claim no greater title, and no less. And they accept no king over them save one of their own choosing."

"A puppet king. An illusion of power, a pretense of royalty." The blind eyes opened wide, fixed upon him as if indeed they could see. Elian's nape prickled. Power gathered like summer thunder, swelling in the smoke-dimmed air, filling the emptiness where minds should be.

"Puppet," whispered the Exile, wind-soft, wind-cold. "Little bantam cock, dressed to seem a king. Men are slaves to their eyes and to a clever song. Let them see and hear the truth. You are nothing. You are an empty thing, a counterfeit, a shape of air and darkness. Long ago I knew you; long have I suffered for that knowing." She raised her hand. Shadow filled it. She cast it outward. "Down, liar, child of lies, begotten in falsehood. Down, and know your master."

That voice froze Elian where she stood: low, vibrant, thrumming with power. Her knees had locked, else she would have fallen. Her eyes swam with darkness.

Mirain swayed in the heart of it, wrapped in it, helpless, powerless, lost. It buffeted him; he reeled to his knees. All his splendid sheen was gone, leaving him stripped bare, a smallish unhandsome man in an extravagance of gold and silk, his face drawn taut with anguish. The little power he had, had been enough to blind simple folk, to erect a semblance of kingship. But against true magery he had nothing: no strength, no magic, no god-born splendor.

His head fell back, as if he had lost control even of his body. The skin stretched tight over the proud bones of his face, grey-pale where they thrust forth, blue-pallid about the lips. A great tremor shook him. His teeth bared, white and sharp and strangely feral.

With an effort so mighty that it seemed to shake the very stones of the hall, he lurched to his feet. His hands worked convulsively, the right clawed, trembling in spasms. Light dripped from it, slowly, like blood.

It snapped shut.

The darkness shattered. The sorceress cried out, sharp and high.

Elian nearly collapsed in the sudden, mind-numbing clamor. All shields had fallen. The hall thronged with thoughts as with men, throbbed with astonishment, quivered with hostility. Only at her back was there a refuge, the strong fierce loyalty of her captain who was her friend, warmed to burning with the love he bore his king.

Mirain stood upon the dais in a cloak of light, head high, strong voice ringing from end to end of the long hall. "Now I see. Now I see it all. As I am called Prince Orsan's puppet, so does Prince Luian dance to your piping. I was most skillfully deceived: I looked for naught beyond mere mortal treachery."

"Not all men are blind to the truth," the Exile said.

Mirain's lips stretched, baring teeth. It was not a smile. "How easily you mouth the words. Truth; falsehood. What would you now? A simple slaughter? A refinement or ten of torment?"

"Neither," the Exile answered him. "I am neither murderer nor torturer." His lip curled; she sensed it. "Nor," she added, "executioner. No longer. You who were a half-mad child have become a king; you are renowned for your honor. I would face you in fair combat. Power against power; mage against mage. Have you the will to face me?"

Elian could say no word; could not even move. Nor was it the sorceress who held her. It was Mirain. Mirain kindling with something appallingly like delight. "I have the will," he said. "I have will and to spare. I have fought body to body against a slave of the dark; I have waged the duel arcane with demon-masters in the lands of the north. But never have I faced an equal in wizardry, servant of the goddess as am I of the god. Formal combat by the ancient laws: To the victor, my empire. To the vanquished, death."

The Exile turned her eyes toward him, as if to search his face. "You would set the stakes so high?"

"You have trapped me. I know that I cannot persuade you, of all women in this world, to let me go; nor will you ever be my ally. I can work free by painful degrees while my people wage war to win me back, or I can risk all on a single cast of the dice." His grin flashed, wide and white and fearless. "I have never been noted for my prudence."

Prince Omian jerked forward. "Treachery!" he cried. "I know the songs. No prison can hold him. He will lull us with false bargains, go quietly to his chamber, and walk out in the night, to bring all his armies down upon us."

The nameless one smiled, undismayed. "Set yourself at ease, my lord. He knows as well as I that he cannot escape the bonds which I have set. Only through battle may he win free; and that, have no doubt, only into death." She turned her voice and her face upon Mirain. "So let it be. The battle of true power, by the laws of the masters. We meet at dawn according to their dictates. Gird yourself well, King of Ianon."

Twenty-five

ELIAN SAT ON THE BED IN THE STATE CHAMBER. ITS splendor dripped with irony, as bitter a symbol as chains of gold. Even, she thought, without the knowledge that its first master had been hanged by his own son.

Mirain was in the outer room, sharing a late meal with the guards. Whatever his intent toward his guests, Lord Garin was not minded to starve them. The food was plain but plentiful and, from the evident relish with which they consumed it, not ill to the taste.

She had no appetite for it. They were all so calm, and Mirain calmest of all, passing round the ale and laughing at a jest. She too was calm, for the matter of that, but it was the quiet of numbness. Her body was leaden, unwieldy, strange to itself.

She stretched out, pulling veil and fillet from her head, letting them fall to the floor. Of their own accord her hands went to her belly. The life there was a Brightmoon-cycle old this very night. Had she been without power, she would have begun to wonder if indeed she had conceived.

Her fingers tensed. She wanted to rip it away, to cast off all of it, to be her own self again: Elian, Han-Gilen's wild lady; Galan, esquire of the Sunborn. She wanted to cradle it, to brood over it like a great bird, to rend any who dared to threaten it.

She lay on her face. Laughing, a strangled gasp, for when she began to swell she would not be able to lie so; choking on tears. And laughing again, because every tale of bearing women trumpeted their mad shifts of mood; but she had always been as wild as a weathercock.

A light hand traced the path of her spine. She raised her head. Mirain sat on the bed's edge, balancing cup and bowl. "Here," he said, "eat." Her stomach heaved, and settled abruptly as she turned about. There was meat in savory stew; warm bread dripping with honey; strong brown ale. All at once she was hungry.

He watched her eat, smiling, approving.

She brushed crumbs from her rumpled gown and drew up her knees, turning the heavy ale-cup in her hands. "Mirain," she asked after a little, "are you afraid?"

He studied his hands. The one that was like any man's; the one that cast a golden light in his face. "Yes," he answered her, "I am afraid. I'm terrified."

"But will you do it?"

His eyes flashed up. "Do I have a choice?"

"Would it matter if you did?"

He followed the curve of her cheek with his fingertip, lightly but carefully, as if he needed to remember it. "If I fall, my enemy wins my empire; and I mean you to get it back again. Whatever becomes of me, our child will rule. It must." She opened her mouth to speak; he silenced her. "The nameless one is very, very strong. I too have great power, but wizardry, unlike the body's strength, grows with age. And in the duties of kingship, in the forging of my empire, I have had little leisure for the training of my power. She has spent long years under the tutelage of masters, to one sole end: my destruction. I mean to defeat her; but it is very likely that I shall not."

"If you die," she said calmly, "I'll die too."

He caught her hands in a sudden, fierce grip. The ale-cup, empty, flew wide. "You must not! What I said to you before you made me wed you, that if I fell the world was well rid of me—that was folly, and cruelty too. That woman has all darkness behind her. She will take my empire and all my people, only to rend them asunder. You must stand against her. You must do as she did: hide, gather your forces and raise our son, and perfect your power until you are strong enough to cast her down. Promise me, Elian. Swear that you will do it."

Her chin set. "Oh, no, my lord king. You can't take the easy road and leave me to finish what you started. Either you win tomorrow, or your whole dynasty dies with you."

He shook her hard. She laughed in his face. "Yes rage at me. The wilder the better. I warned you that your death was waiting; you rode straight for it. Vadin warned you of the trap; you threw yourself into the heart of it. Now you have to choose. You win and save all you fought for, or you lose it all. There are no half wagers in this game."

His eyes blazed; his teeth bared. "I command you."

"Do you?" She tossed her hair out of her eyes, lightly, almost gaily. "We women are different, you know. Even little fools like me, who try to forget, and play at being boys. Thrones and empires, great matters of state, the wars of men and gods—they don't matter. I'd gladly die for you, and I probably will, if you're so determined to get yourself killed. But I won't fight your battles for you."

"I can fight my own damned battles!"

With a quick deft twist she freed her hands, to take his burning face between them. "In that case," she said, "you had better win this one."

His glare was sun-hot, sun-fierce. She met it steadily. With perfect, suspicious coolness he said, "This is deliberate. You're provoking me, to make me fight harder."

"I am," she agreed. "I'm also telling the truth. Your death is my death. If you want your heir to inherit your empire, you'll have to live to see the birth."

"That is—"

"Murder and suicide, all in one. Or your salvation; and the child's, and mine, and your empire's. Until," she added after a moment, "the next time."

His hand flew up. She braced herself for the blow; with a convulsive movement he struck his own thigh. "Avaryan and Uveryen, woman! Won't you let me get through this one first?"

She smiled. "Get through it," she advised him. "Win it. With luck, your army will come to stand behind you. I've bidden Cuthan to take word to the army. He might elude both men and magery. And I think— I almost think—our enemy doesn't know of Vadin. She knows only what she wishes to know. It's part of her madness. It may save us yet."

Muscle by muscle, with skill he had labored long to learn, Mirain relaxed his body. His eyes smoldered still, but his face was quiet, his voice calm. "It may. I'm gambling on it."

"Good," said Elian. Her hands left his face to travel downward, working into the hollows of his robe, finding its fastenings.

"You," he said roughly, "have the instincts of a harlot."

She laughed, half at his words, half at his garments, which came apart in a most interesting fashion. He snatched at them; she twitched them away. "I used to think I should become one. Shall I think of it again? I'll be a wonder; men will come from the ends of the earth for a glimpse of my face. I'll amass the wealth of empires, and pour it all away. All the world will fall at my feet."

"Not while I rule this half of it."

Her fingers found his most sensitive places and woke the pleasure there, while her eyes danced upon his rigid face. "What will you do? Lock me in your harem? Chain me naked to a pillar? Flog me thrice a day to keep me docile?"

"If you touch any other man—if you even look at him—"

Her hands stilled. Her eyes narrowed. "Will you try to stop me?"

He surged against her, bearing her down. She lay motionless under him, laughing silently, but with a flicker of warning. He disdained to heed it. "You are my wife. By law you are my chattel. I can keep you in any manner I please; I can cast you away. Your very life is mine to take."

"Would you dare?"

His eyes were very dark. Deep within, a spark leaped. "Would you dare to test me?"

"Yes."

He laughed suddenly, glittering-fierce. "I could do worse than that. I could find another woman."

"Don't—you—dare!"

"Someone soft. Sweet. Obedient. Living only to please me. Dark, I think, like me. And her hair—"

"I'll kill her!"

His laughter this time was warm, rich, and direly infectious. She fought it. She struggled; she glared. Her lips twitched, her eyes danced, her mirth burst forth. It swept her up, scattering her garments, twining her body with his.

On the bright edge of passion, he paused. "Would you truly dare?"

She set her lips upon his and pulled him down.

He slept as a child sleeps, deeply and peacefully, all the knots of care and kingship smoothed away. That was part of his legend: that he never lay tossing before a batlle. Often he had to be awakened lest he be late to the field.

Gently Elian loosed his braid, combing it with careful fingers, smoothing the heavy mass of it upon the coverlet. She never had given him his answer.

As if he needed it. Born wanton she might be, but as a harlot she had this fatal flaw: all her desire turned upon one man. It had been so since she was too young even to know what desire was.

A small smile touched her mouth. Now that she was an ancient crone, she was lost completely. Such a man to be lost for: an utter lunatic who fancied himself the son of a god. His golden hand lay between her breasts, half curled about one, burning even as he slept: a pain he had never known the lack of. He insisted that she eased it. Maybe; maybe he needed to think so.

Those two, the pain and its lessening in her presence, helped to set a limit on his pride. He could not exult inordinately in his lineage when it tormented him lifelong with a living fire. Nor could he wield his power in a tyrant's peace, not with a sun blazing in his sensitive palm. Sword or scepter he could grip, but only if he wielded them with care. And for what easing the god would grant, he must rely upon a snippet of a child-woman, a maddening tangle of love and resistance and red-headed temper.

Except that the love seemed to have swallowed the resistance. The temper, unfortunately, showed no signs of abating. She could still wish that she had never heard of Mirain An-Sh'Endor, while her heart threatened to burst and her body to melt with love of him.

She traced the whorl of his ear, pausing where it was pierced for a ring, an infinitesimal interruption in the curve of it. He murmured something and smiled, and tried to burrow into her side. She buried her face in his thick curling hair. *Avaryan,* she said in her mind, shaping each word in red-golden fire, *if truly you came to this man's mother, if you played any part at all in his begetting, listen to me. He needs you now, and he needs you tommorow. Stand with him. Make him strong. Help me to make him live.*

There was no answer. No voice; no sudden light. And yet, having prayed, she felt the better for it. Perhaps even, after all, she might sleep; and no dreams would beset her.

After all her wakefulness, it was Elian who woke late in a great tangle of bedclothes. She struggled out of them to find herself alone, the chamber empty. For a moment her heart stopped. No. Oh, no. He could not have.

Voices brought her to her feet. Snatching what was nearest—Mirain's riding cloak, voluminous and almost dry—she opened the door.

They were all in the guardroom, all but Cuthan who was gone, all fully clad, most looking as if they had not slept. A grey pallor sat on their faces; their eyes were sunken, their mouths set tight. Elian did not need to ask. The army had not come. They must face this alone. Win alone, or die alone.

The king stood among them. He had bathed; he was fresh-shaven; he wore a kilt and nothing else, and his hair, drying, seemed thicker and more unruly than ever. As a guardswoman struggled with its tangles, he directed one of his own men in the unrolling of an oblong bundle. Deftly Elian took Igani's place. The bundle, she saw, was a length of leather as pale as fine ivory, tanned to the softness of silk. In the center of it someone had cut a hole.

Her hands faltered. "So," she said as steadily as she could, "you'll do it the old way."

His thought caressed her although his body held still. "The oldest way of all. The shield-circle; the ordered combat."

The first order of which was that the combatants bear about them no binding. No knot or fastening, no seam, no woven garment, only the long tunic of leather, unbelted and unsewn, its sides open to the wind. Thus there could be no aids to enchantment hidden in one's clothing, no spells braided into one's hair. The victory must come through the purity of power.

Elian laughed shakily. "If that's so, my love, you'd better crop your head as close as a desert rover's, or you'll be called down for all your tangles."

"I'll chance it," he said, light and unconcerned. " 'Varyan! I'm hungry. I've been wallowing in luxury too long; I've lost the knack of fasting."

"Think about all you'll feast on when it's over." Igani lifted the long strange garment. Mirain shed his kilt, pausing a moment, drawing a deep breath. She slipped the length of leather over his head.

It settled smoothly, its paleness catching the dark sheen of his skin, its weight falling straight before and behind. For a moment Elian could not breathe. He was going to fight. He was going to die.

She remembered her mother's words, the voice low and sweet in her mind. *A prophecy can be its own fulfillment.* It need not be. It must not be.

They were too somber, all of them; subdued, afraid. Even Mirain. Someone had brought the torque of his priesthood from beside his bed; he held it for a stretching moment, grey-knuckled, eyes too wide and too fixed.

She snatched it from him, and grinned her whitest, fiercest grin. "Yes, Sunborn, put it on. Show them who your master is."

"I am not—" He shut his mouth with a snap. "Put it on me, then."

Slowly she did as he bade. It was pure gold, soft and leaden heavy. Yet he wore it always, putting it off only to sleep, and sometimes not even then; had worn it so since he was a very young man. Even more than Asanion's golden mask or the coronet of a prince in the Hundred Realms, it marked his kingship. The splendor, and the crushing burden. *And my service to the god.* He kissed her hands. *Every priest of Avaryan bears this same burden. No lighter and no heavier.*

"Except that they are plain servants of Avaryan, and you are the king."

"Is there a difference?"

She looked at him. He was smiling very faintly. Strong again, sure again, whatever terrors stirred in the hidden heart of him. "You make me strong," he said softly.

They were nearly of a height. They could stand eye to eye with a palm's width between them, bend forward in the same instant, touch.

She clung with sudden desperate strength, yet no stronger than he, as if he could crush her body into his own, make it a part of him. They said nothing with mind or voice. There was too much to say, and too little.

Elian drew back. Conscious of herself again; aware with a rush of heat that she had lost her covering. No one stared; no one ventured it. With what dignity she could muster, she gathered up the fallen cloak and retreated to the bath.

It was the Lord of Garin who came for the king. And only the king. Elian, scoured clean, dressed again in coat and trousers and boots, was briefly speechless.

The Wolf spoke to Mirain quietly, reasonably. "You are to come alone, sire. I swear on my honor that there shall be no treachery."

Elian's voice broke free, lashing him. "That is not the law! Each combatant is allowed one witness."

He looked her up and down without haste and without judgment. "So it shall be. I am to attend him."

"You!"

Mirain stepped between them. "The law also allows a choice of witnesses. I choose the Lady Elian. And," he added. "the Lord Garin."

The lord pause. Clearly he had not been so instructed. But he smiled and bowed. "As your majesty wishes. Will it please you to follow me?"

Mirain walked lightly beside the Lord of Garin. If it wrenched at him to leave his escort behind, he did not show it. They watched him go with eyes like wounds, open and bleeding. Elian tried to meet them, to heal them a little, to smile and breathe forth confidence. She doubted that they even saw her.

* * *

In the dark before dawn the castle was very still, grimmer and greyer than ever, and bone-cold. Elian shivered in all her riding gear. Mirain, barefoot and nearly naked, might have been swathed in furs. But he was never cold; he had the Sun's fire in his veins.

Lord Garin led them through a maze of passages. Down out of the tower, through the keep, up and round by twisting torchlit ways. Even where the torches failed, he did not falter. Perhaps, like the Halenani or like the wolf of his name, he could see in the dark.

Mirain's hand found Elian's. His grasp was light, fire-warm, and perfectly steady. She could feel the strength in it, quiescent now, awaiting its time.

The passage narrowed and spiraled upward. Elian fell behind Mirain, but his hand kept its grip. Even for her eyes the way was dark, Mirain's tunic a pale blur ahead. The air was cold in her face like the touch of the dead, and dank, heavy with age and darkness.

Mirain stopped so abruptly that she collided with him. Metal grated harshly upon stone. Hinges protested. A gate swung open with rusted slowness.

Dawn was still unbroken, the night at its deepest. Yet Elian blinked, half blinded. All the clouds of storm had blown away. Silver Brightmoon, just past the full, hung low in the west. The great half-orb of Greatmoon rode high above, trailing pallid fire; about it flamed the stars in all their myriads.

Old tales gave Greatmoon to the powers of the dark and Brightmoon to those of the light, calling the huge blue-pale moon the Throne of Uveryen, its god her lover; and singing of the love of the silver goddess for her lord the sun. Some people of late had begun a new naming, and called the brighter moon Sanelin, and set the priestess there, sharing the heavens with the father of her son.

Elian dragged her eyes and her mind from the vault of the sky. There was myth. Here was living legend.

She stood on sere grass in a deep bowl rimmed by mountain walls. In its center glimmered a lake, a pool of ice under Greatmoon, and in the lake a dark curve of islet, a tall shape of shadow: a standing stone.

Lord Garin led them round the lake. Its water lapped upon the shore, infinitely lonely, infinitely sad. Shadow rose upon the far side. As Elian drew closer it grew clearer, taking shape in the moonlight. A building, it had been once; ruined now, no more than a ring of roofless pillars, some tall and straight, some half-fallen like broken teeth. Framed within them lay a pavement of stone.

There waited the Exile. To the eye she was a darkness on darkness, one of three cloaked and hooded shapes. To the power she stood forth in utter and terrible clarity.

As Mirain set his foot upon the level stones, his power stirred and woke. A shimmer of pale light ran upward from sole to crown, and outward through the broken pavement. Elian's gasp was loud in the silence. The stone seemed not stone at all, but sky in the waking dawn, silver flushing to rose and palest gold.

Before the light reached the Exile, it stopped, sharp and clean as if cleft with a knife. That beyond seemed darker still for the brightness so close, a darkness as limitless as the void between stars.

Mirain smiled in the strange light. "Dawnstone," he said with a touch of wonder, a touch of delight. "My keep in Ianon is made of it. And this—would it perhaps be nightstone, that holds the night as dawnstone keeps the glow of morning? I have heard of it in old tales, but I have never seen it."

"It is nightstone," the Exile answered him. "And this is a place older than legend, fane of a people whose works are all vanished from the earth: older than Han-Ianon, older than the Cavern of the God, older even than gods, though not those we serve. Can you perceive the power in these stones?"

It throbbed in Elian's brain, immense, slumbering, yet stirring uneasily in the presence of these small intruders.

"A place of power," said Mirain. "I have never come upon one so mighty."

"Nor shall you or any man, unless you come to the Heart of the World where lie the chains that bind the gods. There are no chains here. Only power. It will not aid us in our battle; it will seek to hinder, and even to destroy, if in disturbing it one of us lacks the strength to soothe it. Do you think still to challenge me, priestess' child?"

"How not?" He advanced a step. "Shall we begin?"

Twenty-six

MIRAIN SPOKE FREELY, EVEN EAGERLY, WELCOMING whatever must come. His enemy stood tall and let fall her cloak. Beneath it she was clad as was he, white hair falling long and free over the shoulders of a tunic as dark as his was pale. Her familiar was gone: fled, hidden, subsumed into her power. For she was strong. She had never pretended to weakness, but her strength now was greater than ever Elian remembered, filling her, mantling her in a shimmer of mingled darkness and light.

The witnesses faded back, retreating from the pillared circle. Well before the shadows took them, Elian had forgotten their existence. She too retreated, but only to the joining of earth and stone. There lay the remnant of a column half-buried in earth and grass and the dead brittleness of a vine. She sank down upon it, her toes almost touching the edge of the dawnstone. Its gleam caught at her eyes; its power sparked her own. In its pale depths she saw the circle shrunken to the breadth of her hand, and two figures upon it, one erect and triumphant, the other fallen utterly. But the image shifted, blurred; now white hair spread across the stone, now raven-dark.

She tore her eyes away. The greater circle opened wide before her, dawn and deepest night. Over it the moons wheeled. Brightmoon sank beneath the mountain wall; Greatmoon thinned and paled. The sky's darkness greyed. Avaryan was coming.

Power gathered. The air hummed and sang. Mage in white, mage in black, both spread their arms. Mirain's voice rang upon the first note of binding. The nameless one took up the second, a high eerie keening. The two notes quivered, distinct and dissonant; eased; softened, drawing together, meeting, merging into a terrible harmony.

At once and as one they broke off. Slowly Mirain's hands met, palm to palm. The Exile's mirrored them. As her palms touched, the circle blazed up, white light and black fire, and dimmed again. But a shimmer lingered, a wall of power, and within it nothingness. Not until one of them fell might that wall fall; nor could any open it, man or mage, god or demon. They were alone, utterly.

Elian reeled upon her cold perch. She was alone, sundered, torn.

She had eyes. And power, though forbidden to pass the barrier, could see all within.

At first there was little to see. They stood motionless, facing one another. Although nothing with mind or power could pierce the wall, a thin wind slipped through the emptiness. It stirred their long tunics; it made witchlocks of the Exile's hair; it blew Mirain's mane into his face. He shook back the heavy mass, to little effect; shrugged; let it be.

The Exile raised her hands. A tendril of darkness uncoiled, reaching, groping for the light.

Sparks leaped. The darkness whipped back.

Mirain stood unmoved. His face was lost in the tangles of his hair. The wind, strengthening, danced about him. Playful fingers caught his tunic, tossing it away from his body, whipping it round and round, binding, tightening.

His swift hands caught and gathered the wildness of his mane, twisted it back from his calm face, knotted it behind him.

The wind fled. His tunic fell loosely to his feet. The knot, which should never have held, kept its place unaltered.

Elian's stiff lips bent in the beginnings of a smile. The first round, it seemed, had gone to Mirain.

He was in no haste to press his advantage. He forsook his rigid stillness, wandering a little in his half of the circle, setting down his feet with feline delicacy. Round, sidewise, back, step and step and step, with a cat's precision, a dancer's grace.

And with each step a glimmer of light grew in the nightstone, a tangled skein of pale fire circling the Exile's feet, weaving among them, drawing together, closing.

Her clawed fingers swept down, rending the web.

He laughed and whirled like a devil-dancer, lithe dark body in a circle of pale leather. The web, torn, spun up the Exile's lank form, knee-high, hip-high, breast-high.

She tossed her head. He spun faster, faster, faster. The web shredded and tattered. A blur of black hummed within a blur of white.

With a vicious, whip-sharp crack, he stopped. His eyes flamed. His hair was free again, witch-wild, his garment a tatter. His breath came hard. And yet he smiled.

The web had melted into the night. His enemy inclined her head very slightly. "You have the beginnings of art," she conceded. "Will you play further? Or shall we do battle at last?"

Mirain fought with light and fire and with his supple voice. The nameless one opposed him with darkness visible, in a wall of living silence. Against his spear of levin-fire she raised a shield of night; against his weaving of subtle melody, a stillness that swallowed all sound. The rising dawn illumined his half of the circle, but in the other, deep night reigned.

At first Elian did not credit her eyes. Mirain's half of the circle was smaller. No—he had moved; her eyes were weary; the growing daylight deceived her, dulling the shimmer of the dawnstone.

He stood as he had stood since the battle began in earnest, and the line of darkness crept toward him. His body swayed; his voice sang three lines of an ancient cantrip. The advance halted.

Elian's hands knotted; her breath caught. The darkness in the circle was a handspan less. But Mirain's face glistened damply; his eyes were squeezed shut, his body rigid. All his strength bent upon the holding of that line.

Slowly, inexorably, the darkness advanced. He trembled visibly with the effort of resistance. His enemy was as still as a standing stone, utterly without expression save for the thin grey line of her lips.

The mark of her power approached his feet. Step by step he retreated. Step by step the dawnstone dulled and blackened. And the line began to bend. Before and beside him, to the full stretch of his arms, the light lingered. But night held the rest. His back touched a pillar. Beyond it he could not go; the shield walled him in. All about him, save only where he stood, was darkness. Slowly he sank to one knee, bowed as if beneath a mighty burden. The light beneath him had lost all its brilliance, flickering greyly, pallid as winter fog.

His enemy came toward him without haste and stood over him, blind eyes bent upon him. She had him, and she knew it. His breath rattled in his throat. Her hand rose, swept sidewise, cast him helpless to the ground.

And she turned her back on him. She faced outward. The circle wavered, stretching. About Elian's feet wove a small furred cat-creature, singing a yowling song. The Exile's power yearned toward it. Elian snatched it up. It came as if it were pleased to come, warm and solid, supple. It nestled in the hollow of her shoulder. And she, tensed to leap back, to cast up her shields, to sunder witch and familiar, could move no muscle of her body. Her scarred cheek throbbed. The beast ended its song and began to purr.

"Yes," said the Exile. "She knows you, my swift one, my dancer in the grasses. We are kin; we are sisters in power."

A shudder racked Elian: deep, pulsing, black-red denial. With terror in it. Because she set all her will to refuse the truth.

The Exile gestured behind her, not in scorn, not without respect. "He was strong, as befit his heritage. But he had not the strength which I have. He will have no part of the dark; he who is born of the burning noon, denies the night with all that is in him. Look now. See. Know what he would make of the world."

Sunlight. Green places. Water falling, and white cities rising, and fields rich with the harvest.

Sunlight. No night. No relief of the cool dark, no light of stars. Green withered, blackened, burned. Water shrank into dust. White walls cast back the light in the blinding splendor, in carrion stench. White bone lay bare beneath fire-ravaged flesh; the land itself was stripped, seared, destryed by the merciless light.

And armies rode through the shattered country. As they rode, they sang a hymn to the Sun; and cursed the dark; and saw only beauty in all that desolation. Faintly within it, something moved: a human figure, gaunt, scorched, staggering with hands held out in supplication. The army fell upon it. It shrieked once, suddenly cut off. The army passed. The dust was dark, dampened with blood; but in a moment the sun had drunk the last of its wetness.

"No," said Elian. A shaft of agony pierced her center. She clutched it, doubling. *"No."*

"Indeed," said the Exile, "no. He has seen the light and the white city. He has not seen its price."

"Not our child. *Not—*"

"Your child?" The woman was astonished. "We do not take the lives of the unborn. That is for the gods alone; or for men who fancy themselves better than gods. Your king's price is for the world's paying. The price of fire, and of the balance's breaking."

The pain was passing, draggingly slow. Elian drew herself up. The familiar had not even shifted its grip. It had solidity but no weight; strength, but very little bulk to house it. She could not force her hands to tear it away. They flattened over her belly. "You will not have our child. I will die before I surrender him."

"Or her," said the Exile. "Or can you not endure the prospect of a daughter?"

"I can endure either, if only it lives to be born."

"Can you?" The woman approached the circle's edge. "You may gather your power to stand against me. You are strong enough; you can will yourself to be blind enough. Or you may stand with me. You bear in your womb both weapon and healing: seal of the balance, seal of the Sun's dominion. What your brother and lover has been, this seed of his shall be a thousandfold."

Elian reeled. Needle-claws brought her snapping erect. The cat mewed softly. Warning. Imparting strength.

It was evil. *Evil*

It was a cat. Small, swift, quick-tempered, centered on itself. Yet when it chose, as it chose, it could bestow its affection. It did not regret its marring of her face; it did not begrudge her battering of its body. It was power, and its purpose was simply to be.

"And," said her kinswoman, "to bolster waning power, of body or of mind."

Elian's eyes squeezed shut against the vision. It blazed within, unconquerable. Traps within traps within traps. Danger and daring and a spice of treachery, to lure Mirain. Mirain, to lure his lifelong shadow. Mirain was to die. She was to suffer it, or to accomplish it. To be seduced. To give her soul to neither light nor dark, but to this thing called balance, that was no god she had ever known.

Mirain was the greater mage, perhaps. She was the greater power. Because of what she was, mage's daughter, royal seed, child of night and fire; and woman, and bearer of a child. This child. Sunborn, mageborn, ruler of the world.

If it lived. Her eyes opened, blinded with vision; met blind eyes which could see beyond sight. The Exile loved her, because she was blood kin; hated her, envied her, but loved her. And would take her life without the slightest qualm, if she chose awry.

"There is no choice," gritted Elian. "There is only the light and the dark. I was born in the light. I cannot embrace its enemy."

The Exile's hand shaped potent denial: a sign in the air, red-gold, gleaming in the waxing morning. "They are not enemies. They are one. Stand with me, sister. Defend them against their sundering."

She pleaded: she, who was as proud as Elian had ever been. She begged. She all but wept for the world that would lie beneath the hammer of the Sun. The wars, the souls cast down into death, the blood poured out in rivers in Avaryan's name. And in Mirain's.

Elian's heart clenched with love of him. And yet . . . and yet . . .

Follow your heart, they all bade her. *Listen to your power. They know. They see what cannot but be.*

Almost she laughed. She had writhed in agony over a pair of lovers, each perfect of his kind. She had not known what agony was.

The cat settled in her arms. She rubbed it soft ears. It purred. It lay against the spark of her child. Defending. Strengthening.

All her understandings swayed and unbalanced and fell. Good, evil. Dark, light. Friend, enemy. Hate, love, peace, wrath—all one, all mingled all lost in a mad tangle of changes. She could not endure it. She would lose her poor wits; she would die. She could—not—

The Exile raised her hand. Offering. Beckoning. Elian's hand moved of its own will. The cat sang its joy.

White fire reared up above the shadow that was the Exile, and swooped down. The world shattered in an explosion of light.

It was very quiet.

Elian swayed in emptiness. She was still afoot; she could not understand why. Nor, for a long while, could she understand why she should not be. The cat was gone. Perhaps she had dreamed the whole of it.

Abruptly and violently her stomach overturned itself. She crouched, gasping and retching; and some of it was hysteria, laughter well past the border of madness, for long shafts of sunlight dazzled her streaming eyes. Morning sun. Avaryan had found his way at last into the mountain's crown.

Sick, half blind, she crawled in a ragged circle. Her hand jarred against an obstacle. A hand, long and bone-thin; an arm; the charred ruin of a face. The eyes had escaped, blind now within as without, opened wide upon nothingness. There was no horror in them, and no surprise at all. Only peace, and something very like triumph.

Elian's breath caught. This was the shape of her vision: white hair spread upon pale stone.

And black beside it. Mirain lay where the last great surge of his power had cast him, limbs asprawl, golden hand flung up beside his face. His eyes were closed, seemly; no mark of burning stained him.

His tunic had fallen awry. Carefully she smoothed it, covering his nakedness. Her hand shrank a little; briefly, from touching him: as if he could loose his fire upon her. Sun's fire.

He had made her choice for her. Or she had, as she always did, in tarrying until it made itself.

She looked at him. She saw a man whom she loved, whom she would gladly die for. She saw . . .

Her mind's eye closed. Her choice was made. She would not seek to unmake it. His truth, the Exile's truth—here and now, it made no difference. All that mattered was Mirain.

"Sweet merciful gods."

Elian looked up. She had heard nothing, seen nothing. Yet it surprised her not at all to hear her brother's voice, to see him there with the Lord Vadin beside him, armored and helmeted and bearing each a sword. The blades, she noticed, had seen use.

Men thronged at their backs. She saw Lord Garin between two grim women of her own Guard, and Prince Omian grey-faced and staggering, and a flocking of men of both Ianon and the Hundred Realms. Cuthan stood in front of them all with his smooth braids fallen in a tangle, and blood on his cheek, and a red blade dripping on the grass.

Elian rose slowly. "You took your time," she said. And cursed her tongue. He stared at her, mute, his eyes dark with misery. She tried to comfort him, but no words would come. She could only touch him. His arm was rigid, but he did not pull away. He had stopped seeing her.

Halenan had sunk to his knees beside Mirain. Somewhere in the ranks, someone cried aloud. Ashan's heir shouted and struggled and suddenly broke free. A dozen swords flashed up. Blood sprayed wide.

Elian turned. She faced Lord Garin. Steel glittered a hair's breadth from his throat, but no closer. "Where is your prince?" she asked him.

The Wolf's eye was steady and fearless and very much amused. "Dead," he answered her, "majesty. It seemed fair enough, upon consideration. A life for a royal life."

She tilted her head, studying him. "Why?"

"Because, your majesty, I am a loyal man."

"Loyal to nothing but his treachery!" Cuthan's voice was raw with hate. "Through him was our king betrayed. Through him was our king destroyed. On his head be it. Murder. Murder of the Sunborn."

A deep snarl ran through the ranks, a snarl that turned to a howl.

Elian ignored it, meeting the despair in Cuthan's eyes. "But," she said, "Mirain is not dead."

Hope made him beautiful again. He looked so young, so easily moved, like a child. Even in her numbness she found the ghost of a smile for him. He turned, stumbling, blinded with tears, but his voice was as splendid as ever it had been. Soft at first, full of wondering joy. "Did you hear?" Louder then, clear and free and glad, ringing in the morning. "Men of the Sun, did you hear? The king is not dead. He lives. An-Sh'Endor lives!"

Twenty-seven

MIRAIN LIVED. HE BREATHED; HE SEEMED TO SLEEP. But he did not wake.

Elian sat by the great bed in the chamber of Garin the elder. People came and went. They tried to be quiet, a sickroom stillness, muting the thud of booted feet, lowering battle-roughened voices. It mattered little to her and less to Mirain whether they whispered or shouted. There were wounded to settle, prisoners to guard, watches to set; and it kept coming back to her. She was the queen. It was her place to rule.

Sometimes her brother sat with her. More often it was Vadin. He was not like the rest; he was quiet, he did not intrude. She could forget that he was there.

Halenan could not efface himself so perfectly. He was restless, like fire. He persisted in chattering. "I have his lordship under guard," he said. He had been drinking ale, from the scent that came in with him; he lowered himself to the floor at her feet. It was not all weariness. He had taken a slight wound in the side, and it had begun to stiffen.

She touched it with hand and healing; he sighed. "Ah, that's better." He swallowed a yawn. "Lord Garin is under guard, but free to go where he likes. The guard is mostly for his sake; the men don't love him. Not in the least."

"Mirain rather likes him." She laid her hand on the still brow. With the women of her Guard, she had bathed and tended him and combed out his many tangles. His braid lay tamed upon his shoulder.

Halenan leaned back against her knee and yawned outright. "I feel as if I haven't slept for a Greatmoon-cycle, what with settling the men in that infernal cave and fretting over you in this infernal castle, and all that's come after. You vanished from power's sight, you know. One moment I looked and you were there, passing Garin's gate. The next, you were gone. I went a little wild. More than a little." Vadin looked at him, brows up. He grimaced. "Very much more than a little. Yonder savage had to knock me down and sit on me, or I'd have sent the whole troop against Garin, then and there. 'Wait,' he said, as if he weren't twitching himself, and starting at shadows. 'Give it time.' I had to: he wouldn't let me up, else.

"We waited till sundown. Just barely. Then we divided our forces. Half we left to guard the cave and Lord Casien's company, and to face any force that might come through the valley. They put on a brave show of numbers, with fires and tents and a wall of tethered seneldi. The rest of us went under the mountain.

"We paused in a cavern only a little smaller than the outer hall, with a deep pool in it. Vadin's people had penned their seneldi there, under guard. We gathered all but a few of the sentries and went on.

"We went carefully, and slowly enough to madden me. But for all of that, we kept going astray, ending in a blind passage or a sudden chasm; or hearing the clatter of armed men, and scrambling for hiding places, and hearing the noises fade away among the tunnels.

"An eon after we began, we saw a light. The rest ran for cover yet again, but I'd had my fill of prudence. I flattened myself into a fold of the wall and tried not to breathe. The light came toward us. It was moving fast, and it was quiet; I could just hear footsteps, booted but running very light. When it passed me, I pounced." He rubbed his side. "I got this for my pains. He was a big lad, that one, and vicious as a cornered ul-cat. We rolled on the floor, snapping and snarling and doing our utmost to throttle one another.

"Until Vadin swooped over us and thrust a torch in our faces. We kept up the fight for a bit, for the fighting's sake, but in the end we stopped and burst out laughing. It was that or howl. I'd been getting the worst of it; Cuthan picked me up and dusted me off and was most apologetic.

" 'Never mind that,' said Vadin. 'What news from Garin?'

"Cuthan sobered all at once. It was bad, I'd known it already; I hadn't known how bad. He'd been lost as we were, and he'd had a guide, a rat of Garin's whom he'd caught and tamed at sword's point. They'd managed to pass the first windings of the maze, which were full of armed men: we'd been hearing them as they mustered, through a trick of the tunnels. We were fortunate they hadn't heard us; or maybe they'd taken us for more of their own.

"Cuthan's rat was killed in a pitfall that nearly took Cuthan with it; he went on by instinct and what power he had. It was enough to take him to us. It just barely sufficed to lead us all on the right path, armies be damned.

"That was a wild march," said Halenan. "The way was steep in places, and it was infernally dark. I prayed to every god I knew, and to Avaryan over them all, that the sorceress wasn't looking for a blaze of power under the earth; because Vadin and I had left off trusting our mortal senses. It was a labyrinth we were racing through, with no way out but the castle, and no time to spare, and precious little light; and enemies all around us." He shuddered. "Avaryan grant I never see such a devil's lair again!

"We met the first of the enemy somewhat closer to the castle than to the cave. They weren't looking for us. We took them by surprise, but they were no fools. No tyros, either. If Lord Garin hasn't tried a little reiving in his father's line, then he has a liking for drilling his troops in mazes.

"He certainly keeps his loot there—and the loot of the past dozen generations with it. If we can haul even half of it out of here, every man of us will be as rich as a lord."

"You always were greedy," said Elian.

He snarled in mock warning; she ruffled his hair and tried to smile.

"Ah well," he said, smiling back, "we weren't paying much attention to the treasure trove while we were in it. We were too busy trying to get out. I was desperate; I could feel morning coming, and I knew when the duel began. I think I lost what little wits I had left. I know Vadin did. We left most of the company to mop up behind us and flamed our way through, clear to the castle.

"Your guards were ready and willing and at least as wild as we were. We had hell's own time to find the way up to the mountain, and a castleful of people in our way, but they weren't quarreling with power. Much.

"We found the door and the tunnel, and we found the open air. And there you were at battle's end. I thought"—he faltered, which was utterly unlike him—"I thought Mirain was dead."

"He . . . almost . . . was."

Halenan caught her hands. "Lia. Little sister. It's over now."

She looked at him. She was very calm; it was he who was shaking. "It's not, really," she said.

His head tossed from side to side. His grip was painfully tight. "It's only exhaustion, and power stretched as far as it will go. He'll sleep the sun around and wake up ravenous and growling, like a cave bear in the spring."

"He'll sleep." Her glance strayed to the bed. "I caused it, you know. The end. She almost had him, but she let him go too soon. She broke the law and the shield and all honor, and turned to me, and tried to make me fight with her. Maybe her mind was breaking. Maybe she thought Mirain was too weak to trouble with; or too strong to stand against alone. Maybe—maybe she knew what she was doing. To him, to me, and to herself. He had power left; she could not but have known it. Enough to wake what slept in the stone, and to aim it when it woke. It carried him with it. It drained him dry, and dropped him when it was done." She freed her hands from her brother's, to take Mirain's slack one. "If he wakes—if he even wants to wake—he'll have nothing left. No power, and very little consciousness. You know how it is when the body uses itself up . . . it dies. Or its life is only a shadow of what it was before."

"No," said Halenan.

"She said he was a danger," Elian said. "To all the world. She showed me what he would do to it. She wanted me to stop him. Because I could. And maybe I did. By listening. By coming so close to betraying him."

She caught Mirain's hand, anchoring herself to it. It was warm, but no strength lingered in it. His life flickered low and slow.

Halenan lurched to his feet, all long limbs and coppery hair, awkward as he had not been since he was a boy. But it was a man who flung down his sheathed sword and swore in a soft deadly voice, the most terrible oaths he knew.

His grief woke something in her. Something she had striven to suppress. Awareness; understanding. Feeling.

She could not feel. She dared not. She had to be strong; to smile; to be queen. They needed her, all these men, these few women, this empire. And this stranger within her, who drifted quiescent, invisible, all but imperceptible, yet mighty in what it would become.

Oh, clever, Mirain, even at the end of all he was. He sat on death's threshold but advanced no farther, nor retreated, binding her to her own flesh, to the child he had begotten and the empire he had won.

Rage she could allow; could welcome. She regarded the still and lifeless face, the lips curved in the shadow of a smile. He thought he had won. He thought he could trick her, bind her, leave her to bear all his burdens.

Better the harem. There at least the chains were visible, the guards solid before the bolted gates.

Her brother was gone, fled. Poor Hal. He loved Mirain almost as much as she. But he could go and weep, and hammer down a wall or two, and whip the castle into order. He was not saddled with an empire and its heir.

She looked up. Eyes rested upon her, dark as Mirain's, deep and quiet. They did not condescend to judge her.

She spoke with great care. "Only once," she said, "has Mirain ever argued me down. That was when he ran after his fate into Ianon, and I knew well enough that mine was in Han-Gilen. He doesn't even have that defense now."

Vadin sat back in his chair. It was a little small for him; he looked extraordinarily long and lean and angular. He was thinner than she remembered; he seemed older. Amid the copper braided into his beard, she glimpsed a thread of silver. He could not have had an easy time of it, abandoning his lordship and his lady and his people on a moment's notice, in the jaws of winter, at the command of a haughty girlchild; with Mirain's death to face if he failed, or even if he did not.

He mustered a smile, although it fled swiftly. "You've looked after Mirain rather thoroughly, haven't you? I didn't say you had to marry him."

"If you had, I wouldn't have done it."

He actually laughed. But again, not for long. Mirain weighted them both like a stone, breathing just visibly, alive and no more.

Elian spoke to him, not caring that Vadin heard. "Ziad-Ilarios loves me still. He'll be emperor in his time, and he'll wed as his duty commands. He'll grow and he'll change, and the change will be bitter, a chilling and a darkening. All his gold will turn to grey.

"But I can go to him. I can tell him I love him. He will believe me, because he longs to, and it will be true. And he won't grow old in bitterness. I won't let him. I can do that, Mirain. I can even make him accept your child, for my sake. Your empire won't last, but I'll see to it that your seed rules in Asanion. And I'll have a man, not a corpse, to share my bed."

No consciousness stirred behind the mask of his face; no power glimmered about it.

"Your empire is dead already. Father will try to keep it alive; Vadin will want to, and Hal. I could, maybe, if I would. Except that I'll be in Asanion and not wanting any rivals. It's rather a pity. There was so much we were going to do. Your city, that would be the most beautiful in the world. Your throne in it, and your tower atop Endros, built with songs and with power. Your priesthood—now you'll never be browbeaten into taking the high seat, and priestesses will go on in their useless fidelity to the god, and the order will fade and crumble, all its promises and all its prophecies come to nothing. I'll never have my company, not only my Guard but a whole fighting force of women, the Queen's Own, that was going to set a few more of us free. You'll never break the slave trade out of Asanion; we'll never climb Mount Avaryan or look on the sea. The Exile will have won after all. We'll never prove that her vision of fire and death was a lie. All because you're too cowardly feeble to face the world again."

Her eyes bled tears. She dashed them away, but they would not stop for that. "Damn you! If you don't come to, I'll kill myself!"

He was far beyond either hearing or heeding.

She seized him, shaking him. His head rolled slackly. His eyelids never flickered. She sobbed, half in fury, half in burning, tearing grief, clutching him, rocking him, blind and mad.

The blindness passed, eternally slow. The madness hovered. Her eyes ached and burned; her throat was raw. She was cold, as cold as death.

Her mind was very clear, her power bright and keen and deadly. To its eyes she was a dark glass full of lightnings, and in its center a pearl of white fire. Mirain was glass only. Empty. Life without mind, without thought, without will. The grass of the winter field shone more brightly than he.

She made a shield of will, glass round burning glass. Stretched it, rounded it, enfolding the emptied other. He who had blazed like a sun in the world of living light—

No grieving. Grieving weakened the shield. She firmed her will, pure guard, pure strength. Joy woke all unlooked for, a pure cold delight. She was young, she was but half trained, but she was strong. Time would make her stronger still, great mage and great queen, equal even to the Sunborn.

Time closed in about her, weighted with death. Her body laid itself down beside the shell of Mirain. Her power slipped free, bright fish in the sea of light. There below swirled the maelstrom, great whirling emptiness, spinning down and down and down. She hovered above it, holding herself still with her power. Pausing, gathering.

Another came to hover beside her, brightness flecked with coppery dark. She arched her supple body; she bared her myriad teeth. This storm was hers to ride. *Hers.* How dared he trespass?

He darted; he twined himself about her. He gripped her fast, and he had hands, a face, a human voice speaking in her human ears. "I go with you. You need me."

She struggled, but he had mastered this seeming; he was himself, great tall Ianyn warlord, mage of Mirain's making, oathbrother, soulbound. She seared him with hate. He shook it off. He smiled, damn him to all the hells. "You need me," he said again. "I need you. Mirain needs us both."

"He needs none but me!" She tore free. She wrought her fish-shape; she poised once more and leaped.

Dark. Dark without sound, without scent, without touch. Void without end, death without life, no light, no air, no strength. Only memory, scattering in a soundless scream.

Remember. *Remember.*

Elian, Orsan's daughter of Eleni's bearing, Mirain's bride: Elian ilOrsan Kileni li'Mirain. Elian who was herself and of herself, free and apart, her own. Longlimb, firehair, fire-tempered and all contrary. Elian.

She stood alone in a dim corridor. It was very plain, floor, walls, ceiling: black stone without sheen, smoothed but unpolished. She wore a long tunic like that which Mirain had worn in the shield-circle, dyed deep green. Her hair poured free and heavy to her knees, a flood of molten copper.

She ventured forward. The passage sloped gently downward. Sometimes it curved; sometimes a door opened upon shadow. She did not turn aside, could not. Some force of will, whether her own or another's, drew her onward.

A wall rose before her, a door in it, opening to her touch. The light beyond was somewhat less dim, like twilight on a day of rain. Before her spread a wide rolling country under a lowering sky. In sunlight it might have been very fair: field and wood, hill and green valley, rising into a wall of mountains. So must Ianon be, where first Mirain was king.

Her body shifted and changed. She spread wide green wings. A sudden wind caught and lifted them; she arrowed upward, pouring forth a liquid stream of song.

The grey land fled beneath her. She outflew the wind; she outflew her own song. The mountains loomed like the world's wall. Singing, she hurtled upon them. Clapped wings to her sides. Soared over them, the bleak stony peaks all but clipping the feathers of her fiery breast.

She swooped down on an endless slide of air into a green bowl lit with dawn: a lake and an islet, a ruined hall, a pavement half of dawn and half of night.

Bare human feet touched the grass. The green tunic settled upon them. In the circle lay a lone figure, black hair spreading upon pale stone.

Slowly she approached him. As she set her foot upon the pavement, it blazed up with heatless fire. Out of it swelled a shape. A woman all of night in a robe woven of dawn, barring the way.

Elian stood still. The woman was beautiful, yet it was not a human beauty. It was too high and too cold and too terrible. The voice was as cold as wind upon ice, as bloodless-pure as the notes of a harp. "If you have wisdom, come no closer."

Elian knew neither wisdom nor fear. She essayed a step. The woman did not move, but said "You seek what is mine. He woke me; he wielded me. Now he pays. All that was his, I have taken. All that was power, I have made my own."

"But," said Elian, "he woke you for my sake. Only give him back, all as he was, and you may have me in his stead."

"I do not bargain," said the woman of night.

Elian's body drooped, but stiffened anew. "So then. Give him to me."

"Why?"

"Because he is mine."

"He is mine now."

Elian stepped swiftly sidewise. The woman did not seem to move, but she was there, inescapable. With the courage of desperation, Elian flung herself upon her.

And staggered and fell to the stones. She had met only air. Mirain lay lifeless. Elian gathered him up, holding him to her breast, rocking him.

A shape loomed over her. A woman of dawn, clothed in night. Elian looked upon her in neither surprise nor awe, only weariness.

This beauty was high and terrible yet not cold, this voice achingly pure yet warm, like a deep-toned flute. And yet it was the same. They were the same, dawn and night: two faces of one power.

Elian turned her mind away. It was temptation. In this place it could be her death, and through her, Mirain's. Her arms tightened about his body.

"He is mine," said the woman of dawn, "and he shall remain mine. Unless . . ."

Elian's breath caught with the agony of hope.

"Unless," said the woman of dawn, "you pay your own price."

"Anything!" cried Elian.

"Slowly, child of earth. I do not bargain. This is the price which the gods set, and not I: the price of one man's salvation. If you will pay it."

"Only name it and it is yours."

The woman of dawn regarded her in what might have been pity. "The name of it is very simple. Your self."

Elian blinked stupidly. "My—"

"Your self. That which makes you Elian, alone of all the children of earth. That which makes you dream that you are free."

Her self. The very power which had snatched her from madness, and flung aside Vadin's strong aid, and brought her to this place. Her strength; her obstinacy. Her reckless temper. Herself.

Mirain lay in her arms. He had never been closer to beauty, or farther from it.

She loved him. Her heart ached with it; ached to see him standing again before her, moving with grace which few men could match, warming her with his rare and brilliant smile.

And yet. To pay so much. Had she not paid enough and more than enough? Other women had lost their loves and gone on. Other women had borne children, served regencies, held fiefs and kingdoms until the heirs could claim them. She could rule Mirain's empire; she had the strength, and the people's love, and her father and her brother to stand behind her. Even Vadin, even he would bow to her for her child's sake.

Or she could simply kill herself as she had threatened to do, and end all her wavering.

Save that life was sweet, and hers had barely begun. And love was the sweetest thing in it, not of the body only, but all the wonder of being two who were one: separate, distinct, yet joined, like gold twined with copper in a fillet for a queen.

If she paid this price, she would lose it all. And Mirain—what would it do to him to wake and find her as she was now? Or worse. Awake and aware, but no longer Elian. Meek and pliant, as the world believed a woman should be, with no thought or word that was her own.

Maybe he would not mind. Maybe he would even prefer it.

Maybe she would not know what she had done to herself.

She trembled, shaking with sickness that was all of the soul. What virtues she had were warrior virtues: courage, high heart, and lethal honesty, and loyalty that could set all the rest at naught. She could be generous with possessions or with power; she had plenty of both. But that great virtue of the priests, that which with bitter irony they called selflessness, of that she had none at all.

"I'm a soldier," she said. "A queen. I was never made to be a martyr."

The woman of dawn stood tall and silent above her.

She bent her head over Mirain's body. She could die. He could die. They both could die. The world would go on without them. Maybe it would be better so. Maybe the Exile had had the right of it, and evil was not only dark alone but light alone, and the world's peace lay in the delicacy of their balance.

His arm slipped from his side and fell, palm up. The Sun shone with none of its sometime brilliance, none of its god-born power. It seemed no more than a folly, a dandy's fashion, an ornament set in the most improbable of places: awkward, impractical, and faintly absurd.

She raised her eyes from it and set her chin. "I'll pay," she said.

Twenty-eight

*T*HE WOMAN OF DAWN BOWED HER HIGH HEAD. ALL pride was in that gesture, yet it was a gesture of respect.

Elian's sudden selflessness, though soul-deep, had no patience in it. "Well. Why do you wait? Take my mind away from me."

"That," said the woman, "was not the price. Nor can I take what you give. You must give it of your own accord."

"But I don't know how!"

That, perhaps, was a smile. The woman of dawn raised her hand. "Look yonder."

Elian looked, thinking to see the woman of night, or some greater wonder still. Seeing—

"You." Vadin said nothing. He was the same here as ever, tall, tired, detested, inevitable. "Of course it would be you. How did you get here?"

"I was always here."

"You were not!" she cried, stung. "I was one with Mirain. You were never there. Never!"

"You didn't want to see me."

The blood flooded to her cheeks. But she had no cheeks here. No blood. No flesh at all. This was but a vision of her mind, a shape she had given to the workings of her power. She was a naked will in the void that had been Mirain's mind, set against the power that dwelt in the mountain. Vadin trespassed, invading where he had no need and no purpose, betraying at last his jealousy of her who had taken his place in his oathbrother's soul. She willed him away.

He stood unmoving and unmoved. If anything, he was more solid than ever. "Don't be more of a fool than you can help. Mirain is trapped, that much at least you have the wits to see. If you want to set him free, you have to give up your stubbornness; banish this illusion; plunge into his mind, and find him, and lead him back to the light."

At last, and terribly, she understood. When she was very young, she had learned: Every mind descended through many levels. The greater one's power, the deeper one could go. Yet even the mightiest of the mages, the master enchanters, the great wizards of the songs, had never dared to plunge to the bottom. For beyond a certain level—Sigan's Wall, her father had called it—there was no returning. One was trapped in the black deeps below all consciousness, beneath even dreams. One's self, indeed, was lost.

And the one gate, the only gate . . .

There was no escaping him. Not through hate, or contempt, or simple refusal to acknowledge his existence. He made it worse; his eyes asked her pardon, but they would not forsake their pride by begging for it. That he was here, deeper even than she had ever gone. That she could not pass save through him and with him. That she must do worse than sacrifice her self for her lover's sake; she must sacrifice it to him whom she could not even like, much less love.

She rounded upon the woman of dawn. "Is there no other way?"

Night flickered over the luminous face. The deep eyes were cold. "None," said the power.

She looked at Mirain, so still upon the stone. She looked at Vadin, whose gaze likewise had settled upon the Sunborn. He knelt; he touched the lifeless brow; he smoothed the hair away from it, as if Mirain had been one of his children.

Hatred roared through her, flaming. And passed, and left her empty. He wept, that haughty lord of warriors. He wept, but he would not plead with her intransigence.

He was the gate, but she was the key. Without him she could not pass. Without her he could not open the way.

His eyes lifted, brimming. Her own were burning dry. "He told me," she said. "Mirain told me—if any man so much as touched me—"

"When did you ever do as you were told?"

She lurched forward a step. Her hands wanted to strike him; to stroke him. Invader, interloper; she hated him. Sharer in Mirain's soul, brother, kinsman; she—almost, she could force herself to—if he were Hal—if it were necessary—

She touched him. Mirain breathed between them, but slowly, slowly, cooling into death. Her breath caught, sharp with pain. "For him," she said. "Only for him."

Vadin rose. Before he could reach for her, she had seized him. Body to body. Mind to mind. Weaving, interweaving, warp, woof, the flash of the shuttle between. He was bright; he was strong. He was Mirain, but he was not. Kinsman. Brother. He shaped himself for her: a strong hand clasping hers, a strong will bolstering her own. Even—even a touch of joy, the delight of a master who has met his master in power.

With joy then, and with Vadin both her armor and her gate, she faced Sigan's high Wall. Which in truth was not a wall at all, but a growing awareness, a swelling of fear. *Back, turn back, or be forever lost.*

The fear rose to a crescendo and shattered. She fell into the void.

Eternity ticked off its ages.

Light.

She thought she was mad. No; she knew it. There was light below. The merest glimmer. Like a candle, pale gold, burning low. Like a star at the end of night, growing larger by infinite degrees. Swelling. Blooming. Enfolding her. With the suddenness of all endings, she struck the heart of it.

Earth. Grass. She stood naked on it, under a sky that was all light. Someone gripped her hand. Vadin. But if she shifted her eyes, she was he; they were one.

They looked down. Mirain looked up. Mirain at his ease, open-eyed yet drowsy, smiling. He beckoned. "Come," he said. "Rest. You look worn to the bone."

Elian was speechless. It was Vadin who snapped, "Of course we are! A fine chase you've led us, down through all the levels of your mind, looking for something resembling intelligence. I should have known we wouldn't find any."

"Ah now," said Mirain unruffled, "there's no need to yell at me. Won't you sit down at least? It's comfortable here."

"Comfortable!"

Elian silenced Vadin with a finger on his lips. "It's a trap, brother," she said, using the word with care; but Vadin was in no mood to notice it. "That's Mirain, but it's not."

The Ianyn's eyes widened, then narrowed. "What are you saying?"

"It's Mirain, but Mirain in part only, walled in his own cowardice.

He'd keep us here in this comfort of his; before we knew it, we'd all be comfortably dead."

Vadin shook himself, and laughed almost freely. "I must be turning foolish in my old age. Of course this is a trap. I've seen the other side of death. It was even more comfortable than this; I hated to go back. But he made me.

"*You* made me," he said to Mirain, who yawned and stretched, sensuous as a cat, and smiled indulgently at his vehemence. "You made me, damn you. It's well past time I repaid the debt."

"Debt?" Mirain asked. "I owe you nothing. I have to linger here for a while. There was something . . ." His brow creased very slightly, as if he sought a memory that eluded him. "It doesn't matter. It's a very pleasant place, don't you think? It will do until the time is past. Whatever it must pass for."

Vadin drew himself up to his full height. Once more Elian stilled him. She yearned to scream, to strike, to run, to do anything but face this travesty of the Sunborn. "It is not Mirain," she told Vadin, and herself. "It is *not.*" She freed her hand, aware that her mind wove still with Vadin's, an awareness as distinct as the warmth of flesh against flesh. She knelt in the grass, and clasped this vapid smiling Mirain-creature, and held it tightly. "Now," she snapped over her shoulder, surging to her feet. "Out!"

Mirain roused. Began to fight. Serpent-supple, serpent-strong. He was too much for her. He was too strong.

She clung. She mustered all her strength. She clutched at Vadin's power; she seized it; she became it. He and she, long powerful manbody, arms hardened by a lifetime of wielding sword and lance and bow, power honed to a bitter edge under the greatest of masters: under Prince Orsan; under Mirain himself.

"Outward!" she cried. "To the light!"

The serpent flared into fire, flowed into water, scattered into air. She flung her power about it, netted it, flasked it, englobed it in crystal. It sprang into an edged blade. The crystal shattered; her hands closed about shards and steel. Pain mounted into agony. She thrust it down. She battled toward the light.

The wall loomed. She cried in despair. No gate. No passage. She must strike, fall, die.

"No." Vadin's voice, strong and quiet, though it shook a little. He led her now, drawing her upward, and in her bleeding hands the thing that had been Mirain. Writhing, snapping, steel-toothed creature, no shape to it at all, only struggle. She clasped it to her breast.

They struck the wall. Faltered. Slipped. Mirain bolted; she caught him. "Help," gasped Vadin. "Help—"

She flung them all forward.

The darkness burst. Stars sang in pure cold voices. Men wept; women laughed aloud. Grass whispered as it grew.

Elian opened her eyes. The world was a blur with a shadow in the middle of it. She blinked.

They smiled down at her. Vadin, his cheeks more hollow than ever, his grin white enough to blind her. And Mirain.

Mirain.

She clutched at him. He was warm and solid and as naked as he was born.

With a mighty effort she unclamped her fingers. They were whole, unscarred, no mark of tooth or claw. "I dreamed," she said. "I dreamed—"

"No dream." She had forgotten how beautiful his voice was. He kissed her brow, and then her lips. She shifted as easily as breathing, and stared at her own bewildered face. And again, from farther away, seeing herself and Mirain together. She wore no more than he. How wanton; how lovely to the eyes of this body. The eyes under the bright brows were Mirain's, laughing, raising a hand to run it down the strangeness in which she dwelt.

She inhaled sharply, and the breath completed itself in her own lungs. Vadin was Vadin, Mirain his unmistakable self. No languor, no madness. "This," she said, "could be confusing."

Mirain laughed. Vadin drew back. At last she saw his proud eyes lowered, and the part of her which was he, knew that he blushed. Why, she thought, he had no more sense than she when it came to considering consequences. Now that it was far too late for any remedy, he was beginning to regret what he had made her do.

"What I did for myself." She took his hand, though he tried to escape; she kissed it. "I was a fool, brother. But not for letting this happen. For letting it take so long." Her lips twitched. "Hal is going to be hideously jealous."

Vadin's eyes went a little wild. "You wouldn't!"

"No," Mirain said. "It's enough that we aren't three anymore; or two. Four in one would be unwieldy. Although," he added, "I can't bring myself to be sorry that you two did what you did."

Elian's thoughts wound through the twinned bright skein of theirs. Hers, Mirain's, Vadin's, all mingled. It was very beautiful.

One skein unraveled. "But I'm still *me,*" she protested.

"And I am I, and he is he, but we are one." Through the splendor of his gladness, Mirain let slip a note of gravity. "It is very unorthodox."

"It's heretical." But Vadin was quieter now, more like the haughty prince whom Elian had thought she knew. He grimaced. "Though I fancy that's not the word most people will like to use. 'Immoral' will sound much more apt to the rumormongers. Not," he said, "that I intend to go so far. Some things are best kept in the inner room where they belong."

He sounded almost prim; Elian laughed, and kissed his hand again. Mirain's eyes glinted, but not with anger, and not ever with jealousy. Her free hand caught his and brought it to her cheek; her eyes flicked from his long-loved face to the one which she was learning only now to love. She smiled at them both.

Yet her brows had drawn together. "The powers in the circle, all the teachings I've ever known . . . they said that if I did this, I'd lose everything. But all I've lost is my stupidity. I've gained a whole world."

"I think," said Mirain, "that none of the masters knew what would happen. None has ever tried this; none has dared. Only you." His hand curved about her cheek, caressing it. "You gave all you had to give. While I . . ."

"I haven't given anything."

"You'll never be free of me again."

She glared at him. "When was I ever free of you?" Sudden laughter shook her. "The day I was born, I decided that you belonged to me. And I to you, although I'd never have admitted it."

"And Ziad-Ilarios?"

"Shall I reckon up all your lovers, O priest of the Sun?" She sat up so abruptly that her head spun. "Look at me, Mirain."

He could do very little else. Rumpled, blear-eyed, and torn between a grin and a snarl, she was the most beautiful creature in all the world.

"Except for Ledi," Vadin said, mischievous.

Her grin won the battle. Beauty she could not judge. But she knew her own fortune. Warrior, mage, and queen; she was all three. Yet greater than those . . .

They waited.

"And greater than those," she said, "I am the sister of Vadin alVadin who came back from the dead. And I am the lover of Mirain who is An-Sh'Endor, who has but to lift his hand to bring all the world to his feet." She paused. Vadin was smiling his white smile. But Mirain waited still. His head had come up, his eyes kindled. Oh, he was vain—as vain as a sunbird, and as beautiful, and as kingly proud.

"But not and never," she added wickedly as she pulled him down, "the Lady of Han-Gilen."

A FALL OF PRINCES

To

The Yale Department of Medieval Studies
The Orange Street Gang in all its permutations
And, of course, all the Faithful

But for whom, et cetera.

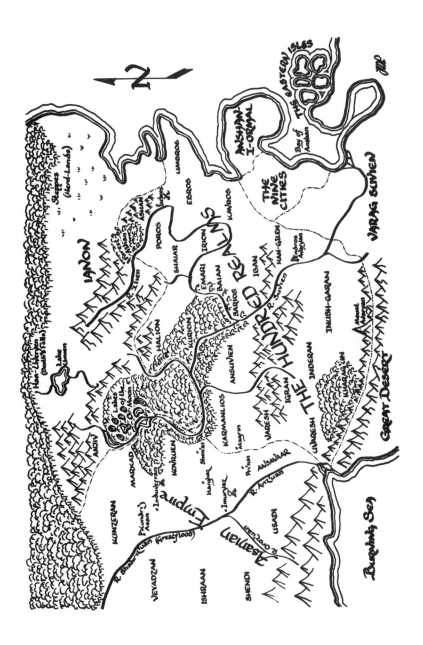

PART ONE

Asuchirel inZiad Uverias

One

THE HOUNDS HAD VEERED AWAY WESTWARD. THEIR baying swelled and faded as the wind shifted; the huntsman's horn sounded, faint and deadly.

Hirel flattened himself in his nest of spicefern. His nose was full of the sharp potent scent. His body was on fire. His head was light with running and with terror and with the last of the cursed drug with which they had caught him. Caught him but not held him. And they were gone. Bless that wildbuck for bolting across his path. Bless his brothers' folly for hunting him with half-trained pups.

He crawled from the fernbrake, dragging a body which had turned rebel. Damned body. It was all over blood. Thorns. Fangs—one hound had caught him, the one set on guard by his prison. It was dead. He hurt. Some fool of a child was crying, softly and very near, but this was wild country, border country, and he was alone. It was growing dark.

The dark lowered and spread wide, shifted and changed, took away pain and brought it back edged with sickness. The sky was full of stars. Branches rimmed it; he had not seen them before. The air carried a tang of fire. Hirel blinked, frowned. And burst upward in a flood of memory, a torrent of panic terror.

Those were not cords that bound him, but bandages wrapped firmly where he hurt most. But for them he was naked; even the rag of his underrobe was gone, all else left behind in the elegant cell in which he had learned what betrayal was. He dropped in an agony of modesty, coiling about his center, shaking forward the royal mane—but that was gone, his head scraped bare as a slave's, worst of all shames even under sheltering arms.

The fire snapped a branch in two. The shadow by it was silent. Hirel's pride battered him until he raised his eyes.

The shadow was a man. Barbarian, Hirel judged him at once and utterly. Even sitting on his heels he was tall, trousered like a southerner but bare above like a wild tribesman from the north, and that black-velvet skin was of the north, and that haughty eagle's face, and the beard left free to grow. But he held to a strange fashion: beard and long braided hair were dyed as bright as the copper all his kind were so fond of. Or—

Or he was born to it. His brows were the same, and his lashes; the fire caught glints of it on arms and breast and belly as he rose. He was very tall. For all that Hirel's will could do, his body cowered, making itself as small as it might.

The barbarian lifted something from the ground and approached. His braid had fallen over his shoulder. It ended below his waist. His throat was circled with gold, a torque as thick as two men's fingers, and a white band bound his brows. Priest. Priest of the demon called Avaryan and worshipped as the Sun; initiate of the superstition that had over-whelmed the east of the world. He knelt by Hirel, his face like something carved in stone, and he dared. He touched Hirel.

Hirel flung himself against those blasphemous hands, screaming he cared not what, striking, kicking, clawing with nails which his betrayers had not troubled to rob him of. All his fear and all his grief and all his outrage gathered and battled and hated this stranger who was not even of the empire. Who had found him and tended him and presumed to lay unhallowed hands on him.

Who held him easily and let him flail, only evading the strokes of his nails.

He stopped all at once. His breath ached in his throat; he felt cold and empty. The priest was cool, unruffled, breathing without strain. "Let me go," Hirel said.

The priest obeyed. He stooped, took up what he had held before Hirel sprang on him. It was a coat, clean but not fresh, tainted with the touch of a lowborn body. But it was a covering. Hirel let the barbarian clothe him in it. The man moved lightly, careful not to brush flesh with flesh. A quick learner, that one. But his grip was still a bitter memory.

Hirel sat by the fire. He was coming to himself. "A hood," he said. "Fetch one."

A bright brow went up. It was hard to tell in firelight, but perhaps the priest's lips quirked. "Will a cap satisfy your highness?" The accent was appalling but the words comprehensible, the voice as dark as the face, rich and warm.

"A cap will do," Hirel answered him, choosing to be gracious. Covered at last, Hirel could sit straight and eat what the priest gave him. Coarse food and common, bread and cheese and fruit, with nothing to wash it down but water from a flask, but Hirel's hunger was far beyond criticism. They had fed him in prison, but then they had purged him; he ached with emptiness.

The priest watched him. He was used to that, but the past days had left scars that throbbed under those calm dark eyes. Bold eyes in truth, not lowering before his own, touched with something very like amusement. They refused to be stared down. Hirel's own slid aside first, and he told himself that he was weary of this foolishness. "What are you called?" he demanded.

"Sarevan." Why was the barbarian so damnably amused? "And you?"

Hirel's head came up in the overlarge cap; he drew himself erect in despite of his griping belly. "Asuchirel inZiad Uverias, High Prince of Asanion and heir to the Golden Throne." He said it with all hauteur, and yet he was painfully aware, all at once, of his smallness beside this long lanky outlander, and of the lightness of his unbroken voice, and of the immensity of the world about their little clearing with its flicker of fire.

The priest shifted minutely, drawing Hirel's eyes. Both of his brows were up now, but not with surprise, and certainly not with awe. "So then, Asuchirel inZiad Uverias, High Prince of Asanion, what brings you to this backward province?"

"*You* should not be here," Hirel shot back. "Your kind are not welcome in the empire."

"Not," said Sarevan, "in this empire. You are somewhat across the border. Did you not know?"

Hirel began to tremble. No wonder the hounds had turned away. And he—he had told this man his name, in this man's own country, where the son of the Emperor of Asanion was a hostage beyond price. "Kill me now," he said. "Kill me quickly. My brothers will reward you, if you have the courage to approach them. Kill me and have done."

"I think not," the barbarian said.

Hirel bolted. A long arm shot out. Once more a lowborn hand closed

about him. It was very strong. Hirel sank his teeth into it. A swift blow
jarred him loose and all but stunned him.

"You," said Sarevan, "are a lion's cub indeed. Sit down, cubling, and
calm your fears. I'm not minded to kill you, and I don't fancy holding
you for ransom."

Hirel spat at him.

Sarevan laughed, light and free and beautifully deep. But he did not
let Hirel go.

"You defile me," gritted Hirel. "Your hands are a profanation."

"Truly?" Sarevan considered the one that imprisoned Hirel's wrist.
"I know it's not obvious, but I'm quite clean."

"I am the high prince!"

"So you are." No, there was no awe in that cursed face. "And it
seems that your brothers would contest your title. Fine fierce children
they must be."

"They," said Hirel icily, "are the bastards of my father's youth. I am
his legitimate son. I was lured into the marches on a pretext of good
hunting and fine singing and perhaps a new concubine." The black eyes
widened slightly; Hirel disdained to take notice. "And I was to speak
with a weapons master in Pri'nai and a philosopher in Karghaz, and
show the easterners my face. But my brothers—" He faltered. This was
pain. It must not be. It should be anger. "My dearest and most loyal
brothers had found themselves a better game. They drugged my wine at
the welcoming feast in Pri'nai, corrupted my taster and so captured me.
I escaped. I took a senel, but it fell in the rough country and broke its
neck. I ran. I did not know that I had run so far."

"Yes." Sarevan released him at last. "You are under your father's rule
no longer. The Sunborn is emperor here."

"That bandit. What is he to me?" Hirel stopped. So one always said
in Asanion. But this was not the Golden Empire.

The Sun-priest showed no sign of anger. He only said, "Have a care
whom you mock here, cubling."

"I will do as I please," said Hirel haughtily.

"Was it doing as you please that brought you to the west of Karmanlios in such unroyal state?" Sarevan did not wait for an answer. "Come,
cubling. The night is speeding, and you should sleep."

To his own amazement, Hirel lay down as and where he was told,
wrapped in a blanket with only his arm for a pillow. The ground was
brutally hard, the blanket thin and rough, the air growing cold with the
fickleness of spring. Hirel lay and cursed this insolent oaf he had fallen

afoul of, and beat all of his clamoring pains into submission, and slid into sleep as into deep water.

"Well, cubling, what shall we do with you?"

Hirel could barely move, and he had no wish to. He had not known how sorely he was hurt, in how many places. But Sarevan had waked him indecently early, droning hymns as if the sun could not rise of itself but must be coaxed and caterwauled over the horizon, washing noisily and immodestly afterward in the stream that skirted the edge of the clearing, and squatting naked to revive the fire. With the newborn sun on him he looked as if he had bathed in dust of copper. Even the down of his flanks had that improbable, metallic sheen.

He stood over Hirel, shameless as an animal. "What shall we do with you?" he repeated.

Hirel averted his eyes from that proud and careless body, and tried not to think of his own that was still so much a child's. "You may leave me. I do not require your service."

"No?" The creature sat cross-legged, shaking his hair out of its sodden braid, attacking it with a comb he had produced from somewhere. He kept his eyes on Hirel. "What will you do, High Prince of Asanion? Walk back to your brothers? Stay here and live on berries and water? Seek out the nearest village? Which, I bid you consider, is a day's hard walk through wood and field, and where people are somewhat less accommodating than I. Even if they would credit your claim to your title, they have no reason to love your kind. Golden demonspawn they call you, and yellow-eyed tyrants, and scourges of free folk. At the very least they would stone you. More likely they would take you prisoner and see that you died as slowly as ever your enemies could wish."

"They would not dare."

"Cubling." It was a velvet purr. "You are but the child of a thousand years of emperors. He who rules here is the son of a very god. And he can be seen unmasked even upon his throne, and any peasant's child may touch him if she chooses, and he is not defiled. On the contrary. He is the more holy for that his people love him."

"He is an upstart adventurer with a mouthful of lies."

Sarevan laughed, not warmly this time, but clear and cold. His long fingers began the weaving of his braid, flying in and out through the fiery mane. "Cubling, you set a low price on your life. How will you be losing it, then? Back in Asanion or ahead in Keruvarion?"

Hirel's defiance flared and died. Hells take the man, he had a clear eye. One very young prince alone and naked and shaven like a slave—if he could win back to Kundri'j Asan he might have hope, if his father would have him, if the court did not laugh him to his death. But it was a long way to the Golden City, and his brothers stood between. Vuad and Sayel whom he had trusted, whom he had allowed himself to admire and even to love. To whom, after all, he had been no more than he was to anyone: an obstacle before his father's throne.

If it had been Aranos . . .

Aranos would not have failed so far of his vigilance as to let Hirel escape. If Aranos joined in this clever coil of a plot, Aranos who by birth was eldest and by breeding highest save only for Hirel, every road and path and molerun would be watched and guarded. Hirel would never come to his city. And this time he would die.

He would not. He was high prince. He would be emperor.

But first he had to escape this domain of the man called An-Sh'Endor, Son of the Morning, lord of the eastern world in the name of his false god. Whose priest sat close enough to touch, tying off the end of his braid and stretching like a great indolent cat. He rose in one flowing movement, and went without haste to don shirt and trousers and boots, belting on a dagger and a sword. He looked as if he knew how to use them.

Hirel frowned. He did not like what he was thinking. He must return to Kundri'j. He could not return alone. But to ask—to trust—

Did he have a choice?

Sarevan bound his brows with the long white band. Initiate, it meant. A priest new to his torque, sent out upon the seven years' Journey that made him a full master of his order. Four disks of gold glittered on the band: four years done, three yet to wander before he could rest.

"Priest," Hirel said abruptly, "I choose. You will escort me to Kundri'j Asan. I will see that no one harms you; I will reward you when I come to the palace."

Sarevan's head tilted. His eyes glinted. "You do? I shall? You will?"

Hirel clapped his hands. "Fetch my breakfast. I will bathe after."

"No," said the barbarian quite calmly, quite without fear. "I do not fetch. I am not a servant. There is bread in my scrip, and you may have the last of the cheese. As for the other, I have in mind to go westward for a little distance, and I suppose I can suffer your company."

Hirel could not breathe for outrage. Never—never in all his life—

"Be quick, cubling, or I leave you behind."

Hirel ate, though he choked. Bathed himself with his own cold and shaking hands, aware through every instant of the back turned ostentatiously toward him. Pulled on the outsize coat and the ill-fitting cap, and found a cord with the scrip, which perforce did duty as a belt. Almost before it was tied, the scrip was slung from an insolent shoulder, the priest striding long-legged out of the clearing. Hirel raged, but he pressed after.

It was not easy. Hirel's feet were bare and that was royal, but they had never trodden anywhere but on paths smoothed before them; and he had done them no good in his running, and this land, though gentler than the stones and thorns of his flight, was not the polished paving of his palace. And he was wounded with thorn and fang, and still faintly ill from poison and purging, and Sarevan set a pace his shorter legs had to struggle to match. He set his teeth and saved his bitter words and kept his eye on the swing of the coppery plait. Sometimes he fell. He said nothing. His hands stung with new scratches. His knee ached.

He struck something that yielded and turned and loosed an exclamation. The hands were on him again. He spared only a little of his mind for temper, even when they gathered him up. A prince could be carried. If he permitted it. And this barbarian was strong and his stride was smooth, lulling Hirel into a stupor.

Hirel started awake. He was on the ground and he was bare again, and Sarevan had begun to unwrap his bandages. Hirel did not want to see what was under them.

"Clean," said Sarevan, "and healing well. But watch the knee, cubling. You cut it the last time you fell."

"And whose fault was that?"

"Yours," came the swift answer. "Next time you need rest, say so. You can't awe me with your hardihood. You have none. And you'll get none if you kill yourself trying to match me."

Hirel thought of hating him. But hate was for equals. Not for blackfaced redmaned barbarians.

"Up," said this one, having rebound the bandages and restored tunic and cap. "You can walk a bit; your muscles will stiffen else."

Hirel walked. Sarevan let him set the pace. Now and then he was allowed a sip of water. They ate barely enough to blunt the edge of hunger. That must suffice, said the son of stone; they might not reach the town he was aiming for before the sun set. Hirel's fault, that was clear enough. While Hirel struggled and gritted his teeth and was ignored, Sarevan sauntered easily in his boots and his honed strength, unwounded, unpampered, inured to rough living. And why should he not be? He was lowborn.

"I'm a most egregious mongrel," he said as they paused at the top of a grueling slope; and he was not even breathing hard, although he had carried Hirel on his back up the last few lengths, chattering as he went, easy as if he trod a palace floor. "I have Ianyn blood as you can well see, and my mother comes from Han-Gilen, and there's a strong strain of Asanian on both sides. And . . . other things."

Hirel did not ask what they were. Gutter rat surely, and a slave or two, and just enough mountain tribesmen to give him arrogance far above his station.

He was up already, prowling as if restless, nosing among the brambles that hedged the hill. In a little while he came back with a handful of springberries, rich and ripe and wondrous sweet.

To Hirel's surprise and well-concealed relief, having eaten his share of fruit and given Hirel the water flask, Sarevan showed no sign of going on. He paced as if he waited for something or someone; he turned his face to the sun he worshipped, and sang to it. Now that Hirel was not trying to sleep, the priest's voice was pleasant to hear. More than pleasant. In fact, rather remarkable. In Asanion he would have been allowed to sing before the Middle Court; with training he might have won entry to the High Court itself.

The sun was warm in its nooning. Hirel yawned. What an oddity they would think this creature: a redheaded northerner, a sweet singer, a priest of the Sun. All the east in a man. He would fetch a great price in the market.

Hirel shivered. He did not want to think of slave markets. His hand found its way under the cap, catching on the brief new stubble. Three days now. And Vuad, Vuad whose mother was an Ormalen slave, had shaken his mud-brown hair and laughed, cheering the barber on. Vuad had never forgiven Hirel his pure blood, or the splendid hot-gold mane that went with it.

"It will grow back." Sarevan's shadow was cool, his voice soft and warm.

Hirel's teeth ground together. "Get," he said thickly. "Get your shadow off me."

It moved. Sarevan stripped off his shirt and rolled it into a bundle and laid it in his bag, apparently oblivious to the offense he had given. He went back to his pacing, tracing precise and intricate patterns like the steps of a dance, humming to himself.

He stilled abruptly, utterly. Hirel heard nothing but breeze and birdsong, saw nothing but shapeless wilderness. Trees, undergrowth, thornbrake; the stones of the slope below him. All the animals they had seen that day were small ones, harmless. None came near them now.

Sarevan made no move toward his weapons. His face in profile was intent but untainted with fear. Hirel was not comforted. The breeze died. The bird trilled once and fell silent. In the thicket below, a shadow moved. Faded. Grew. Hirel's mouth was burning dry. A beast of prey. A cat as large as a small senel, the color of shifting shadows, with eyes that opened and caught the sun and turned it to green fire. It poured itself over the stones, so swift and fluid that it seemed slow, advancing with clear and terrible purpose.

It sprang. Hirel threw himself flat. The grey belly arched over him, deceptively soft, touched with a faint, feline musk. He never knew why he did not break and bolt. The beast was on Sarevan, rolling on the hilltop, snarling horribly. And Hirel could not even make a sound.

The battle roared and tumbled to its end. Sarevan rose to his knees with no mark on him; and he was all a stranger, no longer the haughty wanderer but a boy with a white grin, arms wrapped about the neck of the monstrous, purring cat. "This," he said, light and glad and almost laughing, "is Ulan, and he says that he is not eating tender young princelings today."

Hirel found his voice at last. "What in the twenty-seven hells—"

"Ulan," repeated the barbarian with purest patience. "My friend and long companion, and a prince of the princes of cats. You owe him your life. He drew off the hounds that haunted you, and gave your hunters a fine grim trail to follow. With a bloody robe at the end of it."

Hirel clutched the earth. It was rocking; or his brain was. "You— it—"

"He," said Sarevan pointedly, "caught wind of you before you crossed the border. I tracked you. Ulan headed off the hunters."

"Why?"

Sarevan shrugged. "It seemed worth doing. Maybe the god had a hand in it. Who knows?"

"There are no gods."

One brow went up. Sarevan ran his hands over the great grey body, stroking, but searching too, as if hunting for a wound. It seemed that he did not find one. A sigh escaped him; he clasped the beast close, burying his face in the thick fur, murmuring something that Hirel could not quite catch. The cat's purr rose to a mutter of thunder.

"They think that I am dead," Hirel said, shrill above the rumbling. "Devoured. By that—"

"By an ul-cat from the fells beyond Lake Umien. That should give your enemies pause."

Hirel managed to stand. The cat blinked at him. He unclenched his fists. "They will not know. They will think of forest lions and of direwolves, and maybe of devils; they are superstitious here. But," he conceded, "it was well done."

Again Sarevan loosed that astonishing grin. "Wasn't it? Come then, cubling. Ulan will carry you, and tonight will find us with a roof over our heads. A better one even than I hoped for."

Hirel swallowed. The cat yawned, baring fangs as long as daggers. And yet, what a mount for a high prince. A prince of cats. Hirel advanced with the valor of the desperate, and the creature waited, docile as any child's pony. Its fur was thick, coarse above, heavenly soft beneath; its back held him not too awkwardly, his knees clasping the sleek sides. Its gaits were smooth, with a supple power no hoofed creature could match. Hirel could even lie down if he was careful, pillowed on the broad summit of the head between the soft ears.

Quiet. almost comfortable, he let his eyes rest on nothing in particular. Trees. Shafts of sunlight. Now and then a stream; once Ulan drank, once Sarevan filled the flask. The priest looked content, as if this quickened pace suited him, and sometimes he let his hand rest on the cat, but never on Hirel.

The sun sank. The trees thinned, open country visible beyond, hills, a ribbon of red that was a road. On a low but steep-sided hill stood a wall and in it a town. A poor enough place: a garrison, a huddle of huts and houses, a tiny market and a smithy and a wineshop, and in the center of it a small but inevitable temple.

They were seen long before they came to the gate. A child herding a flock of woolbeasts along the road glanced back, and his eyes went wide, and he flung up both his arms, waving madly. "Sa'van!" he shrilled. "Sa'van lo'ndros!"

The cry ran ahead of him, borne by children who seemed to spring from the earth. They poured out of the gate, surrounded the travelers, danced about them; and several hung themselves about Sarevan, and a few even overwhelmed Ulan. Hirel they stared at and tried to babble at, but when he did not answer, they ignored him.

Their elders came close behind, slightly more dignified but no less delighted, chattering in their barbaric tongue. Sarevan chattered back, smiling and even laughing, with a child on each shoulder and half a dozen tugging at him from below. Obviously he was known here.

Hirel sat still on Ulan's back. He was tired and he ached, and no one took the least notice of him. They were all swarming about the priest. Not a civilized man in the lot; not even the armored guards, who made no effort to disperse the crowd. Quite the opposite. Those few who did not join it looked on with indulgence.

For all the press of people, Sarevan moved freely enough, and Ulan somewhat behind carrying Hirel and a bold infant or two. One tiny brown girlchild, naked and slippery as a fish, had chosen Hirel as a prop, nor did his stiffness deter her. She was not clean. From the evidence, she had been rolling in mud with the dogs. But she clung like a leech and never knew what she clung to, and he was too taut with mortal outrage to hurl her off.

The tide cast them up at last in front of the temple. Small as it was, it boasted a full priestess. A pair of novices attended her, large-eyed solemn children in voluminous brown who might have been of either sex; but perhaps the taller, with the full and lovely mouth, was a girl. They were both staring at Sarevan as if he had been a god come to earth. But the priestess, small and round and golden-fair as an Asanian lady, met him with a smile and a word or two, and he bowed with all proper respect. Her hand rested a moment on his bright head, blessing it. Yes, she was highborn; she had the manner, and she had it as one bred to it.

Half of his own will, half of his body's weariness, Hirel slid from Ulan's back and leaned against the warm solid shoulder. The child, robbed of her prop, kept her seat easily enough, but her wail of outrage drew a multitude of eyes. Hirel drew himself up before them. Dark eyes in brown faces, and Saveran's darkest of all, and the priestess' the golden amber of the old pure blood. Of his own. She saw what he was. She must.

Sarevan spoke, and the eyes flicked back to him, abruptly, completely. He did not speak long. He turned to Hirel. "Come," he said in Asanian. And when Hirel gathered to resist: "You may stay if you please, and no one will harm you. But I intend to rest and to eat."

Hirel drew a sharp breath. "Very well. Lead me."

The crowding commoners did not try to pass the gate, although several of the children protested loudly the loss of their mounts. Sarevan paused to tease them into smiles. When the gate closed upon them, he was smiling himself.

"Ah, lad," the priestess said in Asanian considerably better than his, "you do have a way with them."

Sarevan shrugged, laughed a little. "They have a way with me." He laid his hand on Ulan's head and not quite on Hirel's shoulder. "I have two who need feeding, and one has hurts which you should see."

Hirel could suffer her touch, the better for that Sarevan left them in a chamber of the inner temple and went away with the novices. She did not strip him unceremoniously, but undressed him properly and modestly, with his back to her, and she bathed him so with sponge and scented water, and offered a wrapping for his loins. After the barbarities he had endured, that simple decency brought him close to tears. He fought them, fumbling with the strip of cloth until he could turn and face her.

She inspected his hurts with care and without questions. "They are clean," she said at length, as Sarevan had. She wrapped the worst in fresh new bandages, left the rest to the air, and set a light soft robe upon him. As she settled the folds of it, the bare plain room in which they stood seemed to fill with light.

It was only Saveran. He had bathed: his hair was loose, curling with damp, his beard combed into tameness, and he had found a robe much like Hirel's. He was rebinding the band of his Journey as he came; his quick eyes glanced from the priestess to Hirel and back again.

"You have done all that you should," she said, "and done it well." With a gesture she brought them both out of the antechamber into the inner temple, the little courtyard with its garden, and the narrow chamber beyond, open wide to the air and the evening, where waited the novices with the daymeal. A poor feast as Hirel the prince might have reckoned it, plain fare served with little grace, but tonight it seemed as splendid as any high banquet in Kundri'j Asan. No matter that Hirel must share it with a barbarian and a woman; he had a royal hunger and for once a complaisant stomach, and the priestess was excellent company.

Her name was Orozia; she came of an old family, the Vinicharyas of eastern Markad. "Little thought they would rejoice to hear me confess it," she said, sipping the surprisingly good wine and nibbling a bit of cheese. "It is not proper for the daughter of a high house to cleave to the eastern superstition. And to vow herself to the priesthood . . . appalling." She laughed with the merest edge of bitterness. "My poor father! When I came to him with my braid and torque, dressed for my Journey, I thought that I had slain him. How could he ever explain this to his equals? How would he dare to hold up his head at court?"

"He was a coward," Hirel said.

She bowed her head, suddenly grave. "No. He was not that. He was a lord of the Middle Court whose fathers had stood higher, and he had the honor of the house to consider. Whereas I was young and cruel, burning with love for my god, whom he had scoffed at as a lie and a dream. He was a fool and I was a worse one, and we did not part friends. Within the year he was dead."

Hirel bent his eyes upon his cup. It was plain wood like the others, unadorned. The cap, Sarevan's coarse awkward commoner's cap, slipped down, half blinding him. With a fierce gesture he flung it away. The air was cold on his naked head. "Within the year my brothers will not be dead. They will be shorn and branded and gelded as they would have done to me, and sold as slaves into the south." He looked up. The novices had withdrawn. Priest and priestess regarded him steadily, black eyes and amber, unreadable both. He wanted to scream at them. He addressed them with tight control. "I have no god to make me wise. No dream. No lies. Only revenge. I will have it, priests. I will have it or die."

"They would have been wiser to kill you," Sarevan said.

Hirel looked at him with something like respect. "So they would. But they were both craven and cruel. Neither of them wanted my blood on his hands; and even if I were found and recognized, what could I do? A eunuch cannot sit the Golden Throne. Their misfortune that they listened to the barber who was to geld me. I must be purged, he said, and left unfed for a day at least, or surely I would die under the knife. That night I found a window with a broken catch, and made use of it. Fools. They called me Goldilocks, and Father's spoiled darling, and plaything of the harem. They never thought that I would have the wits to run."

"No one ever credits beauty with brains." Sarevan sat back in his chair, gloriously insolent, and said, "Tell me, Orozia. Shall I take this cubling back to his father? Or shall I take him to mine and see what comes of it?"

Hirel sat still as he had learned to do in the High Court of Asanion, toying with a half-eaten fruit and veiling his burning eyes. Treachery. Of course. Haled off to some northern hill fort, given to a kilted savage, set to cleaning stables for his meager bread. And he was trapped here with a woman who had abandoned all her honor to take the demon's torque, and with a man who had never known what honor was.

"You know what you will do," said the priestess, eyes level upon Sarevan, and she spoke to him with an inflection that raised Hirel's hackles. Not as to the inferior he was, or as to the equal her graciousness might have allowed, but as to one set high above her. "But if I am to be consulted, I advise the latter. His highness is in great danger in the west, and you would be in no less. Avaryan is not welcome in Asanion. In any of his forms."

"Still," said Sarevan, "the boy wishes it."

"When did that ever sway you, Sarevan Is'kelion?"

The barbarian grinned, unabashed. "I should like to see the fabled empire. And he needs a keeper. Demands one, in fact."

"I need a guard," snapped Hirel. "You do not suit. You are insolent, and you try my patience." He turned his shoulder to the mongrel and faced Orozia. "Madam, I shall require clothing and a mount, and provisions for several days' journey, and an escort with some sense of respect."

She did not glance at him. Her eyes fixed on Sarevan. She had changed. There was no lightness in her now, nor in the one she spoke to. "Have you considered what your death would mean? They are killing priests in Asanion. And if they learn what you are . . ."

"What I am," Sarevan said softly, "yes. You forget the extent of it. I will venture this."

Her voice shook slightly. "Why?"

He touched her hand. "Dear lady. It is no whim. I must go. I have dreamed it; the dream binds me."

Her eyes widened. She had paled.

"Yes," he said, as cool as he had ever been. "It begins."

"And you submit?"

"I wait upon the god. That he has given me this of all companions— that is his will and his choice, and he will reveal his reasons when he chooses."

Her head bowed as if beneath a bitter weight; but it came up again, with spirit in it. "You are mad, and you were born mad, of a line of madmen. Avaryan help you; I will do what I can." She rose, sketched a blessing. "It were best that I begin now. Rest well, children."

Two

*H*IREL KNOTTED HIS HANDS INTO FISTS AND BURIED them in the hollows of his arms. "I will not!"

They had cajoled him into the rough garb of a commoner, and given him a cap that fit him properly, and begun to persuade him that he could pretend to be lowborn. If he must. But when the smaller and plainer novice came toward him with a short sharp knife, he erupted into rebellion. "I will not make my hands like a slave's. I will *not!*"

Orozia's patience strained somewhat at the edges, but her words were quiet. "Highness, you must. Would you betray yourself for merest vanity? A commoner cannot make his hands beautiful; it is banned."

Hirel backed to the wall. He was beyond reason. The cap bound his throbbing brows; the harsh homespun garments grated on his skin. The long nails, touched still with fugitive glimmers of gilt, drew blood from his palms. But they were all he had left. The only remnant of his royalty.

Firm hands seized his shoulders, lifted him, set him down again with gentle force. "Look," Sarevan commanded him.

He struck the mirror with all his strength. It rang silver-bright but did not bend or break. In it trembled and raged a peasant's child.

"Look," said the barbarian behind him. Forcing him, gripping his head when he struggled to spin away.

Compelled, he looked. Lowborn. Drab-clad, bare-skulled, wealthless and kinless. But the skull was elegant, pale as ivory, sheened with royal gold; and the face was fine, gold-browed, the wide eyes all burning gold, the thin nostrils pinched white with anger. A peasant with the look of a thoroughbred and the bearing of an emperor— "Who will ever believe the lie?"

"Anyone," answered Sarevan, "who sees the clothing. If you have the hands to prove it."

"Not the face?"

"Faces are the god's gift. Hands are made, and the law limits them." Sarevan raised one of Hirel's easily despite resistance. "Keri."

Woman's name, stolid all-but-sexless face. And the other, sweet-mouthed, had proven to be male; he waited to pounce if his fellow novice had need. Hirel thrust out his stiff hands. "Do it then, damn you. Make me all hideous."

They laughed behind their eyes. Hirel the Beautiful, shorn and clipped, was still a pretty creature, a plaything for a lady's chamber. He spat in the reflected face, blurring it into namelessness.

"You have blessings to count," Sarevan said, cool and unused. "Two, to be precise."

Hirel's voice cracked with bitter mockery. "What! Will you not take them, too?"

"We take nothing which cannot be restored." The priest leaned against the wall, arms folded. "Think of it as a game. A splendid gamble, the seeds of a song."

"Certainly. A satire on the fall of princes."

Sarevan only laughed and flashed his bold black eyes at the priestess, who blushed like a girl. Yet for all of that, when she spoke to him she was grave and almost stern. "Be gentle with him, Sarevan. He is neither as weak as he looks nor as strong as he pretends, and he was not raised as you were."

"I should hope not," snapped Hirel.

They were not listening. They seldom were. The priestess' eyes said a multitude of things, and the priest answered with a level stare. She beseeched. He refused. He had a look about him, not hard, not cold, but somehow implacable. At last he said, and he said it in Asanian which he need not have done. "This is a suckling infant who fancies himself a man. He is haughty, intolerant, and ruinously spoiled. Would you have me cater to his every whim?"

"Haughty," she repeated. "Intolerant. Ruinously spoiled. And are you perfection itself, Sarevan Is'kelion?"

"Ulan likes him," Sarevan said. "I'll be as gentle as I can bear to be. Will that content you?"

She sighed deeply. "I think you are mad. I know he will find no one he can trust more implicitly. Curse your honor, Sarevan, and curse the compassion which you will not confess; and be warned. I have sent word of this to your father."

That had the air of a threat, but Sarevan smiled. "He knows," he said. "I sent him a message of my own. I'm a dutiful son, madam."

"He has given you leave?"

Sarevan's smile gained an edge. "He's made no serious effort to stop me."

Her head came up. Her brows met. "Sarevan—"

He met her eyes in silence, his own level, glittering. After a stretching moment, Orozia's head bowed. Her sigh was deep. "Very well. There will be a price for this; pray Avaryan it is no higher than it must be."

"I will pay as I must pay," said Sarevan.

She did not look up, as if she could not. "Go, then," she said. Hirel could barely hear her. "And may the god protect you."

The road into Asanion stretched long under Hirel's protesting feet. Mounts they had none and were not to get, and Ulan was not precisely a tame cat. He came and went at will, hunted for them when it pleased him, vanished sometimes for an hour or a morning or a day. He was only rarely amenable to carrying a footsore prince.

But Hirel did not press him. *Spoiled,* Sarevan had said. It rankled like an old wound. Worse than Hirel's own hurts, which healed well and quickly, and left scars he did not look at. *Spoiled to ruin.* His brothers had said much the same. It had not hurt as much then, perhaps because they had weakened and paled it with envy and slain it with treason.

Sarevan had only said it once. It was enough. Hirel would show him. Did show him. Walked without a word of protest, though the sun beat down, though the rain lashed his ill-protected head. Climbed when he must, stumbled only rarely, and slowly hardened. At night he tumbled headlong into sleep.

It was a drug of sorts. It helped him to forget. But he had dreams of barbers and of knives, and of his brothers laughing; and sometimes he woke shaking, awash in tears, biting back a howl of rage and loss and sheer homesickness.

Slowly they worked their way westward. They did not strike straight into Pri'nai; they angled north, keeping for an unconscionable while to the marches of Keruvarion. Rough country, hill and crag and bleak stony uplands all but empty of folk, and those few and suspicious, hunters and herdsmen. Sarevan's torque was his passport there, that and the brilliance which he could unleash at will. He could charm a stone, that one.

He tried his utmost to charm Hirel. He told tales as they walked. He sang. He simply talked, easily and freely, unperturbed by silence or shortness or outright rejection. His voice was like the rhythm of walking, like the wind and the rain and the open sky; steady, lulling, even comforting. Then he would fall silent, and that in turn would bring its comfort, a companionship which demanded nothing beyond itself.

"Your hair is growing," he said once after a full morning of such silence.

Hirel had lost count of the days, but the land seemed a little gentler, the air frankly warm. Sarevan had stripped down to his boots and his swordbelt and his scrip, and nothing else. Even Hirel had put aside his cap and unbuttoned his coat, and he could feel the light touch of wind on his hair. His hand, searching, found a tight cap of curls.

Sarevan laughed at his expression. "You're going brown, do you know that? Take off your coat at least and let Avaryan paint the rest of you."

He could say that. Splendid naked animal, he did not burn and slough and darken like a field slave. But the sun was warm and Hirel's skin raw with heat, and Sarevan knew no more of modesty than of honor or of courtliness. With hammering heart Hirel undid the last button, dropped the coat and the shirt beneath, breathed free. And flung the trousers after them with reckless abandon.

He had done it. He had widened those so-wise eyes. He knotted his hands behind him to keep them from clutching his shame, and bared his teeth in a grin, and fought a blush.

Sarevan grinned back. "They'd have my hide in the Nine Cities," he said, "for corrupting the youth."

"What are you, then? Ancient?"

"Twenty-one on Autumn Firstday, infant."

Hirel blinked. "That is *my* birthday!"

"I'd cry your loftiness' pardon for usurping it; but I had it first."

Hirel found his dignity somewhere and put it on, which was not easy when he stood bare to the sky. "I shall be fifteen. My father will confirm all my titles, and give me ruling right in Veyadzan which is the most royal of the royal satrapies."

Sarevan's head tilted. "When I turned fifteen I became Avaryan's novice and began to win my torque." He touched it, a quick brush of the finger, rather like a caress. "My father took me to the temple in Han-Gilen and gave me to the priests. It was my free choice, and I was determined to embrace it like a man, but when other and older novices led me away, I almost broke down and wept. I would have given anything to be a child again."

"A prince stops being a child when he is born," Hirel said.

"What, did you never play at children's games?"

That was shock in Sarevan's eyes, and pity, and more that Hirel did not want to see. "Royalty does not play," he said frigidly.

"Alas for royalty."

"I was free," snapped Hirel. "I was learning, doing things that mattered."

"Did they?" Sarevan turned and began to pick his way down from the sunstruck height. Even his braid was insolent, and the flex of his bare flat buttocks, and the lightness of his tread upon the stones.

Hirel gathered his garments together. He did not put them on. Carefully he folded them into the bag Orozia had given him, in which he carried a second shirt and a roll of bandages and a packet or two of journey-bread. He slung the bag baldric-fashion and shouldered the rough woolen roll of his blanket. Sarevan was well away now, not looking back. Hirel lifted a stone, weighed it in his hand, let it fall. Too paltry a vengeance, and too crude. Carefully, but not slowly, he set his foot on the path which Sarevan had taken.

Hirel paid for his recklessness. He burned scarlet in places too tender for words; and he had to suffer Sarevan's hands with a balm the priest made of herbs and a little oil. But having burned away his fairness, he browned. "Goldened," Sarevan said, admiring unabashed, as he did everything.

"There is no such word."

"Now there is." Sarevan pillowed himself on Ulan's flank, face to the splendor of stars and moons, a creature all of fire and shadow.

It struck Hirel like a blow, startling, not quite unpleasant. Sarevan was beautiful. His alienness had obscured it, and Hirel's eye trained to see beauty in a fair skin and a sleek full-fleshed body and a smooth oval straight-nosed face. But Sarevan, who by all the tenets of artist and poet should have been hideous, was as splendid as the ul-cat that drowsed and purred beside him.

Hirel did not like him the better for it. And he, damn him, cared not at all. "Tomorrow," he said, half asleep already, "we cross into Asanion."

For all the warmth of air and blanket, Hirel shivered. *So soon?* part of him cried. Too large a part by far, for his mind's peace. But the rest had risen up in exultation.

There was no visible border, no wall or boundary of stone, Yet the land changed. Softened. Rolled into the green plains of Kovruen, ripening into summer, rich with its herds and its fields of grain, hatched with the broad paved roads of the emperors and dotted with shrines to various of the thousand gods.

Sarevan conceded to civilization. He bound his loins with a bit of cloth. Hirel put on his trousers and the lighter of his shirts, and hated himself for hating the touch of them against his skin. But he gained something: he could walk barefoot on the road, his boots banished to his bag. It would have been more of a pleasure if Sarevan had not strode bootless beside him, near naked and gloriously comfortable.

People stared at the barbarian. For there were people here, workers in the fields, walkers on the road. There was nothing like him in that land, or likely in the world. No one would speak to him; those whom he approached, ducked their heads and fled.

"Are they so modest?" he asked Hirel, standing in the road with his braid like a tail of fire and the sun swooning on his dusky hide.

"They take you for a devil," Hirel said. "Or perhaps a god. One of the Thousand might choose to look like you, if it suited his whim."

Sarevan tilted his head as if he would contest the point, but he said nothing. He did not make any move to cover himself. No garment in the world could make him smaller or paler or his mane less beacon-bright.

Hirel frowned. "You might be wise to take off your torque."

"I may not," It was flat, final, and unwearied with repetition.

"I can call it a badge of slavery. Perhaps people will believe me."

"Perhaps your father will swear fealty to the Sunborn." Sarevan settled his scrip over his shoulder and began to walk. "I'll not rely on deceptions, but trust to the god."

"To the superstitious lie."

Sarevan stopped, turned lithely on his heel. "You believe that?"

"I know it. There are no gods. They are but dreams, wishes and fears given names and faces. Every wise man knows as much, and many a priest. There is great profit in gods, when the common crowd knows no better than to worship them."

"You believe that," Sarevan repeated. He sounded incredulous. "You poor child, trapped in a world so drab. So logical. So very blind."

Hirel's lip curled. "At least I do not spend my every waking hour in dread lest I give offense to some divinity."

"How can you, a mere mortal, offend a god? But then," Sarevan said, "you don't know Avaryan."

"I know all that I need to. He is the sun. He insists that he be worshipped as sole god. His priests must never touch women, and his priestesses cannot know men, or they die in fire. And if that is not punishment for offending the god, what do you call it?"

"We worship him as the sun, because its light is the closest this world may come to his true face. He is worshipped alone because he is alone, high lord of all that walks in the light, as his sister is queen of all darkness. Our vows before him are a mystery and a sacrifice, and their breaking is weakness and unworthiness and betrayal of faith. The god keeps his word; we can at least try to follow his example."

"Are you a virgin, then?"

"Ah," said Sarevan, undismayed. "You want to know if I'm a proper man. Can't you tell by looking at me?"

"You are." A virgin, Hirel meant. He looked at Sarevan and tried to imagine a man grown who had never, even once, practiced the highest and most pleasant of the arts. It was shocking. It was appalling. It was utterly against nature.

Hirel eased, a little. "Ah. I see. You are speaking of women. It is boys you love, then."

"If it were, cubling, you'd know it by now."

Bold eyes, those. Laughing. Knowing no shame. He was proud to be as he was. He was all alien. Hirel's gorge rose at the sight and the thought of him.

"I serve my god," he said, light and proud and oblivious. "I have walked in his presence. I have known his son."

"Avaryan's son." It was bitter in Hirel's throat, but less bitter than what had come before it. "The mighty king. The conqueror with the clever tale. He is a mage, they say, a great master of illusion."

"Not great enough to have begotten himself."

"Ah," said Hirel, "everyone knows the truth of that. The Prince of Han-Gilen sired him on the Ianyn priestess, and arranged his mating to the princess his half-sister, and so built an empire to rule from the shadows behind its throne."

"By your account, the Emperor of Asanion has that in common with the Sunborn: he wedded his sister. But he at least rules his own empire. However diminished by the encroachments of the Red Prince's puppet." Sarevan's mockery was burning cold. "Child, you know many words and many tales, but the truth is far beyond your grasp. When you have seen the Lord An-Sh'Endor, when you have looked on my god, then and only then may you speak with honest certainty."

"It angers you. That I will not accept your lies. That I will not bow to your god."

"That you cannot see what stares you in the face." Sarevan spun about, braid whipping his flanks.

Hirel wanted to savor the victory, that insufferable mask torn aside at last. But fear had slain all gladness. That he had driven the barbarian away: this alien, this mocker of nature, whose face at least he knew. Whom alone he could dream of trusting, here where he was alone, unarmed, and every stone might harbor an enemy. He ran after the swiftly striding figure.

Sarevan slowed after a furlong or two, but he did not speak, nor would he glance at Hirel. His face was grim and wild. Oddly, he looked the younger for it, but no less panther-dangerous.

"Perhaps," Hirel said in a time and a time, "your Avaryan could be a truth. A way of understanding the First Cause of the philosophers."

It was as close to an apology as Hirel had ever come. It fell on deaf ears. Damned arrogant barbarian. It must be all or nothing. Avaryan with his disk and his rays and his burning heat, and how he had ever begotten a son on a woman without scorching her to a cinder was not for mere men to know. Hirel threw up his hands in disgust. Perhaps that tissue of lies and legends was enough for a simple man, a partbred tribesman. Hirel was a prince and a scholar. And he did not grovel. He let Sarevan stalk ahead, walking himself at a pace which suited him, letting the road draw him westward.

They were coming to a city as it would be reckoned in these distant provinces, a town of respectable size even for the inner realms of the empire. The shrines came closer together now, and many were shrines to the dead, stark white tombs and cenotaphs, hung with offerings. It was easy to mark the newest or the richest: the birds were thick about them, and the flies, and now and then the jeweled brilliance of a dragonel. In the dust-hazed distance Hirel could discern a wall with houses clustered about it.

"Shon'ai," Sarevan said.

At first Hirel tried to make it a word in a tongue he knew. Then he grimaced at himself. It was only the name of the town. People were thickening on and about the road, moving toward the gate, some laden with baskets or bales, or drawing handcarts, or leading burdened beasts.

Hirel saw the haughty figure of a man in a chariot, and a large woman on a very small pony, and a personage carried in a litter.

Swiftly as Sarevan moved, in a very little while they were in the midst of the stream. Hirel kept close to the priest. He had seen no one at all for so long, and then had walked so far apart, and after days of Sarevan's black eagle-mask these round golden faces were strange.

Of course they stared. Children ran after Sarevan, once or twice even dared to throw stones at him. The stones flew wide. The priest glanced neither right nor left. He walked as a prince was trained to walk, as a panther was born to. He towered over everyone who came near him.

The gate of the town was open wide, the guards making no effort to stem the tide of people. It was no mere market day but the festival of a god. Which meant a market indeed and a great deal of profit, but processions with it, and sacrifices, and much feasting and drinking and roistering. There were garlands of flowers everywhere within the walls, on all the houses and the several temples, and on every neck and brow and wrist.

Hirel clung to a dangling end of Sarevan's loincloth and let himself be towed through the crowds. Very soon now he was going to disgrace himself. It was different for a prince. Where he went, the way was always clear, the throngs held at bay. Not pressing in, breathing foul in his face, bellowing in his ear. He could not see. He could not think. He could not—

A strong arm swept him up. Hoofs and horns and seneldi bellings ramped where he had been, clove a path through the press, and vanished. Hirel's arms had locked about Sarevan's neck. His breath came in quick hard gasps. "Take," he forced out. "Take me—"

Sarevan wasted no words. He breasted the crowd, and no one touched him; and in a blessed while the crowd was gone. Hirel raised his head, blinking. It was dark. Sarevan was speaking. "A room, a bath, and wine. Silver for you if you are quick, gold if you fly."

Slowly Hirel focused. They were in a wide room, surrounded by carpets, cushions, tables, an effluvium of ale. An inn. Eyes glittered out of the gloom, many eyes, every patron struck dumb it seemed by the spectacle at the door. One man stood close: a round buttery creature with an astonishingly sour face. "Show me your silver," he said.

Sarevan's grip shifted on Hirel, and Hirel thought he saw a glint of gold. Certainly the innkeeper saw something that satisfied him. "Come," he said.

The room was tiny, no more than a crevice in the roof; Sarevan could stand erect only in the center. But it was clean, it had a window which opened after a blow or two of the barbarian's fist, and its bed-cushions were deep enough to drown in. The bath when it came was hot and capacious, the wine cool and sweet, and cakes came with it, and dumplings filled to bursting with meat and grain and fruit, and a dish of soft herbed cheese.

"No," Sarevan was saying, "it's not catching. He's always been delicate, and the excitement of the festival . . . you understand. With these thoroughbreds, one has to take such care, but the beauty is worth much; and he serves me well, in his way."

Hirel fought his way back to full awareness in time to see the innkeeper's leer, and the closing of the door upon it. He lay in the deep soft nest of the bed, and he was wrapped in a drying-cloth, damp still from a bath he could hardly remember, with the taste of wine on his tongue. The innkeeper had been ogling him. The mongrel had said— "How dare you call me your slave."

"Would you rather I called you my catamite?" Sarevan inquired.

"You did just that!"

"Hush," Sarevan said as to a fretful child.

Hirel raised his voice in earnest. "May all the gods damn you to—"

A hand clapped over his mouth. "The gods do not exist," the priest reminded him with poisonous sweetness.

He choked and gasped and twisted, and found the edge of that quelling hand, and bit hard.

He won all he could have wished for. Sarevan's breath left him in a rush; his hand snapped back. Hirel stared. The priest's skin was not opaque at all. It was like black glass; and a corpse-light burned ghastly beneath. His lips were grey as ash.

But Hirel had not even drawn blood.

Sarevan withdrew as far as he might, which was only a step or two. His hand trembled; he thrust it behind him. It was his right hand. Hirel committed that to memory. This man of limitless strength and overweening arrogance had a weakness, and it was enormous and it was utterly inexplicable, and it was worth bearing in mind. It evened the score, somewhat.

"Cubling," Sarevan said, and his voice did not come easily, "did your teachers never instruct you in proper and honorable combat?"

"With proper and honorable opponents," Hirel answered, "yes."

Sarevan tilted his head. Considered. Bared his white teeth and saluted left-handed, as a swordsman would concede a match.

"And I am not your servant," Hirel said.

"So then, you are my catamite."

Hirel hissed at him. He shook out his hair, laughing almost freely, and availed himself of the cooling bath.

Three

*H*IREL SLEPT A LITTLE. WHEN HE WOKE, SAREVAN was gone. He knew a moment's panic; then he saw the worn leather of the priest's scrip hanging from a peg by the bed. Everything was in it, even the small but surprisingly heavy purse. He had not gone far. Hirel relieved himself, nibbled the remains of a seedcake, poured a cupful of wine and peered out of the window. Nothing below but an alleyway. He wandered back to his cushions, sipping the sweet strong vintage. It was not one he knew; not nearly fine enough for a high prince in his palace. But in this place it was pleasant.

He settled more comfortably. The room was warm but not unbearable. One of his scars itched within where he could not scratch it: one of the deep furrows in his hip and thigh. The guardhound had caught him there, terrifying him for his manhood; he had found strength he had never known he had, and broken the beast's neck. The hound had paid the proper price, but Hirel would bear the marks until he died, livid and unlovely against his skin.

He was changing. He was thinner, with ribs to count. His childsoftness was sharpening into planes and angles. A fleece of down was coming between his legs, and he was not the same beneath it. He was becoming a man.

Perhaps he would call for a woman. That would wipe the leer from the innkeeper's face. Sarevan, poor maiden priest, would wilt with envy.

Hirel frowned. He could not imagine Sarevan wilting. More likely the creature would stand by the door and fold his arms and smile his most supercilious smile, and make of manly virtue a creeping shame.

"Damn him," Hirel said. His voice lacked conviction. "I will go. I will go now and find my own way home. My brothers will fall down in terror when they see me; and I will have my vengeance."

He clasped his knees and rocked. His eyes blurred; he could not stop them. Alone, all alone, with only a demon-worshipping madman to defend him. No one in the empire even knew he lived; and those who cared could care only that he was not safely dead. His mother who had loved him, and yes, spoiled him shamefully, his mother was two years dead by her own hand, and his father was a golden mask upon a golden throne, and his brothers would have sold him a eunuch into the south. And he was going home. Home to hate and fear and at best indifference; to the nets of courtiers and the chains of royalty, and never a moment without the dread of another betrayal.

A shudder racked him. He must go back. What else was left to him?

He knew what he must do. Dress. Gather the last of the food. Take a handful of silver from Sarevan's purse. Just enough to buy a mount and to keep him fed until he came to Kundri'j Asan. When he was done, he would repay the lending a hundred times over: send a bag of gold to Orozia in the town the name of which he had never troubled to learn, and instruct her to give it to the priest.

He went as far as to rise, to turn toward his clothes. They were wet. He was close to tears again.

The door opened. Sarevan had to stoop to pass it. Lean though he was, his shoulders were broad; he filled the cramped space. His face was set in stone. His eyes were burning.

The wall was rough and cool against Hirel's back. He did not even remember retreating to it. Somehow the priest had divined what he would do. Theft; flight.

No. Only true mages walked in minds, and there were no true mages, only charlatans. Sarevan turned blindly about, hands clenching and unclenching. One, the bitten right, rose to his torque and fell again. "They burned it," he said low in his throat. "They burned it to the ground."

"What?" Hirel snapped, sharp with guilt and startlement.

At first he did not know if Sarevan heard. The eyes never turned to him. But at length the voice answered, still low, almost rough. "Avaryan's temple. They burned it. They burned it over the heads of the priests, and sowed the ashes with salt, and set up a demon-stone in the midst of it, cursing Avaryan and his priesthood unto the thousandth generation. But why? Why so immeasurable a hate?"

It was a cry of anguish. Hirel's throat ached with the power of it; his own words came hard, half strangled. "Avaryan is the enemy here, the symbol of the conqueror, of the empire that has dared to rise and challenge us. His priests are suspected as spies, and some have been caught at it. But hatred of that magnitude . . . I do not know."

Sarevan's laughter was frightening. "*I* know. It is politics, cold politics. A game of kings-and-cities, with living folk for pawns. Burn a temple, open the way to the destruction of its patron's empire. They died in torment, my brothers and sisters. They died like sea-spiders in a cauldron."

"Perhaps," said Hirel, "they offended someone in power. No great conspiracy; a personal vendetta. But whatever is the truth of it, you are not safe here, and you should not linger. By now all Shon'ai will have seen your torque."

"Oh, yes, they have seen it. They have all seen me, the mongrel, the monster, the demon's minion. I cast down the cursed stone and laid a curse of my own upon it, and sang the god's praises over it."

"You are stark mad."

"What! You did not know?"

"They must be hunting you now." Hirel's heart raced, but his brain was clear. "We can run. The crowds will hide us. You can stoop, and cover your body and your hair, and feign a limp, perhaps."

"No," Sarevan said. "One at least of my torque-kin remains alive, although the prison is hidden from me. But I will find it. Before Avaryan I will find it." He spoke as if the prison's hiding were an impossible thing, a deep and personal insult. Yet when he looked at Hirel he seemed utterly sane, cool and quiet, reasonable. "You will go. Ulan will come to you when you have passed the gates; he will guard you and guide you and bring you safe to your father. No one will molest you while you travel in his company."

True, all true, and very wise. Hirel had intended to do much the same.

But.

"I will not abandon you," he said stiffly.

"Cubling," said Sarevan, "you cannot help me, you are certain to hinder me, and it is altogether likely that I will get my death in this venture. It was a mage who laid the curse on the temple; he is strong, and he will not be merciful."

Hirel sneered. "A mage. I tremble where I stand."

"You should, child. He's no trumpery trickster. He has power, and it is real, and it tastes of darkness."

"Superstition. I know better. I have seen the mages in Kundri'j Asan. Powders and stinks and spells and cantrips, and a great deal of mystical posturing. It deceives the masses. It enriches the mages. It amuses my father to retain a few of the more presentable in his court. They can do him no harm, he says, and one day they might prove useful."

"That day has come, and the lord of this province has seized upon it. I am going to do battle with the sorcerer."

"You dare it?" Hirel asked, meaning to mock him.

"I dare it. You see, cubling," Sarevan said, "I am one myself."

Hirel blinked at him. He did not sprout horns, or cloak himself in stars, or spawn flights of dragonels from his cupped hands. He was only Sarevan, too large for that cupboard of a room, and rather in need of a bath. The reek of smoke and anger lay heavy upon him.

He gathered Hirel's garments and dropped them on the bed. "Dress yourself. You must be away from here before they close the gates for the night."

Slowly Hirel obeyed. He would be well rid of this lunatic. Mage, indeed. Gods, indeed. A little longer and the barbarian would have had Hirel believing it.

Sarevan saw to Hirel's bag, packed the seedcakes and a napkinful of dumplings, added his own waterskin, and rummaging in his scrip, brought out the purse. Without a word or a glance, he laid it in the bag.

Hirel's throat closed. Sarevan held out the bag; Hirel clutched it to his chest. "Come," the priest said.

Hirel tried to swallow. Time was running on. And he could not move.

Sarevan snatched him up; and he left the inn as he had entered it, carried like an ailing child. The streets were as crowded as ever, the shadows growing long with evening. Hirel began to struggle. Sarevan ignored him. There was a new tension in the priest's body, a tautness like fear, but the press was too tight, the current too strong; he could breast it, but he could not advance above a walk, with many turns and weavings and impasses. It was like a spell, a curse of endless frustration.

At last he could not move at all, and from his shoulder's height the inn was still visible, its sign of the sunbird mocking Hirel's glare. "I will do it," Sarevan muttered. "I must."

"What—"

Sarevan stood erect and breathed deep, and Hirel felt—something. Like a spark. Like a flare of heat too brief to be sure of. Like a note of music on the very edge of hearing. All the small hairs of his body shivered and rose.

"*There!*" Sun flashed on helmets; a senel tossed its horns and half reared, its rider calling out, sweeping his arm toward the priest. Sarevan plunged into the crowd. It parted before him. But against the company behind came a second, barring the broad way, and the throng milled and tangled itself, and no escape but straight into the air. And Sarevan seized it. He launched himself upward.

For a soaring, terrifying moment he flew, and Hirel with him, and people cried out to see it. Then darkness filled the sky. Something like an eagle stooped above them, but an eagle with wings that spread from horizon to horizon. With a sharp fierce cry Sarevan reared back, gripping Hirel one-handed, hurling lightnings.

Hirel saw the arrow come. He tried to speak, even to shape a thought. The dart sang past his cheek and plunged deep into the undefended shoulder. Sarevan cried out again, sharper and fiercer still, and dropped like a stone.

"Fascinating," said the Lord of Baryas and Shon'ai when he had heard his captain's account, inspecting the prisoners bound and haughty before him. Hirel had only a set of manacles, which was an insult. Sarevan was wrapped in chains, his shoulder bound with a bandage, and his face was grey with pain. But he met the lord's stare with perfect insolence.

The lord smiled. He was tall for an Asanian, a bare head shorter than Sarevan, and slender, and exquisitely attired. His slaves were skillful: one had to peer close to see that he was not young, that his hair was not as thick as it feigned to be. But his eyes were not the eyes of a fool. "Fascinating," he repeated, circling Sarevan, lifting the loosened braid and letting it fall. "High sorcery in my own city before the faces of my people, and the sorcerer . . . What is your name, priest of Avaryan?"

"You know it as well as I," said Sarevan with perfect calm.

"Do I?" the lord inquired. He raised a hand. "Unbind him."

Soldiers and servants slanted their eyes and muttered, but under their lord's eye they obeyed, retreating quickly as if the sorcerer might blast them where they stood. He barely moved except to flex his good shoulder and to draw a breath. "Ah then, perhaps I've changed a little; I was somewhat younger when we met. I remember you, Ebraz y Baryas ul Shon'ai."

"And I you," the lord admitted, "Sarevan Is'kelion y Endros. I confess I never expected to see you here in such state, with such attendance."

"What, my boy?" Sarevan grinned and ruffled Hirel's hair. "Do you like him? I found him in a hedgerow; I'm making a man of him, though it's hard going. His old master didn't use him well, and he's not quite sane. Fancies himself a prince of your empire, if you can believe it."

Ebraz barely glanced at Hirel, whose rage bade fair to burst him asunder. "He has the look, true enough. They breed for it in slave-stables here and there; it fetches a high price."

"I had him for a song. The strain is flawed, it seems. It produces incorrigibles. But I've not given up hope yet."

"What will you do with him when you have tamed him?"

"Set him free, of course."

Ebraz laughed, a high well-bred whinny. "Of course!" He sobered. "Meanwhile, my lord, you have presented me with rather a dilemma. By command of my overlord, all priests of Avaryan are outlawed in Kovruen; and you have not only stood forth publicly as a bearer of the torque, you have also wielded magecraft without the sanction of the guild."

"Guild?" Sarevan asked.

"Guild," Ebraz answered. "Surely you know that your kind are licensed and taxed in the Golden Empire." He spread his narrow elegant hands. "So you see, my lord, between emperor and overlord I am compelled to hold you prisoner. I regret the necessity, and I regret still more deeply the circumstances which led to your wounding. You can be sure that I will send to my lord with a full explanation. And to your father, of course, with profoundest apologies."

Sarevan flinched, although he tried to make light of it. "You needn't trouble my father with my foolishness."

"But, my lord, if he discovers for himself—"

"We can take care that he does not. Imprison me if you must, I've earned it, but spare me my father's wrath for yet a while."

The lord smiled in understanding. "I can be slow to send a message. But Prince Zorayan must know; your freedom lies in his hands."

"That will suffice," said Sarevan. He swayed; his lips were ashen. "If you will pardon me—"

"That would not be wise, my lord."

Hirel started. A man had come out of nowhere, a man who looked much less a mage than Sarevan, small, dark-robed, quiet. "My lord," he said, "this weakness is a lie. He plots to deceive you, to cozen you into giving him a gentle imprisonment, and thence to escape by his arts. See, such a fine fierce glare. He knows that his power is no match for mine."

"No?" asked Sarevan, eyes glittering. He no longer looked as if he were about to faint. "I would have had you, journeyman, but for an archer's good fortune. You are but a spellcaster, a slave to your grimoires; I am mageborn."

"Mageborn, but young, and arrogant with it. Arrogant far beyond your skill or your strength."

"Do you care to test me, conjurer? Here and now, with no book and no charmed circle. Come, summon your familiar; invoke your devils. I will be generous. I will hold them back if they seek to turn on you."

"I have your blood, Sunchild," the mage said calmly. "That is book and circle enough."

Sarevan's breath caught. His defiance had an air of desperation. Feigned, perhaps. Perhaps not. "You cannot touch me."

"Enough," said Ebraz quietly, but they heard him. "I cannot afford an escape, my lord. Surely you understand. Your word would suffice, but . . . Prince Zorayan is not an easy man, and he is not altogether certain that he trusts me. I must be strict. For appearance's sake. I will be no more rigorous than I must."

"I will remember," Sarevan said. Warning, promising.

"Remember, my lord, but forgive." Ebraz signaled to his men. "The lower prison. Minimal restraint but constant guard. Within reason, let him have whatever he asks for."

It was dark. It was damp. It stank. It was a dungeon, and it was vile, and Sarevan smiled at it. "Spacious," he said to the guard who stood nearest, "and well lit; and the straw is clean, I see. Rats? Yes? Ah well, what would a dungeon be without rats?"

They had taken off Hirel's chain. He bolted for the door. A guard caught him with contemptuous ease, and took his time letting go, groping down Hirel's trousers. Hirel laid him flat.

Sarevan laughed. "Isn't he a wonder? Protects his virtue better than any maid. But with a little persuasion . . ."

The guards were grinning. Hirel's victim got up painfully, but the murder had retreated from his eyes. He did not try to touch Hirel again.

They left the dim lamp high in its niche, where it bred more shadows than it vanquished. The door thudded shut; bolts rattled across it. Hirel turned on Sarevan. "You unspeakable—"

"Yes, I held your tongue for you, and it was well for you I did. If my elegant lord had taken any notice of you, he would have kept you. He likes a pretty boy now and then. But he likes them docile and he likes them devoted, and I made sure that he thought I might have tainted you with my sorceries. Why, your very face could have been a trap."

"What do you think you have led me into? I could have been free. I could have proven my rank and had an escort to my father."

"You could have been held hostage well apart from me, with no hope of escape."

"What hope is there now?"

"More than none." Before Hirel could muster a riposte, Sarevan had withdrawn, turning his eyes toward the deepest of deep shadows. His breath hissed. He swooped upon something.

Hirel's eyes were sharpening to the gloom. He saw what Sarevan knelt beside. A bundle of rags. A tangle of—

Hair like black water flecked with white. The tatters of a robe such as all priests wore by law in Asanion, torn most upon the breast where the badge of the god should be. The prisoner had on something beneath, something dark and indistinct, but glinting on the edge of vision.

Hirel's stomach heaved. It was no garment at all, but flesh flayed to the bone. And the face—the face—

It had been a woman once. It could still speak with a clarity horrible amid the ruin, and the voice was sweet. It was a young voice, light and pure despite the greying hair. *"Avar'charin?"* It shifted to accented Asanian. "Brother. Brother my lord, *Avar'charin.* I see you in the darkness. How bright is the light of you!"

Sarevan stroked the beautiful hair. His face was deadly still. "Hush," he murmured. "Hush."

She stirred. Though it must have roused her to agony, she touched his hand. His fingers closed over hers, gently, infinitely gently, for they were little more than blood and broken bone. "My lord," she cried with sudden urgency, "you should not be here! This land is death for you."

"It has been worse for you." His voice was as still as his face.

"I am no one. My pain belongs to the god; it is nearly done. But you —Endros iVaryan, you were mad to pass your father's borders."

"The god is leading me. He brought me to you. Give me your pain, sister. Give me your suffering, that I may heal it."

"No. No, you must not."

"I must."

She clutched him, although she gasped, although her broken body writhed with the effort and the anguish of it. "No. Oh, no. They left me alive for this. They left lips and tongue. They knew—they wanted—"

Sarevan's face was set, closed, implacable. He laid his hands on that head with its bitter paradox of beauty and ruin. The air sang; Hirel's flesh prickled. Almost he could see. Almost he could hear. Almost *know.* Power like wind and fire, solid as a sword, ghostly as a dream, terrible as the lightning. Gathering, waxing, focusing. Reaching within the shattered body, willing it to live, to mend, to be whole.

"No!" cried the priestess, high and despairing.

The bait was taken, the trap was sprung. The hunter came in wind and fire, but his fire was black and his wind bore the stink of darkness.

The healing frayed and chilled and broke. Sarevan reared up, and the masks were gone, torn away from purest, reddest rage. He roared, and it was no man who sprang, but a great cat the color of night, with eyes of fire.

Hirel had no pride in the face of a world gone mad. He cowered in the farthest corner. Perhaps he whimpered. He scrabbled at the wall, hoping hopelessly that it would give way and free him from this horror.

As far from him as the cell's walls permitted, and much too hideously close, there was nothing to see, and there was everything. A cat crouched over a shapeless thing that had been a woman. A cat that was also a redheaded northerner, locked in combat with something that was now Lord Ebraz' tame sorcerer and now a direwolf with bloody jaws.

The cat's fangs closed upon the wolf's throat. It howled; it fought. The cat grunted, perhaps with effort, perhaps with the laughter of the prey turned hunter and slayer. The wolf slashed helplessly at air. Cruel claws rent its body. Its blood bubbled and flamed like the blood of mountains.

With a last vicious stroke, the cat flung down his enemy. A man all broken and bleeding, and his blood had still that fiery, sorcerous strangeness. Power, Hirel knew without knowing how. The mage bled his magic at Sarevan's feet. "Thus," said the priest, cold and proud, "do you learn the law. A journeyman does not challenge a master. Go now; reap the reward your folly has won you. Live without power and without magic, and know that Avaryan's line cannot be cast down by any mortal man."

The enemy vanished. Sarevan began to sink down beside the body of the priestess.

Wind swept over him, with fire in its jaws. It caught him unawares. He reeled and fell. Hirel's wandering wits observed the priest's braid, how bright it was as he toppled, bright as new copper, clashing with the blood upon his bandages.

He twisted in the air, supple, impossible, feline. His form blurred and steadied, human shape grappling with living shadow. There were eyes in the shapeless darkness. Terrible eyes: golden, luminous, and infinitely sad. *I must,* they said, as the sky speaks of rain. *You threaten us all. I cannot grant you mercy.*

"Mercy?" Sarevan's wrath had gone quiet. "Was it mercy you granted my torque-sister? Share it, then. Share it in its fullness."

They closed, darkness and darkness, flesh and shadow. The shadow —Hirel giggled, quite contentedly mad. The shadow had the voice of a woman and the suggestion of a woman's shape; a soft curve of cheek, a swell of breasts, a slimness of waist. So close and so fiercely did they do battle that they looked to be locked in an embrace less of war than of love. Hirel's manhood rose in fancied sympathy. His breathing quickened. It was a woman, that shadow, and such a woman, ineffably beautiful, ineffably sad. All Asanion dwelt in her body and in her great grieving eyes.

Sarevan destroyed them. Hirel howled. Now that he must move, he could not. He raged and he wept. He forsook the last rags of his sanity. Yet through it all, his eyes saw with perfect and hideous clarity.

As Sarevan had broken the wolf, so he broke the lady of the empire and cast her down. But she clung to consciousness. She smiled as he set his foot on her. Her smile was beautiful, and yet it was horrible; for it was a smile of triumph. "The battle," she said, "is yours, O slave of the burning god. But the war is mine." She grasped his foot with her last desperate strength, and thrust it up and back. Lightnings leaped from her hands. She laughed, high and sweet and taunting. It was laughter made to madden a man, if he were young and proud and filled with the wrath of his god. It pricked, it stung. It drove Sarevan back; it roused his power anew. He wielded the lightning like a sword. He swooped upon his tormentor and smote her where she lay.

Four

THE SILENCE WAS ABRUPT AND ABSOLUTE. SAREVAN stood empty-handed. His face was grey, his bandage all scarlet. Slowly, stiffly, he knelt. He touched the body of the sorceress. It lay whole and unmarred, as if it slept; but no breath stirred.

Sarevan sat on his heels. "Varyan," he whispered. "O Avaryan."

Hirel, having tasted the warmth of madness, found sanity grim and cold. He stood over the priest and the sorceress. The priestess was gone, if she had ever been aught but illusion.

Sarevan raised his head. His eyes were dull. Even his hair seemed dim, faded, all the brightness gone from it. He scraped it out of his eyes. "I killed her," he said calmly.

"So I see," responded Hirel.

"Do you? Can you?" Sarevan laughed. It was not comfortable to hear. "That was the trap. To make me kill her. To make—me—" His voice cracked like a boy's. He leaped to his feet, staggered, caught himself. "Quick now. Walk."

"Where?"

Sarevan swayed again. He looked about, peering as if he could not see; he drew a breath that caught in his throat. "Walk," he gritted. "Walk, damn you."

They walked. The door melted away before them. No one saw them, and they saw no one. Perhaps they did not walk in the world at all. They came up out of the dungeon, and they walked through a high house richly furnished, part of which Hirel thought he could remember; but not even an insect stirred. And the gate opened not upon the city of Shon'ai but upon greenness and sunlight and a whisper of water. Sarevan stumbled and fell to his knees. Hirel snatched at him; he pushed the hands away. His head tossed from side to side. His eyes were wide and blind. "It's gone," he said. "All of it. All gone." A sound escaped him, half laughter, half sob. "I gave her the death she longed for. She—she gave me worse. Infinitely worse."

"What—" Hirel began.

Sarevan's eyes rolled up. Slowly, bonelessly, he toppled.

Hirel caught too late, managed only to drag himself down under a surprising weight. It ended across his lap, leaden heavy, barely breathing. Trapping him, pinning him to the ground. He struggled briefly and wildly.

Abruptly he stilled. Willing himself to be calm, to think. It was the fiercest battle he had ever known, and the greatest victory.

Hirel regarded the face upturned in his lap. It was much the same as ever, dark, high-nosed, haughty; even unconscious it bore the hollows of exhaustion.

Hirel shivered in the sun's warmth. This creature had called upon a power that could not, should not exist. Had flown without wings, and wielded the lightning, and destroyed two mages who had come against him. Sarevan who had found an Asanian prince in a fernbrake and condescended to be his guard; who never wore more than he must, who was conspicuously vain of his body, who ate and drank and slept and sometimes had bad dreams. He sweated when the sun was hot and shivered when the night was cold, and bathed when he needed it, which was often enough, and relieved himself exactly as every other man must. No showers of enchanted gold.

Hirel bit his lips until they bled. There were mages, and Sarevan was one, and if mages could be, then what of gods?

Perhaps it had been a dream.

The earth was solid beneath him, cool, a little damp. The air bore a scent of sunlight and of wilderness. The weight across his thighs was considerable, and inescapable.

Sarevan. Sarevan Is'kelion, Sarevan Stormborn, Sa'van lo'ndros who could not be what he could not but be. Sa'van lo'ndros, Sarevadin li Endros in the high Gileni tongue that Hirel's father had commanded he learn: Sarevadin the prince.

Hirel had some excuse for idiocy. When a high prince of Asanion was born, all menchildren born that day and for a Greatmoon-cycle round about were given his name. It confused the demons, people said, and spread the gods' blessing abroad upon the empire. And some of the Sunborn's Ianyn savages had taken wives among the women of the Hundred Realms, and many more had not troubled with such niceties, with mongrels enough to show for it. And surely the heir of a very god would not be walking the highroad of his own free will with all his worldly goods in a battered bag.

Sarevadin the prince, son of the Sunborn.

What a hostage.

What an irony.

But there was one wild tale at least—

Hirel lifted one long limp hand. The right, that one which had shown itself to be Sarevan's great weakness. A shaft of sun caught in its palm and flamed. *Ilu'Kasar,* the brand of the god, that he had from his father.

Suddenly Hirel was whitely, gloriously angry. Sarevan had said no word, not even one; had taken a wicked delight in Hirel's stupidity. Letting Hirel look on him as lowborn, driving Hirel wild with his arrogance, laughing all the while at the blind and witless child. Hoping very likely to play the game clear to Kundri'j Asan, and melt away unknown, and rise up in Keruvarion and tell the tale to all who would hear. How the High Prince of Keruvarion saved the life of the High Prince of Asanion, and took him back to his safe nest and his doting father, and won scarcely a civil word in return. "Why," Sarevan would say as he quaffed ale with his father's bearded chieftains, "the poor infant could hardly recall his own name, let alone mine, he was so prostrated by the shock of having to do up his own trousers."

Hirel bit down on the back of his hand. He was going to howl. With rage, with laughter, what matter? He had been a prisoner in the dungeon of one of his own lords, with a sorcery on his tongue whenever he tried to speak his name, and the son of An-Sh'Endor had set him free. Casting them both here, wherever here might be, in a welter of magic and a flood of words that, uncomprehended, roused nothing but dread.

Hirel's eyes flinched from the dazzle of the *Kasar.* It was true gold, bright metal in the shape of the sun's disk, many-rayed, born there, bred in the flesh by a god's power. It burned, the tales said, like living fire. Small wonder that Sarevan had nearly fainted when Hirel sank his teeth into it.

Hirel laid the hand on Sarevan's breast. "Consider," he said to it, "what I know and what I surmise. Your god is being driven from Asanion as quietly as may be, and as completely. The Order of Mages has withdrawn from the Nine Cities and reappeared in Kundri'j Asan under the open protection of the Charlatans' Guild and the secret sanction of the emperor my father. He wields them as he wields every weapon, as a counter to the power of the emperor your father.

"And here we lie, you and I, only your god knows where. Is that the heart of your plot, High Prince of Keruvarion? To bewitch and abduct the High Prince of Asanion?"

Sarevan did not move.

"Sarevadin Halenan Kurelian Miranion iVaryan. See, I know you. I have you wholly in my power. Shall I slay you while you lie helpless? Shall I bear you away to be my slave in Kundri'j?"

Not a sound, not a flicker. Sarevan was alive, but little more; somehow he had thwarted the surgeon's close stitching, and he was ghastly grey, and perhaps there was more amiss that Hirel could not understand. Something uncanny, something sorcerous. And they were alone, foodless and waterless, without weapon or baggage; and a pair of trousers for each, neither excessively clean, and a single torn shirt. And a torque of gold, for what that was worth.

Much, even if it were no more than gilded lead. Hirel had only to unclasp it and run, and hide, and twist it out of recognition and hammer it with a stone and sell a bit of it in the next town he came to. If there was a town. If it was close enough to find before he starved.

What a blow to Keruvarion his empire's enemy, if he left its high prince to die in a nameless wood. No matter if he died himself; he would only make truth of Sarevan's deception, and his father had a surfeit of sons. He might even win free to tell the tale. Magics and sorceries and all.

Carefully, patiently, Hirel extricated himself from beneath the limp body. It was not difficult, now that he was calm. He stood over Sarevan. The Varyani prince sprawled gracelessly in the leafmold that had so bound Hirel, and truly, if he had not died yet, he would die soon.

With a small hoarse sound, Hirel bent over him. The torque gleamed no more brightly than the Sun in the branded hand. Hirel caught the wrist, drew the slack arm around his neck, set his teeth and heaved. Sarevan came up by degrees, so slowly that Hirel shook with the strain, so awkwardly that he almost despaired. Half carrying, half dragging the long body behind him, he lurched and stumbled toward the whisper of water.

Light burst upon him, and treelessness: a broad stretch of lake girdled with trees and sharp stones, ringed with the white teeth of mountains. He lowered Sarevan to the sand that lapped to the forest's edge, and tried to stand erect, gasping, as his sight swelled and faded and settled to a dark-edged blur. Through it he dipped water in his hands, drank what he might, and poured a pitiful few drops into Sarevan.

Hirel lay on the sun-warmed sand. Only for a moment. Only until he had his breath back. Sarevan lay deathly still beside him. He surged up in dread; the bandaged breast lifted, fell again. Clumsily, swallowing bile, he loosened the bloodied wrappings.

The bleeding had ebbed. Whether that was good or ill, Hirel did not know. But the small tidy wound had grown to an ugly gaping mouth. Hirel tore at his shirt, shaking, wanting desperately to cry. He had no skill in this. He had no skill in anything that mattered. The Dance of the Sunbird, the seventeen inflections of the imperial salutation, the precise degree of the bow accorded by a lord of the ninth rank of the Middle Court to a prince of the blood . . .

His hands made a bandage, of sorts. It was not pretty. Perhaps it was too tight. He tied it off with a bowman's knot, which skill at least he had, and sat on his heels, spent. The sun's heat stroked his aching shoulders. He turned his face to it, eyes slitted against its brightness. "What now?" he demanded, as if it could answer; as if it were truly a god and not merely the closest of the stars. "What can I do? I am but a pampered prince. I know nothing but courts and palaces. What use am I here?"

The sun shone on oblivious. A small wind played across the water. Far out, a fish leaped. Hirel's entrails knotted with hunger.

He grasped Sarevan by the unwounded shoulder and began to shake him. "Wake," he said over and over. "Wake, damn you." Cursed barbarian. Son of a fatherless man. Pitiful excuse for a sorcerer, he, who swooned like a maid after the merest wizardly skirmish. Would he die, then, and give Asanion a victory to rejoice in? Hirel reared back and struck him, and struck again, ringing broadhanded slaps that rocked the head upon the lifeless neck.

It rocked of its own accord. Sarevan's body twitched, shuddered. Hirel smote it with all his strength. The long limbs thrashed. Convulsed. Surely Hirel had killed him.

Sarevan sat bolt upright, eyes stretched wide, white-rimmed, lips drawn back from white sharp teeth. Before Hirel could move, the Varyani prince had him, and the strength of those hands was terrible. But it did not hold. Hirel braced Sarevan before he could fall; he said half in a gasp, "I can't—my power—I have no—" He drew a sharp breath, and spoke more faintly but also more clearly. "I have no power to help either of us. When I slew the sorceress, I slew it. That is the law which constrains all mages."

"You never used wizardry to feed us, that I knew of."

"I walked into my enemies' hands. I let my temper master me. I let it destroy me." There was a silence. Hirel did not fill it. Sarevan closed his eyes as if in pain, but he spoke with some semblance of sanity. "What do we have with us?"

"Nothing," Hirel answered flatly.

"Nothing at all?" Sarevan looked about, and his eyes closed again. "I don't remember this place."

For a long moment Hirel could find no words to speak. When they came, they were as faint and foolish as Sarevan's own. "You cannot remember? But you brought us here!"

A spasm crossed Sarevan's face. His hand went to his brow. "My head," he said. "It's an anvil, and Vihayel Smith's own hammer beating down on it. I can't think. I can hardly—"

"We were in prison in Shon'ai," Hirel said, shaping the words with desperate care. The priest's face was appalling, struggling so hard to remember, and in such pain, that Hirel could not bear to look at it. "You fought a sorcerer, then a sorceress. We left, and we came here, and you fell. You slept."

Sarevan touched his bandaged shoulder. His eyes were open, and they had cleared a little; they were no longer quite so bewildered. "This —this I remember. I've served you ill, cubling; I think we're even farther from your city than we were before. This place has a feel of Keruvarion."

"Not of the Eastern Isles? Or the lands beyond the desert? Or the uttermost west?"

"We're not dead quite yet, cubling," Sarevan said dryly; "and even with my well of power gone dry, I know my own country. Somewhere among the Lakes of the Moon, I would guess; though which of them this is, I can't tell you. My power brought us as far eastward as it could before it failed." His brows knit. "Us . . . The priestess. I couldn't heal her. I left her—I forgot—"

Hirel cut across his dismay. "She died before your battle began. She is safe, if death is safety."

Sarevan turned onto his good side, drawing up his knees. Sweat sheened his brow and his breast and trickled down his back. Sand clung to him, dimming the brightness of his beard; his hair was knotted with it. He would have been pathetic but for the sudden fierceness of his eyes. "She's free. I gave her that much. The god will grant her healing."

"Add a prayer for yourself," Hirel said sharply. "You are alive to make use of it. Are these Lakes of the Moon a wilderness, or do people dwell here?"

"There are people, offshoots of the northern tribes. They wander with the beasts they hunt, and breed seneldi, and worship Avaryan in the free places far from the temples."

"Very well," said Hirel. "We look for them. Lie here and be quiet while I search out a way to carry you."

"I'm not an invalid. I can walk." Sarevan proved it. He rose. His lips were nearly white. Stepping with care, as if he walked on glass and not on white sand, he approached the water and waded in.

Hirel was there when the fool's knees gave way. The water lightened him, and he was clinging grimly to his senses; Hirel dragged him out of the lake and into the shade of a tree, propping him against the bole. Wet though he was, he trembled not with cold but with exhaustion. "Power," he gasped. "Power's price is deadly high."

He slept thereafter, or slid into unconsciousness. Hirel looked at him and thought of despair. He would not be walking while this day lasted. Nor could Hirel carry him alone. He was too awkward a burden.

Hirel rose and wandered beside the water. Saplings or long branches; something to bind them with—he could sacrifice his trousers if he must.

He stopped short. He was going to make himself a beast of burden. And he had not even thought of it before he had the first straight weatherworn bough, testing its soundness, snapping the twigs that bristled from it. He was becoming what he seemed. Commoner, servant. Degrading himself for the sake of a greater rival than any of his brothers, the son of the man who had sworn to bring east and west together under his rule: to cast down Asanion and consecrate all the world to his burning god.

"No," he said aloud in the green silence. It was power, of a sort. Revenge of properly royal subtlety. Debt for debt and life for life. A weapon in his hands that hitherto had had none.

In the end he found half a dozen branches that would do. He dragged them back to the place where Sarevan lay, where the shadow was lengthening from noon, and took off his trousers. The sand was warm under him as he sat and began to make a litter.

Sarevan murmured and twitched. When Hirel touched him he was fire-hot, yet sodden as if he had bathed in the lake. He would not swallow the water Hirel brought him. As Hirel dragged and lifted and prodded him onto the makeshift litter, he gasped and cried out and tried feebly to resist.

Girded with the last ragged strips of his clothing, bare of aught else,

Hirel fitted himself between the bars of the travois and set out along the lake's shore. Undergrowth hindered him; hollows opened before him; fallen trees barred his way. Slowly but inexorably the earth bent him away from the water, toward the trackless wilderness. The lashings of the litter wavered and threatened to work free; the ferns and the leaved branches with which he had cushioned it thinned and scattered. His feet bruised, his hands blistered and bled. Thirst rose up to haunt him. Grimly he pressed on.

The land grew rough and stony. Hirel's breath caught in a sob. He was too small. He was too weak. He could not repay this debt which Sarevan had laid on him.

No more could he leave the madman to die. Not now, after so much pain. He shifted the bars in his throbbing hands. Sarevan babbled delirious, sometimes in words Hirel knew, more often in tongues he had never heard.

The slope steepened, leveled for a bit, dipped and began to rise again. Hirel's heart was like to burst in his breast. His sight narrowed to a lone bright circle directly before him, dimming as the sun sank.

The litter caught. Hirel tugged. It held. Too weary even to curse, he turned. Wild green eyes met his glare, and a great grey body weighted the foot of the travois. "Ulan," Hirel whispered in relief too deep even for wonder. "Ulan!"

The cat growled softly, nosing Sarevan, touching his brow with the tip of a broad pink tongue. The growl deepened. Ulan's jaws opened, closed with utmost gentleness about Sarevan's wrist and tugged.

Hirel cried out. "No!" Ulan paused, as if he could understand. "No, Ulan. He is ill. You must not."

Ulan crouched like a pup in a tug-of-war, and backed slowly. Sarevan's body slid from litter to leafmold. When Hirel would have leaped, the slash of Ulan's claws drove him scrambling back. The ul-cat shifted, twisted; and Sarevan lay on the long grey back, face down, and the cat's glance was a command. Cautiously Hirel came to his side, set a steadying hand on his burden. They began to walk.

They were gods. Almost Hirel could believe that there were gods.

Or demons. Ulan led Hirel round a deep cleft in the earth, dark already with night, and down a long hill, and as the land leveled, a hound bayed perilously close. Hirel froze. His scars throbbed. A shriek welled from the very heart of him.

From a deep covert burst a beast of hell: black hide, white fangs, red maw gaping wide. Hirel's scream died behind his teeth.

Ulan raised his head and roared. The hound stopped as if struck. Its pack, bursting from the thicket, tangled in confusion. Hunters scattered them, bright barbaric creatures aclash with copper, resplendent in paint and feathers and embroidered leather. They were as dark as Sarevan, with here and there a tinge of brown or bronze; their hair was braided about their heads and down their backs, and their beards were braided on their chests. Copper gleamed on saddles, on bridles, on the horns of the stallions; one black giant on a black charger blazed with plates and chains and circlets of gold.

They drew in in a running circle, slowing, stilling, staring at the cat and the two princes. Hirel raised his chin and then his voice, sharp and clear above the blowing of hard-ridden seneldi. "Draw back, I say. Draw back! Would you slay your prince?"

The riders murmured. The gold-laden chieftain looked long at the man on the ul-cat's back. Suddenly he sprang down. He seized Sarevan's dangling hand, turning it, baring the *Kasar*. Breaths caught all about him. The giant spoke at some length and with no little intensity; his followers listened, eyes flicking from him to Sarevan.

The chieftain faced Hirel. "We are friends," he said in trader's argot rough with the burr of the tribes. "We follow Avaryan. He sent us to find you."

Hirel wavered, tensed against treachery. The giant's eyes were steady. Hirel shrugged very lightly. Why not, amid all the rest? Why not a tribe of savages running errands for a god? The chieftain raised Sarevan as if the prince had been a child, and mounted again in a graceful leap, a feat that loosened Hirel's jaw. But when a grinning savage swung his stallion toward Hirel, hand outstretched, Hirel vaulted onto Ulan's back. The tribesman laughed and veered away.

They were savages indeed, these folk who called themselves Zhil'ari, the People of the White Stallion. Their tents stood in a scattered circle near a jewel of a lake, and their bold bare-breasted women sang as the hunters returned, a fierce high song that shifted to a wail like the crying of wolves. Hounds and children joined in it, and the deeper voices of the men who had stayed behind, and above it all the belling of stallions.

They took Sarevan away. When Hirel moved to follow, no path opened for him, only a wall of alien faces limned in firelight. Even the children stood as tall as he, or taller. Giant as he had thought Sarevan, here the Varyani prince would be the merest stripling. Again Hirel raised his chin and his voice. "Let me pass."

His tone was clear, if not the words. White teeth gleamed. Someone laughed as one laughs at the cleverness of a child or an animal. Hirel walked forward.

They yielded willingly enough, although some ventured to touch, a brushing of fingers over Hirel's hair and down his back. His skin quivered, but he did not falter. He thought of Sarevan in Shon'ai, and stood a little straighter for it, and turned where he had last seen the priest. The chieftain's stallion grazed before a tent like all the others, a dome of painted hides. Hirel lifted the flap and stepped as if from world to world.

He stood in darkness after the glow of firelight. The air was full of chanting, thick with some sweet potent smoke. It dizzied him, and yet it cleared his brain.

Little by little his eyes focused. He saw the stream of fire that was Sarevan's hair, and the chieftain in his gold and his finery, and Ulan a shadow by the wall; and last of all a woman. She was old, her breasts dry and slack, her swollen belly propped on stick-thin legs. It was she who chanted in a startling, sweet voice; she who fed the fist-small brazier which begot the smoke and the feeble glimmer of light. She did not pause or turn for Hirel's entering, although the chieftain glanced at him.

Hirel moved slowly toward the bed. In this little time someone had combed out that wild fiery mane, and smoothed the tangled beard, and taken off the makeshift bandage. Had Sarevan looked so skull-ghastly under the sky?

Hirel bent close. The wound of the arrow was closing, a raw red scar on the dusky shoulder. The fever—

"He cools," said the chieftain. "The god has spoken. Our lord is not to die."

"I do not understand this sorcery. How he could die from it."

"It is sorcery. It is for sorcerers to understand."

Hirel opened his mouth to upbraid the man's insolence, and closed it again. The smoke, the keening chant, grated on his senses. He fled them for the clean quiet night.

Hirel sat by the water and tried not to be ill. Brightmoon fled westward, pursued by the great pale orb of Greatmoon, and the light they shed together was coolly brilliant. Bright enough to read by, Hirel's tutor would have said. Young girls as tall as tall men, trying to be solemn, had brought him food, drink, salve for his blistered hands, and with ill-suppressed giggles, a garment. His gorge rose at the sight and scent of the meat, the fruit, the strong salty cheese; but his stomach cried out for mercy. Slowly at first, then with ravenous hunger, he emptied the plates and bowls. The cup was full of pale liquid; he tasted it and gagged on its potency, and settled on water from the lake. As the salve worked its cooling magic on his palms, he deciphered the long strip of leather tanned as supple as cloth, wrapping it about his middle. He had not even remembered his nakedness until he was clad, and then he blushed scarlet, here where no one could see.

A sound brought him about. Another long lithe maiden, but this one's eyes were downcast, her gift aglow upon her lifted palms. "Take," she said in halting tradespeech. "Take, see."

It was gold, a crescent of the beaten metal, and from its center hung a claw of golden wire clasping a great teardrop of amber, all frosted under the moons. Hirel took the necklet, held it up. The girl smiled. Her finger touched the pendant and set it swinging, and brushed the lid that shielded his amber eye. "Take," she said, and more in her own tongue, a swift bright stream. When he hesitated, she lifted the jewel lightly from his hands and leaned forward. Her breasts swayed close; gold clasped his neck, rested cool upon his chest. She was very lovely, even with her paint and her braids, her height and her slimness and her tarry skin. Her ornaments were gold and amber. Perhaps she was a princess.

Hirel had thought that he could only sit and stare and drown in nightmare. But she smiled. He smiled in return, shakily. She touched his hair. He touched one of her gold-woven plaits, and her cheek that was richest velvet, and her sweet young breast. She murmured a word. He drew her down to the grass.

"I must go," Sarevan said. Two days in deepest dream, with the shaman chanting and raising her smokes over him, and no sooner had he walked than he tried to leap up. "I must go. I must speak to my father."

Weak as he was, even Hirel could hold him down with one hand. But he would not surrender. "We must ride to Endros. The storm is coming. I must be with my father before it breaks."

"If you ride now, it is you who will break." The wisewoman cradled his head and held a cup to his lips. "Drink."

Sarevan drank with perfect obedience, hideous though the concoction was, herbs and honey boiled in mares' milk. He hardly even choked on it. But as soon as the last of it was gone, he began again. "The day I'm too feeble to sit a senel, that day you can lay me on my pyre. Now let me up; I have bargains to strike with the one who rules here."

"Rise, and you strike bargains with none but death."

"Will you deny a dreamer his dream?"

The wisewoman's lips tightened. Hirel knew that look. His physicians had always had it when he was young and sickly, when he would not lie abed like a mindless receptacle for their potions. Driven by the memory, he slipped out of the tent. Even from outside it he heard her voice raised in expostulation.

Azhuran the chieftain sat in his open tent hearing a dispute, while his wives made him hideous with scarlet paint. When he saw Hirel he rose, scattering wives and warriors. His great arms swept Hirel from his feet. "Little stallion!" he roared. "Little goldenhead, you like my daughter, eh? Woman, be gracious, fetch a cup for Zhiani's man."

Between training and plain shock, Hirel took the massive golden cup. It reeked of mares' milk. He steeled himself to sip, set the thing aside with as much grace as he could muster, faced Azhuran. Seated on the ground, the giant was still taller than he. He knew his cheeks were scarlet. Surely, though he dared not look down to be certain, he was blushing from crown to kilt.

"She likes you," declared Azhuran, loud enough for the whole tribe to hear. "You have arts, she says. You're a lion. A bull. A stallion. A beardless, braidless, girl-voiced lad—miraculous! Are they all like you in your country?"

That Hirel did not die then, he ascribed to the malice of the nonexistent gods. The Zhil'ari were all gaping, and the women were leaning forward with hungry eyes. Traitorous Zhiani was not among them. Serpent-supple, serpent-tongued Zhiani. She had dallied nightlong by the lake, and left him at sunrise with many kisses, only to bring back half a dozen maids nearly as lovely as herself, who fed him and adorned him and made much of him. And again at night they had played together, he and she, in the grass under moons and stars. She was insatiable. She was honeysweet. She was born to the high arts. And she was treacherous. She had trumpeted his prowess to any who could hear. If he left this tent alive, he would kill her.

Her father laughed and prodded Hirel in the most vulgar of places. "*Sa, sa,* little stallion! Did you leave your tongue in your bower by the water? Tell me what brings you here. Would you like gold? Seneldi? Another woman to teach your western dances to? Though that might not be so simple; my daughter has sharp claws, and she's using them on any who even hints at taking a try at you."

Hirel's voice astounded him; it was utterly steady. "Sarevan," he said. "Sarevan would speak with you."

Hirel had conjured rightly. Azhuran was up again at once without question or protest, shortening his stride a little so that Hirel needed only to trot to keep pace, seeking Sarevan's tent amid a straggle of curious folk.

Sarevan sat up in his bed, and the old woman stood well apart from him, and the air between them quivered with tension. Hirel thrust himself into it. "The chieftain is here," he said to Sarevan. "Strike your bargains as you can, but be quick about it. You have need of rest."

He was certain that the witch would cast a curse on them all. But she stood back, arms folded, and glowered in silence. Azhuran bent over the Varyani prince, speaking in a rumble in his own tongue.

The bargaining went on for a very long while. Ulan came in the heat of it, when the old woman had added her own voice to the rest. The cat lay down unperturbed, drowsing with one ear cocked. Hirel settled against the warm solid body and tried to make sense of the words that flew back and forth above his head. It kept him from remembering shame; from resorting to murder.

"Swift seneldi," Sarevan said when the chieftain had gone back to his judging and the wisewoman departed in disgust, "and provisions, and clothing for us both." He had barely voice left to speak, but he looked eminently satisfied.

"At what price?" asked Hirel.

"A concession or two from my father, concerning mainly the freedom of the tribe to hunt on royal lands, and employment in my service for certain of Azhuran's young men."

"I did not mean that. He could ask nothing which your father would not happily pay. At what price to you?"

"None," answered Sarevan. "We ride tomorrow."

Hirel sucked in his breath. He had meant to put an end to the old woman's railings. Not to begin a new madness. "I see that I erred," he said with a twist of scorn. "I credited you with a modicum of sense."

"I have to go," Sarevan said.

"Send Azhuran's young savages in your place, and follow when you are stronger. Surely one of them can be trusted to carry your message."

"Not this." Sarevan sighed and closed his eyes. "Let be, cubling. I do what I must."

"You are a howling madman."

Sarevan smiled thinly. He let the silence stretch; Hirel chose not to break it. It seemed that Sarevan had slid into sleep, until he said, "I've included you in the bargain. We'll go to Endros together."

Hirel went rigid. "We will not. I too can strike bargains; I will find my way to Kundri'j. I am free of you now, as you are free of me."

Sarevan's eyes opened. They were deep and quiet, and there was regret in them, but iron also. "I'm sorry, cubling. I wanted to take you home and have done with it. But now you know who I am, and you guess what I must say to my father. I can't chance your reaching Kundri'j Asan before I come to Endros."

"And what," asked Hirel softly, as a prince must, and above all a prince betrayed, "gives you either right or power to constrain me?"

"Necessity," said Sarevan. "And the Zhil'ari."

"Potent powers," Hirel said, soft still, but never in submission. "But of right, you speak no word, as of honor you know nothing: you who so long deceived me, and cozened me, and reveled in your lies."

Sarevan sighed with all the weariness in the world. "Maybe I did take too much pleasure in it. It's past; I've paid. Now need drives me, and you must come perforce, because you are what you are. You won't suffer for riding with me. You'll be treated with all honor; I'll see that you have occasion to speak for your empire."

"My father will come with an army to free me."

"More likely he'll treat with us for your safe return."

"It comes down to that, does it not? You but played with me while you spied in Asanion. Now you tell the truth. You always meant me to be your hostage. Gods, that I had killed you when I had the chance!"

Sarevan raised himself on an arm that trembled but held. "I swear to you, Hirel Uverias, this is no betrayal. You will see your home and your people again; you will stand again in Kundri'j Asan. But first I must carry this message to my father."

"Must," Hirel echoed him. "Always *must*. And what compels you? You were not your father's only spy. Surely one at least will not be caught as you were caught."

That stung: Sarevan tensed and nearly fell. But he said as calmly as ever, "None of them has dreamed as I have dreamed. None of them is my father's son."

"Speak to him from afar. Wield the magic you are so proud of."

"I have none." Sarevan's elbow buckled; he fell back, with a gasp at the jarring of his shoulder. "I told you, it is gone. You will ride with me. You need not try to escape. Azhuran's warriors are instructed to guard you."

Not ostentatiously. But wherever Hirel went, there were a few hulking tribesmen about, loitering, gaming, blocking every path of escape. When he swam in the lake, half the Zhil'ari came to join him, men and women alike, flaunting their nakedness. One slipped up behind him and tugged wickedly; he yelped more in startlement than in pain. Zhiani's merriment rippled in his ear. She wanted to play, there, in front of everyone. He remembered that he was going to kill her. After he had killed Sarevan.

Her fingers did something exquisite. He groaned aloud, and no one even heard. Close by, between himself and the shore, two men locked in passion, a great grizzle-bearded man and a downy-cheeked boy; little children gamboled over and about them. It was unspeakable. And it held him as firmly as any bars, and Zhiani's hands and mouth were chains, and the world itself his prison.

They were not like his brothers and their accomplices in Pri'nai. No one was careless here, or underrated Hirel for his youth and his prettiness and his sheltered innocence. When morning came, he was still in the camp, and Zhiani made much of his leaving, sighing and kissing him and heaping him with gifts. He had decided to let her live. She was only a savage; she could not know what she had done to him.

Perhaps he might take her with him. She was no fit wife for a high prince; yet she made a remarkable concubine. No one in Kundri'j had anything like her.

If he ever saw Kundri'j again. But he would take her. For comfort. For company. She bathed him, kissing him wherever the fancy took her, nibbling here and there, but when desire rose and he reached for her, she eeled away. "No more," she said in deep regret. She dressed him with a little less playful wantonness, and clearly she did not approve of the breeches which he had insisted on. "Woman," she muttered. "Woman-weak." But she helped him into them, skin-snug as they were, and fastened the codpiece with rather more pleasure, and the heavy plated belt; and settled the embroidered coat, leaving it open so that the gold of her first gift shone clear on his chest. Last of all she brought out the high soft boots, and in her mind they seemed to make up for the effeminacy of the breeches. Small feet were much prized among these broad-footed savages; his, narrow and fine and only lightly calloused, the scars of his wandering beginning to fade, delighted her almost as much as the golden brightness of his hair.

When she was done, he looked like a prince again, cropped head and all. He saw it in her eyes. She brushed his eyelids with royal gold, caressing as she did it; her finger traced a curve upon his cheek. Asking with silent eloquence. Offering paints: gold, scarlet, green. Almost he yielded, but he had a little sense left. "No," he said firmly. "No more."

She sighed, but she withdrew, holding back the flap of her tent. The others were waiting. Nine painted, jangling, kilted giants holding the bridles of their tall seneldi; and Sarevan. Sarevan on his own feet, painted and jangling and kilted like any Zhil'ari buck, with his hair in two narrow braids flanking his face and a long tail behind, and a red-eyed, redmaned demon of a stallion goring the air beside him. He turned toward Hirel; his face was a terror, painted in barbaric slashes of white and yellow, his beard braided with threads of gold. But his arrogance was the same, and the white flash of his teeth. "You took your time, cubling," he said.

"I had help." Hirel looked about. "Am I permitted to ride? Or must I be bundled upon a packbeast?"

"You ride," Sarevan said. He gestured; a boy led forward a tiger-striped mare. She was not as tall as the others, though still no pony, and she was no great beauty. Her like would never have been suffered in Hirel's stables in Kundri'j. But she moved well, and she had a bright wicked eye in her narrow head, and when Hirel took the bridle she snorted and stamped and threatened him with her teeth. He laughed. He liked a senel with a temper.

He vaulted into the odd high saddle with its softening of fleeces, its festoons of straps and rings and bags. But there was a senel under it all, lightly bitted and gathering to test him, and if there was anything he could do, it was ride. Shorn, captive, and thrice betrayed, in this at least he had come home.

The others were mounting. Azhuran had come while Hirel was absorbed in his mount, and Zhiani was close by her father, watching him speak to Sarevan. Hirel nudged the mare toward them. Sarevan ended his colloquy and mounted lightly, favoring his wounded shoulder only a little.

Azhuran saluted Hirel. "Good morning, little stallion," he said.

Hirel inclined his head. "You have been most generous. I thank you; if ever I can repay you—"

"It was nothing," Azhuran said. "We did it for the prince. If anything, we're in your debt. My daughter asks me to thank you with all her heart. You've taught her more than she could ever have hoped for, even from a yellow dwarf."

Hirel would ignore the insults. He would remember who and what these people were. He would—

The chieftain's grin was abominably lewd. "Yes, you're the best teacher she's ever had. Come Fall Gathering, when she spreads her girdle in front of the tent, she'll win a high chief's son; and he'll give a whole herd to lie in her bed."

Zhiani stood beside her father, and she was smiling luminously, not a tear to be seen. Hirel's teeth locked upon the words he would have said.

That he was more than a high chief's son. That she could be a queen; or as close to it as her barbarian kindred might ever come. She had never loved him, only the arts which he could teach her, which every Asanian nobleman learned from his early youth. He was nothing to her but the passport to a rich husband.

"May you wed as you wish," he said to her in his court voice, that could mask anything. Anger. Hurt. Reluctant relief. "May your husband give you many sons."

The mare fretted. Hirel let her dance about, away from Zhiani's heartless smile, toward his captivity.

It would, he vowed, be brief. As brief as wits and will could make it.

He did not look back. The company sprang whooping into a gallop; he kicked the mare after them. She bucked, squealed, and set herself to outpace the wind.

Five

*H*E KILLS HIMSELF," SAID THE SMALLEST OF THE nine zhil'ari, who stood hardly taller than Sarevan.

They were camped by the southernmost of the Lakes of the Moon. Hirel eyed it longingly. If only this great lanky creature would go away, he could bathe and swim and loosen his travel-wearied muscles. But Zha'dan had caught him alone, and was not inclined to sacrifice the opportunity.

Hirel took off his coat and hung it tidily from a branch. With equal care he said, "Sarevan looks well enough to me. He rides without falling. He eats well. He—"

"He keeps the saddle because he refuses to fall. He pretends to eat, but the demon cat eats for him. He paints himself not for beauty as is proper: he hides what the riding does to him."

Hirel loosened his belt. The savage watched with interest. Hirel let his hands fall. He was not ready to strip in front of this glittering meddler; no matter that the whole tribe had seen all of him there was to see. There was no logic in modesty.

Nor in Sarevan's weakness, if it came to that. "His wound is healing. It was healing before we left the village. His wizardry—how can he be dying of that?"

Zha'dan regarded him as one would regard an idiot. Hirel watched tolerance dawn behind the paint. *Ah,* it said. *Foreigner.* Zha'dan took care with his words, stumbling a little with the roughness of tradespeech. "Mages are very great, like gods. But they are not gods. They are men. They pay for their magics. Small magics, small prices. Great magics, prices sometimes too great to pay. The body pays, always. And the power itself pays more. The great one—he fought great mages, and he won, but he killed one. A stone, you throw it, it strikes down the *kimouri*, but maybe it comes back. It strikes you too. It puts out your eye. So with power, and mages who use it to kill. Death's price is power's death."

"And the body's?"

"The power is the body," said Zha'dan. "If the great magics were all mine to use, and I lost them because I let myself fall into a trap, I would want to die."

"What are you asking of me?" demanded Hirel. "I have no power to wring sanity from that madman."

"He is no god to you. You can make him act like a man of sense."

"Sense? In Sarevan Is'kelion?" Hirel laughed almost freely. "Tribesman, you seek a miracle. Pray to your god. Perhaps he will hear you."

Hirel retrieved his coat, with a sigh for his lost bath. While Zha'dan stood in silence, eyes wide and hurt like the eyes of a wounded *kimouri*, Hirel stepped around him and walked away.

The nine Zhil'ari were becoming people, if slowly. There was Zha'dan, who hovered and worried; who painted concentric circles in scarlet on his brow and on his breast, and who liked to sing in a loud unmusical voice. There was Gazhin his brother, who always bellowed him into silence, and who was as burly as Zha'dan was slender. Unlike the others, whose beards were still uncertain of their welcome, he had thick copper-wound braids that brushed his breastbone. There were the twins, Rokan and Kodan, as like as two pups of the same litter, but Rokan painted himself with crimson, Kodan with blue. Sometimes Hirel amused himself in trying to find the faces behind the thickets of hair, and in wondering how their women could possibly endure to kiss those bristling cheeks. Small wonder that Zhiani had taken such delight in learning the arts of love from a beardless Asanian boy.

They had made camp boisterously, as seemed to be their wont, and amid apparent chaos, but it was very well made: a firepit dug, the daymeal set to cook, a guard sent off into the trees. The rest tended seneldi or swam in the lake. Two coupled in the open like animals; Hirel did not think they were the same two whose thrashings had kept him awake all last night.

The one on top saw him staring and grinned, never missing a stroke. He tore his eyes away. This was an art. It had its times, its private places, its rites and its cadences. And always it was to be regarded with reverence as the highest of earthly pleasures. These great hulking shaggy men, with their noise and their contortions—they made of it a mockery.

"This is play. With women, it's as sacred a rite as ever you could wish for." Sarevan stood beside him, perfectly steady, garish in his paint. Hirel saw no black bird of death perched on his shoulder.

"Sacred." Hirel snorted his contempt for the very word. "Sacred enough to buy with gold and amber and to trumpet from the mountaintops."

"No priest enters his rite unrehearsed," said Sarevan. He looked Hirel up and down. "I confess, I didn't believe you were capable. Even after all the tales I'd heard. Is it true that the training begins in the cradle?"

"I am not an infant!" Hirel's voice cracked upon the words.

Sarevan laughed. "Of course not, cubling. But does it?"

"Yes." Hirel's eyes would not lift from the ground. "It is an art. Like dancing, like weaponry, like courtcraft. The sooner begun, the greater the skill."

"Even with that?" At last Hirel could look up. Sarevan looked bemused, and amused, and insufferable. "I suppose I should envy you. I merely learned dancing and weaponry and courtcraft, and the rest was for whispering in corners. For a while I committed a dreadful sin. I went into the minds of people who were loving. Women, even. One day my mother caught me at it. I was mortified, and I knew that I was about to be flayed alive."

"Were you?" Hirel asked in spite of himself.

"Oh, yes. With words so keen, the air bled where they passed. And then I had to serve my penance. I'd been trying to see if I could will a child out of the coupling, and it turned out I had. I lived in the woman's mind throughout her pregnancy, and it was far from an easy one, even in our nest of mages: it was her first, and she was old for it, one of my mother's warrior women who'd never taken time for childbearing until I tampered with her protections. She forgave me. Eventually. After we'd birthed her daughter together."

"But how—"

"I lived in two bodies, and my own was often asleep. My tutors were much concerned. If they had known . . . It was hard sometimes, to know I was a boy of twelve summers, strong and quite disgustingly healthy, but to feel like a woman of thirty with a child growing in her belly. Toward the end I had to watch every moment, or I'd even walk like her. And that was painful, stretching a boy's bones to move as a woman's. But never as painful as hers, that stretched to carry the child."

"Preposterous," said Hirel.

"Utterly." Sarevan lay near the fire, and Ulan came to be his bolster. "When we come to Endros, you must meet Merian. My mother is fostering her, and I when I can be near her. She's a very charming impossibility."

"*You* are impossible." Hirel sat on his heels. Sarevan had closed his eyes. The lids were painted, following the tiger-patterning of the rest, so that his features seemed to blur and shift, eluding the steadiest stare. But if Hirel narrowed his eyes and glanced sidelong, he could see the bones thrusting high beneath the thin-stretched skin. And that was not paint which paled Sarevan's lips, nor dew which gleamed on his brow. For all his seeming ease, his body was taut, its trembling not quite invisible.

Hirel blinked and found himself meeting Ulan's eyes. The cat yawned. His tail twitched and raised and came to rest over Sarevan, protecting, guarding. Sarevan seemed to have slid into a doze.

Hirel went away in silence, found what he needed, came back. As he touched sponge to the damp brow, Sarevan's eyes snapped open. Hirel considered modes of unarmed combat. But Sarevan lay still. With oil and salve, then water with cleanroot rubbed in, Hirel washed away the paint. And having done that, for thoroughness he bathed the rest, as if he were a servant; and Sarevan never said a word. Except, at the end: "You have light hands."

"Training," said Hirel with a touch of irony. It helped to hide dismay. If he had looked on a dying man before the Zhil'ari found them, now he saw one all but dead.

And yet Sarevan rode so well—pretended so well. How could he do that?

"Because," answered Sarevan when it burst out of Hirel, "I must." He smiled, alarming as the grin of a skull. "I won't die. When I come to Endros, my father will heal me. I'm certain of it."

It was well for him that he could be. Hirel lidded jars, wrung out sponges, emptied the basin into the roots of a tree. The sun had gone down at last; the stars were coming out, and Greatmoon waxing to the full, broad as a shield in the darkening sky. Savory scents hung over the camp where the Zhil'ari gathered and babbled and waited to be fed. The lovers were done, sitting by one another; the green-painted one oiled and braided the other's hair.

The lake was all silver and black, glowing with the last of the light. A flock of water birds drifted and murmured, black-waked black shapes on the sheet of silver. Hirel dropped his garments and waded into the water's sudden chill, drew a breath, plunged.

Midway between the shore and the gathering of birds, he floated on his back. The air was cold on his wet face, the water warm about the rest of him. One lone splendid star stared down into his blurred eyes.

Tonight he could do it. Take the striped mare and a sackful of food and run. Last night he had wandered, testing, and the sentry had only grinned and saluted him, taking no particular notice of his rovings. None of them seemed to know who Hirel was, or to care; nor did any keep watch. Feckless boys, all of them. And Sarevan was too ill and too urgent to give chase for any great while. If Hirel slipped away as soon as everyone slept, and rode uncaught until morning, he would be safe thereafter.

He turned onto his face and swam slowly to shore. In camp they were eating, and being uproarious about it. Hirel dried himself, pulled on his breeches, slung coat and cloth over his shoulder.

There was meat on a spit still. Hirel slid round a savage who was not inclined to move. Laughter rumbled; Hirel spun, startled.

The man looked down at him. Very far down. The eyes were very dark in the gaudy face, taking Hirel in at leisure and with unmistakable intent. Hirel bared his teeth, which were very sharp, and let the hulking lout choose whether to call it a grin or a snarl.

The eyes began to glitter. A hand closed about Hirel's privates. With all his strength he held himself still, although his teeth set. "Let me go," he said.

The savage let go, not without a bit of fondling. He said something; the others laughed. Hirel's fingers clawed. The man grinned all over his harlequin face, and went to fill it with roast wildbuck.

"He said," said Sarevan, "that for some things a dagger is more effective than a broadsword."

"Would he know?" Hirel retrieved the spit and addressed himself to its savory burden. Azhuran's hellions drank and copulated and caterwauled themselves toward sleep. Sarevan, having eaten—yes, Ulan was getting most of it, even under Zha'dan's reproachful eye—rolled himself in his blanket and closed his eyes.

Hirel lay down as if at random some little distance from the fire's light, and pretended to sleep. One by one the others succumbed.

Hirel waited. Sleep crept up on him; he beat it back with a litany. Asanion. Asanion and the Golden Palace, and all his royalty restored.

With infinite slowness the fire died. The last rowdy youth dropped like a stone, cup rolling from his hand. Hirel counted, and almost crowed. Their sentry had come back to eat, and had tarried to finish the last of the mares'-milk wine, and they had forgotten to post another. They were all asleep in a tangle by the embers.

Hirel drew a breath. No one stirred. Inch by inch he drew his blanket over his head. Waited. No sound but snoring. Dark-swathed, veiled in night, Hirel crept away from the sleepers. The seneldi grazed near the lake, loose as these tribesmen liked to leave them, trusting to the training that kept each beast within sight of its master.

The saddle was still in the brush where Hirel had hidden it, and the bridle, and the waterskin and the laden saddlebags. He rolled his blanket and bound it to the saddle, and, taking a bit of fruit, went to find the mare.

Darkness surged out of the earth, rolled over him, threw him down upon the cruel hardness of defeat.

"I thought you'd try it tonight," Sarevan said, dropping to one knee beside the massive shadow that was Ulan. Greatmoon made his face a featureless darkness; his eyes gleamed in it like an animal's, his teeth flashing white as he spoke. He seemed more amused than not. "A brave effort, cubling, but alas, perfectly predictable. Ulan, let him up."

Hirel rose slowly, judging distances. One of the stallions was close enough to—

"Don't even think of it," Saveran said softly.

"So that was a lie," Hirel said. "You still have your magic. You can read my mind."

"I can read your eyes. And your face. And your body. I fear I'll have to bind you, for a little while. Until we've gone too far to make escape worth the trouble."

"Then you will have to drag me in chains all the way to Endros Avaryan."

"I brought no chains. Leather thongs will have to do." Saveran bound Hirel's hands in front of him, firmly though not cruelly, and led him back to the fire. No one woke to see. No one needed to. Even the bonds were not entirely necessary: Ulan set himself by Hirel, and Hirel raged and wept behind his frozen face, but he did not fancy bolting for it with the cat on his heels.

Sarevan laid his head on Ulan's flank and went to sleep. Hirel sat wide-eyed, motionless, and watched the sky wheel into dawn. Long before then, he was certain. Sarevan had plotted this. To test Hirel. To seal his captivity.

And Hirel had been within a whisper's span of pitying him, racked with sickness as he was, bereft of all his bright magic.

Sarevan did not make good his threat. In the grey morning he loosed Hirel's bonds and said, "If you will give me your word, I will let you ride free."

Hirel flexed his stiff shoulders, eyes burning upon that hated, mongrel face. It waited without expression. Would wait until the sun fell, in perfect patience. Hirel's gaze dropped. "Yes," he muttered. "I give it."

"It is accepted."

And Hirel was forgotten, left to gather his belongings and tend his mount and fall into the line of riders. Sarevan led, as always; Ulan kept pace with him. The others rode in no perceptible order, except that Hirel took care to hold the rear. They left the lake, winding up a steep wooded ridge, and wound down into a long valley. Trees closed in, but the valley's center was clear, like the last gasp of a road: grass and stones and stretches of barren earth.

Toward midday the vale bent westward, rising into a long gentle slope lightly furred with trees. Stones crowned the hill, a rough circle that held a suggestion of men's hands, but hands long fallen to dust. Hirel slowed his mare as if to stare. No one noticed. He let the gap widen. Sarevan was far ahead, striking for the eastward ridge, and Ulan loped before him.

Hirel clapped heels to his mare's sides, bending over her neck. She bolted toward the hill.

Behind them, a shout went up. Hirel lashed the mare with the reinends; she shifted from flat gallop to full flight.

They were far behind, all his jailers. Hirel grinned into the teeth of the wind.

His jubilation shuddered and died. A grey shadow flowed over the ground, and its eyes were green fire, and it was closing. It was angling. It was moving to cut him off.

"No," he said, not loudly. He bent lower still, singing into the flattened ear, praising, cursing, willing the mare onward. Up the hill. *Up.*

She stumbled. He caught her, bearing her up by main force, driving her forward. Ulan filled the corner of his eye. The great jaws gaped; the white fangs gleamed. The stones. If Hirel could only come to the stones, he could defend himself. Before he fell. As he must. Damn that unnatural cat to the hell that had spawned it.

The circle floated before him. Avaryan sat above the tallest stone and laughed, a great booming roar, filling Hirel's brain. Even in his desperation he could reflect that he was at a sore disadvantage: he had no god to set against this flaming monstrosity. Logic was a very poor defense; philosophy crumbled like a tower of sand. And all Asanion's thousand gods were but a tale to frighten children.

The mare veered. Ulan's jaws clashed shut where her throat had been. Hirel fought with rein and leg, beating her back toward the west. She struggled, stiff-legged, throwing up her head. Ulan snarled. She went utterly mad.

Slowly, leisurely, Hirel wheeled through the air. The earth was a bitter shock. Sharp cloven hoofs flailed about him. He could only lie and gasp and wait to die.

A blur of fire and shadow became Sarevan's face. Hirel sucked in blessed air. Sarevan's expression, a cool corner of his mind observed, did not bode well for him. He had seen it once ablaze with temper, and that had been frightening. But this cold stillness was more deadly by far.

Little by little his lungs remembered their office. The rest of him was bruised but unbroken. He sat up shakily; no hand came to his aid. They were all mounted, staring, save for Sarevan on one knee beside him. Sarevan watched with eyes that granted him nothing. Not mercy, not fury, not even contempt.

Hirel rose dizzily, swallowing bile. He was eye to eye with Sarevan. In spite of themselves, his fists had clenched.

At last the Varyani prince spoke, soft and cold. "You gave me your word."

Hirel laughed, though it made his head throb. "I do not waste honor on animals."

This silence stretched longer even than the one before. Longer, colder, and more terrible. Sarevan stood. He towered like the standing stones, like the god enthroned upon them. He raised a hand.

The Zhil'ari who came at the signal had no illusions of gentleness. He bound Hirel's hands behind him, a tightness just short of pain, and set him in the saddle of the lathered and trembling mare, and bound his feet together beneath her belly. Taking the reins, he mounted his own tall stallion. Sarevan was astride, waiting. They turned again toward the east.

Six

*I*T WAS NOT HURTING IN THE PROPER PLACES.

Hirel steeled himself to endure his bonds. He had earned them; he bore them as brands of pride, that he was neither coward nor traitor to ride tamely into his enemy's stronghold. After the first grueling hours his captors relented, securing him by his hands only, and those in front of him.

He could suffer the constant watch by day and by night. He could face his guards without rancor, the more for that they bore him none of their own. Indeed, they looked on him with something close to respect. They saw that he was fed, that he was clean, that his needs were looked after. "You tried," Zha'dan said once. "That's the act of a man."

No, it was not his captivity that hurt. It was the chief of his captors. Only Sarevan never spoke to him, or went near him, or deigned to take notice of him. The others would be enemies if war compelled it, but they bore Hirel himself no ill-will. Sarevan did not merely hate Hirel; he despised him.

And what had Hirel done, that Sarevan himself had not equaled or surpassed? He was a fool and a child to be so outraged; and Hirel was mad to be so troubled by it. It should not matter. They had been born to be enemies, the sons of two emperors in a world wide enough only for one. Their meeting and their companionship had been scarred with contention. They would come together inevitably in war, that last battle which would raise one throne where now were two.

Yet it did matter. Hirel did not like Sarevan, had never liked him. Nothing so harmless or so simple. This estrangement, this cold distance, with Sarevan riding always ahead, growing thinner and frailer, fighting harder with each hour to remain erect and astride—Hirel wanted to burst his damnable bonds and kick his mare to the red stallion's side and rail at the fool until he smiled his white smile, and bowed his haughty head, and let himself be carried. Or at least until he acknowledged Hirel's existence. And let someone, anyone, bolster his waning strength.

Sarevan entered the Hundred Realms like a shadow of death, but he entered them alive and breathing and guiding his own senel. In one thing only he had yielded to necessity: he had bidden his Zhil'ari to tie him to the saddle. They did not like it, but they obeyed. They understood that kind of pride.

Hirel had it. It had held him aloof and silent, royalty imprisoned but never diminished. It brought him at last to a crux. If he must go in bonds to Endros Avaryan, he would not go with Sarevan's contempt upon his head. Fool or madman or no, Sarevan was a prince. That much, Hirel would grant him. And princes could be enemies, could hate one another with just and proper passion, but scorn diminished them both.

Greatmoon, waning, still filled the sky. Although this was a richly peopled country, the company had camped at a distance from the last town. Sarevan had no wish to be slowed by the duties of a prince. He wore again his paints and his finery, and such a welter of gauds in his hair and beard that their color was scarcely distinguishable. Riding in the midst of his savages, with Ulan wandering where he would, even on the highroad the prince was scarcely remarked. Hirel won far more stares, with his High Asanian face and his Zhil'ari fripperies and his bound hands. People ogled the wild barbarians; they spat on the yellow spy. Sarevan they did not know at all.

Even so, he did not test his disguise in inn or hall. This night they had fish from the swift icy stream, and bread which they had had of a farmwife going to market; and Zha'dan made a broth of herbs and grain and the long-eared *kimouri* which Ulan brought from his hunting, and coaxed it into Sarevan. Hirel watched from across the firepit. Sarevan could not feed himself; he could barely swallow. He was no more than skin stretched over bone. As he lay propped against his saddle, only his eyes seemed alive; and those were dim, clouded. He was not fighting his nursemaid. He had no strength for it.

Hirel stood. Rokan was his guardhound tonight, he of the crimson paint; the Zhil'ari watched but did not hinder as Hirel skirted the fire. Sarevan did not see him. Would not. He sank down beside the prince, letting his bound hands rest on his knee. Zha'dan acknowledged him with a glance. Sarevan was as still as before, but the air about him had chilled.

Zha'dan lowered the bowl. It was scarcely touched. His finger brushed the bandage on Sarevan's shoulder. It was new, clean, startlingly white. "It's festering," he said, not trying to be quiet. "He's been hiding it. Keeping anyone from looking, till I noticed that the wrappings hadn't been changed in days. It needs cautery; he won't let me. He'd rather lose his arm than chance a little pain. Maybe he figures to die first."

"Only cautery?" Hirel asked, reckoning days, and the little he knew of such wounds, from when a slave had pierced himself with an awl in the stable. The man's arm had swelled, and streaked red and then black, and begun to stink; he had lost the arm, but he had died. The surgeon had waited too long to cut.

One could not see the poison's spreading on skin the color of nightwings. But one might be able to feel the heat of it. Bound, Hirel was awkward. He did not try to unwrap the bandage. His fingers searched round about it. The skin was dry, taut, fever-hot, but fevered everywhere the same. It did not flinch away from him.

"If it has spread," Hirel said to Zha'dan, "it has not spread far."

"Must you dicuss me as if I were already dead?"

Hirel was careful not to start, or stare, or blurt out something unwise. He favored Sarevan with a cool regard, and rebuked his heart for singing. "Would you rather we went away and whispered?"

The dark eyes were clear and perhaps not utterly unyielding. "I do not fancy hot iron in my shoulder. My father will heal it more gently and much more completely."

"Your father will heal everything, it seems. If you get so far."

"I mean to," said Sarevan.

"He will fulfill your expectations, or he will answer to me."

The eyes widened. "What right have you—"

Hirel held that burning stare and made it fall. "There is," he said levelly, "a debt or two. And the issue of . . . comradeship."

"Great value that you lay on it," said the cool bitter voice.

"What would you have done in my place?"

Sarevan pondered that, which was a victory in itself. At last he sighed. "I would have found a way to avoid giving my word."

"You demanded my word. You did not stipulate that it embody my honor."

Sarevan stared. Suddenly he laughed, hardly more than a cough. "Asanian oathtaking! Cubling, when I told Baron Ebraz that you were incorrigible, I never knew how right I was. Will you swear again, now that we're so close to Endros? This time," he added, "with honor in it."

Hirel's silence was long enough to trouble even Sarevan's complacency. But his pride had had enough of trying to force nature's relief while a painted barbarian looked on and smirked. He held out his hands and said. "I give you my true word of honor, as high prince to high prince, that I will not attempt to escape until I stand before your father in Endros Avaryan."

"And I give you mine," said Sarevan, "that we will accord you all honor, and return you to Kundri'j Asan as soon as we may." He raised a spider-thin hand. "Cut the cords, Zha'dan."

He did it quickly, with a swift smile. Hirel leaped up and stretched wide, exultant. Sarevan's grin was a white flash in the firelight. Hirel answered it before he could help himself. "Now," he said, dropping down again, "what is this I hear of your dainty stomach? Here, eat. I command you."

Rather to his surprise, and much to everyone else's, Sarevan obeyed. But of course; it took a prince to compel a prince.

When the Zhil'ari in council reckoned that they were two days' ride from Endros, Hirel left his mare to run with the rest, and swung onto Sarevan's crupper. Sarevan cursed him in a hiss, but he took no notice. The body that so brief a time past had seemed so heavy was as light as a bundle of sticks. He was in the saddle behind it, unbinding the lashings, before anyone could move; and Zha'dan came when he called, and took the Varyani prince in his arms. Thereafter the Zhil'ari took turn and turn. "Consider it my revenge," he said to the smoldering eyes. By then he was back on his mare again: she did not take kindly to infidelity.

That night there was a battle. The Zhil'ari would have them lodge in a town called Elei; they were curious, and they had discovered a great liking for southland wine. But Sarevan would not have it. "The temple will know," he said in the whisper that was all the voice he had. "They will come for me. They will drug me to keep me quiet. They will try to heal me themselves before they send me to my father." He struggled feebly in Gazhin's arms. "Let me up, damn you. Let me ride. I can come to Endros sooner by myself."

"But—" Gazhin began.

"No." They all stared at Hirel, except Sarevan, whose effort had robbed him of his last strength. "Better that he rest tonight and ride another day, and gain the tending he needs."

It was not so simple, and at times it was acrimonious, but in the end they rode through Elei without stopping. Beyond the town the land rose in a long ridge like a breaking wave. Trees clothed the ridge and crowded into its hollows, yet high up, almost to the summit, they found a haven: a green meadow, golden with the last long rays of Avaryan, starred with flowers. From a rock near its eastern edge bubbled a spring.

It was early yet. Ulan had come as he always did, bringing a gift for the pot; he dropped it by the half-dug firepit and sought his lord. Sarevan, lost in a dim dream, knew nothing and no one. The cat nosed him from head to foot, growling on the edge of hearing. Sarevan stirred, but at random, unconscious.

"Tomorrow, Ulan," said Hirel through the tightness in his throat. He was not certain, but he thought that he had found a long tongue of greater heat on arm and side beyond the bandage, and the flesh was taut, swollen, unpleasant to the touch. "Tomorrow the Sunborn will work a miracle." He turned away too quickly, striding he cared not where.

The clamor of the camp faded behind him. The way was steep and stony, yet trees clung there, gripping the rock with clawed fingers. He welcomed the pain, the breath beaten out of him, the earth that, though strong, still yielded before him. He was dwarfed here, but only as all men were made small by the immensity of the world.

A shadow sprang past him. He cried aloud in the anger of despair. But Ulan had not come to herd him back to his captivity. The cat climbed ahead of him, sometimes outstripping him, sometimes circling back, bearing him company. Yes, they were in the same straits, they two. Did Ulan's anger match his own, that he could care so much, and come so close to grief, for a redheaded madman?

The summit was a triumph and a disappointment. Hirel had conquered the Wall of Han-Gilen, but he had gained no sight of the fabled City of the Sun. A broad plain stretched away below him, the plain of Han-Gilen watered by the flood of Suvien, but although the sky was clear above and behind him, all before lay under a pall of storm. Clouds boiled; lightning cracked. Rain cloaked the heart of the Sun's empire.

The wind blew fierce in Hirel's face. Challenging him, son of the Golden Throne, trespasser in the land of his enemies. He flung up his arms, defying it. It buffeted him upon his precarious perch. He stood firm; with infinite reluctance it surrendered. With a snap of laughter, he turned away.

He followed Ulan down, slipping and slithering, catching himself on treetrunks. The sun had sunk with alarming rapidity; already it was growing dim among the trees. Ulan descended more slowly, and Hirel caught the thick fur of the cat's neck, bracing himself against a sudden sharp incline.

He did not discover the hollow so much as he fell into it. It was like the one in which they had camped, like many another along this crannied wall of a mountain: an oval of grass hemmed in with trees and watered by a spring. But here the trees crowded close, and a bastion of stone reared up above the meadow, slanting inward into darkness. It was a comely enough place, but Hirel did not like it; and not only because Ulan surveyed it with raised hackles. The cavemouth gaped like a lair of dragons.

Because his body bristled and his heart thudded, Hirel forced himself forward. It was only a clearing growing dim with evening. If anything lived in the cave, surely it was no match for the ul-cat that stalked stiff-legged by his side.

The spring bubbled and sang into a basin of stone. Hirel bent to drink, and froze. Something lay in the water. Something white and shapely, a work of fine craftsmanship, shaped very like a skull. The skull of a child or a small woman, delicate as it was, contemplating the sky with golden jewel-eyes.

Hirel's throat burned with thirst, but he backed away from the water. Ulan crouched before the cave, snarling. Hirel came to his side, moving slowly, helpless to hold back.

If this was a guide, the skull in the spring had belonged to a child. This one had been a boy, one of the red-bronze people of this country, finer-featured than most, his hair the color of tarnished copper. He had not died swiftly, and he had not died easily. In the emptied sockets of his eyes, twin topazes glinted, staring up at Hirel in a horrible parody of awareness.

Hirel had known when he saw the skull, and had not credited what he knew. The darkside rites of Uvarra Goldeneyes were not uncommon in Asanion even in these enlightened days. But he had never thought to come upon them so far east, so deep into Avaryan's country, within sight of Endros itself. The Thousand Gods belonged to the west, and this one most of all, queen of light, lord of the flaming darkness, goddess and god, redeemer and destroyer. Hirel bore her name of the light; his name of the dark had been bestowed upon a lion's cub and the beast sacrificed to Uvarra, that Asanion's heir be proof against all powers of the night.

Superstition, he had always called it. He had better night eyes than most, and he had never been afraid of the dark, but that had nothing to do with gods or demons. Uvarra was naught but that figment of man's mind which, borne eastward, had become Avaryan, and grown from deity of birth and death into sole true god. How like the east to call the bright face male, and to name the dark a goddess, and hate her and fear her and ban all her worship. In Asanion they looked on it as a necessity, however grim, like death itself that was the Dark One's servant.

This was not a sacrifice to distorted and tongue-twisted Uveryen. She did not make use of Eyes of Power. And carved on the boy's breast above the empty cavern of his belly were words in fine curving script, the holy writing of Asanion in one of the older tongues, addressing the one whom Hirel, Lightchild and night's protected, was not supposed to name.

He had done it before, often. He did not do it now. He could not. He was remembering his logic. If there were mages . . .

Ulan moaned deep in his throat. The same keening sound escaped Hirel before he could strangle it. He pulled himself onto the warm comforting back and kicked the long sides as if the cat had been a senel. Ulan snarled at Hirel's presumption, but he wheeled about and bore the prince away.

Hirel saddled his mare with many pauses. She stood quietly for once, as if she knew that he had been sick all night. Blackly, stomach-wrenchingly, helplessly sick. It was not only the hideousness of the sacrifice. All the horrors of the world had come crashing upon his head, all at once, without mercy. And there was no one here who cared enough to minister to him.

Now, in the hour before sunrise, his emptied stomach lay quiet. He was weak, but he felt light, purged, even the sourness in his mouth put to flight by the herb that sweetened the mare's breath. He ran his hand over the black-and-dun silk of her neck. She nibbled his hair. He laughed a little, for no reason, unless that the night was over and the day was coming and he had emptied himself for a brief while of the horror in the clearing.

The mare tensed to shy, but held her ground. Ulan ignored her with lordly disdain. He dropped something at Hirel's feet, turned away.

All the sickness flooded back. Hirel doubled up with it. An eternity, and it passed, and still the hideous beautiful thing gleamed out of the grass. An orb of topaz the precise size and shape of a child's eye. It did not blast Hirel's trembling fingers, and yet he shuddered at the touch of it. He thrust it into the pouch at his belt, where it burned until his mind schooled itself—almost—to forget. Until he must remember.

They rode hard, unsparing of mounts or selves. Sarevan had fallen into unconsciousness like death, passed like baggage from hand to hand, unmoving, oblivious. They scaled the Wall, riding far from the place of sacrifice, and there at last with its veil of storms cast aside was the city they sought: Endros Avaryan, Throne of the Sun, white walls and towers of gold, and the crag above the river, and the magewrought tower a black fang upon the summit. Darkness and light face to face across the rush of Suvien, but both begotten of the mind and the hand of the Sunborn.

They spurred toward it. The mountain shrugged them off; the plain unrolled itself before them, broad green-golden level scattered with villages. They were marked, a wild riding of lakeland savages with a western prince, and one who seemed a savage borne lifeless on a saddlebow. They were not challenged. They were a strong company, and this was the heart of an empire at peace.

Hirel, exalted with emptiness and with the aftermath of illness, gazed steadily upon the walls of Endros. They mocked it in Kundri'j, called it a whitewashed village, an encampment of stone, a rude mockery of the Golden City itself. It was all raw, they said, all harsh stone and bare stripped earth, its white and gold too stark for beauty: the hubris of a barbarian veneered with southern gentility, proclaiming for all to hear: *See, I too can make an empire, and raise up a city, and dare to ordain that it will endure a thousand years.*

And yet, the nearer it came, the lovelier it seemed. Stark, yes, but wrought in a harmony of curve and plane and angle. It looked clean and young, like snow new-fallen in the morning, but not raw; it seemed to grow out of the earth as a mountain does, sudden and splendid and inevitable.

Not that it failed of reality. People lived in it, traveled to and from it, ate and chattered and sang, labored and idled, bought and sold and traded, had need of cesspits and middens and graves. They were a varied people, mannered according to their breeding. Hirel saw black giants, painted and unpainted, bearded and shaven smooth, the women bare to the waist or veiled to the eyes, striding as if they owned the world; almond-eyed folk of the plains, red or bronze or brown, who stared openly and speculated audibly and never knew what the outlanders carried into their city; here and there a white oddity from the Eastern Isles, walking aloof; and many a figure painful in its familiarity, small among the rest, sleek and full-fleshed, with skin in every shade of gold from dun to old ivory, and curling fair hair, and great-irised tawny eyes. Though none had skin as pale as Hirel's had been, or hair so pure a gold, or eyes that often seemed all amber. *They* had courtesy; they did not stare, and they kept their thoughts to themselves, going smoothly about their business.

Ulan was gone again. He shunned cities; even this one, it seemed. Well enough: if he were known, so might Sarevan be, and then would be pandemonium.

But anonymity had its troubles. Hirel, bred in palaces, knew of guards and their office. It had not occurred to him that his companions might come within its sphere. To all appearances they were a ragtag company, a pack of savages from the gods knew where, and Sarevan's name was insufficient passport to the inner reaches of the palace. The outer reaches were splendid enough, to be sure, and quite royally bewildering in their complexity; many persons offered guidance, for a fee, and many more shied away from the redolent corpse in Rokan's arms. Somewhere among the courts, a number of armed men persuaded the Zhil'ari to leave their mounts and their weapons behind, not without a broken head or three.

They would have been ejected then, but for Zha'dan's swift hard words. Hirel had caught a glancing blow meant for someone else; he could not fit his mind properly around any tongue. He heard only the name of Avaryan and the overtones of menace. The guards let them by, afoot and unarmed and drawing close together, with Sarevan shifted to the care of Gazhin who was largest and strongest.

They wandered for an age, to no purpose. "We would see the emperor," Zha'dan kept saying in passable Gileni. He was laughed at, or sneered at, or ignored. "We have your *prince,* damn you. We have the emperor's son!" The laughter sharpened. That? men mocked. That had been a stripling savage before it began to rot, and tricks did not succeed here, and his imperial majesty did not stoop to the raising of outland dead.

It was a brown man who said that, a plump jeweled creature whose every pore breathed forth the air of a petty functionary. Someone else, moved by their desperation if not by the name of their charge, had directed them to him. He sat in his gilded cranny and despised them, and his mind was set in stone. He did not know their painted skeleton. Both its fists were knotted in rictus and would not unclench for proof;

and in any case it was well known that the prince Sarevadin journeyed among his loyal subjects in the west. They were lying in order to get at the emperor, he heard such lies all too often, the whole world would sell itself into the hell of falsehood to gain a moment of the Sunborn's notice. Or of his favor. Or of his fabled magic.

They left him still expounding upon the necessity of protecting the emperor from his importunate people. Most of the Zhil'ari were for storming the inner gates. Gazhin curled his lip at them. "You are perfect idiots. You'll end in chains, and all for nothing. I say we go to the temple. They'll know my lord, and they can bring his father to him. We should have gone there first."

Hirel scowled at the tiled pavement. That was his fault. He had argued for the straight path to the emperor, and the Zhil'ari, ignorant of palaces, had let him have his way. But they had learned quickly enough.

For all their urgency, they paused in the quiet courtyard to which their contention had taken them. A fountain played in it; they bathed their heated faces, and the wounded laved their bruises, and Zha'dan sponged Sarevan's body. Hirel drank a little, found that he could keep it down if he tried, wandered away from them.

In truth this was more garden than court. Tiles rimmed it and circled the fountain; the rest was all grass and flowers and one slender young tree guarding a gate. It opened to Hirel's touch.

Grass again, level, shaved smooth. A groom rode a senel there, a black stallion of very great beauty. It could not but be of the Ianyn breed, that was reckoned the best in the world; although its horns curved in the scimitars of age, it moved like a youngling. Leap, curvet, caracole; sedate sidewise canter and sudden fiery plunge, with always the perfect control of the dancer or the warrior. And yet it wore no bridle, its rider motionless in the light flat saddle, hands upon his thighs.

Hirel's eyes drew him across the grass. He had never seen such riding. He wanted to learn it. Now. Utterly.

He was not seen. The stallion fixed inward upon his art. The man rode as in a trance. A young man, all night-dark, one of the smooth-shaven northerners. He was a priest of Avaryan. Very like Sarevan, in truth, if Sarevan had not had that fiery mane: his heavy braid swinging to his senel's rump, and his kilt threadbare above bare feet, and his chest bare and his torque bright beneath the keen eagle-face. He was not outrageously handsome as Sarevan was, but neither was he ugly; he was simply himself.

The senel gathered himself from a flying gallop into a dance in place, cadenced like a drumbeat, stilling to stone. Hirel's numbed brain struggled. They were stone. Black man on black stallion, with gold about the man's neck and glinting in his ear, and dun-drab paint fading on the sculpted kilt, and rubies feigning seneldi eyes.

The carven rider left the carven saddle, and Hirel stared. For all his northern face and his northern garb, this stranger was no giant; he was merely a tall man. Asanian-tall, middling in the south, small as a child among the tribes. For the first time since he woke beside Sarevan's fire, Hirel felt the world shrink to its wonted size. He was a well-grown stripling, tall for his age, like to overtop his father who was not reckoned a small man; and he could look this man in the eye without strain. "You cannot guess," he said, "how blessed it is to stand straight and look into a face, and not into a breast or a belt or worse."

The rider smiled, and his smile was splendid; it made him look even younger, little more than a boy. "That is quite the most pleasant thing anyone has ever said about my size." He had a marvel of a voice, deep yet clear. Like Sarevan's. Incredibly like.

Hirel was never an idiot twice running. And he had seen enough of magic to credit a stroke of sheerest, blindest luck. But he was all fuddled, and it did not come out properly. "This," he said. "Is this the Mad One?"

"Indeed," said the rider in rags and gold, as the stallion suffered Hirel to stroke his neck. He was hardly warm, for all his dancing. He blew into Hirel's hand, feigned to nip, rolled his wild eye when Hirel smiled. Hirel turned with a hand on the black mane. The man watched him, amused and, it seemed, intrigued. "You've just joined a rare fraternity, stranger: the chosen few who can lay hands on the battle charger of the Sunborn."

Hirel did not bow. If he did, he knew that he would fall; and a high prince did not perform the prostration. "We have brought your son to you, lord emperor. But no one will believe us, and we are turned away wherever we go, and I fear—"

He never finished. The Lord of Keruvarion had vanished. Hirel was alone with the Mad One, who held him up. "But," he said, "the Sunborn is *old*. Older than my father."

He unwound his fingers from the long mane. He had to follow the emperor. The Zhil'ari would not be likely to recognize their lord, ragged as he was. That would be a bitter turnabout; and Sarevan on the very brink of death, if not past it.

Hirel burst through the gate, stopped short. The Sunborn stood in the center of a circle. All The Zhil'ari had fallen back with awe in their eyes. They knew their master, perhaps as beasts might, by instinct. Only Gazhin, burdened with Sarevan, had not moved from his seat on the fountain's rim. His face was blank, blinded.

The emperor looked down at the shape in Gazhin's arms. He wore no expression at all. But he looked young no longer. He was grim, old; worn to the bone by the long hard years.

He took up the lifeless body. With utmost gentleness he cradled it. He did not speak. Perhaps he could not. He turned in silence, and walked through the sudden throng as if it had been empty air, and was gone.

Seven

*H*IREL HAD WON ENTRY FOR ALL OF THEM INTO THE inner palace, and they were accorded some semblance of honor. The poor savages from the Lakes of the Moon, bereft of a battle, were utterly at a loss. They shrank from the hampering walls, and eyed the ceilings uneasily, and jumped like deer when doors shut behind them. The smooth laconic servants terrified them as no armed warrior could; they huddled together, a draggled flock of sunbirds with wary darting eyes.

They fastened upon Hirel as the only familiar creature in an alien world. He saw them through a feeding, which he did not share, and through a bath, which was rather simpler. They were clean people, cleaner in strict truth than most Asanians. The great ever-running stream of water, heated in furnaces, fascinated them; they played in it like children, forgetting at last to be afraid of the men who tried valiantly to serve them. Hirel, who had never seen them without their paint and their braids, was rather pleasantly surprised. They looked almost human with their faces bared under the water-sleeked beards.

Then a man came at them with a razor. Offering, not compelling, but they bellowed like bulls. He retreated rapidly. Gazhin lunged after him, blind with outrage.

Hirel shouted. His voice cracked hideously. Gazhin veered, shocked, beginning to come to himself. The servant escaped forgotten.

Hirel dragged himself out of the water, in which he yearned to lie until it washed away all his troubles. He found the man who seemed to command the servants; who bowed respectfully enough, but not as to a prince. "Let them be," Hirel said, "and quarter them with me. They belong to the Prince Sarevadin; if—when he is able, he will dispose of them as he sees fit."

The man bowed again. Hirel would approve of him, when this creeping exhaustion passed. And still so much to do. He did not know where Sarevan was. No one would tell him. He did not even know if the emperor had come in time: if Sarevan lived, or if he was dead.

With tradespeech and with plain force, Hirel persuaded his unwelcome entourage to remain in the rooms they had been given. A small suite in Hirel's estimation, appropriate for a very minor nobleman, but endurable. The garments given him matched his lodgings, and those would not do at all; he returned to his travelworn Zhil'ari finery and put on a fair sampling of Zhiani's golden gifts. When he left, the tribesmen were restoring one another's paint, and exploring the rooms with affected nonchalance, and taking liberal advantage of the wine which the servants had brought them.

Sarevan would have said that the god guided Hirel. Hirel called it luck, the second such stroke since he came to Endros. He chose a passage at random, and it led him through a court and along a wall and up a stair. One or two servants passed him, preoccupied. There were no guards. It seemed a servants' way, narrow, unadorned, and leading past occasional unassuming doors. The one at the end led to a more public corridor, broad, high, and hung with tapestries which Hirel's wavering eyes did not try to examine.

There were doors, but only one was guarded, and that by two who were high and most haughty, liveried in scarlet and gold. For an astounded instant Hirel thought that the shorter of the two was Sarevan. But this was more boy still than man; his bright hair made his skin seem doubly dark, but it was shades fairer than Sarevan's, like old bronze, and his features were blunter though still very fine, the nose straight, the long mouth apt to laughter. But at the moment it was set hard, the dark eyes glittering with unshed tears.

It was he who leveled his spear on Hirel and spoke the challenge. "Who trespasses in the domains of the emperor?"

Hirel eyed the spearpoint that hovered a handspan from his throat. It was exceedingly sharp, though not as sharp as the voice of its bearer.

He glanced at the second guard, an enormously tall and long-limbed creature who was, for all of that, quite definitely a woman. She reminded him inevitably and a little painfully of Zhiani, even to the look in her eye, the frank appreciation of an attractive young male. She was not as beautiful as Zhiani. Too lean, too firm of feature. Yet as his hope of escape, she was lovely beyond compare.

He addressed her carefully, in the Gileni the other had used. "I would look on the high prince. I mean him no harm."

The spear touched his throat. "Sure you don't," growled the Gileni princeling. "They're getting bold, these cockerels, sending their spies into the Sunborn's own bedchamber."

Hirel swallowed. Metal pricked. He retreated a hair's width. "I was one of those who brought Prince Sarevadin here. We have been companions. I would see him."

"So would all the rest of the world." The woman spoke without gentleness, but also without hostility. "Apologies, stranger, but no one passes. Emperor's orders."

"I would pass. I must see him. I must tell him—"

The Gileni cut him off. "No one will be telling him anything for a long time. Maybe never. Thanks to your kind, Yellow-eyes." He wept openly, without shame, his words spat out in a fire of hate. But the spear had wavered. Hirel slid inside it.

Firm hands caught him, thrust him back, left him where he had stood before, in utter ignominy. "Don't try that again," the Ianyn woman warned him, not without amusement. "You're the westerner he came with, I'll credit that, but no one sees him now. The emperor is working a great magic over him. No one can pass the wards until the working is done."

"He lives," said Hirel. He did not know what he should be thinking. He knew that he should not be as glad as this.

"He may live," the woman said. "He may die. He walks in the shadows; he may not want to come back. Or he may not be able to."

Hirel's heart contracted. "He must not do that. I do not wish it."

They stared at him. The Gileni's scorn was a lash across his skin. He was past caring for it: or for reason or logic or princely policy, or for anything but his own will. "I do not wish it," he said again.

"Are you a mage, then?" the Gileni mocked him. "Can you master even the Sunborn with your power?"

Hirel looked at him, but did not see him. The Eye of Power burned at his belt, burned and sang. "I am high prince. I am his equal. He will not die while I have will to hold him."

Perhaps they spoke again. He did not heed them. He turned away from them, the red Gileni who hated him, the black Ianyn who laughed at him. Barbarians. This alien country, these alien faces, they crowded upon him. They bore him down.

He found a door without guards, that opened on an empty room that opened on light and greenness. A shadow glided from amid the green. Even Ulan languished in exile from his prince. He did not precisely come to Hirel for comfort, but when Hirel's knees, weakening, cast him upon the carpet, Ulan was there to cling to.

Hirel buried his face in the musky fur. He would not be sick again. He would not. He wept instead. Because he was alone, and forsaken, and betrayed. Because his only anchor to this unlovely world was dying or dead, in a welter of magic.

Ulan was patient. He did not upbraid Hirel, or remind him with elaborate tact that a high prince did not cry. A high prince did nothing but bear the deadly burden of his robes, standing like a carven image for an empire to worship, enduring until he should be set upon the Golden Throne in the mantle of gold, with his face forever hidden behind the golden mask.

That was the dream, the nightmare which had haunted Hirel since he was a young child. In it the world was all gold, harsh, yellow, heavier than lead; and he was borne on it, shrouded in it, chained with it, and above him loomed a mask of gold. It lowered slowly, infinitely slowly. It was the precise shape of his face, but it opened nowhere, blind, nostrilless, its mouth but a sculpted curve. Twist, struggle, cry out though he would, he could not escape it.

Sometimes it came close enough to rob him of sight and breath and voice. But always he woke before it touched his skin. If ever it came so far, he knew surely, he would wake and it would truly lie upon him. And his face forever after would be not his own, but the beautiful inhuman mask of the emperor.

Hirel lay coiled with the ul-cat, his tears drying slowly on face and fur. He had not had the dream since he fled from Pri'nai. That much he owed to the kindness of his brothers.

Very softly Ulan began to purr. Hirel let it lull him into a sleep blessedly free of dreams.

When Hirel woke, miraculously hungry, all nine Zhil'ari were there in their paint and their finery. Whatever this room was, they seemed to have laid claim to it and its garden. There were servants about, distraught, but none braved Ulan's claws to eject the invaders. Hirel sent one for food and drink.

The garden had a pool of some size, which one or two of the Zhil'ari were playing in. Hirel bathed lightly, considered, sent another of the hovering servants for garments proper to a gentleman. Those which came were adequate, cut of good plain cloth in the southern fashion; they fit well enough. Ulan growled. A voice babbled. The growl rose to a roar. Hirel, emerging from the garden, found that the cat had cornered a stranger. Save that he had a strong tinge of Asanian gold in his plump cheeks, he was the image of the creature who had barred them from the emperor. "Please," the man said faintly. "Please, sir . . ."

Hirel laid a hand on Ulan's head. The ul-cat subsided to a crouch, but his lips wrinkled still, baring his formidable fangs. Hirel looked his victim up and down. "You have a purpose here?"

The man gathered himself together with an effort that shook his body. "Sir, you cannot— This is one of the empress' private chambers. It is not suited for . . . guests."

Hirel looked about. "True. It needs a bed or two. And a canopy would not be amiss, should it rain when we would bathe."

The servant bridled at Hirel's princely hauteur, all fear forgotten. "You are trespassing in the personal quarters of her imperial majesty. If you do not leave of your own accord, I shall see to it that you are escorted out."

"I think not," said Hirel coolly. "The beds. Fetch them. And wine. The canopy can wait if it must, but cleansing-foam and cloths cannot."

A poor servant, this one, to have risen so high. He lost his temper much too easily, and with it his lordly accent. "This is not a barbarian pigsty!"

"Unless," Hirel mused, "you can provide me with a suite of rooms close by the Prince Sarevadin. Very close. And with service appropriate to my station."

"You'll get service. Direct to the slave-chain that let you loose."

"You are no good to me, I see. Go away, I tire of you." Hirel loosed Ulan. With a joyous leap, the cat drove the fool from the room.

Having tried servants of varying ranks, they resorted to guards, who could not pass a door filled with Ulan and who dared not empty it with bronze. Idiots; they never considered a raid through the garden, for what good that would do, with all the Zhil'ari prowling there, armed to the teeth. Hirel did not ask where the weapons had come from. Savages had ways, and theft was not a sin they knew the name of.

The guards withdrew. Of the services Hirel had required, only the wine came, and food later, when he demanded it again and peremptorily. The Zhil'ari were sparing with the largesse. A game was no pleasure if one were too far gone in meat and wine to play.

Hirel was no longer hungry. He drank a little, for the taste, and played with a fruit. He wandered restlessly, returned to the pool, prowled the room. No word came from the corridor's end. No sound, no scent of wizardry. The guards changed twice. Their faces were somber. They never opened the door, that he could see, nor did anyone pass them. They might have been warding an empty room.

Night loomed and fell. Hirel slept fitfully. A dream found him. He fought it, but it was strong. It seized him and pulled him down.

He walked in a dim country, under cold stars. A shadow walked beside him. They were comfortable, walking, two shadow princes in the shadowlands. Even here, Sarevan's mane was as bright as a beacon.

Something in Hirel was trying to brand it a nightmare: the dim strange hills, the icy stars, the air that was like no air of living earth. But Sarevan was there, and he was as he always was, striding lightly, wrapped in one of his silences. Once or twice he glanced at Hirel and smiled. It was a warm smile, with a touch of wickedness. *We belong together,* it said, *you and I: high prince and high prince.*

Hirel bowed his head, accepting. In this place, one did not deny truth.

The air was full of thunder. Hirel became aware of it by slow degrees. It was strangely like voices calling in chorus. Naming a name. *Sarevadin. Sarevadin!*

Sarevan barely paused in his striding. Hirel looked back. Far away on the edge of sight, light glimmered. He frowned. "They are calling you," he said.

His voice fell soft in the dimness. Sarevan glanced aside, shrugged minutely. It was no matter of his.

"But," said Hirel, "it is. Come, listen. They are calling you to the light."

The darkness beckoned, sweet and deep.

Hirel caught at Sarevan's body. It strained away from him; he tightened the circle of his arms. Sarevan twisted about within them, tensed for battle, but pausing, snared by surprise. "Listen," Hirel said. "For me."

"And what," asked Sarevan. "are you?"

"The other half of you," Hirel answered him.

Sarevan's brows met. Not, Hirel thought, in resistance. As if Hirel had given him something to ponder.

"Listen," Hirel bade him. "Listen."

* * *

Hirel snapped erect. It was deep night, but not the night of the shadow-lands. The air of the empress' garden was cool and sweet; only the snoring of his companions broke the silence. He lay down again in Ulan's warmth and tried to still his trembling. The dream was gone. Nor was there any doubt in him that it had been a dream; but it haunted him.

Morning dawned cool for all the brilliance of the rising sun; the water of the pool was cold. Hirel plunged into it, to wash the night away, to force his mind into wakefulness. He was there when the servants brought that the Zhil'ari fell upon with delight. He was still there when the tall man came.

Another of these damnable giants, Hirel thought as he looked up and up at the figure on the pool's rim. Not a young one, this; his beard was white, his hair iron grey. But he stood as a young man stands, light and alert, and he fixed Hirel with a singularly disconcerting stare. As if he could see through the other's eyes into the thoughts behind, and what he saw made him want to laugh and rage in equal measure. Ulan sat by him. Leaning against him. Purring thunderously. "So," he said in Gileni with a lilt that spoke of Ianon, "you're the invader who's setting the palace on its ear. I don't suppose you've thought to *ask* for what you want?"

Hirel was abashed, and despised himself for it; it made his words rough and haughty. "I asked. I was not given. Therefore I took."

"You demanded the impossible. You took what your temper could encompass." The notherner held out a hand. "Come out of the water, princeling."

Hirel came. He did not accept the hand. He did not blush that he was naked, or that he must dry himself, shivering until his teeth rattled, and dress under the bold stare. Ulan he would not acknowledge at all. The cat was a traitor, precisely like the rest.

The Zhil'ari circled warily. The northerner flashed them a blindingly brilliant smile, and addressed them in their own tongue. They listened; their eyes widened, their jaws fell; they flung themselves at his feet, kissed them fervently, and bolted.

Hirel stood alone, abandoned, and blue with cold, too bitter even to be angry. The tall man's smile shone in vain upon his despair; the warm deep voice was but a grating in his ears. "I told them that they could look in on their seneldi and claim their own weapons, and if they would be so kind, the owners of those they carried would like them back again;

and when they were done with all of that, the captain of the high prince's guard would speak with them."

"That is not all you told them."

"Maybe not." Since Hirel was not inclined to move, the northerner sat cross-legged on the grass. A kilt, Hirel reflected coldly, was an utterly immodest garment. The barbarian did not care. Although he was nothing royal, he could not be, he was quite as supercilious as Sarevan. He raised a knee and clasped it. He was much scarred and not the least ashamed of it, and yet he was good to look on as all these northerners were, with his carven features and his lean long-muscled body and his own, peculiar, gangling grace.

"I thank you for that," he said.

"You are a mage," Hirel said flatly.

One shoulder lifted in a shrug. "After a fashion. I wasn't born to it; I'm no good at all with spells. I've grown into a trick or two, no more."

"You know who I am."

"It's obvious enough. I've met your father; and you're his image. I bring you my emperor's apologies. At first he didn't know you, and then he had Sarevan to think of."

Hirel snatched at what mattered. "Sarevan—is he—"

"He lives."

"He lives," Hirel repeated. He could not even name the force that dimmed his eyes, that set his heart to beating in a swift painful rhythm. "And his—his—"

"His father is recovering. And his mother. It was a hard battle. For a while—for a very long while I thought we'd lost them all."

Hirel regarded the face gone grim with memory, and knew what the mage was not saying. "You were with them."

"We all were, in power if not in body. Even Prince Orsan, all the way from Han-Gilen, and that whole redheaded tribe of his, and every priest in the city. That's how dire it was, and how much we owe you for keeping the young idiot alive for as long as you did."

"I am sure that it delights you to owe such a debt to a yellow barbarian."

The northerner's eyes glinted. "We can survive it. What's driving us wild is that you insist on camping here when there's a whole suite of honor waiting for you. Be kind; take it."

"First I must see Sarevan."

"Of course. He's been asking for you." The man rose, making no attempt to suppress his mirth at Hirel's expression, and beckoned. "Come."

* * *

They had moved the prince, taken him to his own rooms in a high tower of the palace. Hirel entered the topmost chamber slowly, telling himself that he was only cautious. It was a very pleasant place, all light and air, with more in it of taste than of opulence.

The bed was almost demeaningly small, hardly more than a cot set in an alcove. No hordes of attendants fluttered about it, only one quiet person in a torque, who made herself one with the shadows as Hirel crossed the tiled floor. Ulan reached the bed in a bound, all but overwhelming the figure in it, who laughed breathlessly and clasped him close.

This was not Sarevan. This was a boy, gaunt to transparency, with such a light shining out of him as the poets spoke of, that shone in saints or in the dying. His braid lay on his white-clad shoulder and snaked along his side, and the shaft of sunlight on it turned it to red-gold fire, but he had no beard. Even bone-thin as he was, his face was very young and very fine, and almost as pretty as a girl's.

Then he saw Hirel, and his eyes were Sarevan's, bright, arrogant, and thoroughly insouciant. Likewise the voice he raised in greeting, although it was as thin as his body. "Cubling! What took you so long?"

"Inefficiency," Hirel's guide answered for him. "Don't overdo it, children. I'll come back when your time's up."

Sarevan watched him go, smiling with deep affection. "You should be honored, cubling. The Lord of the Northern Realms doesn't often stoop to run errands."

Hirel stared at the closing door. "The Lord of the Northern Realms?"

"Vadin alVadin himself, Baron Geitan, sworn brother to the Sunborn, whom men call the Reborn, and the Chosen of Avaryan, and the Regent of Ianon and the kingdoms of the north." Sarevan's eyes danced. "What, cubling! Is that awe I see in your face? Can there actually be a hero alive whom your loftiness will condescend to worship?"

Hirel schooled his traitor face to stillness. "He is very famous. Notorious, in truth. When nurses need a name with which to subdue their charges, and the Sunborn's has lost it potency, they invoke the horror of Vadin Uthanyas, Vadin who will not die."

Sarevan grinned. "Vadin Uthanyas! What a ring that has. I'll have to call him that when I want to watch him lose his temper. He loses his temper wonderfully. Thunder and lightning, and the sound of kingdoms falling." He raised himself, struggling, his grin turning to a glare when Hirel laid hands on him. He was frighteningly frail. Hirel propped him with cushions and stood over him, hands on hips. His glare wavered. "Damn it, infant—"

"Thunder and lightning, and kingdoms falling." Hirel frowned. "You look appalling. What did you do to your face?"

Saveran's hand went to it. His right hand, moving easily, and under the robe no bulk of bandages. "I've lost flesh, that's all. It will come back."

"Not that, idiot. Your beard."

Sarevan laughed so hard that Hirel thought he would break. When at last he had his breath back, he said, "I bade it a fond farewell. I'm not entirely uncivilized, you know. Only when I'm Journeying, and hot water is hard to come by, and time's not for wasting with a razor and a scrap of mirror. Besides," he added, "it made you so happy; such highly visible evidence of my barbarity."

Hirel's teeth set; but he smiled, honey-sweet. "You look," he said. "somewhat younger than you claim to be. And very . . . comely. I think we are a closer match than you would like."

The bright brows met. Hirel laughed at them. "Insolent whelp," Sarevan muttered. Hirel sat on the bed and refused to be insulted. Sarevan sighed. "I suppose you expect me to be indulgent, now that I owe you my life."

"I did nothing but accept my captivity and see that you were brought where you had promised to put an end to it. I do expect you to drop this game of yours and call me by my name."

"How cumbersome. Asuchirel inZiad Uverias, what an arrogant creature you are. Is there truly a rod of steel in that spine of yours, Asuchirel inZiad Uverias? Ah, Asuchirel inZiad Uverias, how prettily you glare at me."

"Priest," Hirel said with icy precision, "you know full well that I can be called Hirel."

"But that's merely Old Asanian for Son of the Lion. Lion's Cub. Cubling."

"At least it is *Old* Asanian." Hirel folded his arms. "Yield. Or I call you *mongrel* forever after."

"How dare you—" Sarevan stopped. Scowled. Laughed suddenly. "Cub— Hirel Uverias, you are growing into a formidable young man. How long has your voice been breaking?"

Hirel flushed scarlet, and cursed the wit that could spin a new victory out of a clear defeat. "It is not—"

It did, appallingly. His mouth snapped shut.

Sarevan lay back, highly amused. "Avaryan help me, I think I've been growing you up. Small wonder I've got so feeble. It's a task for giants."

"That, having seen the Zhil'ari, I would hardly call you." Hirel's voice held its range, for a mercy. "I am tiring you. Can you rest, now that you know your prisoner is secure?"

The lightness left the worn brilliant face. "Does it gall you so much?"

Hirel considered the question with some care. At length he answered it. "I am not an utter fool; I understand your reasons. But yes, it galls me. How can it not?"

"Do you hate me?"

"No." Hirel stood. "Rest. I will come back later. See that your guardhounds are so instructed."

No doubt Sarevan saw through it. That Hirel left because he could not bear to know the truth: that Sarevan was not yet claimed fully for the world of the living. He could still let go. He could still die.

The tall lord admitted it. He had died indeed with an assassin's spear in his heart, and he had come back at the Sunborn's call, when Mirain An-Sh'Endor was a youth barely set up his throne and Vadin his reluctant squire. But Vadin's wound had been one of the body, with nothing sorcerous in it. This was different. Sarevan had come as far as Keruvarion's magic could bring him. The rest lay with time and the god.

Hirel lingered for a time in the chambers to which the lord had led him. They were fully in keeping with his royalty. They closed in upon him.

He fled. He sought his mare, found her more nondescript than ever among the seneldi of the high lords of Keruvarion, knew that she had few equals for spirit or for swiftness. He was not comforted, even though he rode her for a little, to her great and queenly pleasure. He left her, to wander the palace.

It was all open to him now. People stared and murmured as he went past. Rumor gave him a hundred names, a hundred tales. A few were accurate, or close to it. He found the Zhil'ari; they were content with their barracks, though not with the order that they restrict their paint to a pathetic sigil between their brows. It was indecent, all that bare skin flaunted to the world. Hirel commiserated, and throttled his impulse to laughter, and wandered on. He felt like a shadow, a thing half real, visible yet intangible.

The sun sank. Hirel climbed the long stair to the prince's door, and the strangers on guard did not try to challenge him. Sarevan was asleep with his arm about Ulan's neck. Hirel sat by him in silence as the shadows lenghthened. Faintly, through the open windows he heard chanting. Avaryan's priests were singing their god to his rest.

The priest on deathwatch left; another took his place, settling on the edge of Hirel's awareness. From where he sat he could see the sky flame with sunset and fade slowly. A star kindled. Behind Hirel the watcher lit a lamp, a flicker in the twilight.

Hirel straightened. He was stiff with long sitting. He rose, and stretched each muscle as he had learned to, with grace and precision. Making a dance of it, his tutor used to say. The old man was dead now. He spoke too freely to someone powerful, and one morning there was a new and much younger man waiting to instruct his imperial highness in the proper pursuits of princes.

Hirel turned. The new watcher was a woman, and patently akin to the redheaded princes of Han-Gilen. She did not appear to share her young kinsman's hatred of Hirel. Her eyes admired his figure, and certainly his unconcious display of it.

She was not a priestess, he noticed; she wore no torque, nor any ornament at all. Her gown was green, and very simple, like a servant's. Her bright hair coiled at the nape of her neck. She was well past that first bloom which the poets judged to be the perfection of a woman's beauty, but well shy of raddled age; her features were too strong for perfection, in truth would not have looked amiss on a boy, and her figure in the gown, though far from boyish, was somewhat scant of breast and hip. She was, in truth, too old and too thin, and she was far from pretty. She was the most beautiful woman Hirel had ever seen.

He blinked. She did not vanish. Her eyes had the southern tilt, but they were more round than almond-narrow, long and very dark in the honey-gold face—Asanian blood there, no doubt of it. There were shadows under them. Her cheek was scarred, thin parallel furrows, ivory on gold. The marring only made her more beautiful.

She rose. She was somewhat taller than Hirel. She bent over the sleeper, smoothing his hair with ineffable tenderness. Hirel's heart, ever a fool, throbbed with jealousy. Oh, yes, his brain mocked it. Begrudge a woman's love for her son. Fall instantly, hopelessly, and eternally in love with the Empress of Keruvarion. Why not? His father had done it before him. And been sent packing with courtesy but with great dispatch, because she preferred a fatherless upstart to the heir of the Golden Throne.

It was as well, Ziad-Ilarios had said once. The royal line had clung to its purity against a millennium of alien wives and concubines, had fought an often desperate battle to stem the sullying tide. Ziad-Ilarios had gone home alone to Kundri'j, wedded the sister whom the High Court had allotted as his mate, and begotten an heir of unimpeachable legitimacy. No wild redheaded savage to cast shame upon the dynasty. Hirel shivered. One word from this woman's mouth, and he would never have been. Nor Sarevan. Nor this hour in Endros, full of lamplight and darkness.

She stood erect. A pin slipped free; her hair tumbled down her back. She snatched, and muttered something utterly unqueenly. Her glance crossed Hirel's, bright with temper. His lips quirked. He bit them. Hers were tight, but they wobbled. It burst forth all at once, as laughter must, even in the very midst of grief. "You look," she gasped, "you look exactly like your father."

"So I am told."

Her laughter died. He was sorry: she had a wonderful laugh, rich and full-bodied, like Sovrani wine. "He could do that, too. One look, and all my crotchets would collapse." She paused. "Is he well?"

"He was when I left him."

"I've always regretted that we were what we were. That we had to make choices." Hirel was silent. She smiled quickly. "You are very welcome in Endros."

He bowed. She touched him, a feather-brush of her hand across his cheek. It felt not at all like *lèse-majesté*.

"Yes," she said, "you are his image. He was the fairest of men, and the gentlest, and one of the strongest."

Hirel laughed a little. "I fear I fall far short of him."

"Ah, but he was older. Those shoulders, look, they've inches coming. And you'll be taller than he was." Mischief sparkled in her glance. "Come back to me in a hand of years, and I'll gladly run away with you."

"Need we wait?" asked Hirel. He took her hand and kissed it. "Come now, be my love, and let the empires fend for themselves."

"Why," she said in wonder, "you almost mean it."

"It must be in the blood." He sighed. "They breed us for beauty, for color, and for such size as we can attain; and, it seems, for conceiving mad passions for redheaded royalty."

"No," said Sarevan behind him, "that's not madness, that's taste."

They turned. Sarevan was wide awake. Perhaps he looked a little better; perhaps it was only the warmth of his smile. "Good evening, Mother," he said. "Good evening, O lion of the west. Would either of you be inclined to succor a starving man?"

When Sarevan ate, Hirel discovered that he could share it; and that it would stay quietly in its place. As if his stomach knew what his brain had not yet comprehended. The crisis was past. Sarevan was mending. He would live and be strong.

Eight

HIREL WAS NO STRANGER TO TEMPLES. ASANION'S high prince was high priest of a dozen gods, each with his shrine and his worship and his priesthood, each with his festivals which royalty must adorn. If Avaryan's temple in Endros had been set among the others Hirel knew, it would have been but middling large, and though extraordinarily well attended by both priests and people, not remarkably rich. Folk in Asanion would have looked on it with disfavor, muttering that the god's own son could spare so little of his fabled wealth to adorn the holy place. But here it was of a piece with the rest, simplicity shaped into high art. All that simple pillared hall of gold-veined stone looked toward its center: the altar, and above it an orb of gold suspended in the air, its heart an everlasting fire. Nothing held it up. Nothing at all.

Hirel had come here out of curiosity, and because a novice had brought a summons worded properly and courteously. He stopped to stare at the altar and the orb, and to wonder how anyone could have wrought such a prodigy.

"Magic," said the novice as if he had spoken. "It's nothing in particular, though it makes ignorant people afraid. A few of the novices stole it once and played ball with it. They say it was Prince Sarevan who scored a goal with it, full in the prioress' fishpond, and he not even a novice yet, though he was bound for Han-Gilen's temple that High Summer.

But he was mageborn; he didn't need the spells that all the others had to sing to keep the Orb in the air."

"Are you all mages here?" Hirel asked a little sourly.

The child skipped, tossing her long unruly hair. "Most of us. We're New Order here, under the Sunborn; we're priest-mages, white enchanters."

"You too?"

"I will be," she said from the promontory of her nine summers. Or did she have so many? "I was chosen. The empress says I'm mageborn; she says I'll know it when I'm a woman, and I'm lucky, because by then I'll be old enough to use my power properly."

"Unlike her son."

"Ah well, what can he do? He's not only mageborn, he's godborn; it's a fire in him. That's why he did his novitiate in Han-Gilen. They're Old Order there, no mages, but the Red Prince is the wisest mage in the world. He taught the Sunborn, and he took the Sunborn's son in hand, and tamed him nicely, everybody says." She stopped short. Her eyes filled with tears. "Is it true what they're saying? Is he like to die?"

"Not now," Hirel answered her.

The tears fell; she shook them away, scowling to make up for them. "Thank Avaryan! We've all been praying our hardest. I wanted to do my praying where he was, but no one would let me. It's because I'm still too young; I haven't come into my power. But when I do . . ."

Hirel gratified her with a very visible shiver. She was formidable enough now; she would be a woman to walk well shy of. He narrowed his eyes. "Would you be the empress' fosterling? The one whom Sarevan—"

"Yes, I'm the one who's here because he did something with his power that he shouldn't have. That's why I'm mageborn. A mage made me. When I want to make him annoyed, I call him Mother." She tilted her head, bright-eyed. "He must be very fond of you. He doesn't tell everybody. Only people he trusts."

Hirel blinked. She waited for him to gather his wits. She was another mongrel, a small wiry brown creature with hair and eyes of purest Asanian gold. When she was older she would be striking.

She was going to be very dangerous indeed.

She grinned, gap-toothed, and patted his cheek. She had to stretch to do it. "Poor child, you're shaking. What's the trouble? Is it all too much for you?"

"It is all impossible!" he burst out.

"Of course it is. We're mages." She took his hand without the least suggestion of diffidence. "Come now, we're dallying."

Hirel had not known what to expect. A priest certainly. A mage, from the child's chatter. But not precisely this. The blunt earth-colored face bespoke the Nine Cities, whence had come the Order of Mages; the greying braid, the torque, the white robe marked him a votary of Avaryan. He sat over a scroll in a bare sunlit chamber, companioned by a small bright-eyed creature that sat on his shoulder and purred.

"I had not known," said Hirel, "that a mage of the guild would endure Avaryan's yoke."

The man looked up with perfect calm. His familiar coiled its long tail about his neck and yawned in Hirel's face. The priest stroked it; it arched its supple back. "I had not known," he responded, "that an heir of the lion would endure captivity in Keruvarion."

Hirel smiled with a distinct edge. "It is given out that I am a guest here."

"Are you?"

"I bow to the inevitable."

"Of course." The familiar left its perch to stalk a shadow. Its master rolled and bound his scroll, turned to face Hirel fully. "Have you approached the Asanian ambassador?"

"Is that a concern of yours?"

The wizard-priest folded his hands. To the eye he was utterly harmless, a small aging man with tired eyes. "It concerns me that I be able to trust you."

"Why?"

The man sighed. "The heir of the Sunborn has known betrayal in one of its more appalling guises. He may yet die for it. And you are the highest lord but one, of the people who betrayed him."

"I am no stranger to treason."

"From which side of it, prince?"

Hirel drew himself up, measuring his words in ice and iron. "Much ill can be said of me, and much has been said, by your own prince not least. But of that I am not guilty." He advanced a step; his voice quickened, heated. "What can you know of all that he has suffered? How can you begin to comprehend it?"

"Peace," said the priest, unruffled. "I but do my duty."

"They did their duty likewise, who would have left your high prince to die within call of his father."

The priest rose. His familiar wove mewing about his legs. He cradled his arms; it sprang up weightlessly and curled there, fixing Hirel with a steady golden stare. He glared back, gold for gold.

The mage's voice seemed almost to come from within the creature's eyes, a soft voice, but implacable. "If you had brought him here, there would have been no such contention."

"I brought him to his father as he desired."

"Commendable," the priest said evenly.

"Why have you summoned me?" Hirel demanded of him. "What use can I be to you? Will you make an example of me, and execute me for a traitor?"

"That is the emperor's province. Not ours."

"Why, then?"

The priest looked long at him. Certainly he used more than eyes. Hirel's nose twitched at the tang of wizardry.

At last the priest spoke. "I wished to see you. To know what you are."

"And?"

"You are not what you think you are."

"Folk seldom are."

"Your self-possession is admirable."

"I am a prince."

The priest bowed. Mocking, and not mocking. His familiar purred. "I would not doubt the truth of your birth. But do you know the fullness of it?"

"I have been instructed."

"By philosophers." The priest was above scorn. "Logicians. Men who see with their eyes, but who are blind to the vision within."

"What is there to see, save the reflection of one's own face?"

"What was it that slew your mother?"

The blow rocked Hirel to his foundations. His eyes went dark; his mind emptied. From far away he saw himself, frozen, stunned; and watched his body spring from immobility into deadly flight. The mage fell back, raising neither hand nor power in his own defense.

With all the strength that was in him. Hirel quelled the killing stroke. He withdrew a step, two, three. He remembered who he was, and what he was, and how he had come there. He said, "She died by her own hand."

"Why?"

A prince did not give way to pain. Hirel was surely and entirely a prince, but his training was not yet perfect. He had not learned, yet, not to feel the wound. But he could speak through it with quiet that was only cross-kin to calm. "She failed of her blood. She could not learn to be a queen."

"She looked within and saw only void; looked without, and saw only a cage."

Hirel saw her more clearly now than he saw his tormentor. He was growing into his father's image; in childhood he had been his mother's. Her softness, like his own, had been only for the eye. She was steel beneath, but steel flawed, trammeled in the chains of womanhood and royalty. She had wanted too much: a life of the body as well as of the mind. She had won from her husband the training of her son. She had made him what she herself would have been, had she been born a man.

"They say that she was mad," Hirel said. She faced him in his memory as she had been the day she died: all gold and ivory, perfect in her beauty, with eyes that had forsaken hope. "My father accepted the burden of his birth. She could not. She resisted to the utmost, until she broke. She denied even the gods."

"Often," said the priest, "one denies what one most fears."

"Do not you yourself do the same?"

"I deny your thousand gods. I do not deny the One who embodies them all."

Hirel hissed. Memory was fading; impatience was rising to rule him. "What has my mother to do with you, or with me, or with your god?"

"Little," answered the priest, "and much. She could not bear to face herself; she took refuge in death. What did she see that so frightened her? Not prison bars alone. In extremity, she saw the truth. It slew her."

"Truth." Hirel's lip curled. "I have heard no truth here. Only cruelty."

The priest bowed his head. It was a most convincing semblance of humility. "Truth is cruel. Your mother raised you well, prince, but not well in all. It would have served you better to have learned somewhat from your father. Of gods; of magery."

"Prince Sarevadin has done what he may to fill the void," said Hirel.

"He has indeed. But do you believe?"

"In magic," said Hirel, "perforce. In gods, not yet. I can hope that it may be never. I have no desire to be bound by the caprices of divinity."

The temple did not quake; the priest did not rise up in wrath. "Caprice may prove to be purpose, and chance a design beyond our frail conception."

"Ah," said Hirel. "You have brought me here to convert me. A mighty coup that would be: a servant of Avaryan on the Golden Throne."

"It will yet be so."

"Not while I live."

"Swear no vows, prince, lest they betray you."

"I swear them. I swear that I will not bow to your god. Nor will I surrender my throne to him."

"Even for love?"

Pain drew Hirel's eyes downward. His nails, growing long again, had drawn blood from his palms. He had fallen out of the habit of allowing for them. With great care he unclenched his fists. "I may acknowledge that a god exists, if it can be proven to my satisfaction. It is not reasonable to demand that I love him."

"Love is not demanded. Often it is not even wished for. But it comes."

"Not to the High Prince of Asanion."

The priest looked long at him, but not with pity. "You name yourself truly. You do not know what your name signifies. But that will come. I pray my god that it will not come in pain."

Hirel escaped from that quiet wizard-priest with the bitter eyes and the oracle's tongue. He knew he trod the bare edge of courtesy; he chose not to care. The impudent novice had made herself scarce. He found his own way of the temple—it was much simpler, he noticed, than the path by which the child had led him—and walked slowly back through the city. Anger pricked him. So many words, to so little purpose; and yet they had struck deep, at wounds which would not heal. He had been tested, he knew it surely; but for what, he did not know. He did not want to know.

His mother had fled her lineage and her duty. He would not. He had tarried long enough, both within bonds and out of them. Now he would see what place this world had left for him: if he was a prisoner here, or if he was a free guest; if Asanion was prepared to reject him or to have him back.

Sarevan was up. More, he was walking, with Ulan for a prop, and after a moment's astonishment, Hirel. He tried not to lean heavily. Hirel could feel him trying, shaking with the effort. His face was grim. "Once more," he gritted when they had struggled from bed to wall and back again. Hirel swallowed the words that came to him, and steadied the lunatic with an arm about his waist.

Sarevan fell into his bed, grinning like a skull, panting as if he had run a race. "Every hour," he said with all the strength he could muster. "Every hour I'll do it."

Hirel kept his face expressionless, spreading the coverlet over the wasted body. It shifted, restless already, though it must have been a great labor even to raise a hand, to catch Hirel's wrist. "I'm mending, infant. I'm sure of it. I'm stronger already than I was this morning. Tomorrow I'll be stronger yet. Two days, three—I'll ride."

Hirel's mouth wanted to twist. Such a creature, this was. Not only did he cherish hope; he clutched it with both hands.

He let Hirel go and shifted again, lying on his side. His grin had shrunk to a wry smile. "I bore you to tears, don't I? Why do you keep coming back?"

"I am still your prisoner."

Hirel had not wanted it to sound so flat, or so bitter. Nor had he meant to wipe the smile from Sarevan's face. Not so completely. "You are not," Sarevan said with as much heat as his weakness could muster. "I promised you. As soon as we came to Endros—"

"We have been four days in Endros."

Sarevan closed his eyes. He looked weary beyond telling. "You are free," he said just above a whisper. "You were free the moment you faced my father."

Hirel voiced no thanks. He owed none. As he turned, the thin hand caught his wrist once more. He looked down into a face that had willed itself to life. "What are you going to do?" Sarevan demanded.

"Nothing unduly treacherous," answered Hirel. The dark eyes shamed him with their steadiness; he said more reasonably, "I had in mind to speak with the Asanian ambassador."

"Is it wise?"

"That is what I intend to discover." Hirel sat on the bed. Sarevan reclaimed his hand, turning it so that the *Kasar* caught the light. Hirel slitted his eyes against the flame of it. "Will you stop me?"

"Of course not. Old Varzun is safe enough; he's impeccably loyal to his emperor, and my father says he's been mourning you with honest grief. But some of his people may not wish you well."

"I do not doubt it," said Hirel. "I would send a summons worthy of his rank. May I borrow one of your guards?"

"Avaryan! You're slipping. You actually asked." Sarevan grinned at Hirel's scowl. He raised his voice and called out with surprising strength, "Starion!"

The guard burst in with a mighty clatter, armed for war. Once again Hirel met hostile eyes over the glitter of a spearpoint.

"Cousin," said Sarevan mildly. The spear lowered a fraction; the glare abated not at all. "Cousin, if you can spare a moment from your heroics, we have a task for you."

The young Gileni flushed dark under the bronze. He did not look well in the scarlet of the emperor's squires: it clashed abominably with his hair. Yet he was a very comely young man, and he acted as if he knew it. He grounded his spear with a flourish that came close to insolence, but that was for Hirel; his eyes on Sarevan were a roil of love and grief, anger and anxiety and simple worship. "Is he troubling you? Is he sapping your strength with his nonsense."

"Not as much as you are with yours." Sarevan's smile took some of the sting out of the rebuke. "Do you think you can bring yourself to be civil to Asanian."

The boy's thought was as clear as a shout: *If only it need not be this one.* Aloud he said stiffly, "Stop chaffing me, Vayan. What do you want me to do?"

Sarevan glanced at Hirel, who told him. He listened; repeated his message word for word; bowed with perfect correctness, and left.

Sarevan contemplated the emptiness where Starion had been. "Bless the boy," he said, half amused, half dismayed, "he's jealous. And he's the one who prayed for the day when I'd find someone else to play elder brother to. Or is it—" He laughed suddenly. "I have it! He's afraid you've displaced him as the beauty of the family."

"That," said Hirel, "is not possible. Not while you live to outshine both of us together."

"Ah now, I'm nothing much. This nose of mine . . ."

Hirel snorted. Sarevan wisely fell silent.

Nine

"IDUVARZUN INKERIZ ISCHYLIOS," THE SERVANT AN-
nounced with proper dignity and passable accent; and shattered it
with a grin and a wink which, by fate's own mercy, the ambassador did
not see. Hirel set himself sternly to be as blind.

He received his father's envoy in a chamber small enough for inti-
macy, large enough for dignity; seated in a tall chair, not quite a throne,
with attendants about him and the sun ablaze on his golden robes.
Seven of them, one atop the other, and the eighth, the one which
marked his rank, pouring over the chair and pooling on the floor about
his bare and gilded feet. Its sleeves flowed over his hands, permitting a
glimpse of gilded fingertips; its collar rose high, his face within the
frame of it almost stark in its plainness: barely touched with either gilt
or paint, ornamented only by a single earring, vivid against the darkened skin.

Still though he held himself, his heart thudded painfully as the man
appeared upon the heels of his name. Hirel knew him. He was a kinsman, and the old blood was strong in him; age had bleached his hair to
the ivory of his skin and brought out the fine proud bones beneath, but
the eyes in deep sockets were keen as a falcon's, the gold of them
rimmed just visibly with white. Even as he went down upon his knees,
he stretched the limits of protocol. The face of a high prince was to be
stared at, scrutinized, committed to memory, as an emperor's was to be
hidden forever behind the golden mask; but this stare endured for an

eternity, edged with doubt, and shock, and slowly dawning hope. "My lord?" Varzun whispered.

Hirel beckoned. The ambassador came forward on his knees, with much grace for one so old. At two paces' distance he halted and held up his hands. They trembled as Hirel touched fingertip to fingertip, the greeting of close and royal kinsmen. Varzun looked long at the thin brown fingers with their blunted nails, and up into the altered face. "My prince. What have they done to you?"

Hirel rose and signed a command. Varzun resisted but obeyed, rising also. He was a little the shorter. He blinked, and found a smile to brighten the sudden tears. "Little one, you have grown. But this" —his hand sketched a gesture toward Hirel's hair, toward the sharpened cheekbone— "this is unpardonable. Who has done it?"

"No one in Keruvarion," Hirel answered him. "Indeed I owe my life to the Varyani prince. He found me where my flight had cast me, and preserved me from the hounds that would have torn me, as from the men who would have sold me gelded into slavery."

With each word Varzun paled further; at the last of it he nearly toppled. "My prince. Oh, my prince!" But he mastered himself; he stood straight and spoke clearly. "Your brothers?"

"The slaves' whelps: Vuad and Sayel. And no doubt," said Hirel, "Aranos from amid his priests and his sorcerers, although he would never stoop so low as to take part openly in the plot. That might jeopardize his claim to my place."

"It is rumored that Aranos will be named high prince when the time of mourning is past. But it is also rumored that the princes are quarreling over the spoils."

"They are very certain that I am dead. What tale do they tell of that?"

Varzun lowered his eyes, reluctant. Hirel waited. Slowly the old man said, "It was sickness, they say, my prince. Something swift and virulent, that made imperative the burning of your body and your belongings. They gave you a great funeral, with many sacrifices."

"My slaves? My senel?"

"Sent to bear you company in the Ninth Heaven."

Hirel stood still under the weight of his robes. He was dimly aware of the ambassador's concern. Old fool, the High Court reckoned him, loyal enough and dimwitted enough to suffer exile of honor among the barbarians, blind enough not to perceive that, while he represented the soul of peaceful honesty to the mages of Keruvarion, his servants spied and intrigued and did what harm they might in the heart of the empire.

He was much too direct in his speech to make a courtier, although what Hirel had seen of this court made him seem as subtle as any serpent in Kundri'j. And he had a glaring flaw: he dared permit himself to love his emperor and his high prince. Either of whom would calmly slay him if need demanded.

As Hirel's brothers had slain his servants, that they betray no perilous secrets. And his golden stallion, that they should not seem overeager to usurp the privileges of the high prince. Not that the creature was a great loss; for all his shimmering beauty he had been as placid as a plowbeast. The slaves were only slaves, hands that served and legs that ran. Though Hirel would miss the little singer, and the eunuch whose hands were so clever when he needed easing and had neither time nor inclination for a woman, and Sha'an who alone had ever been able to comb his hair properly and painlessly, and—

They brought it home to him. The finality of it. The Son of the Lion was dead and burned and enrolled among the immortals, with ritual regret that he had not had time to become an ancestor. Ah well, folk would be saying, poor little thing, always sick and never very strong, though he was a pretty one to look at while he lasted. He did seem to have been getting over his youngling weaknesses, but blood and the gods would always tell. Between them they had carried him off.

Hirel let his head fall back, and laughed long and loud and free. Still laughing, he flung off his damnable swaddlings and faced Varzun in the bare sufficiency of silken trousers. The old man looked ready to faint again, more at his prince's nakedness than at the scars revealed upon it. Hirel's mirth died. He rapped Varzun lightly with a finger, driving the poor man back to his knees. "Sit," Hirel commanded him, "and ease your bones. And listen."

Varzun took the chair one of the servants brought, but he took little ease in it. Doubt was creeping back into his eyes. Hirel was not conducting himself as he ought; the old man's scrutiny hardened, searching the altered face.

"Yes," Hirel said, "I am your prince, and I have changed. I wandered the roads for a Greatmoon-cycle and more, companioned only by a priest of Avaryan; I dwelt for a while among northern savages. And what brought me to it, that laid bare a new face of the world. I am not the child who rode trustingly into the claws of his dearest brothers." His raised hand forestalled Varzun's speech. "By now the couriers will be well on their way to Kundri'j with the news of my resurrection. I will follow them. Not at once and not as swiftly, but neither will I ride in imperial state. Have you a dozen of the warrior caste whom you may trust beyond death if need be?"

"My prince, you know that all I have is yours." The ambassador was not an utter fool; despite the blows it had suffered, his mind had begun to work again. "My Olenyai are not all as loyal to me as they pretend, but your dozen I can find. Must you venture abroad with so few?"

"I require speed and secrecy. I shall ride as a lordling who comes to Kundri'j with his Olenyai, to claim his place in the Middle Court. My enemies will not learn the truth of my coming until I am upon them."

Varzun was becoming inured to shock. He did not protest the unseemliness of Hirel's plotting, still less the madness of it. He said only, "Then you will be using the roads and the posthouses, and you will need a token of passage. But, my prince, the lands may not be—"

"See to it," said Hirel. "I must be in Kundri'j by Autumn Firstday." Varzun had the sense to venture no further protests; he bowed in his seat. Hirel returned to the tall chair and vouchsafed his most charming smile. "Now, honored uncle, tell me all that has passed since I left Pri'nai."

Hirel had expected to be summoned in his own turn and called to account for his machinations. He had not expected the messenger to be waiting when Varzun left. He eyed the eightfold robe which would have been proper, settled upon coat and trousers, and followed the liveried squire, holding apprehension firmly at bay. He had no apologies to make and no secrets to keep. Even before Mirain An-Sh'Endor.

But, having summoned Hirel, the Sunborn kept him waiting for a bitter while. He was comfortable enough, it was true: the antechamber was rich, furnished with cushions and carpets in the western manner, and a servant brought wine and sweets and even a book or two, none of which Hirel was minded to touch. He sat, arranging himself with care, and simmered slowly.

He had reached a fine pitch of temper when the squire called him into the emperor's presence. But he was cool to look at, composed, imperial.

The Lord An-Sh'Endor was not even attired for audience, much less set aloft in the Hall of the Throne. He had been standing for a sculptor; the man was there still, measuring living body and half-hewn marble image with cord and calipers. The statue wore the beginnings of state robes. The emperor wore only his torque and his kingship. He had no more shame than his son, and no less form. Over the sculptor's head he addressed a man in full court dress, who seemed unperturbed by the disparity. "By now even they should know what they've brought upon themselves. I am not betrayed twice."

"And their messenger, sire?" the courtier inquired.

"Give him his fee and let him go." The man bowed; his lord shifted at the sculptor's command. "One wing of cavalry should suffice. Mardian's, I think. He's not as close as some, but he's been idle lately. A short campaign should distract his men from the local beer and himself from the local matrons. Write up the order; bring it to me before the sunset bell."

The man bowed again and departed. The sculptor finished his measuring and departed likewise. At last the emperor deigned to notice who stood by the door. "High prince! I pray your pardon. As soon as I'd sent for you, half the empire decided to descend upon me."

Hirel bowed acknowledgement.

A servant brought garments for his emperor: shirt and trousers, heeled boots and richly embroidered coat, the casual dress of a lord of the Hundred Realms. "I do turn and turn about," the Sunborn said to Hirel, easily, as to a friend. "Now a Ianyn in kilt and cloak, now a trousered southerner. It keeps folk in mind that I belong to no one realm, but to all together." He beckoned. "Come, walk with me."

He did not speak as one who expected to be refused. As Hirel moved to obey, he considered his own wisdom in discarding Asanian robes for eastern trousers. The Varyani emperor had the long panther-stride of his northern kin, that Hirel had to stretch to match.

They did not go far. Only to that great hall in which Hirel had expected to be received. It was even plainer than the rest of the palace, austere in truth: a long pillared expanse, its floor of white stone unadorned, its walls bare of carving or tapestry. At its farthest limit stood a dais of nine deep steps, and a broad chair that seemed carved of a single immense moonstone, its back rising and blooming into the rayed sun of Avaryan. Solid gold, all the legends said. Its rays ran from wall to wall and leaped toward the lofty vault of the ceiling. Surely any man who sat beneath that mighty flame of gold would seem a dwarf, an ant, a mote in the eye of his god.

From the hall's end, the throne seemed to glow in the gloom. An illusion: the hall was shadowed, lit only by the sun through louvers in the roof, and the gold cast its reflection upon the translucent stone of the chair. But as the Sunborn drew closer, it grew brighter. Hirel's eyes narrowed with the beginnings of discomfort. Brightmoon itself attained no such splendor, even at the full.

But the emperor did not choose to mount the dais. He stood on its lowest step and eyed the shining throne, his right hand clenching and unclenching at his side. His face was still, young and old at once, ageless as the face of the god. "Do you know," he said quietly, "when I sit there, I come as close to freedom from pain as I may ever come, save only in arms of my empress. But only for a little while. If I linger, if I begin to grow proud, if I consider all the uses of this power I bear, the pain swells until it casts me upon the edge of darkness."

Hirel did not speak. The Sunborn faced him, eyes glittering. "Often as I sit there, I consider my power. I consider life and death, and thrones, and empires. More than once I have sought a way round our long dilemma. Your father has daughters, all wellborn and many beautiful and some legitimate. I have a son. Our empires united, war averted, peace purchased for us all. Who can find fault with such a course?"

"My father has considered the same expedient. For all I know he considers it still, but not with any great hope of fulfillment. Your empire is too young and too vigorous and too close to its god. The union would be all Keruvarion, and Asanion would fall as completely as to any war."

"Would that be so terrible?"

Hirel looked at the Emperor of the East. Remembered the tales. Upstart, fatherless, ruthless warrior and inexorable conqueror, blind, fanatic, driven by his god. His son had been born while he conquered the Nine Cities, born on the battlefield in the midst of hell's own storm; had grown to boyhood in the camps of the army as it spread north and east and south and slowly, with many pauses, west. He had only known peace as his son began to grow from boy into youth, when the empires settled into the uneasy half-amity of warriors who, finding themselves equally matched, see no profit in endless, fruitless struggle. But they maneuvered; they tested. They wielded spies and insurgents and mages, bandits and border lords, even hunters and herders who set no great store by the borders of empires.

The warlord of Keruvarion was warlord still even in the garb of a southern princeling, lean and hard and honed to a razor's edge. And Hirel had seen his people. Outside of Endros the common folk might have become complacent with peace. Within it, lords and commons alike had a look for which only now did Hirel find a name. The look of the falcon: bright, fierce, and poised for the kill.

"The god would have it so," said their lord, not entirely without regret. "Asanion is ancient and it is still strong, but its strength in great part overlies corruption. It has forgotten its gods. Its people embrace mere cowering superstition. Its great ones cleave to the cold follies of logic, or to nothing at all save their own pleasure. In the name of their gods, or of their pleasure, or of this new sophistry which they call science, they practice horrors. Life, say they, is nothing; light is illusion; darkness waits and beckons and proffers the delights of despair."

Yes, Hirel thought. A fanatic. He sounded like a madman in the bazaar. *Woe, woe unto the Golden Empire! A worm has nested in its heart. Soon shall it wither and crumble away.* Madmen had been crying thus for a thousand years. Some had raised armies; some had even claimed descent from gods. But they were gone, and Asanion remained. She had swallowed them. So would she swallow even this greatest of the bandit kings.

The Sunborn laughed. His mirth seemed genuine, if not unalloyed. He ran lightly up the dais, turned. The throne was a blaze behind him, yet he outblazed it. He shone; he flamed; he towered against the image of his father. He sat, and he was a dark slight man of no great height or handsomeness. Yet try though it would, Hirel's eye could not force itself to see aught else. The throne on which he sat, the Sun which rose behind him, seemed but a setting for his royalty.

Hirel raised his chin and set his mind against his eyes' seduction. This man had greatness, yes, he granted that. Power in many senses, and presence, and a mingling of art and instinct that put a Kundri'ji courtesan to shame. How easy to yield, to bow down, to worship the godborn king. Let his armies roll over languid world-weary Asanion, scour it, cleanse it, make it anew in the image of Avaryan. A kingdom of light, where slaves were free and free folk lived in peace and plenty, and lords ruled in wisdom and in justice, and all gods were one god, and that god had sent his own son to sit above them all.

"No," said Hirel. "War is war, even if it be holy war. And conquest is conquest. You stretched your hand toward that to which you have no right."

"I have the right which my father gives me."

"We have the right of our ancient sovereignty. When you were young and bold, you wounded us deeply; you eroded our southern borders, you seized half our northern provinces. Where we were weakest, you struck deepest, until my father's father, worn with war and with the cruel years, sued for peace. Why did you grant it?"

The Sunborn answered willingly, as one who indulges a child's attempts to be wise. "I too was weary, and my army longed to see its homelands again, and my empire had need of a lord who was not always riding to war. The old emperor's death, the masking of Ziad-

Ilarios, lengthened the peace and made it stronger. As it strengthened my empire."

"And now the peace is breaking. I hear much of what my father does to threaten Keruvarion. I hear nothing of why he does it. Your armies gathered and moving. Your spies spreading disaffection even into Kundri'j itself. The revolts fomented in your name among our slaves. Your taking of yet another northern satrapy."

"That was a general grown overbold with power. He has been punished."

"Aye," said Hirel, "with the governorship of your new province."

"No." The Sunborn spoke with an edge of iron. "He was executed. The province we kept. It was no use to you save to feed your slave markets."

"It was ours."

"Was," said Mirain An-Sh'Endor. "So too were the Hundred Realms, half a thousand years ago. Now both are mine, and both are glad of me."

"Of course. They dare not confess otherwise."

"I would know."

Hirel looked up at him and thought of being afraid. "Why did you summon me? To subvert me? To forbid me to depart?"

"Neither." The emperor rose from his throne and came down. Hirel faced him steadily. The Sunborn smiled with no suggestion of strain. "I owe you a debt as deep as any man has ever owed another. I would pay it as I may, though in the end we must be enemies. What aid I can give you in your riding through my lands, I will give; I lay no restrictions upon you, and demand no conditions. I do not even ask that you dine with us before you go. Unless, of course, you wish it."

"You have no tasters here," Hirel said. "Your magic is enough, people say. Poison turns to honey in the cup." He paused. Suddenly he smiled. "I have a fondness for honeyed wine. I will dine with you."

The Sunborn laughed. "Honeyed wine it shall be, and fine company, and for yet a while, honest friendship. Whatever may come after."

PART TWO

*Sarevadin Halenan
Kurelian Miranion
iVaryan*

Ten

SAREVAN HAD NEVER RECKONED HIMSELF A SEER.
That burden was his mother's, and in lesser measure his father's.
They could raise the power at will and at need, and sometimes it would
yield to their mastery. He had no such gift. He had one dream only; but
that dream was true. It shifted and changed, but its import was always
the same. It began in peace. A green country, sunlit, quiet. Yet slowly
he saw the lie beneath the serenity. The green withered. The earth
shriveled, and the sun slew it, beautiful, benevolent, relentless. No cloud
dared veil its face. *See,* it sang, *how fair am I, how splendid, how
merciful. No night shall come to torment my people. No cold shall wither
my lands.* It sang; and endless day destroyed them, and heat unceasing
seared them to the root.

It haunted him, that dream. From the time he first became a man, it
had beset him. It had come perilously close to driving him mad.

Time and teaching had given him, if not mastery, at least endurance.
It had not blunted the edge of the vision. What was veiled came ever
clearer. What began as simple nightmare kindled into the full fire of
prophecy. The sun took on his father's face. The land became his own
Keruvarion. He saw its cities ravaged, its people slain, its dominion
given over to the carrion crow. And his father sat above it and smiled,
and stretched out his hand. Westward the sun sank; westward was
peace, however flawed, and a man in a golden mask, aging and mortal
and indomitable.

It was madness, that twisting of the world's truth. It was maddening. To look for peace to raddled harlot Asanion with its thousand lying gods; to find destruction in the hands of the Sunborn.

Even upon death's marches Sarevan had seen it. Had broken and bolted from it, and fled, and found his father's face; and recoiled in mindless horror. It was not Mirain who had won the battle for his life, nor Vadin whose name and love he bore, nor even Elian who was soul of both their souls. Han-Gilen's Red Prince had brought him back, and taught him anew to bear the pain of his foreseeing. And before Prince Orsan, another. A face beyond memory; a voice he could not name, although he struggled, waging war against forgetfulness. That will without name or face had turned him to the light, and sent him forth into Mirain's hands.

He did not remember all of it. He had fought. He had lashed his father with hatred. He had called him liar and murderer and worse. He had wielded the full force of his seeing; and he had fallen. Mirain was stronger. "It will not be so," the Sunborn said with the force of a vow. "I will not let it be so. I bring peace and plenty, and the victory of light over the ancient darkness."

And Asanion?

"Asanion will see the truth I bear. She is not blind but blinded. I will give her the clarity of my vision."

It was truth, that promise. Sarevan yearned toward it; and yearning, yielded, and plunged at last into healing sleep.

And dreamed. No horror, now; but this was kin to the black dream, and to memory. Nothing so clear as prophecy had led him to a fern-brake on the marches of Karmanlios, and shown him a wounded child: a child who by fate and birth and necessity must be his greatest enemy. And yet, foremost, a child, and sorely hurt. Hirel would never know truly how close he had been to dissolution, or how bitter had been the battle to heal his body and his mind. There was no magery in him, but there was something, a will or a power for which Sarevan had no name, and it was strong in its resistance.

It had found its way into Sarevan's own healing, and somehow made it stronger. It was like Hirel its master. Fierce, heedless, haughty, yet gentle in spite of itself. It neither knew nor cared where it dealt wounds, but it was swift enough to heal them, if only for its own peace. It shaped for Sarevan a vision, a young man's face. Hirel's, perhaps, shorn of its youth and its softness. It was a stronger face than Sarevan might have expected, and more truly royal, with all its pride pared clean. Sarevan could not like it, nor truly trust it. But love—yes, that would not be difficult. Neither did he like or truly trust his father. Mirain was above such simplicity.

The golden eyes opened; the vision raised its chin. Oh, indeed, it was Hirel. No one else had quite that spark of temper. "I am the key," he said. His voice was deep, and yet indisputably Hirel's. "For war or for peace, I am the key. Remember."

"You'll never lose your arrogance, will you?" Sarevan observed.

The dream-image frowned at his levity. "I am no man's pawn. Yet I am the crux. Remember."

Remember. Remember.

"Remember!"

Sarevan started awake. His mind roiled. He clutched desperately at clarity. At memory. Not Hirel's face. Not dreams, not prophecy that must be false or mad. Clear daylight. His own bed, his own high chamber, his own half-mended body. His power—

Nothing. Silence. Utter absence, edged with agony. In dream at least, however terrible, he was whole.

He dragged himself up. Morning flamed in the eastward window. By sheer will he won his way to it. The city spread below, his father's city, his own. Above its roofs, beyond the broad flood of Suvien, loomed the rock from which the city took its name: Endros Avaryan, Throne of the Sun, and on it the tower which the Sunborn had raised in a night with song and with power, his own and his empress' and his oathbrother's. They had faced together all the million stars, and cried to Avaryan beyond them, and made a mighty shaping of magic. All night the rock was veiled in a mist of light, and when at last the sun rose, it rose upon a wonder. The lofty hill had grown more lofty still, and its upper reach was polished like black glass, edged and chiseled into a tower of four horns, with a fifth rising high from their center, and upon this tallest spire a crystal that flamed like a sun. No window broke those sheer walls, no gate divided them. The tower might have been but a deception, an image sculpted in the stone of the hill.

But it was no simple image, nor stronghold, nor monument to imperial pride. It was a temple of its own strange kind, raised to bear witness to the power of the god. While it stood, the tales said, the city of the Sunborn would never fall. A potent comfort while the son of the Sunborn lay yet in his mother's womb.

Sarevan stood by his window, leaning against it, staring at the black tower. Even so early, with Avaryan barely risen, the crystal blazed bright enough to blind a man. Sarevan fixed his eyes full upon it. That much at least he had still, the power to bear the sun's light without flinching. Once he could have drunk it like wine, and fed on it, and gained life and strength enough to sustain his body for a servant-startling while.

It was only light now, bright but endurable. As the earth was only earth, lovely but muted, oddly lifeless; as the air was only simple, mortal, summer-scented air. As living creatures were only bodies, and men no more than their outward seeming: hands and voices; eyes that mirrored nothing but his own face.

Ulan leaned against him, purring. Sarevan looked down. Shadowgrey cat-shape, slitted green eyes. A mute beast that, sensing its master's trouble, strove to comfort him with its body. He watched his fingers weave their way into the thick fur. They were very thin. "Tomorrow," he said, "I call for my sword." His voice, like his eyes, had changed little. It was still—almost—his own.

He straightened. He was not strong, not yet, but he could stand and he could walk, and the rest was coming swiftly enough to make a simple man marvel. He began to walk.

"My lord called?"

Sarevan, caught between window and door, nearly fell. He braced his feet and stilled his face. He did not know this nervous young creature in his own white livery. A new one, fresh from some desert chieftain's brood from the look of him.

Sarevan did not know that he had done it until it was done: the flick of his mind, just so, the gathering of name and lineage, the skimming of thoughts unwarded by power. He had done it from instinct since before he could remember, as a simple man might judge another in a quick sharp glance. He kept doing it, from instinct; he could not school himself to forbear. When nothing came, and then the lancing agony, he almost welcomed them.

One thing he was learning. He did not fall into darkness, although the boy cried out in dismay. "My lord! Are you ill? Shall I fetch—"

"No." Sarevan drew himself up again. The pain was passing. He put on a smile and said lightly, "I must be going to live. I'm down to a single nursemaid. What are they punishing you for?"

The boy's tawny cheeks flushed beneath the patterning of scars, but his narrow black eyes had begun to dance. "My lord, it is a high honor to serve you."

"Two hundred steps high." Sarevan completed the journey he had begun. The squire moved aside, a little quickly perhaps. Sarevan looked out upon the landing and down the long spiral. He knew what had possessed him to live in a tower. High air and young muscles and power that could give him wings if he had need. He had flown straight up more than once, and not always from the inside. One of the gardeners still went about with one eye cocked upward lest he lose his hat to a swooping wizardling.

Sarevan eyed the ul-cat and the sturdy young squire, and counted the steps again. Two hundred and two.

He drew a breath. With a word and a gesture he had them moving, the cat going before, the boy beside him. He walked every step of the two hundred and two, and he did not lean once on his companion. At the bottom he had to stop. His knees struggled to give way beneath him; his lungs labored; his eyes blurred and darkened. Sternly he called them all to order.

The boy faced him directly, a head shorter than he, breathing with perfect ease. The black brows were knit. "You look unwell, my lord. Shall I carry you back up?"

"What is your name?"

The boy blinked as much at the tone as at the question, but he answered calmly enough. "Shatri, my lord. Shatri Tishri's-son.

"I know *your* name, my lord," he added, like an idiot, but his eyes had filled with mischief.

Sarevan studied the bright eyes until they went wide and veered away. Shatri was blushing again. When Sarevan touched him, he started and trembled like an unbroken colt. "Hush now, lad, I won't eat you. Which name of mine do you know."

"Why, lord, all of them. We are required to know. But we must call you *my lord* and *my prince.*"

"Why?"

"Because, my lord. You are."

"Ah, simplicity." But Shari was not simple at all. He would walk as Sarevan bade him, and he would offer his shoulder for Sarevan's hand, but whenever Sarevan spoke to him, he suffered a fit of shaking. It was often like that with the new ones. It had little to do with the terrors of serving mages, and much to do with the terrors of serving kings.

They stopped in the stableyard beside the largest of the stone troughs. Sarevan sat on its edge. For a long while he simply sat, and his sitting was a prayer of thanksgiving that he need not force himself forward another step. His sight swelled and dimmed, swelled and dimmed. His body would not stop trembling.

Yet he smiled at Shatri, and somewhere he found the voice to say,

"My senel. Do you know him? The oddity, the blue-eyed stallion. Bring him to me."

The boy hesitated. Perhaps at last he was considering other orders than Sarevan's. But he bowed and went away. Ulan stayed. Sarevan sat on the damp grass that rimmed the trough, half lying on the warm solidity of the cat's flank. Ulan began again to purr. People came. They remonstrated. Sarevan smile and was immovable. Then someone shouted, and darkness burst from a stable door.

Bregalan was no simple lackwit of a senel. He was of the Mad One's line: he had the mind of a man, a brother, a kinsman born to the shape and the wisdom of a beast. He did not suffer fools, or ropes, or doors that dared to shut him off from his two-legged brother; though for once he had suffered someone to saddle him, for Sarevan's sake.

He was black, like his grandsire. He was beautiful, which he knew very well. He was, as Sarevan had said, an oddity. His eyes were not seneldi brown or silver or green, nor even the rarer ruby of the Mad One and his get. When he was at peace, they were as blue as the sky in autumn. When he was in a rage, they were the precise and searing blue that lives in the heart of a flame.

They found Sarevan. They rolled. Bregalan scattered the presumptuous few who stood in his way; one, slow to retreat, he very nearly gored.

Having cleared the stableyard, he approached Sarevan with perfect dignity marred only by a snort at Ulan. The cat responded with a lazy growl. Bregalan disdained to hear it, lowering his head to examine Sarevan with great care. Sarevan reached up, wound his fingers in the senel's mane. Bregalan sank to his knees. He had never done it before. Sarevan fought the easy tears, mustered the rags of his strength, dragged himself onto the familiar back. "Up," he whispered into the ear that cocked for him.

It was easier by far than walking. Bregalan had soft paces: they were bred into him. He softened them to silk, and he wrought a miracle. He reined in all his wild temper, although he could not forbear from dancing gently as Sarevan woke to something very like joy. He could still converse with his brother, a wordless, ceaseless colloquy, body speaking to body with nothing between. He was no cripple here, no invalid, no precious prize wrested from death. He was a man, and whole, and riding free.

"Is that an art reserved for mages?"

Sarevan looked down. Wide golden eyes, all but whiteless like a lion's or a falcon's, looked up. Alone of anyone in Endros, Asanion's lion cub was brave enough to stand on ground which Bregalan had cleared. He did not seem aware of his own great courage. That was the legacy of a thousand years of careful breeding: an arrogance as perfect as Bregalan's own. And the stallion, like Ulan before him, recognized it and approved it. Ulan had been much amused. From the glint in his eye, Bregalan was no less so. Sarevan smiled. "Riding is an art which any man can learn. Much like loving. With which, I understand, it has something in common."

Hirel was losing the sun-stain of his wandering, returning to the perfect pallor of ivory; even a slight flush was as vivid as a flag. Odd, reflected Sarevan, how a youth of his accomplishments could blush at the merest suggestion of a coarse word. But being Hirel, he covered it with prickly hauteur. "I can ride. I am reckoned a master. But not without a bridle."

"Ah," said Sarevan, "but that's only for the Mad One's kin. This is his daughter's son."

Hirel laid a hand on Bregalan's neck. Bregalan did not warn him away. Sarevan knew an instant's piercing jealousy. An outlander, a haughty infant with no power at all; and Sarevan's horned brother not only suffered him but showed every sign of approving of him. The little fool did not even know that he was honored.

Sarevan slid from the saddle, which was half his penance for thinking like an idiot. The other half he set in words. "Do you want to learn how we do it? Bregalan will teach you, if you promise not to insult him by regarding him as a dumb beast."

The Asanian was cool, but Sarevan had seen the sudden light before he hid it. "What is he if he is not a beast?"

"He is a kinsman and a friend. And he has a thinking mind, though he has no tongue to tell you so." Sarevan gestured, princely gracious. "Will you mount?"

Bregalan was the tallest of the Mad One's line; and while that was nothing remarkable for a stallion of the Ianyn breed, it was a goodly leap for a prince of the old Asanian blood. Hirel made it with that studied, dancer's grace of his, and looked down for once into Sarevan's face. Sarevan grinned at him. "Now begin. You have no bit and no reins, but you have your whole body. Use it. Talk to him with it. Yes, gently. Listen now; he answers. Yes. Yes, so."

Sarevan ended again on the grass with Ulan, voice pitched to carry well without effort. People had gathered: grooms, stablehands, the inevitable scattering of idlers. This was a great rarity, a stranger mounted on one of the Varyani demons; that it was an Asanian, and this Asanian to boot, made it worth a stare or six.

And, Sarevan admitted reluctantly, they had come to stare at him. For their sake he sat upright, cross-legged in his no longer pristine white robe, and leaned on Ulan more than they knew but less than he would have liked to. Another voice slid smoothly into a pause in Sarevan's. "No, don't lean. Sit straight; guide him with your leg. Your whole leg, sir. Heels are merely an annoyance."

How dull the world had grown, that Mirain An-Sh'Endor was only a slight man, very dark, with the bearing of a king. No blaze of light; no high and singing presence in Sarevan's mind, part of it, source of it, anchored as firmly as the earth itself. Even when he came and settled his arm about his son's shoulders, he was only warm flesh; beloved, yes, but separate. Sundered.

Sarevan would not cling and cry. He had done that when he made the long terrible journey from the marches of death's country, and woke, and found himself a cripple. No power at all, only the void and the pain. He had wept like a child, until his blurred and swollen eyes, lifting, saw the anguish in his father's face. Then he had sworn. No tears. He was alive; his body would mend. That must suffice.

"He does well," Mirain said, holding Sarevan up and mercifully refraining from comment on his condition. Bregalan was showing Hirel how a battle charger fought in Keruvarion; the boy had dropped all his masks and loosed a blood-curdling whoop. They were a fine and splendid sight: the great black beast with his blue-fire eyes, his rider all gold and ivory, molded to the senel's back, singing in a voice too piercingly pure to be human.

Until it cracked, and Bregalan wearied of perfect obedience and bucked him neatly into the trough. He came up gasping, more shocked than angry, but he came up in a long leap that somersaulted him over the javelin horns and onto the back that had spurned him.

A roar went up. Laughter, cheering, even a spear smitten on a guardsman's shield. Hirel sat and dripped and grinned a wide white grin. Bregalan raised his head and belled in seneldi mirth.

Sarevan was not regretting what he had done. Not precisely. He had had no strength left to face the stair; his father had carried him up, taking not the least notice of his objections, standing by sternly while his servants stripped him and bathed him and laid him in bed. "And mind that you stay there," said Mirain; and he left Shatri on guard within the door. The squire, transparently grateful to have escaped with a mere reprimand, took his charge all too seriously. If Sarevan moved, Shatri was there, alert, scowling most formidably.

Not that Sarevan moved much. He was discovering muscles he had not known he had. There were not enough of them, that was the trouble. The bones kept thrusting through.

He slept a little. He ate, to keep his nursemaids quiet. When they pressed wine on him, even his sluggish nose could catch the sweetness of dreamflower. He flung the cup across the room. That was petulant, unprincely, and very satisfying. And it persuaded even Shatri to let him be.

Sarevan started awake. Hirel regarded him steadily, without expression. For a moment Sarevan could not choose between waking and the memory of a dream. It was a little unreal, that face, like something carved in ivory. Perfect, without line or blemish, and poised still on the edge between child and man. In gown and veil he would have made an exquisite girl; in coat and trousers he was a strikingly beautiful boy. Sarevan always wanted to stroke him, to see if he would be as pleasing to the hand as to the eye.

Hirel's eyes flicked aside; his brows met. "You drove yourself too hard. I should have seen."

"You couldn't have stopped me."

Hirel answered that with a long look. Abruptly he said, "Roll over."

Surprised, piqued with curiosity, Sarevan obeyed. Quick hands stripped off the coverlet. He shivered a little. The corner of his eye caught Hirel's infinitesimal pause, the widening of the golden eyes.

"Not pretty, am I?"

"No," Hirel murmured, hardly more than a whisper. His hands found one of the hundred screaming muscles. Sarevan gasped and tensed; Hirel did something indescribable; the pain melted and flowed and transmuted into pleasure. The boy's deepening voice spoke just above his head. "No, you are not pretty at all. You are beautiful."

Sarevan's cheeks were hot. Thank Avaryan and his Ianyn ancestors, it never showed. And his tongue always knew what to do. Lightly, carelessly, it said, "What are you trying to do, infant? Make me vain?"

"That," said Hirel, "would be salting the sea." His weight settled on the bed, kneeling astride Sarevan's hips; his hands wrought wonders up Sarevan's back and across his shoulders.

Sarevan sighed from the bottom of his lungs. It was almost sinful, this. Purest animal contentment.

What an artist the child was with those hands. What an innocent, in spite of everything. "You would have made a splendid bath-slave," Sarevan's tongue observed, incorrigible.

Hirel worked his way downward, inch by blissful inch. Then up, and with more ease than he had any right to, he turned Sarevan onto his back. A very faint flush stained his cheeks. His curls were loosening as they grew, falling over his forehead. Sarevan had no will left; he reached to stroke them.

The boy was learning. He tensed, but he held himself still. Only his hands moved. Upward.

Sarevan laughed. "I dare you," he said.

Very slowly Hirel straightened, gathered himself, sat on the bed's edge. His eyes slanted toward Sarevan's middle, and slanted away. Sarevan refused to cover it. Even and especially when Hirel observed to the air, "So very much, to so very little purpose."

"What, child! Envy?"

"Moral outrage." Hirel tucked up his feet and drew his brows together. The line between them was going to be etched there before he was very much older. "Sun-prince, there is that which I must say."

Sarevan waited.

Hirel's hands fisted upon his knees. "This should never have come to pass. You, I. You should have slain me before ever I woke by your fire. I should have taken your life while you lay helpless by the Lakes of the Moon, or held you back upon the journey until you died of your own accord. We cannot be what we are. We must not. For I have heard and I have seen, in Kundri'j and in Endros. I know that two emperors rule the two faces of the world; but when our time comes, only one of us may claim throne or power. And that time is coming soon. Your father makes no secret of it. Mine intends to move before him. Has moved already, subtly. Are you not the proof of it?"

Sarevan's throat tightened into pain. He thrust his voice through it. "I'm proof of nothing but my own stupidity."

"That too," Hirel said all too willingly. "As am I of mine. Your father declares that his god will not permit a peaceful union of our empires. Mine insists that we must not be overrun by the barbarian vigor of the east. Yet here are we. I am not going to find it easy to encompass your death."

"What ever makes you think that you should have to?"

"Bow to me, then. Bow to me now, and swear that you will serve me when I am emperor."

Sarevan sat bolt upright. The last languor of Hirel's ministrations had vanished. His branded hand had flared into agony. But he laughed, though it was half a howl. "You forget, cubling. You forget what I am. Avaryan is not only my father's god. He is mine, and he rules me. He— still—rules me."

Still. Sarevan laughed harder, freer, cradling the pain that was driving him through madness into blessed, blissful clarity. Avaryan. Burning Avaryan. No mere mage could drive him from his only son's only son. He was there. He was pain. He was—

Sarevan's cheeks stung. He rocked with the force of Hirel's blows, blinking, still grinning. "Are you mad?" Hirel all but screamed at him.

"No," said Sarevan. "No more than I ever am."

The boy hissed like a cat, thrust his hand into his coat, held it up shaking and glittering. "Do you know what this is?"

Laughter, joy, even madness forsook Sarevan utterly. The thing in Hirel's palm glowed with more than sunlight, yet its heart was a darkness that writhed and twisted like a creature in agony. Or like a slow and deadly dance. It lured Sarevan's eyes, drew them down and down, beckoned, whispered, promised. *Come, and I will make you strong again. Come, take me, wield me. I am power. I am all the magics you have lost. Take me and be healed.*

Sarevan gasped, retched. "Take it—take—"

It withdrew. Slowly, far too slowly, into the embroidered coat.

"No!" cried Sarevan. "Not there!" He snatched wildly, striking, hurling the jewel through the air. It fell like a star, whispering. He seized Hirel's wrists. "How often has it touched your skin? *How often?*"

The boy blinked like an idiot. "Just now. And when first I took it. I do not like to hold it. But—"

"Never," said Sarevan, choking on bile. "Never touch it again. It is deadly."

"It is but a jewel. The deadliness lies in what it stands for."

"It is an instrument of blackest sorcery." Sarevan dragged himself up, dragging Hirel with him until he remembered to let go. He snatched the first cloth that came to hand, and fell to his knees. The stone sang to him. *Power. Power I bear.* His sight narrowed. He groped. His right hand throbbed.

He fell forward. His hand dropped boneless to the stone. He had no will to rule it. To close. To take, or to cast away.

Gold met topaz. The song rose to a shriek. The pain mounted through anguish into agony, through agony into purest, whitest torment, and through torment into blissful nothingness.

* * *

"Vayan. Vayan!"

Sarevan groaned. Again? Would he never be allowed to die in peace? "Sarevadin." That was his mother, in that tone of her which brooked no opposition. "Sarevadin Halenan, if you do not open your eyes—"

His mind cursed her, but his eyes opened. He was in bed again, and they were there, she and his father, and Hirel green-pale and great-eyed beside them. "Poor cubling," said Sarevan. "We're too much for you, we madmen."

"Mad, yes," snapped Elian, "striking an Eye of Power with no weapon but your *Kasar*."

Sarevan struggled to sit up. "Is it gone? Did I do it? It wanted me to take it. It promised me—it promised—"

They all fell on him at once, bearing him down, holding him, trying to stroke him calm again. But it was his own will that stilled him, and his own wish that laid him back in his bed, somehow gripping three hands in his two. One freed itself: his mother's, strong and slender. She looked angry, as always when her pride refused to weep. "Will you never learn?" she demanded of him.

"I rather think not."

"Puppy." Her slap was half caress. "It's gone. There are aching heads from here to Han-Gilen, but the Eye is broken. As you very nearly were."

"I wish I had been!" he cried with sudden passion. "I wish I had died in Shon'ai. What use am I? Crippled, helpless, weak as a baby—what good am I to anyone?"

"At the moment," Mirain said coolly, "not remarkably much." He won back his hand and turned to Hirel. "Prince, are you well? That was a great flare of power, and you almost upon it when it burst. If you will permit . . ."

Whether Hirel would or no, Mirain searched him with eyes and hands and power. Sarevan, numb to the last, still could know that it was there, and how it was wielded, and why.

But he was forgetting the vow which he had sworn. He willed away the unshed tears and sat up. This time no one stopped him. He set his feet on the floor, gathered all his wavering strength, rose. His knees buckled. He stiffened them. He made them bear him to the eastward window, although he asked no more of them there, but let them give way until he half sat, half lay upon the broad ledge. Night had fallen without his knowing it; the air was cool and he as bare as he was born. He shivered.

Warmth folded itself about him. One of his own cloaks, with his mother's hands on it and her arms circling him. Her swift unthinking smile was for an old jest, of mothers and of great strapping broad-shouldered sons. Her scowl was for the jut of bones in those shoulders. He kissed her cheek, quickly, before she could escape. "I'll be strong," he said as much to himself as to her. "I will be."

Eleven

"*L*ITTLE WHORE."

The voice came from beyond the door into the Green Court. Sarevan knew it, as he knew the one which spoke after. "Yellow barbarian. You couldn't kill him cleanly, could you? You had to make him suffer."

And a third: "But we know. We see what you try to do to him now that he can't defend himself."

"Yes, catamite," sneered the first, "try it. See where it gets you."

Sarevan shot the bolt, blind for a moment in the dazzle of sunlight, forcing his eyes to see. Hirel stood at bay in a cluster of young men, some in the emperor's livery, others clad as the lordlings they were. Sarevan knew them all. Some he even loved.

Whatever Hirel had tried, he had forsaken it in favor of his imperial Asanian mask. Only his lips betrayed him; they were tight, and they were bone-white.

Starion had spoken third and most ominously. Now he spoke again. He sounded as if he had been weeping, or as if he were not far from it. "I saw him yesterday in the stableyard. I saw how he had to be carried away. Your doing, you and your devil of a father. You lured him into the trap that almost killed him. You tricked him into bringing you here. You set your Eye of sorcery in his very hand; and yet you found a way to crawl into the emperor's good graces. But *we* know you for what you are."

"Spy and traitor," said a prince's son from Baian, his round amiable face gone grim, "set here like a worm to gnaw Keruvarion's heart. Is it fools you animals take us for?"

"What's the use of talk?" Ianyn, this great yearling bull of a boy, not quite the tallest but by far the broadest of them all. "He's Asanian; he was born with a serpent's tongue, though he's not deigning to use it on the likes of us. Not when he's got royalty to hiss in the ears of. Here, little snake, I'll tie your tongue for you."

Hirel spat in his face.

Sarevan hardly heard the snarl, or saw the lunge of several bodies at once. He was in the midst of them, striking openhanded, taking at least one blow that all but felled him, until someone cried sharply, *"Vayan!"*

The circle had widened in dismay. Sarevan almost laughed to see their faces. With great deliberation he laid his arm about Hirel's rigid shoulders and said, "So there you are, brother. I've been looking for you."

Starion broke at that. "Don't you know what he *is*, Vayan?"

"Certainly," Sarevan answered. And to Hirel: "Come with me. There's something I want you to see."

"How can you show him anything? How can you trust him? He's here to destroy us all, and you foremost."

Sarevan drew a deep breath. "He's so thin," someone whispered, too low to put a name to the voice; and Sarevan would not take his eyes from Starion. "So weak. O 'Varyan!"

Sarevan swallowed bile and spoke as evenly as he could. "Kinsmen, your concern warms me. But I would thank you to reserve your righteous passion for those who truly mean me harm. Of whom this prince is not one. Touch him again, threaten him, speak one ill word of him, and it will be I who call you to account." He drew Hirel forward. "Come."

"That was not wise," Hirel said.

Sarevan laughed lest the pain lash him into shameful tears. "What's wise? I've pulled rank on that pack of idiots before. Though not," he admitted, "quite so viciously as that. I'm afraid I've not done you much good with them."

"Or yourself either."

"That's nothing. They'll mutter a little, they'll cold-shoulder me for a while, and then they'll come back as if nothing had ever happened. They always do."

"Unless they are driven too far."

"Not yet," said Sarevan with more confidence than he felt. He opened a locked door, passing again from dimness into the heat and the glare of noon in full summer, and had his reward: the catch of Hirel's breath. "This is my own garden. My father and mother made it for me with their power. It's not as big as it looks."

"The pool seems as broad as a sea," Hirel said, sounding for once like the boychild he was. "A sea, and a forest, and a green plain. What mountain is that?"

"The palace wall, painted and ensorceled to look like the peak of Zigayan as it rises over Lake Umien." Sarevan shed his kilt and waded into the water. After a long moment Hirel followed. Sarevan struck his shoulder lightly, challenging. "Race you to the island."

Hirel won, but only barely. They lay on the grass, getting their breaths, back, grinning at one another and at the brazen sky.

Hirel's grin died first; his frown came back. "Sun-prince, I was in no danger, and I was about to escape. You had no need to go to war for me."

"No? It looked as if they were going to war for me." Something in Hirel's face made Sarevan tense, rolling onto his stomach, raising himself on his elbows. "What is it? What aren't you telling me?"

"Nothing."

"Don't lie, cubling. You're no good at it."

"Very well, mongrel. I will tell you. They are indeed going to war for you. And not they alone. It is noised abroad in your empire: my father and I between us fomented this plot to destroy you, and through you your father and all his realm. Your people are crying for vengeance. Your lords and your princes are arming for war. Your wise men are calling for calm, but no one heeds them."

For all the sun's heat, Sarevan was cold to the bone. He had come to Endros for his father's sake, with warning of war in Asanion; with hope, however frail, that he could hold it back. And he had failed more utterly even than he had feared. Coming as he had come, on the very edge of death, he had fanned the spark which he had meant to quench. Now it was a full and raging fire; and all for his own invincible folly.

"No," he said. "Not yet. My father has a little sanity left. He will stop it."

Hirel laughed, short and bitter. "Your father could ask for nothing better. He has you, alive and well enough, and he has the war for which he has waited so long. By next High Summer, he has sworn, he will sit upon the Golden Throne."

"No." Sarevan could not stop saying it. "Not for me."

The boy's face hovered close. He looked frightened. As well he might. Sarevan was losing what little wits he had had. He lurched to his knees; his fists struck the ground. He flung himself into the water.

He must have remembered to dress. His hair had worked out of its braid, but it was drying; and for the first time since he left Shon'ai, his body had forborne to betray him. It carried him he cared not where.

To his tower, in the end. To court dress and the massive weight of his torque and a feast to which he had not been bidden.

Because someone—Shatri, damn his diligence—had made him rest a little, he was late. They were all seated. Emperor, empress, Lord of the Northern Realms, Lord Chancellor of the South, their ladies, their servants, certain of their children. And in the place of honor, still as a golden image, Hirel Uverias.

Their eyes weighed him down. Most were seeing him for the first time since he came back. He read horror in them, and dismay, and pity swiftly veiled. And anger, deep and abiding, most strongly marked in the youngest, who were his kin and his friends.

He gave them his whitest, wildest grin, and said, "Good evening, my lords and ladies. I hear you're having a war without me."

No one spoke. He did not look at his father, or at his mother, although he knew she had half risen. He sat beside Hirel and reached for a brimming cup. He raised it. "To death," he said.

He paid for that, and not cheaply. Not that Mirain dealt him a reprimand. The emperor said nothing, which was infinitely worse. And Sarevan must sit, eat, drink, prove to them all that he was still Sarevan Is'kelion.

He woke as inevitably he must, in a bed not his own. Hirel slept in a warm knot against him. "Damn them," he whispered. "Oh, damn them."

"Damn whom?"

He started up, winced, clutched his stomach, fell back, torn between anger and mirth. "Cubling! I thought you were asleep."

"Obviously not." Hirel settled more comfortably, head on folded arm. His eyes were soft still with sleep. "Damn whom?" he asked again.

"Everyone!" Hirel raised his brows. Sarevan had better fortune in his second rising. He spread his arms wide. "They've made me an object of rage and pity, a banner for their war."

"I know," said Hirel. "It amazes me that you did not. That you came as you did, when you did, in my company—how could it have ended otherwise?"

Sarevan's own thoughts, bitter to hear from a stranger's mouth. His hand flew up to strike; with all his strength he willed it down.

"You should be rejoicing," the young demon said. "You are getting a war. A chance to look splendid in armor, and brandish a sword, and win a hero's name. Is that not the heart's desire of every good barbarian?"

"Barbarian I may be," gritted Sarevan, "but I will not be the cause of this war. I will *not.*"

"Is it not a little late for that?"

"It may not be." Sarevan stopped short. His teeth clicked together. "It is not. I will not have it!"

For a miracle, Hirel was silent. Sarevan's chin itched. His fingers rasped on stubble; he grimaced, rising slowly. His knees were steady. A wave of sickness passed, and it was all wine. No weakness. He stretched each muscle, and each responded, remembering at last its old suppleness. As close to rage or madness as he was, he could have sung.

He availed himself of Hirel's bath and servants, and sent for his own clothing, and ate while he waited for it, for a mighty hunger had roused in him. Which was an excellent sign, better even than the ease with which he moved. When he dressed, he dressed with care, contemplating his image in the tall bronze mirror. Clean, smooth-shaven, his hair tamed as much as it could ever be: yes. And the princely plainness of his boots and trousers, and the understated elegance of his coat, and the rich red gold of the torque at his throat: excellent. His eyes were too large and bright in the hollowed face, but that he could not help; though he had a moment's regret. If he had had all his wits about him, he would not have sacrificed the concealment of his beard.

He sighed and shrugged, and smiled at Hirel whose reflection had come to stand beside his own. Hirel looked him up and down, eyes glinting. "Are you plotting to seduce someone?"

"Keruvarion," Sarevan answered.

The boy tilted his head and vouchsafed one of his rare smiles. He looked like a cat in cream.

Sarevan swallowed. It hurt. "Hirel," he said with great care, "last night. What did I—"

"You were remarkable," said Hirel. "You were the life and soul of the gathering. You were a light and a fire, and you held each man and woman in the palm of your hand."

"Of course I did. That's what I went for. But why was I—" This was hard, and Hirel was making it no easier, going all warm and supple and melting-eyed. Playing some game of his own, and enjoying it much too much. "How did I end in your bed?"

"You do not remember?"

His astonishment was well played, but not well enough. Sarevan fixed him with a grim eye. "All right, cubling. What did I do, and what are you up to?"

Hirel dropped the mask of the courtesan for that of the spoiled princeling, a little sulky, more than a little offended. "You did nothing. Except drown yourself in wine, roister everyone into a stupor, and fall into bed. Mine. Because, you said, two hundred steps were too many, and people were talking, and you were minded to give them something to talk of. Surely you remember."

"Vaguely," Sarevan admitted. "Now answer the rest of it."

"No."

Sarevan gripped that stubborn chin, forced it up. It set against him. With a rush of temper, he bent and seized a long, thorough kiss. Thorough enough to bruise, and long enough to heat them both. He let go so swiftly that Hirel swayed. "Is that what you're angling for?"

Hirel bared his teeth. It was more grin than snarl. "It will do," he said, "for a beginning."

Sarevan's temper subsided; he took Hirel's shoulders, but gently, shaking them a little. "They're only a pack of jealous children. For all their prattle, they know the truth as well as we do."

"But," Hirel asked, "what is the truth?"

"What should it be?"

Hirel tossed his head, swift, nervous, as if he would fling back his lost splendid mane. "The truth," he snapped, "is that I am a whore and a spy, and I was your prisoner, and I contemplated your murder, and at a word, at one lone word, I would fling myself into your arms." He glared into Sarevan's craven silence. "No, I cannot help myself. No, I am not glad of it! I am the worst of all fools. I took you to wield you, and because there was no one else to take. I gave you my trust. I found that I could not hate you, even when you seemed to betray me. And now I am lost. I would be your lover, and I would do it gladly, and I would not ask even a harlot's recompense. But in the end, I remain as I was born. High Prince of Asanion. They know, your kinsmen. They see clearly. I would love you without regret, and betray you with deep regret, even to your death."

"Avaryan," Sarevan said softly. "Sweet Avaryan. I never meant—"

"What an innocent you are," said that most unchildlike child, shaking the slack hands from his shoulders. "You are plotting something, and I know what it must be, and I think that it is utterly mad."

"You can't stop me."

"I would not if I could. I will help you as I can. But I give you fair warning. I will not betray my empire, and I will think nothing of betraying the god to whom you are sworn."

Sarevan laughed suddenly. "I'll take my chances. If I win this throw, there will be no need for betrayal. If I lose it, I doubt I'll be alive to care."

"That is the heart of it, is it not? Without your power, you see little purpose in living."

"I see one, and I am pursuing it. By your leave, sir?" Sarevan asked, mocking.

Hirel bowed, mocking. With a grin and a flash of his hand, Sarevan left him.

It was flight; but it was flight from bad to worse. Sarevan's new strength could not carry him quite as far as he had to go. He paused in a side chamber of his father's antechambers, in a recess that offered a moment's curtained quiet. The press of people did not find its way here; the servants were elsewhere about their duties.

As he gathered himself to go on, he froze behind his arras. Swift feet; the snick of a bolt; laughter barely stifled. It rippled in two ranges, mandeep and woman-sweet. What accompanied it was obvious enough. A pair of lovers had found a haven.

Sarevan did not know whether to laugh or to groan aloud. There was no door but the one the lovers had barred, and no escape except past them; and he was in no state to eavesdrop on their sport. They were most merry in it. He blocked his ears as best he could, and shut his eyes to aid them. Behind the quivering lids, Hirel smiled: but Hirel become a maiden, sweet and wicked. Grimly he began the first of the Prayers of Penitence, with its nine invocations of bodily pain.

The lovers ended before the prayer. Sarevan, lowering hands from ears, heard only silence. He waited, hardly breathing. Nothing moved. No voice spoke. With great care he parted the curtain.

His breath caught. They were there still, in a nest of carpets. Her head lay on his shoulder; his hand tangled itself in her hair. Hair that, had she stood, would have tumbled to her knees, fire-bright as Sarevan's own.

He sank back in his hiding place, hands clapped over mouth. His shoulders shook with the utter and delicious absurdity of it. Lovers, indeed. The Emperor and the Empress of Keruvarion, twenty years wed, trysting like children; and their son trapped without escape, all unwilling to be their witness. Elian would be livid when she knew; he could hope that she would soften into laughter. He did not fancy another nine months' span in a woman's body.

She spoke, a murmur, drowsily tender. Sarevan, moving to uncover himself, paused.

"No one's here," Mirain said. "We have a while yet before anyone looks for me. I told them I was going to ride the Mad One."

She laughed softly. "And no one dares to trouble you then. Alas for me, I never stopped to think. They'll be combing the corridors for me."

"Let them." Properly imperial, that, but with a smile beneath it. "Were you so eager, then?"

"You hardly gave me time to begin. Hot as a boy, you are. And you more than old enough to know better."

"Come now, madam. May not even a greybeard take what pleasure he can?"

She snorted. "Even if you had a beard, which I am glad you do not, there would be scarce enough silver in it to buy a night with a camp follower."

"I found a thread," he said, "this morning."

"Where?"

"Here."

"I don't see—" She stopped. There was a flurry, with his laughter in it, and her mirthful outrage. "Ah, trickster! That's the silver in your robe."

"It's all I have. I'm not aging gracefully, my love. I keep thinking I'm a youth still."

"You are!"

His voice held a smile, for her vehemence. "And you are as wild as ever you were. But not," he added judiciously, "as beautiful."

She growled. He laughed. "O vain! You were nothing in your youth to what you are in this your womanhood. Men sighed for you then. Now they swoon over you."

"Indeed," she muttered. "Flat at my feet, mooncalves all, and blind with it. Though one or two . . . if you were not so fierce in your jealousy . . ."

"When was I ever—"

"When were you not? Vadin you never minded: the world never saw a man more thoroughly married than that one, or more perfectly a brother to his soul's sister. But let other eyes slide toward me, and you turn all to thunder."

"Only once," he said, "and that was long ago; and I had reason." He paused. His tone softened. "Elian. Do you regret it? That you chose as you did, and clove to me, and let the prince go back alone to Asanion?"

"Sometimes . . ." Her voice was softer even than his. "Sometimes I wonder. But regret, never. You are all that I ever wanted."

"Even my damnable temper? Even our battles?"

"What would life be without a good clean fight?"

"He would have given you a spat or two, I think. He was never as insipid as he looked."

"He was not insipid! He was gentle. You were never that, Mirain. Tender, with me, with Sarevan when he was small. But never gentle."

"Ziad-Ilarios was as gentle as a lion sleeping. His son is more like him than anyone might guess, though not so soft to the eye or the mind. There are scars in that child. New wounds; but old ones too, buried deep. He'll be a strong emperor, or he'll break before he comes to his throne."

"If he were going to break, he would have broken before this. Do you know what it cost him to bring Sarevan to us?"

"Not entirely of his own will," said Mirain.

"Less so than he or anyone thinks. He has his father's curse. He's honorable."

"Not all would call it honor, to bring an Eye of Power into Endros."

"He didn't know what he was doing."

"Did he not? He hid it from us. He brought it to Sarevan in his greatest weakness, and very nearly destroyed him."

"In ignorance," she persisted. "He knows nothing of magic; he knows little more of trust. But Sarevan he trusts, though not willingly. He brought a thing that frightened him, to the one person he knew who might know what to do with it."

"If I grant you that, will you grant me this? There was design in what he did. Not his own, maybe. But he found a place of black sacrifice—Asanian black sacrifice—within sight of my city. He brought what it had wrought into the heart of my palace."

"Traps within traps," she said slowly. "Wheels within wheels. It's too obvious. As if someone were trying, deliberately and all but openly, to turn you against the Golden Empire."

"Need it be so complex? Asanion is arming on all fronts. And it has the Mageguild."

"Does it also have Ulan? He set the Eye in the child's hand."

"Oh, come," said Mirain with a flicker of impatience. "You yourself saw a reason for that. He sensed the evil; he cherishes a remarkable fondness for the boy. He trusted Hirel to dispose of the thing."

"You underrate Ulan, I think. If he was ever an ordinary creature, he's one no longer. He's steeped in magery."

"And whose fault is that?"

"Vadin's, for hunting an ul-queen and bringing back her cub. Yours and mine, for letting our own cub out of sight for long enough to lose him. Sarevan's, for finding his way to the cage and witching away the lock and swearing brotherhood with the cat. How were we to know that he had that much power, at five years old? Or that he'd give his heart to the deadliest of all the world's hunters?"

"It's done," Mirain said. "I don't think it was ill done. The beast has played his part more than once in keeping the boy alive. He's part of no conspiracy. But that Asanion has declared war in its own subtle and serpentine way—that, I'm sure of. It chose my son as its target. It will pay." His voice deepened. "It will pay to the last man."

"Someone may be longing for precisely that. Any man in the world can name your weakness: Prince Sarevadin."

"He is my son. He is all that I may have."

"Mirain—" she began.

He silenced her. With a kiss, from the sound of it, a long one, ended with reluctance. When he spoke, he spoke softly, with a hint of sadness. "Of all that I am and have done, this I most regret: that I could give you no more than the one son."

"Sarevadin is enough."

"Surely. But I would have given you a daughter for yourself."

"I need no more than you gave me." Her voice was strange. Sarevan, listening in helpless fascination, could not put a name to the strangeness. It faded almost as swiftly as he noticed it. "I want no more than I have. But I would not have you destroy an empire for his sake alone."

"For what higher cause would you have me do it?"

"You may have no cause!" she cried. "This that he suffers, he did to himself. He knows it. He wants no vengeance. He wants no war."

"He will have both."

"He will die to stop it."

"He will not."

"How can you know?" Her passion rocked Sarevan in his shadow, flung him against the cold stone of the wall. "I carried him in my body. I feel him there yet. He is an open wound; he will do anything, anything at all, to put an end to the pain."

"He will not," Mirain said again, grim as stone. "I will avenge him. He will rule the world with me, and none shall live who dares to stand against us."

"Oh, you *man!*" If Sarevan had been less benumbed by all he had heard, he would have smiled at the depth of her disgust. "Can't you ever see anything but force? You'll settle it all with the sword, and set his will at naught while you do it, and expect him to be glad of it."

"How else can anyone unravel this tangle? I should have struck against Asanion when Ilarios took the throne. I listened to prudence; I had mercy. I gave them peace. Fool that I am. You see how I pay: with my only son. If he dies before this war is ended, I swear to you, I will leave not one stone standing upon its brother. I will raze Asanion to the ground."

"Not before I will." She was as grim as he. "But it will cost you more than Vayan. It will cost you me."

"It will not."

The silence stretched, as after thunder. Sarevan's hand reached of its own accord, drew back the curtain. They did not see. They stood face to face, eye to eye.

"I walk with the god," he said. "He gives me victory."

Her head tossed. All of Sarevan's protests blazed in her eyes. Her hand flew up. Mirain stood steady. She laid her palm against his cheek. "I love you," she said, soft, barely to be heard. "I love you more than anything in the world."

He turned his head to kiss her palm. Their eyes met, held, broke free. Wordless, oblivious to the one who watched, they left the chamber.

Sarevan stumbled from the alcove. The nest of carpets lay forgotten. He stood over it. He was shaking; he could not stop. He said the words with which he had meant to begin. "Father," he said. "Father, consider. What can war do, that words and wisdom cannot?"

He had his answer. Avenge one man's idiocy. End an ancient enmity. Give Mirain the dominion for which he had been born. Which he meant, in its proper time, to pass to that young idiot who was his son.

"Not," said Sarevan, "if I can help it. Not this way."

The shaking had retreated inward. He could move. Hold up his head. Put on the most rakish of his faces. Stride forth into the full and brazen light of Avaryan.

Sarevan wooed Keruvarion with his presence and his smile and a word here and there. He traversed the palace; he sat an hour in the hall of audience; he made himself a magnet for the young bloods of the court.

With Bregalan under him and Ulan striding by his side, he rode about Endros. He traded jests with his father's soldiers, and took the daymeal with his own guard, and had an uproarious reunion with the Zhil'ari who had ridden with him from the Lakes of the Moon.

He sang the sun down from his own tower, and let his nursemaids put him to bed, clucking over him as they did it. He would not let them feed him, but he ate enough to quiet the loudest of them. "And now," he said, "off with you, and let me sleep in peace."

Sleep came fitfully, peace not at all. Behind Sarevan's eyes shuddered the darkness of madness, or of prophecy. Death and destruction; bitter sunlight; a new dread: his mother fallen, his father gone mad over her body. He tossed in his bed, battling, as if his hands alone could drive back the horror that haunted him.

With infinite slowness he quieted. His breathing eased. His mind cleared; his will hardened. But he did not sleep. He dared not. He watched the moons' patterns shift upon the floor. The windows were open to the wind; shadows danced, now lulling, now startling, now alluring his eyes. One was very like a human shape. When it moved, it moved with fluid grace. The rest now approached, now retreated with the wind's turning. This paused often, but never drew back.

It stilled. Its shape was human surely: slender, supple, not tall. It sat at his bed's foot, and its weight was not considerable, but weight it certainly had. It tucked up its feet and settled its rump and regarded Sarevan with wide moon-brightened eyes.

A stare, like a shadow, can have weight. Sarevan fretted under it. It did not waver.

"Cubling," said Sarevan with elaborate patience. "it's late. Haven't you noticed?"

"There are hours yet to midnight," Hirel said. He blinked, which was a small but potent mercy.

"Surely you have better things to do with those hours than sit and stare at me."

"No," Hirel said. "I do not."

Sarevan sat up. "Damn it, cubling! What's got into you?"

"You kissed me."

Sarevan scrambled himself together, cursing the mane that tumbled and knotted and tried to blind him, raking it out of his face. Hirel watched with grave intentness. For once in his life, Sarevan was aware that he was naked: and under a blanket yet, and a heavy cloak of hair. "Damn it," he said again. "Damn it, infant. That was a game I played, to stop your nonsense."

The golden eyes narrowed. "A game, prince?" Hirel asked very softly.

"A game," Sarevan repeated. "That was all. I erred, I admit it. I cry your pardon."

Hirel sat motionless. Sarevan could not read his face at all. He was all alien, inscrutable, like one of his own discredited gods.

"Cubling," said Sarevan, meaning to be gentle, sounding lame even to himself. "Hirel. Whatever you think I meant, I was only playing. Being outrageous, because you were there and being infuriating, and I couldn't help myself. I'm like that. It's the most glaring of all my flaws."

"What should I have thought you meant?"

Sarevan gritted his teeth. "You know damned well—"

Hirel tilted his head. "Would you be so angry if it truly had meant nothing?"

The silence was deafening. Hirel shifted minutely, almost smiling.

"Listen to me," Sarevan said at last. "To you I'm a horror of no small proportions: a man who's never had a woman; nor, for the matter of that, a boy. I won't say it's been easy. I won't say it's easy now. But my honor binds me, and my given word. Can you understand that?"

"It is most immoral," said Hirel. But quietly, as if he considered the matter with some shadow of care.

"What is moral? To those children in the Green Court, *you* are the outrage."

That roused a spark. "They? They would happily die to have what I have."

"You frighten them. They think you have the power to corrupt me, if not to kill me outright."

"And so I do," said Hirel, serene in his certainty. "As do you over me. We are equals. That is what they cannot bear."

"Equals." Sarevan was not sure he liked the sound of it. He, and this epicene creature?

Not so epicene, sitting there, looking at him. It was only youth. Sarevan at not quite fifteen had been pretty enough, eagle's beak and all. Was still rather too pretty for his own comfort, without a beard to mask the worst of it: as he had been amply dismayed to discover, when the razor showed him how little he had changed.

Equals, then. Sarevan lowered his eyes. He had been treating Hirel as a child, or at best as a weakling youth. And weak, Hirel certainly was not.

"So then," said Sarevan, mostly to himself. "What do we do now?"

"You do not know?"

Hirel was mocking them both. Sarevan snarled at him. He grinned back, which was always startling. "Something," said Sarevan with swelling heart. "Something outrageous."

"I will not swear priest's vows!"

"And I won't claim your harem," Sarevan said with a flicker of laughter, though he sobered swiftly. "You can be a moral man for both of us. But harken now—what can a pair of princes do when their fathers foment war?"

"Fight," Hirel said, but slowly, watching him. "What else can we do? We are born enemies. There is not even liking between us; nor, once I leave Endros, any debt of life or liberty."

"And yet there is something." Sarevan held up his hand, the left, which bore no brand. "Equality. A love for this world which one of us must rule; a deep reluctance to see it marred."

"Marring can be mended, if there is peace under a single lord."

"Not such marring as I can see." Sarevan's hand clenched into a fist. "And it is my father who will begin it. Meaning naught but good, in the god's name; seeing only the peace that will follow. Blind, stone blind, to its cost." He let his head fall back, his eyes fix upon the vaulted ceiling. "You don't believe me. No one believes me. Even my mother, who has seen what I see, has refused it: she has sold her soul for love of my father. If she won't listen, how can you? You don't even believe in prophecy."

"I believe in you."

Sarevan's head snapped forward. Hirel was grave, steady. Truthful; or playing a game which could cost him his neck.

"Mind you," the body said, "I do not do this easily. Yet I am a logician. I who have seen magecraft cannot deny that it exists. Prophecy is part of magecraft by all accounts, yours not least. You are outrageous, and you are quite mad, but a liar you are not. If you say that you have seen war, then war you have seen. If you say that it will be terrible, so is it likely to be. I have spoken with your father. I have seen what he is like, and I can guess what he will do when the fire of his god is on him."

"I love him," whispered Sarevan. "Dear gods, I love him. But I think that he is wrong. Utterly, hopelessly, endlessly wrong."

He rocked with it, no longer seeing Hirel, no longer hearing anything but the echo of his own terrible treason.

Terrible, and treason. But true. He knew it, down to the core of him. There was peace in it, almost. In knowing it for what it was. In ceasing his long battle to deny it. He had been no older than Hirel when it began. Maybe, when his power had gone but the dream held firm in all its terrible strength, it had broken him at last.

"I think not," he said. Hirel was staring at him. He mustered a smile. "No, brother prince, I haven't lost the last remnant of my wits. I see a way through this tangle. Will you tread it with me?"

"Is it sane?" asked Hirel.

Sarevan laughed, not too painfully. "Do you need to ask? But it may work. Listen, and decide for yourself."

Hirel waited. Sarevan drew a long steadying breath. "I'm going to Asanion with you."

Hirel's eyes widened a careful fraction. "And what," he asked, "do you hope to accomplish by that?"

"Peace. My father won't attack Asanion if I'm held hostage in Kundri'j Asan."

"Think you so? More likely he will raise heaven and hell to get you back."

"Not if it's known that I went of my own will."

"Ah," said Hirel, a long sigh. "That is blackest treason."

"It is." Sarevan was dizzy, thinking about it; bile seared his throat. "Don't you see? I have to do it. He won't yield for anything I can say. I have to show him. I have to shock him into heeding me."

"What if I will not assent to it?"

Sarevan seized his gaze and held it. "You will," he said, low and hard.

The boy tossed his head, uncowed. "And if I do—what then, Sunprince? I am Asanian. I have no honor as you would reckon it. You are a fool to dream of trusting me."

"You won't betray me."

"No," said Hirel after a stretching pause. "You are my only equal in the world. That cannot endure; but while it does, I am yours. As you are mine."

"We ride together."

"We ride together," Hirel agreed. He stood. "The Lord Varzun has been commanded. I depart on the third day from this. I shall give thought to the manner of your concealment."

"As shall I," said Sarevan. "Good night, high prince."

"Good night," said Hirel, "high prince."

Twelve

THE ZHIL'ARI, LIKE HIREL, HEARD SAREVAN OUT. UN-like Hirel, they did not hesitate. They were apt for this new mischief. He told them what he would have of them; they obeyed with relish, but with astonishing circumspection. No one remarked that the nine most recent recruits of the high prince's guard had vanished from Endros. They might never have come there at all.

Sarevan's own part, for the moment, was an old one. When the new sun struck fire in the pinnacle of Avaryan's Tower, he appeared on the practice field with sword and lance. If anyone took note that the prince chose to confine himself to mounted exercises, he did not speak of it. From the field Sarevan came to his father's council, and to a wild game of club-and-ball in one of the courts, and again to a leisurely meander through the streets of Endros. At nightfall he dined with a youngish lord and a merchant prince and a glitter of courtiers.

The second night of his plotting was quiet, as if his will, having set itself on treason, was minded to let his body rest. The second day brought rain and wind and the empress' presence in the window to which Sarevan had retreated. It was a broad recess, and very deep, and cushioned for ease; it lay in the lee of the wall, letting in neither wind nor rain, only cool clean air.

He started when she laid her hand on his arm; his body gathered itself, coiling to strike. The blow died unborn, but he was on his feet with no walls to hamper him, and she was braced for battle.

She relaxed all at once. He was slower. He made himself sit again, and laugh, and take her hand, and pretend that nothing had changed. "I'm well trained, aren't I?"

"Too well," she said, but she smiled. "You're a perilous man altogether. Do you know, there's a whole bower full of women yonder, and every one is passionately in love with you?"

"Was my chatter that captivating?"

"Not only your chatter."

"Oh, yes. My charming smile. My even more charming title. Who's offering daughters this season?"

"Everyone but the Emperor of Asanion."

It was an old jest. Yet Sarevan stiffened. She could not know what he was doing. No one could walk in his maimed mind. His father, finding it broken beyond all mending, had sealed it against invasion. Even Mirain's power was shut out; only the rebirth of Sarevan's own magics could lower those walls.

She did not know. She could not. Sarevan was doing nothing but what he always did. It was only what he did it for that had changed. And the intensity of it. Perhaps. Time was too short for subtlety.

She was frowning at him. She felt his brow, traced his cheek that was no longer quite so hollow. "You push too hard," she said, "and too fast."

"Not fast enough for me."

"Of course not." She sat by him. She would never admit to weariness, but surely that was the name of the shadows beneath her eyes, and the faint pallor of her honey skin, and the stiffness with which she held herself erect.

He settled his arm about her and drew her to him. "Tell me what it is," he said.

She laid her head on his shoulder and sighed. For a long while he thought she would not answer. When she did, her voice shared not at all in her body's languor. "It's always something. Generals getting out of hand. Governors maneuvering for power. Common people losing patience. Ianon crying that it was never more than a stepping-stone to Mirain's empire, when it should be the first and foremost of all his realms, the only one to which his blood entitles him; but he abandoned it to rule out of the south. As if he never spent two seasons out of every four in Han-Ianon, remote and troublesome as that can be for the ruling of an empire as wide as his. And the Hundred Realms cry now separately and now in chorus that he gives too much of his heart to the north, when it was they who made him emperor. Forgetting that it was the Prince of Han-Gilen who inveigled and threatened and flogged them into it. And the east wants more of him, and the west more yet, and the lords want war, and the commons want peace, and the merchants want their profits."

So much of an answer, and it was no answer at all. "And?" he asked.

"And everything, and nothing. I never wanted to be empress. I only wanted Mirain."

"You should have thought of that before you tricked him into marrying you. Found some well-connected lady with a strong aptitude for clerkery and none at all for the arts of the bedchamber, and tricked him into marrying her, and established yourself as his concubine."

She pulled back, her temper flaring. "Concubine! I would have been his lover and his equal."

"And therefore, empress to his emperor." She glared. Sarevan laughed, truly this time, and kissed her. "I for one am glad you married him. It makes life easier, legitimacy. Now stop evading and tell me what's got you prowling the halls when you ought to be bewitching the council."

"You."

His mind spun on, expecting subtleties, shaping counter-subtleties. The silence shocked it into immobility. She never did what one expected, did Elian of Han-Gilen, the Lady Kalirien of the Sunborn's armies.

She knew. She had come to stop him.

No. Whatever was in her eyes, it was not the horror of one who faces treason. She was blind, as they all were. She saw only her poor maimed child.

Sarevan let his mouth fall open. He knew he looked a very proper fool. "Me?" He inspected himself. He was dressed as a southerner, because the multiplicity of garments covered his bones. But he was less thin than he had been. His body, wonderful creation, wasted not one grain of all he fed it. "Don't fret yourself over me. I'm mending, and I'm mending well, and I was just going to sit in council. Shall we go together? Or would you rather do something else that needs doing? I can speak for us both if there's need."

Now it was her part to stare and pause and hunt for words. She did not look like a fool. She looked more beautiful than ever, and more tired, and more—something. Sad. Angry. Pitying. "No, Vayan," she said much too easily. "I can face it alone. If you won't rest, will you look in on our guest from Asanion? I saw him a little while ago, cursing the rain. He seemed in need of company."

Sarevan sat still. There was a darkness in him, a bitterness on his tongue. She had not used that tone with him since he was still small enough to carry. That tone which said, *Yes, yes, child, of course you may help Mother, but not now; Mother will come back when she's done, and then we'll play, yes?* Which said, *Of course you can't handle the council alone, poor innocent. You have no power to handle it with.* Which said, *You are weak and you are a cripple, and you tear my heart, because you strive so bravely to be as you were before. But you cannot. You cannot, and you must not pretend that you can.*

Sarevan was on his feet again. It could still surprise him to find her so small, no higher than his chin, who had towered over his childhood. Now he was a man, and if not the largest of her redheaded Gileni kinsmen, not the smallest, either.

Among mages, he was nothing at all. "Yes," his tongue said, acid-sweet, "I'll go and play with the heir of Asanion. He wants to teach me a new game. It's played in bed, mostly, and it's fascinating. Though I may be a little old to learn it properly. Am I too old, do you think, Mother?"

She slapped him. Not lightly. Not in play. He swayed with the blow, and met her white fury with something whiter and colder. "Don't treat me like a child, Mother. Or like a simpleton. Or like a broken creature who must be handled gently lest he shatter. I'm none of them. I still carry Avaryan's brand, and the fire that comes with it. I'm still High Prince of Keruvarion. And nowhere," he said, soft and deadly, "nowhere at all does the law ordain that the king must also be a mage."

Her rage had chilled and died. "Vayan," she said. "Vayan, I didn't mean—"

"You didn't, did you? You only believed it. That's your deepest trouble. Keruvarion's heir is no longer fit to hold his title. Keruvarion's emperor refuses to speak of it. Keruvarion's chancellor insists that there's no profit in fretting. The Lord of the Northern Realms, most reluctant of mages that he is, has no sympathy to spare for you. And I —I know that if I don't teach myself to live as a simple man, I won't be able to live at all."

"That's what I'm afraid of," she said.

"Such trust. Such faith in your strong young son."

"Don't sneer. It's unbecoming."

His lip curled further. He raised his chin. "I'll go to my lessons, Mother. Then at least, if I can't rule, I'll know how to beget a son who can."

If she tried to stop him, she did not try hard enough. His temper brought him to Hirel's door and flung him through it.

No one was there to applaud or to jeer. He stalked through the rooms in the dim rainlight. A lamp burned in the innermost chamber, shining on two twined bodies, bronze and gold. Hirel had a woman in his arms, and neither wore more than a bauble or two, and it was clear enough what they had been doing. Even as Sarevan froze upon the threshold, Hirel's hand moved, wandering over a ripe swell of breast.

Sarevan backed away. That was not jealousy, that twisting in his vitals. It was outrage. This was a lady. A baroness. The widow of a high baron. How dared she let that infidel seduce her? How dared he do it?

They saw him. She rose with aplomb. Her eyes sparkled; her cheeks were rose-bronze. She curtsied deeply. "My prince," she said. Her face had no great beauty: broad-cheeked, blunt-nosed, wide-mouthed. But her eyes were splendid, and her body . . .

She covered it, not hastily, not slowly, and took her graceful leave.

Sarevan shuddered and remembered to breathe. Hirel had risen to face him. The boy did not have the grace to look ashamed. "Is that your revenge on Keruvarion?" Sarevan asked him. "The corruption of its nobility?"

"You say it, not I."

"So." Sarevan advanced into the chamber. "Corrupt me."

"No."

"Why? Because I want you to?"

"Not at all." Hirel returned to his nest of cushions, stretching out like a cat, yawning as maidens were taught to do, with becoming delicacy. He propped himself on his elbow and looked up under level brows. "I do not corrupt. I teach, and I tame, and I set free."

Sarevan dropped to one knee, bending close. "Free? Can you set me free?" His hand closed lightly about the boy's throat. "Can you, Hirel Uverias?"

"You," said Hirel calmly, "are in a remarkable state. Are you dangerous? Should I be begging for mercy?"

Sarevan looked at the placid face. At the hand below it. At the body below that. He thought of being dangerous. Of falling upon Hirel; of disdaining to grant mercy.

His hand fell. He tasted bile. He was not made for that sort of violence.

He lay on his face among the cushions. It was that, or run howling through Endros. "I won't," he gritted. "I *won't*, be shunted aside, watched over, indulged and protected like an idiot child. They'd leave

me nothing that befits my breeding or my training. Only pity. Because
they are all mages, and I—and I—"

"Stop it," said Hirel. "Or I swear, I will laugh, and you will try to
strike me, and I am in no mood for battles."

Sarevan thought of murder. Even with power he would have gone no
further than that. But his mind did not know it. It reached for what was
not there, and touched something, and that something was pain.

He dragged himself up. He fought his hands that would have
clutched his throbbing head. "Tonight," he said. "Tonight we ride."

"So soon? But I have told Varzun—two days—"

"Tonight." He turned with care. He set one foot before the other.

He struck an obstacle. It was well grown and strong, and subtly
skilled in the use of its strength. It said, "You are being quite unreasonable."

"Be ready," Sarevan repeated. "I'll come for you."

"You are mad," Hirel said. But he let Sarevan pass.

Sarevan nursed his temper. It had to bear him up until he was well
away from Endros. He nursed it well and he fed it with good food and
ample, and he masked it with his best and whitest smile.

He was not smiling when his father found him. He was in his tower,
bare and damp from the bath, turning a length of white silk in his
fingers. It was naked yet, its mate lost in Shon'ai with its four disks of
gold hammered from coins as custom commanded, pierced and sewn by
the hands of the priest who bore it. No time to make them anew. That
would have to wait until this coil was all unraveled.

He heard the door open. He knew the tread, light, almost soundless.
He had been expecting it. It always happened when he quarreled with
his mother. His father gave him time to cool a little, and came, and sat
by him, saying nothing. His mother did it, for the matter of that, when
he crossed wills with his father. It was one of the world's patterns, like
the dance of the moons.

He had to struggle. To turn his eyes deliberately toward the night
within him, to rouse the vision which told him why he must not yield.

A hand set itself beside his own. Palm beside palm. *Kasar* and *Kasar*.
Sarevan's eyes narrowed against the twofold brilliance. "While you
have this," Mirain said, "you are my heir. I made that law when you
were born, and I will not alter it."

"Nothing was said of altering it. Much was implied of regretting it."

"Only by you, Sarevadin."

Sarevan flung up his head, tossing the damp coppery hair out of his face. "Don't try to lie to me. I'm worth nothing as I am, except to those who would shatter Asanion in my name. For revenge. Because I was too bloody arrogant to know when I was outmatched."

"Not so much arrogant as unwise. And you're no wiser now. All your mother wanted was to keep you from killing yourself with too much strain too soon."

"She succeeded, didn't she?"

"Hardly," said Mirain. "You should have done as you threatened to. You'd have been the better for it."

"I am a sworn priest," Sarevan gritted, to keep from howling.

"So am I."

"But you are a king."

"And you are High Prince of Keruvarion."

"I wish," said Sarevan, and that was not what he had meant to say at all, "I wish he were a woman."

The silence stretched. Mirain's charity. Sarevan wound the Journey-band about his hand and clasped his knees, letting his forehead rest briefly upon them. He was not tired, it was nothing so simple. He ached, but that was more pleasant than not, the ache of muscles remembering their old strength. He shivered a little, not wanting to, unable to help himself.

A robe dangled before him. He let his father coax him into the warmth of it. "We never could keep clothes on you," Mirain said. When Sarevan looked, he was close to a smile, though he retreated all too soon. "We can't keep you here. Even if your Journey would allow it, you wouldn't stand for it."

Sarevan could not move. He hardly dared breathe.

Mirain went on calmly, as if he could not reckon Sarevan's tension to its last degree. "The Red Prince has sent a message. He wants to see you. Soon, he says, and for as long as you please. There's work and to spare for you, if you're minded to do any, and you can prove to Han-Gilen what you've tried so hard to prove to Endros: that you're none the worse for wear."

Sarevan started at that, but he bit his tongue before it could betray him.

"You'd do well to go," said Mirain, "for a while. When Greatmoon is full again, Vadin will be riding to Ianon to secure it and the north. I would like you to go with him."

In spite of himself, Sarevan whipped about. "Why? What can I do that Vadin can't?"

"Speak as my chosen successor. Prove that I haven't abandoned my first kingdom for the decadence of the south. Wield the power of your presence."

The words came flooding. *What power? What presence?* Sarevan choked them down. He had been wielding the latter in Endros without care for the cost.

This much he had won. His father would grant him a Greatmoon-month in Han-Gilen with the man he loved best of all his kin. Who had taught him the mastery of his power; who had brought him back from death. Who had no patience at all with self-pity. And after that strong medicine, a trust as great as any he had been given: to speak for his father before the princes of the north.

His eyes narrowed. His jaw set. "So Grandfather's to be my nurse-maid. And when he's tired of me, Vadin will take me in hand."

"Vadin will ride under your command. He proposed it. It's past time you earned your title."

Sarevan almost laughed. "O clever! You'll bribe me with the sweetest plum of all: the promise of a princedom. No doubt I'll be allowed to rule it as I choose—and well out of the way of your war."

Mirain did not even blink. "You can't stay here. Nor can you wander free as you have until now. The lands are too unsettled; and you are much too valuable. Twice our enemies have sought to snare you. The third time may destroy you."

There was no danger now of Sarevan's temper cooling. He let it flame in him, searing his mind clean even of awe for the Sunborn. His voice was soft, almost light, deadly in its gentleness. "Ah," he said. "I see. You and Mother both—you labor to protect me. I'm your only son. For good or for black ill, I'm the only hope you have of a dynasty. You guard me and shield me and shelter me lest any danger touch me. And where your guardianship has failed, you take most dire vengeance."

"How have I sheltered you?" his father asked, quickly, but calm still. "Have I ever denied you anything you wished for? You wanted priest-hood and training in magecraft. I never hindered you. You Journeyed where you chose, even into deadly danger. I never raised my power to hold you back."

"But you watched me. Your power haunted me. All through Keruva-rion your guards were never far from me. They failed in Asanion; but that was not for lack of trying. I've heard how Ebraz of Shon'ai paid for the trap he laid: paid with life and sanity. I know how you searched for me and never found me, though you combed the empires for me. It drove you mad that I had escaped your watchfulnes; that I had only my own will to guide me."

"My hunters' blindness has been dealt with," said Mirain.

Sarevan raised his clenched fists, swept them down. "Damn it, Father! Am I still a child? Am I incapable even of picking myself up when I stumble? How long are you going to live my life for me?"

At long last, Mirain wavered. His face tightened as if with pain. "I let you do as you would, even when you would do what I reckoned madness or folly."

"But you were there, always, to do the letting."

Mirain stretched out his hand. Not beseeching; not quite.

Sarevan pulled back out of his reach. "Even this war—even that has begun for me. Has it never crossed your mind that I might want to win something for myself?"

"You will have it all when I am gone."

"When you are gone!" Sarevan laughed, brief and bitter. "All signed and sealed, from your hand. A gift and a burden and a curse, and none of my doing. Am I so much less than you? Do you think so little of me?"

"I think the world of you."

Sarevan was trembling. His eyes were open, and he was as full awake as he could ever be, and all his sight was lost in the blackest of his dreams. Elian Kalirien dead in the ashes of the world, and the Sunborn gone mad.

"Vayan," his father said. Had perhaps said more than once. "Vayan, forgive me."

Mirain An-Sh'Endor? Asking forgiveness?

"You are all that I am and more," he said, raw with pain. "And I love you to the point of folly. I never meant to cage you. I only wished to keep you safe, so that you may be the emperor you were born to be."

"Emperor of what?" Sarevan cried from the depths of his darkness. "Dust and ashes, and war's desolation?"

"Emperor of all that lies under Avaryan. I was born for war, for the winning of empires. Peace saps all my strength. But you—you can rule where I have won. You have the strength of will that I have not, to hold in peace what war has gained. Don't you see, Vayan? You are not simply my son and my heir. You are the fulfillment of this creature that I am. You as much as I are the instrument of the god."

"The sword cuts," said Sarevan. "It cuts too deep for any healing."

"Save yours."

Sarevan's sight cleared, a little. He saw his father's living face. It was close, a shadow limned in light, with shining eyes. There were tears in them. He had struck harder than he knew, and deeper.

No, he warned himself. No softening. This man who grieved for his son's pain was king and conqueror; and by his own admission, born and shaped for slaughter.

"I will not haunt you," Mirain said. "No longer. When you go into the north, you go free, to rule in my name but according to your will."

"Even if that will is to oppose you?"

Mirain started, stiffening.

"If I hold the north," Sarevan said, "and forbid it to join in your war, what will you do?"

"Would you do that, Sarevadin?"

Yes, Sarevan was going to say. But he could not. To defy his father by himself—that, he could do. To take a kingdom with him, a kingdom that had been his father's . . .

"I could do it," he said.

"Would you?"

He shivered. "No," he said, slow and hard. "No. That would rouse war as surely as anything else I've done since I resisted you and went into Asanion."

Mirain smoothed Sarevan's hair with a steady hand, worrying out a tangle, stroking beneath where he was cold and shaking. Sarevan tensed but did not try to escape.

"Father," he said after a while. "Must you fight this war?"

The hand did not pause in its stroking. "You know that I have no choice. Asanion's emperor will not yield for words or for wishing. Only war can choose between us."

"If you could see what I see—would that stop you?"

"I see that the darkness has deceived you. Another trap of our enemies' laying. They know what you are; that you are more perilous even than I. They have labored long and hard to ensnare you; to destroy you, lest you become what they most fear."

"What am I, that you are not thrice over?"

"You will be lord of the world."

"I don't want—" Sarevan stopped. That, he knew in the cold heart of him, was false. He wanted it with all that he was: a wanting so deep that it seemed almost the negation of itself. But what it was, and what his father wanted it to be—there they differed. "I don't want it stained with blood and fire."

"Perhaps it need not be. But perhaps," said Mirain before hope could wake, "it must. Will you rule the north for me?"

"Will you stop the war for me?"

"No."

That was absolute. Sarevan drew back, steadying himself. His temper had died; he was, almost, at peace. He found that he could smile, though faintly, and not for pleasure. "I love you, Father. Never forget that."

"Will you rule the north?"

Sarevan let himself sink down in weariness that was not feigned. "I need time," he said. "I'm not—I can't— Give me a day. Let me think." For an instant he knew that he had gone too far. But Mirain said, "Think as much as you like. Your princedom can wait. So," he added more softly, "can I."

Slowly Sarevan turned. Mirain's face was not soft at all. Sarevan hardened his own to match it. "A day," he said. "To set my mind in order."

"A day," Mirain granted him. "Or more, if you have need of them."

Sarevan shivered. His eyes dropped; he could not force them up again. "No," he said very low. "A day will be enough. Then," he said, lower still, "then you will know."

Thirteen

WHEN SAREVAN CAME, HIREL WAS READY. SCOWL-
ing but ready, in plain dark riding clothes, with a long knife at
his side and a scrip in his hand. "I have had the ambassador's message,"
he said with no warmth at all. "You are thorough."

"Of course." Sarevan turned. "Follow me."

They walked quietly but not stealthily. There were secret ways; a
palace was not a palace without them, as Mirain often said. But this
palace was full of mages, and they would be on guard, alert for walkers
in the dark. Walkers in the light, however dim, they might not pause to
wonder at.

Sarevan carried his coat slung over his shoulder and, as by chance,
over both their scrips. He did not hasten; he did not linger. Above all
else, he did not think of mutiny. "Think," he warned Hirel when they
began, "of a restless stomach and an hour's brisk walking, and of deep
sleep after."

Hirel had given him an odd look, but had not protested. He did not
speak at all as they went, until they met a lord with his retinue. The
voices came first; at the sound of them, Hirel slipped his arm about
Sarevan's waist and leaned, hand to middle. His face when he lifted it
was pale. "A little better," he said loudly enough to be heard, "but still
not—"

The company was upon them, large, varied, and warm with wine.
Sarevan almost groaned aloud at the sight of the leader: a baron from

the east of Kavros, rich with pearls and with sea gold, older than he liked to be and less powerful than he hoped. He dandled a girl on each arm; he thrust them away, to bow as low as his belly would allow. "Lord prince! How splendid to see you about, and so strong too, after all I had heard, though you look thin, very thin; that is not well, you must look after yourself, we need you sorely in Keruvarion." Sarevan's smile bared set teeth. "Good evening, Baron Faruun."

"Oh, good, yes, very good, my lord, as the lord your father said to me, just a little while ago it was, he said—"

"I think," said Hirel distinctly and rather more shrilly than he had in many days, "that, after all, I shall be ill."

Sarevan caught at him. He looked ghastly. But his eyes were lambent gold. "You can't," Sarevan said as that shimmering stare dared him to. "I won't let you. Think about keeping it down. Think about the honor of princes."

Hirel sighed, and swallowed audibly. "You are a tyrant, Vayan."

"I'm growing you up, little brother. You can't do this every time you drink a cup or three."

Hirel drooped against Sarevan. "I want to go to bed," he said plaintively. Swallowing in the middle. Nuzzling a little, working mischief with his hands where the watchers could just see.

"You'll pardon us, I'm sure," Sarevan said, flashing his teeth at them all and sweeping Hirel away.

Hirel recovered quickly enough once he had no audience to play to, although his color was slow to come back. He did not let go of Sarevan; Sarevan let him stay. Laughter kept rising and refusing to be conquered. "*You* can laugh," Hirel snarled at him.

Contrition sobered him, somewhat. "But you aren't really—"

"I always am."

Hirel's bitterness was real, and deep. Sarevan pulled him forward. "Quick now; be strong. We're almost out."

They met no one else of consequence. A servant or two; a lady's small downy pet trailing its jeweled leash and looking utterly pleased with itself. Then they had passed an unwarded postern and entered the city. The rain had ended; wind tattered the clouds, baring a glimpse of stars, a scatter of moonlight.

The main thoroughfares of Endros were lit with lamps and tended by honored guildsmen, but its side ways were dark enough for any footpad. Sarevan kept to the latter, daring now to run, dragging the other by the hand. Nothing threatened them save a cur that snarled as they passed. The wall came sooner than Sarevan had expected. By the wan gleam of Greatmoon he groped his way along it, searching for a stone that would yield to his touch. If he had come too far, or not far enough—

It turned under his hand and sank. The wall opened into a tunnel a little higher than a man and a very little wider. Sarevan could just walk erect. Hirel followed him without trouble, gripping his belt.

Another stone, another shifting. They stood on the open plain with the wind in their faces. Sarevan drank it in great gulps. Hirel retched into the grass.

He would not let Sarevan carry him. His resistance was quiet but furious, and he gasped through it, choking, until Sarevan shook him to make him stop. "You're wasting time, damn you! Up with you."

"I am not," Hirel gasped. "I am not—I had to convince—I convinced myself. Put me down!"

He walked, though he let Sarevan hold him up. It was not remarkably far. A thousand man-lengths, perhaps more, perhaps less. There was a hill and a copse and a crumbling byre, and in the byre Shatri with Bregalan and the striped Zhil'ari mare and one more: a rawboned, ugly-headed, sand-colored creature with a bright wild eye and a laden saddle.

"No," Sarevan said. "No, Shatri."

The squire did not even lower his eyes. "He told me, my lord. Your father. Whatever you did, to stay with you."

"Are you his man or mine?"

"Yours, of course, my lord. With all my soul. But he is the emperor."

That, said Shatri's tone, was inarguable. Sarevan drew breath to argue with it.

The sand-colored mare snorted and rolled her eyes. The source of their wildness stalked out of shadow, rumbling gently. Of the seneldi, only Bregalan was calm; but Ulan had been there when he was foaled. The great cat circled Shatri, who stood very still, and came to press against Sarevan and purr. "Go back," Sarevan commanded Shatri. "I am a priest on Journey. I may have no squire or servant."

"But, my lord—"

"In Avaryan's name," Sarevan said, relentless, "and in the name of his priesthood. Go."

"My lord!"

Sarevan turned his back on him and mounted.

"My lord," the boy said, pleading.

Bregalan sidled but would not advance. Sarevan would not turn.

Hirel's voice in the dark was cool and calming. "Your lord has need of you here, to conceal his absence, to divert pursuit. He has trusted you with this most difficult of all our tasks; will you prove his trust misplaced?"

There was a silence, until Shatri broke it. "My lord." He gripped Sarevan's knee. "My lord, I—you never—I wasn't thinking."

"Nor was I," Sarevan admitted, with a glance at Hirel. "If you don't think you can do it—"

Shatri's head whipped up. "I can do it! My lord," he added after a pause. He let go, backed away, bowed desert fashion: dropping to one knee, setting palm against palm. Pride had struck fire in his eyes. "Have no fear, my prince. They'll not come after you while I'm here to stop them."

Sarevan saluted him. His smile was luminous. Then at last Bregalan would heed the touch of leg to side. He sprang forward. The dun mare ran swift in his wake.

Even in the dark before dawn, Bregalan knew this country as he knew his own stable. He set a strong pace, but one the other could match with ease, striking westward across the plain. As it rose into wooded hills, he slowed a little, but he ran lightly still, unwearied.

Dawn rose in rain-washed clarity. Sarevan called a halt to rest the beasts and to see that Hirel took a little bread and a sip or two of wine. By sunrise they were in the saddle again. Their shadows stretched long before them.

They went by paths Sarevan knew, swift enough yet hidden from spying eyes. The shifting armies did not close in upon them; if they were hunted, the hunters did not find them in the wilderness through which they rode. Hirel practiced one of his greater virtues: he was silent, neither questioning nor complaining.

They rode through the first day and well into the night, until at last Sarevan's urgency would let him rest. Hirel's mare was stumbling with exhaustion. The boy's face was ghost-pale in the moonlight. He fell from the saddle into Sarevan's arms, so limp and so still that for a moment Sarevan froze in fear. Then Hirel drew a long breath, shuddering with it. With utmost gentleness Sarevan laid him down, spreading all their blankets for him, wrapping him in them. Cursing that damnable pride which would never yield to its body's frailty.

Sarevan left the child to sleep. He ate a little, drank from the stream by which he had camped. The seneldi grazed, placid. Ulan had gone hunting. Sarevan lay back against his saddle and sighed. He did not want to sleep: the dream waited, armed and deadly. He settled more comfortably. Brightmoon gazed down. Greatmoon had set; she had the sky to herself, for a while. His eyes filled with her cool light.

The sun woke him. He lay under it, eyes closed, neither knowing nor overmuch caring where he was. He ached in sundry places, not badly, but enough to rouse curiosity, and with it memory. He started up.

He had not dreamed it. He was doing what he had resolved to do. For all the sun's warmth, he shivered.

"Don't think about it," he commanded himself. "Just do it."

Hirel stared at him, half asleep still, baffled and scowling and all bright gold. Sarevan laughed at the scowl and leaped up. "Come," he said. "Ride with me."

They rode; and still no hunter followed them. Sarevan was not easy, nor did he trust this quiet, but for a little while he accepted it; he let it think that it had mastered him. Slowly he relaxed his vigilance, letting it pass through thrumming tension to constant quiet watchfulness.

Sarevan gained strength. Hirel went brown again, and his mask slipped, and sometimes he smiled. Once or twice he even laughed.

But for the most part he was silent, somber. "This venture of ours may fail," he said, a camp or four after that first hidden haven, when they had taken to riding at night and sleeping through the burning brightness of the day. "My father can be no less intransigent than yours."

"But," Sarevan pointed out, "even mine isn't likely to attack Asanion while I stand hostage in Kundri'j Asan."

"If we come so far. Even if you are caught and returned to your father, you have less to fear than do I. No one in your empire wishes you dead. Whereas I, and mine . . ."

"We'll face that when we face it," said Sarevan. He lay on his back and laced his fingers behind his head. He was stripped in the heat, his breeches new-washed and spread where the sun could dry them. It was warm on his skin, the air still, pungent with the scent of spicefern. He yawned. His back itched; he wriggled.

Hirel was watching him. Without stopping to think, he rolled onto his stomach, resting his chin on folded arms. It pricked. He was growing his beard again; it was little enough yet to marvel at, and it would grow less lovely still before it remembered what it had been. He rubbed it where it itched, and tried not to feel the eyes on him. In a moment or an age, they granted him mercy. When he looked again, Hirel was asleep, curled on his side, childlike.

And yet he was a child no longer. The swift onset of first manhood was full upon him, working its magic from sunrise to sunrise, almost from hour to hour. He had grown a hand's width measured against Sarevan's shoulder, since he woke wounded and haughty on the marches of Karmanlios; his voice cracked seldom now, and then more often downward than upward. It was going to be deep, that voice, as already he was tall for one of his kind. His shoulders were broadening, beginning to strain his coat, and there was no softness left in him except, a little, in his face: a rounding still of cheek and chin, a fullness of the lips that recalled the girl he might have been. And he was waxing into a man where manhood most mattered.

He was still very young, and delicate in odd ways: in what he could eat, in how much he slept. "Inbred," Sarevan said as they camped in the west of Inderan. "The blood is good, but it's thin. No sister-wife for you, my lad, if you want a son who'll live to be a man."

"What!" said Hirel, and perhaps his indignation was real, and perhaps it was not. "Would you have me beget a litter of mongrels?"

"Mongrel blood is strong." Sarevan grinned. "Look at me, now. Bred of every race that walks the earth; and two nines of days ago I was a rotting corpse, and here I am. Riding all night on a diet of air and wildbuck, up half the day drinking sunlight, and sleek as a seal."

Sarevan had meant to jest. But he looked down at himself and started slightly. Why, he thought, it was true. He was as strong as he had ever been. He felt of his face, suppressing the urge to bring out his scrap of mirror. The angles, were familiar angles, the hollows the old hollows, the skull returned at last to its proper place beneath the skin.

Air and wildbuck indeed, and the sun's fire, and dreams that drove him hard but were no longer a torment; and no pursuit. None at all.

Once Hirel ventured into a town, armed with his brown face and his vagabond's garb and a fistful of Sarevan's silver. He returned with both their scrips full, and even a coin left in his purse. "And news," he said, settling on his heels beside Sarevan, watching as the other fell on the sweetmeats which were his great prize. He nibbled a honeyed nut; he took his time about it, until he had Sarevan still and staring, mouth full of spice and sweetness. "No, Sun-prince, nothing of our riding, and no sign of a hunt. Rumor has it that the Prince Sarevadin is sojourning with his grandsire in Han-Gilen, preparing for a new task: the taking of Ianon's regency. For practice, it is said. To prepare him for a greater throne."

Sarevan's breath caught. Suddenly he had no taste for spicecake. He choked down the last of it. His fingers, unheeded, raked through his new beard. No hunt at all? He could not believe that. And yet he had seen it. And that the common talk should be full of what had been between himself and his father, as if he had never committed this treason, as if he had gone docilely where he was meant to go—there was no sense in it. And yet there was. Frightening sense. If someone knew or guessed what he did, and favored it, or was not minded to stop it . . . if someone was willing to cover his trail, even to lie outright for him . . .

Shatri had promised to do just that, but he had not this measure of power. Vadin? The Lord of the North belonged to his emperor. Even for his namesake, whom he loved as a son, he would not turn against Mirain. Elian—maybe. She was capable of it. But in this he could catch no scent of her. The Prince of Han-Gilen . . .

Sarevan pulled at his beard, scowling. This was his treason, and his alone. He would not share it with some faceless power, some web of purpose and counterpurpose that dared to weave itself into his own. That would not even grant him the courtesy of naming its name or asking his leave.

"You are very well thought of," Hirel said, oblivious to his fretting. "Every idler remembers you, or claims to. Did you know that you spent three seasons in the dungeons of the evil emperor himself? You escaped in fire and magic, took his heir for a hostage, and died in battle with his mages; your body returned to Endros in no less than nine pieces, borne upon the backs of demons. Your father bound the fragments together with his power, and called your soul from Avaryan's side, and made you live again. And when he had done that, he swore a mighty oath: that the Emperor of Asanion would suffer each and every torment to which he had subjected you."

Sarevan would have liked to leap up, to bolt into the woods. To run away from it all; or to run full into it, crying anathema upon all liars and their lies.

He sat still, eyes on Bregalan who grazed unruffled by men and their wars.

"No one hunts us," Hirel said. "No one speaks of it. It is all war and weapontakes and who will remain to bring in the harvest if the war lasts so long."

The fire was rising. Sarevan let it. Words came, slow at first, pale shadows of the rage within. "I don't like this," he said. "I don't like it at all."

"It serves us," said Hirel.

"It reeks to heaven." Sarevan sprang to his feet. "Ulan! Bregalan! Quick now, up!"

* * *

Bregalan was swifter than any stallion had a right to be unless he were of the Mad One's line, and the mare was of Zhil'ari breeding. They thrived on long running and short commons. Like Sarevan himself; but Hirel was not so sturdy. He needed sleep and he needed feeding. Sarevan willed himself to be patient, to stop now and then, to lie quietly while the sun wheeled overhead and his companion slept the sleep of the dead. He himself slept hardly at all. All that had befallen him since he battled mages in Asanion—all he had heard and seen and dreamed— all of it was coming together. Not wholly, not yet. But he saw the first blurred glimmer of a pattern. He had stopped raging at it. He had sworn, and he would fulfill his oath: he would learn the name behind the plotting. Then he would exact its price.

The farther they rode, the quieter the land seemed. But that was only a seeming. Every town had its company of armed guards. Every castle rang with the clamor of men in training and of weapons in the forging. Travelers were few, and those rode armed and watchful. Not all the mem who had gathered meant to fight for their emperor; of those who did, some few had a mind to end old feuds before they rode to war, or else to pick up the odd bit of booty while they waited. Armies took considerable maintenance; if a captain could keep his troops honed with a quick raid and fed with the proceeds, so much the better.

None of them came near to Sarevan. Perhaps he owed it to Ulan's watchfulness and his own caution. He would not have sworn to it.

He rode because he must, drawing the others with him. He did not pause to fear that he rode into a trap: his plots betrayed, the borders held against him. With the fear that rode him now, he would have welcomed so simple a snare.

At last they came to the marches of Karmanlios, and to Asan-Vian gasping in the heat of that cycle of Brightmoon called the Anvil of the Sun. Hirel's mare was close to foundering; even Bregalan showed ribs beneath a sun-scorched coat. Hirel's head was down, his body stiff, bracing at every jolt. There were blue shadows under his eyes.

Vian was the castle which ruled among others the town of Magrin. Its lord had died wifeless and childless; his fief had passed by his will into the care of the Sun's priests. Whose senior priestess in the barony was Orozia of Magrin.

She was waiting for the riders. So too were nine Zhil'ari and a dozen Asanians and a handful of closemouthed servants. Their greetings were various: Zhil'ari exuberance, Asanian reserve, and Orozia's long level gaze that warmed into welcome. "Well come at last, my lord," she said, "and in good time."

Sarevan looked hard at her. She smiled. He saw no deception in her, nor scented any. After a moment, he bowed low. "Reverend sister. All is well?"

"All is most well."

He had not known how tautly he was strung until the tension left him. He staggered. She was there, and nine Zhil'ari with her, desperately anxious. He fended them off. "Here now, don't hover. Look to the lion's cub."

His hellions were obedient. Orozia did not choose to follow them. "I have prepared everything as you would wish it."

He considered her. Her loyalty; her strength. A smile found its way through his new-raised walls. He brushed her cheek with a finger, half in mischief, half in deep affection. "You don't approve, do you?"

"Of course I do not. I am only half a fool. But that half has proven the stronger. It dares to hope that this madness of yours will bear fruit." She shook herself. "Enough now. Time is short and the borders too well watched on both sides. You will rest the night and the day. At full dark tomorrow, you must ride."

No sooner, though Sarevan burned to be gone. Hirel could not ride again that night; they could not dare the armies under the sun.

The company, at least, was excellent, and the food was passable; the wine was cool and sweet. Sarevan finished off a jar with Orozia's aid, sitting late and unattended in the room which had belonged to the old lord.

"You look well," she said when speech had waned into wine-scented silence. "As well as you ever have; as if you were taking your sustenance from the sun itself."

"That," said Sarevan, "I can't do. Not any longer."

"No?"

The wine rose strong in him. It loosened his tongue, but it lightened the words that rolled out, leaching them of pain. "I'm a mage no longer. I've got used to it; I don't waste time in bemoaning my fate. It's even pleasant, when I stop to think. No thoughts clamoring through my shields. No fire begging to be set free."

"No?"

He peered into his cup, found it empty, filled it to the brim. When he had drunk a great gulp, he laughed. "You look exceedingly oracular, O friend of my youth. Of course, no. That part of me is dead. Gone. Burned away. I'm a man among men, no more, if never less."

"No," she said yet again, flatly. "You will never be a mere man. You are the son of the son of the Sun."

"Ah well, that's something I'll have to live down, won't I?"

She slapped him, not hard, but hard enough to sting. He gaped at her. She blazed back with rare and potent anger. "Did we labor so long in Endros and in Han-Gilen to create a fool? Is it true what the philosophers say, that great men by nature can only engender idiots? Are you *blind*, Sarevan Is'kelion? Look at yourself! No mortal man could suffer as you have suffered, ride as you have ridden, and sit as you sit now, no more weary than any man who sits late over wine."

"My father healed me. That's the miracle you see."

"It is not," she said stubbornly. "I watched you from the walls. You had the sun in your face, and it was pouring into you, filling you as wine fills yonder cup."

He drained it. "So then. The god hasn't abandoned me. Maybe he approves what I do, in spite of my father's convictions to the contrary. That doesn't make me a mage."

"What does it make you?"

"God-ridden." Sarevan yawned and stretched. "There's nothing new in that. And for once I'm glad of it. It's high treason I'm committing, Orozia. You can still escape the stain of it, if you move quickly."

She moved. To touch his hand, to meet his eyes. He shivered a little. There were not many who knew her secret: that she was a mage. There was no other power quite like hers, strong, skilled in its strength, yet strangely circumscribed. Of the lesser magics she had few; she could walk in a mind only if her hand lay upon the body of its bearer. But none could walk in hers save by her will.

None at all could walk in Sarevan's. She sighed faintly. Her eyes lowered, although her hand remained. He turned his own, clasping it. "I'll fight," he said, "but I won't blame you."

"You have no need. I too would see this war averted. Though not at the cost of your life."

"Maybe it won't come to that."

She said nothing. There was too much to say; she let it all pass unsaid. In a little while, Sarevan went to his bed. He suspected that she did not follow suit; that she sat there nightlong in the fading scent of wine, staring into a darkness which her power could not pierce.

Sarevan had not known how much he feared for Hirel, until he saw how greatly the princeling profited from a full night's sleep and a full day's idleness. He was even glad when Hirel slid eyes at him—in Orozia's presence, yet—and smiled the most wicked of all his smiles. That was proof positive: there was nothing wrong with the boy but a lifetime of pampering. He would not die of a few days' hard riding.

But those days had been only the beginning. "You can stay here," Sarevan said. "You'll be safe; you can give me a token for your father, to prove that you're alive and well."

Hirel would not dignify that with a response. When night fell, he was ready to ride, clad as a young lord of eastern Asanion who chose to affect the Olenyai fashion: the black robes, the headcloth, the two swords; but never the mask that was permitted only to the true bred-warrior. In his scrip he carried the token of carven ivory that would pass all gates in the Golden Empire and open the posthouses with their beds and board and remounts.

The twelve true Olenyai surrounded him, shadows in the dusk, masked and silent. They did not glance at Sarevan. His part was less simple than theirs, and more perilous. He was to be the young lord's slave, he and Zha'dan who was near enough to his own size to make no matter.

Hirel had taken wicked pleasure in pointing out what neither of them had wanted to remember: that slaves in Asanion kept neither their beards nor their hair. Zha'dan howled in anguish. Sarevan set his chin and his will, and took a firm grip on his braid. "This belongs to the god. I will not give it up."

The boy inspected his hands with studied casualness. He had sacrificed his barbarian claws again to look a proper warrior, as on a time he had tried to look a proper commoner.

"That is different!" Sarevan snapped at him. "Look here, cubling—"

"My lords." Orozia came between them, grave, but clearly trying not to smile. "I can satisfy you all, I think, although my lord of Keruvarion must yet pay a price."

And so he had; but it was one he could pay without undue reluctance. The dye, she assured him, would wash out easily enough with cleanroot and ashes. Zha'dan had assented grudgingly to the shortening of his beard, that the two of them might match; in the same cause, Sarevan lost a handspan of his mane. They put on slaves' tunics and bound their necks with collars of iron—Sarevan's the heavier by far, and Sun-gold beneath its grey sheathing—and stood together before the castle's silver mirror. Sarevan gaped like an idiot. Zha'dan laughed aloud. They looked like more than kinsmen. They looked like brothers of the same birth.

Sarevan rubbed his arm, where no copper glinted to betray him; ran a hand over his many oiled braids, that were as safely dark as Zha'dan's own. "I've never looked like anyone else before."

"You're beautiful," said his image in Zha'dan's voice.

"You are vain," Sarevan said. Zha'dan laughed again, incorrigible. Hirel's expression, when they came out together, had been thoroughly gratifying. He looked from one to the other. Stopped. Looked again. Blinked once, slowly, and drew a long breath. "Very . . . convincing," he said at last, in the face of matched and blinding grins.

Sarevan was still fingering his drying beard, wondering that it did not feel stranger. His other hand gripped a sturdy chain, with Ulan collared and deceptively docile at the end of it. There had been, both Orozia and Hirel had assured him, no other way to bring an ul-cat safely into Kundri'j Asan; and Sarevan would not leave him, even to Orozia's care. They had not been apart since they became brothers. They did not intend to begin now.

Ulan was well content; but Sarevan had not reckoned on Bregalan. Hirel left his wicked little mare behind out of care for her life. The blue-eyed stallion would not be so forsaken. Four years of seeing his two-legged brother only when Sarevan paused for a day or two in his Journeying, or when the court's yearly progress from Endros to Ianon crossed the young priest's path, quite obviously had exhausted his patience.

He was in the courtyard as they readied to ride, trailing his broken bonds. He would not attack a mare who had done him no injury, but he saw to it that Sarevan could not approach the rawboned bay whom he had chosen.

Sarevan seized the stallion's horns. "Brother idiot, you are interfering with my insanity. Move aside." Bregalan laid back his ears and set his feet firmly on the paving. "You fool, you can't come with us. We'll be riding posthaste, with remounts at every stop. Even you can't keep the pace we'll set."

The wild eyes rolled. *Try me,* they said.

"And," said Sarevan, "moreover, O my brother, a slave is forbidden by Asanian law to bestride any stallion, still less a stallion of the Mad One's line. Would you betray me to my death?"

Bregalan snorted and stamped. He had no care for mere human laws. He would go with his brother.

Hirel was watching. Sarevan caught his eye, paused. His own eyes narrowed. "If you go," he said slowly, "you cannot carry me. You must carry the lion's cub."

Bregalan lowered his nose into Sarevan's hand and blew gently.

Sarevan thrust him away in something very like anger, and called for his saddle. Bregalan was all quiet dignity, with no hint of gloating. Sarevan summoned a bridle. The stallion, who had never in his life submitted to a bit, opened his mouth for it and stood chewing gently on it, placid as a lady's mare.

Hirel approached him. He whickered a greeting. The boy was all prince tonight, but standing beside Bregalan, stroking the arched neck, he loosed a little of the delight that was singing in him. Lightly he sprang onto the stallion's back.

Sarevan glared at them both. "Mind," he said to Hirel, sharp and short. "The bit is for show. No more. You keep your hands off it. Tighten the reins one degree, raise one fleck of foam, and if he doesn't throw you off his back, I will."

Hirel's nostrils thinned. He did not speak. His hands were eloquent enough. He knotted the reins on Bregalan's neck, folded his arms, and looked haughtily down his nose.

Sarevan laughed suddenly, at both of them, but mostly at himself. He left them to one another and went to claim his nameless mare.

Eight Zhil'ari watched them go, tall as standing stones about the still form of Orozia. Sarevan looked back once, with uplifted hand. Gold flashed in the torchlight. He veiled it again and turned his face toward Asanion.

Keruvarion's wardens never saw them. By careful coincidence, as Hirel's company neared the border, a pack of young savages fell whooping and laughing upon the border wardens' very camp. One patrol, coming in, stumbled into the very midst of the melee. The other, going out, met it head-on. Asanion's prince and twelve Olenyai and two northern slaves, with an ul-cat loping among them, passed all unseen.

Asanion's guardians might have been more fortunate. There were, after all, only eight Zhil'ari, and they were thoroughly occupied in convincing the Varyani forces that they were a full tribe. But there were a round dozen Olenyai, and Halid their captain, though no greybeard, was old in cunning. While Ulan struck terror among the cavalry lines, the captain laid a false and twisting trail. By sunrise he was riding briefly eastward, to encounter a company in disarray, with lathered and wild-eyed mounts.

"Raiders," their commander said, too weary even for anger. "We lost them, but they were headed west. Keep watch for them, and have a care. There's a lion loose in the woods."

Halid spoke all the proper words, while Hirel waited near him, haughtily indifferent. Zha'dan was shaking with silent laughter. The Olenyai, masked and faceless, were unreadable; but their eyes glinted. Within the hour they rode west again openly: a young lord with his following in a country full of his like. In a little while Ulan returned to them, to suffer again the collar and the chain which his disguise demanded, loping docilely at Bregalan's heel.

Fourteen

NOW I'M SURE OF IT." ZHA'DAN SAID IN THE ANONYMity of a posthouse thronged to bursting. "The god is with us. Else we'd never have come so far so easily."

He spoke in Sarevan's ear, in Zhil'ari, without greater concealment. Sarevan frowned at him. "The god, or someone mortal, weaving webs to trap us in." He glanced about. People were staring in Asanian fashion, sidelong. Halid was settling matters with the master of the house. Hirel had a table to wait at and his Olenyai to wall it and his great hunting cat to guard his person, and his exotic slaves to serve him wine and attract attention. The proper sort of attention, Sarevan could hope. No one would be expecting the lost high prince to appear so, neither in his own person nor in secret.

"I like this," said Zha'dan, unquenched by Sarevan's severity. "I'm not the runt of the litter here. Look: no one's taller than I. I'm a giant."

"You are also a slave," Sarevan reminded him.

He shrugged, but he had the sense not to grin. "Stars! People are ugly here. Yellow as an old wolf's fangs. And fat, like swine fed on oil. And they stink. How can they stand one another."

Hirel spoke from between them, through motionless lips, in tradespeech. "If you are not silent, I will have you whipped."

Zha'dan started, teeth clicking together. Sarevan bent down to refill the barely emptied cup. "You wouldn't dare," he said in the same tongue, in the same fashion.

Hirel's eyes flashed at him, unreadable. His own flashed back in purest insolence.

Even in a posthouse thronged to bursting, a young lord was granted his due: a chamber for his following and a chamber for himself. The inner room had amenities. A flagon of wine; a bowl of sweets. An enormous mound of cushions which in Asanion betokened a bed, and artfully arranged among them, the specialty of the house. She was clad from head to painted toe, but her draperies were little heavier than gossamer. Her hair was butter yellow and carefully curled and, Sarevan judged, owed little more to nature's hand than his own black braids. Her body was riper than he liked but comely enough to make him wish, however fleetingly, that he were free to savor it.

Zha'dan was both repelled and fascinated. He would have hung over her, all wide-eyed wonderment, if Sarevan had not kept a firm grip on him. He almost groaned when Hirel spoke her fair and accepted a moment's intimate fondling and sent her away. Her regret had an air of ritual; her eyes on the seeming slaves were wry and much to wise.

"Did you see?" Zha'dan marveled as she betook her wares to another and more amenable patron. "No fleece at all, anywhere. Not even on her—"

Sarevan stopped listening. Hirel had cast himself among the cushions, and he was trembling, and trying visibly not to. Sarevan knelt by him. His fist clenched convulsively; he pressed them to his eyes.

Sarevan caught them. They did not resist him. Neither did they unclench. He held them to him, first to his breast, then to his cheeks. They were cold, quivering in spasms. "Cubling," he said softly, as he would to a small child or to a frightened animal. "Hirel. Little brother. You will be strong; you will conquer. You will live to be high prince again."

Hirel stilled, but it was not calmness. His fists opened, and then his eyes. "Soft," he said, wondering, like a child. His fingers moved, stroking. "It is soft."

"I'm young yet," said Sarevan, trying to be light. He had not been wise, again. He let go Hirel's hands. They did not fall. Hirel's eyes were all gold.

Very carefully Sarevan eased himself free. This child was more beautiful than the innkeeper's whore could ever be, and infinitely more perilous; and he knew it. He said, "While you are with me, I do not find it easy to endure a lesser lover."

"Then I should leave you," said Sarevan, "lest I condemn you to chastity."

Hirel pondered that, gravely intent, and all the more deadly for it. "Or lest I condemn you to worse. How ingenious, that treachery would be. I need but seduce you as I very well can, and see that your chief priests know of it, and let them put you to death."

"It's not death now," Sarevan said, low, edged with roughness. "I'd only lose my torque and my braid, and suffer a flogging, and be bathed in salt and cast out of the temple in front of all my torque-kin."

"Naked, one can presume?"

"Naked," Sarevan answered. "Body and soul."

"But alive."

"That's not life," Sarevan said.

"And yet you will commit treason, knowing what you do, knowing that you may die for it."

"Some things are worth dying for."

"And I am not?"

Sarevan's lips set. Hirel did not know how to be contrite, but his eyes lowered.

"Child," said Sarevan, vicious in his gentleness, "be wise. Cure yourself of me."

"What If I do not wish to?"

"Then you're a worse fool than I took you for."

"Both of us," said Hirel, rising, seeking the wine.

Hirel was wise. He took Zha'dan to bed with him. Sarevan, curled in a corner with Ulan for blanket and bedfellow, refused to hear what they did; even if it were nothing. He told himself that he was no lover of boys, which was true. He told himself that he cherished his vows to the god, which was truer yet. He told himself most sternly that he had nothing to fret over, and that was not true at all.

Damn the boy for laying open what Sarevan had schooled himself to forget. Damn himself for falling prey to it. It was hard won, this holiness of his. His body knew what it was for; it had no more sympathy than Hirel had with this most painful price of his priesthood. At the very thought of a woman, it could stand up and sing.

At the thought of Hirel, it barely quivered. But his soul, that had never before come even close to falling—his soul was in dire danger.

This was not friendship, this that he had with his brother prince. Often it was very nearly the opposite. And yet, when he thought of leaving, of never seeing that maddening child again, or worse, of meeting him on the battlefield, he could not endure it.

When he was very young, there was one thing in his world that he had never understood, nor known how to understand. Other children had mothers, fathers, uncles: that was right and proper. But no one had a mother or a father or an uncle who were like his own. To power's eyes they were hardly separate at all, though in the body they were most distinct. When Mirain worked great magics, he never worked them without his empress or his Ianyn oathbrother.

"He can't," the Lord Vadin said once, when Sarevan dared to ask. Mirain had been too kingly proud to approach with such a question, and Elian was not the sort of person one asked difficult things of, unless one needed them desperately enough to be snapped at before one was given them. Vadin always managed to have time for a small prince with a great store of questions; and although he was most splendid to look at, taller than anyone else in Sarevan's world, glittering in his northern finery, and his beard gone august silver already though he was not even thirty, he was never either stern or lordly when he was with children.

He sat on the sweet blue grass of Anshan-i-Ormal, on a hill that looked out over the Sunborn's camp, and smiled at Sarevan. After a moment Sarevan decided rather to be content than to be proud; he settled himself in his uncle's lap and played with one of the many necklaces that glittered on Vadin's breast. "Your father can't work high magic without us," Vadin repeated. He had another virtue: he did not mistake Sarevan for the four summers' child he seemed to be. He talked to him as if they were equals. "We're our own selves, have no fear of that; but in power we're one creature. Horrible, some would call it; unnatural. I call it merely unheard of."

"None of you tried to do it," Sarevan said.

Vadin laughed. "We most certainly did not! If you'd told me when I first met Mirain what the two of us would turn into, I think I would have killed him and done my best to kill myself. Or run very far away and never come back."

"Why?"

"I wasn't born a mage," said Vadin. He was not looking at Sarevan now; his eyes were lifted, staring straight into the sun. Sarevan had learned that no one could do that except Vadin and Elian and Mirain, and himself. It was because they were part of the Sun's blood. He was very proud of it, but a little afraid. It turned his uncle's dark eyes to fire, and filled him as water fills a cup. He spoke through it in his soft deep voice, the way he did when he was remembering something long past but not forgotten. "I was a simple creature. I was a hill lord's heir; I knew what my lot would be. I'd do my growing up in my father's house with my brothers and my sisters. Then I'd be a man, and I'd be sent to serve the king for a year or two, to uphold the honor of my house. Then I'd come back home and learn how to be lord in Geitan, and when my father died I'd take his place, and take wives and sire sons and rule my lands exactly as all my fathers had before me. But then," he said, "but then I stood guard at a gate of Ianon Castle, and it was a fine morning of early spring, and the old king was on the battlements above me; and a stranger came to shake me out of all my placid certainties. His name was Mirain; he proclaimed himself the son of the heir of Ianon who had died far away in the south, and the king named him heir in her place, and made me his personal servant. I hated him, namesake. I hated him so perfectly that I couldn't see any revenge more apt than to force him to accept my service."

"You don't hate him now."

Vadin smiled at the sun. "Sometimes I wonder," he said. "We're beyond hate, he and I. I think we're beyond even love. Your mother knows it. She didn't want this, either. She wanted your father, that's true enough; but I wasn't supposed to be part of it. I died for him, you see. An assasin had a spear, and I stopped it, and thereby stopped myself. But he wouldn't let me go. He had his own revenge to take, and we had a wager on whether we'd ever be friends. He said I would. I said never. I'd lose, of course, in the end. He brought me back to life; and he left some of his power in me, and a part of himself. Then in his turn he almost died, waging duel arcane with a servant of the darkness, and Elian and I between us brought him back, and now we were three in one."

"I was part of that," Sarevan said. "I wasn't born yet."

"You were barely there, infant," said Vadin. "Now when we raised the Tower on Endros, that's different. By then you were big enough to kick, and you put something of yourself into the working. That's when we knew you'd be a mage."

"I've always been a mage."

"From before the beginning of time," Vadin agreed gravely, but with a touch of wickedness. "And now you see, power isn't always contained in one mage at a time. Sometimes it's two together, or three. Souls are the same, I think. Some of them aren't made to be alone. They may think so. They may live for years in blessed solitude. Then suddenly, the other half or the other third comes, and the poor soul fights with all it's got to stay alone, but it's a losing fight. Souls and power, they know what they are. It's minds and bodies that struggle to be what they think they are."

*   *   *

Sarevan's mind and body, grown and set on betraying all three faces of that one great shining power, had no power of their own to fight against. But soul they had, and the soul had found its match. The other did not know what it was; he called it desire, and yearned for what he could not have.

"Avaryan," Sarevan whispered. "O Avaryan. Is this how you amuse yourself? Of all the souls in the world, this is the one you've made for me. And you set it in that of all the bodies there are. We can't be man and woman together. We can't share the world's rule. We can't even be brothers, still less lovers while I wear your torque. What do you want us to do? Suffer in silence? Tear one another apart? Kill one another?"

The god's answer was silence. Sarevan buried his face in Ulan's warm musky fur. The cat purred, soft, barely to be heard. Slowly Sarevan slid into sleep.

Zha'dan would never dream of gloating, but he was conspicuously content. "It's true what they say," he said toward the next sunset, "of Asanian arts."

"I'm sure," said Sarevan, meaning to be cool. His tongue was not so minded. "It's me he wants, you know."

Zha'dan did not flinch from the stroke. "Of course he does, my lord. But even he knows better than to stretch so high."

"He's no lower than I."

Zha'dan was polite. He did not voice the objections that glittered in his eyes.

This inn was no less crowded than the last, but its master was more difficult. He took exception, it seemed, to Ulan, or perhaps to the young lord's slaves. Hirel had expressed his will already. The cat was to be neither caged in the courtyard nor penned in the stable. The slaves did not leave his presence.

Halid was making slow headway. Hirel had settled for the siege, drawing prince and savage to the heaped carpets at his feet, which he rested on Ulan's quiescent back. Zha'dan was entirely content to lean against Hirel and be stroked and fed bits of meat from the Asanian's plate. Sarevan was not content at all, but resistance here would have been too conspicuous. He yielded because he must.

Hirel smiled at his rebellious glare and fed him a beancake dipped in something dark, pungent, and hot as fire. Sarevan gasped, sputtered, nearly leaped up in his outrage. His tormentor caught him, bending close as if to kiss. "Do you see those men in yonder corner?"

Sarevan stilled abruptly. His eyes were hot still, hotter even than his throat, but his mind had remembered princely training. He knew better than to turn and stare; but the edge of his eye marked them. Two Asanians sitting together, eating and drinking as did everyone else in the common room, doing nothing that might rouse suspicion. Their hair was cut strangely, shaven from brow to crown, worn long and loose behind.

"Those," said Hirel, "are priests of Uvarra. They were in the inn last night. They watched us then as they watch us now."

"We're interesting," Sarevan said, "and we're on the straight road to Kundri'j. Why shouldn't they be on it with us?"

Hirel fed him wine in dainty sips, a lordling amusing himself with his favorite slave. "Priests of Uvarra do not wear that tonsure unless they serve in the high temple in Kundri'j Asan. Nor do they wander as your kind do, save for very great need."

"They're too conspicuous to be spies."

"Perhaps, like us, they know the virtue of hiding in plain sight."

"But why—"

"They are mages."

Sarevan's teeth clicked together. Oh, indeed that was stretching coincidence. But how could the boy know? He had no power.

Sarevan darted a glance. One's robe was light, and perhaps it was grey. The other's was dark: violet, perhaps. Guild colors. A lightmage and a dark.

"They're sorcerers," murmured Zha'dan, resting his head on Hirel's knee. Sarevan's eyes flashed to him. He would know. The wisewoman of the Zhil'ari was his grandmother. He was her pupil and her heir, and quite as mageborn as Sarevan himself, though never so free with it. Mages of the wild tribes did not wield full power until they were judged worthy of it.

A custom which Sarevan might have been wise to follow. He met Zha'dan's clear stare with the width of Hirel's knees between. "You've set wards?" he asked in Zhil'ari, just above a whisper.

Zha'dan's eyes glinted. "I hardly need to. You're guarded. The veiled ones are invisible to power—I'd pay high to know how they do that."

"They pay high for a spell; it's laid on each of them at initiation. In an amulet." Sarevan was in no mood for teaching, even in a good cause. "And the cubling?"

"Safe," said Zha'dan. "With little enough help from me. He doesn't chatter inside. He knows how to throw up walls."

"He's no mage."

"He's not. But he has shields."

Sarevan scowled blackly at nothing. Hirel had never had shields when Sarevan had power. His mind had been as open and aimless as any other man's, with walls where scars were, closing off memory that pricked him to pain; but nothing a mage could not pass if he chose.

If it puzzled Zha'dan, he did not let it vex his peace. He stroked his cheek against Hirel's thigh, catlike, smiling at Hirel's frown. In tradespeech he said, "We talk about how beautiful you are."

Hirel flushed, but he had perforce to swallow his temper. Halid had won his battle with the innkeeper. The innkeeper himself had been prevailed upon to serve to young lord's pleasure. He occupied them all with his fluttering, until at last they drove him out. By then, Hirel had forgotten Zha'dan's insolence; or simply let it pass.

They were being followed.

It was not always obvious. The roads were crowded with troops, with travelers, with traders. But Sarevan remembered faces, and even where that failed in the likeness of one plump yellow face to another, Uvarra's tonsure and the Mageguild's colors, once noticed, were hard to mistake. He did not see them every day; nor every night in inn or posthouse. Still, he saw them often enough, and perhaps they had allies: men less conspicuous yet oddly tenacious; the same faces, or faces very like them, appearing again and again.

"They're not strong in power," Zha'dan said of the mages.

"Who needs strength?" Sarevan demanded. "They only need to know where eyes have seen two black slaves together."

Zha'dan regarded his hands on the reins of his gelding. "Better black than bilious," he said.

Sarevan bit back laughter. "Oh, surely! But there's no one like us between here and the Lakes of the Moon. We're noticeable."

The Zhil'ari looked about at the Olenyai ringing them, the prince on the blue-eyed stallion in front of him, the traffic of the Golden Empire making way for their passing. "Illusion?" he suggested.

"Too late for that. They'd track us by the scent of your power." A knot of wagons blocked their path; Sarevan muscled his ironmouthed nag to a halt beside Bregalan. The stallion adamantly refused to collapse, or to go lame, or even to look tired. Maybe he had learned to drink the sun. The Mad One could; why not his daughter's son?

Sarevan straightened in the saddle and set his teeth. His head had been aching in spasms for a day or three. Not often; not in any pattern.

He could have blamed it on the sun, but today there was none: the clouds were heavy, threatening rain.

This was no dull throbbing ache. This was pain as keen as a dagger's blade, stabbing deep behind his eyes. It wrung a gasp from him.

"Hirel," someone said, light and bantering, "Hirel, think about last night, and Zha'dan, and the woman with the passion for two lovers at once."

The someone was himself. He was going mad.

Hirel had flushed scarlet, which made Zha'dan grin, but his eyes on Sarevan were steady. Thinking hard.

With crawling slowness the pain faded. Sarevan almost fainted with the relief of it. And with the knowledge.

Now he must suffer not only when he tried to get out of his mind, but when someone else tried to get in.

They had said it, the old masters. For him who slew with power, there was no end to expiation. Even if he had not intended to do it. Even if he had done it in the best of causes. Even . . .

"Stronger shields," Zha'dan was saying in his own tongue. "Dreamwards. I'll post them hereafter. I'll snare our hunters with false dreams."

"Even in our young master?"

Zha'dan laughed. "Even in the little stallion; though he's doing well enough by himself. Maybe when he dies he'll come back one of us."

The lion's cub would have been appalled at the prospect. Sarevan sipped wine from the flask at his saddlebow, washing away the sour aftertaste of pain. They had skirted the wagons. At the head of the line, Halid signaled a quickening of pace.

"Tell me about your brother," Sarevan said.

Asanian modesty had its uses. A young lord could purchase a room in a bathhouse, with a bolt on the door and his own slaves to wait on him. There he could lie on a bench above steaming stones with his head in Zha'dan's lap and Sarevan sitting at a judicious distance. Hirel eyed him with a flicker of amusement. Without his tunic he was an odd harlequin creature, copper-pelted on breast and belly and between his thighs, but all the rest of him safely dark.

The boy sat up suddenly, leaning toward him, and peered. "You will be needing the dye again soon."

"We only touched it up two days ago."

"Your body is not pleased. The black wishes to turn to rust. And thence, I presume, to honest copper."

"Too honest for my peace of mind. The dye is almost gone." Sarevan rubbed his chin. It itched incessantly and with waxing ferocity. He struggled to keep from clawing it. "Maybe I should shave my face and blacken my brows with charcoal and wash my hair clean, and find a hat to cover it. It would be easier. It might work. Who'd recognize me even if I lost the hat? You traveled with me for half a season without the slightest suspicion."

Hirel pulled Sarevan's beard until he hissed in pain. "I was an unconscionable fool. Our . . . friends are not."

"Why? What are they likely to know? I'm a slave. Slaves count for nothing."

Perhaps he sounded more bitter than he knew. Hirel regarded him oddly. Zha'dan said, "I'd dye my hair red for the splendor of it and for the confusion of our trackers, but my beard I'll not give up. I'm no capon."

Sarevan's eyes narrowed. "Would you, Zhaniedan? Would you go from night to fire?"

"With delight. But *not*," Zha'dan said vehemently, "from man to eunuch."

Hirel looked from one to the other of them. "Have you lost your wits?"

"I'm losing my disguise," Sarevan reminded him. "And we'll find precious little black dye here. But copper—that, I think . . ."

Zha'dan was warming to the sport. "Let's do it, my lord! Let's do it tonight."

But Sarevan had cooled a little. "Soon," he said. "Maybe. I need to think. And while I do it," he said, turning his eyes on Hirel, "you can do as I bid you. Tell me about your brother."

For a moment Hirel looked ready to upbraid his insanity. Then the boy sighed, sharp with temper, and lay down again. He took only a small revenge, but it was ample for the purpose: he set his feet in Sarevan's lap. They were very comely feet. "Surely," he said, "you mean to say my brothers. I have half a hundred."

Zha'dan was properly impressed. Sarevan did not stoop to be. "Most of them are nonentities. Even the two who trapped you—you've said yourself that they couldn't have conceived the plot alone. Tell me about the one who matters. Tell me about the Prince Aranos."

Hirel hissed at him. "Not so loudly, idiot. Ears are everywhere."

"Not here," said Sarevan. "Zha'dan's on guard. He's mageborn."

Hirel started, half rising, staring at his nights' companion. Zha'dan was grave for once, level-eyed. Hirel was surprised. That was rare; it made him angry. "Is there anyone in Keruvarion who is not?"

"It's only Zha'dan." And Orozia; but that was her own secret.

"Ah," said Hirel, unmollified. He faced Zha'dan. "That is why you fretted so before we came to Endros. Because you have power, but it was not enough to heal your prince."

Zha'dan looked down, embarrassed.

"Did you fret?" Sarevan asked him. "I'd forgotten."

Zha'dan mumbled something. Sarevan cuffed him lightly, brother-fashion. It soothed him, though he would not look up. Sarevan turned back to Hirel. "Now, cubling. Answer me."

Hirel's brows drew together. Sweat did not presume to bead and streak and stink upon that gold-and-ivory skin. It imparted a polished sheen, salt-scented, with a hint of sweetness. "Aranos," he said at last, "is the eldest of my father's sons. His mother was a prince's daughter from the far west of Asanion. They say she was a witch; I no longer deny that possibility. I do not think that Aranos is mageborn."

"Mages need not be born. They can be made. We call them mages of the book. Sorcerers. They have no native power, but they find it in books; in spells and in rituals; in summonings of demons and elementals and familiar. Does your brother have a familiar?"

Hirel lay back again, shifting until he was comfortable. "I think not. Perhaps it is only, not yet." He raised his head slightly, struck with a thought. "Is Ulan your familiar?"

Sarevan quelled a retort. The child could not know how he insulted them both. "Ulan is my friend and my brother-in-fur. He is neither slave nor willing servant."

"Ah." Hirel's frown was different, puzzled, seeking to understand. "A familiar provides power to the powerless. It is a vessel. An instrument."

"In essence, yes. But any man can't set himself up as a sorcerer. He has to have a talent for it. A desire for power. The willingness to devote his life to the finding of it. Singlemindedness, and ruthlessness, and a certain inborn strength of will. You have it, Hirel Uverias. You have so much of it that you're almost mageborn."

The boy reared up like a startled cat. All the color had drained from his face; his eyes were wild. "I am not a mumbler of spells!"

"It's in your blood. Ulan sees it and approves of it. So does Bregalan. So most certainly does Zha'dan. It's the heart of the lion."

"Ah," said Hirel, relaxing by degrees. "It is royalty, that is all."

Sarevan did not gainsay him. Let him call it that, if it gave him comfort. "If your brother is anything like you, then he may very well be a worker of magic."

Hirel had drawn taut again. "We are not alike. We are—not—"

"He's royal, isn't he?"

"There are," said Hirel with vicious precision, "three ranks of imperial princes, and the high prince above them all. Princes of five robes are sons of slaves and commoners. Princes of six are sons of lower nobility. Princes of seven are sons of high ladies. Vuad, who is a slave's child, is a prince of seven by my father's favor, because his mother is the most favored of the concubines."

"Is? Still?"

"My father is renowned for his constancy." Hirel had recovered himself. It was frightening to see how young he was, and how cold he seemed, and how dispassionately he spoke of betrayal. "There was no perceptible sign of my eldest brother in what was done to me, and yet he must have been the master of the plot, the mind behind the bodies of Vuad and Sayel. He had the most to gain from it. They could not have hoped to seize my titles while he lived, nor to dispose of him as easily as they thought to dispose of me. That they failed, speaks very ill of their intelligence. Aranos would not have failed."

"He may not care, if it gets him what he aims for. It's fairly certain, isn't it? He'll be named high prince on Autumn Firstday. I'll wager that your father won't live long thereafter."

"No wager," Hirel said. "Even before I left Kundri'j I had heard whispers that Aranos was surrounding himself with mages. I do not need to wonder why. To protect him while he lives; to forestall opposition when he has the throne. And yet he cannot have set these mages to spy upon us. A lordling of the Middle Court is no threat to the Second Prince before the Golden Throne. If he knew what I truly am, he would have slain me long before this."

"Maybe he doesn't know. Maybe it has nothing to do with you at all. Zha'dan and I could very well be Varyani spies."

"Perhaps," murmured Hirel. "It is what we might expect of your father: outrageous, and blatant, and insolent. It is not at all like Aranos. It is too simple."

"It looks complicated enough to me."

Hirel's glance was purest Asanian arrogance. "Ah, but you are of Keruvarion. To you I am subtle, a proper golden serpent; and yet in the palace I am reckoned the purest of innocents, a sheltered child who knew no better than to trust his brothers. Aranos was weaving plots in his cradle."

"You were a child when your brothers trapped you. How were you to know that they'd turn traitor?"

"I should have known. They are my brothers. But Aranos . . . Aranos is a very prince of serpents. I shall never be more beside him than a pretty fool."

"And his emperor."

"There is that," said Hirel. He frowned, brooding. "The Golden Palace cannot but know that I live. It has not seen fit to publish the glad tidings, else there would be no mention of a new high prince."

"No," said Sarevan. "They'd be saying that you'd gone over to us, or that you were our prisoner."

"With much outrage and no little relish." Hirel smiled a little. "A banner for their war. My father would not wish that. Aranos most certainly would not. He will be making certain that he receives the title as the empire excepts. Then, alive or dead, I can do nothing: I will have been superseded in law."

"Surely your father won't allow it."

"By law, if I am not present on the day of my coming of age, I forfeit my right to the title. He can do nothing to change that. Even if he would. For then I would prove myself unworthy to rule after him."

"Hard," mused Sarevan, "but fair enough. Maybe it's he who's behind it all. Testing you."

Hirel bridled. Sarevan grinned at him. He leaped up, nearly casting Sarevan upon the stones. "Into the water with you, barbarian. You reek."

"Of what?" Sarevan asked sweetly. "The truth?"

Their attendant mages, whether Aranos' hirelings or another's, seemed not to have found their way to this latest resting place. But someone had; and perhaps he had only been caught by the young lord's unusual retinue, and perhaps there was deeper purpose in it. This was, after all, Asanion.

The messenger was waiting at the door of the bathhouse. "Young lord," he said, bowing and touching his shaven brow to Hirel's foot, "my master, the Lord of the Ninth Rank Uzmeidjian y Viduganyas, begs the pleasure of your company at his humble table."

Even Sarevan, whose Asanian was hardly perfect, could detect the intonation that made the request a command. Hirel's lips thinned. Sarevan, trapped in his disguise, could say nothing. After a pause Hirel said, "Tell the Lord of the Ninth Rank that the Lord-designate of the

Second Rank Insevirel y Kunziad will be pleased to accept his most august hospitality."

The Lord Uzmeidjian was likewise a traveler, but his estate was too lofty by far to suffer the indignities of the posthouse. With his small army of Olenyai and plain men-at-arms, his slaves and his servants and his veiled and secluded women, he had appropriated the house of a magnate of the town.

He himself was a man of middle years inclining toward age. His body was strong yet, for an Asanian's, but softening, growing thick about the middle. His virility, of which he was quite publicly proud, had tonsured him in youth, but he cultivated the fringe of hair that yet lingered, cajoling it into oiled ringlets. He gilded his eyelids, which plainly Hirel did not approve of: it was, perhaps, above his station. Though he stood very high, at the height of the Middle Court.

His manner toward Hirel was that of a great lord bestowing his favor upon a being much lower than himself. Hirel did not bear it with perfect ease.

"Of the second rank, are you, lord-designate?" the lord inquired after the innumerable courses of an Asanian banquet had come and gone. Only the wine was left, and a sweet or two, and a bowl of ices. He had eaten well and drunk deep. Hirel had hardly eaten at all, and only pretended to drink. "Coming to take your place in court, I presume. Commendable, commendable. It is the first time, no?"

Hirel murmured. It might have been taken for assent.

Lord Uzmeidjian took it so, expansively. "Ah, so! I am sure you have been well taught. But the Court of the Empire is unlike anything the provinces might dream of. Even the Lower Court: it is preparation, certainly, but nothing equals the truth."

"Have you ever been in the High Court, my lord?"

That was malice, clad as innocence. The lord flushed. Perhaps it was only the wine. "I have not been so privileged. It is very rare, that dispensation. The High Court is far above us all."

"Indeed," said Hirel.

"Your accent is excellent," the lord observed, mounting again to his eminence. "Indeed it is almost perfect: scarce a suggestion of the provinces."

Hirel bit his lip. His eyes were smoldering. Sarevan damned protocol and laid a hand on his shoulder, tightening it: warning, strengthening.

And diverting the Lord Uzmeidjian most conclusively. "Ah, young sir, such slaves you have! and matched so perfectly. Your slavemaster must be a man of genius."

Zha'dan, who knew no Asanian but who needed to know none, and Sarevan, who was pretending to be ignorant of it, stood perforce in silence. The lord reached for Zha'dan who was closer, taking the young man's arm, feeling of it. "You leave them in their natural state, I see. But cleaner, certainly cleaner, and sweeter to the nose. I had thought that they were all as rank as foxes."

"My overseers were careful to teach them proper cleanliness," said Hirel.

"That is clear to see. They were taken as cubs, I presume; they do not train well else. And left entire—that was courageous. Or did you wait for the beards to come before you had them gelded?"

"They are quite as nature made them," Hirel said.

"So," said the Lord Uzmeidjian, "I see." And so most certainly could he feel. Zha'dan was rigid. Not with outrage at the fondling hand; his own could be free enough, and Zhil'ari did not know that kind of shame. But the talk of gelding had frozen him where he stood.

And now, in more ways than one, his lordship came to it. "I confess, Lord Insevirel, that I am most intrigued. In the high arts I have a certain reputation, yet this I have never known: the embrace of a savage in his natural state."

"They have no art," said Hirel.

"But instinct, young lord—that surely they have. Like bulls, like stallions. So huge, so beautifully hideous: animals, yet shaped like us. Splendid parodies of humanity."

"Their beards are harsh to the hand," Hirel said.

Lord Uzmeidjian proved it to himself, shivering with delight. "O marvelous! Lord Insevirel, I should not ask, I overstep myself, and yet —and yet—"

"Ah," said Hirel, wide-eyed, regretful. "But I promised. My father made me swear on our ancestors' bones. I may not part them, nor may I sell them. I may not even let them wander apart from me. They are our slavemaster's triumph. They are to give me consequence at court."

"Indeed, young lord, they shall," said the Lord Uzmeidjian. "And yet surely, if you should merely lend them for a night . . ."

Hirel was silent. Sarevan's hand tightened on his shoulder. He seemed not to feel it. At last he said, "I promised."

The lord smiled, but his eyes were hard. "A night. And in the morning their swift return, alive and undamaged, with gold in their purses."

Hirel drew himself up sharply. "I am not a merchant!"

"Most surely you are not, young sir. No more than I. We are courtiers, both of us. The court is difficult for one new come to it; but if a high lord should deign to take a young one into his care, what might that young lord become? Your family holds the second rank, and there, alas, it is not the highest, else certainly I would know its name; but it need not remain so forever. A house may rise high under a clever lord. Or," he added, soft and smooth, "it may fall."

Hirel looked into the lord's face. Slowly he said, "Please, my lord. Pardon me. I am new to this; I do not know the proper words to say. Would one of my panthers suffice for you? Then I would break only half of my promise."

Lord Uzmeidjian laughed, all jovial again. "Surely, surely, you must not break it all! This beauty, by your leave, I shall keep; in the morning he will come back to you. You have my word on it."

"With honor?" Hirel asked, innocently precise.

"With honor," the lord answered him with only the merest shadow of hesitation.

Sarevan held his tongue by sheer force of royal will, and held it full into the posthouse, and even into Hirel's chamber. But when their door was shut and Ulan was greeting him with princely gladness and Hirel was moving calmly about the shedding of his robes, Sarevan's rage burst its bonds. He was on Hirel before the boy could have seen him move, bearing him back and down, shaking him until his neck bade fair to break. "You son of a snake! You pimp! You panderer! By all the gods in your sink of a country, how could you think—how could you *dare*—"

Hirel twisted, impossibly supple, impossibly strong. He broke Saveran's brutal hold. He rolled to his feet. A dagger glittered in his hand.

Sarevan sat on his heels, breathing hard. The fire had left him. He was cold; his head throbbed dully. "How could you do that to Zha'dan?"

"Would you rather I had done it to you?"

Sarevan surged up. Hirel was not there; his knife was. With the swiftness of thought, Sarevan spun it out of his hand.

They stood still, wrist crossing wrist, like fencers in a match. Hirel looked up into Sarevan's burning eyes. "I had no choice. He was seven full ranks above what I pretended to be; and he was beginning to suspect trickery, else he would never have warned me that he had not heard of my house. I trod the edge in resisting him even as far as I did. He could have seized you, slain or imprisoned me on a charge of imposture or worse, and had his will of us all; and he would have been perfectly within his rights."

"That is unspeakable!"

"It is the world's way. I preserved your precious virginity, priest. Does that count for nothing?"

"Not when you brought it with Zha'dan."

Hirel lowered his arm. "Do you rate him so low? I do not. He is, you say, a mage; he is insatiable in pleasure; and he has more intelligence than he would like any of us to know. If he does not turn this night entirely to his own advantage, then he is not the man I took him for."

Sarevan tossed his aching head. Hirel had the right of it. Damn him. "That doesn't excuse your peddling him like a common whore."

"It does not," Hirel said wearily, startling him speechless. The boy sank down to the scattered cushions of the bed, half-clad as he was. His underrobe was torn. He struggled out of it and lay in his trousers, closing his eyes. "I did what I had to do. It does not matter that you hate me for it. You will hate me more deeply still before it is ended, if we come to Kundri'j, if I take back my titles."

Sarevan was silent.

"I have told you what I am," Hirel said. "Now do you begin to believe it?"

"You weren't like this in Keruvarion."

Hirel's eyes opened. There was nothing of the child in them. "I had no occasion to be. Your empire is remarkable, prince. It is young. Its emperor is a god's son, and a mage, and a very great king. He can afford to live by the truth; so likewise can his people. I never feared that he would break his word to me while I kept mine to him."

"Nor even when you didn't," muttered Sarevan. He dropped to the cushions. "We're clean in Keruvarion. We're honorable. We don't play foul even with our enemies."

"How fortunate," said Hirel with weary irony. His hand brushed Sarevan's cheek. "I lied a little. Your beard is not harsh to the hand."

"Neither is Zha'dan's."

"There is power in words; particularly in words addressed to a man already well gone in lust."

Sarevan ground his teeth. "That swine. That barrel of butter. I would have strangled him if he had touched me."

"Therefore I did not let him. I would not have liked him to see your true colors."

Sarevan's cheeks burned. He buried them in the cushions. He hated this unnatural child. He hated all this lying empire. And he had trapped himself in it. For its sake he had turned traitor to all that he had ever been.

How long he lay there, he did not know. Pain brought him up at last. The throbbing behind his eyes was mounting to agony.

"Sorcery," he whispered. Even that nearly split his skull. Hirel was asleep, or feigning it. Ulan lay across his feet. The cat raised his head and growled softly.

Sarevan struggled to his knees. If he could think—if he could only think. Plots, counterplots. Zha'dan lured away, his magecraft taken where it could not protect his companions. The Olenyai—

Sarevan gasped, blind and retching, but thinking. Thinking hard, for all the good it could do. This posthouse had no space for a lord's meinie. They had perforce to lodge in the common barracks. The two who should have stood guard at the door had not been there when Sarevan came back. He had been too wild with rage to notice, still less to care.

Sorcery. Betrayal. Deadly danger. This was Asanion. *Asanion.*

Cool. Hands. Cool hands. Cool voice—but not so cool, calling his name, commanding him to answer.

Light broke upon him. He stared into Hirel's face. He was on his back. Hirel was holding his head, looking for once entirely human. He was stark with fear. "Sarevadin, if you die now, I shall be most displeased. Sarevadin!"

Sarevan could not help it. He laughed, though he paid for it in white pain. "I haven't died on you yet, cubling."

"That is not for lack of trying," Hirel snapped.

Sarevan sat up, reeling. All lightness drained from him. "We're in a trap. They've got Zha'dan away from us and stripped us of our Olenyai. You said Aranos hadn't tried to kill you yet. This may be the stroke." He rose, though Hirel tried to stop him. His sight had narrowed, but he could see. He could walk.

"Where are you going?" Hirel demanded of him.

"To confront a pair of sorcerers."

"You are mad! You have no power. You can barely set one foot before the other."

"What would you have me do? Lie quietly and wait for them to slaughter us?"

"They will hardly slay us with their power. I have a little skill in arms; and we have Ulan. We can give a good account of ourselves."

"If any of us kills a man here, we'll all pay in blood."

"So then," said Hirel. "Can you ride?"

"Yes, damn it!" Sarevan paused. Escape now. Yes. But with pursuit on their heels; and Zha'dan . . .

A new wave of agony crested, passed. He snatched up their belongings, flung Hirel's discarded garments at him, scrambled together what food he could find.

The inn was utterly quiet. No one walked the passages. Nothing moved there at all. It was as if it were all enspelled. Sarevan dragged Hirel through it with growing heedlessness, flinging them both from inn to open air to the dark odorous confines of the stable. Beasts thronged it. Sarevan found Bregalan almost by instinct. The shadow next to him was tall enough to carry a tall man, which was not common in Asanion. Sarevan found saddles, bridles.

Hirel waited just past the door with Ulan, who could not enter among so many seneldi lest he drive them all mad with terror. The strange senel, scenting him, snorted and danced, but under Sarevan's hand it eased to a trembling stillness.

They rode slowly from the yard, keeping to shadows. No one challenged them, not even the hound that had welcomed them with yapping and howling. The air was still. The gate was open. Trap?

They spurred through it. Nothing stopped them. The posthouse lay outside the walls of the town, hard by the road; there was no second gate to pass. They kept to the grass on the verge, which made for swift going, and silent. Town and posthouse shrank behind them.

The pain receded slowly. Sarevan's mount was smooth-gaited. In the starless night he could not guess its color, save that it was dark. It was hornless: a mare. All the better. Mares were swifter and hardier and less given to nonsense; and even yet he did not want to be caught on a stallion.

Hoofbeats behind. Sarevan clapped heels to the mare's sides. But Bregalan had broken stride, was turning. Was he mad? Had the spell caught Hirel at last?

Cursing, Sarevan wheeled his own mount. Bregalan had stopped. Sarevan snatched at his bridle; he shied away. "He will not heed me," Hirel said. He was calm, but it was a desperate calm.

The hoofs neared swiftly. It was only one senel. Sarevan, peering, could discern a swift-moving shadow. Metal hissed. Hirel had drawn one of his swords. The other flashed in sudden moonlight. Sarevan caught the hilt. Armed and defiant, they waited.

It was a lone rider, and he was all a shadow. Sarevan's heart knew him before his mind could wake. "Zha'dan!"

The Zhil'ari pounded to a halt beside them. He was breathing hard and his senel was blowing, but he grinned whitely in Brightmoon's gleam. "Thought you could creep out on me, did you?"

"We tried," said Sarevan.

"Good," he said. His grin vanished. "There's death on the wind tonight. Best we not tarry for it."

They rode until Zha'dan would let them stop. The sky greyed with dawn. The seneldi, ridden at the pace of the Long Race in the north, surpassingly swift but not meant to kill, had a little strength left; but none of the riders was minded to squander it. Posthouses would not be safe thereafter; they had no swift hope of remounts.

They found refuge at some distance from the road, in the deep cleft cut by a stream. Its banks offered grass for their seneldi; a thicket offered both shelter and concealment, and a blessed gift of thornfruit to eke out their scanty provisions.

Hirel, having eaten as much as Sarevan could bully into him, fell at once into sleep. The others lingered, crouched side by side. "Was it bad?" Sarevan asked.

Zha'dan shrugged. "He wasn't the little stallion. He was smooth all over. His yard was a bare finger's length. He kept calling me ugly." Zha'dan was indignant. "I may be small, but even Gazhin admits that I'm beautiful. I look like you, don't I? You're the most beautiful of us all."

"Not to an Asanian," said Sarevan. He gestured toward Hirel. "That's beauty here."

"He's not ill to look at. But he's white, like a bone, and his eyes are yellow. That's all very well for an honest lion, but men's eyes are black. And his nose, look. No arch. What's a nose without an arch?"

"Pitiful," Sarevan said wryly, rubbing his own royal curve. "So his lordship has a crooked passion for beautifully ugly barbarians. And then?"

"And then," said Zha'dan. "He didn't last long. He fell asleep, and I was thinking of going, and then the mages struck. They were only trying to read me, to be sure I was well occupied. I gave them something to keep their ears burning for a while. Then they turned on you. And there I was, locked in walls. I couldn't get out. By the time I found a wall to climb over, you were up and running. I borrowed one of the seneldi you left, and followed you." Zha'dan paused. Suddenly he grinned. "They won't follow us for a while, I don't think. I told the seneldi to wait a bit. Then I untied them, and I left the door open."

Sarevan laughed with him, freely, but hit him without gentleness after. "Whelp! This isn't a raiding party."

Zha'dan hit back. Sarevan lunged at him. They rolled on the grass in laughing combat. Ulan made himself a part of it, growling in high delight. At the end of it they lay all together, hiccoughing, scoured clean of aught but mirth.

Sunset brought battle again, but battle of words, without laughter. Sarevan was minded to cross Asanion as he had crossed Keruvarion, in secret, taking sustenance from land and sky. Hirel would not hear of it. "This is not your wild east. The hunting belongs to the lords and satraps, each in his own demesne. Those who hunt without leave are reckoned thieves and punished accordingly."

"Not with Ulan and Zha'dan to cover our tracks," said Sarevan.

Hirel tossed his head, impatient. "And if they do, how swiftly can we ride? How far must we wander, to be secret, to fill our bellies? How careful must we be to spare our seneldi, now that we may find no others?"

"What do you want to do? Take the open road? Invite our assassins to finish what our foolish flight interrupted?"

"Take the road, yes; outrun our enemies. If enemies we have. I saw no daggered shadows. I tasted no poison in our wine. The posthouse might have been abandoned, so easily we left it."

"It was not—" Sarevan's tongue met his mind and froze. He had been too busy running to think. He had forgotten indeed that this was not Keruvarion.

"Speculate," said Hirel, "if you can. Sorcery nearly felled you. You gave way to instinct: you fled it. What if you were meant to do just that? To run into a trap. Or more subtle yet, to abandon the swift way; to take to the shadows. And thereby most certainly to delay my coming to Kundri'j."

"And if you are delayed, Aranos becomes high prince." Sarevan liked the taste of it not at all. It was alien; it burned, like Asanian spices. He spat it out. "But if we ride openly, the enemy will know. He'll lay new traps. I don't think he'll wait long to make them deadly."

"Are you afraid?" Hirel asked.

"Yes, I'm afraid!" Sarevan shot back. "But a coward, I'm not. I don't want to arrive late, but neither do I want to arrive dead."

"That would not be comfortable," said Hirel. "We have Zha'dan and Ulan. We have you, whom sorcery cannot fail to rouse. We even have myself. I have no power and no great skill in hunting or in fighting, but

I do know Asanion. If we vanish for a day or two, press on through the shadows, I think then we may return to the daylight."

"With stolen seneldi?"

"Ah," said Zha'dan, entering the fray at last, "that's easy. We find a town with a fair. We trade. We do it twice or thrice, over a day or two. Then when our path is quite comfortably confused, we go back to the inns and the highroad."

"It won't work," Sarevan said. "We may lose a pair of seneldi, but we can't lose our faces."

"You may," Hirel said slowly. "Sometimes, Olenyai go all masked. It is a rite of theirs. We cannot sustain such a deception: the masked do not mingle with folk in inns, nor speak any tongue but their own secret battle-language. But for a day, two, three—it is possible."

"Where will we find the robes?" demanded Sarevan. He was being difficult, he knew it. But someone had to be.

"I can wield a needle," said Hirel, astonishingly. "For the cloth, we find a fair. I can be a slave for an hour if I must: a slave whose mistress has a fancy for black."

Sarevan opened his mouth, closed it. Zha'dan was regarding Hirel in something remarkably like admiration.

With a sharp hiss, Sarevan conceded the battle. "Very well. Tonight we ride in the shadows. Tomorrow we find a fair."

Hirel did not gloat over his victory. It was Zha'dan who whooped and kissed him, disconcerting him most gratifyingly, and went to saddle the seneldi.

They found their fair: a town with a market, and a wooded hill outside of it, thick enough with undergrowth to shelter the beasts and the two men who could not show their faces. Hirel went down on foot in his underrobe, cut to the brevity of a slave's tunic, with Zha'dan's iron collar about his neck and a purse of Asanian coins hung from his belt. The Lord Uzmeidjian had not missed them or their golden kin, Zha'dan had assured the two princes; and certainly Zha'dan had earned them. Hirel had looked at him and sighed, but said nothing.

The boy was gone for a very long while. Sarevan tried to sleep through some of it. The rest he spent on his belly in a knot of canes, keeping watch over the road and the town. Ulan kept him company. He had shed his damnable tunic; flies buzzed about him in the day's heat but did not sting, and the earth was cool. He would have been comfortable, if he had known how Hirel was faring. The boy had done well enough in his venture into a Varyani town, but this was Asanion. Who knew what niggling law he might have managed to break, all in his princely ignorance? Did he even know how to bargain in the market? Or if the mages after all had not lost him, and had seized him—

Sarevan set his jaw and willed himself to stop fretting. His face itched more maddeningly than ever. He had used the last of the dye this morning. It had stung like fire; he had almost cried out, as much with knowledge as with pain. It was the dye that so tormented his skin: eating at it, burning it, leaving it raw and angry. Even if he could find another bottle, he did not think his face would survive it.

He worked his fingers into Ulan's fur, lest they claw new weals in his cheeks. People passed on the road. Was that a boy with hot-gold hair cropped into a wild mane, coming up from the town?

Not yet.

He set himself to his vigil. The sun crawled to its zenith.

Ulan growled, the barest murmur. Sarevan shook himself awake, peered. A slave with a pack on his back trudged slowly toward the thicket. A slave with dust-drab hair.

Dust in truth, and a handsome bruise purpling his cheekbone. He started as Sarevan rose out of the thicket; his eyes widened at the bare body. He did not speak. He looked both furious and pleased with himself. He strode into the thicket's heart, tossed down his pack, greeted Zha'dan with a vanishingly brief smile.

"You've been fighting," Sarevan accused him.

He knelt to uncover his booty. Coolly, without looking up, he said, "I have been defending my honor."

Sarevan seized him by the nape and hauled him up. "What did you do, you little fool? Were you trying to get us all killed?"

Hirel twisted free, all angry now; a white heat, rigidly restrained. "I was trying to be what I seemed to be. I did not heed the taunting of the market curs. But when they seized me and sought to strip me, because they had a wager, and they wished to see what sort of eunuch I was— was I to let them see that I am no eunuch at all?" He tossed his hair out of his eyes. They were fiery gold. "I had already let it be known that I served a lady; and the law is strict. One of my adversaries had a knife, if perchance it should be needed. Should I have let him use it?"

Sarevan said nothing, quenched for once, beginning to regret his hastiness. Hirel was white and shaking. He was worse than angry. He was on the thin edge between murder and tears.

He calmed himself visibly, drawing in deep shuddering breaths. "I defended myself well enough. Better certainly than they looked for. They chose to seek meeker prey elsewhere; and I won a modicum of respect from the merchants. They did not drive as hard a bargain as they might have."

"You liked that," Sarevan said. "Maybe you should have been born a merchant."

"Better a tradesman than a worthless vagabond. Or," said Hirel, bending again to his unpacking, "a eunuch. Of any sort."

Zha'dan looked ready to ask how there could be more than one. Mercifully for all of them, he held his tongue.

Hirel had needles and thread and cutting blades. He had bolts of black linen and bolts of fine black wool. He had belts of black leather, and black gauntlets, and boots that proved not to fit too badly; and marvel of marvels, four black-hilted swords in black sheaths. They were Olenyai blades; but he would not tell how he had found them. He looked both proud and guilty.

"He stole them," Zha'dan translated, with approval.

Hirel flushed. "I appropriated them. As high prince I am overlord of all warriors. I claimed my royal right."

Zha'dan applauded him. He flushed more deeply still and attacked the somber linen.

The others found themselves pressed into service. With Hirel directing them, they transformed themselves into *shiu'oth Olenyai:* warriors under solemn vow. When they were done, the sun was westering, and Sarevan was sucking a much-stabbed finger. Hirel slapped down his hand. "Mask yourself," the boy commanded. Sarevan obeyed rather sourly.

Hirel stood back, hands on hips, head cocked. "You will do," he judged, "for a while. If no one examines you too closely."

"You comfort me," said Sarevan.

Hirel ignored the barb. For himself he had stitched a headdress to match the rest: the filleted headcloth and the mask that concealed all beneath it, even to the eyes. A panel of thinnest linen set over them was easy enough to see out of, but from the outside seemed all featureless darkness.

"We look alarming," Zha'dan said. He sounded highly amused.

Sarevan was stifling already. At least, he reflected wryly, he would not find it so easy to claw at his itching cheeks.

People had stared at a dozen Olenyai and a young lord and his two barbarian slaves. They did not stare at three *shiu'oth Olenyai.* Their eyes slid round the shadowed shapes; their voices muted; their bodies drew back, smoothly, as water parts from a stone.

It was almost ridiculously simple to exchange the stolen seneldi for a pair of black mares. The seller did not haggle at all. He almost thrust the beasts at them, his eyes rolling white, his plump face sheening with sweat. He asked no questions. When they left him, he looked ready to weep for relief.

So with the next seller, and the next. Most often it was plain fear. Sometimes it was fear poisoned with hate. Then Sarevan's back would twitch, dreading a stone or a hurled blade.

Zha'dan was swift to lose his pleasure in the game. In the night, when they camped, he was unwontedly silent. He would speak of it only once. "I've never been hated before. It hurts."

Hirel comforted him as only Hirel could. Sarevan lay apart and tried not to hear them. The trying only made it the more distinct. Whispers. A flicker of laughter. A breath caught as if in sudden pleasure. The rhythm of bodies moving together: the oldest dance in the world.

For the first time in a long while, he was aware of the weight of his torque. He took it off, straining a little, for the iron sheathing stiffened it. The night air was cold on his bared neck. He rubbed it, feeling of the scars, the circle of calluses that had grown from old galls. A bitter smile touched the corner of his mouth. An Asanian would not have known that he was not a slave, that he had not been one for long years. The first had been the worst. He had lived with numbroot salve and no little blood, and wounds that festered, and no bandages. Bandages only prolonged the agony.

He turned the blessed, brutal thing in his hands. Disguised, it looked liked what it was: a badge of servitude. He held it to his breast. It was a cold lover. It granted no mortal peace.

Yet there was peace in it, bounded within its circle. Peace that came neither easily nor quickly, and yet it came. He was still Avaryan's priest. Neither murder nor treason could rob him of that.

The hunt had lost them. Sarevan marked it in the passing of pain.

"For a long while I could feel them looking for us," said Zha'dan. "They followed the seneldi we stole, I think, and when that trail proved false, cast wide for scent of us. Now there's nothing."

"They will wait ahead," Hirel said. "In Kundri'j."

He did not sound unduly cast down. The Golden City was far away yet, and they were advancing at a good pace, under a clear sky. The brilliance of autumn had begun to touch it; the land beneath was like and yet wholly unlike anything Sarevan had known in the east.

Hirel had been wise, he conceded now, to demand that they take the open road. In this the heart of Asanion, there were no shadows to hide in: no wilderness. The broad rolling plain was a pattern of walled towns joined together by roads, each town set like a jewel in a webwork of fields. The streams here ran straight and steady, wrought by men and not by gods; the trees were planted in rows that guided and guarded the wind, or in the artful disarray of the high ones' hunting grounds. And always there were the gods, the small ones and the great ones, worshipped in shrines at every milestone, and often between.

This was a tamed land. A company could not ride free over the fields, or wander from the highroad upon a path that though narrower might prove a shorter way to Kundri'j. Even the road had its laws and its divisions, its hierarchy of passers, from the slave on bare feet to the prince in his chariot. For *shiu'oth Olenyai* on swift seneldi, there was the broad smooth verge and an open way, but they might not stray into a field or onto the road itself. And even they had to stop for the passage of a personage, or slow to a crawl in traversing a town.

Now and then as they crossed Asanion, and more often as they drew near to the imperial city, they had seen caravans of slaves shuffling in chains from market to market. Hirel had seen, but he had not seen, as was the way in the Golden Empire. Zha'dan learned that custom quickly enough: his people had captives and the odd bought servant, though never whole market-droves of them. Sarevan, raised to abhor the thought of men kept like cattle, took refuge in the schooling of a prince. What one could not alter, one endured. And though it shamed him, he was glad for once of his mind's crippling, that he could not sense the misery that throbbed about the chained and plodding lines. He could look away and make himself forget.

But he had not had to ride within sight and sound of a slave market.

Sarevan did not ask the name of the town. He did not wish to know. It was large; it trumpeted prosperity. The road ran straight through it, dividing its market, so that travelers might pause to trade a wayworn senel for a fresh one, to satisfy hunger or thirst, to buy a weapon or a garment or a jewel.

Or a slave. There were, it seemed, a number of purveyors of such goods. Some did so within the privacy of walls, marked only by a sign above the door: a gilded manacle or an image carven in the likeness of a particular breed. Others set up tents, open or half open or enclosed. And here and there stood a simple platform, perhaps canopied, perhaps not, with a man crying the day's wares to a throng of buyers.

The three of them rode close together with Hirel in the middle. Even behind his mask, the boy seemed much as always. A little stiff, a little haughty, disdaining to take notice of the world about him. His mare was moving very slowly.

She stopped. Sarevan's glance strayed. When he looked back, the saddle was empty.

Bregalan spun on his haunches, breasting a current turned suddenly against him. Sarevan raged, but the stallion could advance no swifter than a walk, and for that he was jostled and cursed, even threatened by a charger with bronze-sheathed horns. He snorted and slashed; the destrier veered away. He plunged through the gap which the other had left.

Hirel's rough-coated mare stood abandoned and beginning to wander. Beyond her the road gave way to a broad shallow space filled with people, focused upon a platform and a huddle of slaves. They were all boys, the youngest perhaps nine summers old, the eldest a little older than Hirel. They were naked, collared, their hands bound behind them that they might not seek to cover their shame. Most were Asanians, slight and tawny; two were pale-skinned green-eyed Islanders; one was a tribesman of the north, haughty and sullen, and several standing close together had the faces of desert wanderers. They were all eunuchs, every one.

Sarevan found Hirel easily enough. He was taller than many, and he was the only one in Olenyai black. He stood on the edge of the crowd, straight as a carven knight. His mask was crumpled in his hand. Beneath the dusty headcloth his face was bloodless.

Sarevan followed his eyes. One of the Asanians stood a little apart. The others were chained together, neck and ankle. This one had his own chain and his own guard; his collar was gilded, and from it hung a written tablet.

"A thoroughbred," said Hirel. "He will be offered last, and the seller will accept no price unless he judges it sufficient. See, how fair his skin, how pure a gold his hair, how flawless his face; how perfect his age, the very flower of boyhood. I wonder that he is sold in the open market; that is not common for slaves of his quality. Perhaps his lord has a debt to pay."

It was too calm, that voice. His eyes were too wide and too pale. Sarevan gripped his shoulder; it was rigid, impervious. "It's not you, Hirel."

"A season ago," said Hirel, "it was. It would have—I would have—"

Sarevan pulled him close. He did not resist. He was shaking; his brow was damp. But he would not turn away from the boy who was so much like himself: himself as he had been when Sarevan found him, a child poised on the very brink of manhood. He had passed it in the season since. This one never would.

"He is not you," Sarevan said again. "He is brass and painted bone. He is soft; he is pretty; his eyes are not the eyes of the lion. He is nothing beside you."

"He is myself," whispered Hirel.

Sarevan slapped him. He swayed, but his face did not change. "You are beautiful," Sarevan said to him, "and very certainly a man. No one now can make you like him. No one ever could. He is false coin. You are true gold."

Hirel did not hear him. Something, at last, had broken him; or something had roused that had been long and safely sleeping.

"He's gone away." Zha'dan, won through to them. Even muffled in the mask, his voice was deeply worried. "I can't find him at all."

Sarevan reached to touch Hirel, to wake him, to lift him, he hardly knew which. The boy, who had been so limp and lifeless to look at, turned demon under his hands. Steel slashed. Sarevan recoiled. Hirel whipped about in a swirl of robes and bolted.

They bolted after him. He ran like a deer. The crowd parted before him but closed behind, hindering the pursuit, jarring it aside, even challenging it. Sarevan drew one of his swords. The challenges stopped. The hindrances did not.

Hirel twisted and doubled and darted. His face when Sarevan glimpsed it sidelong was chalk-white. His eyes were blind.

The throngs thinned. The pursuit began to gain on its quarry. A procession swayed and chanted from a side way, full across their path: marchers innumerable, linked hand to hand, eyes closed, trancebound. All the narrow street was clogged with them. Even at his wits' end Sarevan could not bring himself to cut a path with steel.

The procession wound away. Hirel was gone. Zha'dan caught Sarevan's arm. "There!"

They sped from the narrow way down one narrower yet, walled in the stink of cities; past blind gates and blinder walls. There was no sign of Hirel. Zha'dan slowed to a stumbling trot, then to a walk. He swayed against Sarevan. He tore at his mask, rending it, flinging it away. His face was grey and sheened with sweat. "Hard," he whispered. "So many people. So many walls."

"Hirel?" Sarevan snapped at him, cruel with desperation.

His head tossed. He halted. He leaned on Sarevan and trembled. "Can't," he gasped. "Can't—"

Sarevan would have given his soul for a few breaths' worth of power.

He had only pain. No Hirel, anywhere. The seneldi were lost and forgotten. Ulan had withdrawn to circle the town. Unless he too was bewitched, led astray, ensnared.

Zha'dan staggered erect. Both his swords were out. He whirled. Sarevan backed away from him, raging at heaven. Not Zha'dan too. One madman was more than enough. "Zha'dan!" Sarevan lashed out with all the power of his voice. "Zhaniedan!"

The Zhil'ari checked, turning slowly. His lips were drawn back from his teeth. "Caught," he said. "Trapped. Sorcery—it has the little stallion. I can't win him back. I have not that much power. I can't even stop them. I can't—" He broke off. The swords fell from his slackened fingers. With a low cry, of anger, of despair, he whipped about, spinning. The air filled with a thin high keening. He was drawing in his power.

Sarevan cried out, protesting. Zha'dan never heard. Light gathered to him. Lightnings cracked.

The walls were as bare and blank as cliffs of stone. The street darkened. From either end of it, men closed in. Grim men, armored, with drawn bows.

Sarevan knew an instant's bitter mirth. Whoever the enemy was, he was taking no chances. Not even Olenyai swords could stand against a whole company of archers.

An arrow sang past Sarevan's ear. It kindled. Zha'dan flung darts of power against the darts of mortal making. He laughed in the sweet madness of magery. Setting his teeth, making all his body a prayer, Sarevan flung himself at the young fool.

They went down together. Over them hissed a rain of arrows. Power spat and flared about Sarevan, but it did not touch him. Nor did it shield him. Sarevan knew the blow before it fell. It was neither spell nor weapon. It was a bubble, drifting over them. It broke. His body had gasped it in before his mind could act: gagging, cloying sweetness; and in it, irresistible, a heavy weight of sleep.

"Not sorcery," he tried to say. To instruct Zha'dan. "Not magic. This is alchemy." It was very important that Zha'dan know it. He did not know why. He only knew. "Alchemy," he repeated. *"Alchemy."*

Fifteen

ALCHEMY; BUT MAGEBORNE. THEIR HUNTERS HAD found them, and were not minded to let them go.

Sarevan did not remember all of it. He saw the mages, the dark and the light. No doubt he gave them defiance. They gave him nothing. Zha'dan was there. They looked closely at both; they were not pleased. Their armed companions pried hands from sides, fingers from palms. The *Kasar* startled even the mages, although surely they had been looking for it. Perhaps they had not known how brightly it could burn.

They left Zha'dan to drugged dreams. They stripped Sarevan, though they did not take his torque; they scoured him without mercy. His body howled with the pain of cleanroot and ashes on his raw skin. They finished with something that was purest agony, and then it was blessedly cool, with a scent of herbs and healing.

They drugged him again. He fought it: the bruises lingered. Useless enough. They were too strong.

He woke at last from a black dream. He was cold and sick, and he hurt wherever a body could hurt. The earth rocked; he clutched at solidity.

Walls, closing in upon him. They rattled and shook. Cushions narrowed the narrow prison. He was naked on them, his hair loose and tangled, and for a moment he did not understand why he was startled. It was a copper-bright as it had ever been.

He was not alone in that hot and breathless space. Someone else strove with him for what air there was. Someone as bare as himself, as pale as he was dark, coiled in all apparent comfort at the utmost end of the box.

Only Hirel's face held Sarevan to sanity. It was calm to coldness; it was entirely conscious, and sane, and princely proud. It was not the face of one whose will had broken.

Sarevan struggled up. He could sit; he could kneel, if he crouched; he could not stand. Light came through intricate lattices, one on either side of him. It shifted, changing. They were moving.

He pressed his face to the lattice. Air brushed it, warm, heavy, but cooler and cleaner than what filled the box. Shadows passed. Trees, perhaps. Towers. Mounted men.

He dropped back. He wanted to claw the walls. He drew himself into a quivering knot and glared at Hirel.

The boy uncoiled, stretching. "You look like a panther at bay," he observed.

Sarevan snarled at him. "You did this. You led us into this."

Hirel's ease shattered. "I was tricked and trapped. I was"—he choked on it—"bespelled. I knew what they were doing to me. I could not stop it. Because—because I had seen what I would be, if I did not run then, run as far and as fast as I could."

"You may be a eunuch yet."

"I may die for this, but this much I have been promised: I will not die unmanned." Hirel had calmed himself again. "We are in a litter," he said, "like ladies who must travel swiftly. You see how we are prevented from escaping."

Sarevan did not. He found a door. He set his nails to the crack of it. It groaned but did not yield.

"If you succeed," said Hirel, cool and maddening, "where will you go? An armed company surrounds us. We are unarmed and unarmored. We are also," he pointed out, "unclad."

"What difference does that make?"

Hirel looked as if he could not choose between laughter and shock. "To you, perhaps, none. To me, enough. I am not a spectacle for low-born eyes to see."

"Why? You have nothing to be ashamed of."

"I have a body," Hirel snapped.

Sarevan was mute. Hirel withdrew again, barricading himself with cushions. The silence stretched. The walls closed in. Sarevan set all his will to the task of enduring. Of keeping himself from going mad like an ul-cat in a cage.

After an eternal while Hirel spoke, low and taut. "The people must not see. That I am mortal. That I wear flesh like any man of them. That my blood is as red as theirs, and flows as freely. I am royal; every inch of me is holy. My nails were never cut save by priests, with many prayers and incantations. My hair was never cut at all. The water of my bath was preserved for the anointing of the sick."

"What did you do with nature's tribute? House it in gold and give it to the gods?"

Hirel's breath hissed. "I did not say that I believed in it! I meant to change it when I could. But until I came into my power, I was my power's slave. I served it most dutifully. I was a very proper prince, O prince of savages."

"Wise," said Sarevan. "Did anyone ever know how much of your mind was your own?"

The golden eyes hooded. "A prince's body belongs to his people. His mind does not enter into it."

"But they aren't supposed to know you have a body."

"Flesh," Hirel said. He trust out his arm. Sunlight shattered on the lattice, turned the fine hairs to sparks of gold, found a bruise and a healing cut and an old white scar. "Blood and bone. Humanity. When I am emperor, I will be not even that. I will be pure royal image."

Sarevan shivered in the breathless heat. He felt very mortal. His throat was dry and his face itched and he ached. He said, *"When* you are emperor? Will you come to it now?"

Hirel smiled. It was not a comfortable smile. "I will come to it. I am captive; I am not dead. And I do not surrender. Nor do I ever forgive."

"I pity your enemies."

"Do that," said Hirel, still smiling.

With the sun's setting, their prison halted. Sarevan had not spoken for a very long while. He dared not, lest he howl like a beast. He had been imprisoned before; he had been shut up in close walls, for punishment, for training as mage and priest. But he had had power. He had not been trapped within himself. He had not had to fight to breathe, to think, to be himself and not mere mindless panic.

With a scraping of bolts, the door opened. He had no will left. He burst into the light. Bodies barred him. He swept them away. He struck stone. Wall. Gate—

Men closed upon him. He fought them. They were too many, and they were armored. His hands could only rock them; could not fell them. They caught him, bound him, dragged him into quiet.

Hirel sat in it, robed from throat to toe, sipping from a cup. The walls about him were blessedly far away.

Sarevan's captors flung him into the chamber and bolted the door upon him. He lay on musty carpets, gasping, beginning to be sane again. The cords were twisted cruelly tight. His arms throbbed.

Hirel knelt by him and began to worry at the knots. "Our jailers are most impressed," he said, "with the perfection of your savagery."

"It's not the cage," Sarevan said carefully. "It's that I can't get my mind out of it. I can't breathe inside; I can't breathe without."

Hirel could not possibly understand. Or perhaps, and that may have been worse, he could. "You are not a creature of sealed palaces," he said.

Sarevan shuddered. He tried to be light, to turn his mind away from the dark. "Are our captors hoping I'll maul you to death?"

"It would be convenient," Hirel said.

"To whom?"

The boy shrugged. "I asked. I was not answered."

One by one the knots yielded. The cords fell away. Sarevan lay and tried to make his numbed arms obey his will.

Hirel sat on his heels, watching. After a moment he caught one of Sarevan's arms, bringing it back to life again with those clever fingers of his. "I have not seen our mageling," he said. "Nor our grey hunter."

Captivity had weakened Sarevan's wits. He had to struggle to understand. Hope leaped; died. "Dead. Or fled."

"Perhaps." Hirel exchanged one arm for the other. "We are wanted alive. No one moved to cut you down when you broke free. They gave way rather than wound you."

"Hostages?" The irony struck Sarevan; he laughed, though it hurt. "It may be well enough for me, as long as someone in Asanion is holding me. But for you . . ."

"I think they do not know me," said Hirel. "Yet."

He stood abruptly. Sarevan sat up, opening his mouth to speak. Hirel strode to the door and spoke. He raised his voice barely enough, Sarevan would have thought, to pass the panel, but its inflection raised Sarevan's hackles. He had never heard the twelve tones of High Asanian wielded with such deadly subtlety, by one bred to the art. "O thou who guardest this door, send to thy master and tell him. The prince who is above princes would speak to him."

No sound came back from without. Hirel returned to the chamber's center, settled himself on the mound of cushions there, picked up his cup again. His free hand indicated the table beside him. "Eat," he said.

Sarevan was more than glad to obey, though warily, mistrusting Asanian sauces. He found himself yearning for good plain roast wildbuck, or fruit untainted with spices, or simple peasant cheese. Even the language in which he had always been pleased enough to address Hirel had grown to a mighty burden. He ate in silence, to quiet his stomach, tasting little. He drank sour Asanian wine. He prowled the space, which was endurable, wide but windowless. He was going to break again. Anger did not help him. Should Keruvarion's high prince go mad like an animal, simply for a few hour's confinement?

Bolts rattled. Sarevan spun, poised. The door boomed back. Armed men poured through it. They passed Hirel without a glance, spreading to surround Sarevan.

"Thou wilt not touch him," the boy said, again in that mastery of tones which came close to sorcery.

The guards paused. Sarevan did not move. They leveled their spears, but neither touched him nor threatened him. His back was to the wall. He grinned suddenly, leaned against it, folded his arms. The men were not, he noticed, staring at him. They were working very hard at it. The tallest came barely to his chin. The smallest had to look up or sidewise, or close his eyes altogether, lest they fix on what he was trying hardest not to see. "What's the matter?" Sarevan asked him. "Haven't you ever seen a man before?"

The Asanian flushed. He did not take vengeance with his spear. Sarevan admired him for that, and said so. He flushed more deeply yet, and scowled terribly.

With the chamber well and most valiantly secured, the captain of guards stepped back from the door, sword raised in salute. All of his men who were not hedging Sarevan with bronze clapped blades to shields and knelt.

Their master entered at his leisure, escorted by a pair of Uvarra's priests, one in silver grey and one in dusky violet. Sarevan almost laughed. He carried himself like an emperor, and yet he was as small as a child. He might have been taken for one, fair and smooth as his face was, all perfect ivory: a nine years' youngling of indeterminate gender, wrapped in fold on fold of midnight silk. But his eyes were never a child's. They were like Hirel's, clear gold, seeming whiteless unless they opened very wide; and they were bitterly bright.

Hirel rose. He was tall here, even young as he was; he stood a full head above that perfect miniature of a man.

Sarevan, watching, smiled. The other carried himself like an emperor.

Hirel Uverias had no need to. It was beautifully played. "Brother," he said, cool, unsurprised.

Indeed. They were very like. Hirel, sun-painted, thinned and hardened with travel, looked almost the elder.

"Brother," said the silken mannikin. His voice was sweet and nearly sexless. "I rejoice to see you well."

Hirel inclined his head. Then he paused, as if he waited. His eyes were very steady.

For the merest flicker of an instant, the other lost his poise. Hirel never moved. Slowly his brother knelt. More slowly yet under those quiet relentless eyes, he prostrated himself. His mages followed him.

Hirel looked down at them all. No smile touched his lips, but Sarevan found one in the light behind his eyes.

The princeling rose with grace, the mages with relief. Hirel did not offer his hand. He sat and tucked up his feet and said, "Your bravos should be whipped. They have given insult to a prince."

"That has been remedied," his brother said. Aranos, Sarevan was prepared to name him.

"It has not," said Hirel.

Aranos followed his eyes. Sarevan smiled at them both. The lesser prince regarded him with interest and without visible embarrassment. The fine brows went up. Aranos approached. His spearmen drew back, not without reluctance. He put out a hand. It was child-small; its nails were fully as long as the fingers from which they grew, warded in jeweled sheaths. Sarevan shivered at the brush of those glittering claws, but his smile held. "Little man," he said, purring, "I give you leave to touch me."

The hand paused. Aranos had to tilt his head well back to look into Sarevan's face. He was not at all afraid. "You are splendid," he said.

He meant it; or he was far too subtle for Sarevan's outland innocence. Or was simplicity another kind of subtlety?

"Are you insulted?" asked Aranos.

Sarevan thought about it. "That," he answered in time, "is not what I would call it. But here . . . yes. It is an insult."

Aranos bowed his head. He gestured. A garment came quickly enough to interest Sarevan. It was a robe like Hirel's, of heavy raw silk. It fit, which was more interesting still. The servant who brought it brought also a comb, which, when Sarevan had been persuaded to sit beside Hirel, he plied with a master's skill.

Aranos watched and waited. He did not sit. His robes, Sarevan thought, must have been deadly heavy. There were seven of them, one atop the other, each cut to show the one beneath.

Hirel, at his ease in a single robe, leaned back upon his cushions. "You will explain the meaning of this," he said. "We are taken like criminals. We are transported in a litter like women, but set within like slaves, in robeless shame. And yet you pay me homage. Is it," he asked very gently, "that you mean to mock me?"

"Errors have been committed," said Aranos with equal gentleness. His mages were pale; their eyes had lowered. "They will not be repeated."

"We are therefore to be set free?"

"I did not say that."

"Ah," said Hirel. Only that.

"You mistake me," Aranos said. "The Olenyai who rode with you were sworn to betray you; to complete what was left undone by Vuad and Sayel. Your companion they were to treat likewise and to send back to his father with the compliments of the Golden Empire."

Calm though he willed himself to be, Sarevan shuddered. Hirel was white about the lips. "That would not have been wise of them," he said.

"Indeed not. My mages had word of the plot; they were undertaking to warn you. But matters moved too swiftly, as did you. You mistook their sending, but it saved you. When the traitors came to seize you, you were gone."

"Even should I believe that there was a conspiracy to destroy me," Hirel said, "still I would wonder. A loyal man does not drug and abduct his high prince."

"There was no time to do otherwise. Your betrayers were closing in upon you. It was most ill-advised, that disguise of yours. No true Olenyas could have been deceived by it; and word passed swiftly that three impostors had taken the road to Kundri'j, and two of them extraordinarily tall, and one on a blue-eyed stallion."

"I do not see one of them, though he was caught with us. Nor have I seen the stallion."

"You shall see them," Aranos said. "Come now, my brother and my lord. You have always suspected me of hungering after your titles: of lying and deceiving and even slaying in order to gain them. And yet the brothers whom you thought you loved, whom you went so far as to trust, turned against you. Can you alter your vision of me? Can you begin to see that I may not be your enemy?"

"You were the heir apparent until I was born."

"Apparent only," said Aranos. "It was known to me even before our father wedded your mother that I would be supplanted by a legitimate son. When our father went in pursuit of the Gileni princess, there was open fear in the High Court, and no little resistance to the prospect of a halfblood heir; but heir most certainly that child would be. When he returned alone and rejected, to drown his sorrows in his harem and thereby to sire his mighty army of sons, I knew that in the end he would surrender to necessity. As indeed he did. He took the sister-bride who was chosen for him. He sired your sisters, those who died of their frailty and the one who lived to be her mother's image. Then at last he sired you. I would have been glad; I would have been properly your brother. But your mother would not abide me. The others she feared little or not at all. I who was eldest, whose blood was high and quite as pure as your own, in her eyes was deadly. Neither of you ever sought to learn the truth of me."

Sarevan looked from one to the other of them. He did not try to speak. Hirel was white and rigid. Aranos was pure limpid verity.

Very slowly Hirel said, "I do not know whom to trust."

"You trust yon outland prince."

Hirel's eyes flashed on Sarevan, white-rimmed as a startled senel's. "He is not Asanian."

"Do you therefore mistrust yourself?"

Hirel's fists clenched upon his knees. He drew a swift sharp breath. "Prove yourself to me. Ride with me to Kundri'j. Stand behind me on Autumn Firstday. Name me living man; proclaim me high prince before our father."

Sarevan watched Aranos narrowly. The princeling seemed unshaken and unstartled. He said with perfect calm, "So I had meant to do."

"If you lie," said Hirel softly, "then you had best destroy me now. For if I live, even if I live unmanned, or slave, or cripple, I will have your life in return for your treachery."

"I do not lie," Aranos said. He went down once more, prostrating himself, kissing the floor at Hirel's feet. "You are my high prince. You will be my emperor."

Aranos kept at least one of his promises. His guards brought Zha'dan to them. The Zhil'ari was unharmed save for a goodly measure of Sarevan's own trapped terrors, and quite as bare as Sarevan had been. He had refused a robe; they had refused him a kilt. He greeted his companions with a cry of joy and a leap that brought blades leaping out of sheaths. Hirel had to fend off the guards. Sarevan had had the breath crushed out of him. Zha'dan had lost even tradespeech; he babbled in his own tongue, too fast for Sarevan to follow, until Sarevan shook him into silence.

He drew back, searching Sarevan's face. "They caged you," he said. There was no lightness in him; none of the bright reckless temper with which he liked to mask what he was. "I heard you. I thought they had broken you."

"Am I so fragile?" Sarevan asked him, the sharper for that he came so close to the truth.

He frowned. "They think they know what you are. They're fools."

"Are they treacherous?"

"They all are, here." Zha'dan looked as if his head hurt. "They don't want to kill you. Either of you. Yet. The ivory doll—have you seen him? He has more in that tiny head of his than anyone might imagine. I don't like him," said Zha'dan, "but he thinks it's to his advantage to serve the little stallion. For now."

"I wonder why," said Sarevan.

He was thinking aloud, but Hirel answered him. "Convenience. And cleverness. If all is as he has told us, we owe him a debt for our escape. That can be parlayed into very great power."

"But not imperial power."

"He is my heir until I sire a son."

"You'd best get about it, then, hadn't you?"

Hirel blushed, but his tongue had not lost its sting. "Can you preach to me, O priest of the Sun?"

Sarevan grinned. "A priest can always preach. It's practice he has to walk shy of." He shook off levity. "Are you going to trust him?"

"I have little choice."

Sarevan bowed to that. "We can all walk warily. I'll guard your back; will you guard mine?"

"Until it behooves me to betray you," answered Hirel, "yes."

Hirel armed himself and rode in the free air as one of Aranos' men-at-arms. He did not even need his helmet unless he wished to wear it: his face was pure High Asanian, but there were others like it in the company.

Sarevan and Zha'dan had no such fortune. Sarevan refused flatly the concealment of the litter, and shied away from Aranos' great curtained chariot with its team of blue dun mares. He was betraying his cowardice, he knew it, but he could not master himself. He insisted on his freedom and the sweet familiarity of Bregalan's back. He won it, and Zha'dan won it with him, but as always, at a price. He wore armor from head to foot, magewrought to his measure, with a great masked helm. It was ridiculously ornate and ridiculously uncomfortable, but it matched him to the small company of the princeling's personal guard; and it hid all his strangenesses.

The mages rode with their master. The forging had wearied them; they slept, perhaps, behind the swaying curtains. Sarevan did not like to think that a darkmage had had a hand in the making of his armor. It seemed perfectly earthly gilded bronze; no stink of evil clung to it. Only when he first put it on did his branded hand throb as at the touch of power; thereafter he had no pain, of hand or of head.

If a lordling of the Middle Court or a riding of *shiu'oth Olenyai* could win free passage on the roads, a prince of the High Court could empty them before him. To him all inns were open, all posthouses his own to command; if that did not please him, he had his way of the local lords. No one impeded him; no one ventured to question him.

That Hirel had not chosen to ride in comfort with his brother was a mild scandal in the guard. Sarevan and Zha'dan were endurable: they were only outlanders, however royal they might consider themselves, and they did not inflict their barbarian faces on good human men. Hirel was more than human, and they all knew it. They liked not at all to have him riding knee to knee with the least of them, cropped head bare, helmet on saddlebow in the heat, looking as mortal as any man.

He did not seem to notice, still less to care. Often he rode by Sarevan at the tail of the princeling's personal guard and the head of the company of men-at-arms. Sometimes he reached across as if he could not help it, and stroked Bregalan's neck. He did not ask to ride the stallion, nor would he let Sarevan offer it. He was turned in upon himself. He spoke, sometimes, in the beginning, but the Asanians would not answer him. After the first morning he did not speak at all.

On the fourth night of the compact with Aranos, three days yet at swift pace from Kundri'j Asan and four days shy of Autumn Firstday, the princeling took an inn for himself. Its patrons left perforce, with no objections that they let him or his small army hear.

It was not fitting, Sarevan had been told the first night he tried it, that he bed down with the guard. He suspected that they were not pleased to bed down with a barbarian. He was given a chamber of his own; he was allowed to keep Zha'dan with him. Tonight he had been offered his choice of the house's women, an error which had not been committed before. Someone must have forgotten to warn the innkeeper. He was interested to witness Hirel's swift and scathing refusal on his behalf. It was much swifter and more scathing than his own would have been. Everyone looked at Zha'dan and thought he understood. Some looked at Hirel, longer, and grew very wise. The boy quelled them by choosing the most comely of the women and departing for his chamber, from which neither of them returned.

Sarevan went slowly to his solitary bed. Zha'dan took station across the door, too wise to long for what he could not have, too fastidious to sample the innkeeper's culls. "Once was enough," he said as he spread his blanket. "They're not clean, these people. No wonder they shave themselves smooth. Else they'd crawl with vermin."

"They say much the same of us, I think," Sarevan said.

Zha'dan snorted. Even if he had not bathed every day, more often if he could manage it, he would not have deigned to entertain small itching guests. Vermin did not like mages, even apprentice mages of the Zhil'ari.

Some air of it must still have clung to Sarevan. He was in comfort, in that respect at least. He lay and closed his eyes and tried not to think. It was hard. Last night, after a blessed respite, he had dreamed again. The old darkness; the old fear. But at the end of it, strangeness, which he both hoped and feared was not prophecy but plain dreaming born of wish and fear and the day's living.

It was clear in him even yet, try though he would to blot it out. After the lightning-torn blackness of foreseeing, a soft light. Lamplight on walls of grey stone; a tapestry, rich and intricate, alive with myriad figures: beasts, birds, blossoms, a jeweled dragonel. He was lying on softness, languid, free for a little while of either horror or urgency; although there was a strangeness in him, in the way he lay, in the way his body felt, it did not trouble him. Stranger still was the way his heart was singing.

A light finger caressed his cheek. Its touch was very distinct. It made him shiver with pleasure. He turned his head. In his dream he knew no surprise at all, nor any of the alarm that in waking would have cast him into flight. It was perfectly and properly right that Hirel should be lying there with all his masks laid aside, smiling a warm and sated smile. Sarevan's mind had not even troubled to transform him into a woman. He was a little older and a great deal larger—as large, impossibly, as Sarevan himself—and quite incontestably a man.

Perhaps he would have spoken. Sarevan never knew. Zha'dan had awakened him, calling him to the sunrise prayer and the day's riding.

All day, as they rode, Sarevan had caught himself shooting glances at the boy: not a simple feat in the heavy gilded helm. Hirel showed no signs of growing suddenly to match Sarevan's Gileni height. Sarevan's body did not yearn toward him as it had in the dream, although he was most comely in the plain harness of a man-at-arms, erect and proud, sitting his mount with the easy grace of the born rider.

It was the mind, Sarevan told himself as he lay alone. It confused the body with the soul. He did not want Hirel to his bed.

Then why, asked a small wicked portion of his self, was he tossing in it like a thwarted lover?

Because he was dream-maddened. Because on Autumn Firstday he would be one-and-twenty, and his body had never known either woman or man, but his mind—his wild mageling's mind—had known them both very well indeed.

The Litany of Pain frayed in his head and scattered. He tried to mock himself. It was the Asanian air. It was full of lechery. He offended its sense of rightness; it struggled to make him like all the rest of the Golden Empire. Would it then turn his copper to gold and bleach his skin to ivory?

He rose on his elbow, regarding himself in the nightlamp's flicker. He was quite as perfectly a mongrel as he had ever been, and rather more rampantly male than he was wont to be. He covered it, somewhat, with the robe which one was expected to wear to sleep here: odd constricting custom, but useful if one were in a state which one did not wish to proclaim to every eye.

Zha'dan did not stir when Sarevan stepped over him. Sarevan prowled softly through the passages. Movement cooled him a little. No one else was abroad. Aranos' guards eyed him warily but did not challenge him.

The kitchen's fires were banked, cooks and scullions snoring in concert. A grin of pure mischief found its way to Sarevan's face. Royal prince and man grown he might be, but he was young yet; and it took more than a year or six to forget old skills. He uncovered a trove of sweet cakes and a flask of the thin sour wine that was all they seemed to drink here. He filled a napkin, appropriated the flask.

A small door opened on starlight and coolness. He had found the kitchen garden; a breeze was keeping at bay the stink of the midden. Near the wall stood a bench overhung by a tree in full and fragrant fruit. He sat back against the bole, filling himself with cakes and fruit, drinking from the flask. His body's heat had all but faded; the ache of it was passing. He stretched to pluck another sweetapple.

His hand stopped. Someone was walking toward him among the beds of herbs. A remnant of youthful guilt made him tense to bolt. The rest of him remembered that he was a wild boy no longer; no one would dare now to thrash him for his thievery.

He finished plucking the apple. His eyes sharpened. Not one figure approached him but two. The other paced on four legs, a great graceful shadow with eyes that, turning upon him, flashed sudden green.

He forgot guilt, manhood, gluttony, even the very fruit in his hand. Ulan met him in midleap, singing his joy-song. "Brother," Sarevan sang back in a loving purr. "O brother!"

Ulan butted him full in his center. He dropped to his rump half in the path, half in pungent herbs. He clung to the great neck and laughed, breathing cat-musk and silversage, while Ulan feigned with mighty snarlings to devour him. It was love, purely. He lost himself in it.

He remembered the sweetapple first. He was still holding it. He laughed at that, using Ulan for a handhold as he pulled himself to his feet.

He was almost body to body with Ulan's erstwhile companion. It was, his skin knew utterly and instantly, a woman. He drew back swiftly, not quite recoiling, shaping a spate of apologies.

None of them passed his tongue. The stranger had become a shape he knew: plain epicene Asanian, he had thought the creature, or even a eunuch. Tonsured for Uvarra's service; robed as a mage. The darkmage.

Knowledge and starlight limned her face, transformed eunuch softness into very feminine strength. She was not beautiful. She did not need to be. She made his body sing.

And yet his heart was cold. She had come with Ulan. A black sorceress. She had seen him in naked joy. She knew, now, the most mortal of his weaknesses.

Ulan purred against him. The cat was not bewitched. Sarevan would have known. There was no mark on him; no stink of evil.

Perhaps she sensed Sarevan's thoughts. She seemed amused. "He is a great hunter, your brother," she said. "Did you know that he tracks by scent of power? He marked mine. He cast me from my bed, that I might conduct him to you."

All of Sarevan's training cried to him that she lied; that no servant of darkness ever told the truth. And yet he knew that it was so. Ulan could scent magery. It would be like him to seek out a mage, to demand an escort to his lost brother. He knew how a simple man would see him; he did not like to be shot at.

And yet, a darkmage. Sarevan glared at the cat. He felt betrayed.

Ulan sat, yawned, began to lick his paw. His nose wrinkled. He did not like the scent of silversage.

Yes, the witch was amused. "I see," she said, "that the tales are in error that give you the readiest tongue in Keruvarion. Or is it that a priest of your order may not address a woman?"

Sarevan's cheeks flamed. "What do I have to say to you? You are a slave of the dark."

"Are you any less a slave of the light?" she inquired calmly.

"Your kind should be scoured from the earth."

She sat on the bench which Sarevan had abandoned. Her robe was belted loosely; it opened as she moved. He caught a glimpse of full and lovely breasts.

His own was not belted at all. He clutched it about him.

She smiled. "One always fears most what one knows least."

"I know all I need to know."

That was feeble, and they both knew it. She took up a cake, nibbled it with visible pleasure. "Avaryan was Uvarra, long ago. She has kept her two faces. He has bound himself to one alone. That I serve the night, that my power is of the moons' dark, does not bar me from either the arts or the worship of the light."

"There, priestess, you speak false. No servant of Night can abide the Sun."

"Is it so among your people?" She sounded both shocked and sad. "Is it all so twisted? Do you know nothing of the truth?"

The hand with the apple in it whipped back. She sat still, clear-eyed, unfrightened. She looked horribly like Hirel. With a curse he spun away from her, flinging the apple with all his strength. It arced high over the wall. He never heard it fall.

"You know," she said. "In your heart, you know. If you did not, you would not have come to Asanion."

A shudder racked him. "I came to stop a war."

"Just so."

He whirled. "You came to stop me. You find I can't be ensorceled. You think I can be seduced. First with my brother; then with your body."

She laughed in pure mirth. "See what Avaryan's vows can do to a man! If I seduced you, prince, it would not be to destroy you. It would be to heal you."

Asanian cant. It sickened him. "What makes you think that I could want you?"

"In your condition," she said with sweet malice, "any female would suffice." She looked him up and down. "You will prosper in Kundri'j. The High Court will find even your rudeness delightful."

"I'm going to be allowed to get so far?"

"We have labored long to see that you do."

"Why?"

"Rude," she mused to herself, "or perhaps simply unsubtle. And young; and ill taught; and I think, though you are no coward, afraid. It is not easy to learn that all one believed in is a lie."

"Not all," he whispered.

"Most." She laced her fingers in her lap. "I am not what you expected, am I? I am almost human."

"Your power stands against all that I am."

"Does it? Have you ever encountered a true darkmage?"

"I have taken the power of one. I slew his ally; she took my power with her. She was," said Sarevan tightly, "very like you."

"They were a testing. You failed it."

He shut his eyes. His fists were clenched. He should turn and walk away, for his soul's sake. He could not. "I have faced an Eye of Power. It was evil beyond conceiving. No sane mind could endure it, still less hope to wield it."

"Not all power is either easy or pleasant. Some of it must be neither; just as the summer requires winter's cold for its fulfillment."

That was the truth of his dream. She mocked it. For if she did not, then all that he had done had been to serve the dark, and he was worse than a traitor: he had betrayed his god.

"We of the Mageguild know what is," she said, "and what must be. I tell you a secret, Sun-prince. Every mage is one of two. Every initiate is chosen by a facet of the power, dark or light; and every one finds his match in another who is his opposite."

His eyes snapped open.

"So," she said, "are we complete. No dark without light. No light without dark. Balance, always."

"Then the other priest—is—"

"My brother. My other self."

He tossed his head. His voice shook; he could not steady it. "You should not have told me that."

"You will not betray us."

He laughed. It was half a sob. "I am the blackest traitor who has ever been."

"I trust you," she said. She stood and bowed in Asanian fashion, hands to breast. "Good night, high prince. May the darkness give you rest."

Sarevan gasped, shuddered. When he had his voice again, she was gone.

Sixteen

*T*HEY CALLED HER QUEEN OF CITIES, HEART OF THE Golden Empire, most ancient of the dwellings of mankind, sacred whore, bride of emperors, throne of the gods: Kundri'j Asan. She sprawled across the plain of Greatflood, Shahriz'uan the mighty that bore the heart's blood of Asanion, flowing from the wastes of ice to the Burning Sea. There was no greater city, none older and none more beautiful. Its walls were ninefold, sheathed each in precious stone: white marble, black marble, lapis, carnelian, jasper, malachite and ice-blue agate; and the eighth was silver, and the ninth was all gold. Within the circles of the city were a thousand temples, domes and spires crusted with jewels and with gold, and among them the mansions of princes, the hovels of paupers, the dwellings and the shops, the forges and the markets, tanneries, perfumeries, silkweavers and netweavers, stables and mews and shambles, side by side and interwoven in the ordered disorder of a living thing.

Sarevan saw little enough of it, his first day in it. Aranos entered it like a storm off the plains, cleaving its crowds, thundering up the Processional Way on which none might ride but princes or the followings of princes. They were not acclaimed as a high lord would be in Keruvarion. Silence was Asanian reverence. It was eerie to Varyani senses, to ride in that wave of stillness; to be the only clamor within their ears' reach. And as far as their eyes could stretch, only a sea of bent backs, bowed heads, bodies prostrate upon the stones.

The Golden Palace opened to embrace them. Its arms were splendid and cold. Its secrets were impenetrable.

Not for long, Sarevan promised himself. He had to leave Bregalan, who was not pleased; he had Aranos' word of honor that the stallion would be accorded the reverence due a king. Ulan and Zha'dan clung close to him, pressing against him, darting wary glances from under lowered brows.

They were led in haste to Aranos' chambers and there secluded, with picked guards at the door. Aranos left them with a warning. "Be free of these rooms," he said. "But do not wander abroad, nor eat nor drink aught but what these my slaves shall bring you."

None of them answered him. Hirel stood very still and watched him go. Then, slowly, he turned about. Sarevan very nearly forgot all his wisdom. Came perilously close to pulling the boy into his arms: stroking him, shaking him, shouting at him—anything to warm that slowly chilling face.

A great anger rose to fill Sarevan's soul. It was not his wonted, fiery temper, as swiftly calmed as provoked. It was cold; it was bitter. It found its echo and its spur in Hirel's eyes. No man should live the life these chambers spoke of. Splendid, remote, and chill. Forbidden human warmth, forbidden even the touch of a hand, because he was royal, because he was sacred, because he would be emperor, and the emperor must be more than a man.

And less. As the image of a god is more, because it stands high and apart in its perfection. As that same image is less, because it has no heart. It is only gilded stone. Lifeless and soulless, mere empty beauty, cold to the touch and comfortless.

Flesh yielded under Sarevan's fingers; blod pulsed, muscle tautened in resistance. But the eyes were jet and amber. "Let me go," said Hirel.

"I will not," said Sarevan.

The eyes measured him. He knew to the last degree what their judgment would be. Outlander; barbarian. Blatant and improbable mongrel. Mage who had been, cripple who was. And against all of that: Prince. Emperor's son. Son of the son of a god.

He was, perhaps, worthy to kiss one of those slender and surpassingly comely feet.

Sarevan laughed suddenly, opened his hands, dealt the boy a cuff that was half a caress. "Cubling, stop trying to glare down your nose at me."

Hirel's nostrils flared. "You—"

"Bastard?" Sarevan suggested helpfully. "Son of a hound? Slave's whelp? Sensible man?"

"Sensible man!" Hirel spat the words. Caught himself. Struggled for composure. Failed dismally. *"You?"*

"Are you? You let Aranos bring us to this place, after all. What were you hoping for? That the rest of your brothers would be here to arrange your convenient disposal?"

"Aranos may have gone to do just that." But Hirel was calming, and not into that cold and terrible stillness. He turned about again, more quickly than before. "I have never been here," he said.

"What, never?"

Sarevan won a burning glance. It comforted him. "Are yours different?" he asked.

Hirel shrugged. "Mine are white and gold. And larger, a little. He is Second Prince before the Golden Throne. I am high prince. Will be. Tomorrow."

"Tomorrow," Sarevan agreed, setting all his confidence in it.

They wandered through the rooms. They were somber in their splendor, black and silver and midnight blue. There were very many of them. Zha'dan was round-eyed. "Ostentatious," Sarevan said to him, deprecating room on room of nothing but clothing. One whole chamber held only gloves. Gloves for dancing. Gloves for riding in one's chariot. Gloves that were all a crust of jewels, for dazzling the High Court. Gloves that were finer than gossamer, for receiving one's concubines.

"For receiving one's concubines?" Sarevan repeated, holding one up to the lamp's light. It was like a doll's glove, tiny and perfect and utterly absurd.

Hirel snatched it out of his hand and flung it against the wall. "Do not mock what you cannot understand!"

They stared at him. He seemed to have forgotten them. He confronted a mirror. It reflected a young man in plain armor with the dust of travel thick upon him, and his face white beneath it, and his eyes wild. "Look at me," he said. They were mute, looking. Hirel raised a clenched fist, bit down hard. Blood sprang, sudden and frightening. He did not heed it. He drew breath, shuddering. "I shall be a disgrace. They will mock me, all of them. My head shorn, my body grown lank and awkward, my voice less sweet than a raven's. I have dwelt among the lowborn; I have broken bread with them. I have walked in the sun, all bare, and the sun has stained me. And I have touched—I have touched—"

Sarevan did not stop to think. He pulled him in. Stroked him, shook him, murmured words forgotten before they were spoken. And Hirel suffered it. For a very little while he clung, trembling.

He stiffened. Sarevan let him go. His hand was still bleeding. He sucked on it; saw what he was doing; thrust it down. "You see," he said, faint and bitter. "I am not worthy."

"You're more worthy of princehood now than you ever were." Sarevan took the wounded hand between his own. "Listen to me, Hirel Uverias. You've changed, yes. Inevitably. You've grown. The child I found in a fernbrake was a soft thing, plump and pretty like a lady's lapcat. Even after his few days' suffering, he knew surely that the world belonged to him; he was the center of it, and all the rest existed to serve him. He was an insufferable little creature. I had all I could do not to throw him across my knee and spank him soundly."

Hirel flung up his head in outrage. But he did not say what once he would have said.

Sarevan saluted him, not all in mockery. "You see? You're not a man yet, not by a long road, but you're well started on it. You'll certainly make a prince."

Hirel's lips thinned. He raised his chin minutely. He began to speak; stopped. He spun on his heel and stalked toward the outer rooms, and Aranos' slaves, and a bath and food and a bed for his weary body.

The slaves had no little to endure. Hirel they seemed delighted to serve, but the outlanders and the great cat both shocked and terrified them. Sarevan began it in the bath, by stripping and plunging into the great basin and swimming from end to end of it. Hirel, being scoured clean on the grate beside the pool, allowed himself the shadow of a grin.

Sarevan folded his arms on the basin's rim and floated, and grinned back. Zha'dan was watching the scrubbing and the pumicing with real dismay. One or two of the slaves eyed him; one had a razor in hand. Zha'dan took refuge with Sarevan in the pool. "He hardly has any fleece yet," the Zhil'ari said of Hirel, "and look: they're taking it. How can he let them?"

"It's the custom here," said Sarevan.

"Not for us!"

"Certainly not," Sarevan said, baring his teeth at the slave with the razor. The eunuch blanched and backed away. "We're outland princes. We keep our own customs."

"If that's so," said Zha'dan, "I want a kilt. And paint. And gauds. I want to look like a man again."

Aranos' slaves were ingenious: they found all three. Sarevan did his braids for him. It was not a thing a slave could do; it were best done by a lover. A Sun-prince sufficed. Zha'dan was almost purring, at ease with himself for the first time since he came to Endros Avaryan.

His contentment coaxed a smile out of Hirel, which passed too quickly. The boy would not eat, though he would drink: too much, to Sarevan's mind. He would not hear of stopping. When Sarevan pressed, Hirel drove them all out, cursing them with acid softness. Sarevan let himself be driven. Hirel was in no mood to accept any comfort that he could give. Perhaps wine and solitude would calm him; steel him to face what on the morrow he must face.

The bed to which Sarevan was led was a very comfortable one, a proper eastern bed hung on a frame of sweetwood and covered with scarlet silk. Sarevan buried himself in it. Ulan poured himself across the foot of it. Zha'dan set himself, as was his wont, across the door.

Sarevan worked his toes into Ulan's thick fur and sighed. Tonight, he thought, he could sleep. It made him smile, though with a touch of bitterness. They said it of his father: he always slept in perfect peace before a battle.

He did not want to think of his father, whom tomorrow he would betray before the High Court of Asanion.

He rubbed the healing skin beneath his beard, lazily, yawning. His eyelids fell of their own weight.

A supple body lay beside him. Wise fingers found the knots of tension in his back. Warm lips followed, and a nip of teeth.

Sarevan thrust himself up on his hands. "Damn it, who told them I wanted—"

Hirel slid beneath him, all gold in the nightlamp's glow. Sarevan pulled away with tight-leashed violence. "What are you doing here? Zha'dan's not here; he's over yonder. Get out of my bed!"

"Prince," said Hirel, and he sounded not at all like the boy whom Sarevan had thought he knew. This was a man, weary to exhaustion, with no strength left for temper. "Prince, forbear. Or I swear to you, I will weep, and if I weep you will see me do it, and if you see me I will hate you for it."

The tears had already begun. Sarevan wanted to groan aloud, to thrust the young demon away from him, to shout for Zha'dan. Who could give Hirel what he wanted; what he needed on this night of all nights. Who could dry those damnable tears.

Hirel buried his face in Sarevan's shoulder and clung. Sarevan's arms went round him. He was fever-warm; his skin was silken; he smelled of wine and musk and clean young body. He was slender and strong, like a warrior woman. But he was no woman at all.

He was an Asanian courtesan, and he knew precisely what he was doing.

Sarevan lifted him bodily and bore him to the door, kneeling burdened beside Zha'dan. The Zhil'ari lay motionless, wide-eyed. Sarevan pried the arms from about his neck and held them well away from him, meeting the burning golden stare. "You know I can't," he said.

Hirel tore his right arm free and struck, backhanded. Sarevan swayed with the blow. "You are no man," Hirel spat at him. "Virgin. Limpyard. Eunuch!"

"When the wine's worn off, little brother, you're going to be sorry you let it rule you." Sarevan let go the boy's left arm. It did not strike. He brushed away a tear that crept down the rigid cheek.

Hirel shivered convulsively. "Damn you," he said. "Oh, damn you."

Sarevan stood. "Zha'dan. Love him for me." He turned. It was wrenchingly hard. His torque, gold and iron both, was strangling him. He cast himself down and cursed them all.

Sarevan had seen splendor. He had seen the festivals with which the Sunborn had regaled his armies. He had seen the lords of Keruvarion riding in triumph to the Feast of the Peace that ended the great wars in the empire. He had seen the consecration of Endros Avaryan, and the games of High Summer there every year after, and his own confirmation as High Prince of the Sun.

He had seen splendor. This did not blind him, but it widened his eyes a little. The Asanians granted to the gateway of autumn that preeminence which belonged to Keruvarion to the gateway of summer. Then were all the gods worshipped. Boys became men, girls became women; marriages were made, children named and presented in the temples, heirs proclaimed and lordships allotted and princes taken into their princedoms. The emperor held full court in the great hall of his palace, the Hall of the Thousand Years with its thousand carven pillars upholding a roof of gold. So huge was that hall that an army could array itself therein; armies had, for festivals, for the pleasure of emperors: even mounted warriors whirling upon the sand that lay beneath the inlaid panels of the floor. At the hall's farthest extent the panels were lifted from a moat of glittering sand: dust of gold, and a kingdom's worth of jewels crushed and strewn beneath the armored feet of a hundred knights. These were the Golden Guard of the Golden Throne, princes of the princes of Olenyai, a living wall about their emperor.

He sat alone within the circle of his knights, raised high upon his throne. It was no eastern chair but a great bowl of gold set upon the backs of golden lions. Even its cushions were of cloth of gold. He sat erect, banked in them, a golden image, masked and crowned and robed in the ninefold robe of the highest of all kings.

His sons held the foremost rank of the court, and Aranos foremost of them, standing with his guards and his mages and his priests before the emperor's face, three spearlengths from the Golden Guard. The prince wore full court dress, almost too heavy to stand in: the robe of seven thicknesses to which his rank entitled him, with its hood woven of gold and silk laid on his shoulders, baring his artfully painted face. He was expected to stand but permitted to lean on the arms of his two most favored mages.

Sarevan, fantastically armored and viciously uncomfortable, had taken station with Aranos' personal guard. As the tallest of the line save for Zha'dan who stood beside him, he had been given the place of honor directly behind the prince. Hirel was farther down, invisible unless he turned his head in the stiff and blinkering helmet. Which he did, more than once, damning discipline. Hirel's armor was as ridiculous as his own, his visor a dragon mask with darkness in the slits of its eyes. Of Hirel there was nothing to be seen.

When the boy woke to a pale dawn, he had been quite as catastrophically sick as Sarevan had expected. Aranos' slaves had brought him a potion with which he seemed unhappily familiar. He took it with distaste, grimacing as he swallowed it, but it brought the light back to his eyes and the color to his cheeks. He even ate a bite or two, under duress. Thereafter he seemed much as he always was, facing what he had to face with admirable steadiness.

Sarevan was not sure he trusted it. Hirel had not spoken to him since the night's bitter words. He had not let Sarevan touch him in his sickness; when Sarevan tried to speak, he turned his back. He had put on his haughtiest mask, at its most insufferable angle.

Sarevan sighed and faced forward. He could not see the army of Hirel's brothers, but he could feel them behind him. Aranos had come in last and most royal; they had had to bow as he marched in slow procession before them. Sarevan had had time to number them, even to consider faces. Forty, he had counted, which could not be all of them: the rest, no doubt, were too young or too indisposed to stand in court. Boys and youths and young men of every shade from umber to ivory, clad variously according to degree in robes of five and six and seven, bull-broad and whip-thin, twitching with nervousness and motionless with hauteur, beautiful and unbeautiful and frankly ugly, but all marked with the stamp of their lineage. It might be as little as the set of the head. It might be as complete as Hirel himself, whose portrait graced the Hall of the High Princes; but that portrait was his father's before him, and his father's father's.

Sarevan had marked two princes most clearly. They stood highest but for Aranos; like him and like no other save a handful of very young children, they wore the sevenfold robes of princes of the first degree. They were not the least comely of the emperor's sons. Indeed Vuad might have surpassed Hirel but for the misfortune that had given him hair the color of old bronze. That was reckoned a flaw here, and a tragedy; Sarevan thought it very handsome. But he was only a tarry-skinned barbarian with no eye for beauty.

Sayel he liked less, at least to look at. He was a pale creature, handsome enough if one were fond of milk and water, attired unwisely in gradations of crimson. His eyes were sharper than Vuad's, his tension less readily apparent. He was watching Aranos as a bird watches a cat: in fear, but mindful of its beak and its claws. He had noticed the prince's following. Too carefully. By the pricking of Sarevan's nape as the ceremonies crawled on, he was still noticing it.

Sarevan shifted infinitesimally. His back itched. His bladder twinged. He cursed them both, and his armor into the bargain: steaming hot, hideously heavy, and far too ornate to trust in any battle. If its weight did not fell him, its curlicues would, catching blades and hampering his arms.

He would not have to fight. Not here. Not in front of the Asanian emperor. Courtiers waged their battles more subtly, with poisoned words and poisoned wine.

It was close now. He dared a twist of his body, a sweep of his eyes within the helmet. The princes had tensed subtly. Their eyes were wide and bright.

A very young lord was being presented to the emperor with the full rite, even to the nine prostrations. He performed them with grace and composure, although his face was ashen.

He rose for the last time, said the words which he must say, backed from the presence. When he had taken his place among the ranked nobles, there was silence. Bodies shifted, eyes flickered. Only Aranos did not move.

With imperial slowness Ziad-Ilarios stood. Not dignity alone constrained him: his robes were heavy, as heavy as all his burden of empire. He rose like an image ensorceled to life, and his face was no face at all, but a mask of beaten gold.

It was custom, Hirel had told Sarevan. The mask was the mask of a god: ageless, flawless, impervious to human frailties. How simple then, Saraven had said, to murder an emperor in secret and to take on his mask and his name and his power. Hirel had been far from amused. The common crowd was not to know when an emperor was old or ill or uncomely. Indeed the emperor who had begun the custom had been an outland invader with a terribly scarred face and the gall to have won his predecessor's confidence, wedded that emperor's only daughter, and disposed of his marriage-father by means more foul than fair. But no one in the years since had succeeded in perpetrating an imposture. Not only were the princes and the queens and certain of the High Court entitled to see their lord's face; his identity was attested at intervals by a council of priests and lords, aged and wary and incorruptible.

So had they attested at the beginning of this endless festival. Sarevan did not need to be told. His skin knew who wore that mask; the void behind his eyes was sure of it.

Save only when he spoke of matters of the highest import, the emperor did not speak even to the High Court. A Voice spoke for him, a shadow-speaker, a herald in black whose mask was black and featureless but whose voice was rich and full. "It is time," he proclaimed, "and time, and time. The throne is filled, its majesty is strong, may its bearer live forever. But even highest majesty, which makes the laws, must also obey them. So was it decreed in the days of Asutharanyas whose memory is everlasting: Every lord must name his heir. If that heir be of full years, one naming suffices. If said heir be yet in his minority, whether babe newborn or youth well grown, he must himself, upon attainment of his manhood, request and receive the name of heir from the lips of his lord. Then only may his title be affirmed." The herald paused. The silence deepened. Even the myriad sounds of a myriad people living and breathing and standing close together had sunk into stillness. "On the first day of autumn in the thirty-second year of the reign of the divine emperor, Garan-Shiraz Oluenyas, whose memory endures forever, to the High Prince Ziad inShiraz Ilarios and to the Princess Azia of pure blood and great worship, was born a son: Asuchirel inZiad Uverias, highborn, chosen heir of the chosen heir of Asanion. In the eighth year of the reign of his majesty, the great one, the Lion, the golden warrior of Asanion, Ziad inShiraz Ushallin Ilarios, came word of the death of his chosen heir. In the night it came, in the spring of the year, in grief immeasurable.

"But the law endures; it knows no grief. Every lord, even to the very lord of lords, must name his heir. It is time; it is time and time. Hear and attend."

The silence focused, stirred, began to thrum. This was the highest of moments. The emperor must speak as the law commanded; he must name a name. The princes waited, even Aranos standing erect, alert, forsaking his pretense of ennui. It smote Sarevan then, almost felling him. How cruelly, how bitterly they had failed. The *emperor* must name the name. If Hirel had gone to him, made himself known, assured himself of the naming—but they had obeyed Aranos. They had trusted him; they had let him seclude them all. And thus, serpentinely, he mocked them. Ziad-Ilarios did not even know that his true heir was there to be chosen. Before Hirel's very face he would name Aranos the heir of Asanion.

In the mighty silence, metal chinked on metal. Sarevan glanced aside, cursed the helmet, turned half his body.

One of Aranos' guards had left his post. He stood on the glittering sand all alone. The Golden Guard lowered their spears, warning. He had discarded his own.

The emperor seemed not to see him. He was only a lone madman, a nonentity; beyond the sand, only the princes could know that he was there. The Guard would deal with him; the court need never know what had passed. The golden mask lifted.

The man on the sand moved swiftly. His hands caught at his corselet. The emperor's knights began to close in upon him. Sarevan left his place, elbowing through startled guardsmen, shrinking slaves, the odd inscrutable mage.

Within the elaborate armor, hidden clasps gave way. The whole clever shell opened at once and fell clattering to the sand. Robes gleamed beneath, white on white on white: simplicity of purely Asanian complexity. There were seven of them. And over them, a shimmer of gold. The eighth robe, the imperial robe, the robe of the high prince.

A grey shadow sprang from air, or perhaps from among the mages. It crouched before Hirel. Its snarl was soft and distinct and most deadly. The emperor's knights paused.

Sarevan won his way to Hirel's back. Zha'dan was with him. They stood, warding him.

He seemed aware of none of them. His back was straight, slender still for all the waxing breadth of his shoulders; proud and yet ineffably lonely with all the staring eyes behind him and his helmeted face turned toward his father. He set his hands to the helmet's plumed extravagance. He flung it aside with sudden and most uncourtly force, shaking out his shorn hair. He raised his chin and fixed his eyes upon the emperor.

Sarevan's mouth was dry. He would have given much to be able to see the faces of Vuad and Sayel. But more, infinitely more, to see the emperor's. The mask betrayed nothing at all of the man behind it. He had half a hundred sons. Would he even recognize this one, altered as he was, grown from child into man? And even if he did, would he name the boy his heir?

Hirel did a thing that could only be perfect courage, unless it was perfect insanity. He walked forward. Ulan walked with him. He walked straight and unwavering toward the lowered steel. Just before the first spearpoint touched his breast, he raised a hand.

The spears hesitated. Suddenly they swung up. The Olenyai stepped slowly back.

The princes could see all of it. Perhaps some of them understood it. In the hall beyond, the silence's length had begun to rouse wonder. A murmur grew.

Hirel set his foot on the first step of the dais. He went no farther. He stood, waiting, eyes lifted still to his father. People behind the princes saw him now, and the beast with him, and the two tall guards. Their voices were like a wind in the forest, swelling to a roar.

Still the emperor did not move. His mask was bent upon his son. His Voice wavered, at a loss.

Sarevan was beginning to twitch. This had gone on much too long. If the man in the mask did not soon make up his mind, if mind he had to make up, there was going to be a riot in the hall.

Sarevan tore at the catches of his armor, shook off the shell of it, kicked it out of the way. Were those gasps behind him? He had had his own splendor of folly: he had demanded, and received, full and imperial northern finery. It would seem very nakedness to these people. White sandals laced to the knee. White kilt. A great burden of gold and rubies hung wherever an ornament would hang. It left a remarkable quantity of bare skin. Zha'dan had twisted his hair into high chieftain's braids: the Zhil'ari did not know the Ianyn royal way, and there had been no time to teach him. No one here would know the difference; and it did not matter. The color of the many woven plaits was proof enough of his station.

He tossed down his helmet, shook out all his braids, looked the emperor's mask in the eye and bowed his head briefly as king to king. "Lord emperor," he said, clear and cool above the rising tumult, "I bring you back your son." That won a spreading silence. Incredulous; avid with curiosity. Hirel was whitely furious. Sarevan hoped devoutly that Aranos was the same. He smiled. "Your son, lord emperor. Your heir, I believe. Will you name him, or shall I?"

That was boldness beyond belief. It awed even Hirel. It struck the High Court dumb.

The emperor did a terrible thing, an unheard-of thing. In all his casings of silk and velvet and cloth of the sun, in his mask and his crown and his wig of pure and deathly heavy gold, he stepped away from his throne. He moved with mighty dignity, with ponderous slowness. Yet he moved. He came down. On the step above Hirel, he stopped. He raised his hand. His knights tensed to spring. His son stood unmoving, braced for the blow.

The hand fell in its glittering glove. It closed upon Hirel's shoulder. He caught his breath as if with pain, but he did not waver. His eyes met the eyes within the mask.

It came up. A voice rolled forth from it. It was a beautiful voice, rich and deep, more beautiful even than his imperial Voice. "Asuchirel," said the Emperor of Asanion. "Asuchirel inZiad Uverias."

That was not, by any means, the end of it. Hirel and Sarevan between them had seen to that. They had shattered the ritual; they had shocked the High Court to its foundations.

It was rising to a riot when the emperor's knights swept them out of it. Hirel resisted. "We are not done," he said. Loudly, above the uproar. "I must take their homage. I must—"

"They'll take your hide," Sarevan said, laying hands on him, because no one else would. He was too furious to struggle.

Silence was blessed, and abrupt. Sarevan took in the chamber to which the Olenyai had herded them. It must have been meant for the emperor to rest in between audiences, or for hidden listeners to take their ease in while peering through screens at the throne and the hall. The screens were closed and barred now; one of the Olenyai drew curtains across it. There was something familiar about him; about his eyes above the helmet's molded mask.

Sarevan clapped hands to his swordless belt. All his weapons lay lost and useless on the floor of the hall. "Halid!"

The Olenyas bowed. His glance was ironic, his right-hand sword drawn and most eloquent. His companions ringed the walls: a round dozen.

Very slowly, very carefully, Sarevan turned back to Hirel. Ulan was alert but quiet. Likewise Zha'dan who had shed his armor, who was all

Zhil'ari beneath, painted with princely richness. "We seem," said
Sarevan, "to have made a mistake."

"Several mistakes."

The Olenyai snapped to attention. A man had entered through the
inner door. He wore a robe of stark simplicity, for Asanion. It was
merely twofold, overrobe and underrobe, plain white linen beneath,
amber silk above, with no jewels save the golden circlet permitted to
any noble of the High Court. He was not young, but neither was he old.
The years had thickened his body and furrowed his face, and the hair
cropped shorter even than Hirel's was shot with white, and his skin had
a waxen pallor which narrowed Sarevan's eyes; but he was handsome
still, with the strength of the lion that, though aging, remains the lord of
his domains. Hirel went down on his knees before him.

He laid his hands on the bowed head. Hands stiff and swollen and
grievously misshapen, trembling on the edge of perception. Yet it was
not his sickness that shook them. His face was carven ivory; his eyes
were burning gold.

Hirel raised his head. They had the same eyes, they two. The same
blazing stare in a face scoured of all expression. It could have been
deadly wrath. It could have been apprehension. It could have been deep
joy, bound and gagged and held grimly prisoner. "My lord," said Hirel,
"call off your dogs."

"My son," said the Emperor of Asanion, "call off your panthers."

Swords hissed into sheaths. The emperor's Olenyai knelt before their
lord. Zha'dan did not see fit to follow suit; and Sarevan knelt to no one
but his god. He let his hand rest on Ulan's head and regarded with
interest his father's rival. Ziad-Ilarios was not at all the bloated spider
that legend made him, but neither was he the splendid passionate youth
who had wanted to run away with a Gileni princess. Youth was long
lost, and innocence, and the gentleness for which the Lady Elian had
loved him. Passion . . .

For Hirel, briefly, it had flared with all its youthful heat. But the ice
of age and royalty had risen to conquer it. He raised his son, and they
were eye to eye, which widened the emperor's by the merest fraction.
He stepped back. He said, "Sit."

Hirel sat stiff and still upon a cushion. His father sat raised above him.
Sarevan stood with his cat and his Zhil'ari. He doubted very much that
he was wanted here. He doubted still more that Hirel would pass that
door again unscathed. The very silence was deadly. Ziad-Ilarios had
said no word for an endless while. He had glanced more often at

Sarevan than at his son, cool measuring glances as empty of enmity as of warmth.

When Sarevan had had enough of it, he smiled, white and insolent. "Well, old lion. Now that you have us, what are you going to do with us?"

Hirel's shoulders stiffened. Ziad-Ilarios let his gaze rest on Sarevan. For the first time in a proud count of days, Sarevan's longing for his lost power passed the borders of pain. To touch that mind behind all its veils and masks; to know truly what that silence portended.

The emperor raised a hand. "Come here," he said.

Sarevan came. He did not wait to be invited; he sat, returning stare for stare. "Well?" he asked.

Ziad-Ilarios leaned forward. His hand gripped Sarevan's chin, turning it from side to side, letting it go abruptly. He sat back. "You favor your father," he said.

"It's the nose," said Sarevan. "It conquers all the rest." He tilted his head. "If you want to play games, I'll play them. But I'd rather come to the point. Of this meeting, or of yonder sword. If you don't want to tell me what you intend to do with us, will you tell me what mistakes you think we've made?"

"I will and I can," answered the emperor directly, without visible reluctance. Perhaps he was amused. "You should not have made it so painfully clear that Keruvarion's heir is here, and that he is here by his own will, and that he must be thanked for the return and the naming of the heir of Asanion."

Sarevan leaned against the emperor's divan, cheek propped on hand. "You weren't in any great hurry to name him yourself, and there was a riot brewing. I had to do something."

"Thereby beginning a riot indeed," said Ziad-Ilarios.

"They'll see sense soon enough. You named your heir. Once the shock wears off, they'll be content with him."

"Do you think so?"

"I know so," said Sarevan. He was not as confident as he hoped he sounded.

"And you? What will they say of you?"

"The truth. I come indeed of my own will, lord emperor. I make a gift of myself to you."

Ziad-Ilarios was neither startled nor dismayed. Of course not. Halid was his man. He knew everything; had known it, most likely, from the beginning. "There are two edges to that sword, Sun-prince. I can use you as a pawn in my game. I can barter your life for your father's empire."

Tension contracted to a knot in Sarevan's middle. He smiled. "Don't trouble. He won't play. Alive I can keep him from you. Dead I can give you your war. Keruvarion you'll never get, from either of us."

"And if I desire war?"

Sarevan tilted his head back, baring his throat. "I'm yours, old lion. Do as you please."

"You are young," mused Ziad-Ilarios. His tone excused nothing. "I am not a man who whips his sons. But were you mine, I would consider it."

Sarevan sat bolt upright. Ziad-Ilarios regarded him sternly, yet with a spark beneath. "Young one, your folly has placed me in a very difficult position. I have considered returning you forthwith to your father—"

"You can't!" Sarevan burst out.

The emperor's brows met. He looked more than ever like Hirel. "Do not tell me what I can and cannot do. Your father suffered my son to return to me, great though his advantage would have been had he held the boy hostage. For that, I stand in his debt. I might choose to repay in kind. Or," he said, "I might not. I do not know what use you may be, save to cause dissension in my court. You may be better dead or in chains."

"So be it," Sarevan said steadily.

Ziad-Ilarios looked long at him. For all his fixity of purpose, for all that he had had long days to firm his will, Sarevan had all he could do to sit unmoving, his face calm, his hands quiet on his thighs. His heart beat hard; his mouth was dry. A cold trickle of sweat crept down his spine.

The emperor said them, the words he dreaded. "Do you propose to betray your empire?"

"No!" cried Sarevan, too swift, too loud, too high. Grimly he mastered himself. "No, Lord of Asanion. Never. I propose to save it." He spread his hands, letting Ziad-Ilarios see them both, the one that was human-dark, the one that was burning golden. "I offer myself. Hostage. Peacebond. A shield against my father's war."

"Are you so certain that he cannot win it?"

"I know he will."

"Why, then? Surely you have no love for Asanion."

"I know what that victory will cost." The emperor raised his brows. Sarevan swallowed. His throat seemed full of sand. "I was never the seer my mother is. But I have seen what my god has given me to see.

War, Lord of Asanion. Red war. Two empires laid waste, the flower of
their manhood slain, the strength of their people broken." Sarevan was
on his feet. "I will not have it. If I must die to prevent it, then let me
die. I will not be emperor if that empire is ruin."

"That," said Ziad-Ilarios, soft after Sarevan's passionate outcry, "is
the heart of the matter. You will turn traitor rather than face what you
fear will come. Even in Asanion we have a name for that. We call it
cowardice."

"Old lion," purred Sarevan, "I am young and I am a fool and I have
no courage to speak of, but you cannot test my mettle by twisting the
truth. My father let your son leave Endros because he has no intention
of keeping peace and no taste for cold murder. He never dreamed that I
would go as far as I have."

"Do you believe that I cannot have you put to death for my realm's
sake?"

"I believe that Mirain An-Sh'Endor will hesitate to invade Asanion
while you hold me hostage. I am, after all, his only son. His father has
decreed that he may never have another."

"But if war is inevitable, your death may move him to act in haste,
before he is well ready. Then may I claim the advantage."

"He was ready when I left Endros. I may have delayed him by escaping his vigilance, but if I die at your command, he will fall upon you at
once and without mercy." Sarevan rose and stepped back, freeing Ziad-
Ilarios from the weight of his shadow. "Lord emperor, I came willingly,
in full knowledge of the consequences. I am yours to hold. I will serve
you, whether you use me as prince or slave, guest or prisoner, if only
you do not ask me to turn against my people."

"What surety have you that I will not keep you and turn against your
father? He has no child of mine in his power."

"In that," Sarevan said levelly, "I trust to your honor. And to the
size of my father's army."

The emperor stood. "Asuchirel," he said. "Judge. Do I keep him? Do
I put him to death? Do I send him back to his father?"

Hirel was slow to answer. Not for surprise, Sarevan could see that.
He looked as if he had been expecting the burden of judgment; and it
was heavy. Perhaps too heavy for his shoulders, however broad they
had begun to be.

At last he said, "Death would be wise, if we would consider the years
to come and the enemy he must inevitably be, but he has warned us
clearly against such foresight. If we send him to Endros, it must needs

be in chains, or he will not go. I counsel that we keep him. We may gain time thereby, and we will certainly discomfit his father."

"And you can always kill me later," Sarevan pointed out. He bowed with a flourish. "I am your servant, my lord. What will you have of me?"

"Respect," replied Ziad-Ilarios, with a glint that might have been laughter. "And now," he said, "I would speak with my son. My captain will guide you to a place of comfort."

It was indeed very comfortable: a suite of princely chambers, with slaves for every need, and a great bath, and its own garden. Halid, having guided Sarevan there, was not disposed to linger. Sarevan did not try to detain him. There was no tactful way to ask a captain of guards if he had intended to murder his charges.

When the man had gone, Sarevan rounded on Zha'dan with such fierceness that the Zhil'ari leaped back. His hand was on the hilt of his sword; but he had not drawn it. "Truth," Sarevan spat out. *"What is the truth?"*

"I don't think there is any," Zha'dan said.

Sarevan paced, spun, paced. "That was Halid, laughing at us. If he is the emperor's man, why did he plot to kill us? If there was no plot, why did Aranos tell us there was? What is this web we're trapped in?"

"I don't know," said Zha'dan. "I can't read these people. Even when I think I can. They keep thinking around corners."

Sarevan stopped short. Suddenly he laughed. "The sword and the serpent! And what does the sword do when the serpent coils to strike?"

Zha'dan caught the spark of his laughter. "It strikes first."

"Straight and steady and clear to the heart. We'll master this empire yet, brother savage."

They grinned at one another. It was sheer bravado, but it buoyed them up.

They were still grinning when Hirel found them, the two of them and the ul-cat, all nested most comfortably in the mountain of white and golden cushions that was the state bed of Asanion's high prince. He stopped in a cloud of slaves and hangers-on, motionless amid the dropped jaws and outrage. Sarevan watched him remember with whom he was quarreling, and with whom he was not, and why. Watched the mirth swell, perilously. "Good evening," he said in his beautifully cadenced High Asanian, "my panthers. Are your chambers not to your liking?"

"Good evening," said Sarevan, "brother prince. Our chambers are very much to our liking. But we had a mind to explore. I see you have your place again."

"It was inevitable. It is my place." Hirel raised a finger. His following scattered. Not without dismay; but perhaps there was something to be said for Asanian servility. No one argued with a royal whim.

When they were well gone, Hirel dropped his robes and stood in his trousers, drawing a long breath. His shoulders straightened; his eyes sparked. He grinned. He laughed. He leaped.

It took both men to conquer him. He had not their strength, but he was supple and lethally quick, and he knew tricks they had never heard of. And some they had, and called foul. Loudly. He laughed at them. Even with Sarevan sitting on him and Zha'dan pinning his hands.

"Beard-pulling," Sarevan told him severely, "is not honorable."

Hirel sobered. Somewhat. "It is not? Groin-kneeing, surely, but that . . . it is so irresistibly *there.*"

"I didn't pull your hair."

"Ah, poor prince."

Sarevan growled. Hirel lay and looked almost meek. After a moment Zha'dan let go his hands. He flexed them, sighing. Sarevan gathered to let him up.

The world whirled. Hirel sat on Sarevan's chest and laughed. His fingers were wound in Sarevan's beard. "Never," he said, "never call an Asanian conquered until he yields."

"What happens if *I* won't yield?" Sarevan demanded, not easily. His chin had too keen a memory of anguish.

Hirel bent close. "Do you wish to know?"

Sarevan twisted. Hirel clung like a leech. His fingers tightened. "I won't," gritted Sarevan.

Hirel swooped down. He did not kiss like a woman. He did not kiss, for all Sarevan knew, like a man. He was simply and blindingly Hirel.

When Sarevan could breathe again, Hirel was on his feet, wrapping himself in a simple linen robe. It was voluminous enough, but a good handspan shorter than it should have been. Hirel looked at it, and Sarevan forgot anger, outrage, fear that was half desire. More than half. He struggled in the endless clutching cushions.

Hirel tried to pull the robe down over his feet. It yielded a bare inch. He raised his eyes to Sarevan. "I am not the same. I am—not—"

Sarevan could not touch him. Dared not.

He bent, took up the first robe of his eight. It was silk, and rather more elaborate than practical, but it fit him. He put it on slowly, discarding the other. He straightened, worked his fingers through the wild tangle of his hair. "I am not the same," he said again. "I can laugh. I can—I could—weep. I am corrupted, Sun-prince."

"And I," Sarevan said, barely to be heard.

Hirel laughed, not as he had before. Short and bitter. "You are purity itself. A kiss—" His lip curled in scorn. "That was vengeance. For what you gave me. Now do you understand? Now do you see what you did to me?"

"But it was only a kiss."

"Only!" Hirel jerked tight the belt of his robe. "My father warned me. It is a Gileni magic. It has nothing to do with mages, and everything to do with what you are, your redmaned kind. A fire in the blood. A madness in the brain. You do not even know what you do. You simply are."

"But you did the same to me!"

"Did I?" Hirel smiled slowly. "So, then. It can be given back in kind. Perhaps, for that, I may concede the existence of gods." He drew himself up, settled his robe and his face. "Enough. I have been remiss; I have let myself forget who I am. Go, be free. I have duties."

"What sort of duties?"

Hirel bridled. Sarevan refused to be cowed. He lay and waited and willed the boy to remember who he was.

Hirel remembered. He eased, a little. His outrage faded. "Prince," he said. It was an apology. "My father gave me a gift. A judgment. I must make it tonight."

"Your brothers?"

The faintest of smiles touched Hirel's mouth. "My brothers."

Sarevan regarded him, long and level. "I don't like what you're thinking," he said.

Hirel tilted his head. There were diamonds in his ears; they could not match the glitter of his eyes. "What do you think I am thinking?"

Sarevan stretched the aches out of his muscles and yawned. His eyes did not shift from Hirel's face. "You're contemplating revenge. Sweet, isn't it?"

"Sweeter than honey," said Hirel, standing over Sarevan. "Would you make it sweeter? Linger as you are, half naked amid my bed."

"Hirel," Sarevan said, "don't do it."

"Can you forbid me?"

"Believe me, prince. The sweetness doesn't last. It turns to gall, and then to poison."

"How wise you are tonight." Hirel's smile was bright and brittle. "But I am wiser than you think. Watch and see."

"Hirel—"

"Watch."

They came boldly enough. Only the two: Vuad and Sayel, without attendance of their own, escorted politely but ineluctably by half a dozen of the emperor's Olenyai. They were putting on it the best faces they might. Sarevan was not half-naked in Hirel's bed; he sat with Hirel, robed like the other, his hair free and his brows bound with gold, with his ul-cat and his Zhil'ari mageling at his feet. They played at draughts upon a golden board.

Zha'dan straightened, at gaze. Ulan raised his head from Sarevan's knee. Hirel pondered the board. He was losing. He was not frowning, by which Sarevan knew that his mind was not on it. Sarevan made no such pretense. He turned to regard the princes; they stared back in a fashion he was learning to name. High indignation that a dusky barbarian should presume to conduct himself as their equal. He belonged, the curl of their lips declared, in the slave-stables with the rest of his kind.

It was hard to pity them. Even when, at very long last, Hirel condescended to notice them. Their bravado shuddered and shrank. "Good evening," said Hirel, "brothers. I trust that my summons did not inconvenience you."

"We are always at your disposal," Sayel said. "My lord."

Hirel smiled. Sarevan thought of beasts of prey. "No expressions of joy, brothers? No hymns of thanksgiving that I am returned safe to my kin?"

"Hirel," said Vuad, dropping to his knees and catching at Hirel's robe. "Hirel, we never meant it."

"Of course you did not mean to let me escape. Your guardhound was fierce. Would you like to see my scars?"

Sayel sank down coolly, with grace. He even smiled. "Surely you understand, brother. We were forced to it. We did not intend to slay you."

Hirel looked at them. The one who clung to his hem and sweated. The one who smiled. "I loved you once. I admired you. I wished to be like you. Fine strong young men, never at a loss for a word or a smile, never ill or weak or afraid. You never fainted in the heat at Summer Court. You never fasted at banquets lest you lose it all at once and most precipitately. You never paid for a few days' brisk hunting in thrice a few days' sickness. You were all that I was not, and all that I longed to be."

Sayel's smile twisted. Vuad's tension eased; he raised his head. "You do understand," he said. "After all, you do. We knew you would. It was circumstance; necessity. There was no malice in it." He managed a smile. "Here, brother. Send your animals away; then we can talk."

"We are talking now." Hirel stared at Vuad's hands until they let go of his robe.

"At least," said Sayel, "dismiss the beast with the firefruit mane." He was easing, falling into a manner which must have been his wonted one with Hirel: light, familiar, very subtly contemptuous. "Rid us of it, Hirel'chai. Our council has no need of Varyani spies."

Hirel laughed, which took Sayel aback. "I am not your Hirel'chai, O Sayel'dan, my brother and my servant. Bow to the lord high prince, who is my guest and my brother-above-blood. Crave his pardon."

Sayel looked from one to the other. His brows arched. "Ah. Now I see where your manners have gone. Is it true that his kind ride naked to war?"

"On occasion," Sarevan replied. "Our women especially are fond of it. Beautifully barbaric, no?"

"The beauty is questionable," said Sayel.

"Bow," Hirel said very softly. "Bow, Sayel."

Vuad, less clever, was relearning fear. Sayel was still rapt in his own insolence. "Come now, little brother. Am I, a prince of the blood imperial, to abase myself before a bandit's whelp?"

Hirel was on his feet. No one had seen him move. Sayel fell sprawling; Hirel's foot held him there, resting lightly on his neck. "You are not wise, Sayel'dan. The Prince of Keruvarion was inclined to intercede for you; but you have shown him the folly of it." Hirel beckoned to his guards. "Take them both. Rid them of their manes; chain them. Bid the gelders wait upon my pleasure."

"I watched," Sarevan said with banked heat. "I saw nothing wise in what you did."

"You did not speak for them," Hirel pointed out coolly.

"You never gave me time."

Hirel said nothing, only looked at him.

He rose. "Go on, then. Take your revenge. But don't expect me to condone it."

"And what does your father do with those who betray him? Embrace them? Kiss them? Thank them for their charity?"

"You keep my father out of this."

"I will keep him where I please. We do not love him here, but we fear him well; we know how he deals with his enemies."

"Mercifully," snapped Sarevan. "Justly. And promptly, with no cat-games to whet their terrors."

Hirel tossed back his hair, eyes narrow and glittering. "Is that your measure of me?"

"You are High Prince of Asanion."

"Ah," drawled Hirel. "I break my fast on the tender flesh of children, and beguile my leisure with exquisite refinements of torture. There is one, prince; it is delightful. A droplet of water upon the head of a bound prisoner: one droplet only at each turn of the sun-glass. But sometimes, for variation, no droplet falls. It drives the victim quite beautifully mad."

Sarevan's teeth ground together. "If you're going to kill them, at least kill them cleanly."

"As cleanly as the armies of the Sun took our province of Anjiv?" Hirel advanced a step. "As cleanly as that, Sun-prince? They slew all the men of fighting age. They put the women to the sword, but not before they had had their fill of rape. They made the children watch, and told them that that was the fate ordained for all worshippers of demons; and the menchildren they put to death, but the maids they took as slaves. But no," said Hirel, "I cry your pardon. There are no slaves in Keruvarion. Only bondservants and battle captives."

"They are your brothers!"

"The worse for them, that they would destroy their lord and their blood kin."

Sarevan turned his back on Hirel. "That's not justice. That's spite." He walked away. Hirel did not call him back.

Sarevan did not know where he was striding to. He did not care. Sometimes there were people; they stared. No doubt they thought him indecent: all but naked, with one thin robe and no attendants. Ulan and Zha'dan had forsaken him; had stayed with Hirel. Faithless, both of them. Traitors to their master.

He found a tower. He climbed to the top of it and sat under the stars. They were the same stars that shone on Keruvarion, in the same sky. But the air was strange, Asanian air, warm and cloying. He choked on it.

"I did it," he said to the pattern of stars that he had made his own, the one that in Ianon was the Eagle and in Han-Gilen the Sunbird. "I confess it freely. I brought it on myself. I cast away my power and my princedom. And for what? For a dream of prophecy? For peace? For the empire that will be?" He laughed without mirth. "For all of those. And for something I never looked for. For the worst of all my enemies."

He lay back, hands clasped beneath his head. His temper had passed. He was calm, empty. "I think I hate him. I'm afraid I love him. I know we quarrel like lovers.

"And what hope do we have? If he were a woman I'd marry him, if I didn't kill him first. If he were a commoner I'd make him a lord and keep him by me. Even if he were a lord . . . even an Asanian lord . . ." Sarevan surged up, crying out, "O Avaryan! Why did you do this to us?"

The god was not answering.

"No doubt," said Sarevan dryly after a starlit while, "I've solved everything with tonight's performance. If he's even civil to me hereafter, I'll count it an honest miracle."

The stars were silent. The god said nothing.

"I hate him," said Sarevan with sudden fierceness. "I hate him. Haughty, corrupt, cruel—damn him. Damn him to all twenty-seven of his own hells."

Seventeen

THE GOLDEN COURTS SETTLED SWIFTLY ENOUGH UN-
der the emperor's strong hand; and, in the way of courts, went on
as if they had never risen up in near-revolt. Hirel was solely and certainly their high prince. Sarevan was neither spy nor upstart; certainly
he had never presumed so far as to ordain whom they would accept as
their lord. Matters of such indelicacy were not discussed.

He was their new darling. He would have been their new pet, but like
Ulan, Sarevan Is'kelion was not a tame creature. He did not trouble
himself with all the intricacies of protocol; he would not keep to the
paths ordained for a royal hostage. He rode his blue-eyed stallion wherever he pleased. He crossed swords with guardsmen. He wrestled up-
roariously with the painted savage who was his shadow, and sometimes
he won, but sometimes, resoundingly, he lost. He discovered that certain courtyards looked upward to the latticed windows of the harem,
and that if he lingered there alone, in time soft voices would call to him.
They told him of unfrequented passages, of walled gardens and of
chambers where a handsome outlander might go to be stared at through
hidden screens. But never suffered to stare in return. Even if he were
minded to chance the loss of his eyes for letting them rest on a royal
lady, not to mention his manhood for daring to be aware of her existence, his sweet-voiced companions grew almost shrill in forbidding it.
It was sin enough that he heard them speak.

Their kinsmen were enchanted with him. He frightened them, deliciously. They reckoned him a giant; they waxed incredulous at skin so dark and hair so bright and teeth so very white; they called him Sunlord, and Stormborn, and Lord of Panthers.

He was as vain as a sunbird, but he knew what the flattery of the courtiers was worth. Wizard's gold. While one labored to maintain the spell, it glittered brightly. But a moment's lapse, a few breaths' pause, and it withered away.

Avaryan knew, there were wizards enough here. The charlatans were everywhere: men of little power but great flamboyance, who wrought illusions and told fortunes and found lost jewels for the credulous of the court. But they were only a diversion. While they persuaded the skeptics of Asanion that there was nothing to fear from their kind, the true mages passed unseen and unregarded. Nondescript persons, seldom noticed but always in evidence, robed in grey or in violet, often accompanied by a beast or a bird. Sarevan did not know that any of them had the emperor's ear. They did not confess it and Ziad-Ilarios did not admit to it, although he was free enough with Sarevan in other matters. When Sarevan appeared in his council and in his courts of justice, he said no word, though eyes glittered and lips tightened at the enormity of it. The emperor refused to see, refused to restrain the interloper; who had a little sense, when it came to that. He never tried to speak where he listened so avidly, though often his eyes would spark or his jaw tense, as if he yearned to burst out in a flood of outland interference.

People were calling him the emperor's favorite. Some, in a country where tongues were freer, would have called it more. Would have remembered who his mother was, and what she had been to his majesty. Would, perhaps, have spoken of bewitchment.

There was one who did not speak at all, nor in any way betray that he had had aught to do with the return of Asanion's high prince and the presence of Keruvarion's high prince in Kundri'j Asan. Aranos had made no public appearance since Autumn Firstday. That, it seemed, was perfectly usual. He was known for his strangeness. His name, when it was spoken, was spoken most often in a whisper.

It was very cleverly done. As much as Asanian courtiers could love anything, they loved their bright and haughty high prince. Aranos they feared.

"He doesn't even have to do anything," said Zha'dan. "Just hide in his walls and refuse to come out. And let people talk."

"Serpent ways," said Sarevan. He smiled at the guard who stood before Aranos' gate. It was his most charming smile. "I will speak with your lord," he said in Asanian.

The man surprised him. He bowed with every evidence of respect. He stepped back from the gate.

A mage was waiting. Sarevan was painfully glad that it was not a darkmage. The man bowed and was most courteous. He led Sarevan into the black-and-silver chambers.

Aranos did not see fit to keep Sarevan waiting, although an Asanian would have reckoned him indisposed. Perhaps it was its own kind of insult. He had bathed; he lay on sable furs as a slave rubbed sweet oil into his skin, while another combed out his hair. His mane, unbound, was longer than his body.

He was, indeed, a perfect miniature of a man. Rumor had cast doubts on it. He had begotten no children that anyone knew of; and that, in an Asanian prince some years Sarevan's elder, was frankly scandalous.

Sarevan, looking at him, knew. His eyelids lowered, raised. He almost smiled. "I, too," he said.

Sarevan glanced at the slaves. Aranos' smile came clearer. "Deaf-mutes," he said. "Most useful, and most discreet."

"But why would an Asanian choose to—"

"For the power in it."

Sarevan sat on the edge of Aranos' furs and frowned. "I've heard of that. I never found it to be true. Maybe my kind of power was different."

Aranos was gravely astonished. "It did nothing for you, and yet you suffered it?"

"For the vows and the mystery. For the god."

"Ah." The essential Asanian syllable: eloquent of volumes. "And yet you knew me."

"No one in your harem has ever told anyone?"

"They are women," said Aranos. He did not even trouble to be contemptuous. "Every one believes that another enjoys my favors. Some have even lied to claim them, to gain what can be gained. I indulge it. It serves me; it quiets my so-called concubines."

"And you? Have you gained anything?"

Aranos shrugged slightly. "I am an apprentice still. The full power, I am told, comes with full knowledge."

"You're not mageborn."

For an instant Sarevan saw the man beneath the mask. The prince cast him down. "I am not. I must learn to fly with wings of wax and wire, where you were eagle-fledged in infancy."

Sarevan quelled a shiver. In that moment of Aranos' nakedness, he had seen desolation, and hatred, and corroding envy. And yet, beside it, he had seen compassion. Even the unmasked man was Asanian. Webs within webs. Sarevan made his tongue a sword to cleave them. "I fly no longer. I walk as a man walks, and no more. But this much of power I have left: I can see the snares about my feet." Aranos was silent. Sarevan thrust, swift and straight. "You promised to stand at your brother's back; to name him heir before your father. You did not. You accused our Olenyai of treachery. They have proven to be loyal, and to your father. How do I know that you did not lie in all the rest?"

"My brother is high prince as he was born to be."

"For how long?"

The golden eyes hooded. "For as long as he can hold."

Sarevan considered seizing him; chose not to move. "You wanted us away from Halid and his men. Why?"

"I cannot tell you."

"Cannot or will not?"

"Both."

"I can beat it out of you."

"Can you?"

Sarevan measured distances, boltholes, the prince and his two silent slaves. He smiled.

Aranos smiled back. "Beautiful barbarian. How you must tempt my brother!"

Sarevan fitted his long fingers to that delicate neck. "Tell me how I tempt you. Tell me what you plot against us."

"Truly," said Aranos, undisturbed by the hand about his throat, "I cannot. I have my own designs, I admit it freely; perhaps my brother will not be emperor as long as he would like. But this that concerns you . . . I am part of it, but I do not rule it. I am not free to tell you more."

Cold walked down Sarevan's spine. "You're lying."

"As I have never known a woman, I swear to you, I am not."

Sarevan looked at him more than a little wildly. It had been so clear. So obvious. And if he lied—but he did not. It was enough to drive a man mad. "Then, if not you, who?"

"I am forbidden to tell you."

Sarevan's teeth bared. "You are the Second Prince of the Golden Empire. How can anyone presume to forbid you anything?"

"My father can."

Almost—almost—Sarevan fell into the trap. But he knew Ziad-Ilarios. Liked him. Loved him, maybe, a little. None of it was enough to blind him. Ziad-Ilarios was a strong king, a good man as far as an emperor could be in Asanion, and an intriguer of no little subtlety. And yet. "This is not his weaving. No more than it is my father's. Neither could have done what has been done in the other's empire. Even the shattering of my power—I blamed him for it once. No longer. It was too magelike a trick. Too—much—like—"

Sarevan stilled, suddenly, completely. Aranos' eyes were wide and clear as topazes. "Mage," Sarevan murmured. "Like." A sweet wildness rose in him. Under the sky, he would have let it out in a whoop. "Ah," he said tenderly. "Ah, little man, how cleverly you plan this game. Do they know it, your fellows? Do they guess how very dangerous you are?"

"Any man is dangerous."

"Don't babble." Aranos said nothing. Sarevan smiled at last and let him go. Already the bruises were rising on his ivory neck. His skin was as delicate as a woman's was supposed to be, yet almost never was. "You are dangerous. Your brother is dangerous. I—I am violent, and therefore dangerous."

"And subtler than you think, Sun-prince."

"Avaryan forbid," said Sarevan. He rose, bowed without mockery. "I thank you, prince."

"Perhaps in the end you will not."

Sarevan paused. He could not read the princeling at all. He shrugged. "That will be as it will be. Good day, little man."

The Mageguild had settled itself in an unprepossessing quarter of the city, in the fifth circle between the cloth market and the high temple of Uvarra Goldeneyes. There along a narrow twisting street that ended behind the temple were the sages and the diviners, the sorcerers, the necromancers, the thaumaturges, the enchanters. They had divided the power into the light and the dark. They had named the greater powers, which were prophecy, and healing, and ruling of men and of demons, and mastery of the earth, and walking of the road between the worlds, and raising of the dead. They had named the lesser, which were mind-speech, and beast-mastery, and firemaking, and flying, and cloudherding, and all the arts of shifting the world's substance by will alone. They had even made a craft of the naming, turning a gift of the inscrutable gods into a scholar's pursuit.

Sarevan found the guildhall by scent, as it were: by the throbbing behind his eyes. Its door was neither hidden from sight nor blazoned with the badge of the order; it was a plain wooden panel behind a bronze gate, with a porter who eyed Sarevan through a grille. Taking in the man in plain lordly garb of the Hundred Realms, with a cap on his head but his bright hair plain to see below it, and an ul-cat beside him and a painted Zhil'ari guarding him. The eye betrayed no surprise. Gate and door opened; the porter, an Asanian of no age in particular, bowed and said, "If you will follow, prince."

It seemed a house like any other. No twisting shadowed passages. No stink of potions or moaning of incantations. No shimmering sorcerous barriers. Through open doors Sarevan saw men and a few women bent over books, or deep in colloquy, or engaged in instructing apprentices. Nearly all the masters were earth-brown easterners or bone-pale islanders. Most of the apprentices were Asanians. Some glanced at him as he passed. Curious, even fascinated, but unsurprised.

Sarevan had expected to be expected. He had not expected to be piqued by it. They could at least have pretended to be amazed that the son of the Sunborn dared to show his face among them.

He followed his guide up a stair and down a corridor. One door in it stood open. The chamber within was a library: shelves of scrolls, rolled and tagged, and a long cluttered table, and a man working at it. There was no telling his age. His hair was white but his skin was smooth; his back was bent but his eyes were bright; and the fingers that held the stylus, though thin to emaciation, were straight and fine and strong. Sarevan saw no familiar; he knew that he would see none.

He bowed his aching head. "Master," he said. No more. No name. Mages of the order gave their names only as great gifts.

The guildmaster bowed in return. "Prince," he said. "Your pardon, I pray you; I cannot rise to greet you properly. Will it please you to sit with me?"

The porter had gone. Zha'dan established himself by the door; Sarevan sat across the table from the master, with Ulan at his side, chin on the table, watching the master of mages with an unblinking emerald stare.

They all waited. Sarevan did not intend to speak first. He glanced at the scroll nearest: a treatise on the arts of the dark. His grandfather the Red Prince had made him read it. "A mage must know all the uses of his power," Prince Orsan had said.

"And its abuses," Sarevan had countered.

"The dark arts are not abuse of power. They are as native to it as the arts of the light; but where light heals, the dark destroys."

"I would never fall so low," Sarevan had declared. "My blood is Sun-blood. The dark is my sworn enemy. I will always heal; I will never destroy."

He smiled now, bitterly, remembering. He had been too proud of himself. And now he was here, traitor to Keruvarion, facing the master of that guild which had turned its back on his father.

"Because," said its master, "he would have constrained us to his will alone. We will not deny the dark; we will not ban the practice of its arts. That would be to deny the world's balance."

Sarevan held himself still. The man had read his face, that was all. His mind was barred as firmly as ever, despite all assaults upon it. "I have heard," he said, "that you will ban the arts of light and turn all to the dark."

"There are those who would do so, out of greed or out of bitterness. I am not one of them."

"And yet you suffer them."

"While they obey me, I do not cast them out."

"Even though they work abominations in the name of their magic?"

"What are abominations, prince? Refusal to deny their gods and worship Avaryan? Insistence upon their own rites and prayers? Resistance to laws which they reckon tyranny?"

"If it is tyranny to forbid the slaughter of children," answered Sarevan, "yes. I know what rites you speak of. The Midwinter sacrifice. The calling up of the dead and the feeding of the gods below. The making of Eyes of Power."

The master folded his long beautiful hands. He wore a ring, a topaz. Sarevan shivered a little. He could no longer abide topazes. Quietly the mage said, "The world is not gentle. Nor are the gods. If they must have blood, then blood they will have. It is not for us to judge them."

"We contend that they demand no blood. That that is human avarice and cruelty and grasping after power."

"Is your Avaryan pure, prince? Has he spurned the blood shed in his name? Did he spare even his bride the pain of death?"

"Human cruelty, guildmaster. Human envy and betrayal."

"The worse for those who perpetrated it, that they had no god to make their bloodshed holy."

Sarevan sat back, stroking his beard: sure sign of his tension, but he could not stop it. "Maybe we're wrong. Maybe you are. Balance could be another name for spinelessness. Avaryan has made himself known in the world; no other god has done that. No other god will. There is none but the one."

"Save, by your belief, his sister. The dark to his light. The ice to his fire. The silence to his great roar of power. The other side of his self."

"That is Asanian teaching. We say that they are separate. He has chained her, lest she plunge the world into everlasting night."

"Or lest she prevent him from tipping the balance. The sun gives life, yet also destroys it. Excess of light condemns a man to blindness."

"Not if he be pure of soul."

"Are you, prince?"

"Hardly." Sarevan smiled, little more than a grimace. "If I were, I wouldn't be here. I'd be Journeying in blissful ignorance, or kinging it in Ianon."

The master was silent. Waiting.

Sarevan let him have that victory. "Yes. Yes, I doubt my god. I wonder if my father is mad. If the Asanians, after all, worship the truth: twofold Uvarra who is above the gods."

"Have you come to me for an answer?"

Sarevan laughed sharply. "I spent an hour in Uvarra's temple. It's much like all the others. Crusted with jewels, fogged with incense, infested with priests who know no god but gold. The image of the deity would rouse blushes in a Suvieni brothel. And yet," he said, "and yet, for all of that, when I bowed down and prayed to Avaryan, a madness struck me. I thought it was Uvarra who heard. Uvarra of the light and Ivuryas of the dark, all one. And the dark was beautiful, guildmaster. It called to me. It offered me my power, the dark power which I refused and which is still within me, if only I will free it."

"There is no law which forbids the gods to lie."

"Precisely my response," said Sarevan. "But if I can taste a lie, I can also taste the truth. And there I tasted truth."

"There is always a price."

"Of course. And for this, my mother's life and my father's heart. I refused. It was too easy, mage. Much too easy." Sarevan leaned across the table. "Choices should be difficult. I think I've yet to be given one. I know you have something to do with it."

"And how do you know that?"

Sarevan frowned. It hurt. He cradled his head in his hands. "Maybe the god drives me: whichever god is the true one. Maybe I'm mad. I think I've been chosen for something. If only for a traitor's death."

"Are you asking for a foreseeing?"

"I am asking for the truth. I know what I've done and why I did it. But it's been too smooth, mage. Too simple. I think I've had help that hasn't chosen to uncover itself."

The master raised his brows. "Indeed?"

"Indeed," said Sarevan, throttling his impatience. The tactics of the sword worked wonders with Asanian courtiers, but this was a mage, in that mage's own demesne. He chose his words with care. "Consider. A trap laid in Asanion; a prince's pride caught in it, his power taken from him. A hunt through two empires by a mighty master of power, who could find nothing; but an Eye of Power found the one for whom it was meant. Chance, maybe; a god's inscrutable will. But for two princes and two seneldi and an ul-cat to pass through the very heart of Keruvarion, under the eye of the Sunborn, with treason on their minds—for them to pass so, with no whisper of their passing, no rumor of their betrayal, no sign of a hunt raised against them, that is not chance. That is magecraft."

"Or skillful deception."

"No," said Sarevan. "It takes power to lie to my father. Power, and great bravery. And someone has done it. Someone ventured to cover my going; to open my road through Keruvarion."

"We are not the only mages in the world."

"You are the only mages, aside from the Sun-priests in Endros, who gather together under a firm rule. And they would never have woven this web: it smacks too much of treason against my father. The little prince is part of it. He professes not to be the master of it; and that's unlikely enough to be true. He's no servant, he's serving himself and no one else, but at the moment it suits him to be a loyal conspirator. He'd not be loyal to anyone whom he didn't at least pretend to respect."

"You see great complexities in what may be no more than luck and chance and a prince's plotting."

"Maybe I do. I'm a prince myself; I'm an only son. I'm spoiled. Indulge me." Sarevan smiled his whitest smile. "Your people can have no love for my father. He was too inflexible with them. Either he would rule them or they would leave his empire. They chose exile. Now suppose," he said, "that some of them have seen a path of both revenge and peace. A conspiracy. To deny him his war, to rob him of his heir, and in the end, it may be, to have their own country back again. With the Sunborn safely dead and someone young, malleable, and comfortably powerless to stand in his place."

"Logical," the master said.

Sarevan bowed to the tribute. "My insanity has been a godsend. I'm not only well out of the way; I'm in debt to your plotting. Don't you think it's time for a truth or two? A man can't pay a debt if he doesn't even know to whom he owes it."

"If you knew," inquired the master, "would you be willing to pay?"

"That depends. There may be more to this web than I've been allowed to see. It may lead to a blacker infamy even than I'm willing to stomach."

"Have your deeds been as vile as that?"

"I'm here, aren't I?"

The guildmaster smiled. "I was warned, Sun-prince. Your father is called the greatest courtesan in Keruvarion, but there are many who would contest that primacy; who would give it to Sarevan Is'kelion."

"Would you?"

The smile widened a fraction. "The Sunborn does not know that he is beautiful."

"He knows that he has never betrayed a trust."

The silence sang, hurting-sweet. Slowly the master said, "He has never been forced to choose. I envy that certainty. I would that it had been granted to me."

"Neither of us is the son of a god."

The master's head bowed. "This much, high prince, I can give you. A web has been spun about you. I will not say that you are the center of it. There is more to the world and the power than a pair of warring empires. Yet what you have done has been woven into the pattern."

"And the pattern?"

"You have seen it."

Sarevan rose. He leaned on his hands, keeping temper at bay, willing a smile over his clenched teeth. "You have told me nothing that I did not already know. Do you expect me to leave and be content?"

The master looked up at him, resting cool eyes on his burning face. "You were not born for contentment. I would give you what you ask for, or as much as concerns you, yet I may not." And as Sarevan straightened, thunderous: "Not yet. I am the Master of the Guild. No more than the Prince Aranos do I command my allies. That is given to no one of us. I must speak with the rest; I must win their consent before I uncover our secrets."

Sarevan snorted in disgust. "What did you model this mummery on? The Syndics of the Nine Cities?"

"Any tribe in the north is so ruled. Keruvarion's emperor himself pays heed to his lords in council."

"But in the end he rules," said Sarevan. "So. You have to agree to make me part of what I've been part of since it began. You'll pardon me if I feel used. And ill-used, at that."

The master spread his hands. "Prince. It shall be redressed. That I promise you."

Sarevan turned his hand palm up on the table. It burned and blazed. "On this?"

The master drew a breath as if in apprehension. He touched a finger to the *Kasar*. A spark leaped; he drew back. "Upon your power," he said.

Sarevan's fist clenched. Its pain was no greater for the mage's touch, though the man looked pale and shaken, as if he had gained more than he bargained for. "I accept your promise."

"It shall be kept," the master said. "And you shall have as much of the truth as you may. I will speak with my allies. When it is done, have I your leave to summon you?"

Sarevan considered the mage, and his words, and his honor. "You have my leave," he said.

Sarevan had his honest miracle. Hirel had been not merely civil to Sarevan after their quarrel. He had been magnanimous. He had been princely. He had chosen to forgive even the most bitter of Sarevan's words.

Sarevan found it harder to forgive himself. It was not Hirel who told him what had become of Vuad and Sayel. A courtier related it, half in admiration, half in incredulity: how the princes had languished shaven-headed in a cell of the emperor's prisons, and how after a night and a day in which they went well-nigh mad with dread of the gelders' coming, Hirel himself had come with a choice. A life of ease and power as eunuchs of the Lower Court in the far reaches of the empire, or a tour of duty as officers of the imperial army, with the strong likelihood of falling in battle, but the chance also of surviving to regain their rank and their brother's favor. Vuad had found the choice ridiculously easy. Sayel, it was said, had wavered. But Sayel was not well loved in the Golden Courts. He had gone with his brother to serve on the marches of the east; and before they left, they swore great oaths of loyalty to their high prince.

Hirel was in the harem when Sarevan looked for him, doing his duty by his twice ninescore concubines. It was just, Sarevan conceded, that he should have to wait, and for such a cause. He did not have to like it.

He prowled his own rooms. He prowled Hirel's. He drank rather more wine than he needed, and worked it off in a heated mock battle with Zha'dan, and came very close to deciding that Hirel did not deserve an apology.

The wine was stronger than Sarevan had expected. It made him see what he should do: and that was outrageous. It kept him from hanging back.

He had a little sense. He left Zha'dan in Hirel's rooms, rebellious but subdued. Ulan would be guard enough, and would be less likely to pay in blood.

They passed the empty courtyards, traversed an unfrequented passage. Today no sweet voices called through hidden lattices. Sarevan strode beyond them on ways which he had not taken before.

The Golden Palace stood in two worlds. The outer was all of men and eunuchs. The inner was all of women and eunuchs. The unmanned walked freely in both. A whole man walked within only where he was unquestioned master: only among the women who were his own.

Sarevan was alien in the outer world. In the inner, there was no word for him. The women who dwelt there had never seen sky unbounded by walls. They had never stood face to face with any man but father or brother or master. Husband, few of them could claim. Not here, where every one of fifty princes had his proper number of concubines.

Sarevan had learned what every concubine prayed for. That her lord might marry, for then by custom he might set her free. Or better far, that she might bear him a son. Then was she not only freed; she gained honor and power among the ladies of the palace.

If he had not known it was a prison, he would have found the harem no stranger than the rest of the palace. It was opulent to satiety, it was redolent of alien unguents, it was labyrinthine in its complexity. Its guards were eunuchs, but eunuchs both tall and strong, with drawn swords. Black eunuchs. Northerners all strange with their beardless faces, their shaven skulls, their eyes like the eyes of oxen: dark, stolid, and unyielding. Sarevan was nothing to them. He was a man. He could not pass.

Almost he turned away. But having come so far, he could not surrender like a meek child. "The high prince will see me," he said. "You may impede me. My furred brother may not be pleased. I cannot answer for what he will do then."

Two swords lowered most eloquently, to pause within an arm's length of Sarevan's middle.

Ulan growled deep in his throat.

The edge bronze dropped a handspan.

Sarevan essayed a smile.

Behind the eunuchs, the door opened. Asanian, this one, and flustered. He paid no heed at all to the guards. He beckoned with every evidence of impatience. "Come, come. Why do you dally? Time's wasting!"

Sarevan stared, nonplussed. The little eunuch clapped his hands in frustration. "*Will* you come? You're wanted!"

Sarevan looked down. The swords had shifted. Carefully, restraining an urge to protect his tender treasures with his hands, he edged between the guards. The Asanian hardly waited for him.

Long as his stride was, he had to stretch it to keep pace with his guide. The harem's corridors passed in a blur. No one was in those through which he was led: deliberate, perhaps.

Bemused as he was, he found himself wondering. Was he being rapt away like the wise fool in the bawdy song? Made a prisoner among the women forevermore, his manhood slave to their every whim.

He laughed, striding. Softly; but it startled him. It was so very deep.

His guide all but flung him through a door, into a chamber like any other chamber in this palace. A space neither large nor excessively small. A low table, a mound of cushions, a flutter of silken hangings. No odalisque awaited him. He was disappointed.

There was wine. He stopped short, remembering Asanion and Asanians. Sniffed it. It was thin and wretchedly sour: superb, to Asanian taste. If there was poison in it, surely the sourness had killed it. He poured a cup, drained it, prowled. Ulan, wiser, had arrayed himself royally atop the cushions.

One of the hangings concealed a latticed window. He tensed, remembering a litter and a long day's madness. Grimly he made himself forget, set eyes to the lattice. A courtyard opened below. There was something of familiarity in it. If one set a man just beneath the window, a very tall man as men went here, with wondrous bright hair; and set a woman behind the lattice, or a handful of women, taking high delight in the pastime . . .

He turned slowly. Words began, died. New words flooded to the gates. Hirel in gown and veil, eyes dancing, mocking him, driving him to madness.

Hirel was a boy of great and almost girlish beauty. But no boy had ever had so rich an abundance of breast, so wondrous a curve of hip within the clinging silk. Hirel had never walked as this creature walked, light and supple, yes, but swaying most enchantingly, smiling beneath her veil. She was all sweetness, and ah, she was wicked as she laughed at him: great outland oaf with his jaw hanging on his breastbone. Her head came barely so high. She stood and looked and laughed as a bird sings, for the pure joy of it.

He had to sit. His knees gave him no choice in the matter. He clung to Ulan and stared, grinning like the perfect idiot he was.

Her mirth rippled into silence. She stood and smiled at him.

"You look," he said, "exactly—"

"How not? He is my brother."

Her voice. He knew it. "Jania!"

She curtsied. "Prince Sarevadin. You are . . . much . . . more imposing without a lattice between."

He had not felt so large or so awkward since he grew a full head's height in a season. He was painfully aware of his long thin feet and his long thin limbs and his great eagle's beak of a nose. All of them blushing the more fiercely for that no one could know. "Jania," he said. "How did you know I was here?"

She pointed to the lattice. "I saw you. Then I heard you at the gate."

"And you had me let in." He drew his breath in sharply. "You shouldn't have. Your duennas will flay you alive."

She tossed her head, fully as haughty as Hirel. "They will not. Even before I knew that you would come, I informed my brother that he would give me leave to speak with you. He was wise. He granted it." Her eyes sparked. "Sometimes it profits him to remember: I could have been a man. Then he would not be high prince."

Sarevan blinked stupidly. He had known her spirit, and delighted in it, even through a lattice. He had not known who she was.

Suddenly he laughed. "If my father only knew!" Now she in her turn was speechless, caught off guard. "You could have been given to me. It was thought of: to ask the Asanian emperor for his daughter."

"He has a legion of them," she said.

"But only one born to the gold."

"Do you think that you are worthy of me?"

This was princely combat. Sarevan lounged in the cushions, Sarevan Is'kelion again, with his bold black eyes and his wide white smile. "Your brother has called me his equal."

"Ah," she said. "My brother. He has always been besotted with fire."

"What, princess! You don't find me fascinating?"

"I find you conceited." She laughed at his indignation. She leaned toward him over Ulan's body, bright and fearless, and ran a finger down his beard. He had kept it when his face healed, because no one in the court had one; this morning Zha'dan had plaited it with threads of gold, taking most of an hour to do it. "And beautiful," she said.

"Truly? Have the poets changed the canons?"

"Damn the canons."

She was a little too reckless in saying it. Defiant; outrageous. Sarevan laughed. "Have a care, princess. You might make me fall in love with you."

"I should fear that?"

Fine bold words, but they were neither of them very steady. Her fingers seemed scarcely able to help themselves, weaving among the braids of his beard. No woman, not even his mother, had ever touched him so. So soon. So perfectly rightly. "Gold," he said with dreamy conviction, "is the only color for eyes."

"Black," she said. Firmly. They laughed. Her breast was full and soft and irresistibly there. Her lips were honey and fire.

His torque was light to vanishing. He was in no danger. This was only delight. His mind remembered what one did. His body was more than glad to learn it.

Her hair was free, a queen's wealth of gold, cloaking them both. She never heeded it. She was drowning in fire and copper.

He could circle her waist with his two hands. She could bring him to his knees with her two bright eyes. He laughed into them and snatched another kiss. And another. And another.

He did not know what made him pause. Ulan's growl, perhaps. The quality of the silence. Still kneeling, still veiled in gold, he turned.

He would not again mistake Jania for her brother. They were very like; but a world lay between them. The woman's world, and the man's.

His mind, spinning on, took thought for what Hirel could see. His sister, standing with her arms about a kneeling man. Her gown and his coat and trousers were decorously in place. But her veil was gone, her hair all tumbled, and his wild red mane was free of its braid. They looked, no doubt, as if they fully intended to go on.

And did they not?

Sarevan rose. Jania did not try to hold him. Her voice was cool. "Good day, younger brother."

Hirel inclined his head. He wore no expression at all. "Elder sister. High prince."

It was cold at Sarevan's height, and solitary. The wine of his recklessness lay leaden in his stomach. A dull fire smoldered beneath his cheekbones.

Hirel was clad for the harem. Eight robes of sheerest stuff, one golden belt binding them all. He looked calm, and royal, and impeccable. His duties had not even smudged the gilt on his eyelids. He said, "You will pardon me, prince. I was given to understand that I was looked for. I shall await you in my chambers."

"No," said Sarevan. "Wait. It's not—"

He had waited too long to muster his wits. Hirel was gone. Sarevan glared after him. "Damn," he said. "And damn."

"And damn," said Jania. She meant it, but there was still a thread of laughter in it. "My eunuch will lose somewhat of his hide for this."

Sarevan looked at her, hardly hearing her. "You are meant to be his empress."

"What, my eunuch?"

He ignored her foolishness. "You shouldn't, you know. It's gone on too long. The strain is growing dangerously weak."

It was very stiff and prim, reflected in her eyes. "Are you proposing an alternative?"

His finger traced her brow, her cheek, her chin. Ebony on ivory. "Would you consider it?"

"You ask me that? I am a woman. I have no say in anything."

"I think you do, princess."

She wound her hands in his hair and drew him down. But not for dalliance. That mood was well past. She began to comb out the many tangles, to weave again the single simple plait that marked his priesthood. "They say that you know nothing of the high arts. That you are sworn to shun them. And yet you are very much a man."

"It's you," he said. Pure simple truth.

"Is it?" Her fingers paused. After a little they began again. "If my brother were a woman, would you even trouble to glance at me?"

Sarevan twisted about. Her eyes were level. Eyes of the lion. Royal eyes. "But he's not," he said, "and you are."

"And you are the most splendid creature I have ever seen." She kissed him lightly, quickly, as if she could not help it. "Go now. My brother is waiting."

He stood. He was holding her hands; he kissed them. "May I come back?"

"Not too soon," she said, "but yes. You may."

Hirel was not waiting in his chambers. He had been called away, his servants said. They did not know when he would return.

Sarevan had had enough of tracking him down. The next hunt might not end so perilously, but neither could it end in such sweetness. "If he wants an apology," Sarevan said to his cat and his mageling, "he'll have to come and get it."

He went early to his bed. Part of it was weariness. Part, paradoxically, was restlessness. There was nothing that was allowed to him, that he wanted to do. What he wanted most immediately was a certain gold-and-ivory princess.

Now at last he comprehended the prison to which he had sentenced himself. Ample and gilded and most gracious, and yet, a prison. He could shock the councils of the empire with his exotic and insolent presence, but he was given no voice in their counsels. The intrigues of the court meant nothing to him. Keruvarion he had forsaken. He was neatly and most comfortably trapped, fenced in like a seneldi stallion of great value and uncertain temper. He could not even rage at his confinement. He had brought it on himself.

And like a seneldi stallion shut off from the free plains and the high delights of battle, he turned inevitably toward the other purpose of a stallion's existence. He had been mastering himself most admirably. He was not prevented from performing the offices of a priest on Journey, the prayers and the ninth-day fast; these had sustained him. And Hirel was coolly and mercifully distant, absorbed in his princehood. Women heard through lattices were intriguing and often delightful, but hardly a danger to his vows.

"Am I lost?" he asked Zha'dan. The Zhil'ari sat on the bed beside him, listening in fascination to his account of the harem.

"Does she look exactly like the little stallion?" Zha'dan asked.

"Exactly," Sarevan said. Paused. "No. The beauty, it's the same, white and gold. And the face. She's smaller, of course. A woman, utterly. What he would be if the god had made him a maid. But not . . . precisely. She's not Hirel. She's herself."

Zha'dan gestured assent, paused. His eyes were very dark. "He likes me; I please him, and he pleases me. We play well together. But I'm not . . . precisely. I'm not you."

Sarevan shook that off. "I've seen so many women, Zha'dan. A prince can't help it. Before he was, there was the dynasty, and it has to go on. If a woman is unwed, unmarred, and capable of bearing a child, she's cast up in front of me as the hope of my line. It doesn't even matter that I wear the torque. That only keeps me from playing while I look for my queen."

"Have you found her?"

"I don't know!" Sarevan rubbed his hands over his face. "I was full of wine and plain contrariness. But I never fell so easily before. Or with such perfect abandon. I didn't care what I did, or how I'd pay for it; and yet I wasn't in any haste at all to consummate it. It was as if . . . we were outside the world, and nothing that mattered here could trouble us there."

"Magic?"

"Not magery." Sarevan smiled wryly. "But magic, maybe. She's not only a beauty, Zha'dan. She has spirit. She's a golden falcon, and they've caged her. I could free her. I—could—free her."

He took it into sleep with him, that singing surety. She lay with him in his dream, and they were both of them free; he wore no torque and she no veil. She was all beautiful. She said, "If my brother were a woman, you would not glance at me."

Sarevan swam slowly from the depths of dreaming. Warmth stirred in his arms, murmuring. Dream above dream. This was dimmer than the last, and yet wondrous real. He stole a drowsy kiss.

It tasted strange. Strange-familiar. His hand, seeking, found no firm fullness of breast; but fullness enough below.

Sarevan's fingers had closed. He willed them open. Hirel blinked up at him, still more than half asleep, but frowning. He was most solid, and most certainly not a dream. "What are you doing here?" Sarevan demanded, sharp with startlement.

Hirel's frown deepened to a scowl. "Do you know no words but those?"

"Do you know no tricks but this?"

"Was it I who set your hand where it is now?"

It snapped back. "I was dreaming," Sarevan said.

"Ah," said Hirel. "Surely. And not of me."

Sarevan gaped. Suddenly he laughed. It was madness, but he could not help it. It was all too perfectly intolerable. "You're not jealous of me. You're jealous of her!"

Hirel struck him. It was not a strong blow; Sarevan hardly felt it. Hirel rolled away from him, drawing into a knot, spitting words to the wall. "A man who has never had a woman is an unnatural thing. A prince in that condition is an abomination. She has done her duty by you; she has made you a virtuous man. It was my duty to you as my brother and my equal, not only to allow it but to encourage it. But it is not my duty to be glad of it."

"Hirel—" Sarevan began.

"She is the jewel of the harem. I do not need to ask if she pleased you. She is a great artist of the inner chamber; she has taught me much of what I know. And all the while you lay with her, I who am royal, I who by birth must be your enemy, I who can never be aught to you but lust and guilt and in the end revulsion—I could not rest for that you lay with her and not with me." He drew his breath in sharply. It sounded like a sob. "I give her to you. It is she for whom you were born, she and all her sex."

"Asuchirel," said Sarevan. This time Hirel did not cut him off. "Hirel Uverias, I never lay with her."

"Surely not. You knelt with her. Or did you mount her stallion-wise?"

Sarevan went briefly blind. When he saw again, Hirel was under him, and the marks of his open palm were blazoned on the boy's cheeks. "Never," he gritted. *"Never."*

Hirel was not fighting him. He began to cool, to be ashamed. He drew back carefully. "I'm sorry," he said. "For all of it. Your brothers, your sister . . . all of it."

Hirel said nothing. His face was rigid, at once haughty and miserable. His skin in the lamplight was downy, a child's. It would bear bruises where Sarevan had struck it. Sarevan's hand laid itself with utmost gentleness upon the worst of them. "Hear a truth, little brother. Jania is very beautiful. I think that I would gladly give my torque and my vows into her keeping; I would rejoice to make her my queen. And yet that gladness rises not simply out of Jania who is woman and beauty and high heart. It rises out of Jania who is her brother's image." Hirel was silent. Sarevan pressed on. "I can't be your lover, Hirel. I'm not made for it. But what my soul is, what it longs for—Jania is nothing to it. Hirel is not. Hirel is most emphatically not." He swallowed. "I'm afraid I love you, little brother."

Hirel flung himself away from Sarevan's hand. His eyes were blazing; his cheeks were wet. "You must not!"

"I don't think I can help it," Sarevan said.

"You must not!" Hirel's voice cracked. "You must *not!*"

"Hirel," said Sarevan, reaching for him. "Cubling. We can be friends. We can be brothers. We can—"

Hirel was very still in his hands. Cold again, and far too calm. "We cannot." The tears ran unheeded down his face. "I have not told you the truth. While I embodied the jealous lover, word came. Your father has received my father's message. He has answered it. His armies have begun the invasion of Asanion."

Sarevan frowned. "That can't be. He wouldn't—"

"He has. And you must die, and even if I could prevent it, I would not. And it is the custom—with royal hostages, it is the custom that the high prince commands the executioners."

It was not real. Not yet. Not that Sarevan had failed more utterly even than he had feared. That the war had come; that he would die. But

Hirel's pain was present and potent. He held the boy, rocking him, wordless.

Hirel allowed it: that was the depth of his pain. "Clearly your father does not believe that we will slay you. He will expect us to shrink from the threat of his vengeance; to bargain with your life. Therefore," said Hirel, "you must die."

"Tomorrow?"

Hirel began to tremble. "I do not know. By all the gods, I do not know."

"There's still the night," Sarevan said.

"You do not believe it, either!" Hirel cried. "You think we will not dare. But we will, Sarevan. As surely as I hope to sit the Golden Throne, we will."

"I know." Sarevan played with the tumbled curls, smiling at their refusal to go any way but their own. "I'm not afraid to die. I don't even have much to regret. Though I would have liked to know a woman. Just once. In my own body."

Hirel pulled back. "I shall bring her to you."

"No," said Sarevan, holding him. "I can't do it to her. Even for my line's sake—and she would conceive, Hirel. That is certain. I can't abandon her to bear a Sunborn child in the heart of Asanion."

"I would raise it as my own."

"As your heir?"

Hirel would not answer.

Sarevan sighed, smiled a little. "You see. And yet he would overcome any heir you begot, any heir you named. There would be no stopping him. We are born to rule, we Varyani princes. We suffer no rivals."

"No," said Hirel. "You conquer them. You make them love you."

Eighteen

"SAREVAN. SAREVAN IS'KELION."

They had come for him. So soon. He was up before his eyes were well open, hissing fiercely, "Don't wake him. Don't make him do it. Take me now and get it over."

"Sun-prince."

The voice was—baffled? Amused? Sarevan glared through a tangle of hair; he raked it back. Prince Aranos regarded him with great interest. He eased, and yet he tensed. "Good. You can do it. Don't tell him till it's done."

Aranos said nothing. Slowly Sarevan's mind recorded what his eyes were seeing. The silken chamber had vanished. These walls were stone, stark and unadorned, and the floor was stone spread with woven mats, and the ceiling was a grey vault from which hung a cluster of lamps. None was lit. The light that filled the room came pouring from a high round window. Sunlight, bright, with little warmth in it.

Sarevan turned completely about. The bed was intact, rich and foreign in this stark place, with Hirel coiled in it. The scars on his side and his thigh, though paling with age, were livid still. The light was cruel to them.

On the wall above him was a tapestry. Beasts, birds, a dragonel. Sarevan had seen it. Somewhere. He could not, in the shock of the moment, remember where.

He faced Aranos again. The prince had companions. One was a mage clad in the violet robe of a master of the dark. The other was a priest of Avaryan, torqued and braided, with his familiar on his shoulder.

Sarevan stilled. He was remembering a promise made, and his leave given, and the part which the Mageguild had played in all of this. "I think," he said, "that I should begin again. Good morning, my lords. Where is the guildmaster, and what is this place?"

Aranos bowed slightly, but he was not choosing to answer. The mage said, "You will please to come with us."

The chief priest of Avaryan's temple in Endros said nothing, but he smiled. It was a smile that reassured Sarevan, yet frightened him. He was all a tangle.

He took refuge in vanity. "Must I go as I am?"

"Come," said the mage.

None of them would say more than that. The way seemed long; it was dim and cold, all stone, with now and then a lofty window. Whatever this place was, it could not be Kundri'j Asan. The air was too icily pure.

He was entirely out of his reckoning. It made him want to laugh. All his plotting, his betrayals, his multiple sins, and nowhere but in a dream which he had all but forgotten, had he seen himself in this place.

His companions would not answer his questions. They would not speak at all. After his third failure he desisted, not entirely gracefully. He was not used to being ignored.

This was a castle, perhaps. The stone and the steep narrow stairways had a flavor of fortresses. The end was a hall like the great hall of a lord, with its central fire and its stone-flagged floor and its walls hung with faded tapestries. Yet unlike a lord's hall, it was all but empty. The pillared bays about its edges, where men slept and gamed and kept their belongings and often a woman or two, were dark. There were no hounds, no hunting cats, no falcons on perches. No singers sang by the fire; no guards stood at attention, no servants waited on those who sat together in the warmth.

Sarevan stopped short. There was the master of the Order of Mages. There was the witch of the Zhil'ari with her grandson mute and motionless at her feet. There, in a moment, were the priest and the mage and the prince. And there was Orozia of Magrin, and beside her the last man whom Sarevan had ever thought to see. Orsan of Han-Gilen, his bright hair gone all ashen in the scarce three years since Sarevan had seen him, but his body strong still, and his eyes darkly brilliant in the black-bronze face.

A more complete conspiracy could not have gathered. Except—

"Aren't we missing someone?" Sarevan asked. "An emperor or two, maybe?"

"We suffice," the Red Prince said. For all his training in the necessities of princes, Sarevan almost cried his hurt. Even at his sternest, even in the midst of just punishment of a scapegrace grandson, Prince Orsan had never looked as he looked now. Cold. Remote. A stranger.

Sarevan stood straight before them all. "Well? Am I going to have my answers? Or am I on trial for my sins?"

They were going to drive him mad with their silence.

It was Aranos who spoke, as if he too were losing patience with this mummery. "You are not on trial, prince."

"Ah now," drawled Sarevan, "I'm not a perfect idiot. I've killed with power. I've betrayed my father and my empire. I've sold my soul to my greatest enemy. Now I've dared to look on the faces of your mighty and hidden alliance, for which I'll surely die. And you plainly intend to give me no answers, and I'm not given even a moment's grace to make myself decent. You can't tell me that you merely want to feast yourselves on my famous beauty."

Aranos glanced at his companions. They were like stones. He sighed just audibly. "You have committed no crimes that I know of, prince. Unless it is a crime to wish for peace."

"The priests would argue that," Sarevan said.

"You have sinned as all men must while they dwell in living flesh," said the priest whose name was hidden behind his magecraft. In Endros they called him Baran, which was simply, *priest*. "You will atone for it; have no fear of that. But now we ponder other matters." He raised his hand, commanding. Orozia came quietly, eyes lowered. She halted behind Sarevan. He felt her hands on his hair, braiding it with much patience for its tangles. She bound it off and returned to her place. He thought he saw tears on her cheeks; but that was not likely. She had never been able to weep stone-faced as she wept now.

He swept his eyes around the circle. "You grant me my priesthood. Now grant me your courtesy. Tell me what I see here. Have I guessed rightly? You are a conspiracy?"

"Just so," answered Aranos. "A conspiracy of mages. Of the guild, and of those outside the guild. Of the light and of the dark. Of all those who foresee only ruin in the Sunborn's war."

"Even you?" Sarevan demanded of his grandfather.

"Even I." Orsan had warmed not at all. "I who began it by snatching a priestess from the Sun-death and by fostering the child she carried. I saw even then that in him lay the seeds of the world's salvation; yet also those of its destruction. He is truly the son of the god. Of the true god, who is both life and death."

Sarevan was not astounded. He had heard it before, if never so explicitly. But he set his chin and his mind and said coldly, "You and all your line made Avaryan supreme long years before my father was born. Are you repudiating your own doctrines?"

"I am not. No more than are you."

"I don't have any doctrines. I'm merely selfish. I don't want to be lord of a desert."

"And you love him."

"Yes!" cried Sarevan with sudden heat. "I love him, and I think he's trapped himself, and he knows what he has to do, and he knows what will come of it, and he has no escape. But at least he can die in a blaze of glory, with Asanion in ruins under his heel."

"It need not be so."

"Of course it need not. But now it must. Even for me, he wouldn't stop it." Sarevan tugged viciously at his braid. "Maybe we're all fools. If I'd succeeded, what would I have done except to postpone the inevitable? I love the heir of Asanion; I love him as a brother. But he would no more bow to my rule than I would to his. The world simply will not support two such emperors as we would be."

"Granted," said the Red Prince. "Be patient for a moment now. Believe that we shall return to your dilemma; but first, hear a tale." He paused. The young Zhil'ari rose. Like Orozia, he would not let Sarevan catch his gaze. He brought a warm soft robe which Sarevan was glad of even so close to the fire, and set a chair for him. Sarevan sat as much at his ease as he might and waited with conspicuous patience. Something flickered in Orsan's eyes, too swift to be sure of, but perhaps a smile. After a moment he said, "As you see and as my lord prince has affirmed, we are a conspiracy. A reluctant one, truth to tell. I cannot say who began it. It seems that we came independently to the same conclusion: that both Keruvarion and Asanion were advancing toward an inevitable conflict, and that that conflict would be one not only of weapons but of wizardry. Many wielders of power would welcome that: a final battle for the mastery, light against dark, with the god's own son on the side of the light, and arrayed against him all the cult of the goddess and of the gods below.

"But a very few of us have seen past the names and the divisions. The true masters of mages, and with them the shamans of the tribes, have always known that it is not a war of opposing powers, but a balance. I have learned it slowly and against my will, for it flies in the face of much that I thought I knew.

"Some few years past, I had a sending. It was you who brought it, Sarevadin, with your dream of destruction repeated night after night until we feared for your sanity. For you were and are no prophet, and it is your mother who is the Seer of Han-Gilen; and if she has had such a foreseeing, she has not seen fit to reveal it to any of us."

"She has," said Sarevan. "She refuses it."

"So," said Orsan steadily. "I know that I wished your dream to be a nightmare only, the midnight fancies of a boy on the brink of manhood. But the truth came surely, if slowly. I saw what you have come to see. I knew that I must do all in my power to avert the destruction. First I spoke with trusted priests. Then I spoke to Baran of Endros, who sent me where I would never have gone of my own accord. He sent me to his shadow in the guild: to the one who was matched with him at his initiation, darkness to his light, black sorcerer to his white enchanter. We spoke, and it was slow, for there was no trust on either side. But at last we agreed. We would fight together to keep Avaryan within the bounds ordained for him. Which he ordained for himself before the world was made."

"Why?" cried Sarevan. "Why can't my father see it?"

"He can. He denies it. My fault, my grievous fault. I raised him all in the light. I never taught him to comprehend the dark. Nor did he ever learn it from all the wizards whom he vanquished. They turned to the dark, and they did it without wisdom, and he laid them low. When the guild would have taught him, he called it falsehood and drove them from his empire."

Sarevan's throat ached with tension. "They say," he said, low and rough, "that Avaryan is not his father at all. That you came to his mother in your magic. That you begot him upon her."

"Look at your hand, Sarevadin. Look into your heart. What do you see there?"

"Gold," grated Sarevan, "and doubt. My father is wrong in one thing. Why not in all the rest?"

"A man may err once, even if he be half a god. If he is a great man, he may commit a great error. It does not negate either his lineage or his greatness."

Sarevan let his eyes fall. His fingers flexed about the anguish of the *Kasar*. "What do we do, then? What can we do?"

"We have you," Orsan answered, "and we have the heir of Asanion. By now that is known. One hostage was not enough; two may well be."

"For a while," said the guildmaster. "This is the Heart of the World, the hidden place which only our masters may know. I will not tell you where it is. It may not be in the world at all. Certainly neither your father nor his loyal mages, nor the sorcerers whom the Asanian emperor has sworn to him, can find you and so snatch you free."

Comprehension dawned, late but still almost comforting. Sarevan's head came up. "He was going to do it. My father. Take me before they killed me."

"But we came before him."

"I would have refused. I would have killed myself to stop him."

"You would have. It would have been a great waste and a very great folly. Now that danger is averted. The Asanian prince will sleep until we wake him. For you we have a choice."

Sarevan sat very still. They had all tensed. He remembered what he had said to the guildmaster. Chance? A remnant of foresight beyond even dreaming?

It would be hard. They were not all in accord over it. The younger mages were losing their composure, and beneath lay a fire of protest. It might be hard enough even to suit Sarevan's madness.

He smiled with remarkably little strain. "So now we come to it. You've plotted this from the beginning, haven't you? Aimed my every stroke; guided my every move. To bring me here before you." None of them denied it. He sat back. He almost easy now. Almost comfortable, here at the heart of things, with the truth within his grasp. "Tell me now, O bold conspirators. How shall we escape our dilemma? Is there any escape? I can die. That will leave my father without an heir. You can protect Hirel, and when it's over, produce him to rule the ruins."

"Or," said the Zhil'ari witch, "we may slay him and leave you alone to live. But we will not."

Sarevan shivered. He did not want to die. Yet he was ready for it. He had been ready, perhaps, since he left Endros. "So, then. Hirel lives. I die. May I ask you to kill me quickly?"

"You may not," Prince Orsan said.

Sarevan had no words to say. The Red Prince looked long at him. He stared back. He could read nothing in those hooded eyes. He was beginning to be afraid.

"There can be but one emperor," Orsan said. Steady, quiet. "Another emperor may not share his throne. But," he said, "an empress may."

Sarevan stared at him, incredulous, almost laughing. *"That* is the summit of all your plotting? Even I know it's not worth thinking of. I could marry every princess in Asanion, but the emperor would still have sons. Unless you mean to kill all forty-odd of them."

"Fifty-one," murmured Aranos. "There was no mention of their murder, and no intention thereof. Nor any, of your marriage to my royal sister."

That was a shrewd blow. Sarevan hardly felt it. If there had ever been any logic in this council, it had fled. He sat back under the force of their stares. He was quick-witted. Too quick, many would say. He had never felt as slow as he felt now. He should know what they were telling him. He could not begin to guess.

Zha'dan sprang up. "Tell him, damn you. Stop torturing him. Tell him what you want to do to him!" No one would. He smote his hands together. Lightnings cracked; he started. Sarevan would have smiled if he had had time. Zha'dan gave him none. "It's you, you fool. It's you who'd be the empress."

Sarevan laughed, sudden and full and free.

No one else laughed with him. The silence was thunderous. His mirth shrank and fled. "That's preposterous," he said. "I know shapeshifting is possible, though it's not supposed to be. But you can't—"

"We know we can," the guildmaster said. "It has been done. It has been done to me."

This was not illogic. It was madness. Sarevan could only think to ask numbly, "Why?"

"It was one of the tests of my mastery. Not the greatest and not the most perilous, but great enough and perilous enough, and not easy for the mind to endure."

Sarevan closed his eyes. When he opened them again, nothing had changed. He thought of the woman whom the master must have been. Of the girl whom Hirel could have been, to no purpose; not with fifty brothers. Of himself. Great, gangling, eagle-nosed mongrel of a creature: comely enough as a man, but as a woman—

He gripped the arms of his chair until the wood groaned in pain. He could not take his eyes from the master. He dared not; for that would slay all his courage.

"It is not easy," the master said. "There is pain. Great pain in the working and great pain after. But the foreseeings have shown us. If you do it, if you wed Hirel Uverias, if you bear him a child . . ."

He went on and on. Sarevan stopped listening. This was worse than death. Worse even than death of power.

"It is not so terrible to be a woman," said the Zhil'ari witch. Her eyes glittered, perhaps with anger, perhaps with mockery. "Less terrible than to be a man. To be a man, and to rule over ruin."

"At least I would be—" Sarevan throttled his tongue. He had never been like Asanians, who were said to thank their gods on each day's rising that they had not been born women. He knew that they were not lesser beings, or weaker vessels, or pretty idiots to be pampered and protected. He had known his mother; he had spent long hours with her warrior women. He had been one. Almost. When in Liavi's mind he had shared the bearing and the birthing of her daughter.

But to be one in truth. To face his father, his mother, his kin. To face his empire. A eunuch could not rule. And that, very broadly and very brutally, was what they would call him.

"That will be a lie," the witch said, reading him with almost contemptuous ease. "You will be a woman whole and entire, in all respects. You will unite the empires; you will lessen the destruction."

"But not stop it."

"Not what has already begun. More than ruin will remain." She folded her arms over her breasts. "No one will be astonished if you refuse. You will live, whatever befalls. You need not live maimed."

Sarevan's own frequent thought, mercilessly twisted. He flashed out against them. "I'm maimed already. A woman is anything but that. But I was never made to be one."

"We can see to that," Orsan said.

Sarevan surged up. "You. Even you would consent to this?"

"I proposed it," said the Red Prince.

Sarevan sank down, all strength gone. He had thought his world was broken when he woke without power. He had not known that it could break again. And again. And again. Or that his mother's father, his master and his teacher, his blood kin, could grind the shards beneath his heel.

"Would it be so terrible?" asked Aranos. "You longed for a solution. This one is simple. It gives you your empire and your peace. It gives you my brother whom you love."

"Will he have me?" Sarevan demanded. "Will he want me?"

"How will you know unless you do it?"

"I can ask him."

"No," Aranos said. "That is not part of the bargain. You and you alone must choose. No other may make your choice for you."

Sarevan laughed in pain. "It comes to that, doesn't it? Myself, alone. Courage or cowardice. Peace or war. Life or death. You think you know what you ask of me. Do you? Even you, master—do you?"

"Yes," the master answered levelly. "We do not compel you. It is not a simple magic, and the pain of it is terrible. All your body will be rent asunder and made anew; so too your mind and your soul. You will pass through the sun's fires, slowly, infinitely slowly, with no mercy of unconsciousness."

Sarevan shivered in spite of himself. But he said, "Hirel will survive, you say."

"And your father," said the mage who had been silent for so long. Sarevan spun to face him. It was truth he spoke. He spoke it without joy, as one who knows he must, for the truth's sake. But he was a servant of the dark. His stare raised Sarevan's hackles. Strangeness roiled in it. Darkness. Warmthless, sunless cold. And yet, woven into it, something which Sarevan had never expected to see: acceptance. He could endure the survival of the Sunborn, if the balance was kept.

"You're lying," Sarevan said to him, a soft snarl.

"Not in this," said Baran, the light of his shadow, who never lied.

Mirain alive. Hirel alive. The war ended.

For a price.

Such a price.

Sarevan gathered his body together. His beautiful proud body, just now awakened to the delights of a woman's embrace: one woman, who might have been, who might still be his lady and his queen. He had been more vain of it than of anything but his power. He had lost the one. Now must he lose the other? Would he have nothing left?

Mirain. Hirel. Two empires made one. Peace. A child. They had all but promised that. An heir of his body.

Even if it must be a woman's body. He was not afraid of that. He had birthed a child already.

They waited. He could read them. Even Orsan. Even the darkmage. They would not scorn him if he shrank from the choice. Orsan could not have made it. None of them could. The master, who had, had begun as a woman. Had passed in the world's eyes from lesser to greater.

Sarevan stood again. His knees melted; he froze them with his terror. They asked too much. He could not do this. He was royal; he was a warrior trained. He could die for his empire. He could even betray it for its own salvation. But he was no great selfless saint, to give up all that he was and to live on after. Death was frightening, but it was final. This . . .

"I suppose," his tongue said, hardly stumbling, "that you'll do it now, before we all have time to turn craven."

Damn his tongue. *Damn* it.

No one smiled. No one looked triumphant. Orsan rose as Sarevan had never seen him rise, as an old man, stiff and palsied. "We will do it now," he said.

They brought Sarevan to a high bare chamber. Its many tall windows were open to the wind; its center was a table of stone. Dawnstone slab on nightstone base, stones of the light and the dark brought together in balance. They took his robe; they freed his hair from its braid and combed it carefully; they took the gold from his beard and the emeralds from his ears and the torque from about his neck. With no knot or weaving on him, bare as he had come into the world, he lay upon the table. And started a little. His skin, braced for cold stone, recoiled from a warmth as of the sun in summer. The dawnstone knew his lineage; it kindled for him although it was full day and not rising dawn, flushing with the splendor of the morning sky.

Blessed numbness had brought him so far; now it was forsaking him. His brain screamed and struggled, battling for escape. His body lay meekly where it was bidden. He could not even move to bid it farewell.

The mages stood about him, a circle of shadows against the windows' brightness. One bent. His grandfather kissed him very gently upon the forehead. No word passed between them. *Make me stop,* he tried to plead. *Don't let me do this.*

The Red Prince straightened. His hands rose. Power gathered in them.

Sarevan closed his eyes, breathing deep. He could still see. Witchsight. They had given it to him: thinking to have mercy, perhaps. But they had forgotten how bitterly clear it could be.

Slowly his breath left him, and with it fear. He had chosen. Not his tongue, not his madness. His deepest self. There had never been such a choosing, for such a cause; nor would there ever be again.

Avaryan, he prayed in the center of the power, *take me. Hold me fast.*

Light wove with dark. Chanting fused with silence. Mage and sorcerer wrought together.

And there was beauty in it. There was rightness. Balance. Perfection. A strength that, wielded, could alter worlds.

He would remember. He swore it, even as the power took him. He would remember the truth.

Then there was no memory. Only pain.

PART THREE

Hirel Uverias

Nineteen

*H*IREL COULD BELIEVE THAT SORCERERS HAD
snatched him away from Kundri'j. He could easily believe that he
was a hostage. He could even find it credible that his captors were a
conspiracy of the world's mages.

But this.

At first they would not tell him what they had done with Sarevan.
Then he heard them: the cries of a man in mortal agony. His jailers, a
pair of young mages, one in violet and one in grey, insisted that they
heard nothing; that all was silent. No force of his could shake them.
When he lunged for the door, their power caught him and bound him.

The cries went on unabated. They tore at his heart; they rent his
sanity. They came from everywhere and from nowhere. They echoed in
his brain.

Night came. The guard changed. A man and a woman, these, older
and considerably stronger. They brought silence. They forced sleep
upon him, from which he woke to a cold and relentless fury. And, with
crawling slowness, to what they called the truth.

They broke it gently. Too gently. At first Hirel heard only that they
had wrought some unspeakable sorcery upon Sarevan. That they hoped
by it to end the war. That they had slain him.

"No," said the woman. "He is not dead."

He was worse than dead. Hirel commanded; for a wonder they
obeyed. They took him to a chamber almost princely in this barren

fortress. They set him before the bed and left him to stare. A dark lithe body; a flood of molten-copper hair.

A body. Hirel's mind struggled against the impossibility of it. Liars, they were liars. This was a stranger. A stranger who was a woman.

"It is Sarevadin," said the mage in grey, unmoved by Hirel's rage. She was as splendid as Sarevan had ever been. She was fire and ebony, strength and delicacy melded together, the eagle's profile smoothed and fined into a stunning, high-nosed beauty.

Hirel rounded on his jailers. The guard had changed again. High ones indeed now: Han-Gilen's prince and the Mageguild's master. He addressed them almost gently. "Undo your magic."

"We cannot," the prince said.

"You must," said Hirel, still without force, still with the semblance of reason.

"It cannot be done." The master leaned heavily on a staff; nor was it only the twisting of his legs which so weakened him. "This magecraft is perilous to endure even once. Twice is deadly."

"Undo it," Hirel repeated, obstinate. "Change him back. I command you."

"No."

It did not matter who said it. Even now Hirel could recognize finality. And hate. Hate as pure as that profile. "You will pay for this," he whispered. He turned face and mind away from them. "Get out," he said.

In time they obeyed. Hirel sat, cold and still, waiting with the patience of princes. He waited long and long. The changed one slept. Sometimes she stirred. Once she murmured. Her voice was low, but it was most certainly a woman's.

Hirel knew when she woke; knew it beneath his skin. Carefully he drew back.

For a long while she neither moved nor opened her eyes. Her face betrayed nothing. When the lids lifted, the eyes were dim, clouded. Slowly they cleared. Her hands wandered amid the coverlets. One crept up. She stared at it, turned it. Gold flamed in the palm. She flexed slender fingers, eyes wandering along the fine-boned rounded arm. She touched her thigh. Raised her knee. Frowned at it. Turned it, peering at her foot. Not a remarkably small foot, but narrow and shapely.

She was long in coming to her middle. Hesitant. Perhaps afraid. She felt of her face; of her neck. Ran fingers through her hair. Brushed a breast as if by accident, and recoiled, creeping back, trembling. Her frown deepened. Her lips set. She sat up, glaring down at the altered

lines of her body; breasts high and round and firm above the narrow
waist; hips a gentle flare; and where her thighs met, the worst of it. She
touched it. No miracle transformed it. It was a miracle itself, frightening in its perfection; and no memory in it of the man who had been.
That was all within.

She rose, awkward-graceful, feeling out the balance of this new shape.
Flexing narrowed shoulders, swaying on broadened hips, essaying an
uncertain step. Little by little her gait eased, though it was taut still,
wary.

A shield hung on the wall, polished for a mirror; she faced it with an
air of great and hard-won courage. She turned slowly, twisting about,
knotting her hair about her hand, peering over her shoulder at her
mirrored back. She touched her shoulder where the deep pitted scar
should have been. It was gone. She was all new, whole and smooth and
unmarred.

She confronted herself, face to reflected face. Her hand rose to her
cheek. "I'm not ugly," she said in wonder. Starting at the sound of her
voice, speaking again with an air of defiance. "I'm . . . not . . .
ugly."

Hirel's body moved of itself. She spun, quick as a cat. Hirel gasped
under the force of those eyes. They had changed not at all; they were
black-brilliant as ever, sweeping over him, flashing to his face. "You,"
she said. "You look different."

His jaw was hanging. He retrieved it. Laughter burst from him: hysteria certainly, and incredulity, and something astonishingly like relief.
For a moment she only stared. Then she echoed him, a great ringing
peal, tribute to perfect absurdity.

They hiccoughed into silence. They were holding one another up, eye
to streaming eye. She was a hair's breadth the taller.

She stiffened all at once, going cold in his hands. He let her go. She
drew back. Her back met the mirror; she whirled upon it, tearing at it,
flinging it wide. It rang as it fell. She sank down shivering, veiled in the
bright cloud of her hair.

Hirel stood over her. Touched her.

She did not erupt as he had half expected. He sat by her, wordless.
When she did not heed him, he stroked her hair. Her ear beneath it was
exquisite. He kissed it.

She pulled away with the swiftness of rage. "Stop pitying me!"

"That," said Hirel, "I had not begun to do."

His flatness gave her pause. For a moment. She flung back her hair.
"Not yet. Oh, no. Not yet. I merely disgust you. I did the unspeakable.

I who was a lord of creation, I who was nature's darling, I let myself be twisted into *this.*"

"A woman of great valor and beauty."

"Don't lie to me, cubling. I can taste your anger. You think I was tricked, or forced. I was neither. No one made me do it. I chose it for myself." She scrambled to her feet. "Look at me, Hirel. Look at me!"

Hirel had learned to measure beauty by Sarevan Is'kelion. This that he had become was fairer still. Fair and wild, with the recklessness of despair. "I am angry," he said. "They had no right to demand such a thing of you. None even to conceive of it."

"They demanded nothing. They tried to dissuade me."

"Surely," said Hirel with a curl of his lip. "They warned you of the dangers, and spoke of the faces of courage, and named all the lesser choices. It was cleverly done. I applaud them."

"It was the only choice with hope in it." She clenched her fists. "It's no matter to you. You can wed me, bed me, get the child who will bring the peace, and go back to your twice ninescore concubines."

Hirel regarded her. She looked very young. As indeed she was: scarce a full day old. But Sarevan Is'kelion lived yet in her. It was in her eyes, and in her bearing, and in the tenor of her words. "Am I to wed you?" he asked. "I was not consulted."

"Did you need to be? It should be easy enough for a man of your attainments. You're not asked to love me. Only to beget a son on me."

Hirel frowned. She stiffened; he frowned the more blackly at himself, cursing his wayward face. This was going all awry. He tried to choose his words with care. "You are too certain of my thoughts, Sunchild. Must I be revolted by you? Might I not find you as beautiful now as you ever were? Perhaps I even find endurable the prospect of contracting a marriage with you. After all, it is logical."

"Of course it is. Else I'd never have done this."

"But," said Hirel, "I would that you had spoken to me before you submitted yourself to the mages."

She heard none of his regret. She heard only the rebuke which he had not intended. The glitter of her eyes warned him; he faced her, pulling her to him, holding her too close for struggle. She was no soft pliant woman. She was strong in her slenderness, like a panther, like a steel blade. In the instant of her surprise, he kissed her hard and deep. She tasted much the same. A little sweeter, even in resistance.

For a long moment she was rigid. With suddenness that startled them both, she kindled. Her arms locked about him. Her body arched. Her sweetness turned all to fire.

He laughed, breathless. She did not laugh with him. Her eyes were wild and soft at once, and more than a little mad. "Lady," he said. "Lady, I have wanted this, I have dreamed of this, so long, so long . . . Bright lady, I think I love you."

The softness fled; the wildness filled her. "Damn them," she whispered. "Damn their meddling magic."

He drew breath to speak. To protest, perhaps. But she was gone.

Hirel started after her, stopped. She was all raw, looking for pain wherever she turned. Pain had brought her to the choosing; pain had made the choice, and pain had wrought the woman where a man had been. Time would heal her; he could only hinder it.

He left the room slowly, letting his feet bear him where they would. He was not surprised to gain a companion, nor, at all, to recognize the man who walked beside him.

Aranos was as coolly wise as ever, and as full of serpent's sympathy. "She is a woman, brother," he said with the suggestion of a smile. "These moods will beset her."

Hirel kept his anger at bay. Saving it. Hoarding it for when he should have the power to wield it. "You have made a woman. You have not unmade the Sunborn's heir."

"Indeed we have not," said Aranos. "But we have assured that you will live to rule not Asanion alone, but with it Keruvarion."

"Do you believe that?" asked Hirel.

"It will require tact, of course. She was born a man and raised to rule. She will not accept meekly the woman's portion: the harem and the bearing of children. But her body will aid you. It will guide her on the path of her chosen sex; it will yield to your mastery. Get her with child and keep her with child, and she will be glad to surrender her power into your hands."

Hirel knew that he should be calm. Aranos spoke simple wisdom. The philosophers proclaimed it. Women were begotten of a lesser nature, of flawed seed, with no purpose but to nourish the children which their lords set in them. And of course, the sages averred, to give pleasure in the seed's sowing. Beasts might do as much. Beasts did, some believed; for what was the female but a blurred and bestial image of the male?

"No," Hirel said. "Lies and folly, all of it."

Aranos looked long at him. "Ah, Asuchirel. You have fallen in love."

"So I have. But I have not lost my ability to see what lies before my face."

"The better for you both," Aranos said undaunted, "if you are besotted with her, if only you remember who you are. And what this marriage can gain you."

"I am not likely to forget," said Hirel.

Aranos was too well trained to lay hand on a high prince, but he raised that hand athwart Hirel's advance. "See that you do not. Yon conspirators dream that they have won great victories: the Varyani that Asanion is theirs in the person of a malleable child, the mages that they have found a way to lessen Avaryan's power and to increase their own. I know that you are not the pretty fool which you so often choose to seem; I believe that the victor can be Asanion. If you press your advantage. If, having lost your heart, you do not lose your head."

Hirel smiled, honey-sweet. "My head is entirely safe. You might do well to be concerned for your own." He stepped around his brother's hand and stretched his stride. Aranos, in robes and dignity, did not see fit to follow.

They had a fine nest of mages here. One or another was always within sight, although none accosted Hirel once he had rid himself of Aranos. He paced off the limits of the fortress; much of it was carved into living rock, the rest built upon the summit of a mountain. Beyond it was all a wilderness of stone and cloud and sky. Some of the thronging peaks were higher, clad in snow. Many marched below in jagged ranks, black and red and grey and blinding white. No green. No sign of human habitation.

Water rose bitter cold from a spring within the mountain. Food came by the will of mages: solid enough for all of that, and plentiful if not rich. The cooks knew no art but the art of spiceless stews and boiled grain. The wine was little better.

But there were compensations. The purity of the air. The splendor of the heights, and at nightfall the stars, great flaming flowers in the perfect blackness of the sky.

Mages found Hirel at a high window, set a robe on him, and led him to the hall. After the vault of heaven, the chamber of stone was dim and cramped. Hirel struggled to breathe its heavy air.

The conspirators had gathered. They had a haggard look; the Red Prince was not among them, nor had they left a place for him. The Varyani sat a little apart from the mages, and Aranos stood with his brace of sorcerers. They were saying little.

The Sunchild stood alone by the fire. Her hair was loose down her back; her robe was plain to starkness, white girdled with white. She was not wearing Avaryan's torque. The Sun-priests' glances deplored it, but her shoulder was turned firmly away from them. She played with the flames as if they had been water, letting them lick at her fingers.

Hirel sprang toward her. Her glance halted him. It was a stranger's stare, cool and composed, with no spark of recognition. Hirel stiffened against it. The fire had done her no harm. Of course; she was born of it. He had tasted the anguish of the birthing.

She did not even choose to know him.

Hirel stood beside her. He knew that the mages watched. He was past caring. He spoke quietly but not furtively, and reasonably enough when all was considered. "Lady, whether we will or we nill, we are bound together. We can make of that bond a misery, or we can transform it into a triumph."

"Such a triumph," she said. The words were bitter; the tone was remote and cold. "You with all your women. I in the harem's chains."

Aranos' satisfaction was distinct, like a hand on Hirel's shoulder, a voice murmuring complacencies in his ear. He twitched them away. "You would be a fool to choose that, lady."

"I have already."

He looked at her then. At the bowed bright head; at the suggestion of her body within the robe. At the hand half hidden in her skirt, knotted into a fist, trembling with repressed violence. "Yes," Hirel said, "it is a great pity that the spell's weaving did not slay you as you wished it to. And that, having condemned yourself to life in a woman's body, you should have waked to find yourself fair. And greatest of all, that I cannot find it in me to shrink from you. That I find you beautiful; that I desire you."

"Of course you desire me. I'm female. I'm dowered with an empire."

Hirel paused. "Perhaps," he said, "I am at fault. To your eyes I would be no great marvel of a man. I shall never be more than small as your people reckon it; I am pallid away from the sun and sallow in his presence; and I am years too young for you."

"Now who's talking like a fool?"

Hirel spread his hands. "Is it folly? You insist that you repel me. Since you do not, then surely it is I who repel you. Did they fail, your meddling mages? Did they make you a woman who can love none but women?"

Her head flew up. Her eyes were wild.

"Look at me," he said. "Touch me. What does your body say of me?"

She would look. For a long moment he feared that she would not touch. Her hand trembled as she reached, as it traced his cheek. "It sings," she whispered. "It sings of you."

"Of me? Not merely of men?"

She drew a breath fierce-edged with temper. "Of you, damn you. It never—it didn't—I still don't want just any man. Or—or any woman. But you, I want. I want you with all that is in me."

"So always," murmured Hirel, "have I wanted you." His voice rose a little, clear and calm. "It is not the shape of you from which I recoil. It is that it was done to you. That, I can never forgive. Since it is done and is not to be undone, I bide my time; I wait upon my vengeance. And while I wait for it, I am minded to love you. I will share the world with you."

"If I am minded to share it."

"Half of it is mine, my lady."

"But half of it is not." She smiled. Hirel was comforted, a little. He hoped that Aranos was not. It was a white wild smile, with no softness in it. "You'll free your concubines, prince. You'll swear solemnly to take no other woman as bedmate or queen. Else you'll not have me."

"The concubines," said Hirel, "I can agree to. But the rest—"

"Swear."

Hirel struggled to master his temper. "You must be reasonable, my lady. There will be times when you do not want me. Would you have me force you?"

"So then. We compromise. When you don't want me, I'll find another bedmate."

Hirel flung up his head. "You will not!"

"Why not?"

"It is unthinkable. It is forbidden. It is a breach of the marriage contract."

"Exactly."

"I do not understand you," Hirel said with heroic restraint. "You suffered all of this for one sole end: to contract an alliance with me. Now you demand of me a concession which you know I cannot grant."

"Can't you?"

"I have no need of you. You need me, or your sacrifice is worthless."

"Without me, you die and your empire falls, and I live to rule."

"Who will follow you?" demanded Hirel, the more cruel for that his cruelty seemed to wound her not at all. "Who will accept the rule of a woman?"

"Who will be left to claim the power? I have the *Kasar* still; Keruvarion's law binds the empire to the bearer of the brand. Asanion will be harder, I grant you. But I can rule it, and I will. With you or without you."

"You will have to slay me with your own hand."

"Or marry you. On my terms. I'll not be your veiled and big-bellied slave, Hirel Uverias. Nor will I wait my turn with all your other slaves, contending with them for a night of your favor. Unless you agree to do the same for me."

It was to be expected. She still thought like a man. She did not know how to be a woman.

She would not lower those bold black eyes. The same eyes that had transfixed Hirel on the first night of their meeting, refusing to accede to the laws of nature: of race then and of caste, as now of gender.

She spoke almost gently. "It's hard, I know. But it's not unheard of. My mother bound my father to the same."

"Your father had been a priest; and he was never an Asanian high prince."

"So? Can you do any less than a bandit king?"

"I would not stoop to it."

She laughed. It was cruel, because there was no malice in it. It turned all Hirel's resistance into the petulance of a spoiled child.

She was glorious when she laughed. She had no shame of this that she had chosen; she had nothing resembling a maiden's modesty. In front of all the staring mages, she took Hirel's face in her hands and kissed him.

Hirel's heart thudded; his head reeled. Sarevan, mage and priest though he was, wild and half mad and as near a giant as made no matter, had never frightened Hirel more than a little. A prince could match a prince, though one be descended from a god.

This was still Sarevan, little changed once one grew accustomed to the single great change. Yet her touch woke Hirel to something very like panic. A prince could match a prince. But what of a Sunborn princess?

She drew back slightly, searching his face. It flamed under her gaze. She smiled. "I think I love you too, youngling. Don't ask me why."

"If there are gods," Hirel muttered, "they laugh to hear you."

"They do." She reclaimed her hands. Her smile took on an edge of iron. "But I am not marrying a man who refuses to grant me the full freedom which he grants himself."

Hirel's breath escaped him in a rush. "I never said that I would bind you. You need not take the veil, nor shall I imprison you in the harem. You may even," he said, and that was far from easy, "you may even bear arms, although for that we must change the law in Asanion."

"And?" she asked, unmollified.

"Is that not enough?" He knew it was not. Her brows had lowered. He glared back. "I cannot bind myself to you alone. My nature forbids it. I am a man; I am made to beget many sons. My desires are strong, and they are urgent, and they are not to be denied. Whereas a woman is made to bear a few strong children; her lusts are less potent, her needs gentler, her spirit shaped for the loving of a single man."

She laughed again, and now she mocked him. "Hear the wisdom of a child! I almost hate to disillusion you. But alas, it is illusion, and I will not be swayed by it. Bind yourself, Hirel, or set me free."

"And raise another man's son as my own?"

"Only if you demand the same of me."

He tossed his aching head. "You will drive me mad."

She would not even pretend to regret it. She only waited, unshakable. She was very beautiful. She was not the only beautiful woman in the world. She was certainly the most obstinate, and the most unreasonable, and the most maddening. And she brought with her the greatest of all dowries.

It was not worth the price she set on it.

And what price had she paid to offer it?

"Be free, then," he snapped at her. "But do not expect me to acknowledge your get."

"Even when it is yours?"

"How can I ever be sure of it?"

"You will," she said, "I promise you."

She held out her hand with its flame of gold. He stared at it until it began to fall. Then he caught it. Raised it. Kissed it. "Lady," he said, "whatever comes of this venture, certainly I shall not perish of boredom."

Now she looked as a maiden ought, eyes downcast, demure and shy. Struggling, no doubt, to keep at bay a grin of triumph. Hirel could not even be indignant. Aranos' expression was too intriguing a study.

Twenty

THE MAGES HAD WROUGHT WELL. HIREL GRANTED them that. The hall blazed with magelight: sparks of white and gold, blue and green, red and yellow, set like jewels in the roof. Flowers bloomed on the grey stone and wound up the pillars; hangings shimmered behind, light and shadow interwoven, shaping images that shifted and changed whenever he glanced at them.

He stood by the undying fire in a circle of mages, clad as a prince who went to his wedding, in an eightfold robe of gold and diamond. The mages of the guild stood two and two, each servant of the light with his dark companion. Zha'dan loomed over them, painted and jeweled and braided, outblazing the fire itself with his splendor. He flashed Hirel a white smile, which Hirel returned with the faintest of flickers.

He glanced at his companion. Aranos held the place of the honored kinsman, attended by his priests with the scroll of the contract. Han-Gilen's prince faced them with Orozia and the guildmaster. They had words to say: ritual challenges, ritual concessions. They called the lady Sarevadin. Odd to hear it as a woman's name. One might have thought that the empress had known, to choose a name which would serve for a daughter as for a son.

He marshaled his wandering wits. It was a very long contract, and very complex. But its heart was simple. The heir of Asanion took to wife the heir of Keruvarion. He granted her full freedom, as in turn she granted him. When he came into his inheritance, he must share his throne with her; so too must she share the throne of Keruvarion. The first child of their bodies would stand heir to both empires.

He set his name where he was bidden. When he straightened, he went rigid.

An Asanian bride did not show herself at the exchange of legalities that was the wedding proper. When her kinsmen had sold her with due ceremony, slaves bore her in a closed litter to her husband's house. There she would feast among the women until he had done feasting with the men. Then, and only then, would he see her: swathed and veiled and weighted with jewels, enthroned amid the riches of her dowry.

She wore a veil, a shimmer of royal white upon her bright hair. Her gown was of a northern fashion, shocking to Asanian eyes: a skirt of many tiers, white and gold, broad-belted with gold about her narrow waist, and a vest of gold-embroidered white, and a kingdom's worth of gold and emeralds about her arms and her neck and her brows, suspended from her ears and woven into her hair. None of it sufficed to cover her breasts. Her nipples, like her lips and her eyelids, bore a dusting of gilt.

She took the pen from Hirel's stiff fingers and signed her name next to his, in the characters of the Hundred Realms and again in those of Asanion. Hirel bit his lip lest he disgrace himself with laughter. Aranos was appalled. Even Prince Orsan seemed mildly startled by her coming, if not by her presumption.

Having sealed the alliance under Asanian law, they faced the prince and the priestess in the rites of Keruvarion. Orozia demanded Sarevadin's torque of priesthood, held it up in her hands, raised a long chant in a tongue which Hirel did not know. She ended on a high throbbing note. Her hands lowered. She set the torque again about Sarevadin's throat, with much solemnity and no little resistance from the Sunchild. But the prince quelled her with a stern word. "You may not repudiate your calling. You are High Princess of Keruvarion; you will continue in Avaryan's priesthood. As your father has done. As many another ruling queen has done." She bent her head then, submitting without humility.

Hirel spoke the words which he had been instructed to speak, but as soon as he had spoken, he had forgotten them. They were only words. This was reality. The hand he held, no warmer or steadier than his own; the voice that murmured in his silences; the eyes both bold and frightened, and once the glimmer of a smile. He was rapt. Bewitched. He the prince, the logician, the master of his royal will.

He hardly tasted the wedding feast. Some he must eat, and some he must drink: it was the rite. They drank from the same cup, ate from the same bowl. She ate and drank for them both.

She kindled under all the eyes. She had even cold Aranos falling into her hand, hanging on her every word, dwindling when she turned her eyes away from him. Sevayin, they called her. Sevayin Is'kirien, the Twiceborn, the Sun's child.

Then it was past, and they were alone, locked in a chamber with a hearth and a winetable and a bed broad enough for a battlefield. Hirel did not know where to go. She—Sevayin, he must resolve to call her—had lost a little of her brittle brilliance. She filled a cup with wine and held it out. Hirel declined it. She toyed with it; sipped; hesitated; set it down. "It's not done, you know," she said. "There's still the crux of it. I hope you haven't lost your courage. Because," she said, and her voice shook, "I don't think I ever had any."

She looked most valiant, standing there in all her beauty, trying not to tremble. Hirel let his body act for him. It went to her; it held her, or she held it. They clung together like children.

It was she who broke the silence. "I dreamed this," she said. "And you."

"And you call yourself no seer?"

"I'm not. I'm merely mad." She laughed as she said it, unsteadily. "And to crown it all, now I can't escape. Now I have to begin my lessons in the high arts."

"I shall take delight in teaching you." Hirel held her at arm's length. She smiled shakily. He smiled back. "I confess, I have somewhat more skill as a lover of women than as a lover of men. And rather more inclination for it."

"I . . . incline . . . very much toward you." She swayed forward, brushing his lips with hers. Her hands sought the fastenings of his robes. They were wedding robes; they parted, slipping away of their own accord. He wore no trousers beneath. Her breath caught. "You've grown again, cubling."

"How fortunate you are," he said. "No one can know when you wake to desire."

She lowered her eyes. "I can," she said very low.

He touched her. She quivered. It was not wholly true, what Hirel had said. Her breasts were taut. He freed them of encumbrances; the vest, the necklaces, the golden pectoral. He loosed the clasp of her belt. It sprang free. Her skirts fell one by one. There were nine. He appreciated the irony.

She cast off the ornaments which he had left her, and the drift of veil. Only the torque remained, and a single jewel: a chain of gold about her hips, thin as a thread, clasped with an emerald. He set his hand to it. "Not yet," she said, her laughter half a gasp. Her heart was beating hard. "That's the maiden-chain. It has to wait until you've made a woman of me."

She was. Entirely. A maiden, and then a woman. As he breached the gate, she cried aloud. For pain. For exultation. They sang in him. They wrought a great and wondrous harmony, a symphony of bodies joined together. He soared upon it. He made himself one with it.

They descended together, he and she. He laid his head upon her breast. She wove her fingers into his hair. Slowly their hearts quieted. Her cheeks were wet, but the tears were none of grief.

He let his hand wander down her belly and her hips to the clasp of the chain. It parted. His fingers found their way between her thighs. She kindled, but she shifted slightly, away from him. He yielded to her will; his hand came to rest again upon her hip.

"Hirel," she said after a few tens of heartbeats. He turned his head to kiss her breast. "Hirel, where were you when the mages loosed their power on me?"

He raised his head, frowning that she should speak of it now of all times. But he answered her readily enough. "I was locked in a chamber, and no one would let me go to you."

She met his eyes. "Where were you, Hirel?"

"I told you, I—" He broke off. She knew what he had said. She wanted more. "I was locked away, but I heard your cries. They all denied that there was aught to hear."

"There was nothing. I was silent, Hirel."

"I heard you," he insisted.

"You did." She scowled. Damn these witches and their paradoxes. A smile flickered; she bit it back. "You were in my mind. You and the mages. You've been in and out of it ever since."

"That is preposterous."

"Have you ever had a better night's loving? Or a stranger?"

"You have a gift for it. And I am besotted with you."

Her smile escaped. "And I love you, my proud prince. But something is happening with my power. I should have suspected it long ago. I began to when I found you amid the pain, and your presence eased it a little. It's been growing stronger since; it's strongest when you touch me. I've been afraid to believe in it. Afraid I only dreamed it. But now I know. We're mages, Hirel. Both of us."

He thrust himself to his knees. *"You* are a mage. I am glad for you. It was bitter, your power's loss. But I have no part in it."

"You are the heart of it," said Sevayin, relentless. "You were there when I lost my power. You were with me when I almost died; it was you who turned me back to the light. You found the Eye of Power. You were almost on top of it when I destroyed it. We came to love one another; we faced death together, as we faced life. Somehow, in the midst of it, my magery bound itself to you. It's part of you now."

"No," Hirel said. "I can believe the improbable, but not the impossible."

She seized his hands. He could never accustom himself to her strength, even though he knew what she had been and what she would always be: born of warriors, trained for war. He glared into her eyes, and lost his battle thereby.

It was a sharpening of all the senses. He could see through stone; he could hear across worlds. His skin knew every nuance of the air. He tasted love and fear and gladness. He scented wonders.

Power, she whispered. Her lips never moved. *This is power. I thought that I had lost it. I wanted to die for lack of it.*

"I am not made for it!"

She drew back. Hirel reeled, blind, deaf, all but bodiless. By slow degrees his senses grew again, but dimmed and dulled, mere earthly senses. The only brightness was Sevayin lying beneath him, her face a vision of lamplight and shadow, crowned with fire. With great care he touched her cheek. The power roared and flamed about him.

Her smile was sad and joyous at once: warmth and coolness mingled, scented with flowers. Flameflowers, burning-sweet. "Oh, yes, my love," she said, "you are made for it. It flames in your blood. It takes its strength from you."

"Ah," he said, wry, not yet angry. "I am your familiar."

Her eyes glittered. "You are much more than that!"

"Certainly. I am your lord and husband."

"And my lover." She stroked him until he quivered with pleasure. Her joy made his heart sing. She was whole again and growing wild with it, leaping up, sweeping him with her, spinning like a mad thing. She reached for the fire that was in her; she set her will upon it.

Hirel groped through the blinding pain. He found her huddled on the floor, too stunned even for temper. "Crippled," she said. "Still—after all—"

"You are not!" Hirel cried.

She barely heard him. "I was so sure. I *knew.* My power has come back. It has been coming back ever since the change; and you are its focus. But the pain is still there. The walls are as high as ever." She raised her head. Her lips drew back from her teeth. "I will break them down. By Avaryan, Hirel, I will."

The Red Prince was gone again. So too was Aranos. The mages would not tell Hirel where. The how he could guess. Even a little of the why, if he set his mind to it. There was trouble. The war did not go well. But for which side—that, they refused to say.

He could not find Sevayin. She was present in his mind, an awareness as of his own body, a glimmer of night and fire; in time, she had promised him, he would learn to follow the presence to its source. But he had not yet learned, and she had hidden herself well. He spared a moment for temper. A wife should hold herself at her husband's disposal.

This one did as she pleased. Which was nothing but what she had always done, insofar as she could in this wintry eyrie.

Hirel could do nothing that befit a prince. There were no servants but the mages, and they performed none but the most essential of services. He must bathe and dress and amuse himself. There were books, a whole great vault of them. None could tell him what passed between the empires. One of the mages condescended to a match or two of weaponless combat; he would speak of naught but holds and throws and falls.

At length, driven by his mighty restlessness, Hirel came to the heart of the castle, to the chamber of power denuded of its wedding splendor. Its fire burned unabated. If it failed, Sevayin said, the fortress would fall; for the fire was the power that held stone upon stone.

Hirel sat on the floor in front of it. It looked like a simple mortal fire. Its warmth caressed him; its dancing soothed his temper. He closed his eyes. The flames flickered in the darkness. "If you are power," he said to them, "serve me. Tell me what my jailers will not have me know."

"Are you strong enough to endure the telling?"

Hirel glanced over his shoulder, unstartled. The fire's doing, perhaps. The guildmaster leaned on twin staffs. His robe, which had never seemed to be of any color in particular, in that light seemed woven of silver and violet together, shimmering like imperial silk. "I must know," Hirel answered him. "Has Asanion fallen?"

"No."

"Is my father dead?"

"Indeed not."

"Have I been stripped of my titles?"

"You know that you have not."

"Then," said Hirel, "I have nothing to fear."

The mage sat by him. Why, thought Hirel, the man was young. It was the twisting of his body, and the pain of the twisting, that had aged him so terribly.

It was no less than he deserved.

"Indeed," he said calmly. "It was my payment for the power I wield. I had great beauty once, and great strength, and grace such as few of mortal race are given. I was a dancer in the temple of Shavaan in Esharan of the Nine Cities."

"But they are—"

"Yes. They are all women. What I did to your beloved, I did to myself. And more. All that I had been, I surrendered, to be the master of mages."

Hirel considered that broken body, those clear eyes. "What price will you demand of me?"

"Not I, prince. The power. It will do with you as it chooses."

"I do the choosing, guildmaster."

The master smiled. "Perhaps you do. Perhaps you have. Are you not inextricably bound to the Sunchild? Do you not accept the reality of magic?"

"Perforce," said Hirel, "yes." He narrowed his eyes. "Tell me."

The master bowed his head, raised it. "Perhaps, after all, it is not so terrible. It is merely a wielding of power. We are out of your world, prince, and out of your time. It is still autumn there; the war has barely begun. Mirain An-Sh'Endor has taken Kovruen. Ziad-Ilarios has announced that he will lead the Asanian armies in his own sacred person, as he led them before he took the throne."

Hirel bared his teeth in a smile. "Scandalous."

"Is it not? But that is nothing to the greater scandal which now rocks Asanion. The emperor your father will not only command his own forces in the field. He has sent an embassy to the Sunborn, proposing an alliance."

Hirel stiffened, incredulous.

"Truly, prince. An alliance against us who dare to hold you hostage."

Hirel laughed suddenly. "Thus is the biter bit!"

"If either of them can find us."

"They will," said Hirel. "You are not the master of all mages."

"I am not," the guildmaster conceded. "The Sunborn is greater than I. But if he accepts your father's embassy, he will have fulfilled our purpose. They may find our gate; they may besiege it; they may even conquer it. It does not matter. You are here, with your lady who bears the heir of the empires."

"And they fight together." Hirel frowned. "If all is turning to your advantage, why are your mages so reluctant to boast of it?"

"It is too early yet for certainty. The Sunborn may refuse the alliance. The Golden Courts may turn against your father. Ziad-Ilarios himself may choose to act alone in despite of his ambassadors."

"And," said Hirel, seeing clearly now, "we their children may manage to escape you. What will the Sunborn do when he discovers that he is father to a daughter?"

"He will discover it. In good time. When it will best serve us all."

"How long, guildmaster? How long will you imprison us here?"

"As long as we must."

"As long as you can." Hirel stood. "I should be compassionate. Your order will bear the brunt of the emperor's wrath. Does it trouble you that even as your people suffer, certain princes will enjoy the full trust of their lords?"

"That trust serves us well," the master said.

"Trust us, magelord. Let us share in your counsels. We are your great weapon; should we not have a voice in our wielding?"

"What sword is given such grace?"

"What sword has a will to oppose its bearer?"

"Your lady will not. She has foreseen what will be. She will not betray her prophecy."

Hirel heard the echo behind the words. "You fear her even more than you fear me. You struck a bargain of desperation with a prince bereft of his power. A mageborn princess is a new and frightening thing; for she may choose to disregard the fears and follies of her elder self. Is it you who give her such pain with each new flexing of her power? Is it you who would strengthen each wall as she casts it down?" Hirel stood over the mage, wielding his presence with all his royal skill. "Trust, we meet with trust; and there may be much that we can do to aid you. But if you persist in treating us as captives, we will do all that we can to set ourselves free."

The guildmaster sat silent, uncowed. Hirel refused to let the silence diminish him. At last the mage said, "Perhaps we have erred. We meant but to spare you anxiety."

Hirel folded his arms and bulked a little larger.

"Would you rather have heard rumors and half-truths from the mouths of our apprentices?"

"There are no apprentices here."

The guildmaster shifted his body, sighing. "Prince Orsan warned us. My fault that I would not listen. I am not greatly skilled in dealing with princes."

"Young princes. Children who refuse to be children. Apprentices with the arrogance of masters."

The mage smiled. "Just so, high prince. Will you pardon me?"

"If you will trust me."

"I can try."

"I will know if you do not." Hirel stepped back. "Good day, sir."

It struck Hirel as he left the hall behind. A lady who bore the heir of empires.

Already.

How could they know?

Of course they must. They were mages.

He began to run. Stopped short, mindful of dignity. Damned it all and bolted toward the whisper of her presence.

It was not hard, with necessity to drive him. She was on the mountain, perched on the tip of its fang, calling to eagles. Hirel dropped gasping at her feet. Heights had never troubled him overmuch, but this was loftiest lunacy. For a long while he could only struggle to breathe. Then he looked down and nearly lost his senses. He clutched at unheeding stone and forced his eyes to open. She filled them. In the bitter cold she wore torque and trousers and an armlet or three. Her feet were bare. Her mantle she wrapped about Hirel, wrapping herself about that, firing him with kisses. "I can talk to them," she said, exultant. "The eagles. They're bronze, have you seen? They know no white kin."

Hirel glared at her. "Are you going to face the courts of the empires as you face yonder eagles?"

She followed his glance downward to her breasts. "They don't like coverings."

"Have you paused to wonder why?"

It was Hirel who blushed. She shrugged. "It's common, I suppose. I may be more sensitive than most. Or maybe I'm simply not used to it. Other women grow into it gradually."

"Yes," said Hirel, "it is gradual. Twice nine Brightmoon-cycles, more or less."

There was a very long silence. She drew back, sitting on her heels, staring down at her body. She weighed her breasts in her hands. She spanned the faint curve of her belly. She reached inward, a quiver of Hirel's newborn senses. Her head came up. Her face was blank, shocked. "I am," she said. "I . . . actually . . . am." She still did not believe it. Even though she knew. Even though she had wedded him for this very purpose.

She had begun to shiver. Hirel spread her cloak over them both, holding her in silence. Her mind was walled and barred. How far he had come in so little time: he floundered in its absence, like a man struck blind. It was easier when he was apart from her; then he could endure to be alone. But to be body to body and shut away . . .

Anger flared, warming him in the wind. Was that how he must live? Crippled when he walked alone, whole only when he lay in her embrace. Living for the touch of her hand. Pining for the lack of it.

Suddenly she flung him away from her. "I don't want it," she said. Her voice rose. "I don't *want* it! I want my body back. I want to be what I was born to be!"

Hirel's temper collapsed into terror. He hardly dared breathe. One step and she would tumble from the precipice. He watched her ponder it, poised on the edge, hands clawed as if to rend this flesh which had imprisoned her.

She whipped about. She laughed, and that was frightening. "Not me alone, my husband. That's the heart of it. Now I know why so many men try so hard to keep their women locked in cages. We're weak. We're fragile. We're strangers to reason. And we have this mighty power. Without us, none of you would be. Without our consent, granted freely or by force, none of you would have a son to brag of."

"So too must we consent," Hirel said, treading with care.

She swayed backward. His heart stopped. She bared her teeth. "Such consent! A few moments' pleasure and you can walk away. It's the woman who faces twice nine cycles of steadily worsening pain, with agony at the end of it, and all too often death."

"Not always. Far more often there is great joy."

"Maybe." She tossed her wild bright hair. "I endured this once, Hirel; and even then I could take refuge in my own body. I can't endure it again with no such escape. I'll break. I was made to hunt, to fight, to face death edged or fanged: for man's courage. Not for this."

"I never marked you for a coward."

"Of course I'm a coward. I'm a woman." She leaned toward him. "You are a bold brave prince. You carry this child."

"I cannot."

"No; you can't. You shrink from the very thought of it."

"Sevayin—"

"Sevayin!" she mocked him. "Sevayin! Sarevadin who ever was, with all the bloom worn off, and grim reality staring her in the face. It was a splendid game when it was new. A body my old self would have lusted after; freedom at last to be your lover; my power born again all unlooked for. Wouldn't you think I'd paid enough for all of that? Couldn't I stop now and go back to what I was before? I can even face the war. Nothing I've done seems even to have delayed it, let alone put a stop to it."

"Would you give me up, Vayin?"

She left the brink. She swooped upon Hirel. He tumbled backward. She raged; she laughed; she dropped beside him, hands fisted over her eyes, tears escaping beneath them. "You must despise me."

Gently he drew her hands down, holding them against his breast. "I love you."

"The god alone knows why."

"Yes." He kissed her. She tasted of salt.

Her head twisted away from him. "You like me better this way. You're freer with me."

"Because you are freer with me."

"That's not I. That's this body I'm trapped in."

"But surely your body is as much your own as is your mind."

"You don't understand, do you?" She faced him. "You love me because the mages have bound you to it. I desire you because they set the same spell on my body."

"No mage alive," said Hirel, "can compel a man to love. My body has desired you since first it saw you, all exotic insolence beside a gangrel's fire. My heart was yours soon enough thereafter." She curled her lip. He fixed her with a cold stare. "Yes, what heart I have. Do not belittle it. It belongs to you."

"You are beyond hope." She freed her hands, to clasp them behind him. "We both have matters to settle with the mages."

"We do indeed," said Hirel. "Promise me, Vayin. You will not begin without me."

She hesitated. Hirel firmed his will. Slowly she said, "If I can."

"You will."

She set her lips and would not speak. Hirel drew her to her feet. "Come back to prison with me."

"We do keep meeting in chains, don't we?" She led him down from the pinnacle, surefooted as a mountain cat, fearless as any madwoman born. It was her good fortune that Hirel loved her to distraction. Else he would have hated her cordially for daring so to best him.

Twenty-one

THE WALLS OF THE HALL OF FIRE WERE SOMETIMES stone, sometimes tapestry, sometimes windows on alien worlds. Worlds utterly strange or strangely familiar; worlds that were hells and worlds that were paradises; worlds held motionless in time, worlds plunging headlong into the glittering dark. None was Hirel's, no more than this one with its brilliant moonless sky.

Sevayin was learning to shift the worlds, to call up new visions and to bring back the old. It passed the time; it honed her power. It diverted her from wilder pursuits: scaling peaks, herding clouds, challenging mages to combat with swords or staves or bare hands.

Hirel found her there on a day like every other day, white-sunned and bitter cold. She sat staring at one of the gentle places: green, with flowers and bright birds and falling water. Her eyes upon them were anything but gentle.

He sat on his heels beside her. She had had to forsake her breeches; it would have been like her to go naked. But she had wrapped herself in a robe the color of the sky at sunrise. It glowed against the midnight of her skin; it showed clearly the shape of her body. She insisted that she was ungainly. She had lost none of her grace. It was merely changed, deepened: not the hunting panther now but the ul-queen growing great with her cubs.

Hirel's hand found its way to the waxing curve of her belly. Heels drummed a greeting; he laughed, struck with wonder. "He knows his father, that one."

"If it's a she, what will you do? Disown her?"

"Spoil her to ruin." Hirel set a kiss in the corner of Sevayin's mouth. She did not pull away, but her mood was not to be lightened by either joy or desire.

"They'll bind us here," she said, "for the full twice nine cycles, if they can. And keep our child for their own purposes."

"So they dream," said Hirel, calm because he must be. Refusing to consider that a little more than half of that span had driven him perilously close to breaking. They must not break, either of them.

Her eyes burned upon him. "You haven't heard, have you? You know my father has been up to his old bandit's tricks: running like a fire through the whole of eastern Asanion, driving the satraps' armies before him; or pretending to retreat and leading his pursuers into the full might of his army; or simply conquering with the fear of his name. And always managing by sheerest chance to escape engagement with your father's forces.

"Ziad-Ilarios' ambassadors had a bitter chase, but at last they found the Sunborn. He kept them about for days while he took a baron's surrender, rested his men, raided a fortress which had threatened resistance. But when he deigned to receive his guests, he barely heard them out. He refused the alliance. 'My son is safe,' he said, 'where none will dare to touch him. I will give him the world to rule.' "

Hirel was silent. He was not surprised. But the pain robbed him of words. Her pain.

She had honed it into anger. "And then," she said, choking on the words, "and then he began the conquest of Asanion. All the rest was merely prelude. The armies of the north have swept over the mountains. The armies of the south have flooded the plains of Ansavaar. Ziad-Ilarios is beset, driven back and back, battling for the heart of his empire."

"But surely it is winter now, even there. The rains—"

"They have not come. Avaryan rules the sky. The mages say that that in part is my father's doing. His weathermasters are stronger than Ziad-Ilarios'; and the earth is his ally." She thrust herself to her feet. "And we sit here. Moldering."

"Growing an heir."

"An heir of what? My father has been wise in one respect: he's made little use of power beyond the encouraging of a cloud or two to shed its rain outside of Asanion. His armies have been enough; and his generalship that can leap from mind to mind across a battlefield or across an empire. But your father has unleashed his mages. Black mages, most of them, vicious with hatred of the Sun's son. Even now their master is hard put to restrain them. The city of Imuryaz is gone, and every living thing within its walls; Avaryan's banner rules the emptiness. And that is only the beginning."

Hirel had known Imuryaz. It was called the City of Spices, for there where Greatflood divided into Oroz'uan of the mountains and Anz'uan of the desert, the three great southward roads came together. Its market was the gateway to the spicelands of the south and west. It had been a city of the Compact: no wars could be waged in or about it, and within its boundaries all enmities were void. It was frighteningly close to Kundri'j Asan.

"Gone," said Sevayin, "shattered in the clashing of power. I can wish that a mage or two shared in the shattering."

Hirel was up, circling the hall, striding swifter and swifter. Trapped. Trapped and helpless, while cities fell, while barbarians destroyed the labors of a thousand years. Barbarians of both sides, and mages, always mages. Even his father had cast off the shackles of his rank to defend his realm: to take the place which should have been Hirel's. Because Hirel could not take it; because a foregathering of traitors had walled him in their prison. "How long?" he cried in a flare of passion. "How low must Asanion fall? How close must I come to madness before they let me go?"

He spun to a halt in front of Sevayin. Her face was a blur of darkness. This he had wedded, this he had bedded, this creature of sorcery. His hand was white against the shadow of her. The child that swelled her body would be like her: outland, alien, barely human. In older days they would have drowned it lest it defile the purity of the dynasty.

His head tossed. He was breaking. To think such thoughts: to shrink from Sevayin; to dream of slaying his own child. The heir of the empires, the seal of the peace.

"Peace!" Laughter ripped itself from him. "There is no peace. There is no hope of it."

"There may be," she said.

She spoke quietly, yet she shook him from his despair. He tasted blood. He had bitten his fist. The pain was only beginning.

She was calm, eyes narrowed, thinking deep within the walls of her mind. Hirel eyed her with growing wariness.

"Plots within plots," she said. "Magics within magics. Our jailers have not told us all that they know or intend. But of this we can be certain. They will do all they may to set themselves at the center of their balance."

"Whoever falls in the doing of it." Their hands met and clasped. Hirel contemplated them, hers long and slender, his own shorter, broader, with the blood drying on it. "It would serve them well were we dead and our heir newborn, raw clay to be shaped as they would have it. It would be logical. We are all set firm in our gods and our enmities, and none of us has ever yielded to any will but his own."

"What makes you think our offspring will be any different?"

Hirel's free hand rested again on her belly. Her own covered it. Her smile echoed his, slow to bloom, edged with wickedness. "The guildmaster," said Hirel, "has little knowledge of princes."

"You could never have been the hellion I was."

"I was worse. I was civilized."

Her mirth deepened and brightened. "He's mageborn, Hirel. Mageborn and twice imperial."

"He?" Hirel asked.

"Can't you tell?"

He could. He had called the little one *he,* because an Asanian did not consider the possibility of daughters, and because it irked Sevayin. But it was *he,* that body stirring beneath his hand. Mageborn and twice imperial. "He will be a terror to his nurses."

"He will," she said, and she said it as a vow.

"And it shall be we who raise him." Which was his own vow, sworn to any gods who were.

Sevayin had found it. Their own world, surely, incontestably. Twin moons looked down upon it. The winter stars filled the sky. And on the broad bare plain, replete with the flesh of plainsbuck, drowsed a green-eyed shadow.

"Ulan," whispered Sevayin.

The slitted eyes opened wide. The great head came up, ears pricked. Ulan growled softly.

"Brother," she said. "Heart's brother."

He flowed to his feet. The tip of his tail twitched. His eyes burned.

He shattered. Sevayin cried out in pain. Hirel was all but blind with it. She stumbled against him; he sank down beneath her.

"That was unwise," said the mage who was the Sun-priest's shadow. He stood over them in a dark sheen of power. Sevayin bristled at it, her own power rallying, rising, sparking red-golden.

He damped it with a single soft word. She shrank in Hirel's arms.

The mage regarded her coolly. "It was clever to think to forge a gate through your brother-in-fur. But it was blindest folly. Has no one ever taught you what the wielding of the greater powers can do to an unborn child?"

"No doubt it would please you to teach me." Her voice was faint but far from subdued.

"I do not take pleasure in the destruction of a soul."

"But you would do it, if it served your purposes."

"At the moment, it does not. We need you, and we need your heir. We will not let harm come to either of you." She bared her teeth. He blinked once, slowly. "You may look upon the worlds to your heart's content. You will not attempt to meddle in them."

"Or?"

"Need I say it?"

"I hope," she said, shaping each word precisely, "that your manhood dies of the rotting disease."

He said nothing, with great care. When he had said it, he walked away.

Sevayin began to laugh. Softly at first. Sanely. But she did not stop. Nor would she, even for the mages, even for the Red Prince's coming. Her laughter turned to a torrent of curses in every language Hirel knew and several he did not. It was Orozia who dosed her at last with wine and dreamflower and saw her laid in her bed. Even under the drug she tossed, muttering, clinging desperately to Hirel's hand. One of the mages had tried to separate them; he did not try twice.

What price the darkmage paid for his mischief, Hirel did not ask. It was enough that he saw no more of the man. He had done Sevayin no lasting harm; when she woke from her drugged sleep she was as close to sane as she ever was. But she was slow to return to her hunting of worlds.

"I still have it," she said.

Hirel's mind was empty of aught but pleasure. Her skill had begun to approach art; and that art was all her own, at once wild and gentle, shot through with sudden fire.

She traced her words in kisses round his center; they sank through his skin, trickling slowly to his brain. She followed them, nibbling, stroking, teasing. Her eyes dawned on his horizon. They were wide and wickedly bright.

His breath shuddered as he loosed it. "What do you have? My heart? My hand? My—"

She tugged it; he gasped and snatched, rising, rolling. She lay under him and laughed. "O perfect! There is no world but you."

He glared. "You rob me of my wits, and then you ask me to use them?"

"Ah," she said. "I had forgotten. You strong wise men have to choose: the brain or the body. Whereas we who are women, however that came about—"

He silenced her with a kiss and a long, lingering caress. "Now," he said sternly, "what have you done?"

"Hoodwinked the mages."

He widened his eyes.

"You believed it, didn't you? That one black sorcerer could threaten my sanity."

"You gave me no reason to doubt it."

"It was my grandfather. The others don't know me; they see the body and forget what is in it. But I had to make the Red Prince forget. I had to convince even you."

"He has been gone for a hand of days."

She pulled Hirel's head down. "Don't sulk, child. Do you want to escape from here?"

"There is no escape."

"There is," she said. "And it's not insanity. I've held the link with Ulan. It's still there; it's been growing stronger. I think it's strong enough to ride on, if you give me your strength."

"You are mad." She grinned. He shook her. "You cannot do it. I am not the idiot you take me for—I know how great a magic is the building of gates from world to world. Your power is still remembering its old mastery; and the child saps it as he grows within you. This that you contemplate will slay you both."

"How wise a mage his father is." She kissed Hirel long and deep. Her mind flowed burning into his own. *They're going to kiss us, Hirel. I saw it in the necromancer's mind when he thought I was too well conquered to see. But first, our fathers will die. It's all prepared. They only needed my grandfather's consent.*

Hirel's body was rousing to her touch. It had no interest in words. He made it shape them. "Why do they need—"

Because he has the power to stop them. She turned, drawing him with her until they lay side by side. Her lips withdrew; her power plunged deeper. *He won't help, but he's been persuaded not to hinder. They'll kill him with all of this, and regret it sincerely enough, and sigh that a man so old should have been caught in a war so bitter. But we are far from old, and we have power, and no one has persuaded us with logic or with threats. We will stop them.*

"We will die," Hirel said.

They've overcome you without a blow struck. They had only to hint at harm to your son.

Her scorn was like a lash of sleet. He hardened himself against it. "Very well. Work the magic. But I will pass the gate alone."

You can't. It's I whom they need to see, and I who can make my father see the danger in time to stop it.

"But—"

Would you rather die now or later? Me they'll keep alive; I'm valuable. Until I whelp their royal puppet.

Hirel let the silence swell. She played with his hair, unraveling its many tangles. He glared at the ceiling. "Power," he said. "It is all power. My brothers began this dance with their lusting after the name of high prince. Our fathers contest the rule of the world. Our jailers conspire to rule the world's ruler. And we play at magecraft and dream of thrones, and fancy that we have a right to either."

She was in his mind, mute, listening within and without.

"I would curse the day I met you, Sarevadin. If I were the child I was. If you were even a shade less purely yourself." He raised himself on his elbow. She lay all bare, tousled, swollen, glorious. "We will die together. Lead me; I follow."

He was a reed in the wind of the gods. He was a leaf in the tossing of the sea. He was the sword and she the swordsman; he was power, she power and mastery. Through him and in him she raised the shields. She laid bare the bond like a thread of fire. She sang it into a road, fire and silver, with a glitter of emerald.

They stood upon it hand in hand. He felt most solid. His heart beat; his palms were cold, his mouth dry. If he was not careful, his stomach would forget that it belonged to a man grown. A very young one. A youth. A boy.

A bark of laughter escaped him. Sevayin tugged him forward. He followed. He had begun naked; somewhere in the working of witchery he had gained boots and breeches, coat and cap, even a scrip: all his old traveling gear. But she was clad as any free Asanian woman must be who presumed to walk abroad, in the grey tent of the *dinaz* that veiled even the eyes. She passed as a shadow, laden with power.

And the worlds passed them by. The mages had wrought a new number in the reckoning of them: a thousand thousand; a million worlds. The road pierced them, or they swept over it, or perhaps somewhat of both. She did not vary her pace. Faceless, voiceless, all but shapeless, she might have been a dream, save for her hand in his. It was hot to burning.

They walked, not swiftly, not slowly. They did not pause. Not even for the strangest of the worlds: for creatures of fire swirling heatless about them; for creatures of ice with no power to chill them; for a battle of dragons in a sky of brass, and a dance of birds about a singing jewel, and once even a single human figure. He could almost have been Asanian, fair as he was, reddened by the sun of his world which could almost have been Hirel's own; but his eyes were as blue as the sea which lapped his feet. They lifted, narrowed against the glare. They met Hirel's. The man drew breath as if to speak, stretched out his hand. Before he could touch, Sevayin had drawn Hirel away.

Hirel looked back. The stranger was gone with all his world. The road stretched into bright obscurity. Uneasiness knotted Hirel's shoulders.

The bright way quivered, rippling like water. It fascinated him.

He stumbled and almost fell. Sevayin held him up by main force, flinging him forward. Her strides stretched. Her hand had gone cold.

He resisted. She was too strong, and ruthless with it. She cursed, low and steady. He twisted out of her grip.

The road was mist and water. The world was dust and ashes. The air caught at his throat.

Iron hands gripped him. He gasped, coughing, eyes streaming. "Fool!" she gritted. "Idiot child. Let go again and you die."

They were on the road again. They breathed clean air, neither hot nor cold, characterless, safe. About them lay a desert of black sand, black glass, black sky with stars like shards of glass. Behind them was mist. Shapes coiled in it.

"The mages," said Sevayin. "Damn them. Damn them to all the hells." She began again to walk, swift now, dragging him until he found his stride. He had neither time nor breath for anger. The road was narrowing, weakening. It yielded underfoot, like grass, like sand, like mire. It dragged at his feet. The mist had drawn closer. The worlds had dimmed about them.

Sevayin faltered. Her shape blurred beneath the robe. She was a shadow edged with fire, and fire in the center of her. For an instant she was not she at all, and the fire struggled, dimming, dying. Hirel clutched it in a surge of terror. The mist billowed forward. Sarevan shrank into Sevayin, doubled in Hirel's arms, arms wrapped about her burden. She flung defiance into the dimness. "Will you kill, then? Will you shatter all your machinations at a stroke?"

Hirel did not pause to think. He gathered her up. He staggered: she was a solid weight, she and their son. He pressed on.

A voice boomed behind them, mighty with power. "It is you who slay him. Who already may have slain him in your madness."

Hirel could not listen. The road was a twisting track, treacherous, now solid underfoot, now falling away into a seething void. A wind had risen. It plucked at him. He tightened his grip, set his head down, and persevered.

The worlds went mad.

There were dragons. There were eagles. There were ul-cats and direwolves and seneldi stallions. And every one a mage; every one in grim pursuit. Some were hideously close. Some had begun to circle, to cut off the advance. *Capture.* The world rang in Hirel's mind. *Capture, not kill.*

Even the boy? A whisper, the hint of a serpent's hiss.

We may need him, the great voice said: a master's voice, calm in the immensity of its power. *If the child is damaged or dead. To beget another.*

Hirel laughed in the midst of his struggle. There was the simple truth. A prince served but one purpose: to engender his successor. Perhaps the empires should dispense with the charade of ruling dynasties: put all their lords out to stud and let the lesser folk fend for themselves.

"Yes," breathed Sevayin. "Go on."

He faltered. Was the road a shade broader? The wolves were closing in. But they had slowed. They cast as hounds will who have lost the scent. Yet Hirel could see them with perfect clarity.

Sevayin had won her feet again. "Don't stop. Nonsense distracts them. Do you know any bawdy songs?"

Hirel stopped short, mortally and preposterously affronted.

She laughed. Their pursuers had tangled in confusion. "Levity," she said. "It's a shield. It scatters their power. Did you ever hear of the Sunpriest and the whoremaster's wife?"

It was outrageous. It was scurrilous. It widened and firmed the road and quickened their pace.

Dragonwings boomed. Dragonfire seared their shrinking flesh. Dragons' claws snatched at them. *"Run!"* cried Sevayin.

Hirel took wing and flew. Worlds whirled away. Sevayin, linked hand to hand, was singing. Even in wind-whipped snatches, the song set Hirel's ears afire.

A blow rocked him. The pain came after, runnels of white agony tracing his back. His will found a minute, impossible fraction of strength. The next stroke fell a hair too short. The third wrapped claws about his trailing foot.

His training was all a tatter. He had forsaken sacred modesty, and he had learned to believe in magecraft, and his careful princely manners had gone barbarian. But he could still meet agony with royal silence, and with royal rage. He turned on his tormentor.

He flung Sevayin off. She gripped his wrist. She was as strong as the dragonmage. Stronger. He was the link and the center, and they were rending him asunder. He twisted, desperate.

His desperation had substance. It was dark, round, heavy. It lay cold in his lone free hand. Without thought, he flung it.

The dragon howled and fell away. Hirel whirled through madness. The road was lost. He was lost. He was not afraid; he was intrigued. So this was damnation. Now he had proof beyond doubting: the logicians were ignorant fools.

A few moments more and he would be worshipping Uvarra.

Something tore. Sevayin cried out, sharp and high. Hirel fell headlong into darkness.

He did not know why this dream should be pleasant. It had all the trappings of a nightmare. His back and his foot were afire; his wrist throbbed. His every bone cried for mercy. And yet he lay on that tortured back, and he saw the blue vault of the sky with the sun pitiless in it, and he knew without seeing, that the solidity under him was earth, a barren fell, bitterly cold. The wind keened over him.

It was the sweetest song he had ever heard. And the shadows that rose above him, the most beautiful he had ever seen. Sevayin's faceless, shapeless shape; Ulan's dagger-fanged grin. He flung arms about them both.

Together they drew him up. He could stand, with cat and Sunchild to hold him. He glanced once at his foot. Only once. The boot was a charred remnant. The flesh . . .

He did not want to know what the mage had done to his back.

"I was beautiful once," he heard himself say.

Sevayin tugged. He swayed. Ulan crouched. He understood. He was inordinately proud of that. He bestrode the supple back; the cat rose. His legs dangled. His foot screamed in a voice of fire.

"Vayin," he said quite calmly. "Vayin, I do not think I can—"

"Be quiet," she said, and she was not calm at all. Ulan began to move, and she with him, swift and smooth. But never smooth enough for his pain.

The sun shifted. The fell had grown a wall. Hirel heard water falling; and, sudden and sweet and improbable, a trill of birdsong. He did not wonder at it. Worlds changed. That was his new wisdom.

The wall spawned a gate. It swallowed them.

There were always voices when one dreamed. These were fascinating. One was Sevayin's, cold and quiet. "I did not escape one prison simply to cast myself into another."

"I could not let you die as you intended." Hirel knew this deep voice with its whisper of roughness. The name would not come. Merely a memory of power, a vision of fire dying to ash.

"I have no intention of dying," Sevayin said. "How can I? You made me a woman; and I have two children to think of."

"Do you believe that, Sunchild?"

"*I* do not!" Hirel would have cried, had his body been his own. Sevayin said, still calmly, "I know that if I die, they both die. And I love them. Whatever magnitude of idiot that makes me."

Hirel's eyes dragged themselves open. Sevayin confronted the Prince of Han-Gilen: old and young, man and woman, he drawn thin with age, she ripened and rounded with the child; yet, for all of that, blood kin. Redmaned Gileni mages with tempers tight-reined behind the rigid faces. Hirel was the foreigner here, half the bone of their contention. The lesser half, he suspected. He saw that she cradled her belly as if to guard it. "Let us go," she said.

"Your prince can go no farther without healing."

"Then give it to him. It was your servant who wounded him."

"It was not."

She bared her teeth. "Don't quibble, Grandfather. So it was your ally. Who bore firmly in mind that a man needs very little of his body to beget sons. And who did all he could to leave very little else."

"Sevayin," said the Red Prince, "I had nothing to do with it."

"Are we deluded? Is this not your summer palace? Did we not come to it from the heart of the Golden Empire?"

"I knew when you made your gate. I knew where you would come if you were not taken; I feared that you would be in sore straits. Thank Avaryan, you are unscathed and he is but little hurt."

"You call that little?"

"Flesh wounds," the prince said, "as you would see, were you less blind with fear for him." He bent over Hirel, meeting the boy's level stare, unsmiling. To Sevayin he said, "I will heal him."

"And then?"

"We will speak together."

Hirel struggled to rise. He came as far as his knees; he held himself there. He was naked. He had not noticed. He had no time to notice now. "We will speak before you touch me. You will tell us why we should trust you. A man who would sacrifice his own grandchild in the name of a god."

Prince Orsan's eyes considered Hirel. Reckoned the count of his forefathers. Widened at the sacrifices some had made, in the name of a god, or a throne, or their own pleasure. The Red Prince said, "You have no choice but to trust me. The mages could not keep you: they did not know your true measure. I know it, and I know that while I may not be the stronger, I have the greater skill. You will not escape me."

"We can try," said Sevayin.

"And then?" Her own words, set coolly before her. "What do you fancy that you can do?"

"Stop the war."

"No," the Red Prince said. "Tell me the truth, priestess."

She stiffened at the title. Her nostrils thinned; she would not speak.

"I will tell you," he said. "You foresee what I foresaw; what sent me from the Heart of the World. The circle of deaths which must encompass the peace."

Still she was silent.

Not so Hirel. It was all bitterly, brutally clear. "It will be soon. Within days. If it has not already befallen."

"Not yet." The Red Prince looked very old. He lowered himself stiffly into a chair, bowing his head with infinite weariness. "I was to keep you here if you came so far. I thought I had the strength. I thought that I could countenance it all, for the world that will be. Even the murder of my heart's son."

"Why not? Your body's son is safe enough. He'll have the regency when the birthing kills me." Sevayin tossed the fire of her mane, fierce with despair. "Let be, old man. You'll heal my prince, because you know you'll get no peace until you do. We'll do our utmost to get out of your clutches. Meanwhile our fathers will die, and the war will end, and the mages will have their victory. What use to say more?"

"Yes," said Orsan, sharp enough to startle her. "What use? Your heart is set on hating me. I am the one you loved most, who betrayed you most bitterly."

"Just so."

Hirel let himself fall. Let a cry escape him. At once they were beside him. The fear in Sevayin's eyes was little more than that in the Red Prince's. He quelled a smile. So then: he was worth a moment's anxiety. He lay on his face, masked in pain, and let them fret over him. The heat of their anger abated, and with it the fire of his wounds. It was fascinating. It was pleasant, like the first movements of the high art. Very like.

Sevayin's hands stroked where the prince's had passed. Her kiss brushed his nape; her whisper sighed in his ear. "You were too clever, cubling. You tried the merest shade too hard."

He yawned. His foot itched; he rubbed it. It was all healed. So too his back. It could be convenient, this magic. "I shall remember," he said drowsily to Sevayin, "when next you quarrel."

She nipped him. He only laughed, and that for but a moment. Her kinsman was watching. Hirel said, "I do not trust you, Red Prince. I do believe that you will let us go. My lady is in no danger while she carries the child; and she may work a miracle: end the war without ending the lives of its principals."

"You are clever," Orsan said, "and cold, and wise. If you did not have the grace to love my grandchild, I would crush you as I crush a scorpion."

Hirel smiled. "And I detest you, old serpent. I do not make the error of despising you."

They understood one another, as true enemies must. The Red Prince vouchsafed the glimmer of a smile. Hirel saluted him as a warrior will who grants his opponent due respect. But no quarter. Not now, not ever.

PART FOUR

Sevayin Is'kirien

Twenty-two

N O ONE WOULD EVER KNOW HOW MUCH SHE HATED
this body. Hated it and loved it. Its softness. Its roundness. Its
downy skin. Its heavy swaying breasts; its grotesquerie of belly; its
limbs like a spider's, thin and strengthless. It knew what it was made
for. To receive a man's seed. To carry his children.

To carry this child, this alien, this stranger growing and dancing and
dreaming within her. She hated him as she hated the body that had
conceived him. She loved him with an intensity that made the *Kasar*'s
fire seem a dim and warmthless thing. When on the road she had nearly
lost the bonds of her being, and her son with it, she had known surely
that if he died, she could not bear to live. She still reached often for him
with hand or mind, assuring herself that he was well; that he had not
suffered, that he was prospering. She loved only Hirel more. She loved
her body but little less. Because one of them loved it, and one of them
waxed within it, and she had chosen it in full awareness of what she did.

As full as it could be, when she was he. She did not know the whole
of it yet. She was too new to it.

But the heart of the matter was purest simplicity. The shape had
changed; the self remained the same. She laughed in the darkness,
knowing it. There was no escape from the tangle of loves and hates and
fears and joys and flaws and perfections that were Sarevadin.

She hated it. She loved it. She was beginning, slowly, to accept it.

She lay beside Hirel, that last night before they faced their fathers, and watched him sleep. There was no sleep in her. She had done all her shaking; she had caged her myriad terrors. She was calm, resting her eyes on his face. He looked like a child.

She could go. Leave him there, safe and hidden, and soothe his anger after. She did not need him. It was not his father who would accept no end but his own and utter victory. She only needed herself as she was now, carrying the heir of the empires.

He stirred, seeking her warmth. His hand found her middle. Even in his sleep he smiled. His dream saw a bright-headed manchild, night-skinned, with startling golden eyes.

She buried her face in his hair. No. She was lying to herself. She could not leave him. She needed him. Her dream had seen it long since. He was the key to her power. She could not even hate him for it: there was too much else to hate.

Prince Orsan would not ride with them. He had turned his coat too often; this last turning had broken him. The man who faced them in the dark before dawn was become a stranger, ill and old, leaning heavily on a staff. He was their servant in spite of their resistance. He led them. He led them to bathe. He offered them clothing: garments fit for princes who must face their people, splendid to garishness but practical enough under the crusts of gold and gems. The eightfold complexity of Hirel's robe went on all together, like his wedding garment; this was divided for riding, its folds as supple as good armor. Its diamonds adorned his every point of vulnerability; a great collar of gold and diamond warded his throat, and his coronet was of an ancient style, shaped as a crowned helmet. He smiled when he put it on, an edged smile.

Sevayin's own finery was less warlike, if no less antique. Men and women both had worn it a hundred years ago in Han-Gilen. Its ornateness bespoke the Asanian fashion. Its simplicity was of the east. Boots heeled with gold, their soft leather dyed deep Gileni green. Trousers cut full, cloth of gold with Asanian velvet within. A breastband, which she was wise enough to put on in silence. A shirt of fine linen. A tunic, knee-long, stiff with embroidery. A great glittering overrobe, half coat, half cloak, which would pour beautifully over a senel's back, and ward off arrows with all its gemmed embroideries, and merely in passing disguise both her sex and her condition. Her torque guarded her throat; for crown she had her hair, woven with strings of emeralds and coiled about her head in the helmet braids of the Ianyn kings. Hirel helped her: she would not let Orsan touch her. She almost pitied him, such pain she gave him, and he grown too feeble to conceal it. But she could not stop herself.

Mounts awaited them in the court of the green silences. At sight of the smaller, Hirel nearly forgot his princely hauteur. Time had done little for her beauty and less for her temper, but the Zhil'ari mare had gained back all her strength. She greeted Hirel with the air of one who has waited much too long for a dawdling child; her nostrils trembled with the love-cries which she would not utter. He greeted her with a tug of the girth and, under lowered lids, a shining eye. They were made for one another, they two.

Sevayin forced herself to walk forward. Ulan was waiting, soul's kin, and no foolish man to care whether she was one who bore children or one who begot them. Bregalan stood prick-eared beside him. For all the splendor of his caparisons, the stallion wore no bridle; his saddle was a tooled and gilded offspring of the flat training saddle, no high pommel to mock her ungainliness. His gladness sang in her. Come, his eyes called to her; come and ride, run, be free and together, soul and soul and soul, beast of prey and beast of the field and mage of the bright god's line.

He was a poet, was Bregalan, although he scorned mere rattling words. She smiled and thought warmth at him, but her heart was cold. For he stood in the center of a guard of honor. Nine Zhil'ari in the full panoply of their people. Nine proud young men who had known the Prince of Keruvarion. Their eyes glittered in their fiercely painted faces. Fixed on her. Level, bitter-bright, relentless.

"We are yours," said Gazhin. Great Gazhin-ox who never lied, because he never saw the need; who never bowed, because a true king knew who revered him and who did not. "You are the great one. The Twiceborn, the dweller in the two houses, the mystery and the sacrifice. We are yours. We would die for you."

Sevayin laughed like blades clashing. "Don't. I'm not worth it."

Nine pairs of eyes refused belief. Zha'dan said, "We belong to you."

She looked at him. He was wearing his best air of innocence, the one with the wide liquid stare. "And what does your grandmother say to that?" she demanded.

The mageling's eyes held fast. They had laid aside their innocence. "Sometimes," he said, "one has to make choices."

She paused a breath, two. She bowed to that, to all of them.

Bregalan pawed the turf lightly, barely scarring its mown perfection. Before she could think, she was on his back. No one troubled to marvel

at her feat. She was not maimed, or ill, or too old to master her body.
She was simply with child.

Self-pity was a curse. Her grandfather had taught her that. She would
not look at him as she rode past him, or bid him farewell. It was Hirel
who did both, rebuking her with his graciousness.

At the gate she turned back. Or Bregalan turned. Orsan stood alone
on the trampled grass, bent and frail but mantled even yet in his power.
It held open the mage-way into Asanion. It asked nothing of her. Not
understanding, not acceptance, and certainly not forgiveness.

"Not now," he said. "Now is not the time for that choosing. Go with
the god, Sarevadin."

She could not answer him, either to bless or to curse him. She raised
her burning hand. Bregalan spun away.

The Army of the Sun and the Ranks of the Lion stood face to face
across a field of desolation. It had been a city once: Induverran, the City
of Gold, which guarded the gate of Asanion's heart. Mages had cast it
down, warring over it: a blast of fire; a wind out of the dark. Its towers
were fallen, its walls laid low. The shrines of its gods were smoking
ruins. Its men were slain; its children were dead, or wandering, or
wailing in the emptiness. Its women lay in the ashes and wept.

Sevayin paused at the summit of a low hill, drawing a cloak of power
about her company. The air was heavy with the reek of death. Death,
and magery. They had loosed the power; it had tasted blood. It roamed
now like a living thing, hungering.

This was worse than dream. The sounds of it. The carrion stench.
The beast that walked the ruins, neither shadow nor substance, fed by
the hatred of warring mages.

They had ceased their open battling. The emperors who wielded them
had reined them in. The bonds of royal will strained sorely: the beast
snarled as it stalked the domain it had made.

Sevayin saw them all with eyes and power. She saw the armies arrayed upon the smoldering field. Asanian gold, Varyani gold and scarlet, brave and splendid. They stood ranked and ready, poised on the
edge of battle: that moment when all rituals were done; when the heralds had withdrawn from the game of threat and parry, and the companies taken their places, alert, braced for the signal. The generals played
at patience. Even the beasts—seneldi ridden or yoked to chariots,
warhounds, fighting cats, eagles of battle—even they were still, waiting.

It was like a game upon a board. Perfect, frozen, comprehensible.
Ziad-Ilarios had chosen the classic opening of the west: the Three

Waves of the Great Sea. First his infantry, serfs and slaves and half-trained, half-armed peasants, driven like cattle before scythed chariots. They would die to hinder the enemy's knights, while the chariots mowed down friend and foe alike, and the archers in the second wave sent down a hail of arrows. Third and last and irresistible would ride his princes: cataphracts in massive armor on stallions as huge as bulls, and the swifter, lighter Olenyai lancers on racing mares, and a wall of the terrible chariots.

Before that formidable precision, Mirain's army seemed scattered, each company setting itself where it pleased. Sevayin, who had been born and raised in his wars, saw the order in the careful disorder. Three wings of manifold talents, three armies trained to fight as one, taking their shape from the necessities of the battle. Against the Three Waves they offered a shieldwall, and a wall of mounted bowmen, and a shifting fringe of foot and knights and chariotry. The center beckoned, its line a shade thinner, with a flame of scarlet waiting in it. His crowned helmet caught the sun; his black stallion fretted, goring the air. Green glowed beside him, green knight on red-gold mare: his empress riding as ever at his right hand, and behind her, her warrior women.

Sevayin's eyes were burning dry. The Lord of the Northern Realms commanded the right under Geitan's crimson lion; the left looked to the flame and green of the Prince-Heir of Han-Gilen. How brave they looked, those mighty princes, with their knights about them and their panoply glittering and their armies straining to run free.

Brave fools. Children gone mad in the wreck of worlds.

Hirel sat his senel knee to knee with her. His hand closed about hers. He was half a child who pleads for comfort, half a man who comforts his woman. She could not find a smile for him. He kissed her fingertips. "Consider," he said with royal Asanian steadiness. "We are not—quite —too late."

Not quite. She glanced at the Zhil'ari. They waited, patient. On the field below, a horn rang.

"Now," she said. Bregalan plunged down the hillside.

Hirel rode still at her knee, his mare defending valiantly the honor of her sex. The Zhil'ari fanned behind. Ulan wove through them, settling at last on Sevayin's right hand. He laughed his feline laughter, drunk on the sweet exhilaration of danger.

Her own fear had burned away. The child was quiet within her, but his soul was a white fire, exulting, exalted. She looked about her and knew that the battle had begun. A sound escaped her, half laughter, half curse. She cast aside all concealments.

The armies surged toward one another. Arrows fell in a sparse rain. Horns blared, drums rattled. Men sang or shouted or howled like beasts. Where the air had bred nine Zhil'ari and two princes, the battle eddied. But like the storm and the sea, once it had risen, it knew no mortal master.

She was no mortal woman. They were hers, all her barbarians. She drew their wills together. She set her power above them, burning through the glass that was her prince. She forged a weapon like a blade of fire. It clove the armies, flung them back. It swelled, billowed, grew. Arrows fell in a shower of ash. Beasts veered and screamed and fled. Men struck the wall and could not pass. Could not pierce it, though Varyani pressed face to face and all but sword to sword with Asanian warriors.

The melee ground to a halt. On both sides seethed the chaos of a rout. Men had died, were dying still, crushed in the confusion.

But most, having barely begun the charge, or having waited in reserve for the second assault, had fallen back in good order. These were the cream of their empires: seasoned fighters who knew how to face the unexpected, and who knew when to wait.

There were mages among them. Sevayin felt the pricks of their power, testing this working of hers, measuring her strength; goading the beast that haunted the field, deepening the shadow of it. It crouched, catlike. Its eyes were madness visible. It began a slow and sinuous stalk.

It was not even a tool, that creature. No mage had willed to make it. It was pure raw power. Neither dark nor light; neither good nor evil. Death was its sustenance.

Power only fed it. Lightnings only swelled it. The wall was nothing to it. It had never lived, therefore it could not die.

She gave it flat denial. It was not. It had never been. It had no power to touch her.

It stretched forth a limb like the shadow of a claw.

She refused its existence.

It closed its claws about her.

She felt nothing. She saw nothing. There was nothing.

The sky was clear. A shadow passed: a bird, a cloud, an eyelid's flicker. Sevayin wound her fingers in Bregalan's mane. Night and raven, woven. The stallion danced gently. "Yes," she said. He gathered his body, held for a singing moment, loosed it.

She rode headlong between the armies, flaming in the sun. One bold bowman loosed an arrow. She caught it, laughing, and flung it skyward. It kindled as it flew, flared and burned and fell.

Now they knew her. The roar went up behind her, followed her, rolled ahead of her. *"Sarevadin!"* And in the army of Asanion, someone had counted robes and marked a crown and raised the cry: *"Asuchirel!"*

Army faced army once again across the no-man's-land, the broad expanse of ash and ruin made terrible with power. In its center, Sevayin halted. Her Zhil'ari spread in a broad circle. Hirel set his mare side by side with Bregalan, facing his people as she faced her own. The thunder of their names rose to a crescendo and died.

Gazhin circled the circle, his stallion dancing, snorting at shadows. He halted a little apart and raised his great bull's voice. The clamor sank into silence. "The heirs of the empires have come before you. They command you to lay down your arms. They bid you lay aside your enmity. They say to you: 'We must rule when the war is ended. We will not rule a realm made desolate. If you will not give us peace of your own will, then we will compel it, as we compelled the sundering of the armies.' "

Never had such words been spoken on any field of battle. Never had the heirs of two great kings not only refused to fight, but put an end to the fighting by sheer force of wizardry. It was presumptuous. It was preposterous. It was highest treason.

Sevayin was well past caring. She could not sustain the wall. The Zhil'ari were flagging. Hirel had begun to waver. Healed though he had been, he was but newly come from a bitter wounding. Already the power was escaping his control, sending darts of fire through brain and body.

With infinite care she loosed the bonds. Too swift, and the power would run wild and destroy them all. Too slow, and Hirel would break and burn and die. He knew, because she knew. His fear, rising, sapped her strength. It fed the power. He struggled in vain to quell it. She could not touch him; dared not. He was a shell of glass about a rioting fire. A breath would shatter him.

The last bond melted. Sevayin nearly fell. Hirel snatched. Sparks leaped, startling them both. He recoiled in horror; but it was only power's fierce farewell. Sevayin gripped his hands and laughed. He scowled. "I am a disgrace to my lineage."

"You are indeed. Practicing high sorcery, interfering in imperial wars—"

"Turning coward at the crux and nearly destroying my consort."

"You'd be worse than a disgrace if you hadn't, cubling. You'd be truly, heroically stupid."

He glared at her. She remembered the lesser world, and turned to it. It had gone mad. Much of it was howling for blood. Some was roaring for the emperors' destruction and the enthronement of their heirs. A vanishing fragment was striving for sanity. The battle looked fair to begin again, true chaos now, man against man, mage against mage, and no commander but the beast-mind of the mob.

She raised a cry with more than voice, a great roar and flame that cowed, that quelled, that fixed every eye and mind and power upon her alone. She made of them all a summoning. *You who would rule this waste, come forth. Answer to me.*

She could not see the emperors. They were lost, walled and buried in furious princes. Asanian, Varyani, they thought for once with one mind. They cried treachery. They dreaded a trap. And in it the bait: the heirs of the empires. Prisoners still, or illusions of magery, set to lure even greater hostages than themselves. Or set to lure the emperors to their deaths.

She shifted infinitesimally. Her bones ached with the passage of power. It took most of her strength to sit unmoving, to keep her head up and her mind shielded. Mages sought to pierce it; their touch was pain. With each swift stabbing probe it mounted higher, with no blessed gift of numbness to grant her ease.

The end of it came all at once. In white flame among the Varyani; in a scattering of Asanian princes. The Mad One burst from the lines. Ziad-Ilarios' chariot rolled past the last of his attendants, his twin golden mares matching stride and stride.

Sevayin's lips stretched in a grim smile. They were alone, both of them, without attendance: Mirain with only his Mad One, Ziad-Ilarios with only his charioteer. Yet neither came without defense. Mirain needed none but his power. A thousand archers stood in the forefront of the Asanian army, bows strung, arrows nocked, aimed, waiting.

The emperors advanced without haste, moving slowly, yet all too swiftly. The Zhil'ari drew back before them.

They halted. Mirain was not quite close enough to touch.

Sevayin held herself rigidly still. His anger was hot enough to feel on the skin. Too hot to let him see aught beyond a dark face, a bright mane, a defiance the more bitter for that it was his own child who defied him. He flung it back in her face. "What have you done? You young fool, what have—you—"

She watched it strike him. Watched him refuse it. Watched him struggle to see the truth. His truth. His son who was young enough still to change remarkably from season to season; who had gained flesh, but who had needed it desperately, and who even gaunt to a shadow had looked much younger than his years. It was not impossible that in full health he should look more like a beardless boy than a man grown. A very beautiful boy. A boy as lovely as a girl.

She sensed rather than saw Hirel's moving away from her, dismounting, advancing to help his father from the chariot. She knew when Ziad-Ilarios laid aside his mask: Hirel's pain was sharp within her. The emperor had aged terribly. He walked because he must, but his every step was anguish, his every joint swollen and all but rigid; his face had lost the last of its beauty, his hair gone white. But he embraced his son and let himself weep.

Mirain had not changed at all. He was a little leaner, perhaps; a little harder. He looked as he had when his heir was a child, when he waged his wars in the outlands of the world. Although Sevayin knew with mage's certainty that he was mortal, she could comprehend the tale men told of him, that he was a god incarnate; that he would never age or die.

Good bones and good fortune, and hair that was slow to go grey. He dismounted slowly, calm now: a quivering calm. His eyes never left Sevayin's face. He took off his helmet, hung it from the pommel, shook down his simple braid. Their minds could not meet while hers was barred.

She touched Bregalan's neck. He knelt; she left the saddle. Her knees buckled briefly. The child kicked hard, protesting; her breath caught. She drew herself up.

He could not deny it now. It was as obvious as the shape of her under the archaic robe.

He stepped toward her. She stiffened, willing herself to stand fast. She was not as tall as he. His army saw it; they were slow to understand it. His hand brushed her hair, her cheek. "What have you done?" he whispered. *"What have you done?"*

"Given us hope."

He flinched at the sound of her voice. He touched her again. Set hands on her shoulders, gripping cruelly tight. Tears of pain and weakness flooded to her eyes; she would not let them fall. "Why?" he cried out to her in pain at least the match of hers.

"It was possible," her tongue said for her. "It seemed logical. Should I simply have killed myself?"

"You should have killed the lion's whelp."

"I love him."

"You—" He stopped. His eyes were wild. "You fool. You bloody *fool.*" He shook her until she gasped. "You have betrayed us all."

"I have saved us." She tore his hand from her shoulder, pressed it to her middle. "This is our hope, Father. This is our peace."

He tensed to break free. The child kicked. He froze.

"Our son," she said. "Mine; the young lion's. He shall be mageborn, Father. Mageborn and doubly royal."

He said nothing. He seemed transfixed.

She laughed, sharp and high. "Yes, go, disown me. It's your right. I'm an attainted traitor. I've sinned against you; I've sinned against nature itself. But you can't deny your grandson his inheritance."

"Do you think that I can deny you?"

She started, swayed. He held her up. There was no gentleness in him; his wrath had diminished not at all. He said, "I do not revoke the laws which I have made. Nor do I call you to account for this latest of many madnesses. Not yet. But if I come within reach of those who laid it upon you . . ."

"There," Hirel said, "I am your ally." He stood with his father, the emperor's hand on his shoulder, two pairs of burning golden eyes. Hirel moved slightly. Warning, as a cat will, or a wolf: *This is my mate. Touch her at your peril.*

Mirain regarded them steadily. "You have gained much," he said to Hirel. "Are you regretting it?"

"Never," Hirel answered. "Nor shall I forgive those who wrought it."

Sevayin set herself in the cold space between them, filling it with the heat of her temper. "You'll both have to wait until I'm done with them." All three would have spoken. She overrode them. "Have you forgotten where we are? Or why?" She spread her hands across her swollen middle. "Here lies the end of this war. Will you leave him a world to rule?"

The emperors did not move, and yet they had drawn away. "It is not so simple," said Ziad-Ilarios. And Mirain said, "You cannot buy peace with love alone."

"Why not?" she demanded. "Why ever not?"

"Child," said Mirain. "Lady," said Ziad-Ilarios.

She flung up her fists, swept them wide, taking in the ruin about them. "I will not hear you! One of you must rule. You hardly care which. You care not at all what price the land pays for your rivalry."

"I care what price Asanion pays," Ziad-Ilarios said. "And it has paid high. Our most grievous fault. We are men of reason. We have little defense against the fanatics of the east."

"And what is reason," Mirain countered, "but blindness of soul? You deny your own gods. You refuse aught but what your eyes can see, your hands touch. You call us fanatics who are merely believers in the truth."

"Are you?" They both rounded on Hirel. He folded his arms and regarded them coolly. "There are times and places for the settling of old grievances. I do not believe that this is one. You have seen us; you know that we come of our own will, and that we have made our own peace. Will you accept it? Will you agree at least to consider it?"

The emperors eyed one another. Sevayin saw no hate in either, nor even dislike. In another world they might have been brothers. In this one, neither could yield. Too much divided them. Too many wars. Too many deaths. The world was not wide enough for them both.

She came to Hirel's side, even as he came to hers. They stood shoulder to shoulder. "You can kill one another," she said. "We will live, and we will do what you refuse to do. Now or later, Father, Father-in-love. Choose."

There was a long silence. Hirel, so calm to look on, was trembling just perceptibly. She shifted, leaning lightly against him; his arm circled her waist. She tasted the emperors' bitter joy. Every man rejoiced to see his line's continuance. But that it must continue thus—that was not easy to endure.

Slowly Mirain said, "I can consider what you have done. I cannot promise to accept it."

"And I," said Ziad-Ilarios. "My people must know, and I must think. You will come with me, Asuchirel. You will tell me, at length and before our princes, why I should yield to your presumption."

Hirel drew his breath in sharply. "How do I know that I can trust you? I have seen enough of betrayals, and more than enough of prisons."

Anger sparked in Ilarios' eye. He spoke with deadly softness. "You are my son and my heir. Neither title is irrevocable. Remember that."

Hirel started as if struck. Sevayin held him tightly. "Trust him," she said. "He may try to lure you into his war, but he won't compel you. He knows there's no profit in turning you against him."

"I will not go without you," Hirel gritted. "I will not."

"You must." The Sunborn's voice was velvet and steel. "Someone must face my army. Someone must tell them what has become of their high prince. I am not minded to lie to them, and I am even less inclined to give my enemies a hostage."

Sevayin had been expecting it. She did not have to be eager for it. "I must go, Hirel," she said as steadily as she could.

His face set in imperial obstinacy. "I will not hand you over to our enemies."

"They are my people," she shot back. "And no one hands me over to anyone. I go where I choose to go."

"You are my wife."

"I am not your property!" She wrenched away from him before she struck him. "Damn it, cubling, now's no time to get unreasonable. Go with your father. Beat some sense into his head. And be sure of this: I don't intend to do my own arguing from a cage."

He was stiff and haughty, lest he break down and cry; angry, lest he blurt out the truth: that he could not bear to be apart from her. He would never know what it cost her to kiss him lightly, flash him her whitest grin, and turn her back on him. She was on Bregalan's back before anyone could be solicitous, dispatching her Zhil'ari to guard Hirel. On that, she was adamant. She had Ulan, who was worth a dozen men, even men of the White Stallion. She did not watch them ride away. Her eyes and her mind were on the army. Her father's army. Her own by right of birth.

If they did not rise up to a man and cast her out.

Twenty-three

*T*HE TRUTH CRESTED SLOWLY, LIKE A WAVE: RISING, gathering, poising long and long at its summit. It crashed with deadly and inexorable force.

The Sunborn's tent was an island in the torrent. The empress' women guarded it with their full strength, which was potent, but which was sore beset. They could not abate the roar that overlay and underlay all that passed in the cramped and crowded space.

Sevayin stood against the central pole with Ulan for wall and guard, facing her father's princes. She had expected revulsion. She had been braced for bitter recrimination. She had known that a precious few would begin to accept her, and that all too many would reject her out of hand. But her foresight had failed her. That their high prince should sacrifice his manhood for his empire, that, they could endure. It was the act of a hero, of a saint; it had a certain tragic splendor. And she was very beautiful, they said, seeing her there, glittering, growing desperate.

They could endure a woman's rule. They would not contemplate an Asanian consort. "I carry his son!" she had raged at them while she still had strength to rage.

"You carry a Sunborn prince," said the Chancellor of the Southlands. His Gileni temper was well in hand; he was struggling to be reasonable. "Sarevadin" —he said it gingerly as they all did, not wanting to slip and wound her with her old usename, not ready yet to call her by her new one— "Sarevadin, we cannot grant Asanion so much power. We are too young and too raw; it will overwhelm us with the strength of its thousand years. Keruvarion will shrink to a satrapy, a dependency of the Golden Empire."

It was not the first time he had said it. It was not the last. They all said it, singly and in chorus. They spoke of Asanion. Of the Golden Empire. Of *it* and *they*. Never of Hirel Uverias, or of Sarevadin who had no intention of dwindling into a mere and ornamental queen. When she cast the truth in their faces, they took no notice of it. She was a woman. Of course she would yield, or she would die. Asanion would make certain of it.

"No," the chancellor said at length, as weary as she. "It is not that you are a woman. It is that you are Varyani and their high prince's mate. They will not suffer equals. They will assure that their prince holds all the power."

"Are you any different?" she demanded of him.

He smiled wryly. "Of course not. We wish you to rule; we cannot let you share your throne."

"What will you do, then? Poison my husband? Strangle our son at birth?"

"We do not murder children," he said.

"Hirel is hardly more than that."

"He is old enough to father a child. He is more than old enough to rule an empire."

"He'll never be old enough to rule me."

"His empire—" the chancellor began.

"Uncle," she said. "Halenan. If he dies, I die. You call yourself a mage. Look within and see. We are soul-bound. There is no sundering us."

He looked within. He was gentle and he was skilled, but she was a tissue of half-healed wounds; and he had not his father's mastery. He all but blinded her with pain. "You fool," he said. "Oh, you lovestruck fool."

"It was not her doing." The empress had been silent throughout that bitter hour. The princes had all but forgotten her. Sevayin had not. Elian had said nothing, done nothing, revealed nothing behind the walls of her mind. She had scarcely glanced at the child she had borne. She did not raise her eyes now, but gazed into her folded hands, her voice cool and remote as when she spoke in prophecy. "Brothers, you accomplish nothing. The lady is weary; and she has another to think of. Let her be."

"But—" said Halenan.

"Let her be."

In time they left, all of them. Mirain was the last. He paused to kiss Sevayin lightly, without ceremony. Accepting her. It nearly broke her. But she was his child. She stood firm and watched him go.

When he was gone, she let her body have its way. It crumpled to the threadbare carpet.

"They're right, you know." She started, glared. Vadin had done what he did all too often: effaced himself to invisibility, and so escaped both notice and dismissal. It was one of his more insidious magics.

He paid no heed at all to her temper. He knelt beside her, easing off the gaudy robe, tugging gently but persistently until she lay back against Ulan's flank. "Stop fighting, infant. Do you want to lose the baby?"

Sevayin drew up her knees and sighed. Vadin watched, studying her. "You knew," she said.

"I guessed. A mage, even as reluctant a mage as I am, can always tell whether a woman is carrying a manchild or a maid. With you we never could. We were afraid you'd be a monster: both and neither."

"I am," she muttered.

"Stop it, namesake." He was stern but not angry. Calmly, deft as any good servant, he began to unbind her braids. "Your mother knew, I think. She wasn't as glad as we were when you proved to be as fine a little man as ever sprang out yelling from his mother's womb. She insisted on bringing you up with both men and women. She made you live in Liavi's mind while she carried her little hellion."

"She did her best to beat the arrogance out of me." Sevayin laughed thinly. "Though in that at least, she failed. I'm still intolerably proud."

"Royal," said Vadin.

Sevayin fixed her eyes on the tent wall. "Father is taking it well."

"What else can he do? He can't disown you. You're all he has."

She flinched. Anger flared. "That's why it was even possible. Because I'm the only one. The only heir he could ever beget, the sole and splendid jewel in the throne of Keruvarion. Do you think it's been easy for me? Do you think I welcome all the stares and gasps and cries of outrage? Do you think I don't know what battles I'll have to fight all my life long, because I gave up my very self for love of an Asanian tyrant?"

"Not your self," said Vadin. "But there is a little truth in the rest of it. Your uncle sees it. Keruvarion will never accept a western emperor. Too much of it has fought too long to avoid just that."

"Hirel would never—"

"Your young lion is as charming as his father ever was, and as honorable, and as perfect an epitome of Asanian royalty. He was bred to be
an emperor."

"But not a monster."

"Maybe not." Vadin combed Sevayin's hair in long strokes, intent on
it. "Old hatreds die hard. Asanion is Asanion: the dragon of the west,
the vast devouring beast with its insatiable lust for gold and souls. The
only defense against it, most people would tell you, is its destruction."

Sevayin bared her teeth. "They say much the same of us. It's the
same hate and the same fear. But they reckon without me and without
my princeling."

"I was young once," said Vadin.

Sevayin thrust herself up; Vadin reached for another plait. She shook
him off. *"Damn* it, Vadin! Stop treating me like a child."

"That," he said, "you're not. But you're carrying one."

She was mute, simmering. He reached again. Sevayin suffered him,
holding to Ulan for comfort, drinking calm through the cat's drowsing
consciousness.

"You are going to rest," Vadin said firmly. "Then you are going to
face your people."

"Naked, I presume. So that they can be properly outraged."

"Why? Are you hiding something?"

"Only an unborn lion cub."

He looked hard at her. Her heart stilled. She had told them that the
Mageguild had held her prisoner; that the master had wrought the
change with the aid of Baran of Endros. She had not cried Prince
Orsan's treason before the army. She did not know why. Certainly not
because he was her mother's father, her father's more-than-father. Nor
had he set a binding on her.

But she could not say the words that would condemn him. She
strengthened her mind's shields; she put on a tired smile. The tiredness
was not feigned. "I've told you all I can. Except . . ."

"Except?"

Sevayin drew a breath. Vadin looked ready to seize and shake her.
She straightened with an effort. "There was more to the mages' conspiracy than a plot to unite two royal houses. When our son was born, Hirel
and I were to be killed." Vadin said nothing, only waited. "But first, our
fathers were to die. Are still to die. It will be soon, within days. I have
hopes that our presence here, close by the emperors, will hold them
back. They dare not lose me now, and they know that if Hirel dies, I
die."

"Assassins are no rarity," said Vadin, "and we've met sorcerous assassins before."

"But never a full circle of mages, led by the Master of the Guild himself." Sevayin's body levered itself up, driving itself round the tent, evading cot and clothing chest, skirting the low table with its maps and its plans of battle. Abruptly she stopped, turned. "Uncle. I know the way to the Heart of the World."

Vadin rose. "Are you as mad as that?"

Sevayin grinned at him. "Do you need to ask?"

"It will be guarded."

"With Father's loyal mages, and with Ziad-Ilarios'; with you, with Mother, with Father himself, we could conquer worlds."

"Clever," said Vadin. "This world may not be wide enough for two emperors, but if there are many . . ."

Sevayin hissed her impatience. "One world or a thousand thousand, what use to a dead man? You yourself taught me that it seldom profits a commander to wait for the enemy to attack. Better to stike the first blow, hard and fast, before he can gather his forces."

"What makes you think the mages aren't armed and waiting?"

"They may be." Sevayin took up a stylus, turned it in her fingers. In Ianon they jested that a pen was a waste of a good dart. She almost smiled. "But I don't think they know what I'm capable of."

"By now they do."

She tossed her freed hair, sweeping her body with her hand. "Look at me, uncle. This is all of me that most of them have ever seen. They know why I ran away from my prison. I was afraid to die; I had my prince to be my courage and my son to make me desperate. That I succeeded—ah then, I'm a god's grandchild, and luck is his servant."

Vadin's grin was wry. "And you are quite astonishingly beautiful, and when has beauty ever needed brains?"

"Avaryan knows, I never have."

"And here I was, thinking what a marvel you were, to have learned so quickly how to play the princess."

"It's not so different to play the prince. It was much harder to teach myself to walk. I kept wanting to make my body balance like a man's."

Vadin laughed freely then, pulling her in. She let her arms close the embrace. The child kicked hard; Vadin started. For a moment all merriment dropped away. But not for grief. For wonder; even for awe. "He's strong," the Ianyn said. "And much too pretty for comfort." His laughter rang out anew. "I think your father's nose is immortal."

"And his darkness," said Sevayin, "and my mother's hair. You know this should be a brown child, or amber. So for that matter should I."

"They knew what they wanted you to be."

"This?" asked Sevayin, braced for pain.

"This," said Vadin. He smiled with a touch of wickedness. "Here's a secret, namesake. Men want sons; how can they help it? But every one of us, in his heart of hearts, prays for a daughter."

"However he gets one?"

"However he gets one." Vadin stood back, stern. "Now, namesake. Lie down and let your baby rest."

She obeyed meekly enough, lying on the cot which was barely wider than a soldier's. Vadin left to be a lord commander again. Sevayin breathed slowly, swallowing past the ache in her throat. Here in solitude, with the army's roar as steady as the sea, her sight was bitterly clear. She had solved nothing yet. She might have slain them all.

She met Ulan's green stare. The cat blinked, yawned. He did not like all this crowding and shouting; he needed the free air. But if she was about to go to lair with her cubs . . .

"One cub," she said, "and not quite yet, brother nursemaid."

Ah, then. He would go. She laid her golden hands on his head; it bowed beneath the weight of the god. With a last green-fire glance, he slipped from the tent.

Sevayin lay for a few breaths' span. Abruptly she rose. There was wine where it had always been, in the chest at the bed's foot. She filled a cup, stared at it. Her stomach did not want it. "My courage needs it," she said, downing it. It was proper Varyani wine: sweet and heady, sharpened with spices. It steadied her.

She turned to face the one who stood in front of the tent's flap. It had been a goodly time since they stood eye to eye. She had never seen in those eyes what she saw now. In Prince Orsan's, yes. When he offered her the choice which even yet might be the end of her. But not in the eyes of his daughter.

It went beyond pain. "Mother," she said, calm and quiet.

Elian came, took the cup from her fingers, filled it and drained it herself. Choking on it, but forcing it down. Sevayin stared at her.

She stared back. The cold distances were heating, closing in. "I hope you're pleased with yourself."

Sevayin snapped erect. Here was all that she had expected. From the one in whom alone she had thought to find understanding. In her mother, who had foreseen this. Who had trained her for it.

And would not, could not accept its fulfillment.

"You've set the army on its ear," said Elian. "You've shown them what in fact they've shed their blood for. You've shaken your father and all that he has made, to their very foundations. Are you content?"

"Are *you?*" Sevayin shot back. "You saw all that I saw. What did you do to stop it? What did you do that even slowed its advance?"

"I did not strangle you in your cradle."

Sevayin began to tremble. "The others are finding that they can bear what they have no power to change. You can't. Why? Does it matter so much to you whether I walk as a man or as a woman? Are you afraid I'll be a rival?"

Elian slapped her. She did not evade the blow, nor did she strike back. "Oh, splendid, Mother! You always hit what you can't answer. I've betrayed you, haven't I?"

"You have betrayed your father."

"That," said Sevayin, "is not for you to judge. I've betrayed *you*. You loved the shape I used to wear. You hate me for giving it up."

"I could never hate you."

"Scorn, then. Contempt. Outrage."

"Grief." Elian was weeping. It was bitter to see. Her face was rigid; the tears ran down it unregarded. "That you should have hurt so much. That you should have given up—all—"

"Whatever I gave up, I have gained back. I have my prince, Mother. I have my son. I have my power, and it grows stronger than it ever was before."

"But the price," said Elian. "The pain."

Sevayin was quite thoroughly a woman, and almost a mother. But she could not understand this woman who was her mother.

Elian laughed, still weeping. "That's a great secret, child. Women don't understand women, either. I was so sure that I could face this. When it came. If it came. And then I saw you, and I couldn't bear it." She laid her hands flat upon her middle. "I was very ill, not so long ago. I lost a child. It would have been your sister."

Sevayin staggered with the pain of it. Reached, to heal her, to grieve with her.

Elian eluded her hands. "She should never have been. We knew it, your father and I. And yet we dared to know joy. To hope that maybe, somehow, we could have it all: that we could be victorious, that you could be healed, that we could live in peace with our daughter as with our son. Then," said Elian, "then the pains came. Nothing that we did could stop them. They were more terrible than anything I had ever known. As if my very substance were being rent from me."

Sevayin sank down, cradling her own substance, her child who would be, must be, born alive.

"The god took her," Elian said. "And mages. I knew, Sarevadin. I knew that they were birthing you. Wielding my power. Taking my child that would be, to transform my child that had been. It was godly cold, that taking. It was divinely unspeakable."

Sevayin rocked, shivering. If she had died in the working, her sister would have lived. Would have grown to womanhood. Hirel would have survived the war; would have had to wait, in grief, perhaps in captivity. But would, in the end, have had his Sunborn queen.

"Avaryan," she said. "There is no Avaryan. There is only Uvarra." She raised her head. Her mother regarded her without pity. Pitiless. "No wonder you hate me."

"I told you, I do not." Elian sat beside her, but out of her reach. "You didn't know what you were doing; you wanted to save us all. You paid higher even than I did, and in greater pain. I never stopped loving you. I'm trying to forgive you."

Sevayin drew a sharp and hurting breath. "I don't want your forgiveness. I want your acceptance. I want you to stand with me when I face Keruvarion."

She looked at Elian and knew that she had asked too much. It had taken all the empress' strength to come here, to face her alone, to tell her the truth. More than that, Elian could not give.

Sevayin bowed her head, hating defeat, knowing nothing that would alter it.

"I do not know that I can accept you," said Elian. "But I will stand with you."

Sevayin started, half rising. Elian held her down. It hurt, that light touch. It hurt bitterly, as a touch can, when it bears healing in it.

The empress drew her into a swift embrace. They were trembling, both of them, with all that roiled in them. "Come," said Elian. "Your people are waiting."

Sevayin did not face her people naked, but she faced them as a woman, and a priestess, and a queen. She needed all her pride. She could have done without her temper.

It was not the common folk who tried her sorely. They had needed most to see her, to know that she was well and strong and triumphant in her sacrifice. She knew how to make them her own.

But no lord yet born had sense enough to listen and let be. It was the same fruitless battle. Keruvarion's lords and captains would not ally themselves with Asanion. They would not suffer an Asanian prince. They would not acknowledge the legitimacy of the union: not without contract or witnesses.

That broke her. She did not fling herself at the idiot who had said it. She dared not; she would have killed him. But she rose from her seat in front of her father's tent. She smiled a clenched-teeth smile. She inquired very softly, "Are you calling my child a bastard?"

She did not heed the scramble of denials. Commoners had sense. They understood logic; when they hated, they hated with reason. Lords were like seneldi stallions. They bred and they fought; they snorted and they gored the air, and they raised their voices at every whisper of a threat.

They had fallen silent, staring. Some looked frightened. And well they might be. "I have heard you," she said. "I have heard all I need to hear. It changes nothing. I have taken as consort the High Prince of Asanion. Refuse him and you refuse me." She faced her father. "Now the beast has danced for all your people. Has it danced well? Has it pleased you? Must it return to its cage, or may it go back to its mate?"

Mirain was not angry. He seemed more proud of her than not; and he had never been one to meddle where his heir was faring well enough alone. He sat back, arms folded, and said, "We have matters to consider, you and I. They need a night's pondering. Will you tarry for it?"

She could refuse. He offered that, to her who had betrayed his trust. But Mirain An-Sh'Endor always granted a second accounting. Then he had no mercy.

"I will stay," she said, "until morning."

He bowed his head. She moved without thinking, knelt, kissed his hand. Her eyes rose. His own were clear, steady, and filled to bursting with his power. She shivered. He was king and emperor, great general, mage and priest: death had always ridden at his right hand. But now when she looked at him, it lay upon him like his own dark-sheened skin.

"Sarevadin."

She stood on the edge of the cavalry lines, gazing over the shattered city, watching the sun set behind the Asanian camp. Hirel lived; she knew that. But no more. A shield of power lay between them. She ached with trying not to batter it down.

When her father's voice spoke behind her, she was perilously close to mounting Bregalan and damning all promises and storming to her prince's rescue. She whirled, as fierce with guilt as with startlement.

Mirain's gaze rested where hers had been. There was no one with him, he could have been a hired soldier in his plain kilt, his cloak of leather lined with fleece against the chill, his hair in its plait behind him. He stroked Bregalan's shoulder, and the stallion raised his head from cropping the winter grass, snorting gently in greeting. Mirain was rare in his world: a two-legged brother. Like Sevayin herself. Like Hirel.

She shivered a little. The wind was rising as the sun sank, and her robe was less warm than it was splendid.

Mirain spread his cloak over her. She thought of resistance, sighed, submitted. It was warmer within than without, and she had nothing in truth to hate her father for. He was only doing what he must.

She closed her eyes. He was doing it to her. Again. Being the Sunborn. Luring her mind into acceptance of his madnesses. It was he who had begun this war; it was his intransigence which had brought her here, and which was all too likely to be his death.

"Why?" she demanded of him. "Why are you doing this?"

He was slow to answer. "Because," he said "I am my father's son. I was born for this: to subdue the Golden Empire. To turn the world to the worship of Avaryan. To bring light where none has ever been."

"By invading a country in the face of its ruler's pleas for peace?"

"I gave him peace. I gave him a decade of it. And watched him strengthen his armies, and rouse my outland tribes to revolt, and free his slavetakers to raid within my borders. He lured the Mageguild into Kundri'j; he sent his sorcerers as far as Endros, to whisper in the ears of my people, to rouse them to their old dark rites, to slay as many as they might in the name of gods long and well forgotten."

"While you did almost exactly the same in Avaryan's name."

He sighed at her back, folding his arms a little more tightly about her. "There were no slaves taken and no children sacrificed at my command."

"No. Only cities leveled with sword and power, and their children slaughtered to sate your armies."

"War is ugly, Sarevadin. But I bring justice where none but princes have ever had it, and one god where a thousand had stripped bare the land and its people."

She twisted to face him, hands knotted on his chest, trembling with the effort of keeping them still. "It would have come without your war. Don't you see? Don't you understand? We did it, Father. While you great emperors glowered and threatened and called up your armies, Hirel and I forged our own peace."

"I see," he said levelly. "I understand that the Mageguild seized upon a potent and mutual infatuation, and wielded that infatuation entirely for its own ends." She would have cried a protest; he silenced her. "I have no objection to a love match. I made one myself; I swore long ago that if the god granted you the same, I would not stand against it. Nor do I object to the one you have chosen. Under other circumstances I would have urged you to take him. But we have gone well past either logic or simplicity. We were past it before you submitted yourself to the mages."

Her throat had swelled shut. She forced words through it. "You don't want a bloodless end. You want to set your foot on Ziad-Ilarios' neck; you want to see his people die. Because they pray to the wrong gods. Because they dare to call your father a lie."

He touched her torque. "Your god also, Sarevadin."

She struck his hand, flinging it from her, breaking his grip and his spell. "My god is not your god. My vision is not your vision. You call my hope simplicity, as if I were a child who would put an end to death with a garland and a song. But it is you who are the child. You strive to shape the world in an image as false as the desolation of the black sorcerers. You blind yourself to any enemy but the one who would choose to be your ally."

"Asanian friendship is the friendship of the serpent. Jeweled beauty without, poison within."

She breathed deep, willing herself to be calm, to think. To remember that men had died for words less bitter than these which she had cast in his face. Which he was suffering with almost frightening forbearance.

"Father," she said. "Suppose that you let us try our way. It can't harm you. If it succeeds, you become the begetter of the great peace. If it fails, we children forced it on you with magery and with sheer youthful heedlessness; and you can go back to war again. You know you'll win. You have a god to fight for you."

"So do I now," he said.

"But you have no son."

He stepped back. His face was very still in the dying light; his eyes were like the eyes of one of his images, obsidian in ivory in ebony.

"I can't go back, Father. Not only because the trying would kill me. I have too much pride."

"You always did."

"And whose fault is that?"

"Mine," he said, "for begetting you." He did not smile. "If my death is ordained, Sarevadin, what right have you to hinder it?"

"Every right in the world." She raised the white agony of her hand. It cast its own light, sparks of gold in his shadowed face. "This is how I endured the change. I had a pain to match it, and years to learn how to bear it. It is not the same with my dream of your death. Yours and my mother's, Father. I saw her die before you. And though the years stretch long and the pain never falters, it never numbs me. It only grows more terrible. Therefore I chose this path. It offered a grain of hope: a chance that you would live."

"And yet," he said, "if I die, I assure your peace. Living, I can only stand against you."

"Not if I can persuade you to stand with me."

"Why? Why prolong the agony, when I can be lord of the world by tomorrow's sunset?"

"Lord of the world, perhaps. But Elian Kalirien will be dead."

He tossed his haughty stubborn head. "You are no prophet, Sunchild."

"In this," she said, "I am."

There was a silence. She fixed her stinging eyes upon Bregalan, who had raised his head, drinking the night wind. Her father was a shadow on the edge of her perception.

After a long while she said, "Tomorrow you may renew your war. I shall not be here to see it."

"Indeed you will not. A bearing woman has no place on the battlefield."

"Not in armor, no. There's none that would fit me and no time to forge it. I have another battle to fight. I shall go back to the Heart of the World and stand against the mages who have plotted to take you."

She heard his swift intake of breath, but his voice was quiet. "You know you cannot do it."

"With power enough, I can. The Asanian mages may be willing to ally with me to preserve their emperor. Some of your own may choose the same. You give them little enough to do while you wield your armies."

"On the contrary. They hold back the Asanian sorcerers; they ward my army against attacks from behind."

"No need for that if there is truce; if all of us are joined to break the conspiracy."

"Light and dark together?"

"Why not?"

"You cannot do it."

"I can try."

"You must not. Your child—"

She laughed, but not in mirth. "How you all do fret! And yet I don't think any of you knows what power can do to an unborn child."

"We know all too well. It destroys the waxing soul. If the body is fortunate, it too dies."

"Human soul. Human body. What of the mageborn? What of a bearer of the *Kasar?*"

"You would be more than mad if you sought an answer."

"What choice do I have? They will kill you otherwise, and Mother with you. I would free you at least to find your own deaths in battle."

He seized her. "You will not!"

"You can't stop me."

"No?"

She met his glittering eyes. "I will do it, Father. You can't bend all your power on me, and keep your army in hand, and wage your war against Ziad-Ilarios. He has a message from me: if I fail to appear here by sunrise tomorrow, he is to disregard any word you speak, even of peace, and fall on you with all his conjoined forces. He has more than you think, Father. His sorcerers aren't holding back out of weakness, still less out of fear of your mages' shields. They're grateful for the favor: it frees them from the need to maintain protections while they set about opening gates. Worldgates, Father. The dragons of hell will be the least of what comes forth to face you."

His hands were iron, his face lost in night. She had no fear left. She had given her second accounting. Now she would see the face which he turned toward treason.

His fingers tightened. She set her teeth, against the pain. Abruptly his grip was gone. The pain lingered, throbbing.

"What," he demanded roughly, "if you are here and I am not?"

She hardly dared breathe. She could not have won. Mirain did not lose battles.

He could, on occasion, retreat. To muster his forces. To mound a new attack.

He could indeed. "I will face these traitorous mages. I will end their plotting."

"Alone?"

"My enchanters will follow me."

"Not without me. Alone of anyone outside of the guild or the conspiracy, I know the way."

He was silent for so long that she wondered if he had heard; or if she had at last gone too far. Then, startlingly, he laughed. "Oh, you are mine indeed! You have me dancing to your music; now will you command that I dance with the Asanians?"

"Can you bear to do that?"

He pondered it. "For this cause . . . perhaps. But it can only be a truce, Sarevadin. I will not end this war until Asanion bows to me as its overlord."

"But now you need Asanion's strength. Without it you can't face the full power of the Heart of the World. With it, you may be able not only to face that power. You may be able to overcome it."

"No certainty, princess?"

"What is certain?" She wanted to hit him. He was yielding, but in his own way. Meaning to rule even where he was vanquished. "I'll lead you to the Heart of the World. I'll stand with you there against all our enemies."

"With half of our enemies fighting at our side." He took her hands, held her gaze. "You will guide us. You will not join in the battle."

She freed her eyes from their bondage, cast them down. "If I can."

"You must."

"I'll go," she said. "I'll fight if I have to. I'll fight you as hard as any of the mages, if you try to stop me. That is my solemn oath, by the god who begot you."

His anger seared her within and without. She stood firm against it. Not fighting unless he forced her to it. Simply refusing to yield.

And he drew back. She held, lest it be a trap. He said, "On your head be it, O child of my body. May this mere and humble emperor request, at the least, that you take thought for the child of your own?"

"Always," she promised him.

It was hardly enough. But he let it suffice.

Twenty-four

SEVAYIN DROWSED, ALONE AND LONELY IN A TENT set wall to wall with her father's. Through the tanned hide she could hear the voices of mages and captains. She had banished herself from their colloquy: they could accomplish little while she was there to cloud their wits. And she was deathly tired. Alone, she could admit it. She was too tired to play the royal heir; too tired to think, too tired even to sleep.

Shatri had mounted guard outside her door. He had been appalled to see her, until he had decided to worship her. It was bearable, that worship; it demanded nothing but her presence and, on occasion, her smile. Later she would teach him that she was neither saint nor goddess. Tonight she had no strength for it.

She lay on her side, shivering under the heaped furs, and tried to shut out the murmur of voices. The child was restless; young though he was, he kicked like a senel. Her hand calmed him a little, the power of the *Kasar* over the spark that was his presence.

A familiar weight poured itself over her feet. Familiar warmth fitted itself to her body, hand slipping to cup her breast, kisses circling her nape to the point of her jaw. The child leaped no higher than her heart.

She turned carefully. Hirel scowled at her. She scowled back. "Couldn't you live without me for a night?"

"No." His hand was gentler by far than his voice, tracing the line of her cheek, smoothing back her tumbled hair. "Have they been cruel to you?"

"My people," she said, "are still my people. And yours?"

"I remain High Prince of Asanion."

"In spite of your unspeakable consort."

"By edict of my father, you are a princess of the first rank. Who dares speak ill of you, dies."

"How absolute." She looked at him in the lamplight. He wore Olenyai black, the headcloth looped under his chin, stark against the ivory of his skin. His eyelids were gilded. She brushed them with a fingertip. "You shouldn't be here."

"I cannot be elsewhere." He was angry, but suddenly he laughed. "One fool berated me for falling prey to a succubus. Ah, said I, but there is no sweeter enslavement."

"I hope he lived to hear you."

"My father had not yet spoken." Hirel kissed her, drew back. "Vayin," he said, "I must speak with your father."

"That's dangerous."

"What is not?" He rose, drawing her with him. She drew breath, considered, swallowed the words. In silence she took up the robe of fur and velvet which her mother had given her, and wrapped it about her. Hirel's impatience mounted, dancing in his eyes. She took his hand and led him out of the tent.

They had ample escort. Ulan leaving his warm nest at the foot of her bed, and Zha'dan with a great black cloak and a wide white smile, and Shatri. The boy bowed to Hirel with deep and revealing respect. Sevayin loved him for it.

Mirain's council had shouted itself into stillness. The princes took refuge in their winecups, the priest-mages in lowered eyes and folded hands and carefully expressionless faces. Sevayin's coming brought them all about, staring. It had always been so, she told herself. Gileni mane atop a Ianyn face, and the sheer awe of what she was: heir of the Sunborn. She showed them her most ourtrageous semblance, white teeth flashing, black eyes dancing, red mane tumbling over the somber robe. "How goes it, my lords? Trippingly?"

Mirain met her with a bright ironic eye and a grin as fierce as a direwolf's. He bowed his head to Hirel who had come from behind to stand at Sevayin's shoulder.

The rest, mages or no, were slow to know him. They marked the Asanian face and bristled at it, but even Prince Halenan at first did not see more than the barbarian warrior. Hirel played for them; he braced his feet and set his face and gripped the hilts of the twin swords belted crosswise over his robes. Sevayin tasted the wickedness of his pleasure. "I bear a message from my emperor," he said, speaking Gileni, which was courtesy bordering on insult. "Will the Lord of Keruvarion deign to hear it?"

"The Lord of Keruvarion," said Mirain, "would gladly hear new counsel."

It was dawning on the rest of them. Vadin was amused. One or two of the priests were appalled: the more for that they could see how the power ran between Sevayin and her prince. A simple man could have seen it, strong as it was, growing stronger in the face of all their magecraft. Hirel's eye were molten gold. She could not resist and did not wish to; she poured herself into them, and out again, effortless as water.

"This is an abomination!"

No matter who said it. It burst from a Sun-priest's torque, child of a mind grown narrow, blinded by the light. Sevayin remembered the fire's heart and the darkness which dwelt there. She spread her hands, black and burning gold, and spoke as sweetly as she had ever spoken. "We are your peace. We who were born for undying hatred; we who without power could never have been. The god has willed it. He is in us. See, my lords. Open your eyes and see."

"I see it," Mirain said, and he did not say it easily. "Speak, high prince. What brings you here?"

"Your daughter." Some of them grinned at that. Hirel grinned back. "And of course, Lord An-Sh'Endor, my father. He proposes a two days' truce, a pause while his mages settle a certain matter. He bids me assure you that the matter is nothing of your making, and that your people will not be harmed in the resolving of it."

"There is truce until morning," Mirain pointed out.

"And a pair of cold beds." Vadin said it lightly, but his eyes were level upon Hirel. "Why, prince? What do they need to do that will take the night and two days after?"

"It may not take so long." Hirel met a captain's eyes until the man slid out of his seat. Coolly Hirel set Sevayin in it. She let him, mainly out of curiosity, to see what he would do next. Little enough, for a breath or ten. He sat at her feet, considering those whom he faced, letting them wait upon his pleasure. At last he said, "While I spoke with my father's princes, my eldest brother appeared with little escort and no fanfare. He was not astonished to see me. In part indeed he had come for my sake, with news of great and urgent import. The mages know not only of my escape with my lady but our coming to this field and of our actions thereon. They are far from pleased. Peace they profess to seek, but it must be peace as they alone would have it."

"Aranos told you this?" asked Sevayin. She could easily believe it; she wanted to be certain of it.

"None other," Hirel answered her. "He has, he said, grown weary of that particular conspiracy. It serves Asanion no longer; it threatens to destroy us all. The time and the place are set, the mages prepared. Both emperors are to be slain at their meeting; you are to be taken, I to be held in sorcerous confinement lest you seek again to win free."

A snarl rose; wordless and deadly. Sevayin spoke above it. "I don't trust that little snake," she said.

"Who does?" said Zha'dan, coming into the light. "But its truth he's telling."

"How much of it, I wonder?"

"Enough." Mirain met all their stares. The rumble of anger quieted. "So then, prince. You would seek out the mages, end their plotting, leave us free to choose our own peace." He leaned forward. "Why is it only truce for which you ask?"

"I," said Hirel, "do not ask it. My father has no hope of more and no will to suffer your refusal. If you will not grant the truce, he asks at least that you restrain your mages while his own are engaged in preserving your life."

Mirain laughed across the mutter of outrage. "What if I offer him my mages? Will he take them?"

"Can he trust them?"

"My presence will keep them honest."

Hirel rose to one knee. "So I told my father. I vowed that I would bring you back with me."

"And you say you are no mage." Mirain stood over him, drawing him up and embracing him with ceremony. "I will keep your vow for you."

They rode into the Asanian camp in the deep hours of the night: four priest-mages who bore within them the gathered power of their order, and Mirain, and Elian and Vadin and Zha'dan, and Prince Halenan with Starion who was the strongest in power of all his children; and Hirel leading them with Sevayin. She had lost her weariness in the exhilaration of danger, the light keen madness which comes before a battle. They all had it. Hirel thrummed with it, vaulting from his mare's back, swinging Sevayin to the ground. She snatched a kiss. He drank deep of it before he pulled free.

Ziad-Ilarios was waiting for them. He sat like a golden image within his golden pavilion, in its center where the roof lay open to the stars: a court of fire and darkness. His mages stood about him, nine men and women garbed variously as priests, as courtiers, as guildsfolk, but all mantled in power. It rose like a wall before the Varyani. They halted, drawing together. Their power gathered, flexed. Ulan growled softly despite Sevayin's calming hand.

The air breathed enmity. Sevayin thrust herself into it. Made herself face that shadow of her own power and see it as it saw itself. Born of the god as was her own. Necessary; inevitable. Her body did not want to accept it. Her mind wanted to fling it away in revulsion. Only her raw will drove her forward. Opened her mind. Embraced the darkness and the fire in its heart.

She stood before Ziad-Ilarios. Ulan was with her, and Hirel standing at her right hand. She bowed as queen to king.

The emperor took off his mask, met Sevayin's eyes. "Help me up," he said, "daughter."

She was as gentle as she could be, and yet she caused him pain. He had worsened even since the morning. Death had lodged deep within him. "No," she whispered. "Not you too."

He smiled, touched her cheek with a swollen finger. "Present me to your escort," he bade her.

She named them one by one. They bowed low, even Starion under Mirain's stern eye. Elian did not bow. She came to the emperor, her shock well hidden, her smile warm and no more than a little unsteady. He took her hands, raised them to his lips. Neither spoke. There was too much to say, and too little. Sevayin, watching, swallowed hard. She knew what they had been once. The songs were full of it. She had known that he still loved this one whom he had lost. She had not known that her mother loved him a little still. Perhaps more than a little.

Elian drew back. Her smile died; she averted her face so that he might not see her brimming eyes. Sevayin saw and held her peace; but she reached for her mother's hand. It was thin and cold. It did not pull away, but closed tightly about Sevayin's fingers, drawing from them a glimmer of comfort.

Mirain faced his rival. He was all that Ziad-Ilarios was not: hale, strong, young in body and great in power. But they were both imperial. Mirain acknowledged it. He bent his head, sketched a gesture of respect. "It seems that we are allies after all," he said.

"And kinsmen," Ziad-Ilarios responded, "after all. I find that I am not displeased."

"My daughter has chosen well, if not entirely wisely."

"My son has chosen as he could not but choose. So too must we."

"And your eldest son? I do not see him. How has he chosen?"

"For himself." Ziad-Ilarios' irony had no bitterness in it. "He has returned to his old allies, lest they suspect that he has betrayed them. He will aid us as he can."

"He might have been better dead."

Ziad-Ilarios smiled with terrible gentleness. "Perhaps. But he has yet to betray me openly. Even were he not my son, I would not condemn him to death for simple suspicion." He raised his hand, ending the matter, inviting Mirain to his side. "The gate waits upon our opening. Will you begin, son of Avaryan?"

Mirain bowed to his courtesy. The mages of the Sun went where their lord's will bade them, weaving into the Asanian circle. It strained, resisting. Eyes glittered; tempers sparked.

It was Starion, wild Starion, who broke the wall. His mate in power was young and comely and very much a woman, and by good fortune, a lightmage, a priestess of Uvarra. His body drew him toward her; his hair caught her eye and his face held it, and won from her a blush and a smile. They had met before they knew it, clasped hands and power, and laughed both at once, both alike, for the wonder of the meeting.

The rest moved then. Light met dark, thrust, parried, struggled and twisted and locked. Their very hostility was strength, their sundering a bond as firm as forged iron, holding them ever joined and ever apart.

Out of the weaving rose wonder, and a flare of joy that was half terror. They were strong. They were *strong*.

The terror was Sevayin's. Body and power shaped the center of the circle, her body clinging fiercely to Hirel's, her power drawing its potency from his presence. And they were the strongest. Mirain himself, great flaming splendor, was less than they.

It was the two of them, and the child they had made. Because she was what she was and had been, and because Hirel was what he was: the Sun and the Lion mated before all gods who were. The third made them greater than any three apart.

The circle was in her hands. Had fallen into them. She could not even feign raw strength without skill. She wielded that skill to gather it all. Tensed to thrust it into her father's hands. Paused.

He had no part in the weaving with the dark, although he rested within it, accepting it as grim necessity. There was a sickness in him that he must do even so much. He could not raise the gate. He could not will himself to hold the dark together with the light.

Her love for him touched the borders of pain. From that pain she drew strength to hold the circle. To make it her own. To call on its manifold potencies, and from them to build the gate of the worlds.

Stone by stone she built it, each stone a mage's soul, mortared with power. Such magic had wrought the unfading gate at the Heart of the World, the highest of high magics, the blackest of black sorceries: sacrifice of souls for the gate's sake. This need not endure so long. Only long enough to shatter a conspiracy. The lesser powers that were her stones would know no more than weariness and an ache or two, and perhaps a little more. Starion was very much taken with his companion of the lintel. They met with force like love, and held with joyful tenacity.

She smiled in the working, even through the beginnings of weariness. Only the capstone remained. She chose him with care, knowing that he would resist. He was part of Mirain. He would not be condemned to helplessness while his foster brother cast dice with death.

Halenan. Her voice rang within the circle. *Halenan of Han-Gilen, you must permit it. No one else has the strength. No one else can hold the gate against the full force of the mages.*

With the eyes of the body she saw his head come up, his body stiffen, his eyes burn with the fire of his resistance. But he submitted. He bowed that high head. He yielded his power into her hands.

She accepted it as the great gift it was, and set it at the summit of the gate. The power flowed full and free. She brought her hands together; she bent her will. What she had wrought with bare power took shape in the living world: a gate indeed, because she saw it so, white stones set on black, and the capstone of its high arch all burning gold.

The mages of its making lay in a circle, linked hand to hand, seeming to sleep. One tawny head lay pillowed on Starion's breast. Power shimmered over them.

Twelve stood within them, four who were royal and four who owed allegiance to the Asanian emperor, and Vadin and Zha'dan and Ulan, and Ziad-Ilarios himself. He had no power, but he had his firm will. He would go. He would witness this great working and see it to its end.

Hirel was his prop, set against all protests. Sevayin had no strength to spare for them. Ulan's mind touched hers, with no power to offer, but the full and potent strength of his kind. It bore her up. She turned her back on fate and her face to the void and cast them all into it.

* * *

Void, Prince Orsan had taught her long ago, *seeks ever for form, as form seeks ever to return to void.* She heard him say it now, clear as if he stood beside her, cool and dispassionate, and yet, somehow, loving her. She thrust the love away. She wrought sanity from his words: knowledge; comprehension. Suspended in nothingness, nexus of power, she focused her will. They were mighty, these mages of her circle. They acknowledged no fear. She touched each briefly, imparting strength even as she drew it forth.

The road was simple and sparing of power, and she knew with soul's certainty that it was guarded. But there was another way. A shorter way by far, but harder, and if she took it, perhaps she would spend all their strength before ever they came to the battle.

Take it. Mirain, and Elian with him, fire and prophecy, and the weft on which they were woven: the Lord of the Northern Realms in the full and quiet surety of his power.

The echo rang sevenfold, with a touch of desperation, private, Hirel-scented: *Father cannot endure the long road. Go swift, Vayin. Go now, and damn the cost.*

Formless, she willed assent. Shaping. Forming. Compelling. The void, gaining substance, gained will to shape itself. She raised the full force of her power. Chaos roared rebellion. She smote it down.

Cold stone. Air cold to bitterness. The warmth of fire. She could not see. She could not hear. All her power was draining away. She clutched at it. Not again. By all the gods, not again.

"Vayin." Hirel, tight with urgency, yet calming her. He was in her mind; she had not lost him. Light grew, limning his face. She always forgot how beautiful he was. She smiled. He scowled, lest he weaken and smile back. "Vayin, it is done. We stand in the Heart of the World. But—"

"But?"

"It is empty," a stranger said, an Asanian, a priestess in black-bordered scarlet. Sevayin wondered fleetingly which deity she served. It mattered little here.

Sevayin struggled to her feet. She had fallen by the fire, which burned as it had always burned, unwearied. Between the fire and the circle shimmered their gate; most of them stood near it, close together, taut and wary. Mirain roved the hall like a cat in a strange lair, and Ulan walked as his shadow, growling softly at the shifting world-walls.

"It is an ambush," said Ziad-Ilarios. He took the seat which Prince

Orsan had so often favored. His voice and his face startled Sevayin, for they were strong, as if the power in its working had given him sustenance. His eyes were clear, bright, fascinated. They flicked round the chamber, taking it in. "Mark you," he said. "They tempt us with emptiness. They wait for us to betray ourselves; to become complacent; to let our guard fall."

Mirain halted, spun on his heel. "Yes. Yes, I sense them." He returned to the fire. It bent toward him. He laughed, spread his arms wide. "Come, my enemies. Come and face me."

"Enemies not by our choice." The Master of the Guild stood in the hall, leaning on his staffs. Behind him a worldgate shimmered, changing. So with each: thrice nine gates, thrice nine mages, light joining with dark as the circle closed. Sevayin knew Baran of Endros, and the witch of the Zhil'ari, and Orozia refusing to meet her eyes. The rest were familiar strangers, faces from her captivity, silent and nameless. Some smiled. Some were only implacable.

Last of them came Aranos in his princely finery. He neither smiled nor was implacable. He wore no expression at all.

Mirain set fists on hips and tilted his head. He looked like a boy: a young cockerel with no wits to spare for honest fear. "What, guildmaster! Were you compelled to plot my death?"

"You have compelled us," the master said.

"Because I would not abandon my truth for your fabric of lies?"

"Because you will destroy all that is not of your truth."

Mirain laughed, light and easy. "Such destruction! A little matter of war and conquest; a city or two fallen. I have preserved life where it has consented to be preserved, and bidden my mages to heal when they have done with destroying. If I have been ruthless, I have been so only where mercy has failed. That is a king's fate, guildmaster, and his grim duty."

"Granted," the master said willingly. "You have ruled well, little corrupted by the immensity of your power: which alone would prove to me that you are the son of a god. Yet still you are our enemy. You have destroyed all worship but that of Avaryan; you have slain or driven out all mages but those of the light. And not only of the light, but of your light, which bows to your god and names you sole and highest master. Your Avaryan suffers no god before him; your magecraft suffers no power beside it."

"All others are corruptions of the truth."

"Corruptions? Or true faces? You thunder denunciations of Uveryen's sacrifices. What of all her temples sought out and destroyed, her priesthood slaughtered to the last novice, her rites and her holy things ground into the dust? For every temple, one man would die, perhaps, in a year; or if the observance were strict, one in each dark of Greatmoon. Abominable; horrible; and no matter that few of these sacrifices were aught but willing. And how many died in your purgings? Hundreds? Thousands? How many went to the fire, how many to the torture, for the mere invoking of the goddess' name? And all to save one life in every Greatmoon-cycle."

Mirain's lightness had gone all dark. He straightened; his face hardened. The boy was gone. The king stood in his majesty, his masks forsaken. "I cast down darkness wherever it rises."

"But what is darkness?" the mage demanded. "Can it be no more than that which dares to oppose you? You are a just king; you temper your justice with mercy. You even suffer your people to contest your judgments. Save in one thing only. Avaryan must be worshipped as you worship him. Power must be wielded as you wield it."

Mirain's voice came softer still, scarcely more than a whisper. "And for that I must die? That I do not wield power as you wield it?"

The mage smiled sadly. "To your eyes, no doubt, it would seem so. You have shown yourself incapable of comprehending the truth which lies behind all magics. Light is mighty, and it is beautiful, and it is most congenial to the human spirit. But no man can live forever under the sun. It burns him; it withers him; at last it consumes him. Remember the Sun-death of your order."

"It was swifter by far than the cold-death of the goddess."

"Extremes, both. And necessary. The day must have its night. The light must have its dark. The worlds hang in the balance; it is delicate, and its laws are ineluctable. For every flame there is a spear of night. For every good an evil; for every day of grief a day of gladness. One cannot be without the other."

"Sophistry," said Mirain, cold with contempt. "The goddess slips her chains. I would bind her fast for all of time."

"Do that, and you destroy us all. It is the law. If the light rules, so in its turn must the dark. Win us a thousand years under your god and you gain a thousand more under your goddess. We can live in the light, though in the end it burns us. In the dark we would wither away."

Mirain closed face and mind against that vision. "I will chain her. From the world's throne I will do it, and none shall stand against me."

"First," said the master, "you must come to it." He advanced slowly, and his circle advanced with him, closing upon the allies and the shimmer of their gate.

Mirain drew back into the circle. He was calm, alert, unfrightened. His power gathered to his center. Elian, Vadin, lent theirs to it. And after a moment, Sevayin, drawing in the others. Ulan set himself on guard by her side, Hirel by his father's. Wise child. She sat on her heels to ease her body's burden, and let herself be power purely, hilt and guard of the sword in her father's hand.

The mages struck hard and swiftly, and full upon Mirain. He staggered. His hands caught at the two who stood with him, Ianyn lord, Gileni lady. The mages took no notice of them, recked nothing of the unity which they made. The power struck at their center. Again. Again. It left no time to parry, no breathing space, no hope of subtlety. No need. They were many, the mages; they were strong; they willed Mirain's destruction. They did not care how they wrought it, if only he was destroyed.

Sevayin could not even cry protest. A great blow sundered her from the weaving, cast her into the living world. She crouched, struggling to breathe. All her mages were fallen, her father and her mother and her name's kin stricken to their knees in a whirlwind of power. With a mighty effort they brought up their hands. Fires leaped from them. The wind shrieked, buffeting them, beating them down.

Laboriously Sevayin straightened her back. Ulan sprawled beside her. His mind was dark, his flanks unmoving. Men hemmed her in. Mages. Strangers.

One came to face her, and she understood. Aranos was not smiling. Not quite.

Her eyes flashed beyond the circle. There was another. Ziad-Ilarios sat in it. Hirel struggled in strong hands. She lashed out with her power.

The blow recoiled upon her. It laid her low. Sundered from her kin. Sundered from her brother-in-fur. Sundered from her prince. Sundered, all sundered.

Hands stroked her. Meant to soothe; drove her all but mad.

Mages held her. They were strong. She spat in Aranos' face.

He regarded her coolly, still smiling. "I chose," he said, "long ago. My brother has served his purpose; he has begotten the child who will rule our twofold empires. You may keep him if it pleases you, though we must draw his claws. Excise his power; render him fit for service in the harem."

"Only if you suffer it first."

He was amused and slightly scandalized. "I shall have to keep you in lovers, I see. And keep you with child, until it tames you."

"You'll kill me before you tame me."

"I will not. I require you alive and obedient. Have you no gratitude? My erstwhile allies would have slain you. I not only let you live; I grant you your beloved. I will cherish you, Sunlady, and raise your children as my own."

He was pleased with himself. He thought that he was generous. He expected her defiance; he did not let it prick him. That a great war of magery roared and flamed without him, concerned him not at all.

"Come," he said, "be wise. Your father must fall, as you yourself have endeavored to make certain. Mine is dead already. My brother dies unless you accept the inevitable."

She stared at him, loathing that miniature mockery of Hirel's face. "You did it for me," she said.

"I did it for a twofold throne. But also," he conceded, "once I had seen you, for your own sake. I will not taint you with fleshly desire. I wish only to possess you. To feast, on occasion, upon your beauty."

She lunged. Her captors were caught off guard. She fell upon Aranos. He was a serpent indeed, stronger by far than he looked, and fanged. Steel flashed past her eyes. She snatched, caught a wrist as slender as the blade. She wrested it from his grasp. Thrust herself up, graceless, whirling. Men fell back. She laughed. She slashed through the second circle.

Hirel spat a curse. He was—almost—free. Blades flashed. Sevayin darted toward him.

A knife's edge lay across his throat. She halted, gasping. The blade eased a fraction. Its bearer smiled, approving her prudence. She hardly knew. She saw only the bead of blood swelling on Hirel's neck.

She turned slowly. No one touched her. Ziad-Ilarios had fallen from his seat onto his face. He lay unmoving. There was blood on his hands, pooling from beneath him.

Aranos had regained his feet. He was amused no longer. "You have a man's spirit," he said. "Still. Be sure of this, my lady: I will break it."

He approached her. The circles parted for him. He cradled his hand. Perhaps she had broken it. He paused to regard his brother, coolly, without either hatred or pleasure; paused longer over his father. "I regret this," he said. "He deserved a better death."

"Better? How better? In bed, of poison?"

"In bed, in his palace, of the sickness which had all but taken him."

"Which, no doubt, he owed to you."

"No," said Aranos. "I would never have slain him so slowly, or in so much pain." He held out his unwounded hand. "Come."

He set power in the simple word; and compulsion; and unshakable will. She knew the shape and the taste of it. The mystery and the sacrifice. And no god to make it splendid; to give back warmth where warmth was forsaken. Cold heart, cold purity. Cold self turned inward upon itself, forgetting joy, abandoning desire.

She was light to him. Light and fire. He recoiled from her. He yearned toward her. He bent all his strength upon her.

It crushed her down and down. Alone, sundered from her power's center, she could not stand against him. He stretched out his hands. His power wrought chains to bind her. His fingers curved to close upon her arms; to claim her. He smiled, tasting the sweetness of his victory.

She struck with steel. He recoiled. Too slow. The blade bit flesh: brow, temple, cheek. Blood sprang.

The mage with the knife cried out, abandoning his prisoner. The weapon flew from his hand. Slow, slow. They were all crawling-slow. It keened past her neck, cleaving air where her throat had been.

Aranos made no sound. He leaped; he bore her back, down. Her arm struck first, brutally. The knife fell from shocked and senseless fingers. His power took its edge from pain, its strength from blood. It closed jaws upon her mind.

Beauty without will was beauty still. Beauty without mind, without spirit, without resistance. "I will have you," he said. "I will own you utterly."

She raked nails across his bleeding face.

He gasped, but he laughed. She had barely raised a welt: her nails were cut warrior-short, the better to wield dagger and sword. He raised a single jeweled claw and set it gently, gently, just below her eye. "Will you yield after I have blinded these lovely eyes? Or will you yield now, while you have all of your senses?"

She closed teeth on his arm. Her power rallied, reared up.

Shadow loomed behind him. She throttled despair.

He stiffened: pain of body, pain of mind. Shock. Incredulity. He arched backward, tearing his arm from her teeth. She gagged on blood. He twisted, clawing.

Ulan squalled in rage and pain, and tossed his wounded head. He snapped; caught the slender throat; tore.

Aranos' eyes were wide, astonished. His hands closed uselessly on shadows. He fell broken, a fragile thing of bones and blood and tattered skin.

And yet he smiled, as if it were a mighty jest: that he of all men living should die as a beast dies, and for this. An outland beauty; an outland fire.

Hirel was there. Love that she could understand; desire without taint of corruption. He dragged her up, or she dragged herself. She had no strength to waste in caring which it was. Aranos' servants were scattered: lost, wavering, waking to fear. Some already had fled. None of them tried to recapture their prey.

Sevayin first, Hirel after, fell upon Ulan. He was bleeding, yet he was grimly content, as ever at a kill well made.

He gave them strength. They linked hands over his back. Hirel's grief struck her, wrought of fire, edged in royal ice. Not only for his father. For the one who, after all, had been his brother.

It was a weapon. She sheathed it in her power. Grief, wrath—there was no time. Aranos had reft Mirain of all her strength; and through it of the bond, the union of mages. They were all fallen, their power taken or held prisoner. He was alone, he and the two who shared his soul.

He held. Battered, beaten, he held. Mages had fallen before him. Their power had gone to swell his own.

But it was ebbing fast. They were too many and too strong; too ruthless. Neither hatred nor vengeance drove them. They were cold and they were steady, implacable, willing him to fall.

Sevayin's teeth bared. She hated. She hated with crystal purity. She raised her power through the burning glass that was her lover. She loosed it in the fire of her hand. She joined it to Mirain's. The pain was terrible; unbearable. But she had borne greater in the fires of the change. She remembered. She firmed her will with the memory.

And the mages wavered. Their blows fell awry. One toppled, keening: a youth in violet, seared by the Sun's fire.

Sevayin left Hirel half lying on Ulan's back, rapt in the perfection of power. She inched toward Mirain. The mages dared not strike her. Her child was too precious. They raised their power like a hand, closing about her wrist, forcing it down, driving her back and back. She let them quench the *Kasar*. She twisted round their hindrance, flung herself toward her father. The floor caught her; she cried out, short and sharp, more in surprise than in pain. But her hand gripped his. She drew herself to him, wrapped her arms about him, held fast.

The silence was thunderous, in mind as in body. Sevayin lifted her head, met the guildmaster's stare. "Now," she said, "kill him."

"Let him go," said the master.

She set her body the more firmly between them. Mirain knelt motionless, his eyes closed. His branded hand lay half curled on his thigh, trembling a very little. Its pain was the twin to hers.

For a long while no one moved. One by one, Elian and Vadin stumbled to their feet. Hirel came dreamwalking toward them, yet clear-eyed within it, smiling, being power purely. They linked hands like children in a dance, and were still.

"Sarevadin," the guildmaster said, "you swore a vow. Have you forgotten it?"

"I have sworn nothing," she said.

"You have," he said. "In accepting the change. In shaping yourself for peace. Now you see that the balance cannot endure while he lives, nor can the war be ended. Will you honor the compact? Or will you be forsworn?"

Her body was leaden heavy; Mirain had turned to stone in her arms. "I never agreed to watch you slaughter my father."

"We are sworn to peace. We cannot gain it while he lives."

"You will not—"

Mirain's hands closed upon her wrists, prying her free, thrusting her back. His eyes tore her soul. "You have sworn," he said. "Honor your oath."

She struggled uselessly. "I have not! They promised me. You would live."

"You gave yourself into their hands. You surrendered your manhood for peace. Their peace. Which is only assured if I am dead."

"You are all mad!" She broke his grip, wheeled. "I will have *my* peace. Two emperors upon two thrones; myself wedded to Asanion's heir; our son heir of the empires. No war. No killing. No constant, relentless, implacable resistance. Will you be sane or must I raise my power?"

"It is too late for sanity," the guildmaster said.

"Far too late," said Mirain, lifting his hand.

The mages whirled to the attack. Daggers glittered; Hirel cried out. Blood fountained over his hands. Vadin sagged in them.

Sevayin cried out in rage and despair. They had come for a clash of power, not for a battle of bronze and grey iron. Only Ulan was glad. He roared and sprang. Mages fell. Blood stained the stones.

She clutched at the rags of her magery. Hirel left Vadin lying, sprang to ward her with his body. He had his two swords, Olenyai weapons, lean and wicked as cats' claws. She snatched one, won it from his startlement.

No one would touch her. Ulan crouched at bay on the very brink of the fire. Mirain stood back to back with Elian, blades in their hands.

Vadin was up. Bleeding, staggering, blessedly alive. Smiling at the mages, a bared-teeth smile. "So," he said. "This is the honor of your guild. Sword-honor. Traitors' honor." He laughed and swept out his blades, sword and long wicked knife. "Look you! I can fight as foul as any mage."

He whirled still laughing, leaped, cut down the Zhil'ari witch. A mage, death-driven, sprang full upon him. Elian's knife caught the man in the air. He fell sprawling, clutching at her. She stumbled, swayed. He dragged her with him as he died.

She struggled wildly in his deathgrip. Broke it. Surged up.

She was forgotten. They were all forgotten. Knives closed in upon Mirain. Power sang in discord, pitched for his mind's ears, dulling them, sapping his strength. Alone, he could not match them. There were too many. He crouched, eyes glittering, lips drawn back in a fierce panther-smile. He had always loved a battle.

Elian caught a blade as it licked toward Mirain's back, turned it, closed with its bearer.

"No," whispered Sevayin. She had dreamed it. Just so. The hall of stone, the figured walls, the fire. The guildmaster standing apart, dispassionate. The Asanian emperor sprawled before a wooden throne. Mirain beset, battling for his life. Vadin Uthanyas down once more, wounded unto death; and in his lord no strength to bring him back, no time to begin. Hirel flung out of the battle, wavering against the great grey cat, stunned in the shattering of power's bonds.

And first and last and most terrible, Elian Kalirien locked body to body with a black sorcerer, a man tall and strong and skilled, fierce in his hatred of all that she was.

"No," Sevayin said, louder. She shifted her grip on the swordhilt. It balanced well. She could not say the same for herself. The combatants twisted, twined. Elian's hair had escaped its net; she whipped it across the mage's face. He recoiled. Sevayin tensed to spring. A strong body thrust her aside, wrenched the blade from her hand. She stood gaping. She had seen Ziad-Ilarios fall. She had seen him die.

He should be dead. His wound was mortal. He moved on will alone, and on something very like a seer's certainty. He had come for this. He had lived for it. He sprang, blade shortened, stabbing. The mage bellowed, spun, slashed. Elian lunged for the hand, Ilarios for the heart. Their eyes met across the straining body of their enemy. They smiled the same swift smile. Bright, wild, daring death itself to touch them.

The fine Asanian steel plunged through flesh and bone, drinking deep. The mage gasped, astonished; and toppled.

Ziad-Ilarios sank down. His golden robe was scarlet. His life ebbed with the tide of his blood. His smile had died, his last sweet madness faded. But he was content. "She lives," he said distinctly. "I have died in her place. I could not have died a better death."

Sevayin swayed. Her heart thudded. The child was too still, in a stabbing of small pains. She quelled them with stiffened hands and stiffened mind. She could not see her mother.

Under the cloaked and lifeless bulk, a body stirred. Sevayin heaved the carrion away. Beginning to understand; crying out against the understanding.

Elian lay on her back, pooled in blood. But the man had hardly bled: the blade was still in him. Sevayin dropped to her knees. Elian looked up at her and smiled. She was all scarlet.

Her throat.

Sevayin's mind was very clear. For a timeless moment, she thanked all the gods that Ziad-Ilarios had died before he knew that he had failed. For even as the mage fell dying, he had remembered his weapon. Perhaps Elian had aided him: snatching at his hand, casting it awry as his weight bore her down, averting it from eyes or heart to the undefended throat. It had cut deep. Her life poured out of her, driven by her frantic heart. Sevayin could not stop it.

Mirain. Mirain was a greater healer than Sevayin would ever be. If she could only slow the torrent. If he could—

A wolf was howling.

It was Mirain. Battling to break free, trapped, hedged in bronze and in power. Going mad, beast-mad.

"Father!" cried Sevayin. Her power lashed through the white agony of magewalls. Struck his, seized Hirel's, sucked in the magegate itself.

Blades flared molten, dropped. The gate could not endure the force of it. Not her power flaming through it, and the mages rising against her, and the magefire itself roaring to meet them. Its stones writhed in agony. They were not strong enough. They could not give as she demanded.

For Mirain they would give it. She wielded them without mercy. They writhed in her grasp. One rose above them, separate, yet binding himself to them. *Vadin,* her mind whispered, protesting. He was dying. He could not. He must not.

He fitted himself to her hand. He was strong in this his second death; he had no fear of it. He wielded her as she wielded him, to set his oathbrother free.

The gate wavered. A little more, she begged it. Only a little. She fed the fires with her own substance.

No. Vadin, clear in her mind. *Will you kill your son? Back, now; this fight is mine.*

She struggled. He had not her strength, even now, but he had learned his skill from Mirain himself. He eased her out and away. He poised, paused. He made himself a spear, and plunged full into the mages' wall.

It burst in a shower of fire; the spear burst with it, exulting.

Mirain bestrode his lady's body and cried aloud. The gate was gone. Vadin was gone. Elian died even as Mirain bent to heal her.

But he who had raised the dead had no awe of death. Her soul eluded him; he pursued it. He was the Son of the Sun. He would not let her die.

You must. Hers was no witless flitting soul, befuddled with its freedom. She barred the way to him, even to him who was half a god. Perhaps she grieved that she must do it. She was stern before him and before all the silent helpless mages. *The gods are not mocked. Go, Mirain An-Sh'Endor. Leave me to my peace.*

He fought the truth of it. All death's ways had closed against him, save only his own. He contemplated it. He yearned for it.

But he was the Sunborn. He had been that before ever wife or brother came to share his soul. He was the high god's son, the Sword of Avaryan, the lord of the eastern world. The lord of the west was dead. He had a world to claim.

In the looming silence, he turned. No madness marred his face. He looked quiet and sane and worn to the bone. His hands opened and closed. No hilt came to fill them. Sevayin had destroyed them all.

He sank to one knee. With utmost gentleness he lifted his empress, his brother. He cradled them. He murmured a word, two. Sevayin did not try to understand. Gently again he laid them down, straightening their limbs, smoothing their hair, closing their eyes. He kissed them both, brow, lips, lingering.

He rose. Sevayin shivered. He was utterly, terribly calm. He raised his hand.

Twice nine mages yet remained. Most were wounded. But they had no fear of him. They had robbed him of the greater part of his soul.

Limping, halting, they came together. They raised their shields. They waited for the lightning to fall.

PART FIVE

Hirel Uverias

Twenty-five

*T*HE WORLD WAS ENDING. HIREL WAS NOT UNCOM-
fortable, contemplating it. His neck stung where the knife had cut,
but the bladesman was gone, felled or fled. No one else had touched
him. He was the merest shadow of nothing: the Sunchild's familiar. He
had no power in himself; his steel they would not face. He could not
make them face it.

He had been angry, a moment or an age ago. It did not matter now.
Nothing mattered but that his death was waiting. It was strangely beautiful. It had Uvarra's face.

If he lived, he would grieve: for his father, for the Lord Vadin, for the
Lady Kalirien. But if he must die, he preferred to do it by his lady's
side. His empress' now. He smiled a little at the irony of it, setting his
hands upon her shoulders. She scarcely knew that he was there, but her
body let him draw it back against him. Tremors racked it: exhaustion,
fear, more pain than Hirel could easily bear. He caught his breath, set
his teeth, held fast.

And the lightning fell.

There was splendor in it. Like mountains falling; like a storm upon
the sea. The castle rocked beneath their feet. Whips of levin-fire lashed
above their heads. The magefire roared to the roof; the world-walls
writhed with visions of madness.

Mirain was a white flame in the heart of it. They had erred, the
mages, in their lofty wisdom. They had slain the two who shared his

self: thinking so to weaken him, to bring him into their power. So had they done with that part of him which was mortal man, that part which had seemed the whole of him. Which had been but the veil over the truth: the bonds that bound the light.

The son of the Ianyn priestess was gone. Avaryan's son stood forth in all his terrible splendor. He was pure power and pure wrath, bodiless, blinding. He would destroy those who had destroyed his empress and his brother; in the doing he might well destroy himself; and he would not care. No more than does a god when he has risen in his rage.

"Father," Sevayin said, soft yet clear. "Father." She kept saying it. Her own power had touched his once, seeking to calm him; much of her pain was the payment. He heeded her voice no more than he had her mind-cry. Mere human need, mere human strength. Not even for the light of the god in her would he turn from his course.

"Mirain." His name rang like a gong. "Mirain An-Sh'Endor."

The flame of him flickered, turning, bending toward the magefire. He spat power. The fire drank it like wine. Again the deep voice spoke. "Mirain An-Sh'Endor."

Amid the terrible brightness that had been the Sunborn, a face flickered. Eyes, dark and almost soft, entranced. The lips smiled. The power caught a handful of lightnings and cast them into the fire.

A man walked out of it as out of a gate. A young sunbird in Zhil'ari finery. His name hovered on Hirel's tongue. Zha'dan. Hirel had thought him dead. He limped: he bore a wound. But he was still bright irrepressible Zhaniedan, giving way with deep respect to the one whom he had brought. An old man, bent and grey, cloaked in black.

The old man straightened. He was tall, broad of shoulder even in his age, and perhaps stronger than he seemed.

The Prince of Han-Gilen let fall his cloak, which was not black but deepest green, and faced the pillar of fire. His hand brushed the peak of it, lightly. A breath escaped him: his only tribute to that awful strength.

Hirel reeled in sudden darkness. The flame was snuffed out. Shadow filled its place. Mirain on his knees in his black kilt, the gold of belt and armlets, torque and earrings and braids, a pallid gleam after the splendor that had been. He raised his head. His face was a skull, stripped of youth and of hope, but never of strength.

The Red Prince passed him, dropped to the floor beside Elian's body. "Daughter," he said with all the sadness in the worlds. "Ah, daughter, if you could but have waited, this would never have been." His voice died of its own weight. He kissed her brow and rose, laboring. They watched him. Hirel wondered why the mages had not struck him down.

"Because," Sevayin said, clear and bitter, "he is one of them." She dragged herself up. "Go on, Grandfather. Kill him before he gets his senses back."

The old man did not look at her. He faced Mirain, who frowned like a man in the throes of bafflement. Trying to remember. Trying to remember why he should remember.

"He led them!" Sevayin cried in a passion of despair. "He began it all. Now he ends it. Now it is all ended."

Mirain studied his foster father's face. He bowed his head a fraction. "Of course it would be you." He smiled faintly. "It has always been you. I saw your mark upon my daughter's soul. I thought only that it was her love for you, and the teaching which you gave her when she was my son. Who but you could have wrought the change?"

"No one," Prince Orsan said. "It was all mine, all this making. Now, as my lady says, I must end it."

"Or I." Mirain stood, light and swift and deadly. "Thrice nine mages could not fell me. Would you venture it, O prince of traitors?"

"I have no need. The Asanian emperor is dead. His successor stands at your daughter's back, soul-woven with her. Will you slay them? Or will you grant them the peace for which they have fought?"

"There is no peace but death."

"For you," said the prince, "there is not."

Mirain laughed bitterly. "How you all must hate me!"

"No." The prince was almost gentle. "No, Mirain. Will you not bow to defeat? In truth, it is a victory."

"My lady always told me that I had no grace in defeat. And truly I have none. I do not lose battles, prince. I do not know how."

"Perhaps it is time you learned."

"No," said Mirain. "I would have made our world a citadel of the light. You have condemned it forever to the outlands of the dark."

"So be it," Prince Orsan said.

Mirain sighed, drooping, as if weariness had mastered him. The Red Prince stretched out a hand. Perhaps in compassion; perhaps in warning. Mirain reared up like a serpent striking.

Sevayin tore herself from Hirel's hands. She sprang between her father and her mother's father. Her power roared through Hirel's brain.

The choice consumed but the flicker of a moment. It endured for an eternity. Father, grandfather. Light, light and dark together. Love, love turned to hate. Grief and grief, and no joy in any of it, no comfort and no hope.

She struck. It nearly slew her. But Mirain's power wavered the merest degree. In that weakened instant, Prince Orsan pierced his shields. Plunged deep and deep, and seized his heart, and closed.

His eyes opened wide, fixed upon his death. He knew it. He comprehended it. All of it: betrayal, and necessity, and bitter choosing. With his last desperate strength he lunged, seized the prince, seized his daughter, cast them all into the fire.

Someone howled. Hirel's throat was raw. He was blind, deaf, stunned. She was gone. He had nothing left.

Only death.

He laughed in the emptiness. For if she saw truth, he would have her back; if his was the way of the worlds, and death was mere oblivion, it would not matter.

No reasonable man would love a woman so much.

No reasonable man would have given his soul to Sevayin Is'kirien.

He was still laughing as he fell into the fire's arms.

It hurt. By all the nonexistent gods, it hurt. But it did not burn. It was bitter cold, fiery cold, and it struck him a millionfold: each atom of his being tormented separately and exquisitely, in endless variety. And yet his scattered being laughed. What a splendid irony it would be, if the end of this pain found him in woman's semblance. Then it would all begin again, the whole mad comedy.

Pain did not like to be laughed at. It flung his body together with claws of ice, thrust his mind all battered into the midst of it, cast him down in stillness.

He was all a great bruise. Did the dead know such petty pain? He counted his bones; he had them all, etched in aches. The head was his own, the hands, the body blessedly his own. Even dead, he was the beginning of a man.

"If this is hell," he said to the silent dark, "it is a poor thing. Where are the mighty torments? Where are the agonies of the damned?"

"Perhaps," a deep voice responded with a touch of irony, "we are in paradise." A body moved; a hand groped along Hirel's arm, tightening on it. Hirel's mind quivered at a sudden mothwing touch. Slow light grew. "Ah," said Prince Orsan with a scholar's cool pleasure. "You are stronger than I thought."

Hirel spat the shortest curse he knew. It was also the most appalling. "What am I? A candle for any mage's lighting?"

"Hardly," said the prince. "I am your lady's master. Her power is woven with mine. As, therefore, is yours."

"We are not dead." Hirel's voice was flat. He rose, letting his body protest itself into speechlessness, and glanced about. It was a little disconcerting: he was the center of the light, a sheen of gold that waxed as his strength grew.

If one stood in the heart of a diamond. If that diamond's center were a flaw, black without light, a shape as simple as an altar. If two stood frozen, face to face across the altar, man and woman both in black, and a grey shadow-cat crouched at its foot. If any of it were possible, it would be this place.

"Andal'ar 'Varyan," Prince Orsan said. "The Tower of the Sun atop Avaryan's Throne in Endros of the Sunborn." He spoke the names with a certain somber grandeur, and a suggestion of despair. "We stand in the very heart's center of the Sunborn's power."

Mirain turned. The man and the god had come together. Once before, Hirel had seen him so, standing in front of the Throne of the Sun. His grief had not diminished him. His loss had not cast him down. He remained Mirain An-Sh'Endor, the mighty one, the unconquerable king.

Hirel's soul knit with a quivering sigh. Sevayin was beside him. He had not seen her come. He looked at her, and she was all that her father was. And more. Because her mortality bound her; because she was she, Sarevadin.

He laid himself open to her, for the battle which now must come.

"No," Prince Orsan said. "The great wars are ended. The reign of the Sunborn is past."

He had come to the center of the light. He was no stronger here, no younger, and no less powerful.

"Tell me now," said Mirain, soft and calm. "Here at the end of things. Who is my father?"

"You are Avaryan's son," the Red Prince answered him.

Mirain held out his burning hand. "Swear on this, O weaver of webs. Swear that you had no part in my begetting."

"I cannot."

Mirain laughed. It was light, free. "You dare not. I think that you created me as has so often been proclaimed. The Hundred Realms had need of a king to rule them all; therefore you wrought me, setting me in the womb of an outland mother, casting upon her a spell of lies and dreams. But your spell succeeded beyond your wildest hopes, beyond your blackest fears. The god himself came to fill you. Thus indeed he begot me, but through your flesh and your seed."

"I summoned him," the Red Prince said. "It was the rite, as well you know: the calling of the god to his bride. My foresight brought me to it; the god named his chosen through my power. Beyond that, I do not remember. Perhaps indeed he wielded me. Perhaps he had no need. I do not seek to define the limits of divinity."

"Your working," said Mirain. "Your working still, for all that you deny it. The world has shaped itself as you would have it. Now dare you dream that I will do the same?"

"What is left in the light for you? Your lady is dead. Your soul's brother has gone back to the night from which you called him."

"Before they were part of me, I was Mirain."

"You can live without them? You can endure the emptiness in heart and power?"

Mirain stiffened. His eyes closed; his jaw set. A spasm of grief twisted his face. It passed before the strength of his will. "My armies wait for me. My war is not yet ended."

"I think," said the Red Prince, "that it is." His hand took in the two who stood in silence: Hirel because he had no part in it, Sevayin because she could not find the words to speak. Her hands were locked in his, braced above the child in her belly. "There is the end of it. You have refused it. Be wise at last, son of my heart. Accept this that you yourself have yearned for."

"And I?" Mirain demanded. "Am I to fall upon my sword?"

Sevayin started forward, breaking away from Hirel. "No, Father. You can rule as you have ruled, until the god comes to take you. Keruvarion is yours. Asanion is mine to share with my emperor. Our son will hold them both."

He could see it. It was in his eyes. Almost, they smiled.

But the prince said, "How long will you be content? How long before it begins to rankle in you? You have struck deep into the heart of Asanion. Will you insist that all you have won is yours?"

"He has won nothing yet," said Hirel.

Sevayin spun upon him. And back, furious, upon her father.

"Yes," Prince Orsan said. "There is no peace while you live, Mirain An-Sh'Endor."

"You will have to kill me with your own hands," said Mirain.

And Sevayin said very softly, "You will have to slay me if you hope to touch him."

The Red Prince looked at them all. His eyes sparked at last with Gileni temper. "Was ever a man beset by such a brood of royal intransigents?" In three swift strides he was before Mirain. He was very much the taller, and he was not to be towered over, even by the Sunborn. He did what Hirel would not have done for worlds: set hands on Mirain's shoulders and held them, looking down into the Sun-bright eyes. "I will slay you if I must. I pray that I may have no need."

He could do it. Mirain smiled. Knowing surely, as did they all, that he himself could take that life which beat so close, end it before the prince could set hand to weapon. And yet, loving him, this master of the masters of kingmakers, this weaver of plots which could dazzle even Asanian wits. Loving him and hating him. "Foster-father." His voice was almost gentle. "Tell me."

Prince Orsan met his smile with one fully as wise and fully as implacable. "There is another way."

"Of course," said Mirain.

"An enchantment." The prince paused. "The Great Spell. The long sleep which lies upon the borders of death."

"But not full within its country." Mirain tilted his head back, the better to meet the prince's gaze. "What profit is there in that? Better and easier that I die. Then at least my soul will be whole again."

"For you, perhaps, there may be no profit. For this world which you have ruled, which you may yet destroy . . . Your daughter has waked to wisdom. She sees that light and dark are one; she knows in truth what power is. To that truth you may come. And if the years pass as I forebode they will pass, a time will come when again the balance is threatened: when Avaryan shall need the Sword which he has forged."

"Thrifty," said Mirain. "And hard. Have you ever laid an easy task on anyone?"

He asked it of Prince Orsan, but he asked it also of one who could not be seen. He did not sound either awed or frightened. Hirel could admire that.

"If I won't do it," he asked, and now he spoke only to the prince, "what will you do?"

"I will do my best to kill you."

"You could fail."

"I could," the prince agreed calmly.

Mirain laughed, sudden and wonderfully light. "And if I do it—a wonder. A splendor of legend; a deed beyond any that I have ever done. But the cost . . ." He sobered. "The cost is very high."

"The great choices do not come cheaply."

Mirain's eyes flashed beyond the prince to Sevayin. They softened a very little. "No," he said. "They do not."

There was a silence. No one moved. Mirain stared wide-eyed into the dark. His mind was as clear to Hirel as if he spoke aloud, its vision shimmering behind Hirel's own eyes. Sleep that was like death, but was not death. Long ages passing. Dreams, perhaps. Awareness trapped in unending night. And at the end of it, a hope too frail to bear the name of prophecy. A foreseeing that might prove founded on falsehood. A waking into utter solitude, utter abandonment, in a world beyond any seer's perceiving.

Better the simple way. A battle of weapons and power. Death if he fell, life and empire if he won. The prince was strong, but he was old; he had never been Mirain's match in combat. Nor even yet could he equal the Sunborn's power.

Mirain drew a long shuddering breath. He looked at his daughter and his daughter's lover. Their hands had met again without their willing it, their bodies touched. Pain swayed him. His hands reached as if to seek the ones who were gone; his power wailed in its solitude. Alone, all alone.

But to die—

He had no fear of it. He knew wholly and truly what it was. And yet . . . "I'm young," he said. "I'm strong. There are years of living left in me."

None of them spoke. Years indeed, Hirel thought. Years of war.

Mirain flung back his head. It burst from him in pain and rage and royal resistance. "I am not called!"

"You are not," Prince Orsan said. "The god will accept you if you go. But he does not summon you into his presence."

Mirain closed his eyes, opened his hands. Hirel's eyes could not bear the brilliance of the *Kasar.* "I am summoned," the emperor said softly. "But not to that.

"Father," he said, "Father, you are not merciful."

"But just," said Orsan, to whom he had not been speaking, "he has always been."

Mirain smiled as a strong man can, even in great pain. He held out his hands, the one that was night, the one that was fire. "And now you see. To the will of a god, even the Sunborn can submit." He bowed his head. "I am yours, O instrument of my father. Do with me as you will."

The Red Prince bowed low. "Not for myself, my lord and my emperor. For the god who is above us all."

Mirain lay upon that table that could have been either bier or altar. Prince Orsan did nothing for an endless while, gazing into darkness. He gathered power, yet not as Hirel had known it, in light and fire. This was quiet, inexorable, immeasurable. Mirain did not move under it, save for his fist, that clenched once, and slowly unclenched.

The Red Prince stood over him. His eyes sparked. Rebellion. Repentance of his choice.

Sevayin trembled under Hirel's hands. Remembering. Living again the terror of great magic chosen and not yet begun. Seeing once more that stern dark face bent above her, pitiless as the face of a god. Hirel tried to think calm into her; to give her strength.

Prince Orsan laid a hand on Mirain's brow and a hand on his breast. Mirain drew a shuddering breath. "Now," he said, low and rough. "Do it now."

The prince bowed his head. "Sleep, my son," he said. "Sleep until the god calls you to your waking."

Mirain smiled. The air was full of power. Throbbing, singing. It filled Hirel. It poured through him. It reft him of will and wit and waking.

He caught at solidity: dark, fire-crowned. She brought back the world.

They bent over the man upon the stone. He woke still, though dimly; he saw them. He smiled. "Children," he murmured. "Children who loved beyond hope and beyond help. I see—I am glad—after all—" His voice faded. "Love one another. Be joyful. Joyful . . . joy . . ."

Sevayin broke down and wept. He never knew. He was kingly in his sleep, and young, and at peace; and on his face the shadow of a smile. Even as she wept she straightened his kilt so that it was seemly, folded his hands upon his breast, laid his braid with care upon his shoulder. She shook off the hands that would have helped her.

Slowly she straightened. Her eyes burned, emptied of their tears. "There has never been anyone like him. There shall never be his like again."

"He was a strong king," Hirel said, "and a true king, and an emperor."

"He was Mirain An-Sh'Endor," the Red Prince said.

Sevayin kissed him. One last tear fell to glitter on his cheek. "Sleep well," she said softly. "Dream long. And when you wake, may you have learned to be wise. To face the dark. To know it; to transcend it."

"Or may you never wake." Prince Orsan signed the still brow. Where his hand passed, light glimmered, shaping words of blessing and of binding. "Remember, O my soul's son. Remember that I loved you."

He turned slowly. He wept like a king, strongly, out of a face of stone. "He has gone beyond us now. His end I cannot see. Perhaps for him there shall be none.

"But for us," he said, "the world is waiting." He bowed low and low.

"Empress. My soul is yours, my body, my power, my heart. Do with me as you will."

Sevayin shuddered at the title. At his oath, she raised her clenched fists. He waited, mute. His life was hers for the taking. His title, his power, all that he had been, hers. She could slay him, she could exile him, she could leave him here to go mad and die. For this was the crag of Endros Avaryan, and he was a mortal man, and the curse was strong about them all.

Her hands fell; she breathed deep, trembling. She stepped toward him. He did not move. "I chose you," she said, "in the end. It will be a very long while before I can forgive you. I may never trust you fully. But love . . . love has no logic in it." Her voice cleared, sharpened. "Get up, Grandfather. Since when have you ever bowed to me?"

"Since you became my empress."

"You never bowed to Mother. Or to Father, either. Stop your nonsense now and help me. I don't have the strength for a magegate, and there is no other way out of this place."

"There is one," he said, rising. He took her hand. It stiffened against him, eased slowly, opened. He turned the palm up. The *Kasar* flared and flamed. "Here is that which opens all doors."

"But there are no doors," she said.

"Save this." He met her eyes. "The way is simple. Inward through the *Kasar*. Outward through the Heart of the World."

She frowned. She was very close to the end of her strength. Hirel lent her what he had, hardly caring how he did it. Little by little her mind cleared. "Inward," she said, fitting her will about the word. "In." Gathering their threefold awareness. "Ward." The *Kasar* swelled and bloomed and closed about them, a torrent of fiery gold. The worlds whirled away.

PART SIX

Sevayin Is'kirien

Twenty-six

THERE WERE NO ENDINGS. THAT WAS THE TRUTH which ruled the gods. Sevayin would have been a great sage, if she had cared a jot for wisdom.

Inward through the *Kasar*. Outward through the Heart of the World. Simple; inevitable. When she came out of the darkness, it was all changed. The mages laid themselves at her feet and called her empress. She looked down at them and saw no sweetness in revenge. She glanced at her consort. "Hirel?"

He eyed his Olenyai blades, measured the bowed and humble necks. Remembered all the hatred he had borne them.

He raised his empty hands to her, angry, yet bitterly amused. "It is gone," he said. "All of it, I cannot even despise them."

"Nor I. But," she said, "this we can do. We can rule them."

"That has been all our intent," said the guildmaster.

She did not believe him; she did not trust him. But he was hers, he and his mages, while she had strength to bind him. She made them swear fealty to Hirel as to herself; she won from them an oath, that they would do no harm to herself or to her consort, or to the child which she bore.

They made her sleep, all of them together, there outside of the world's time. She wanted to fight them. Her body refused. It was fordone, and it had a child to think of. A living child, dreaming in his warm dark womb, his flame of power burning diamond-bright. The mages had been afraid of him; they would learn to be afraid of him. If he had ever been a simple mortal infant, this night's working had put an end to it.

He would be something new, this heir of Sun and Lion. Something wonderful.

"But of course," said Hirel with his inimitable certainty. "He is our child."

She was not ready to laugh again, not quite yet. But she smiled: she kissed him and said, "I do think I love you, Hirel Uverias."

She slept in her old chamber, cradling her son as Hirel cradled her; and if she dreamed, she remembered nothing of it. When she woke, she ate because she must, but her mind had leaped far ahead. She hardly saw who followed her from the chamber to the hall of fire.

Her worldgate had fallen. She had felled it herself. Vadin, Starion, her poor mages—

Inward through the *Kasar*. Outward through the Heart of the World.

Avaryan was rising. His light lay gentle on the dead. Vadin Uthanyas who had died at last, died fearlessly and joyfully so that the rest might live. His body lay in royal company: Asanian emperor, Varyani empress. Sevayin would mourn. Later. She would reckon up her guilt, when there was time for reckoning. Two armies waited, hating one another. Two herds of princes hot for war. Two empires, two royal cities, two palaces with all their flutter of courtiers. Two lifetimes' worth of battles to make them all one.

She laughed, standing over her dead, because she wanted most to howl. They were all staring. All her mages now, those who would have slain the emperors and those who would have defended them. Each had half succeeded. One alive as wicked fate had promised her, one dead as he had wished to be, both gone where no harm could reach them; where they themselves could do no harm.

So much to do. She opened her arms. "See," she said. "The morning has come. The war is won. We have a throne to claim, my prince and I. Who dares to gainsay me?"

"I."

She spun upon Hirel in shock and sudden rage.

He stood before her, gold-maned in the morning, his robes in tatters and his eyes black-shadowed and his will indomitable. The mask of his father was in his hand. He raised it; he held it before his face. His voice came forth from it, a stranger's voice, cold and quiet. "I," he repeated. "I am the Emperor of Asanion. I yield my power to no man."

She stalked him, cat-soft. "No man," she said, "certainly. But a woman, Hirel Uverias? A woman of the bright god's line. Mage and queen and bearer of your son."

The golden face was still, inhuman, imperial. It granted nothing. It yielded nothing.

It lowered slowly. She saw his eyes over it, and then his living face, more beautiful than any mask. "And my lover? Are you that, madam?"

"That," she said, "always and ever. But before all else, I am Empress of Keruvarion."

"So." He looked her up and down. His brows met. He bent his eyes upon the mask, turning it in his hands, pondering long and deep within the walls of his mind.

She held herself still. Not even for love of him would she surrender her half of the throne.

"Only half?" he asked her.

"No more," she answered, "and no less."

He raised his hand. She raised her own. His eyes narrowed against the flame of it. He set palm to burning palm. His face was still, but his eyes were all gold. "So be it," said the Emperor of Asanion.